Enemy Unknown

Journey of Selvorne: Enemy Unknown

Series 1
Book 1
Volume 1

First Edition
Unabridged

by David Stephenson

Journey of Selvorne: Enemy Unknown
by David Stephenson

First Edition, Unabridged
Paperback

ISBN 978-1-922422-01-9

205091.10

This is a work of fiction. Names, characters, places, events, locales, ideas and incidents are the products of the author's imagination. Any resemblance to actual events, or persons, living or dead, is purely coincidental.

Should you know any such persons, kindly send them to me, as they would be fascinating. Or at least mildly amusing.

Devotion

For Ann, my wife – the luckiest, in all the world. I am. We are. This was not possible without you. The best of my life is not possible, without you.

For Luke and Lara, our children. Beautiful in all ways, wonderful and kind. Hilarious, and fierce. A million words could not describe you both. This is my gift, to cherish. Wisdom, and love.

For my parents. The greatest gift – to appreciate reading, thinking, understanding. My hope is to pass that on. My gratitude, that I have the chance.

For family. Those who came before, all of whom missed this, all the way back, through the ages. Some never met, well before my time. Others greatly missed, and remembered. For those who shall follow, none yet met, some could never be. Through this, may I be remembered. Through the ages. For some while.

For all who have influenced me, greatly, or slightly.

For myself. I have enjoyed this, more than anything I have written or read. I would do it again a dozen times, if it was read by only me. I have done it again, a dozen times, and enjoyed it, every word.

For the characters within. They live, now, if only in my mind. They live. In my mind. Their hopes, dreams, losses and loves – alive, but only in my mind. I hope, soon, also in yours. And so, finally,

For the readers. You. Though I may not know you. Might not meet you. Might never be able to meet you – though you may not yet be born. May the characters within begin to live, in your mind. May you enjoy it, a dozen times or more. May it influence you, if only slightly, perhaps greatly, to bring the best of life to you.

David Stephenson

Contents

A thought is not a thing

a map is not the land.

It is a song just when you sing

you cannot hold it in your hand.

Of our journey, this is all

we have

to understand.

Once Upon a Bridge

Under, standing. A lone oak tree – shade, beside a barren cliff road. The end of a hot spring day, travellers parting ways at the start of a long wooden bridge. One youth remained, waving a warm farewell. Not returned by the three crossing the bridge, riding a waggon of wine along the road to home. Friend. Father. Other ... a lumbering ox. Selvorne instead was to the lake, to fish for their meal – hungry, eager, yet feeling almost alone as his final wave was ignored. Unnoticed? Not likely. Unmissed? They seemed merry enough without him, as the ox plodded along. Unwanted? Could ... no. Briefest doubt became a frown. Unfooled, he waited. They grew distant, a hundred feet across the bridge. He watched, raising a brow when they finally turned. Feigned disinterest, ended – one waved back. One laughed, absurd as it was to be amused by something so silly as pretending poor manners. Taunting, or whatever nonsense they shared amongst themselves. Selvorne could not help but smile, and likely would a few times that day, to think of it as he fished. Until they met again that night for a meal, freshly speared. Soon. Yet missed, a little, already. Three men, two loved, one dearly. Four faces of horror at the sudden cracking of wood.

Down. Staring. Gone – truly. Men. Ox. Wine and waggon, barrels and bridge. Down, not across. In only a moment of breaking wooden beams. Snapping, and screams. Ended. Alone. Standing – over.

Silence.

The crash must have made a noise. Selvorne had not heard it. Could hear nothing, other than water and wind. His heart stopped – gone. His heart pounded, though crushed, or hollow, or torn. There was no noise beside the cliff, no unusual sound, it was still. The screams remained, in his mind. He breathed hard, three times, clenched his fists and ran to the edge.

No bridge. The road that once led to it was the same. The cliff, the same – the bridge far below, the same they had crossed so many times – scattered pieces in river and rocky gorge. Part of it remained beside Selvorne, where he stood at the very edge. Carefully. The path ahead was perfect, for a few yards – then nothing. The bridge had broken, snapped and failed – fallen entirely, with ox, waggon and men upon it. All in pieces, broken where they landed below.

He planted his spear in the ground and began to climb down as fast as he dared. It was the easier side, on the south, for a rapid descent – but to slip and fall, he surely would be dead. Then could bring no help to those who might have lived. He moved fast, but it seemed forever to clamber down. Rough and clumsy, even with care. He kept looking below as he went – no movement. Not even the ox, which was stronger than men. Barrels were shattered. Slabs of granite, cut fine and thick at the quarry, snapped. Both were harder and tougher than men. There were no cries for help or wails of pain, not even creaking or settling of shifting wood. No sound other than the stones he dislodged, and the trickling waters of a river turned red by lost wine.

Selvorne almost did not turn from the cliff when he landed at last. He hoped, somehow, it was a prank to make him look the fool, as any of the three might play upon him. To turn and see them laughing, only having pretended, only making jest. He wondered, he wished, but knew it was not to be – no man could feign such a thing. He would not see their laughing faces. A deep breath, he turned to look on the horror of the gorge – he saw only stillness and death. A few moments of pain, to locate each man, then he ran at once.

Three men lay – it should have been four. It could have been him. Three men, and an ox that did not move. Crushed by the waggon, it was the end of a beast that served so well. It, at least, could not have realised the horror of its fate as it fell. The others knew it, Selvorne had seen it in their faces at that last brief moment. He could see it still. All fell at once, but not all the same way. Girradehn, their guard, landed by the river, half in water, half on rock. Arnlausa Laehtene must have leapt from the waggon, far, but to no avail, for it was the stony river edge where landed his old friend.

One more man lay broken. One more, most dear. Ended by two falls – first, his own, to land upon the rock – then the waggon, to crash upon him by half. It would have been fast. Final. There would be no pain. For him, at least. For his son it was deep anguish, as Selvorne stood and stared. Uhlsko Skelorne – his father, his friend. His only family, and his greatest loss.

Last of his family, dearest to his heart. Dead. It was certain, even from yards away, though he was oddly unbloodied. Selvorne knew it was wrong to go first to the dead at such a time, but he could not help himself. Uhlsko did not breathe, move nor watch with his open eyes, so Selvorne closed them. Injuries, but no blood. He seemed as though asleep, with the great weight of the waggon as a blanket, and the riverside as his bed. Perfect, as though asleep – just as his mother had been, so long ago, before the covers were drawn. The waggon would be turned, the body carried, taken to be laid beside her in the ground. Together again, as he wished. Too early for him, he was not greatly old. Too early for her, she had been very young. Too early for Selvorne, were it one hundred years later – they were gone. Lost, his only family, and he was alone.

It was not like Selvorne to anger, but he clenched one fist to punch the waggon hard, as though it was its fault. It did not help in any way, removing none of his pain, only adding more. He did not care, and punched with the other fist as well. No, it was no use, other than to shake his wits, so he went to the river, shoved both hands in the waters, and splashed coldness to his face, to clarify his thoughts.

The other – he went fast to Arnlausa, who was half on stone and half in the river. To his astonishment, his friend breathed. Harder than stone, some said of Arnlausa, who was an ageing man still young enough to take offence at being so called. Or feign it, chuckling in mirth, or yelling his displeasure, as he fancied. Both could be frightening, either could be amusing. Blood was at his mouth, he otherwise seemed unbroken, but he did neither speak, scream, nor stir when prodded. He might have been choking, so Selvorne dragged him to where the ground was flat and pebbled, laying him carefully so he might more easily breathe.

One dead, one lived – great friends of each other, and of Selvorne. Beside them he should lie, and would have done, also broken, but for a fish. A fish he meant to kill, which had strangely saved his life. Three would lie, battered and – Selvorne breathed in hard, and bit his lip in horror.

Girradehn – he had forgotten him. In his grief he ignored the third man, who was not so much a friend as he was an annoyance, usually. He could not feel ill for a man in need, so ran at once to where the guard had fallen upon smooth river rocks. A few more yards and Girradehn would have landed in water. A few days of rain, and the river would have been higher – the young man before him would have lived.

He did live, and stirred where he lie – a broken leg, it seemed no more, but the worst break Selvorne had seen, or imagined, and the only time he had seen living bone. And so much blood he fancied that it, not the wine, was making the river red. Quickly he stopped it as best he could with Girradehn's own trouser leg cut to ribbons, and he wondered if the man would ever walk again. Girradehn the Mighty. So he called himself, and was by those who also adored him. He hardly deserved it for size, strength or skill, each of which was good at best, and that was hardly a better title than mighty. Girradehn the Vexing, Selvorne called him, and Girradehn the Bore. All would call him Girradehn the Lame, or something similar, just as insulting. His misfortune would make him all the more sour, as he dwelt on his woes, and not the wonder that he lived at all. Selvorne finished his poor bandaging, ashamed at his lack of skill, and at the wish that it was his father, instead, lying there merely injured.

Selvorne stood and gathered his thoughts, looked over the wreckage and wondered what had happened. The bridge had failed. Not the cliff, not the rock – the beams of the foundations stuck proudly out from the cliffs, on both sides of the ravine. It seemed not as a bridge broken, but one about to be built. It was not lightning, then, nor fire, nor worms. Selvorne knew the bridge well, for he had helped build it, not so many years ago, when he was a young boy. Carrying wood, and even cutting it, in places, with the best instruction from the most skilled craftsmen. It should not have failed. It never had. He checked it was sturdy and undamaged every time they crossed it, which was at least twice a year. Not one month ago, since he last ... looked ... and then he realised he had not checked it that very day – that hour – that time. Had he done ...

He breathed hard and slow, staring up at the cliff top, then down at the bridge. Had he done, such horror would not have befallen them. Instead, he had wished to hurry ahead by another road – rush to the lake, to fish. His spear, his knife, his meaning to bring dinner – all in haste, which saved him, and slayed them. Had he checked, it would not be crossed. Had he delayed, only a little. Waited. It was his fault, and there was nothing he could do for it.

Blame for its failing, and disturbed to realise what might have happened instead. Two things worse – for one, he could have fallen with them, and the other, he might have run ahead to the lake without saying farewell, caught his fish and returned to town, wondering where the other three were, and why they dallied along the road. He would have gone looking that night, likely, to find there was no bridge – and that the two who might have lived had perished. Left unattended, to die slowly without help, or ... be eaten by a bear.

Whatever blame he felt, he buried, there was no time for pity. Not for the dead, it would not bring them back. Not for the wounded, who needed care, instead. And not for himself, though his loss was great and fault was severe. Wits, not sorrow, was what he needed, so he steadied himself and thought of a plan.

Help – he needed men. The only way out of the ravine was to climb, and he was not sure he could, carrying a limp man on his back, not even on the easier southern cliff. The north was almost sheer in places, and required a jump at the start. Cliffs to the east were impossibly smooth, as was most of the west, and to the west it went for miles before any way out could be found. And, apart from that – there were no people anywhere but to the north, miles to his own town, on a good road, but too far to carry even one wounded man. He had to run, bring others with ropes, buckets and carts, and anything of use for the wounds, and go at once.

~

A terrible scream echoed in the ravine, as though a pig had caught its leg in a gate. A screech he knew well, though it was no pig, but Girradehn, who had woken to find his leg broken. Selvorne ran to him at once and tried to make him comfortable, for which he received much abuse, yelling and spluttering snarls, until Girradehn settled on his side, angry and hurt. Grim, but calm.

"Father?" Girradehn asked.

"Dead."

Girradehn was silent, and seemed to bow his head – perhaps he felt for Selvorne's loss. It was only moments before he looked up again, and seemed puzzled.

"Arnlausa?"

"Very badly hurt, and I think he sleeps," Selvorne replied.

He breathed in slightly and tensed with pain, then stared, at nothing. At first, for a few moments, then at Selvorne, until his gaze began to focus, and he narrowed his eyes.

"How is it that you are unhurt?"

"I – was not on the waggon."

"Why not?"

"Girradehn – I was going to the lake, to fish," Selvorne said. Girradehn kept staring for a while, until he seemed to ease. His head lowered, and he winced in pain. Reaching for his lower leg, he prodded it, doing his best to stifle a yell when he moved it most oddly. A few more agonising adjustments until he could take no more pain, then he spoke again, in a grim tone.

"I will not survive this. Unless someone, somewhere in the lands knows how to rebuild a leg, or remove it and close the wound. And unless we meet that person soon. I know of no such person, not weeks from here. Not ... now."

"Who? Can I run to them? Could I – cut it off, and burn it closed?"

"If it was my foot. This leg is ruined – it is my ruin. Never has a man survived such a wound. I have only days. Or less. No ... more."

Girradehn then was silent, and Selvorne thought he was surprisingly accepting of his fate. It was not usual for him, a man who Selvorne never considered particularly brave, although Girradehn was not usually broken at the bottom of a gorge.

"You must move the bodies from the water," Girradehn said after some time.

"That is the last thing I – "

"It is the law, Selvorne – do it. What – time is it? How long – what day?"

Selvorne frowned – then took a deep breath.

"You have been here only moments, it is the same day as you fell. No more than an hour, at most."

Girradehn winced – pain was on his face, then changed to a strange relief.

"Move us. Find a cave or crack, away from the water – light a fire, gather what ... drink there is, then ... take to the town, fast. Your father, also. Now!"

His last words were a command, but it was given weakly as Girradehn fell back into a sleep, almost as he spoke. He lay there, unmoving, as though dead.

And there Selvorne could lie, so easily mistaken for Girradehn by looks, at least at a distance. Neither was the same in face – neither was tall, nor short. Both were broad, and strong, for young men. One from idle fighting, trained as a guard – one from working in the quarry, far from an idle life of ease. The rougher man made fancy, the gentler man made hard. Different, though similar. One to make fun, and one to be made fun of, and when that reversed, the first to make a fist and punch

Selvorne when he teased. It was many years since the fear of a punch would stop his fun, for Selvorne had grown bold, and Girradehn's blows either more restrained, or Selvorne's body tougher. Girradehn's hair was kept shorter, so it appeared closer to brown than blond – Selvorne's hair he kept deliberately longer, to be different from the man of whom he was not fond, and so he seemed more fair – usually. But after the past weeks of travel, they were much the same, young broad men of fair hair, who could be mistaken for cousins, perhaps. Looking on the wounded man who did not stir, Selvorne saw what could be himself, feeling a strange sense of sorrow, and relief. For both he felt ashamed.

At the order, he felt some anger. Commanded, as though he served Girradehn, who was often so demanding. At such a time, Selvorne should obey. Girradehn knew better, he was trained, his advice was good, and Selvorne knew the law. They were of the Waehter – a people who revered the waters of the land. Rivers admired, lakes were adored. The sea was feared, and all were treated with utmost respect. The Waehter people, led by the Waehdric in spirit and wisdom, in all such matters of living and death, of custom and command. Never must a body be left by water. Not a pond, a bog, a marsh – not a stream, and certainly not a river, whether it flowed then to another town, or not. It was a crime that would be punished – but worse than that, to break it would bring shame. Rivers and streams must run clear and clean, untainted by any means. They were the blood of the land, and must be honoured as the blood of family – those still living, and those who had come before. It was the duty of all the people, accepted as custom and common practise. For lords, it was an oath sworn most sacred, to be upheld at any cost. That was the quandary facing Selvorne as he looked on the river turned red – for Arnlausa, and Uhlsko, his father – were both lords. So the duty fell to Selvorne to uphold their oath, as would the shame for breaking it.

Shame he did not want, but laws were not made for shame, and he had to admit some fear. The reason for the oath, which was never said, but always suspected, was that the dead, left near the river, would draw creatures of the woods to the towns where people lived. Bears. Wolves. Other things, worse. Bears, he thought, were very rarely seen. It was the only explanation that made sense, for there were no towns downstream at that river, all the way to the sea, and it should not matter how many bodies were thrown to the gorge. But for the smell to bring a bear close to the town – worse, to the ravine, from where Selvorne could not quickly flee, and where the two wounded men were trapped – Girradehn's order would be obeyed at once.

~

Caves would be safest, surely creatures would avoid such dark places. There were some away from the water, he knew, for the land seemed ripped apart where the ravine was, and in places the crack extended at angles, far from the river. In other caves the river must have once been high, carving the cliffs smooth, and wandering. He cursed that the water was not deep that day – the waggon and barrels would float, the granite would sink and stay, and the men, with luck, would have been battered and wet. Laughing, and living. Then angry at his neglect for not checking the bridge – he would have been taunted, forever more. But ... living, and ... he had no time for sorrow.

Nor much time to run to his town and return, so he hurried to find a safe cave. He skipped over the shallows where low water left stones exposed, and went to where he knew a cave might be. It was suitable, so he returned at once. He saw wood on his way, driftwood which had fallen into the gorge. Some from over the cliff near, but not so much. Most had fallen in the east, into the lake, then swept down the waterfall to the ravine. Caught on rocks in higher waters, stranded and left as waters fell, dried in the sun, and so was ready to burn. Years of fallen wood, and that of the broken bridge, providing kindling and slow burning beams to last a week, if he wanted. He should be running to his town, not making fires, but Girradehn knew better and his order, though spluttered in pain, was clear.

All the men to be moved, his father also, though he was dead. Not left by the river, and a grim thought came to Selvorne as he lifted Arnlausa and made his way. Chosen first, for he lived – first, for he wished to delay the next, more painful task. Arnlausa was a man not old, but past his prime, and at his greatest weight, having lost none of his strength, and adding perhaps a little more fat than he would admit. Selvorne heaved him to his shoulder and struggled over the crossing, taking him yards from the water to leave him in the cave.

The next was his father. Selvorne checked again whether he lived. He did not. The waggon he strained to lift, just a few feet to free his father. It rocked, and he shoved until it was half on its side. Barrels toppled, those that were not tied wriggled free and rolled. Heavy – wine perhaps was spared. He did not care. He checked again, his father remained dead. Not even water could wake him. Selvorne lifted him gently, as though the moving might disturb his sleep. Older than Arnlausa, not as heavy as he might once have been, he was carried with all the honour he deserved, and placed in the cave beside his greatest friend.

One dead, one asleep – two lords, best of friends. Selvorne was not sure what would bring greater grief to Arnlausa when he stirred – that he was hurt, or his friend had perished. They looked no way the same, Arnlausa a larger man, Uhlsko older, not feeble in any way, but clearly not the stronger of the two. One man once was fair, turned grey with woe and age – the other, once grey, made dark of hair with vanity and dye. Brothers in arms, they had served together as guards, long ago. Brothers in heart, they were merriest when together. It was good they had one last adventure that year, journeying south. A grim end, though, and as Selvorne looked down on his greatest friends, he winced as he remembered he had forgotten Girradehn once more, and ran out of the cave.

Girradehn was the most difficult – he always was – for he complained furiously at every step. Selvorne was sure it was not pain, for he did not yell, and as he carried him, he began to wish it was, and that Girradehn would scream. Not because he wanted him to suffer, but because he knew what it must mean. Girradehn was not that tough. He was injured severely, perhaps more than he had realised or would admit to himself. His feeble yells were made to convince himself he could feel – that he could not, was worse than pain. Selvorne carefully left him in the cave near where the fire would be, then went at once to fetch wood.

Fire. Selvorne had thought earlier he should run at once to the town, but stayed, obeying the order of Girradehn, not entirely understanding why, until he saw the ox. Dead, enormous, it could not be moved. It bled to the river, and the smell was growing strong in the hot afternoon sun. That would bring bears, and fire, he hoped, would keep them out of the cave. Flame and smoke, the only defence for three men in a cave who could not move. Bears, or other things of the woods that Selvorne did not know. He had not seen a bear, he only knew they were large, hungry and impossible to fight. He did not know what else might be there amongst the trees, perhaps wolves, in many ways worse. Selvorne hurried to gather wood, for fire would be their armour, guard and sword.

Where the actual swords were was a mystery. Girradehn's was broken, it had landed poorly between rocks, then been smashed by granite blocks that fell upon it. The other swords were gone. Usually carried in the waggon, unfastened, but lying flat and safe, they must have been thrown to the river as it tumbled. The small axe was gone as well, and that would have been useful. Most other things had fallen well, not far from the cart – a tinder box was in the sack he spied, with cooking things for their camp. He snatched it all in one passing as he carried wood, and left it in the cave. The seals of the lords and writing tools – in their fine box. Strong and well made, the best thing Arnlausa had ever bought, he once said. He said the same of anything he paid too much for. It seemed safe enough attached to the waggon, in that hidden place that was never meant to be seen, though the waggon was never meant to be turned on its side, either. Selvorne unbuckled it and took it with him, hanging by its belt as he gathered armfuls of splintered wood and returned to the cave.

No animal would come and face the flames he was preparing – dry river wood to start, he had the flames dancing in moments. Larger branches to build it, and then the best wood of the broken bridge, which would burn strongly for hours. Long beams as well, which Girradehn might use as flaming spears, should such creatures come. Selvorne's own spear was left atop the cliff – no time to fetch it, and it would be little use. The flame was the thing animals feared, and it alone would keep them warm and safe.

Water, should they need to drink, in bladders that had not burst. Wine also, though he was not sure if it was wise to be drunk when so badly hurt. Selvorne made it comfortable in the cave, though for food they had only oats that none would bother cooking, and week–old salted ham, which sorely needed to be either cooked well or thrown away. None of them had planned another night in the wild, they were almost home, where food would be fine. Where Selvorne would have brought a fresh fish. Mere hours to home, after weeks being away on their yearly journey south. No food remained, and likely, no appetite. Not for the wounded, not for Selvorne who felt ill, and certainly not for the dead.

Selvorne returned to the broken waggon to gather what he thought might matter. There was not much. A few belongings, nothing that could be considered treasured. Wine that his father and Arnlausa had brought from the south – many barrels broken and spilling, some were unharmed, having fallen in the river. Some were of finest quality, undamaged despite landing on rock – the best barrels, which were prized, once emptied. Worth more than the wine, Arnlausa said, though he never offered to sell them full at a price that suggested he meant it.

Granite, also, was mostly unharmed. Great slabs cut by Selvorne, and the quarry men he knew well. He never joined his father on the journey farther south for wine, but for many years remained in their own lands, in a quarry near the sea, working with stone, for good profit. He had little desire to go south to lands that were never spoken of well – he had no wish at all to do so with Girradehn, not for an entire month. And so in the far west, two days' journey along the top of the ravine, he parted from his father, Arnlausa and the annoying guard, to work for weeks with stone, waiting until they returned. It had been a long wait that year, he had made many slabs, hoped for good profit selling them, and planned to buy a new spear. All such plans in ruins, even though many stones might be saved. It did not matter. He would have preferred them all smashed, instead of the men. As he looked upon them scattered about the gorge, he wondered if their weight had made the bridge break.

More fault, more blame. From the south they had returned later than expected, and not well prepared, meeting Selvorne at the quarry where stones had accumulated as food dwindled. An unexpected week of poor food had caused Selvorne's hurry for the fish – a fine fish, of great size, which he had tried so often to spear. Cautious, cunning, clever and fast – it always outsmarted him, somehow.

Suddenly, he laughed – then bit his lip with woe. A thought of something funny said, and the realisation that he who said it never would again. The fish was welcomed to dinner – and often refused to come. Uhlsko had said his son needed a new invitation, and Selvorne laughed, for he knew he meant spear. A new spear – lighter, faster, and not damaged from hitting stones, being sat upon or dropped. Bindings fraying, edge dulled or a dozen other things Selvorne had a habit of doing to his things to wear them away. A new invitation, to the fish to join them for a meal. A new spear, and the hint – the promise – of a present from the Festival of Tavalehk. Selvorne wanted to laugh, as he had when it was said, but it was all he could do not to cry.

Had the fish saved his life, by drawing him away – or caused the accident, by distracting him from his duty to check the bridge. Both. Neither. There would be no fish for them that night, no meal of trout – nor would there be a meal for fishes, in the river where they had fallen. Nor for bears, or wolves, or foxes or ... ground bears, of which he had heard. Smaller, but no less fierce. He gathered what he thought might be useful for the men in the cave, looked over the waggon once more, then returned to check the men, one final time before his long run to get help.

They were the same as before, and Selvorne's heart was heavy from checking his father, in the hope that somehow he had lived. He was much colder than he should be – so was Arnlausa, though, and Girradehn, despite the fire. There was nothing more he could do other than drape cloaks over them as blankets, and he pondered his journey ahead.

Vaskatohr town – his own, miles to the north. The one man of the town who could certainly treat the wound was lying in the cave, dead. The town was very small, more of a mining village, and a pig farm. The miners could do no more than Selvorne, but they would lift the men out of the ravine by way of bucket and rope. Enough men to carry them all, and carts to take them back to town, then onwards to Tavalehk – that town was a day's journey farther, and though there were likely some there who knew what to do, it would be two days before any treatment could be had.

Uhlsko was Lord of Vaskatohr. Arnlausa was Lord of Tavalehk. There was nothing either town would not do for either man – no expense, no lack of men, all would run at speed through the night. But it was no use, for no desires of man could change the distance from ravine to town, or call them to come at once. Selvorne felt grim as he realised he would be leaving them alone for so long – dragging them out, then running with carts, to perhaps cut half a day from the time they had to wait. There was nothing he could do otherwise, so he decided to check one more time that they were comfortable and safe.

"Why are you here?" Girradehn asked.

"I am leaving – but – your leg?"

"Is fine, unhurt."

Selvorne frowned – shook his head – stared. Girradehn was chuckling.

"Is this some – "

"But the other leg is lost," Girradehn said, and began almost to laugh – it hurt him to do so, but he could not help himself, and Selvorne shook his head in astonishment, "one last laugh before The Sea."

"And not a very good joke. Does it – hurt?"

"Yes. A lot."

"That is ... good, then."

"Though I should thump you for saying it – I know what you mean. He spoke," Girradehn said, jerking his head to one side.

"Arnlausa?"

"No, your father – of course Arnlausa, you idiot."

"What did he say?"

"Wait," Girradehn said, and at that, he groaned.

Wait – it could be nonsense. Arnlausa did not look like he could talk, or if he had, it might have been mumblings that were unintended, from an injured man, asleep. Selvorne examined him carefully – blood was spat on his shirt since he had been sat against the wall of the cave. He was limp and did not respond to prodding, but clearly he had said something – and "wait", though not a plan, was an order that had to be obeyed.

"You must wait," Girradehn said, "is it night? It is dark."

"You are in a cave, it is ... not night yet."

"How long?"

"Sunset in hours. If I wait here, it will delay any help you could – "

"Selvorne, stop talking – he spoke. His order. He – if he wakes, he can fix me, if he ... or you can, though I shudder to think what you might do with your mallet hands. Knives, water, bandages, wine – wood for the fire, bring ... my sword, where is it?"

Selvorne winced – it was broken, he had seen it. Fallen, crushed and snapped. He said nothing, but nodded and went at once to fetch all that was required, for though little was said, it was clear what had to be done.

~

Clothes might be used as bandages, tied tightly to stop bleeding that could only become worse. Knives, unharmed by the fall, already sharp, not yet cleaned. The sword Selvorne fetched, for Girradehn kept asking for it. If he was to die, which he claimed was likely, for Selvorne took too long, he wished to die with it in his hand – as any fighting man would. It was nonsense, for men who said such a thing meant to die in battle, wielding their sword, not cradling it, complaining in a cave.

And he did complain. He had good reason to, yet the moans of Girradehn were for anything other than his wound. The cave was damp, the floor was cold. Neither was true. The fire was too hot or too far – either could be true, there was no way to tell. He sat upon pebbles, unbearable as a seat, though Selvorne could find none to remove. It was all a distraction, all very annoying, and Selvorne at last gave him the broken sword to make him silent.

It worked. Girradehn was silent as he stared at the hilt in one hand, the end of the blade in the other. Not bent, but cleanly snapped – perhaps it could be mended. Selvorne did not know of such things, except that the fittings of the hilt could be used once more, and the iron itself might be worked into something else, perhaps two daggers. Nothing truly was lost, and it was merely a sword – in his family for a long time, but a sword, and nothing more. And yet, as he stared at it, Selvorne thought it was the first time that day Girradehn almost cried. Once fine, once strong, meant to be passed on to his children, and theirs – the sword was broken, and if not discarded, would never be the same again.

"Never again," Girradehn lamented, "will the sword of Radehn swing – made for he who fought the men of Rigan first. Passed to Darradehn, Enforcer of Law in Hartlehk town. Passed to Jarradehn, woodsman who delivered the murderous robbers on the road – Hero of Tavalehk, most proud. Passed to Girradehn, Guard to Arnlausa – who fell off a bridge, and died. Childless. Loveless. Without coin, and the sword broken. Remembered in mourning for a week – then forever, in jest."

Selvorne looked down on his grim friend – he was right. It was sad. Sorrows of a life lost, too young, no greatness achieved. Broken. A bridge, a leg, a life – a line. Selvorne felt like kicking him.

"I shall remember that," Selvorne said, "and carve it on a stone for you – one of those in the ravine that broke in the fall. I will put it over your grave, and another near the Lordstone of Tavalehk – so all can remember you forever, as you wish."

"As a joke?"

"As a fool," Selvorne said.

"Thank you, that would be most kind," Girradehn said – and Selvorne's eyes opened wide. Was he ... making a joke? Again? Two in a day, and not his usual, made with malice towards another. Girradehn chuckled, and it clearly hurt.

"You are very odd today," Selvorne said.

"Climb the cliff – leap down, crawl back here, and tell me how odd you feel."

Selvorne bit his lip, and Girradehn chuckled until it hurt too much. He spluttered, then grew solemn.

"I – well, I am ... sorry," Girradehn said, "your father was more than good. Mine ... there is much death today, I fear. He said wait. I have some hope. How is he now?"

Selvorne checked Arnlausa, and found him stirring, but not waking.

"Not worse."

"Good. Pots and pans, and ... I guess the blade will have some use, after all. And perhaps can be mended. I am amazed none of the gems fell out, they were held so gently, I thought, apparently not. The blade, hard as steel – broken. Silver and steel, I would have put my coin on steel."

"Girradehn, I – "

"You are sorry? So you should be. I had plans for my life – live or die, they are no more. Taken from me, for the fancies of a stupid boy, for a ... fish. Wait – that was the order – it does not mean stand idly, Selvorne. Get the things I said, and go."

Selvorne felt fury – a boy, indeed, he was only years younger than Girradehn. Not even his father called him a boy anymore, even in jest. Arnlausa did, but he called men the same, though some were older than himself, so it was no insult. From Girradehn, it was, and ... perhaps not entirely undeserved. He left the cave almost angry, then stood in the ravine and breathed deeply. Anger was no use. He would not fail them twice in the day.

The sun was low in the sky, and behind the ravine walls it had already set. In the lands above there was perhaps another hour of sunshine, then twilight, with a first quarter moon. Enough to see a little, but he would need to gather more wood. Light to see, true, but it was for fire to ... burn. That would be unpleasant. Painful. As annoying as Girradehn was, Selvorne did not want to remove his leg, certainly not by the light of the moon.

Pots and pans they had used to cook with, none of them damaged in their sack when they fell. Most of Selvorne's things were in the river, and only a strap kept them from being washed away, mere yards from the broken waggon, in the waters where everything was catching on the rocks. Not all was lost, and it gave him hope. Perhaps Arnlausa was unharmed. He was, they said, as hard as stone, and many of the stones had not broken in the fall. He might yet live, and he could help Girradehn, who would also survive, with a limp and reason to whine. He already whined, so with one leg gone, if anything he might seem more reasonable. A grim jest, to make light of the day. Some loss. Great loss, but not all – and of the wine, some had not spilt.

Many drunk fishes downstream, however, but barrels could be recovered. Some unharmed completely, standing neatly on one end, as though rolled amongst rocks by a master barrelman. The waggon, it was damaged, one wheel smashed, and it was almost upside down. The waggon could be righted – the wheel, wrighted – all damage mended, made good once more. The ox ... it could be eaten. Not left, not by the water, that was law. He was not strong enough to drag it away without rope and pulley. Perhaps in pieces, but then the blood would bring creatures from the woods. No more, he guessed, than it already was, for the ox had bled into the waters. Selvorne took his knife and went to where the meat would be best.

Few regrets for the ox, though it had served them well for years. For most of its life he had known it, not hours before he had patted it. He mused on the changing fortune of the beast that was promised rest and hay, and instead was slain and butchered. Guilt, though it was not his intention. Guilt, regardless. A meal was needed, if he was to stay the night. River stones in the fire would cook the meat quickly and well, and it was fresh, if the beast quite old. A meal might lift their mood, he thought, and so the ox could serve them once more. The next day the pig farmers of Vaskatohr would come, and when all was done for the men, they would take the ox to pieces, turning it entirely to meat.

Then – a feast, to use the meat that could not be kept – in honour of his father. Sensible, if not in celebration. Celebrate his sensibility, he would have wanted that. Selvorne was hungry, but in no mood for feasts. Quite hungry, as he cut the flesh, for he had not eaten since the early day, and the smell only made things worse. A feast – what would the town think. To celebrate their dead lord. The grim accident, the broken bridge – one road remained, by way of lake and a shallow ford, the old road. A most excellent way to travel in the rain, if travellers wished to sink their waggons in the mud. Not a good road, then, and the ravine bridge would need rebuilding, within the year, before their next journey ... south ... the following spring.

Selvorne stopped cutting. He stared at the flesh, and blinked, then sighed. There would be no trip south the next year. It was their last. His father was dead, his only journey would be to his grave. Arnlausa was injured, and would not go south without his lifelong friend – the pain of memory would be too great. Girradehn would not go anywhere limping, save to the taverns to drink. No more the guard to Arnlausa, some simple task would be found for him, and he would be well paid and miserable, more than usual. Even Arnlausa would no more be the merry Lord of Tavalehk, he would be grim. And no more the Lord of Vaskatohr, Uhlsko would be ... was ... lost.

Slicing flesh for food. Had all the others died, Selvorne would be sitting there in misery. Likely doing much the same. Remove the bodies, make fire and food. Alone, with neither urgency or eagerness. But he was not alone, and he had tasks ahead, which were grim. Slicing flesh for meat, cutting meat for ... life. To cut, to cook, to eat – to cut, to burn, to prevent the bleed that would end a man. There was no time for sorrow, so he grasped the meat for their meal, and moved with speed to the cave.

Two large river stones into the fire, the meat was placed upon them at once. It was not the best way to cook, for they should be hot first, but he did not care. Not the usual sizzle, but soon the hearty smell. The fire was too slow, too cold, so he went for more wood.

Barrels – even split, could be repaired, and so were spared. The waggon as well, and so he chose the broken beams of the bridge, as large as he could lift. He returned with two great struts that he had once helped cut and carve, years before, as a young boy learning something of the craft. Oak from the north, highest quality, great expense, larger than needed – they should not have failed. They did, and he cursed the tree from whence they came, shoving them into the fire to serve some final purpose. He would find the men who had felled the trees, dried the wood and shaped them ... it could have been himself, though, those beams might have been his poor work. They began to burn, and he went outside to find more.

Gathering many loads, it was more wood than he could possibly need, but he almost wanted to destroy the bridge in flame, piece by piece, burning them to ash. He gathered more until it was too much, then he stood before the cave and wondered at their fate.

A simple journey south, the same as every year. South for him to quarry, for them to return with wine. They planned to be back home for a night, the next day to the Festival of Tavalehk – wine sold at great profit, and stone sold for a fine sum. It was a joyous journey, usually, and had been that year, despite delays and strange weather, and ... it had been, until that day. They should be dining on fresh fish, in his father's house, resting the night for one more day's journey to Tavalehk town. A fire, a feast, the townsfolk asking questions that never would be answered. Except with mysterious smiles, from his father, and mischievous jokes from Arnlausa. Likely boasts of Girradehn, also, and no way to determine if he spoke lies or truth. It should have been a fine ending to a great journey – the best time of the year, for his father, who had not so much joy since Selvorne's mother died, so long ago. He had, at least, one last month of joy before meeting his end ... before joining her once more.

Selvorne returned to the cave. The sun was soon to be truly set, for the ravine was growing dim. The quarter moon was up, but in the crevice only the fire lit the walls. It was growing large and hot, so he moved the wood away. He checked on Arnlausa, and he was the same as before. He checked on Girradehn – asleep, but stirring. He checked the meat – and turned it to the other side. He checked his provisions for the task ahead, then did the same again, then sat, staring at the flames, all things ready. Dreading what he might have to do in the night, and it occurred to him it might not be wise to eat first. Or perhaps after, either.

"I must have slept well," Girradehn said, making Selvorne almost jump at the sudden sound of a voice.

"Good, you need it."

Girradehn stared into the flames.

"Too hot?" Selvorne asked.

"Not hot enough. I did not hear the axe. I thought ... my ears were gone."

"Your – what? Why would your ears be – what axe?" Selvorne asked, frowning, and Girradehn nodded at the fire.

"I smell," Girradehn said.

"Is – this a joke?"

"I can smell the meat burning. And the fire – oak? It smells – wonderful. I thought ... is the fire loud?"

He was making no sense, so Selvorne put his hand to his forehead, and Girradehn slapped it away the first time, but not the second.

"You are hot," Selvorne said.

"I feel cold."

"Well, you ... are not. I might – water?"

"Leave it. I feel – yes, a drink," he said, and Selvorne gave him a drink, "I feel cold. Thirsty. The smell – I smell it. And ... the meat. And more. I should like to taste it, but – I thought I was to die."

"You talk a lot for a man to die," Selvorne said, hoping to lighten his mood. Girradehn just stared for a moment.

"I feel nothing."

"Pain?"

"Pain – yes, not ... much. A lot."

"You make no sense at all."

"No, I ... had none. Senses – I thought them gone. Silence. Numb. Then, the smell – the taste. I hear you, but ... the fire is quiet, and I heard no axe."

Girradehn must have truly lost all sense, for he made none. Selvorne looked into his eyes, and thought he seemed confused, staring into the flames. Not in agony, not ... Selvorne breathed in as he realised what he must have meant.

"Girradehn ... oh, friend – there is no axe. I have not found it, so you heard none. Are you – is it too late?"

"No axe?" he asked.

"No, it is likely in the river. It will not wash away, nor rust, if – no, I will look now," Selvorne said, and he felt grim.

It was horribly clear what Girradehn meant, and why he might have wanted his sword. Not for vanity, not for pride. Their axe was small, but so much faster than a knife. Neither axe nor sword were fast enough to be painless – neither could have been used to do the deed without him knowing. Even if asleep, even if completely numb. Girradehn was cold, and felt no pain – he felt no leg. He thought it had been removed already – he hoped, perhaps. All that agony was yet to come. Reluctantly, Selvorne began to rise.

"Halt," Girradehn said, then he spluttered. It was an order, and though Selvorne was no guard, he knew he had to obey.

"What?" Selvorne asked.

"What wood is in the fire there?"

"What?"

Girradehn nodded to the fire, then spluttered and coughed. Selvorne stared at the fire – oak. It smelled good to burn, and his friend was being most odd.

"Oak."

"Waggon? Barrel?"

"Bridge."

"No axe?"

"I will look for it. Before it is too dark, and – "

Girradehn held up a hand weakly, shaking his head so slightly it was barely noticed. Unspeaking, he pointed to the fire.

Selvorne stared again – bright, warm, burning well, made to last the night. Large beams of wood from the bridge, long, so that when burnt at one end, he could ... push them in farther. He could ... but he instead pulled one out. He lifted it – inches only, then feet, then stood and took it, making the fire spill across the cave, a little. He stared at the end of beam – it was not as he had made it, not those years ago. Not as any man would make it. It was not broken, it had not snapped, and it was not as long as it should have been, that strut. That beam. That most important piece of the bridge – that part which shifted weight, in ways he only partly understood. That support. He stared at it in silence, for the oak at one end, where it needed to be most strong, had been roughly hacked to weakness by an axe.

When Darkness Comes

Selvorne stared at the end that was cut, then looked along the length of the beam that once held up the bridge. A few feet long, thicker than his arm, less than his leg – good wood, and heavy. Not so polished as furnishings might be, but well smoothed, to shed damp that might gather beneath the bridge. It was a beam he knew well, one of many that crossed each other, their placement and well–cut joints gave greater strength than their size would suggest. The craft of clever men, one beam of many. There was another like it in the cave, set aside from the flames.

He dropped one and snatched the other, looking to the end – the same. The same kind of beam, and the same kind of cut – in a different place, more to the middle. Whoever chopped at it was not a master builder of bridges. He threw it down and found another – no marks of an axe, it had splintered. Snapped in the middle, broken by weight it was never made to bear alone.

Disbelief rose within him to battle confusion, and he turned to Girradehn – his face was the same, though more grim. Selvorne looked to the wood – three beams meant for the fire, all familiar, similar, save for two that were cut. It could not be, and yet, it was – the beams he knew, the mark of axe he knew – the two together was something new. As impossible as it was, he had to accept it – some fool who built the bridge had used damaged, weaker beams. Fury began to burn within him ... for moments – then it froze.

No. Not a fool. Not a builder being careless, nor saving coins with lesser wood. It was not done years ago, but recently, and in malice.

Selvorne stared at the fire and felt ill. He would need more than anger to avenge what was done. Shaking a little, cold, a little, though the fire was hot – he stared until he heard a voice.

"Your face – it can only mean one thing," Girradehn said, "are you sure?"

Selvorne nodded and looked to Girradehn, who bowed his head, then, trying to take a deep breath, he coughed.

"Orders," Girradehn said, with all the authority of a commander of guards, "and you will obey – arm yourself. At once, and – "

"Should I get the swords? Can you use one? I ... they cannot be far, I will – "

"Be silent – where are the swords?"

"I do not know."

"Do not – look if you can. At least do not let them get them."

"What ... do you mean?" Selvorne asked. Girradehn raised one hand as a sign to be silent, and spoke in a low voice.

"Arm yourself, now, with whatever is here – leave the cave, look for enemies outside – do not be caught. If they come ... for us, flee. You should do that well. Avoid men if they are here. If it seems ... safe, if none come, if none are here now – then return, and wake him."

Selvorne looked to Arnlausa and wondered if he would wake.

"He does not seem to wake easily, and – "

"And wake him – if you have to cut a finger off to do so – his, or yours. Go, now. Selvorne – do not be caught. Do not be caught – whatever happens. They may be here – they may be watching. If you flee to towns, take care. Go, now, remember what I said."

Selvorne at once snatched one knife, then another, and moved through the shadows of the cave looking for anything he might otherwise use. Finding nothing, he began taking strips of cooked meat until Girradehn spluttered at him to go. He went to the entrance, looked out on the growing dimness of the ravine – searching for any who might be watching from the shadows – then slipped into them himself. Heart pounding and hands shaking, he was angry, but dared not let it control him – he had none of the advantage, knew nothing of the enemy, and the best he could do was hide.

The order was wise. A retreat, to hide and observe. If men were upon them, he would need to flee, and mere moments dallying in the cave could have been his last chance. If men were upon them, if they were about to charge.

To hide and wait – if men were near, they must mean to observe, perhaps coming in the late night when those in the cave slept. Girradehn gave good orders, which should be expected from a guard. To retreat and watch, and secure the area against all foes. Return if it seemed clear – be wary, at all times. Something about a retreat ... his father spoke like that often, but in his fear Selvorne could not quite recall. A planned retreat, and a plan for the plan that failed.

Who were the foes, though, who would do such a thing – cut a bridge and leave it to fall, to take the lives of men unknown. Girradehn must have thought brigands were on the roads. As a guard, that was what he would think at once – more than robbers, they were killers, and would murder without regret, then merrily pick through the treasures a traveller might have. The thought of such men was not new to Selvorne. Fear of them was, for he had never travelled dangerous roads without dangerous men beside him – his father, Arnlausa, and Girradehn. Or the quarry men of Tawlehk town, strong and bold, they could not be easily defeated, nor their stone treasures simply taken. Selvorne thought the same of his father and Arnlausa – and Girradehn – though their things of value might be easily taken, be it coins or cart. Not easily defeated, usually, yet one was dead, one asleep, and one could not stand. And the last might have had two knives, but had little idea how to use them against a dozen brigands. Or even a few. Or one, he guessed, who would likely know far better than himself what to do with a blade. Such fear was new to Selvorne, as was the feeling he was being watched, and hunted.

~

Across the river he went once more, to hide in the shadows of the southern cliff. Away from the moon that had already risen, away from the cave entrance where the fire was glowing. Into the shadows where enemies might wait. To think, to hide and watch, and wait himself in silence. Armed with two knives, few wits, and no plan.

He had thought to take the remains of the sword – a few inches of blade, but sharp enough, and the hilt was good. It might have been some use. Girradehn kept it near, it might have been some use to him as well. Selvorne wished he had his spear, but it was planted in the dirt, high on the southern cliff. He was glad, though, that he thought to snatch some of the meat that was cooking, for he had only been waiting moments before hunger began to take hold.

Odd that he thought of it, or stranger still that he did not – think not to starve, his father had warned him, be sure to sleep when one can, to be rested and well fed, but not overly so. Wits leave a man for hunger or fatigue, and blades without wits may as well be blunt. So his father had said, and most guards agreed. Selvorne ate and it gave him strength, and he pondered his situation from the shadows.

He did not know how long to watch and wait. He did not know what to do if any men came – flee, he was told, that he could do well. Was that some insult? A jest, even at such a time. Likely it was, Girradehn was not one to praise. And yet Selvorne had not felt mocked, and did not detect malice in the voice of the man who often taunted him, on a usual day. Flee, and he should do it well. Selvorne nodded, for he could, none knew those lands better than he, and they were lands that presented trouble to any who did not know them well.

West – along the ravine, no escape. Only waterfalls and pools, smooth walls with the odd crevice leading up to thick, impassible woodlands on the north. To the south, above the side of the ravine, was the road leading west, all the way to the sea. Neither was a good place to flee, for the woods had wandering paths and hidden, dangerous bogs, and the western road, though clear – well, that was its problem. Mostly treeless and barren for days, to flee that way, a man would be seen, tracked, and caught.

East along the ravine floor – much the same, with one great waterfall that could not be climbed. The end of the ravine, with no way out other than dangerous ascents – for a fleeing man, it was an end in which to be ended.

North led to the road that would take him home – but such a road, if brigands were about, had to be their place of hiding. The climb on the north cliff was harder than the south, but not impossible, save for a beast. The bottom of the ravine wall was smooth, and required a jump to find holds that only a hand could grasp, and only a strong man could climb. Doing so led up to where the bridge should have taken them, to the road leading north, where he could run along at speed. Perhaps he could run faster than the enemy, or perhaps he would run into their waiting blades. Had he not waited ... he might have done so already that day. Had Arnlausa not woken, not commanded, not ... noticed. Perhaps. He was no fool, and though hurt and broken, his mind was clear, and with the one word he spoke, he had saved Selvorne's life.

Wait. The simplest order, and the wisest advice, when a man knew nothing of what was happening. Girradehn had scolded him – wait – it does not mean stand around – those were his words, and Selvorne knew them well, for his father and Arnlausa had said the same, many times. To wait upon the tables of noble men dining – it did not mean idly watch them as they ate, it demanded service and attention. To wait for pigs to be herded home required calls to tempt them to their pens – food, mud, a roll in the hay, a gentle stroke or tickle. To wait for love, Arnlausa had said, was not to idly sit nor stand, and not to ignore the lady, but to seem as though one did – again, to tempt them to your pens, he had joked, the desires of ladies little different to pigs. Men were also much the same, he added, if the women present were offended, and men laughed – the men, however, were often lured to the pens by women, roasting pigs.

So he said, in taunts and jests and mirth to pass the time. Selvorne waited in the shadow of the ravine, and in the boredom, felt the pain of loss. He tried to fill his mind with memories instead, of the men and what they said, unsure if it eased the pain.

Uhlsko had said the same of love, though less crudely. It had not seemed to be a deceit, where Arnlausa often spoke of romance as though it was some measure of cunning mixed with delight and delivered by trickery, charm and desire. That was not truly love, Uhlsko had said, which was most wonderful, and the greatest unknown, at first – and then the most certainly known, at last. A stranger never met – then a bond, forever set. There was no greater knowing, than that another loved one back. Years to find, moments to realise – or the reverse, or the inverse, if all was jumbled about, as was the way of love. Wait – that was the only thing a man could do – and waiting was not done idly, but carefully – watching, learning, discovering who the lady truly was, and what it meant to know her, and she you, and then from strangeness to adoration, and a certainty like no other.

So he spoke of love, for Uhlsko was, perhaps, the most devoted man Selvorne had ever met. To think of it made Selvorne's heart ache, even when it had been said – more that day, to think the man who said it was dead, left in a cave. But even then, years ago – for Uhlsko to speak of waiting, it was a taste of all he had been through. A great love, for Selvorne's mother Vorlisi – a great life, what brief time they had together – a terrible sorrow, when sickness took her from him. Then the waiting began again, though not for love in life, but to join her once more, in the Sea of the Dead. Years apart. Uhlsko had finally gone – there he was with her, perhaps, that very night, united in death. The thought of it gave Selvorne little joy, and what little it gave soon faded. He had become the one waiting – he would do so through the rest of his life. Waiting to join those he loved once more, in the Sea of the Dead. The thought of it was grim.

Dim was the light in the ravine, and with killers about, perhaps he would not wait long. Uhlsko had not only spoken of love, but waiting to learn – a man who faced the unknown must wait until something is revealed. Waiting must not be idle – cautious, cunning, hidden. Be unseen by those you cannot see – be unknown, if you are unknowing. Wait. Let others show themselves first, let them not know the face that held the blade, when grim work was needed – as a man may end a pig.

Very grim words from a man who was otherwise known to be lovely. Kind, and warm when he was not sorrowed by thoughts of his lost wife. Uhlsko was a good lord, and a good friend to the people of his small town. He was, however, once a guard, and guards did grim work at times. As did farmers of pigs, so Selvorne was not surprised by such talk, especially since he had heard such things his whole life. Only in the ravine did it begin to make sense, for he knew nothing of his enemy, and his only hope was to be as hidden as they. Neither the greatest swordsmen nor largest army could hurt a man, if they did not know where he was – and so he hid.

And hiding, he realised it was a lie – the enemy had done just that, by knowing where they might be – the road they were to use – the bridge they were to cross. The town to which he might return. The trap had been waiting, with patience beyond measure, and mercy, none at all. Not hidden truly, in their usual lives – not safe, anyway. Selvorne was hidden in the shadows of the cliff, he was certain no danger would come to him there, at least not without him seeing it first – but Selvorne was not going to live his life in a cave. Or a ravine. He would have to leave, sometime, and he did not know what was waiting for him. The thought of danger ahead disturbed him, and he watched the far ravine wall in silence.

Could it be a mistake – no, the axe marks were clear. Could it be unintended, then – he hoped it was – men had come to take down the bridge, meaning to build another. No, it could not be – it was his father's bridge, paid for by himself, and none would take it down without good reason. Even then not without permission – or at the very least leave a sign to warn others. A rope, a red cloth, a fallen tree trunk shifted to block the road. Even on the far side it would be seen, the ravine was not so wide. No such warning placed, it was not done by guiltless men. The only hope of innocence was that men had meant to do such a thing, but an animal of the woods came and chased them away – how likely that was, Selvorne guessed not at all. Such men would have been armed at least with axes, and, fleeing, would have left some sign such as a cart, or at least a bag.

And there were no such beasts – not likely. Not in the day, anyway, and never seen in the area. Talk of bears and wolves and ... ground bears, he was not even sure they were dangerous. He had never seen one. He had no doubt they might come if they could smell blood in the water, for that was the warning, but to attack a man cutting a bridge – it was nothing but a fanciful explanation. His last hope to find some innocent reason for the accident that had to have been done in malice. He could barely think that any could be so cruel ... despite the tales of such men, thieves and killers on the road. He had not believed it, and he thought it gave him almost as much despair as the loss of his father, to realise it was done for greed.

How long had he waited – he had eaten all the meat and was growing thirsty and bored. An hour? Perhaps. Or half. Initial fear had turned to cunning, and silence. And hunger, then plotting, reasoning – watching. Yawning, and at that he felt ashamed, though it was honest fatigue, and true tedium to stare into the dimness of the cliffs. Both were dangerous, his father warned – at such times enemies struck. His father said many such things, and Selvorne thought he saw the wisdom in it, but had never truly tested himself against such boredom. Waiting was the main task of the guards – waiting, and boredom, through which they must be alert. It was much harder than he had guessed, for though his grief should have shaken him to tears, and though his anger should have made him shout in rage, and though enemies might be near, wishing him dead – he was cold, thirsty, bored and restless, and the need to do something useful was filling his thoughts.

Movement at the top of the cliff – his heart pounded. A change – an enemy. No, just a creature in the woods, it was not a man. A creature come to hunt at night, though what it was he dared not think. A bear – it had to be – or some fear of his imagining. A bush in the breeze, perhaps. Too tall for a man. A bear? If so, very shy. No bears had been seen there, in those woods, but he remembered the warnings of blood in the water, and began to question the wisdom of waiting in the shadows. Men would not see him – a creature would smell him, and perhaps would wonder at the meat fresher than the ox.

He moved away from the foot of the cliff, to the edge of shadows, and waited some more. A different angle of view on the ravine, and by the moonlight he saw nothing. Not to east or west or across the way – not on the top of cliffs or on their face, scrambling down. Surely any men who set the trap knew the bridge had fallen – or perhaps they meant to return in the morning and see. He had enough of it, and decided to return to the cave – carefully, creeping, making his way through the shallows of the river, slipping from stones to wet his boots. Miserable, and shameful to be upset by such a small thing – he had his legs, both of them, and lived. On the northern side of the river he stopped, looked around once more, then made his way to the cave. No enemies were about, or if they were, they were far better than he at waiting.

~

Selvorne returned to the cave entrance with caution, listening for enemies that might have been waiting for him to do just that – once inside, there would be no fleeing, and ended there, no witness to what was done. He stopped when he heard voices, and his heart pounded to think foes might have already entered, unseen, killed his friends and were waiting his return.

"I did not want to spend this last night arguing," a muffled voice said from inside, and Selvorne bit his lip.

"And I did not want to spend the last in a cave, and – "

"Would ask – would risk – to carry – you – "

"As son of a lord – "

"The son of a lord," the first voice said, "should know better. As should a guard, who would realise what matters more."

It was then silent, and Selvorne knew the voices – Arnlausa and Girradehn – so he moved quickly into the cave.

"Where have you been?" Arnlausa asked as he looked up at Selvorne.

"Chasing shadows," Selvorne said, "there are no others here – I should run for town – or – you both seem well?"

Girradehn snorted and coughed. Arnlausa took a deep breath – he had moved, somehow, for some reason, pulling himself along the wall – a piece of meat was near him, out of reach. Selvorne picked it up, washed it and put it near the fire to warm it. The others stared at him as he did, then he examined Arnlausa's face, neck and arms, prodding and testing his strength until he was slapped away.

"Well, you are in a grim mood," Selvorne said.

"And you are rather cheerful for a man who has lost his father," Arnlausa said.

"Ask me tomorrow how cheery I am – what are you both fighting about?"

"Report," was all Arnlausa said, and Selvorne took a deep breath – he knew what he meant – to say all that mattered, and nothing more.

"None seen, outside. Sunset over an hour ago, the moon is up – I saw something move to the north, at the top of the cliff – a bear, I think, it was large enough. Not a man, I am quite sure, or if it is, he has not come down to see, and likes to walk near the edge of the cliff, stand like a bush there in the breeze, then leave."

"Very funny," Arnlausa said, then spluttered.

"I – did not mean it as a joke. You know of the cuts?"

Arnlausa nodded once, though it was more of a bow of the head, for it fell to his chest.

"Cut, to kill," Selvorne said, "and it is clear you agree on that – cheerful? I am not – angry, and – "

"Oh – stop talking," Girradehn said.

"And it shall make my grim task easier," Selvorne said, "though I have not the axe. Arnlausa, you cannot move, can you?"

"I can a little. I cannot cut – the bone is out?" Arnlausa asked. Selvorne nodded, and Arnlausa turned to Girradehn, "And you feel nothing?"

"Just an horrific pain that makes me wish to be ill," Girradehn said.

Arnlausa nodded, or half nodded, and there were a few moments of silence.

"Good. It means there is hope. Selvorne, you will obey me as though I was – "

"My lord?"

"Your father. I doubt you would obey me as a lord, or anyone, in fact, but him –
I speak for him now, and you will obey. I need to know two things – first, how far
are we from the fall – how easily would we be found in this ... it is not a cave, is
it?"

"Crevice in the rock, deeper than it seems, but narrow. A roof in parts that I
think is only soil. We are less than one hundred paces from the waggon, I think."

"Paces or yards?"

"Paces. As I said."

"That is not good. Mind what you say, time is ... how long, since ... the fall?"

"It might be five hours. It might be six?"

"I think seven," Girradehn said.

"I think not," Arnlausa said, "and you think poorly, for the pain – Selvorne, you
ate just once? Are you hungry?"

Selvorne nodded, then shook his head.

"Five or six hours, or he would hunger again. That is good. Now – "

"How is that good?" Girradehn asked.

"I have a mind to ask you, Selvorne, to bandage his mouth as well as his leg – it
must be wounded, for it makes strange sounds. Mind not to cover his nose, would
you?"

"Mind I do not bite when you try," Girradehn snarled.

"And mind you do not use his trouser leg as bandage, lest you then discover by
chance his great secret – that he is a girl. For he makes the sounds of one, yet has
such a slight wound, it must be so, a girl amongst the guards – even I was fooled.
Though, barely," Arnlausa said, then chuckled. Girradehn only bowed his head.

A joke – a taunt – that was Arnlausa, Lord of Tavalehk. Even when injured, no
matter how grim the situation might be – and Selvorne knew that it was, though
Arnlausa pretended it was not. He hardly moved, and no unwounded man could
be comfortable sitting that way against the stone. So either he was very tough and
did not care to shuffle slightly, or he felt nothing, and would not say. More grim
than jokes would suggest, and Girradehn's wound was far from slight.

Arnlausa was tough, however, and once was a guard. Tall, and perhaps not as
broad as he was in his youth. Selvorne thought him old, though his father was
older, and neither man was remarkably so. Dark hair, quite lush – still dark,
despite his age, though it was greyed at one time. Some trickery was suspected
long before dye was discovered in his house. Handsome, apart from his hooked
nose and long chin, his dark gleaming eyes, and – actually, Selvorne never
understood why he was considered handsome, but he was, and all agreed. His hair
was his best feature, and though tall, he stooped just a little – or bent low, to be
closer to others, perhaps. Charming – yes he was, in all ways. Mischief and mirth,
and well liked – apparently, not by everyone. Unless the killers wanted Girradehn
dead, or ... Selvorne's father. Likely Girradehn, he was not at all charming –
disarming was a better word, for he seemed to enjoy putting people ill at ease.

Arnlausa was tough enough to joke despite his wounds, but not tough enough to stop himself shuddering at times. Unable to do anything about it, he clenched his teeth. He was hurt, and spluttered as he laughed. Whatever good he had suggested – whatever hope he saw in the situation – likely it was not for himself. He suffered to regain his composure, and they waited on his thoughts.

"Be silent, and listen," Arnlausa commanded, "it may be that the bridge was cut to be removed. Taken down, and nothing more. Unlikely. No such order, without our consent, could be given – unless there was a war, and it was to stop an army. I doubt that – if there was, they would leave the bridge standing until the last, and it would be guarded."

He spluttered, and Selvorne nodded in silence – Arnlausa wanted to speak, and not be questioned or interrupted.

"It may have been cut – axe marks left – from when it was built, long ago. I doubt that. It fell today. It was strong before, many years, now. It fell just as ... others have. When cut ... a trick, deliberate, to take a heavy waggon. Ended by wine – how cruel by weight carried, not quantity drunk. Paid for, too – how much is lost?"

"More than wine," Selvorne said.

"True. Much more than all the wine of the world. Some left, to drink?"

Selvorne nodded, and went to bring some in a bladder, but Arnlausa waved a hand to stop him.

"Not yet. A trap – for us? Or others. No enemy to finish us – no hurry, then, to kill. Or they did not know when we would come. So, unwatched, both road and bridge. I doubt they think us dead if they watched, perhaps they are afraid. I doubt that also."

"This makes no sense, then," Selvorne said, "and why would – "

"You speak when I said be silent?"

Selvorne bit his lip.

"You are not a guard. You should be. A shame – but, untrained, and in danger, so listen. My first warning – beware any man who claims it was my order to break the bridge. Or the order of your father – it was not. Such a man means you ill, do you understand?"

Selvorne nodded.

"To break a bridge so, it is a trick of brigands – who care nothing for the cost of it. Broken, we are now easy prey for thieves. And – what?"

"Brigands?" Selvorne asked, for he had been frowning at their mention, "Still here, after being driven out of our lands?"

"Kill one, two more take their place," Girradehn said from his side of the cave.

"Sadly true, and none believe all were driven out," Arnlausa said, "but perhaps these were only thieves, after the wine."

"How?" Selvorne asked, "Half the wine is lost, and all is now at the bottom of a ravine?"

"Only half remains?"

"Well, most is lost. Barrels split and spilt."

"Ahh – the barrels, then, as I thought. Some were made cheaper, not the usual, and the better ones held. True, it is not easy, such a theft. But no danger to them, not from us – and barrels float well – down the river to the sea, then to the road there, north to Veksehl. A few at least of good value. And our gold, and anything good we owned. All evidence also washed to the sea. Not a bad trick, actually, to rob in such a way."

"It would be better to have attacked us and taken the waggon back west," Selvorne said, "all of it – easily done."

"Unless it was just two men, who feared us – Selvorne, think. One desperate man, one man alone, with an axe and no heart – he could break the bridge, then take all our goods. Why are they not here – they wait, likely near. Few men, afraid, cautious, not knowing if the four in the cave are dead, or having a feast. They may be just outside, listening."

Selvorne jumped up, and Arnlausa chuckled, amused despite spluttering.

"You jest?" Selvorne asked.

"I find jest in your eagerness to run out and fight. Who? Where? What – with knives? Do you even know how?"

Selvorne had some idea of how – at least to kill. A pig. Or a man, though ... not one he could not see. Perhaps it was not a bear he saw atop the cliff.

"The life of a brigand is not an easy one," Arnlausa said, "nor one to to admire, or envy. Most of the time, it is wealth and opulence, from that which was stolen, taken from those who must work."

"Like a lord," Girradehn said.

"Very unlike a lord," Arnlausa said, "and yet – yes, in a way. Both lord and brigand fear – both are in danger. One from the other, perhaps. The brigand can disappear into a town and seem as any man, and live an ordinary life. The lord is known wherever he goes – there is no hiding, wherever he goes, danger is always. The brigand, desperate at times, does things ... most cruel. Theft, when needed – murder as well. He cannot hide from that, he may not be able to hide that. Such men are rare, even in the past, not so many as you might think. It has not been – for a long time, no groups of them, but when there were, they were not together, usually only a dozen at a time, in the woods. Hunting. Planning to steal. On the roads – it seems they are back."

"We must go," Selvorne said, and Arnlausa nodded.

"Not yet. Listen first – to rob us, a waggon, how would you? You could – no, be quiet, that was not a question. Listen. When do we pass? It is known we would come from the south, everyone knows it, we go each year – but never do they know the day of our return. Even we can only guess when that might be. So, a trap, which waits forever – one we could not expect, and it would stop us. They would check – my guess is, each morning – one day, find our things and send them west. Very easy, and no danger to themselves. A clever plan."

"Unless he checked the bridge for weakness or traps," Girradehn called out, coughing, and Selvorne's heart sank.

"If I had, then – "

"You could have done," Arnlausa said, but to Girradehn, "so be quiet. Yes, had we checked – what then? Suspicion to find it cut, and likely we would go by way of the lake, but ... I fear an ambush prepared there, or at some other place. Or we would have checked, and not noticed the cuts. These were the beams from the middle, yes?"

"They could be the ends," Selvorne said.

"I doubt it. The middle, unseen by any usual check, and only a heavy waggon, as was ... ours. I have no doubt it was intended, now only can guess at what they have done besides – boredom. Their great enemy. Perhaps a man watched and waited for us, but I doubt it. A check each day or other, few come this way, it is a clever theft. It may be they last checked this morning, or a week ago, or at lunch. It may be a week until they come, or a day, or this night – likely not at night, it is too dangerous walking along the cliff tops, even by the moon."

Arnlausa seemed pained, and clenched his teeth, then spluttered. Selvorne offered him water, wine and food, and he took only water, then coughed it up. Girradehn also seemed in pain, so Selvorne took the wine to him, and the meat, but he only drank, then looked up at Selvorne.

"They also might mean to kill us," Girradehn said.

"You speak now?" Arnlausa asked, "Is that your wish?"

"None of this is my wish – can you continue?"

"Yes."

"Then hurry."

"Always in a hurry, always ... Selvorne, yes, they might not mean to rob us at all. Despite the river headed west, allowing them to float barrels away, all this – in the ravine – it is not very convenient. Half the wine is lost to the river. That is my fear – not theft, but our deaths is what they wanted. Two lords, and a guard not well loved, by some."

"By few," Girradehn said.

"It only takes one. Your enemy – our death," Arnlausa said, and Girradehn winced in pain.

"And how likely is that?" Selvorne asked.

"Not very. None hate him enough to kill. For us, though, your father, he was – "

"Loved well by all," Selvorne said, and Girradehn coughed.

"Not all," Arnlausa said, "by me, though. And many. Not all – and it takes just one. Yes, your father – or me – or even Girradehn. One enemy afraid – murderous, ruthless. It may be your father they wanted, and, seeing him dead – they left. Or me, thought to be dead, and they are gone. Or perhaps they thought wounds were enough, for revenge, or as a warning – I do not know – what I fear, though, is that they are waiting, and plan to come and finish us. A rock to our heads would look like it happened in the fall – no lords would come in anger to avenge us, no guards would be sent by those who loved us.”

“Except that I would – oh,” Selvorne said, stopping himself as Arnlausa tried to nod. He had meant, of course, that the killers would kill them all, leave no witness, arranging things so it would seem an accident to any who found them.

“Perhaps wrong,” Arnlausa said, “but if right – and if you have been seen – you are dead. We all are, and you must keep this in mind for what I am to ask you to do. Go unseen, to the guards of Tavalehk, and you must – ”

“No,” Girradehn said, and Arnlausa tried to take a deep breath, and continued.

“He is right. Go unseen, to Senylehk, then, to Tarbo, and – ”

“Father,” Girradehn said, then coughed, and Selvorne frowned.

“Ugh – he is right,” Arnlausa said, “your father, Selvorne ... complicates things. Even Tarbo is ... a problem. Selvorne – you must find Cienn, and no others – you understand?”

Selvorne nodded. Cienn Reganai Doethmoud – Lady Cienn. Leader of the Waehdric, perhaps the most powerful woman in the land. Very old, and rarely seen. More than a few wondered if she still lived. To send him to her, Arnlausa's fear must have been great – or for all others he had a terrible lack of trust. Finding her was not an easy task, to be granted an audience, or even to send word, for she had taken leave of duties years ago. Difficult to find, dangerous to be seen – Arnlausa had to have very grave fears for who had wanted them dead.

“Do not go yet,” Arnlausa said, “listen. Unseen, to Cienn. Not fast, if there is danger – not in haste. Now we must leave this ... crevice. Listen very carefully, these are the orders of a lord – find a better cave, farther down the river, and – ”

“Done,” Selvorne said, “I know one.”

“Far?”

“Far enough for what?”

“Far down the river, a cave – a good one, where we may go. Carry us all there, where we may not be found. All our things here of use – take. Leave signs we were here – let the fire burn low, with little wood. Signs we came, ate – laughed, drank to our good fortune that we were not harmed. Three merry men, glad to be alive, but angry at the loss, and dangerous to confront. Once here, then disappeared. No sign of where we went – so when the others come, they will ... you know what.”

“Think we left.”

“Yes. And we will have done, but wounded, and only as far as the cave. We will need fire there, not large, not seen – you must find the seals of mine, parchments and all such things of importance. No others must find them. I would never leave them, leaving them will let them know something is wrong. All swords, all spears – where is your spear?”

Selvorne bit his lip – he had left it at the top of the cliff, he did not bring it down, thinking he would not find fish in the river, being unable to climb with it, and in such a hurry – he told Arnlausa it was stuck in the ground at the top of the cliff, beside the broken bridge, and to his astonishment, Arnlausa began to chuckle.

"That is ... most amusing. Leave it there. That is an order. It will serve you better there than here. Swords, though – do not leave anything we would not. Whoever did this, and for whatever reason, when they come they will not know anything but fear."

"Unless they find us in the cave," Selvorne said.

"And then they shall find death," Arnlausa said – very grim, as though he meant to kill them all, and Selvorne had no doubt he would, if he was well. The thought of it made him glad. Sad, as well, for the brigands truly would find death. Selvorne turned to the place where his poor father sat, cold against the stone.

~

There was no time for sorrow, so Selvorne left at once to prepare. It was not easy finding the cave in the growing dark, though he knew where it was well enough. Selvorne hoped it would be just as difficult in the day – impossible to those who did not play in the ravine as a child. It should be, he thought, for the entrance was raised a little from the pebbled riverside, and bent at once, so only from the west did it seem an entrance at all. There were other caves, not so deep, and though he was glad for the quarter moon's light, he did not enjoy the many trips back and forth, through the cold water to his knees, carrying one man after the other who could not walk. He was glad the water was not deep, until he realised that if it had been, two at least might only have been made wet from the fall.

Arnlausa was heaviest, and unable to walk. Selvorne was strong from working at the quarry – used to walking on uneven rocks, his boots were tough, and he was determined not to drop a man who he loved almost as much as his father. Every step was a danger unseen – rocks below that could twist an ankle, enemies above, watching, perhaps, and it was all he could do to make his way carefully, burdened by the heavy man over his shoulder. His strain was nothing compared to the agony his friend was hiding, and when he took him to the cave, Arnlausa had fallen back into a sleep.

Girradehn could help a little, with a stick to lean on and his arm around Selvorne, he made a brave effort to walk, but could not – not alone. He yelped at the cold water, then laughed – at least he felt that – and Selvorne had to carry him for fear of getting his bandages wet. In the cave he immediately felt cold, so the next trip was to bring wood and burning sticks – not what Arnlausa would have recommended, but Selvorne reasoned that if anyone was watching they would have already seen him half a dozen times, flaming torches or not.

A fire was burning well in the new cave, and he left for the worst – his father. Dead and unable to help, but not as heavy as Arnlausa, carrying him broke his heart, not his back. Over his shoulder, as he knew he was carried as a child, laughing – swung and tumbled, tickled and chased. His mother had carried him also, she who was fine, but strong. Merciless when heaving him about. The two of them tortured the child with laughter and unstoppable fingers to his ribs. Often, and always. Until the bog sickness came, and took her away.

Vorlisi – Lady Vorlisi, being wed to a lord. Beautiful, and not only from his fathers account of her face. Not only from the memory of a child, who would think any mother wonderful to see, despite her awkward smile that he since learnt was astonished love. She had a severe frown, which he discovered was the same as his own, and made in jest, teasing, and delight. Beautiful, by all accounts of those who knew her, and by solemn assurances of Arnlausa, who explained it was her who gave Selvorne his face, thankfully, not his father. It was one of Arnlausa's few taunts of his father that he never made when Uhlsko could hear – indeed, no one mentioned Vorlisi before his father, for it always made him sad. The sickness took not only her life, but much of his joy, and left a hidden sorrow behind his smile, which remained always, until ... that day.

Such sorrow was with Selvorne also, but not the same. He was very young when his mother was taken, and it could not have been helped. Sickness was a foe difficult to fight. Only care could prevent such illness – and not only the weak had died from it. There was no way to do battle with it, no means of vengeance, against an unseen vapour from the bogs. The bogs themselves were to the north, a mile or so, in the woods above the ravine. Drain them, other bogs might form. Cover them in weeds, plants would sicken also and die, and perhaps the illness would be worse. What year it might come, or from where, none knew, and anger could do nothing more than sorrow or despair, against illness.

Against murder, anger could do more. A bridge cut to fall, the axeman could be found. The thief, killer, fool – whoever did it, for whatever reason. Murder, or stupidity. Selvorne took care as he crossed the river – not to fall, in fear of hurting himself, but also for his father's last dignity in death. On the other side of the water he took care to dry his legs, to not get ill. Care, also, he took – not to be found – care as though to avoid all sickness, discovery, delay, injury or death – care as he sought to bring that vengeance to the killers. For both parents, he would be doubly cruel. And for himself he would not be merciful when the chance was before him – until then, he would take the greatest care.

To the depths of the cave he took his dead father, leaving him by the firelight – all three there seemed to be asleep. Outside to the ravine he went – to the wreck, to find anything of value that no unharmed man would leave. Nothing was of much consequence, it was the seals more than anything that must not be left. Those of Tavalehk, those of Vaskatohr – those of Arnlausa, those of Uhlsko. Pressed to wax, such seals could grant favours, land, finalise arrangements or issue commands, for either town. A reason to kill, perhaps. But also, a reason to wait for the kill, and then to quickly find them. Nothing else mattered amongst the wreckage. He found a good sack and returned to the first cave.

There were the seals, in their magnificent box. He shoved it in the sack as though it were a loaf of bread, and though they were the authority of two towns, he almost wished he had bread instead – then shook his head at a strange, half remembered meaning, known only to lords, and not quite understood. Loafing lords – perhaps it was only a joke.

No matter, he was to weave a deceit amongst the stones. A tedious task, for he was cold and wet, but with some delight he left the smaller cave with a dying fire, and no sign he could see by a torch that the men were more than a little inconvenienced from the fall. Blood was washed away by wine – merry men, spilling more and caring less for lost profits than their own great luck in being alive. Such a scene would frighten killers to think that two lords and a guard yet lived, made light of the accident – yet likely would seek revenge, to learn it was intended. Selvorne made sure the wood that had been cut by axe was removed with all other things – a broken sword, the bladders and pots, pans, bandages – all in sacks to be carried away. Killers would enter that crevice cave and find fear, and Selvorne grinned as he left, making his way one last time over the cold river to stand before the larger cave, its narrow mouth hidden in the shadows of its stone.

Moon lit the ravine. No rain, a clear sky. The sound of water over rocks, nothing more. A strange world he stood in – a world between lives, for above, his town, and below, far to the west – the sea. The Waehter people believed that was where the dead would go – the spirits of men, like rain, fell to the land. They flowed – their lives, like rivers to the sea. By many ways and turns unexpected, sometimes unchosen, but always to the sea, where all things ended. The Sea of the Dead. Such were their teachings. Not all thought it true, and Selvorne rarely gave it much thought, but standing there he could not help notice where he was.

A river, headed to the sea. Above, to the south – where he had been. Ahead, climbing up, to the north – where he was to go. But the ravine was between what was and what would be, and the river there led only to death. He was between worlds, as they said, in that place of choosing paths, to go one way or another. A barrel floated past – it had been trapped against rocks, yet somehow was suddenly freed. It tumbled and bobbed on the waters, low in the waves, it had to be heavy still. Lost, then, to the river and then the sea – a waste of a barrel, still full of wine. Filled with joy that never would be had, not by those who would have shared it, in festivities. He watched it leave, and wondered at its fate, then breathed in deeply and considered his own.

Some found comfort in such thoughts – the Sea of the Dead. Where all loves lost would wait, to meet again. Others did not believe it to be true, thinking it only a tale spoken to make men wise. To help men make better choices – to keep part of their mind, at least, on what was before them, and not merely on what was around them.

Selvorne was not sure he believed it as truth, but he felt some comfort in it, regardless. The moon on the water of the river was beautiful – the sea would be magnificent. He had seen it so, mere days before. To think his mother waited there, with her half smile and mocking frown, her bright eyes and warm embrace – waiting for his father, returned to her at last. It gave him some joy.

Some hope for what was otherwise a broken body of a man, sat in a cave against his will, devoid of life and joy and warmth. Return to her, in love. Return to Selvorne, in hate, and join him in vengeance upon those who had brought death and wasted wine – no, Selvorne did not believe that much. The dead did not return. It was a pleasant thought, mixed with a grim fury. He knew the loveliness of it was mere fancy, but the anger he knew was real – his own – and would be with him, should the spirit of his father return from the dead or not. Quiet, like the moon on the ripples of the river – silent and unseen. Vengeance had a beauty of its own. With that thought, and a final glance at the ravine for foes, he turned to the cave and entered the darkness.

No More Remains

Darkness at the bending entrance to the cave – shadows on dull rock, the way turning, lightening, then glowing from the fire. Burning low, it warmed the cave, but the mood could only be grim. As best he could, Selvorne made the others comfortable for the night, and assessed their place of hiding. The smoke might be seen in the morning, if it drifted outside, so he had water to douse the embers before the sun rose. The smell of fire should frighten beasts, and hopefully draw no enemies near. They were otherwise hidden, and he hoped safe. At dawn he would certainly be awake, he was not sure he could sleep – at first, but then exhaustion took him. The long journey of the day, the lifting of the men, and the sorrow of it all made him fade to sleep, and then, in dreams, the same memories shocked him to wake.

"Are you to judge?" came a voice from beside the fire, and Selvorne shook his head clear of sleep – Arnlausa, stirring, so Selvorne rose and examined his friend. Half asleep – half alive, and half a man who could not properly move. He did his best to seat him well, and all the while Arnlausa stared at him with wide eyes.

"Are you ... the judge?" Arnlausa asked.

"Of the dead? No," Selvorne said, "only of how well you sit. Is there pain?"

"No," Arnlausa said, then lowered his head, "I thought ... that was why."

Selvorne frowned, then bit his lip when he realised what was meant – he thought he had joined the unfeeling dead – so he patted the shoulder of his old friend.

"I did not think you believed such things?"

"And now am so close, I wonder if I was wrong."

Selvorne nodded, but then frowned and shook his head.

"And yet were certain it was nonsense," he said, hoping to ease Arnlausa's worry, "and, I think, you said that if a man believed that, he may as well believe in witches, enchantments, and giant men."

Arnlausa gave a strange half smile, then nodded. He coughed, and it became a chuckle, and Selvorne thought he might fall to sleep before he spoke again.

"Not quite what was said," Arnlausa said at last.

"Witches with enchantments to make men large," Selvorne corrected.

"Was said – not meant. No matter. The Judge of the Dead – last guard of the Sea. Teachings of old, and the fancy of a dying man – such men near death are, by the living, considered wise. All hear the dying words, they must be true, what has he to hide, what wonders has he seen, on the other side."

"Have you seen any?" Selvorne asked, more than a little curious at what might have made Arnlausa so solemn, other than his terrible wounds.

"In life, yes. After – who knows. I think ... away, at least, one part of the Sea for me, one for women who never forgive, if they are judged at the very last. Some rest, then, for me. Witches – wives. Women, locked in war. Women ... "

Selvorne was not sure what was wrong with his friend as he drifted back to sleep. Tired, confused, dazed by his wounds, whatever they were – he was quite sure Arnlausa could not move his legs even a little, for they were heavy and swollen. Selvorne dared not examine them, but could not help stare for some time, for he could not sleep, and he wondered if Arnlausa might ever wake again.

~

He did wake, after a while, stirring as though from a nap, yawning – spluttering – remembering. Selvorne moved to tend him, but Arnlausa waved him away.

"I am quite fine," Arnlausa said.

"Never better."

"Than you?"

Selvorne smiled – a game his father played, which he had no desire to play, so he only nodded, but Arnlausa looked pained.

"Please? Than you – "

"May find," Selvorne continued, reluctant, but ... it seemed to cheer Arnlausa.

"So gloat."

"You goat."

"You ewe's."

"Behind."

"A ram to bite you back you find," Arnlausa said, then chuckled until he spluttered, and Selvorne could think of nothing to do but offer water.

"Do not let it die," Arnlausa said.

"You – it does not go like that – I do not – the poem?"

"Yes."

"I – do not even know what it means," Selvorne said, which was true, his father and Arnlausa had said it to each other for longer than he had lived, and it made no sense at all.

"Nothing, it means nothing. Remember it."

"I am not sure I could ... forget ... oh, Arnlausa?" Selvorne asked. He began to breathe heavily as Arnlausa looked at him, nodding once, "How long?"

"Not the night."

"And you ... have known how long?"

"When I woke and tried to move. I am broken, I am ended. Selvorne – you must promise me this, and it is an order, an oath, and – everything now is the most serious swearing. Do you understand?"

Selvorne nodded.

"When I die – and your father, also – you must seal us in barrels and hide us, perhaps here, I do not know ... how well hidden we are – you must not leave our bodies by the river, and we must not be found."

"I will take you back to the town, and – "

"How is that obeying? Do not make your own plans – barrels, here, sealed. Hidden. Not to town, not to ... just obey, will you, for once?"

Selvorne bit his lip – the law, not to leave bodies by the river. But more than that, or fear of bears – not to leave bodies for enemies to find, for then they might ... he did not know what they might do.

"You know why?" Arnlausa asked.

"Yes – but – do you fear bears? Wolves? Are we ... safe here?"

"We are ... as safe as can be, with men searching, meaning to kill us all."

"Do you think – "

"Yes."

"And if not, bears?"

"Fear fire. But love caves. But no bear is here, and I think the chance of one looking for a home tonight are low – and the ox is still in the river?"

Selvorne nodded.

"It cannot be helped. It will be gone soon enough – if any men come, and ... you kill them, the same – put all dead in barrels and seal them. Be there wine or not, be certain they are sealed, and – "

"What? Why?"

"You know the law."

"But there are no towns to the west along the river, and – the enemy? Also in barrels? As well?"

"All the dead, leave none. If you – but you should not fight. You must flee, carefully. Swear you will put all dead in barrels, sealed and hidden?"

Selvorne nodded, but Arnlausa made him say it, and then he sighed.

"Your mother played as well," Arnlausa said.

"I know, but – what?"

"The game – the goat's behind."

"I thought it was sheep?"

"Goat, sheep, cows – it goes on a while. Very dull, being a guard, sometimes. I must ... tell you something of her," Arnlausa said, and then was quiet.

"Well?"

"The shirt ... your father is wearing. She made it – he always ... you know he always wears it when travelling away?"

"Yes. It needs repairs – again."

"He meant to die in it, he meant to be buried in it – with her. See to it."

"Oh – I ... will. Anything else?"

"So many things, I cannot start to ... time, Selvorne. It is going."

Selvorne knelt beside Arnlausa and put a hand to his shoulder.

"Not yet – soon. Soon, to sea – all to sea," Arnlausa said, and then, coughing a little and trying to take a deep breath, he spoke.

"Have no grief for the father gone,
dead to Sea, all shall we.
I follow soon, sons follow me,
and after them, sons not born,
friends unmet, lives unwet,
so the Waehdric wise do warn."

He coughed again, but seemed pleased.

"The Waehdric are grim," Selvorne said.

"No – wise. And foolish. They are not grim, nor their songs – do you feel grim?"

"No. Angry."

"No, you are not. And not fear, and not ... you are unaware, as am I – so, cautious, careful. Pained, though – we are not as other men."

"What? Do – oh," Selvorne said.

"Guards."

"I am not."

"Son of a lord – you are, in a way, and not as other men. Not from birth, not by blood – by what you have lived with – you are not in the back of the cave there, weeping with your ... though I also ... would weep for my lost friend."

Selvorne nodded, and Arnlausa tried to take his hand, but could not lift his own, so Selvorne held it – and to his surprise, felt his own almost crushed by Arnlausa's grip.

"Ha! Some strength left in me – cheer, my friend, I at least shall join him soon. I will tell him how brave you were, and that you live, and I hope there are women there, in the Sea of the Dead, and also ... they have never met me, or remember me fondly, or have had a long time to forgive me any quarrel we might have had."

"You are a brave man, Arnlausa."

"Indeed, to face the scorn of three dozen dead women, I hope the Waehdric are wrong on this, for – "

Selvorne put a finger to Arnlausa's lips to silence him, and shook his head.

"Even now you joke?" Selvorne asked.

"What better time, indeed – what time. Alas, I do not joke, and fear what I might face there – such is life, and such is death. And such is the duty of a lord that only ends in death – I command you, now, and you obey. Tell me what you plan to do."

"I will ... all the dead in barrels, as early as I may, being sure to be unseen. I might search in the moonlight for barrels to fit, but ... the moon is close to setting. I will – "

"Not tonight – what do you plan to do when you ... are away? Join the guards?"

"What?"

"Do you mean to join the guards?"

Selvorne frowned – join the guards? Why would he – but then he realised, perhaps that would be best, in such a situation. He had not given any thought to what he might do, he had no chance to think of anything other than danger, vengeance, and grief. What he might do in weeks to come was not at all important compared to what he had to do that night.

"No," Selvorne said.

"Well, what do you want to do?"

"Sleep. Rise. Go to the lake with spear and fish, have an early lunch of it. Home, to wash and change. Then head to the Festival of Tavalehk for several days, and have a wonderful time."

Arnlausa almost shook his head, and blinked many times.

"A joke?"

"No – that is what I want to do. Attend the festival – with you, and father, and ... him. As we always do, and now – never again. To hear you mock your townsfolk and make them laugh, to see a play, or tumblers, or hear a song, and ... that is what I want. That is all I want, and that is all now gone. I shall go, regardless, and see who is there."

"Cassini?" Arnlausa asked, and Selvorne screwed up his face.

"What?"

"Cassini Cassub, you ... do you still like her?"

"What has that got – no. I meant whoever did this," Selvorne said in a low voice, almost a whisper, waving his hand at the three men fallen.

"I am quite sure they cannot hear us, if here – forget that. Think past it – Cassini? Something felt for her, still?"

Selvorne could not believe it, but – yes, he could. Arnlausa, to the last, teasing and taunting Selvorne over a young man's fancy. A young boy, if he remembered correctly how she called him, and Arnlausa said he was – no, said Selvorne was a fine man, truly ready for romance. Arnlausa's mocking confidence for Selvorne who was, in truth, merely a young boy at the time – when he had felt such adoration, for a young woman who was old enough to laugh, instead of take offence. Selvorne bit his lip, and Arnlausa rumbled as he chuckled.

"Teasing – are you ever going ... to ... " Selvorne said, almost without thinking, and Arnlausa raised an eyebrow.

"What? Stop? Soon, I think."

"I ... did not ... "

"Mean it? Yes you did. You speak before thinking, sometimes. Thankfully you do not speak fast, who could guess what you might say if you did – and Selvorne, I do not tease. Not now. Cassini is a fine woman, I do believe you were fond of her? You are older, has it been one or two years?"

"Yes."

"Yes – two years – or yes, an interest?"

"Yes, I am astonished you would either remember or care, and no, I ... do not know. I have not seen her in two years since ... then."

"She has a hearty laugh."

"I prefer not at me."

"A fine woman – handsome, too."

"And the only woman you have ever called handsome, instead of delightful, magnificent, adorable, or delicious."

"I meant you, you idiot – no matter. Women like stupid men. And a handsome man – I should know," Arnlausa said, then, though wounded, he tried to raise his chin to the side, to pose most strikingly, and Selvorne almost chuckled.

"You should know, should you?" Selvorne asked, "Last I heard, you were unwed – unless you have charmed some lady of the south?"

Arnlausa shrugged, then coughed as he laughed.

"Yes, a few years yet, for you," Arnlausa said, and he seemed to grow quite solemn.

"If you are so fond of her, you should have wed her yourself," Selvorne suggested, almost as a tease to cheer his friend, but Arnlausa seemed suddenly thoughtful, and nodded.

"Believe me, I have tried. None are good enough," Arnlausa said, more solemn and thoughtful than before, despite Selvorne's attempts at jest.

"And you are now grim – even speaking of her, even teasing me, and – not for your wounds – why?"

"She is a fine woman, Selvorne, and ... your wedding would have been grand, at my expense."

"You have been thinking of ... my wedding? To her?"

"Or any ... lady. Just the celebration, you understand – it would be – yes. Grand. Soon, I guess. A few years. Some thought. Always ahead, you must ... think of the future. Not only of ... revenge. Cassini is a fine woman, a man should be proud of her, and ... were you to – be kind to her, and noble."

"Do you think I would be otherwise? To anyone?"

Arnlausa nodded, and though Selvorne thought he was teasing still, he could tell by the eyes of his good friend he was not, as just for a moment he narrowed them, but nodded once more, and seemed relieved. There was silence between them, and Selvorne began to fear his friend might fall back to sleep – to sleep, and never wake, so he spoke.

"That was what I wanted, wished – all now has changed."

"No – now, all will change," Arnlausa said in a low voice.

"I will, tomorrow, return to the town by ways no man could know, other than me, and bring men – many, to lift you on a sheet," Selvorne said.

"A sheet? Please, you could at least think to bring a cart."

"I meant to get you out of the ravine."

"Oh ... I forgot we were here."

Selvorne bit his lip – to forget such a thing, it was a bad sign – but Arnlausa shook his head, and continued.

"I mean – well, I did not walk down here. It seems as though we are still on the road."

"In a cave?"

Arnlausa said nothing.

"Two carts for you both, far apart so you do not have to hear him complain," Selvorne suggested as he jerked his head towards Girradehn.

"I doubt I would. I doubt he will."

"Well, if he does, it will be far from your bothered ears. Back to Tavalehk, and then – who will take over your town when you are ill?"

"Some fool, of that I have no doubt."

"Oh – well, until you recover, then."

"Until I recover," Arnlausa said, quite slowly, "but should I not – if we all die, other than my orders before – to find Cienn – you should go to the festival. Will you promise that?"

Selvorne winced – it was not pleasant to think of it, no matter how good the festival was, nor how eager he had been to go.

"You will go – that is an order," Arnlausa said.

"A strange one, then."

"Is it? You will obey regardless, or I shall swim back from the Sea and follow you as a Spirit of the Dead."

"I will go if you command it, though my mood will be grim – and if you can swim back from the dead, bring father, and then as a spirit you can both fight by my side, and I shall be feared by all who defy, threaten me or attack – you will be needed when I find whoever did this."

Arnlausa did not chuckle or laugh, or splutter, but nodded once. He stared at Selvorne in silence, then shook his head as if waking from a dream.

"What – is it?" Selvorne asked.

"Nothing."

"Pain?"

"Of a sort – you remind me of someone."

"Someone handsome, I hope."

"And there, again – thought so by some, yes."

"My father?"

"Ahh – yes, always. And your mother, at times. But I meant – you remind me of me."

Selvorne frowned, and Arnlausa laughed – then frowned as well. Selvorne bit his lip, and Arnlausa chuckled at it.

"That is a most cruel thing to say, even without the injuries to your face," Selvorne said.

"Indeed. Had I yours instead, a thousand women would be mourning this summer, this fall, this winter and spring. Your frown is mine, your biting lip is that of your mother, though I doubt you remember."

"I do remember her face – you had better not tell me now that – "

"No," Arnlausa said, "only that you have my nerve, boldness, cheek – and not your father's gloom."

"And now have a reason for it, as did he."

"And that is what I warn you of, I see no sign of it, yet – mourn him and live in sorrow, he would not be pleased. It is one thing to mourn a wife beloved, quite another to throw a life to sorrow over a father. I know none who would wish it – would you, for your son?"

Selvorne bit his lip – Arnlausa nodded once. Selvorne had no son, of course, and so he had not thought of it like that – he had not the time to think on his grief at all, not that day. To lose his father was reason to mourn. His mother, lost, was painful – but he was then very young. His father never completely recovered, but was not always in grief. Some sorrow was always there, but not always. Selvorne felt anger more, and the danger of the day had not yet passed.

"Good – you see it," Arnlausa said, "your whole life ahead of you – which might be just one day. You live – he realised that as we fell, I am sure of it. A great relief, a joy. Victory, a final defeat of enemies, through luck alone, his son survived. If you die – your sons, not yet born, die with you. All that could have been will be lost. You must live, and listen to me well."

"I am listening."

"Tell me your plans – for life. Now, after this, or before ... you never properly said – tell me now, without jest."

Selvorne told of the plans he had from before that day, for he had no time to make any new. The town of Vaskatohr was very small, it could grow, doubling the men at the mine, and the efforts, it still had years of copper left for profit. Perhaps two lifetimes, it was hard to tell with mines, but provisions had to be made for those born to an empty hole in the ground. Water was plentiful and fresh from the spring, and some houses might be built near the lake, which was not far from the town, to fish and cut wood. Pigs could be farmed by the lake as well as in the town, and there they would be less effort to tend, for they could not escape from the woods at the foot of the mountains, not unless they learnt to climb sheer rock. A natural pig pen, wooded and rich, and the pigs of the town would outnumber people. All surplus to Tavalehk town markets, by a waggon of pigs, not herding, to keep them fat and prevent them wandering along the roads – or escaping, as they tended to do at times. Perhaps goats on the side of the mountain, also, for milk and hair. It was a good plan for a town of a few dozen people – perhaps Vaskatohr would triple in size, and double in wealth. For each person, that was, all who lived there would be pleased with such a plan.

"Are you ambitious? To grow the town?" Arnlausa asked.

"No – but there is opportunity to do so, and I am sure some would be willing to cut wood. Great woodlands near – is not Tavalehk running low on forests?"

"Some ... problems. How to get trees there, then? From your town to mine?"

"I would not send trees, only what is made of them – cut, dry, and shape things at Vaskatohr, and a family or two who make furnishings could send them to be sold at the festival."

Arnlausa spluttered and Selvorne thought he choked, but he was laughing.

"You think that is stupid?" Selvorne asked.

"I think the limit of your ambition is delightful."

"And you mock me for it," Selvorne said, quite annoyed – it was not his fault the town was small, and it would be a very good life for any who wanted to join his ... limited ambitions.

"No," Arnlausa said, "I praise you. More highly than you realise."

Another jest, and – no, he meant it. For once he meant it and did not joke, despite ... the chance to do so. Arnlausa could be blunt, and might say a truth that hurt, where others might be shy – say it harsh, tease it in jest, but say it, he would. Selvorne was quite sure he never lied, or if he did – as a jest – it was a deceit that contained a greater truth. He certainly was unafraid to speak his mind, and to hear such praise – Selvorne felt great sorrow, and pride, and was more than a little confused.

"Who is heir to Vaskatohr? Lordship of the town, and all that is owned by the lord?" Arnlausa asked rather suddenly, and Selvorne bit his lip.

"You are," Selvorne replied, then frowned, "but ... now?"

"Still it is me, I am not dead yet – I was not sure you knew. Who is heir to Tavalehk?"

"Oh, Arnlausa ... "

"Well? Who? I have not got all night."

"Father told me – it is he," Selvorne said, then lowered his head.

"And did you tell others?"

"Never. I would not, he – "

"Told you not to? You just told me."

"And you did not know?"

"Of course I did – who, then, is my heir? After your father? Now he is gone?"

Selvorne shook his head – he did not know, and as far as he knew, no one did – and nobody knew Uhlsko was the first heir, either. Such things were often assumed as obvious, sometimes wrongly, and rarely known for certain, even by the heir himself.

"Unknown," Arnlausa said, "and for good reason. But ... unexpected, this – both at once. Unexpected, but not unplanned for, with much effort for us both – it is far better that only one of us died first. Do you think yourself heir to Vaskatohr?"

"I – what? You are, I have already said?"

"After me – who is heir to Vaskatohr?"

Selvorne frowned, then shrugged.

"You?" Arnlausa asked.

"Am I?"

"I was," Arnlausa said, "I, alone. Not you. Each of us heir to the other town. His town to me, mine to him – were one to die. As I said, much effort to ... arrange. You would not believe how much of a battle it is to get anything done with the foolish record keepers, or Waehdric. Anything simple, let alone complicated."

Selvorne nodded and Arnlausa watched him carefully.

"You are not disappointed? Yet ... you do not seem confused?" Arnlausa asked.

"Do I look confused?"

"No, you look more grim than me."

"With a mirror you might not think that," Selvorne said, "to not be heir – no, how can I be disappointed by something I knew before? Each heir to the other, one lord of two towns, once ... when the time came. Vaskatohr is hardly a town, though, it should be part of Tavalehk."

"It has its own river and stream and spring – no, it should be more than a town. More than Tavalehk. Several towns, perhaps. What were your plans, if not to be lord? You just told me you meant to expand the town?"

"With my father's guidance, with him as lord – or yourself," Selvorne said, and Arnlausa nodded, but then frowned.

"And with us both gone? If others took both towns? What, then, were your plans?"

Selvorne shrugged, then shook his head – he had no such plans, and did not care for such talk, and could think of nothing to say. Arnlausa nodded his head at the silence of his response, and seemed oddly pleased.

"I owe Uhlsko my life," Arnlausa said.

"I know. Many times. As do I, you realise, and – "

"Selvorne – quiet. No, you do not – you have no great friend of your own, and are young. You are only his son – he, and I, were as one. Many times saved, from many dangers. Though we do not ... did not see each other so often, of late. To lose him is to me as to lose a wife, almost, a son, not quite – but more than a father, though a father is dear."

Selvorne clenched his jaw – it took him some time to determine the meaning, but when it was clear, he was not sure if he was angry or hurt. Arnlausa was saying that for him, the loss of Uhlsko was greater than it was for Selvorne.

"And there I see you do not agree," Arnlausa said, "your face is easy to read – good, for now, bad, for later. My loss is the greater – he was my closest friend. But ... if my pain to see my friend dead is greater than yours, it does not make yours any less than terrible."

"He was my father."

"And I also lost a father, Selvorne, and then it was an old man who had lived well – and I remember how his good friends mourned. Were you dead this day, we both would weep – either of us would change places with you. He, or I, would prefer to die – father or friend, to save a son. A hard choice we would make – some joy to think you live, but grief, to lose a friend. In time you will know my pain – for lost friends of your own."

Selvorne breathed in slowly – he was losing a friend. His father was also a friend, and father. Great loss, but Arnlausa was right, Uhlsko would rather he die, than Selvorne, and though he wished his father lived, he was not sure, if given a choice, he would die in his place. Uhlsko would not want it, Selvorne would not do it – for his own son, if he had one, he would. Or wife, he imagined – but no great friend he could think of, other than the man before him, who was old, had lived, and was lost. And would never wish for Selvorne to die in his place. It was not shame Selvorne felt, but the weight of his grief, his fear, and their wishes. He bowed his head, but when he raised it again, Arnlausa was shaking his.

"You, however – do not weep," Arnlausa said.

"Nor do you. Yet claim you hurt more than I."

"But why do you not?"

"There is no time. No use. And danger – and your grief is likely worse, I admit, but only because you have your own woes as well – yet you also do not weep."

"And your grief?" Arnlausa asked.

"Might soon be doubled."

"Or worse. Selvorne, your father – a great friend. I have known him longer than you, before you were born, and we have faced danger and ... great joy. Each the other saved – I he, and he me – many times. To have had one last great journey, one victory, one ... not so bad a way to end it. One last ... all is owed, one to the other – and to the last. And now, to you."

"I wish I could ... do something."

"Yes, as do I. He saved me more than I he, many times in the past – and I repaid him by enchanting his only son, teaching you to taunt him with jests of poor humour, intolerable to endure."

"What?" Selvorne asked, and Arnlausa smiled.

"So he said, bemoaning the curse I placed on his son, wishing I had taught him manners of refinement, not boldness of jests."

"He ... did he?" Selvorne asked, horrified to think that he had overly taunted his father somehow, for Uhlsko was a man who might not complain of such a thing, but bear it quietly. Selvorne fancied he remembered the pain of it in his eyes.

"Yes, he did say it, but smiled as he did," Arnlausa said, "but – yes. My charm, passed to you – a favour, and a curse. Better than his sour moods, and glum half smile. My magnificence – that, at least, I see is going to live on, and do mischief. It must be a wicked spirit that lived within me, which now resides in you – you have my tongue, I hear."

"I wish I did, then you would not be able to talk such nonsense," Selvorne said. Arnlausa coughed and spluttered until he calmed himself.

"And you are killing me with it."

"I will save it, then, until tomorrow."

"No – but now is not the time ... Selvorne, I owe Uhlsko, for my life, and more.
Many times and not only ... today – I have something for you."

Arnlausa nodded once and Selvorne frowned, then looked around the cave
where his wounded friend sat, and wondered what he meant to give him.

"Is it a rock?" Selvorne asked, "I see nothing else in this cave, and I have plenty
of those already."

"In your head, it seems – I have but words."

"A joke?"

"A joke – no ... not a joke. Selvorne – you did not check the bridge before we
crossed today, and now we are dead."

Selvorne breathed in hard – he was silent, and stared – not a joke. He was ...
accused. Condemned. By a lord, which was the same thing, and by accusation
would be guilty. Arnlausa had every reason to do so, for Selvorne's guilt was clear.
He had failed, neglecting a task, to save moments, in his eagerness to fish. He
could not speak.

"Girradehn thinks, for that, you should – "

"I know," Selvorne said.

"You agree?"

"He is right. Had I checked, we – you would be unhurt. Please ... do not remind
me of it."

"Remind you ... a good choice of words, I agree."

Selvorne frowned – Arnlausa was being oddly coy.

"With ... what?"

"You should have checked it – had you done, your father would live."

Selvorne nodded slowly, and felt ill.

"He agrees, I agree, your father also, had he lived," Arnlausa said.

Selvorne stared at the dark cave floor. Shadows from the fire that was burning
low, very little light, just a flicker every so often. Arnlausa was right.

"Nothing can change that now," Selvorne said.

"No. Nothing can change it now. Guilt – to remain with a man the rest of his life,
for such a small thing let slip. You did not check the bridge. In too much of a
hurry, to fish – to run off at speed – to save moments, you cost lives."

Selvorne clenched his jaw, and felt weak.

"You are guilty – I see your eyes, you condemn yourself with your gloom."

"My punishment?"

"Is clear."

"Is – what?"

"Selvorne – you should have checked the bridge."

"I know. I – "

"Selvorne," Arnlausa said, trying to shift, but being unable, he just shook his
head, "you did check the bridge."

Selvorne blinked – Arnlausa was speaking nonsense.

"What?"

"Weeks ago, when last we crossed. Under you went, as always – looking for rot, for damage, for weakness caused by bugs or water. As taught, as shown when we built it."

"That was weeks ago."

"Yes. Weeks. No storm, since then – no great wind. No lightning – no reason to think it would be any different than before."

"No men were there at the time with axes, waiting to chop it down. I should have checked they had not come by since."

"True. You could have checked it today."

"I know, I feel – "

"But – should you have? Truly? Perhaps. You were to fish – Selvorne, you are just ... not a boy. I do not tease. A young man – Girradehn is a guard. I was, your father was – three great guards. Three great fools. And we both lords, more than any should have been careful – we are the ones at fault, a dozen times more than you, and for reasons that we should especially ... have checked. Guilty. We are – were – past our best. Wisdom of age has become the weariness of – the laziness of neglect."

"And so, as old men, I could not expect you to climb under a bridge and – "

"Please! We are hardly that old. Just stupid. And lazy – and we would have sent him. If he was not so ... "

"Defiant?"

"His guilt is far worse than yours, Selvorne, so he pushes more upon you."

"His wound is worse, and I should have checked, and not left it to others – you know this."

"His fault is worse, and his wound, and his duty so much greater – my guard, to protect me. Not you – you are just ... "

"A boy?"

"Not a boy. And not to blame. You must keep that in mind – remind yourself if – you are without guilt, in this – that is my decree."

"My wound is ... terrible, though."

"Guilt? So you think. In time you will realise it is not guilt, but grief. It is because horrors happened you wish you had stopped – helpless, now – blame is all you think you can do. Better that, than nothing. It does not make a difference, it only makes you suffer. Then you fear for other faults to follow – for those who mean you harm, that you hope to defeat. And they will follow – and grief, and blaming yourself will not defeat them, either. Check the bridge – next time. For yourself, as best you can – you cannot do all, for all, at all times – but you must try to, as best you can. It is the way of guards, of lords – and of great men. That is my gift."

Selvorne nodded, but felt awkward.

"Not much of a gift, then – guiltless, threatened, helpless."

"Wisdom – caution – and help more, not less. There is no other way – if you think being carefree and blameless, irresponsible and ignorant, and then – hope that others will come to save you – then you have a grim time ahead, and you are doomed," Arnlausa said, and Selvorne nodded.

"Father always said the same."

"And is now dead. And you have inside you the beginnings of a fury that is not out of your control, but growing, grimly, plotting – and I see it. Even now when you seem calm. For today, women would weep, men – most – would be swinging their swords in anger, cursing, had such a thing fallen upon them. The loss of wine alone would make men rage – but you are calm, and – where are the swords?"

"I could not find them."

"Do so, or – they might be in the river. We threw them so they would not break – look to the waters."

"You ... threw them? You should have thrown yourselves."

"One of us did."

"Girradehn?"

"No. He jumped to save himself. Look to the water – if too deep, leave them, it is too dangerous to ... if men are watching. Yes – the river, I remember now, to the deepest part, I saw them fall."

Selvorne frowned – it could only have been moments from the time they fell to the time they landed.

"How did you see that?"

Arnlausa spluttered before clearing his throat.

"You would be surprised what a man might see, as he falls to his death, Selvorne, and what he might realise with clarity he could have used in life. Moments for you, years for me – that fall. I am now as old as Cienn, I think, and half as wise."

"Very wise, then."

"Very – you think my gift is nothing? You need to think on it more – I have taken a lifetime of remorse from you, if you were so stupid to dwell on it. And ... I hope that I have saved your life as well. Taken, all the gloom you would burden those you love with, for guilt that is undeserved. Your wife and family may know a merry man, not a sullen misery who ruins their home. A great gift. Now, however – from now until you die – be more cautious."

"As a guard should."

"And you should join the guards."

"And – I have never wished to do so."

"And now?"

Selvorne looked over to Girradehn, who was asleep. He seemed peaceful, and Selvorne winced.

"Would I ... have to serve under him?"

"Girradehn?" Arnlausa asked, frowning as he did.

"Yes."

"No – is that your fear?"

"You know we – do not get along."

"I know. And so you killed him."

Selvorne drew his mouth back so far it hurt, and Arnlausa's laughter only made him feel ill.

"That is not even slightly funny."

"And not meant as a joke. No, Selvorne, you will not have to serve under him, I realise you do not like him, he is annoying, but I think shall not be, after this."

"For the wound ... you think it will change him? I ... do not think he will be more pleasant with a limp, more likely he will be more angry, less tolerable, and quick to find fault with anything I do."

"He will not limp."

Selvorne's eyes widened – no limp – the wound, then, was not so bad. It was some joy to think of it. Arnlausa was watching him as carefully as he could, from the ground where he sat, his eyes narrow and unwavering as they stared, and Selvorne grew uneasy.

"I thought it was much worse," Selvorne said, "he can be healed? That well? To not limp?"

"No."

"You mean – he will not walk," Selvorne said slowly, feeling ill once more.

"Not walk. Not complain – nor talk. Not limp, not say unpleasant things, in jest or cruelty – nor breathe. I mean that he will not live."

Selvorne stared into Arnlausa's eyes – it was not a joke. It was no exaggeration, as he had hoped before – it was certainty that Girradehn, untreated, would die.

"We must go – and now," Selvorne said.

"In the dark? Up the cliff? With you lifting him – with enemies watching?"

"Enemies are not here, I can bring men from the town, back by dawn, an axe and – the leg, removed and burnt, he will live. I know he can."

"And who, Selvorne, would you bring? Who can set a bone back in the flesh? Clear the wound or chop the leg – seal it at the end?"

"My – "

"Father?"

"Yes. No – someone – you?"

"Do I look like I could do any of those things? If I knew how?"

"I thought you did?"

"I have seen it done – I have watched it tried."

"We will try."

"What I saw failed. Left, or tried – fast, or slow – both ways lead to death. It is too late. He should have tended it at once."

"He – he should have?"

"He could have. He knew how, as well as I, but hoped – wished it was not so, and his grief – his stupidity has killed himself. But ... few men are so bold to cut their own leg – he could have told you. He wanted to keep it, he hoped to do so, now he has lost all. To spare a leg, lost his life."

Selvorne bit his lip – Girradehn had spoken of dying at the first, and it was taken as his usual moaning. Not at once – he was believed, at first, but then, as he seemed unexpectedly brave, Selvorne assumed he was going to live, despite complaints he was to die. He had ... he was sure he said he would, and his hope for healing ... perhaps he was just complaining. No, Selvorne did not believe that – the wound was terrible, but in the cave he thought it was a one–legged Girradehn facing pain and fearing death, not a man who knew he was going to die. Girradehn knew then, and said nothing. Arnlausa knew as well – but said there was hope, to which Girradehn did not argue, and ... it was what he did not say that Selvorne suddenly realised.

"You have saved my life," Selvorne said, "to spare me, you lied. To keep me here until dark. Stop me fleeing into a trap, stop me rushing to get help for Girradehn. His life, for mine."

Arnlausa said nothing.

"Am I right?"

"He is a guard. You are not. His life for yours – though, truly, his life for the vanity of a leg, or fear of what he had to do. You are fast."

"And could have run, and – "

"I think, been caught."

"And so hid, and now must live with it for – "

"And slow, at times, not to realise the truth in it. By all means feel remorse – guilt – sorrow – do not let it get in the way of surviving. And then, living a good life. Do you think our time in the guards was all fun?"

Selvorne shook his head.

"I did not mean that you run fast – I meant you are fast to think of that, Selvorne – few would. So quickly. Most would be sitting here weeping over their poor luck, useless and annoying, though such poor company might ease my passing to death. We three are dead – do not follow us. I meant all I said – the barrels for bodies – three. Remain hidden. There is not one person who can save him now, not even Cienn, and I have seen her work when she was much younger, and her skill, though greatest, is not good enough. Not with the delay – the leg is spoilt, the blood, the wound. I am not sure he will wake."

"Is this the truth – or are you trying to comfort me, and remove my guilt?"

"Ask either of us tomorrow, and in our silence you will have your answer."

Arnlausa was grim, but had good reason to be, and Selvorne nodded. He knew his friend well enough to be almost certain he spoke no lies.

"Truth, Selvorne," Arnlausa added, "guards do not lie to each other for comfort. Not – old guards, anyway. Your life is spared, though, by my lie – and now you owe me."

"I – anything. What do you want?"

"Anything? Good. A few things – first, learn to fight. I see fear in your eyes, at times."

"Would I be wise to be unafraid?"

"No, fear is good – but better felt by your foes, than you. If they are here, watching, they will fear – three guards thought not dead, waiting to start their vengeful hunt – yes, fear is good. But you have not the skill with weapons to turn your own fear to ferocity, and you may need just that."

"I agree. If men came to the cave, I would not know what to do."

"And any one of us three would – and that alone should keep them away. And you will, also, once trained."

"Do you think they are out there?" Selvorne asked, staring at the dark mouth of the cave.

"No. But likely soon will be, and wonder where is Uhlsko, Arnlausa and Girradehn – any of us they would fear greatly. Unfound – terrifying," Arnlausa said, then spluttered a chuckle.

"And – me?"

"No."

"A fourth man, also dangerous, if instructed to – "

"No – they would not think you are here, unless they saw you – and I doubt they did. Had they done, they also would have seen we were helpless, being carried, and would have come down for us, fearing nothing."

"But – my father – they would expect me to be with him, and – "

"No."

"Not with him?"

"No. Never. Only if they saw you. Or if they knew your father well – perhaps. If it was a man from your town who did this."

"Never would any in our town do this, but I see – "

"No, you do not. And yes – it could have been a man from your town. Be quiet. Promise to learn to fight."

"I promise. Now?"

"Now?"

"Learn to fight now?"

"Now – in the cave? Who would teach you – me?"

"I meant – "

"Are you sure you did not fall? Hit your head, somehow? Not here, not now, but one day – soon. You must escape and you must learn – promise."

"I promise. We must escape, at dawn, when – "

"You escape. If men come – flee. Stop ... talking. Nonsense. Live – escape – it is your second promise, and must be made above all others. Now."

"I – promise. To ... live?"

"Die – and what has happened here might not be known. You must live to take a report, or none will be delivered. Also, you would be dead, and that alone is not at all good for you. Promise to live."

"Agreed, and a promise I do not mind keeping at all. You know more of this than you say."

"I suspect more than I can say, in the time we have, and likely I am wrong, and I know nothing, but that we were attacked. It might be a mistake – a theft – not for us, I do not know. We must assume it was. Promise to live – and find who did this, and judge them."

Selvorne nodded.

"Revenge. I swear it."

"Some would say justice. But – yes, revenge. With all the care of justice – find the truth of it, do not kill a man thinking him the killer – a man who was sent with some absurd order to cut the bridge for the Waehdric – they do stupid things at times, especially lately."

"Why would they destroy a bridge?"

"To build a new one in stone – yes, a stupid thing, when the wooden one is good. Expensive, unnecessary. Hiring fools to save coins, half cutting the supports to save time. But this ... swear it. Revenge – with care."

Selvorne nodded.

"Good – third, you must put our bodies in barrels."

"Keep making me swear that and I will put you there before you die," Selvorne said.

"I might not mind, if dropped into one with wine – do they call me the Wining Lord, still?"

"I – have never heard it before?"

"No matter. For my singing, much improved with age."

"It must have been truly dreadful, then, in your youth."

"It was. In a barrel – for me, burnt or buried, I do not care. Girradehn, buried, with a gathering of as many as you can – speak of him with honour. All will wish to see his face, unless he has terrible wounds, then – "

"But – his face is unwounded?" Selvorne asked, and as he did, he realised what was meant – it was unwounded as yet. If enemies came, horrors might happen, and Selvorne breathed in hard, clenching his fists as Arnlausa narrowed his eyes.

"Eager to fight and yet – you must flee. You swore."

"I swear. This is now more grim, and I thought that was not possible."

"This is not near the worst I have seen, though this time it is me dying, and I cannot move my legs, Selvorne. You know the wishes of your father?"

"By her side."

"Yes. And that shirt, conveniently worn already. I would not ... mind being buried near her, as well."

"My mother was – loved by you?"

"Your father. And yes, Vorlisi was loved by all. Mourned by all. Put me near your father, but not beside. I shall watch them both, from a distance. As a guard. I think I would like that – as would they."

"Very well – but you are not yet dead, and I have had enough talk of it."

"As have I – but Selvorne, the bodies, in barrels, then buried as instructed. When it is safe to do so."

"I swear."

"And the seals, hidden."

"They are."

"Hidden again – from all. From ... everyone but yourself. Well, unable to be found – only known to you, no others, and ... "

Arnlausa stopped, then groaned, and seemed in pain. Selvorne offered water, but he waved his hand.

"Bring them to me."

"The – seals?"

"Yes."

"Now?"

"Yes, now – first, swear you will hide them? Once all is done?"

"I swear," Selvorne said. Arnlausa nodded, which was a command, so he went to get the seals.

Certain and Sealed

Selvorne left the cave as carefully as he could, for if men were waiting, he did not want to be surprised. He had not hidden the sack of their things very well, in a hole near the cave. It was his one hope that if found and killed inside the cave, at least the killers might not find all their most precious things – and his second hope was that they were lazy men who would not bother searching boulders and hollows near. Foolish, he knew, to rely on hope, but he had been distracted at the time, and he swore to himself he would find a better place for them where they could not be found.

When he returned to the cave he thought Arnlausa asleep – or worse – but he stirred. Prepare – it was all that he said, and it was a command, Arnlausa wanted all made ready to issue written orders. The box was opened – so elegant, the best thing he had ever bought, Arnlausa swore, and though it was a praise for many things he had bought, the box was truly magnificent, being made of finest wood and tightest fittings. A candle was lit, both for light and its wax, then positioned so Arnlausa could easily see what he might write. The box was folded to be used as a small table, on his lap – held steady by Selvorne. A fine pencil, itself costing quite a coin – a charcoal shaped thin enough to be threaded through wood – no expense was spared by Arnlausa, Lord of Tavalehk.

To see a lord write orders was a rare thing for any man, be they family, friend or trusted advisor, for the lords often had secret ways of making signs and seals. Arnlausa cared nothing for secrets that night, only for his coughing that made his hand unsteady, and Selvorne marvelled to think he complained not of his wounds, but the shame that his final written words would not be elegant. He wrote one parchment after another, then told Selvorne to seal them all with wax and his great stamp – great for its fine detail, not its size, as it was made for travel. Arnlausa scrawled a sign on each where the wax should go, as if Selvorne might forget and seal the wrong place. One parchment after another had wax dripped upon it and was stamped, then left to dry, and it occurred to Selvorne he was likely breaking some unwritten law, for he was sealing them as though he was the Lord of Tavalehk.

As they all dried, Selvorne wondered what he had sealed, what they all said, and what could be of such important complications that it had to be done that night, and yet could not have been prepared in advance. Final orders of a living lord who expected to die, and writing them exhausted Arnlausa, who collapsed against the rock to recover.

"Now should I hide it all?" Selvorne asked.

"A promise to hide them if – at the end. Until safe to retrieve, until you have men by your side who you trust. And only show who is trusted."

"Cienn?"

"Yes. Or her man who has replaced her, if she is also dead."

"Or woman?"

"Or ... woman. I guess ... another woman it may be. You understand why?"

Selvorne nodded – her alone, for whatever was written there was of greatest importance, and if discovered by others, its intentions would be undone. Not urgent, though, not if it was to be taken to Cienn alone – by himself. Uhlsko had explained it to him, years ago, it seemed Cienn was not easy to contact. But to do so would be to speak with a most trusted ally, and she would be sure that all others told after could be trusted as well. His father always spoke of her with the most solemn respect, perhaps even ... fear, though awe might have been a better word. To think that he was to deliver such a message to her made Selvorne tremble.

"And – should I know what it says?" Selvorne asked.

"Are you going to break it open to read it?"

"No, I would never do that."

"Then you are a fool, if you present it to her and it says to put an end to your life," Arnlausa said.

"Does it?"

"In a way, yes."

"That is not funny."

"And it is not ... exactly a joke. Selvorne, I will not last to dawn."

Selvorne was silent for a moment, and Arnlausa looked to the fire.

"And ... is this a joke?"

"No."

"And Girradehn?"

"Do you think all this has been a joke?"

"No, but I hoped."

"That I have been having fun with you? All night – even now?"

Selvorne nodded.

"None of it a joke, I fear," Arnlausa said, and Selvorne knew he was speaking the truth. He had hoped – he knew the hope was vain – but he clung to the slightest that his friend would last the night. Sleep, wake – joke once more, and tease in the morning. Something about the barrel being too small, meant for a woman – or the wine too foul, not to his standard, and then complaints the merchants cheated him. Or delight he was to drink forever of the best. Anything but silence. To think there might be mere hours left of his friend made his heart ache, and he did not want to believe it.

"You seem not very grim for a man about to die?" Selvorne asked, hoping a little more that his friend might laugh.

"And you – not very – for a man who saw his father die."

"Or so grim I cannot think of it."

"Yes. I have seen that before. At least you do not wail like a woman."

"Which would bring death upon us."

"On you – it is on me already. But that is not why – you have seen death before, you have had loss, and you know already that tears do not help."

Selvorne nodded.

"Later – tears may help," Arnlausa said.

"Not you, and not him."

"And not Girradehn – do you hate him so much? That you do not mention him?" Arnlausa asked, and Selvorne winced.

"I do not ... hate him at all. I might miss him – a little. If it were he dying, and not you, and not father, then my grief would be for him alone, but not as great. It is a little loss, compared to you both – I only forget him for the pain of you. I know it is not ... I am ashamed for it, as well. Arnlausa, please – tell me you joke of this? A cruel joke to cope with the pain?"

"I wish I did. I feel no pain. Nothing. And nothing of where I sit, though I know beneath my leg is a stone – I cannot bend to remove it, and once moved, would not know it gone."

"Your legs move, though?"

"No. I push them, with my hands, not by my will. I cannot stand. My cough – that I swallow – is blood. I can taste that, at least. I am not sure if ... I prefer to be here knowing my fate ... or to be as good Uhlsko there, at peace. It is better, I think."

"There is no good in it."

"Oh, but Selvorne – there is."

Selvorne gave a painful smile, and Arnlausa looked up at him with wide eyes.

"Did you cut the bridge to make us fall – to kill us?" Arnlausa asked, and Selvorne widened his eyes in horror.

"What?"

"No," Arnlausa said, "you did not. Strange, she was right, a dying man sees true ... good."

"How could you think that I would – "

"And how can you think I would not? And you must think, Selvorne, and not like a boy. It would not be the first time such a thing was done – do you know who did it?"

"Do you think I would let them live if I did?"

"No. And they would be stupid to let you know, and ... things will soon be clear, as you think it over."

"You think it was to kill you – my father? Girradehn?"

"You know I do. Killers came for us, not wine, and not ... with petty anger, for an annoying guard."

"But you more than suspect – you expect it. What are you not telling me?"

"Many things. And there is no time, so ... "

Arnlausa was silent, and Selvorne waited for an answer, but there was only strained breathing and the sound of the fire in the cave.

"Arnlausa?"

"Selvorne," Arnlausa said, "by dawn, perhaps a little more – but then I am no more. Girradehn – a week, but painful. He knows ... hide the seals from him."

"Why? You – do not suspect him?"

"Do you?"

Selvorne was not sure – no, certainly not if he was also dying, not even if he was wounded. Girradehn was annoying, but not such a fool to have brought death upon himself as well as men he might have planned to kill, even if he was so heartless to want them dead.

"A fool, if so," Selvorne said, "but you suspect someone?"

"Selvorne – I suspect everyone except those who are in this cave. Now – after this – I suspect everyone."

~

Selvorne took a deep breath, then let it go – Arnlausa did not have to trust anyone. He was dying. He would soon be dead. It was not his fear that troubled him – it was that Selvorne did not share it, and so might not be as cautious, wary, and afraid as he needed to be – Arnlausa feared for him. Selvorne did not know why, other than that killers might be after him. That alone should have been enough, and yet there was something more.

"Who can I trust?" Selvorne asked.

"Good. You think. Cienn. No others. No others – not one other person, no matter how much you love them, trusted them before, want to ... trust them."

"No friends?"

"Do you even have any? Who would you call friend – children in your town?"

"Miners at the quarry, who are not children. The stone workers of Tawlehk."

Arnlausa frowned, nodded once, then winced.

"Not even them, Selvorne – if I lived, perhaps I could test them, but you cannot. Deceit is easy for some, and long planned for others who might have become your friend years ago, knowing ... or may meet you tomorrow, and seem harmless.

Lovely. Kind – beautiful. Trust no one. Trust especially no lord – trust least of all, a friend. Only Cienn.”

“Who is very difficult to find.”

“Yes. Or speak to once found, though, she likely will find you first, I think.”

“And if she is dead?”

“Likely. Possible. She is very old, and has not been seen in a long time – she could be already dead, and none were told. Deliberately, to hide it. If so, you must be careful to determine who has replaced her, as Leader of the Waehdric, for whoever she might have chosen perhaps was not as well picked as she thought.”

“I thought she had already chosen – ”

“No. Not him. Not ... yet. Selvorne, there are men in the lands I would swear are true – men I would name as close as brothers. Until today. Now I do not know, so – not one person, but Cienn, or the man she has chosen as her replacement. And that is not Taffoanan – if you knew him, you would understand why – if you meet him, you will realise at once.”

Selvorne nodded – a signal he would obey, but he did not like the warnings he was being given.

“That is not many allies, though.”

“One. The most important – and she has an army of guards. Do not trust who leads them – or them – or any who work for them – or who present themselves to you. Do not trust my guards, although ... I love them dearly. The men of Tavalehk are good.”

“And untrusted? Your own men?” Selvorne asked. Arnlausa took a deep, strained breath.

“Cannot trust, cannot risk. My men chosen – tested – selected – good men. Guards. Others. Capable, not for this. Involved? Unlikely. Watched? Almost certainly. Even the best of them brings a danger unintended ... for this. You can only trust the men here – the dead, the dying. And Cienn. Swear it.”

“I – very well. I swear it. You must suspect something – ”

“Terrible? Could it be much worse?”

“No,” Selvorne said, and it could not – murder was bad enough, if deliberate and planned. Murder of a lord suggested something far worse than the death of a few men. More than life was lost – power and authority were disturbed, the lords would be replaced, further plans might unfold. Arnlausa had a darkness in his eyes that was not from the wound – not fear for himself, not sorrow for his loss. His suspicions and caution hinted at something the lands had not seen in a very long time – his mood suggested war.

“I am to take the scrolls to Cienn?”

“Yes. Or the man who has replaced her.”

“Or woman.”

“What?”

“Or woman – who has replaced her?”

"Yes – or woman. I suppose another woman might be likely. There is one other you must tell, though ... not entirely trust. Be wary – tell Rerleden."

Selvorne frowned – Rerleden was an old man who lived in his town, and he cared for the pigs and chickens, though – he had once worked for the guards.

"Of Vaskatohr?"

"Yes. I hope he can be trusted. Your father ... has kept him near for such a time as this, but I – you must not tell him all. Argh!"

Arnlausa groaned and rubbed his side as best he could, so Selvorne helped – or tried, but was not sure it did help, so he offered wine that was eagerly drunk. Arnlausa settled and calmed himself, and for the first time that day looked afraid.

"I consume it, it will consume me," he said of the wine as he dropped the bladder and it began to spill. Selvorne snatched it and held it up, closed it again and put it aside, "tell Rerleden just this – we are dead. The bridge was broken. You are to ... no, say you are going to get help. He will know what to do. But be wary, he could have – been involved. I think not, but ... tell him no more."

"What, exactly, is more to tell? That is everything, is it not?"

"No. But tell no others even that – nothing. Tell – what name do you use in the town?"

Selvorne frowned at the odd question, then nodded. Uhlvorne, Uhlvorsk, Vorgarve, Ahrvorne – when young, he thought that all boys were to have their names changed when they became men. He soon learnt that was not true, and wondered if his parents had either argued over what name he might have, or were fond of so many that they could not decide. At times they might use one or the other, until he responded merely to the sound of their voices. Selvorne was the one he liked most and had stuck with – defiantly, at the end, and there would be no changing it against his will, and if they dared try to make it Uhlvorgarvorsk, as they once had threatened, he had a plan to run away. When he was four years of age, before his mother was lost. Only a threat, but the plan of his father was, one day, likely soon, to change his name to Uhlvorne.

"Selvorne, still. I ... am not sure I want the – "

"Want or not, I care not," Arnlausa said, "time is ... Selvorne. Your name now, remains. Use no other – do not say your last, and do not mention mine or his, or your mother or any – you are from the quarry, the men there – will vouch for you. You know this."

Selvorne nodded, but did not know what Arnlausa was talking about.

"What is in the scrolls I wrote?"

"I ... do not know?"

"Answer!" Arnlausa demanded, as firmly as he could, yet it made no sense.

"I – Arnlausa, I did not look. I do not know, I swear it."

Arnlausa's head dropped, resigned, exhausted. Selvorne put a hand to his forehead to lift it up – still awake, his face was cold, and he gave a half smile.

"Good," Arnlausa said, "good. What they said – one, my word, that you did not do this, to save you from trial, or suspicion. Two – matters of a private nature. Not concerning you. Not for you to pry. Three – lordship."

He coughed again, and Selvorne offered wine and water, but he wanted neither. His head rolled and he spluttered and spat – blood, then coughed again and spat once more, until he looked very ill.

"Wine!" he managed to say, but he did not drink, just rinsed his mouth and spat, then breathed heavily for a while.

"At least I can taste – how cruel. Wine like blood. Blood like ... death. Taste, and think. No time, it is gone. Selvorne, listen."

"I am."

"Of the Will of Arnlausa NohcLehk Laehtene – concerning the Heir to Tavalehk and Vaskatohr. By agreements made before, by law of duel, grant and succession – I, Arnlausa Laehtene, Lord of Tavalehk, pass Lordship to Selvorne Skolerne, known as son of Uhlsko Skolerne, who was Lord of Vaskatohr. I, Arnlausa Laehtene, on behalf of Uhlsko Skolerne, who was Lord of Vaskatohr, by agreements made before, pass Lordship to Selvorne Skolerne, known as son of Uhlsko Skolerne, who was Lord of Vaskatohr. By this I – "

At that, Arnlausa began to cough again, and almost choked on blood. He spat some out and Selvorne held him up as he regained his breath.

"You made me heir?"

Arnlausa coughed again, then took a strained breath.

"Did you do this? Did you kill us all?" Arnlausa asked.

"You ask me that now? Now your will is written and sealed? Would it make a difference if you – oh," Selvorne said, nodding, "and that is why. No, I did not. Arnlausa – I would rather have you, than all the towns of the north."

Arnlausa gave an odd smile, and Selvorne felt pained.

"For my father, or you – all the towns of all the lands. Or for Girradehn, though I never liked him much – his life, before lordship. No, I did not do this. But I will do this to whoever did this, I swear it."

Arnlausa put a hand to Selvorne's as his head flopped in a nod.

"It is good to hear, and my thoughts ... are clear. Pain is back, I feel more sick than before. The wine, perhaps. Not a good idea. I think ... I may have a leak."

Selvorne looked down – no wine was spilt. Arnlausa meant inside. He also meant more by his questions than Selvorne had first thought.

"You test me ... even now," Selvorne said in a low voice.

"Yes. Even now – son of my friend most trusted. As lord now, named and known, you must not trust ... anyone. Only Cienn."

Selvorne nodded solemnly, and Arnlausa raised his head once more.

"Who never lies?" Arnlausa asked.

"The dead."

"Yes. Your father, now – you will not find a more honest man. You may find, though, that he speaks from his death."

"What?" Selvorne asked with a frown.

"Selvorne – who can you trust?"

"Cienn. And Rerleden, only ... oh. You mean ... only trust the dead, and the dying. What are you trying to tell me?"

"Do not always trust the dying," Arnlausa said, "not all believe they are, and so may lie, in hope of recovery, of deceit ... to fool you. I am dying. You must listen to me. And you are not dying, but now, at the last – I must trust you."

"Do you?"

"Yes. And have ... always, but to be sure ... not me, not you, but far more ... important matters. Uhlsko died knowing you lived. I die, knowing you live – and I live in you, in a way."

"Remembered," Selvorne said, nodding.

"Influenced. Strange, this death – the pain, the clarity – it comes and goes. Now I know what they meant ... things are seen differently, now. You are trusted – and tested."

"I understand."

"Not completely," Arnlausa said in a low voice.

"No, but you asked me often enough if I planned this."

"Yes. Direct, then, as you often are – you have reason to have killed us all. Many will think the same."

"And so you wrote a pardon, which must not be lost," Selvorne said.

"Ambitious – only for your townsfolk, and not overly. You are a good young man, Selvorne, and sensible – with some clever ideas ... that must never be done, for reasons you could not possibly know, or you would not have suggested them – look to Tavalehk, as well as Vaskatohr. Do not tempt my ... your people from there to the south. Not without good reason. There are things of which you do not know."

"I would never do anything without good reason – I would not move people to Vaskatohr merely for fun," Selvorne said, and Arnlausa smiled.

"Oh – but fun is a good reason, if there is no harm in it. Never forget that, my boy. Work alone does not make a life worthwhile."

Selvorne nodded, and Arnlausa studied his face, until he nodded once as well.

"True sorrow," Arnlausa said, "and for us all. Even for Girradehn, who you did not like – you had no intention of stealing the seals."

Selvorne nodded again.

"And true anger to get revenge. I saw that at the start, but remember, always – never without thinking. Be cautious. An angry, hurt man seeking vengeance might rush in – almost wishing death himself, if the pain is great. Some do so and realise their mistake only when it is too late. Violent in desperation, blinded by pain."

"I would not rush in, I would – "

"Oh – I am sure you would go carefully," Arnlausa said, "nevertheless, heed my warning. Many men rush in anger, die in fear. You tend to fear, then rush. It may be as dangerous – be careful. Do not rush one man to kill, only to learn your true enemy led you to it – you know the stories.”

“Of Molarklod, yes, the foolish guard,” Selvorne said, and Arnlausa nodded.

“You also realise it will take time.”

“Yes, I know, I – ”

“Selvorne – I know that you know. It is not quite patience, is it?”

“Resignation.”

“As with splitting stone – I know the lesson quarrymen teach. A thousand blows of hammer and stone, a thousand times to break a boulder.”

“When I find the man who did this, death by a thousand blows, then,” Selvorne said, and Arnlausa seemed to shake his head.

“Make it fast – and certain. Not cruel. The thousand blows ... it may take a while, and cunning, and help. Not wounds, but learning what was done, and why – it may take ... like a thousand blows. You cannot fight – you must learn how. Unless ... if it was one man only, and he comes here alone, and you are sure – push him in the river, and spear him like a fish.”

“That I can do well.”

“Very well. Be sure he is not some poor traveller passing by, and to do so, you will need your spear.”

“I know where it is, and I will be sure, if it is one man, I will – ”

“No,” Arnlausa said with as much strength as he could, “do not. Leave the spear. Do not challenge one man – a poor joke. To try, and fail – and die – all is lost. Do you hate Girradehn?”

Selvorne bit his lip, and shook his head.

“I will weep for him as well.”

“But do not like him?” Arnlausa asked.

“You know this.”

“Yes. He thumped your nose, years ago.”

Selvorne winced, and clenched a fist, but Arnlausa chuckled.

“Yes, to look at it – none would know, for it is perfect, straight, and hard,” Arnlausa said, “and you do not know how difficult it is to punch a man so.”

“Nor why it needed to be done so often,” Selvorne said.

“No – you do not. But you may, in time. Not only your nose, and though you do not know how to fight, you know how to be beaten, which is a better start, some believe.”

“Better the start than the end,” Selvorne found himself saying, and, as Arnlausa smiled, he wondered if that was some secret plan he and his father had for him, and he frowned. It made Arnlausa chuckle, but then he became solemn once more.

“You,” Arnlausa said, “your father, and Girradehn – the only men I trust. And myself. And soon the three of us will be gone.”

“Which is why you made me heir?”

"No," Arnlausa said, and then was silent, gathering his thoughts, as Selvorne wondered what he was about to say.

"Arnlausa," Selvorne said, unable to bear waiting for his friend to speak, wondering if he would again, "what would you do – if we were all dead, and you were unhurt today?"

Arnlausa was stirred from his thoughts, and frowned.

"Why do you ask? Do you mean – how would I fight them?" Arnlausa asked.

"Fight them? No – I mean, what would you do, as lord?"

Arnlausa's face eased, and Selvorne thought, if he had the strength, he would have put hand to chin and stroked it as he pondered what he might do. For a few moments he considered his answer, then nodded once.

"Good – a wise question. Selvorne, I would want to fight. Unhurt, and you all dead – I would wait, and I would kill. If I was strong and unharmed – and if you three were dead. Dead friends is very different to wounded men. You ask to hear my advice, but the very fact of me living changes everything – it suggests I was not to die, but you, or him, or your father. A very different thing, Selvorne, and you are not me, and cannot take my place in battle, yet."

"And I did not mean to, I only wanted to know – "

"What I might do – you need to know what you should do. It is very different. Think on what we know, which is little – on how things are, which is unknown. Someone is smart enough to have killed your father and myself. Smart enough to have a second plan, no doubt, and wise enough to wait. We know nothing of who they are, let alone where they are – what traps lay ahead, not even the reasons for such vengeance."

"Vengeance?"

"Not even that is known. Theft, or desire for power are also possible. We do not know – to guess is dangerous, to lack preparation is worse. To start imagining something very different – you dead, me living – that is a foolish waste of time. My advice to you, Selvorne, is this – disappear."

"Hide?"

"Hunt. Hidden, as if stalking a boar."

"I ... have never stalked a boar."

"A pig, then, that has fled into the woods and needs capture to return to the pen. With more cunning and care. Can you?"

Selvorne nodded.

"In stealth to your home, speak to Rerleden alone. Then onwards to Cienn – you swear?"

"I do," Selvorne said, and Arnlausa seemed to ease.

"Had I lived instead, I would have fought," Arnlausa mused, "fair and fast, certain and deadly. But had your father lived – and you died – I dread to think what he would do."

"Weep and mourn," Selvorne said, "he would be heartbroken."

"Mourn – yes, he would ... break hearts. You have not seen him weep."

"I have, he – "

"No, Selvorne, you have not."

"He wept when my mother – "

"Only on his return. You think him a quiet man – a man of sorrow. To seem as one thing, to be another – I cannot speak of this, our past is grim. Our enemies could be any ... sometimes, to hide ... is best where all can see."

"You make no sense."

"Yet. Find Rerleden, go in secret, unseen. He will explain, once you tell him what you must – we are dead, the bridge is broken. Nothing more."

"You do not trust him?"

"I trust you," Arnlausa said, "and that you will obey. You must trust me – more than you already do, perhaps. What do you know of Krogarve?"

Krogarve – a man of battle, of cunning, a hero – a story, nothing more, to inspire young boys with tales of adventure and daring – but with a lesson in each tale.

"Of the stories?" Selvorne asked, and Arnlausa seemed to wince.

"And Torlor?"

"The clumsy? Kludbo Torlor Molarklod rue?"

"Rue?" Arnlausa asked, then almost chuckled, "Oh – that poem. He hates that."

"In ... the stories?"

"In the stories, yes – be like Krogarve, and not like Torlor. Be clever, cunning, cautious. Not a fool rushing in – to doom."

"He never was doomed, though," Selvorne said, and Arnlausa tilted his head.

"Not in the stories, which were not all true. But truth is in them – remember Torlor at Troltohr?"

"He attacked the brigands, armed with rocks," Selvorne said, "though – survived."

"In the story. The tale was true, though not of him – a guard who had all his life before him, who, seeing the foe, and seeing them unarmed – leapt out with spear and sword and a stupid grin. One stone, Selvorne – picked from the ground by a brigand, and thrown to his head. He died. There was no fine glory about it, only a lesson, contained in the tale. Do not be reckless. Be as Krogarve, as best you can."

"As fine as the greatest guard," Selvorne said, meaning Arnlausa, who had been very skilled, as a guard – so he had said. Arnlausa nodded once with no modesty at all, then took a deep, wheezing breath.

"Selvorne – to be lord, it is a great task."

"I know."

"I know ... that you do. Others would not. Sons of lords have some idea, not all of it, not of the danger, the work, the – "

"I know," Selvorne said, and Arnlausa nodded once.

"What is the reason, then, to be lord? Power – wealth – glory?"

"Danger – toil – to be alone," Selvorne said.

"Then ... why would a man be lord?"

"To spare the same for others, who do not know, and should not endure the task."

At that, Arnlausa smiled, and bowed his head.

"Few know this," Arnlausa said, "few who are not lords. Long ago, men fought to rule – others came and took it from them, only to lean the truth of the duties. Danger – from those who would take it, from those who resent what power you have. Toil – for little wealth, truly, perhaps in coin, but not in freedom. A lord is wed to town, first, to wife, second, to himself last of all, after all his people and all their woes. There may be some glory in it – my name on the Lordstone, to be forgotten, as are all those before me. Who was Arnlausa, children will ask in one hundred years – was he not the handsome lord, so magnificent to see, mourned by all the ladies? There is no joy in such glory, Selvorne. Danger, toil, and then to be forgotten."

"Never forgotten," Selvorne said, and Arnlausa smiled.

"No, not ... now."

A silence fell over the cave as Arnlausa rested his head. He might have slept, but when Selvorne checked, he realised he merely sat there, lost in his thoughts. He went to Girradehn – asleep, unmoving, but breathing. Not bleeding much, and some blood was a better sign than none, perhaps, but Selvorne looked on the wounded man with a new sorrow. He had known death was coming, his hope for help to be brought by Selvorne was abandoned, for the risk to the living was too great for the dying. Were he a normal man, it was wrong – but, as a guard, he was not to risk the lives of others for himself. An oath once taken that he likely never thought he would have to keep. Not so completely, so finally, so cruelly, and by his own choice, with no actual choice to be made. He could have lied. When Arnlausa slept he could have chosen to send Selvorne to the town for help. But he could not, not truly – no choice, and yet he chose death for himself, chance for Selvorne, and silence at the very last. Proven, then, finally, as a noble man. All his past vexations were forgiven.

Selvorne checked on his father, also, though no longer with the hope he would find him living. Unmoving, except when prodded – loose, which seemed quite odd. Dead, and gone, and the next morning at dawn, to be placed in a barrel and his face seen no more. Only the very best barrel would suffice, for in that he would be buried. Three barrels of the best, of the older style that was preferred. Unbroken – some of the wine removed to make way for the men to take its place. Men consumed by wine, then laid to rest.

Arnlausa was checked again, and Selvorne's heart pounded as he detected no breath. No movement of chest, no spluttering – he was dead – his friend lost – gone, and no more would he hear his joking taunts. Never again would he –

A spluttering and laugh, Arnlausa choked until he breathed once more. Chuckling and straining, smiling – a joke. He had held his breath and feigned death, and found it most amusing. Anger became pain before Selvorne also laughed.

"One last jest, I fear," Arnlausa said.

"And not so amusing."

"Take my place as lord – make men laugh. It costs little, and warms the heart."

"And lightens the head."

"And fills the bed, my boy, there is no greater beauty than a twinkling eye and a sly wit."

"Was it not a sly eye and wrinkling wit?" Selvorne asked, and Arnlausa chuckled a little.

"Even an old man may be thought amusing to a young lady, be he rich," Arnlausa said, "sly eye or no, wrinkled, or no, and wrinkles soon go, if the man is youthful, below."

Selvorne smiled. The kind of nonsense Arnlausa often said, which made many laugh as they could find no meaning in it, but dared not look a fool. The man fancied himself a poet, and though at times recited terrible verse, none complained, and many had their hearts lightened by the folly of it all. Mirth amongst the powerful men and women of the town – not trust, though, it seemed, and Selvorne wondered how much was tease and how much taunts, of people not entirely liked, and the poems might have contained hidden meanings none dared reveal – secret insults, and accusations directed at many by his side. Selvorne felt a new sorrow for Arnlausa, and wondered if his life was very lonely, with so few he truly loved and trusted – his father only, perhaps. And himself.

Or it was all merely nonsense. No insult, no meaning, just Arnlausa being silly. He usually was far from serious. Opposite to Uhlsko in so many ways, and yet, beside him in so many others. Trust, more than anything – to have both slain at once, one reason for it was clear and needed no other explanation – each lord was to the other a great friend. One slain, the other would seek revenge, never to rest. Neither one could be killed without bringing death to whoever did it – unless both were slain at once. And by such an accident, it could be done, and no others would be the wiser.

None, that was, but Selvorne, who was there and unknown. Had he been seen – had the killers been near, they likely would have come already, for the night was late. Perhaps morning, the middle of the day. He wondered how lazy they were, or cautious. He would live – escape – hide. After the bodies were to barrels, then he would seek Cienn. Learn to fight, as promised. Take his time, be cautious, more than his enemy, thinking themselves safe – and their mistake in overlooking him would be their ruin. The third vengeful man, who loved both of the dead, and would allow nothing to hinder his revenge, no matter what it took to bring it to them unexpected.

"I must sleep," Arnlausa said.

"Now?"

"Now. Though I fear I shall not need to be well rested tomorrow."

"Must you ... sleep?"

Arnlausa let his head fall in a nod, and Selvorne lifted it once more by his chin.

"Early to bed," Arnlausa said.

"Early to rise," Selvorne said.

"No rise for me, never again."

"I will help," Selvorne said, though he knew not how. Arnlausa gave a half smile, then tried to shake his head.

"Oh – Selvorne – when you say such things, I do not know if you tease, or if you truly are so very young. Despite your years."

"What?"

"Yes – you will help. Not me. The town. And ... those I love. More than you know, as best you can."

"I ... promise. I vow all that I promised. I swear."

"I know."

At that, Arnlausa closed his eyes, and Selvorne thought him dead – he was not. His head was made as comfortable as it could be, as was his body, though, as Selvorne took away stones upon which he sat, and moved his legs to more pleasant positions, he wondered if his friend truly felt anything at all. He slept. He likely would not wake. His life would end in dreams, they likely would not be pleasant. His life would end in knowing, though, that he had secured final preparations – a plan for revenge against the killers – and few murdered men had such a chance as that. It had to be some relief to Arnlausa at the last, but Selvorne could feel only sorrow, anger and hate. And frustration, more than anything else, for what he did not do, what he did not know, and the many things he did not understand.

Both To Barrels

Selvorne woke to the pain of a poor bed, its cold stone rough beneath the cloak on which he slept. The air was cool and still. No breeze. Not much light, from a low fire, or a lower sun. Or perhaps it was the dawn of a misty morning, for all around seemed grey.

The distant sound of a river, he was sure of it when he stirred and blinked – a wall of rock, a roof – a cave – the cave. The ravine, and ... all that happened came back to him at once.

He took a breath as he lay on the rock. One shallow breath, not as deep as he had meant, not as easy, and not a relief. There was no relief from the grim sorrow. No distraction, except – danger – that woke him truly. It had to be considered first, before sorrow or comfort or fear. He was wise enough to think to look around before moving, remaining still, unnoticed, or seeming dead. No enemies were there in the cave, no shadows of men, come to kill. He rolled over and sat, looked into the dark, and, seeing poorly, he rose and went to the others.

Arnlausa was not dead. On his side, breathing. He had lasted the night, but he was cold. Selvorne put his cloak over the one he already wore, and hoped it might help somehow. He might, perhaps, recover, the pain of his wounds may have affected his mind. It could be that he exaggerated ... and he might live. So Selvorne told himself as he tucked around the sides of his old friend.

Girradehn was asleep, and did not sleep well. Little blood near his leg, but Selvorne was not sure if it was a good sign after so long, and when he checked the bandaging, Girradehn did not stir. No feeling and no bleeding, it had to be grim.

Uhlsko looked to be asleep, and seemed to be the most at peace. Seemed almost to smile, in the dim light of a burning stick. A trick of the shadows, he looked either grim, or pleased, as the flame was moved before his face. Otherwise he did not move, breathe, sigh or flinch, and Selvorne thought for all his father had done for him, he could do nothing more – not without the help of his son. Not move, not sit, not lie down, though he could fall – he was helpless. His body remained, but truly he had gone to the Sea.

Promises made. Oaths sworn. There was no time for grief, there would be years for that, later. Selvorne took two knives – no, three, one for each man – that meant to kill, that meant to cut, that meant to carve. Perhaps three was too many, but Selvorne took them regardless, two at his belt in well–made sheaths, the carving one in its leather wrap, strapped badly to his leg. He stirred the fire to greater warmth, and positioned two large sticks to burn through the day. They would be flaming clubs if he had to return, if he had to fight – he was not sure if he hoped to, so when he left the cave he looked for his foe, but perhaps not as carefully as he should have done, more hunting than hiding.

No man or creature moved amongst the rocks. The sound of the river was heard, and nothing more. It was peaceful, and not so early in the morning as he had thought. The sun had risen, but, being in a cave at the base of the southern cliff, they were in shadow. Hidden – not a bad place to hide, it would be in shadow all day. He made his way carefully from corner to boulder, staring to the distance in all directions, searching the ravine floor and top of cliffs as he went.

The wreckage seemed almost to belong there, it had settled, it made no sound. Barrels had shifted, by wind or water, only one was in the river, floating low – wine was in it still, it had not split. It was caught by a small group of boulders and bumped against them, as gently as a cradle, a babe inside, asleep. It seemed strangely at peace. The wine within it would be valuable, but Selvorne thought he liked the way it had almost escaped from being drunk. When he checked it, it was unharmed, and of the finer sort of barrel, so he prodded it free and let it flow down the river, following to keep it moving from the shallows to the depths. A few times he had to push it, roll it, or chase it as it went too fast, and soon it was near the cave, so he stopped it.

Few of the barrels that year were fine. Most were of the ordinary sort, sealed by a bung hammered into the hole, and not to be opened until ready to be used. Annoying, for the merchants who would buy them at the festival. Also for Arnlausa, who preferred the more expensive kind of barrel, which had a strong iron latch on the head hoop, allowing the entire end to be removed. Very costly, but it meant they could open the barrel and taste the wine at the purchase, and it also meant the barrel, once empty, could be used for other things ... and he would not need to buy barrels from the north, something that always gave him grief, both for the vast expense and dislike of the barrel makers there.

So Arnlausa bought barrels of wine in the south, took them north and sold them at the Festival of Tavalehk. It was a good trade every year, and an adventure together for two old friends. No others journeyed south to do the same, and that only made it more profitable, but it was not for coin that they went each year. It certainly did not discourage them, indeed, that year it had not gone so well for profit, and yet they seemed pleased for reasons they would not reveal. Different sellers had been met in the south, not the usual merchants, and sharper deals were made against them. They were not unhappy, even though speaking of it with some anger. It had taken a longer time than usual, they had returned later than expected, and each had bruises, almost faded, and the hint of smiles that had not yet left their eyes. Especially when asked of their wounds. A fight must have happened, but his father would not speak of it. Nor would Girradehn, which was most odd of all. When Selvorne tried to trick them to talk, all three merely grinned. All three – even his father – and that was very strange. Selvorne decided that, if he could think of no trick to make them talk, he would demand an answer. That was his plan the day before, if they did not speak of it freely, but all had changed, and he did not think he would ever know.

There was no time to think on it that morning, and if it was important, they surely would have said. He looked to the other barrels, and found some were fine – very good quality, for very good wine. Large enough for many sales by the cup, at the festival. Large enough for ... a new purpose. None of his friends could have realised weeks ago they were purchasing their wooden tombs, or that the wine they had then tasted would return to the barrels once more, in their bellies, and in their blood.

Nor did Selvorne think he would be heaving one up from the river to a cave. Pushed, tumbled, rolled, he should have emptied it first, but could not bear to waste more wine, even though it would be lost forever in the wooden tomb. With all his strength he lifted it when he had to – the weight of a heavy man, which was not too great an effort, for it had good edges to grab, unlike a man. He headed into the cave, where they slept, and he wondered as he caught his breath if the effort might make him join them. He did not fall, nor collapse exhausted, but rested until his strength returned.

So began his first task promised. Three would be fetched, though only one needed the barrel that morning. Arnlausa slept and breathed, Girradehn stirred and wanted wine – Selvorne was not sure if wine was wise, so he gave water.

The second barrel was chosen. He poured half the wine to the river, then sealed it again. The finer ones with a removable end were very well made, and few were hurt from the fall. Only one had broken completely, having flown free to hit a rock, but even its wound was only a deep cut, and the wine flowed only emptying half. The cheaper barrels had burst the bung or completely split – even those still in the waggon, though it had fallen at an odd angle and they should have had some protection. Strange, but they were poorly made, as was their wine. Only the finest barrels would do for a tomb, and once he had made his selection he floated, rolled and heaved the second barrel to the cave.

A strain – though less weighty than the first, he was growing weary. No food, no time – poor rest, and the unpleasantness of the task, the day, the situation – only the fear and necessity kept him going. Despite the urgency, he had to rest.

~

To the back of the cave he rolled the first barrel, positioning it so it would be hidden the best, and removed its top. The smell of wine, already on his clothes – the cave filled with it. Some would spill. Some could be saved, so he filled a bladder with it – and hid it there for a better time, when he would return, victorious, he would drink of it to honour his father. He was sure it should keep well for a few weeks, let alone days, hidden at the back of a dark, cool cave.

By the light of a burning stick, and a candle held in one hand, he examined his father – unbruised. Unhurt – asleep. No – not as pleasant as the day before, he seemed grim. Selvorne felt the same as he looked on the face of Uhlsko one last time. No smile. No frown. No eyebrow raised in silent astonishment at his silly son – none of the looks that Uhlsko would usually give. No hint it was all a wicked jest – no sign it was one of his tests. No joy, and not even disappointment. For any of those, Selvorne yearned, but instead, by the light of a candle in a cool dark cave, he saw only death.

As hollow as it was, what he began to feel was duty. His father was the best of men, and deserved dignity at the end. Selvorne put down his candle and burning stick, arranged so he could see, and grasped the shirt of his father – made by his mother – well made, he realised as he did not tear it, despite the strain. It must have been almost as old as himself, and he felt some pride that his mother made such a thing – that his father wore it – and that, if they were to meet in the Sea of the Dead, it would please her to see it again.

Both might be proud to see their strong son, for Selvorne, having worked with heavy stones for many years, and doing his best to complete his grim task with refinement, managed to lift his father from under the arms before him, up from where he sat, to almost standing – then heaved him up higher, in a way to swing his body and make his feet land over the edge of the barrel. Bumping hard, but not spilling. He lowered, it was awkward and strained him, but he did so and Uhlsko descended into the wine. Lower he sank, held in Selvorne's hands – lower, to his chest, then wine began to spill. He held his father until his arms were strained, until the edge of the barrel dug into his flesh for the weight of the man. Until he could no longer bear the effort or sorrow of staring into the face of the man he loved his whole life. Then Selvorne let him sink.

Uhlsko rested under the wine, causing spillage like a gentle fountain, for a few moments. Then ripples – then stillness. Selvorne used the candle to peer down – slumped to the bottom of a barrel large enough to hold two boys, he thought, or one man snugly. His father seemed comfortable. At least, he did not complain. Selvorne winced at his own thoughts, then took the lid to seal the wooden tomb. Uhlsko was gone, and if Selvorne did not wish to join him, he would have to hurry. He almost left, but it seemed wrong to leave him there, alone. Stooping, he chose three small stones from the ground, then placed them nicely on top of the lid. One for his mother – one for his father – one for himself. Together, in a way, the best marker he could make for the tomb. For the time – and he knew he must hurry, so with just a single nod of farewell, he gathered the candle and burning stick, and left the back of the cave.

The third barrel was the worst to fetch, the hardest to find, the most pain to bring – not for weight, as Selvorne drained it more than the others. Not for lack of choice, though few remaining seemed suitable. The hurt of it was the realisation of what it would mean to the man who saw it there in the cave, made ready and waiting for him.

Girradehn knew he would die. Arnlausa said he did. He might have hoped otherwise at first, or perhaps to die, but not in the cave. Not alone. Carried by men to Vaskatohr, making it to Tavalehk and there – friends at his side, to mourn him as he languished. Some small hope, but it was a lie, he must have known that as well. If killers wanted them dead, if they waited and watched and meant to catch Selvorne, there would be no carrying him to towns. He might have hoped other men might be sent to carry him away, told by Selvorne, once he was safe. Many could come, all who loved him, tend him in the cave, perhaps, not leave him alone – but the barrel could mean only one thing. The order of Arnlausa was to let him die in the cave, put him in a barrel, then leave him there until it was more convenient to roll it away. Alone, save for Selvorne, and neither man liked the other much.

Selvorne found a fine barrel already emptied. It had a break at the bottom, and was sitting nicely, the correct way up – how it had fallen that way instead of toppling to its side, he could not guess, though it was empty because the bottom had split and all the wine drained away. The ravine stunk of it – and worse. Blood and death, stronger than before. The ox made the smell – he thought to cut meat for breakfast from it again, but wished he had done so the previous night, when it was fresh, when it did not smell, when it was – headless?

Selvorne stared at the ox – headless. There was the cause of the terrible smell, and that – it made no sense. It had a head, he ... could not have been mistaken. No, he was not – crushed by the waggon, half turned as it fell – the poor beast had caught the all of it. Barrels and slabs and the weight of its body, falling in shallows between waggon and stone. Its horns bending its neck, that alone should have killed it fast. He remembered it well, but that morning its head was gone. No horns, no head. No look of fear frozen on its oxen face – it all was gone.

Almost into the waters he crept, to determine how it had been lost – perhaps, so broken, it hung by a thread of neck, then was worked free by the current – but it was not there, in the river. Very well, it had floated away. Did ox heads float? Perhaps it was gnawed by rats, then ... eaten. That was nonsense. A fox? Or ... a bear. In the ravine? None had ever been seen, but – and then he realised – the thing he had seen the night before, it had to be, atop the cliff when he watched from shadows – larger than a man, silent and dark. A bear had come.

There was the mystery solved at once. The Waehdric law was clear – no bodies by water to be left. Selvorne bit his lip to think that such a creature had been so near. Terribly ferocious, silent – and strong. Fire would keep it away – fires did not burn forever, though, and that ox was going nowhere. Not by his hand. Nor was Arnlausa, or his father – not carried by him, as he had to avoid being seen on the road. No more delays, no fear of what Girradehn might think, he went to the barrels to find one at once.

As if he did not have enough to trouble him, bears were about, and he had only a small fire and a long dagger, a small cutting knife, and one for carving. If he did manage to kill a bear with the first, he could slice it with the second and serve it with the third. Any enemies who came upon such a mighty hunter having breakfast would flee. No, they would come to the ravine and find his wounds ... unbearable, Arnlausa would say – knives were no use. No spear, only a broken sword – the others were likely at the bottom of the river. His own spear, there on the cliff – and what use against a bear, which could take the head of an ox with ease, and go unnoticed in the night.

At night they came, so he was told – never seen. By day as well, though, and rarely seen, and few dared hunt them. In the far north, in the mountains, none had been seen near his town for his entire life – clearly they were there, and either no one knew or none had warned him. All those times he slept alone outside by the lake – wandered in the woods, poorly armed – herded pigs, with nothing but a stick, a bell and a horn. Bears, and only miles from home. One more thing he should have been told and had not. Anger mixed with fear as he poured wine, from the only fine barrel that seemed strong enough to keep such creatures out.

A crashing rock, and he froze. He heard it – he was sure – over the sound of the river, which was not so loud there where it was deep – over the sound of breeze that was gentle that morning – over the noise of his own thoughts that ran fast through his mind. A rock – falling – a creature, approaching – but the fear of bear became that of man, as the sound was followed by laughter, and one calling to another atop the cliff.

Selvorne slowly crouched. Not hidden well, if at all – foolish, but hopeful. Voices, from the northern cliff, where the bridge once joined the road leading to his town. Friends – townsfolk – come to help – why would they laugh, then, to see the bridge broken, fallen to the ravine, and all its wreckage below?

Towards the waggon he crept, unsure if moving slowly or staying still would be best. A man was atop the cliff – and another. No more laughter, and the two began a descent – one, two – three? No, there was no third. Not that he saw, but one might be watching.

Selvorne did not care, he moved fast to the one fine barrel he knew to be empty. Men clambering down would face the cliff, not the ravine – he had no other choice, or chance. No bushes there to hide, no boulders large enough to conceal a man, and no time to run back to the cave, which would lead enemies to the others and trap himself – and running the other way, east, would lead him to a small lake, a cold swim, and a large waterfall. The start of the ravine, with smooth sides and no escape.

Three knives, one long – at belt and boot. Neither weapon nor skill enough to do battle against two men. The barrel was light and empty, and once opened he put the lid aside. Silent and swift, he upended it and lowered it over himself as he crouched, as though it were an enormous hat. Darkness was all around him, until his eyes adjusted to the light at the broken end, where there was a small hole through which he could see. He rotated it until it faced the men, then wondered if that was wise. Two men – three knives – no skill, but he was hidden, and he almost hoped they would find him, for a plan began to form as he realised that as both lifted the barrel expecting wine, they would instead discover a blade in each of his hands.

The thought of it made him tremble in fear – or something else. What had his father said – he was not sure, but he felt ... something. It should have been silent in the barrel, but he heard his heart pounding, and his breath. Not the men, he could only see them, and the ravine was quiet as they made their way quickly down the cliff.

Why was he there – he should have hidden. He was, just not very well. Anywhere would be better, but ... even a boulder would be circled, by men in each direction. There was no choice, his barrel was the best he could have done. But why had he ... his promise was to live, to flee. Broken, and at the very first dawn. He calmed himself, his breath slowed, and though crouched and cramped, he did not move for fear the barrel would be noticed. Though ... it was not quite fear, he realised, and he felt strange.

Two men came. The waggon blocked his view, but across the river, then up the rise – there they were, he saw them at times. Silent. To attack, sudden – knives, fists, or the broken beams of the bridge – he would beat them soundly. The thought kept coming to him, but he remained quiet. What had Arnlausa said – and his father – fear and caution, and ... be aware of the enemy. Seeing them was not enough, he had to watch them, he had to be sure.

Selvorne breathed deeply, and put himself at ease, and as he did and watched them across the river, he began to smile. Fear – yes, there it was, he had no doubt – in them, not himself. They were more than cautious. He felt delight. Furious delight – anticipation, not fear, as would a hunter feel, watching his prey.

A promise had been made to be careful, but the realisation they were afraid gave him joy. Every step they took was silent – looking, waiting to be attacked. Selvorne was not sure if that was an advantage or not, in the barrel. To be so cautious, they might suspect he was there, and kick him over. His plan began to seem stupid as he thought more upon it, and the men more deadly as he saw they were armed – his heart began to pound once more as he wondered what might happen. And then he realised he did not know if they were enemies – two innocent travellers would also be cautious, seeing such a wreckage in the ravine. So would thieves, who had nothing to do with the bridge falling, who happened by and wondered what had occurred there, and if danger remained. The killers would be just as afraid, but they also might have others watching and waiting, ready to charge out from where they hid. That would mean clambering down the cliff, and Selvorne could flee – unless they had already done so. A dozen plans and twice as many problems ran through his head, and he regretted once more hiding instead of trying to run.

The men went west. Not to the wreckage, they headed west on the other side of the river. Selvorne watched in horror – why west – why were they not taking the easy crossing in the shallows? What men would head that way, unless ... the wreckage was nothing new to them, and ... why were they sniffing the air?

Along the bottom of the cliff they went, to the crevice where Selvorne had first made the fire, and he realised what they were doing – they smelled the ash. Their entry to the crack in the cliff wall was silent and deliberate – knives drawn, both men were there to kill, if needed. That was not how friendly men moved – nor frightened travellers, he thought, though he was not so sure of that – would good men call out? A greeting, expecting good strangers to be met? Or would they be fearful, and killers calm – Selvorne was unsure. He was quite certain, though, that they were not surprised to see the wreckage, for no smell of smoke would draw men to a cave when there was a broken waggon and barrels scattered in a ravine. Killers, most likely – and their intention seemed deadly as they disappeared across the river, into the cave.

His hiding place – stupid. His plan – foolish. His only hope was that they would not see him – that they would not be curious as to how one barrel opened itself and turned upside down to stand neatly on its end. That they would not peer into the hole, looking for wine or valuables there – not start gathering all they could to steal. All such things would happen, and he began to think again how he might fight. A jump, a stab, the barrel as a shield – surprise, unlikely – but he could shove and charge and dive to the river, and swim well, and though not far across, should they follow, he might be able to wrestle – that was just as stupid. As soon as he was swimming, they would throw rocks at his head. The promise to Arnlausa – to learn to fight – also broken, and the morning was early. Never again would he be so stupid to hide so poorly, if he had the chance. He swore it as he sat crouched and uncomfortable, then the men appeared from the cave, calling to each other and jumping over the crossing. He watched as they approached, seeming more dangerous with every step.

One man appeared quite tall, with long black hair, tied back behind his head. He wore all grey in various shades, and seemed very elegant for a man who might be a killer, walking with his head held high and not at all afraid as he approached.

The other man seemed quite average in all ways – not tall, not short, not fat nor thin, brown hair of medium length, which seemed wet by water or sweat, although it could have been styled by spit. His shirtsleeves were rolled to the elbows, and he wore leather bindings on his wrists, as a man might if he was not used to heavy labour, and had strained his hands lifting. Of the two, he had the most trouble climbing down the cliff, the harder time leaping from stone to rock at the crossing, though that could have been from the difference in height to the other, who almost stepped over. The shorter man had seemed the most afraid, at first, and yet was the most confident as he approached the wreckage. Any fear either man had was gone when they were there, and that only made Selvorne uneasy, for no innocent man would stand before such a thing and remain so calm.

"Touch nothing," the shorter man called out to the taller man. He stooped to a barrel that was dribbling wine, and Selvorne could only half see him there.

"Would you like some wine? A morning taste, it goes to waste, none will miss it, none will see?" the taller man asked – a clear voice, refined, and – delighted?

The other took wine to his hands and drank, both agreed it was good, and, standing, they looked at each other.

"A shame to waste it? A fine drink – it flows, it is lost – do you think?" the tall man asked, and the other nodded, removed his bladder from his shoulder and emptied it – water, Selvorne thought – and then began to fill it from the leaking barrel. The taller man tilted it so it would hurry, and at the end, they both seemed pleased.

"Touch nothing," the shorter man said, and the taller one nodded – an order, repeated and acknowledged, but Selvorne suspected the shorter man was not the one being obeyed.

They peered around the wreckage – creeping, staring, touching nothing – but searching for something. From all angles – it was odd behaviour for thieves. Or brigands, or whatever a man might be called who meant to take what belonged to another. Strange behaviour for a traveller, also. Not strange for men in fear, and Selvorne began to wonder if it was being attacked that they feared – or being careless.

For a brief moment one came close, passing the barrel, he may have looked down, might have suspected Selvorne hiding there, it was hard to tell for a man crouched beside a man standing tall. Only a moment near – less than a moment was the desire to jump and strike. Only moments would Selvorne last, in such a battle, he would surely – no, he might win. It was not impossible – for a young man he was stronger than most, clearly more than the smaller man, and had both weapons and surprise. Just for a moment he wondered, and he sat in silence. Even if he succeeded, he would not know who he was attacking.

Men sent to help – hope rose within him – who would come and not touch anything? It had to be men sent to look for the injured. Someone had seen the wreckage, someone who was travelling to the Festival of Tavalehk, though ... that would mean someone coming from the south. Very unlikely, no one ever came from the south anymore. Not a traveller, then, unless ... people had come from the north. That was just as rare, but the order made no sense for travellers. Touch nothing – disturb nothing, unless helping, they had to have been sent – and later, others would come to investigate, and wanted things left as they had fallen. Touch nothing – do not steal. An order to two men sent running to assist. Help if you can, if men are injured – no men there, they instead helped themselves to some wine that would be lost. Hope rose in Selvorne and he thought to announce himself, but something seemed wrong, so he remained hidden, and bit his lip.

"By my reasoning," began the shorter man, "I have determined the truth of it."

"Oh? And is this your famed reasoning, a far – or, for that matter, the actual truth?" the taller man asked, but Selvorne misheard some of what he said.

"Aha – you have your doubts. Explain, then – the headless ox."

There were murmurs from the taller man that Selvorne could not quite hear, then the shorter man laughed – standing nearer, his voice was clear.

"Indeed. I think not, my friend, float or sink we would see it there – no. A stubborn ox, as is the way of such beasts – led half across. It stopped. They do, you know – then the sudden crack."

"You think they fled afar?" the taller man asked.

"Saved by the very ox, that not moments ago they whipped – forcing them to walk – enabling them to run."

"I admit, it makes sense."

"More than sense – good reason. A stubborn ox that will not walk, and so, the delay – first days, then moments."

"And a chance to flee, afar – I am not so sure. They did not flee."

"Your conclusion, not mine," the shorter man said, "only to the sides, north or south, I think south. There is left a sign."

"Perhaps they did not cross?" the taller man asked, and the shorter man laughed.

"My, friend, clearly they did, or – "

"At the top," the taller man said, and he seemed proud, "the ox stopped before the bridge. The men, they waited – perhaps to eat. Then, it crossed of its own, and fell."

Selvorne was facing the north – the light of sun would not shine into the crack in the barrel, not reveal his astonished eyes peering out. The shorter man seemed thoughtful, and began to nod – the other was grinning wide, then bowed a half bow, not complicated or formal, though it was quite elegant.

"I am impressed, your time with me has made you clever," the shorter man said.

"By your side, any man might seem clever," the taller man said – and they both laughed.

Laughter was not what friends would do – not friends of Arnlausa, or men of the town. It was not an amusing thing to discover such death, not even if they thought the men were unhurt. The poor ox alone was a cause for sorrow. The cost of it alone should make friends glum.

"But what of the head?" the taller man asked.

"Ahh – you now realise the truth of it," the shorter man said, "the head of the ox, destroyed, gnarled – gone. From the fall? I think not – and there, a crevice with a fire, and see the shoulder, cut for meat."

"Surely not eaten – taken afar?"

"Taken. Eaten, yes, a lunch of fresh meat. The stupid ox – what cost to them, but see, nothing of value left – the head, a trophy to show, though."

"A strange, heavy trophy for men with no waggon – why would they bother?"

"Again, my friend – allow me. Destroyed, gnarled – anger at first, and a meal. Then, wine, sour at first – yes, quite sour. The cost, the loss – but not of their lives. How long, with wine, to realise the beast saved them – how long before – "

"Are they here?" the taller man asked suddenly, and Selvorne clenched his teeth. The shorter man raised a hand – Selvorne's eyes widened as he peered through the crack – that was a sign, a signal, an order. The other man obeyed in silence, as Selvorne's heart missed a beat.

"Do you see them?" the shorter man asked.

"No."

"Eaten, well fed, drunk – perhaps a second waggon followed, or a cart. One fallen, one saved. Them saved – by the beast, it would not take long to realise, and then decide to keep its head in honour, and displayed – or kept for luck. Loss of profit, some has remained. Wine and ... these odd stones. Slabs cut for carving, I believe, for writing with a chisel. Lives saved, and a tale to tell – a head to hang at a tavern, all would ask, and then perhaps more wine would be sold in days to come. At the tavern of the Lucky Ox. Profit returned, to the wise man. Danger, though, remains."

"We must go afar – but – why have we not seen them?"

There was silence for a few moments, and it seemed both men nodded. Selvorne felt uneasy – signals were given that he could not see – a look, or glance or sign with the hand. He was sure of it, but not certain they were not signalling that he was seen.

"And of course, more difficult to the north," the shorter man said.

"Faster to climb there than go around, though. Do you think – how many?"

"Few."

"And – how do you think that?"

"The waggon – no room to sit for many. The fire, not so large. The food taken, not so much – the best parts left, though, I am not so sure of that, I admit. Some like the cheek of ox, and the tongue."

"And tail," the taller man said.

"And tail – all of which may keep a day for soup, if left here, and so – we must hurry. They might want soup tonight."

"We must go afar – I – I am not sure of this," the taller man said.

"I am as sure as can be – come, some are ... not all, that would look suspicious. A few. By chance, and one to be caught and left. Hurry!"

Selvorne eased a little as the men moved away, until he realised they had taken to a barrel, working it free of the waggon where it had been tied and stuck. It crashed to the ground, as did others, once there was room. The men then pushed the barrels into the river.

Touch nothing – they had an odd way of obeying that order. Barrels filled with wine or not, they were pushed to the river, one after the other, and began to float to the west. Just as Arnlausa said they might do, were they thieves. Guilty, then –

there was his proof – there was the sign of it, and there was his knife, ready – push his barrel to the river, and they would have a nasty surprise.

Four barrels only were pushed, then the taller man protested. One more was placed near the river, as a clue to where the others went – and one of the four was pushed until it became stuck on rocks. The other three were prodded and moved until they floated down – they floated not too well, and had to be rolled over river stones where the crossing was shallow. That part of the ravine where the bridge had been was narrowest, the river, deepest, except at the crossing. Much farther downstream barrels would be rolling and tumbling, all the way to the sea – but it was a strange river, at one time fast, and other times slow. For a mile at least barrels would need to be shoved and guided, from one deep pool to the next. If the men meant to head that way to secure their theft, they might find the cave.

"Better that we go afar, I think, and now," the taller man said.

"I agree – they ... later we may ... no, they are stuck once more. Come, quickly."

"It is too – the village is not far."

"Quickly then!" the shorter man said, and though both headed to the crossing, the taller man crossed and the shorter man ran farther, pushing the barrels into the deeper waters and then, farther still – calling, until the taller man joined him. They disappeared to the side where Selvorne could not see – to the west, their voices grew more distant, until he heard them no more.

Selvorne could have killed them. He was sure of it. Speed and surprise, they seemed unable to handle either. But he was not sure who or what they were – if thieves, the strangest he could imagine. Or perhaps the cleverest, if they meant to steal and not be caught, by floating barrels west before hoisting them up the cliff. A lot of effort and danger, for three mere barrels. Almost everything they said made little sense for thieves, or killers, or passersby, who happened upon the wreckage. And least of all for friends.

No sense at all. The two men showed neither worry for the death of those who might have fallen, nor concern for the failed killing. They feared something – that was clear. Not to be attacked, not there, in the ravine, and they did not seem keen to meet with those who owned the waggon. It was all quite odd and confusing, but what worried Selvorne more than their strange behaviour was the realisation that it all could have been a performance done for him – that they had detected him, seen him from above, spied him in the barrel, or somehow knew he was there, and they said things to make him come out from hiding.

Seen him, but suspected others – perhaps. But to steal barrels, and the things they said – surely it would have been wiser to lure him out by feigning sorrow? It made no sense. None of it. Except the theft of barrels, which were being floated towards the cave as he sat there wondering.

To the west he could not see, not through the crack in the split oak. He dared lift the barrel an inch – turned it – set it down and looked – there they were, far away, not standing behind him, as he had feared. Hundreds of yards of shallows where the river was wide, then some deeper pools, but a maze of water until it became a river again. That would take them a mile, followed, perhaps, by many more miles to the next falls, where barrels would be stuck on stones. Either would take them dangerously close to the cave, and Selvorne could not risk them finding all that was hidden there.

Up and over went the barrel in which he hid, heaved away from him like a great wooden cloak, and it crashed down. Searching the cliffs – no sign of other people. Should any come, he would climb the south side, apparently fleeing, then wait with spear for their heads to appear, near his feet, as would a fish in a lake. No sign of men, though, and no danger – just two odd fellows pushing barrels west. For a moment he felt like freeing the one they had set against the rocks – ruin their plan, whatever it was, but such revenge was petty. He needed to capture them, and he was not sure he could. There was one thing he could do, and if he had to, he would.

Carefully he followed – it was not difficult. They were occupied with the barrels, and all Selvorne had to do was stay far away and behind any stone or shadow he could find – the south side was mostly in shade, and the men rarely looked his way. They also were moving slowly. West they went, cheering when the three barrels floated, cursing when they were stuck. Quite a fortune in wine, they were large barrels – properly called drums, though Selvorne thought the name stupid, as drums were much smaller and made for music, not wine.

The cave – there it was, and perhaps if Girradehn was stupid enough to yell out for help, men might hear. But he should not, unless asleep and in pain, and unaware of what he was doing. The fire was out, but it might smell of smoke, perhaps. Selvorne was not sure, but his own clothes must have done. Then again, most men travelling smelled of smoke often, so perhaps the others would not notice – they had noticed the remains of the fire in the crevice, but that was deliberate, and the ash was near the entrance.

They passed. Not a moment of pause to look to the dark cave – one of many crevices and cracks, not at all interesting. No care, except for their boots threatened by water, they did their best to remain dry. The taller man had a long stick and the shorter one encouraged him to use his long arms as well. Farther they went, but only to the first waterfall, then the river ran deep almost to the sea – days of travel, surely they would not go so far ... no, they would not. They had nothing with them for days of travel, but if they had – Selvorne could take them in the night. One at a time, as they slept, thinking themselves unseen and safe.

Selvorne stood near the cave. That was his plan, which he almost dared not admit. He had hoped they would go in the cave. Into the dark – fearful, and astonished. Out to the light – and in goes his knife. When entering or exiting their eyes must adjust – his would not, and they would be blind. He almost hoped ... almost followed – but instead he looked for other foes, west, east, on the cliff and anywhere they might hide. He saw no one, and entered the cave alone.

~

Girradehn was asleep – Arnlausa still lived, also asleep, but he would not wake when prodded. Girradehn did, and was not at all pleased as he complained loudly.

"Be quiet," Selvorne said.

"Why are you still here?" Girradehn demanded.

"Men have come – two – armed with knives," Selvorne said, and Girradehn shook his head to wake his mind, "they looked over the wreckage, they have stolen three barrels, floating them down the river."

"Father?"

"Dead," Selvorne said, frowning – worrying – Girradehn was not thinking clearly.

"Arnlausa? Dead?"

"Alive, asleep. He will not wake."

Girradehn sucked in a breath and looked down to his wounded leg. He stared and was silent, and Selvorne wondered if he might fall back to sleep.

"Was it them?" he asked at last.

"Who?"

"Did – they – cut – the – bridge?" Girradehn asked – very slowly, as was his way when suggesting Selvorne could not keep up.

"I – do – not – know," Selvorne replied.

"You are an idiot."

"And you are clearly feeling better, so go out and do what guards do," Selvorne said, regretting it at once, for Girradehn was crushed, "I did not mean it. Ignore me – advise me. Thieves? They only seemed interested in the wine. Arnlausa suspected ... killers had come for us."

"Not for you – for us, perhaps. Stealing barrels – two men – thieves. Killers would look for us, not the barrels. Kill them both. Or bring them here."

Selvorne stared and blinked.

"What?"

"Kill or capture – there are your orders, off you go."

"Are you joking?"

"Do I look like a man in the mood for jest? My leg is gone, I feel nothing of it – only the creeping sickness that comes, and though there is no pain now, I know what that means. I am dead. But I should like to see them die before I do, indeed, where is the hilt of my sword? Still lethal with no blade, and I think I can swing it hard, if you hold their heads low."

It was grim – Girradehn was not joking. Selvorne agreed with him, in all ways except one – he did not know who the men were, and doubted they only wanted the barrels. He told everything that he had seen and heard, as best he could, and Girradehn grew frustrated.

"You are just a boy," Girradehn said.

"I am."

"What, no argument, for once? Have I finally defeated your defiance – now, at the last?"

"Yes. Arnlausa said not to confront anyone – that we do not know who they are – clearly we do not. What do you ... I am not going to capture them, I have not the skill."

"I know," Girradehn said.

"And I will not pretend I do – I might be able to kill them, or might die trying."

"Or might have to, if we wait here and they come in, hearing us argue."

"Then you can help me fight."

"Trip one to me and I shall. Selvorne – leave me with tinder and food, water and wine, and cover Arnlausa for warmth – give me clothes as blankets. Give him the cloaks. Make haste – then go carefully, to Vaskatohr. Careful – do not be a fool. They likely have others, though I think not many. They likely fear being caught – that is good. Do not fight them – but find men of Vaskatohr, the strongest, four should do, leave some to protect the women, tell all to be careful – come for me. I might last. I would rather die in Tavalehk than in a cave – or anywhere, other than here. I cannot order you, but these are my wishes."

"I will do my best, but this may take many hours."

"Well, I shall stay here then, but I cannot vouch for Arnlausa, his eyes wander and feet follow," Girradehn said.

It was not amusing, but Girradehn seemed to think it was – for a few laughs, which became almost sobs. Then he was grim once more. One barrel was near Arnlausa – Girradehn knew what it was for, and seemed to look around for another. Selvorne prepared as instructed, did the best he could – said his farewell to each of them, briefly to those not awake, a mere wave towards the barrel with his father inside – then moved out to the ravine, to make his way home, northwards to the town of Vaskatohr.

~

Brigands, killers, thieves – whoever the two men were, they could not be seen as he cautiously left the cave, wondering if they were prepared to attack him. Not seen, not heard, not to the west, nor the east. He made his way carefully, knowing well that a third man or more could be waiting.

He did not expect it, the two men had seemed alone. It made sense – they had come to check that the bridge had fallen, and had expected the waggon to come. A delay of days, one of them had said – and after their initial caution, the two men had become bold. Neither of them had made signal or sign to any who might be waiting on the top of the cliffs.

No such thoughts made Selvorne less cautious. He had the anger to fight them, but was unsure of his skill – he had wrestled and fought his father, at times – and Arnlausa. Win or lose, he never thought they tried their best, and Girradehn always pounded him to the ground. Men he worked with in the quarry had let him win in mock wrestling, and likely thought it most amusing, to praise a boy. Just as they had him convinced he was the strongest of them all – a trick, to make him do more of the work carting stones. False flattery and jests, but his time with them made him stronger than a young man might usually be, and capable, if not skilled. The two men come to the ravine were not friends and not family, and they were used to the dangers of the roads. Selvorne was willing to kill, but not sure how he would do, and so moved with all the care of a man who could see his enemy, added to that of a man who could not, but knew they were there, and expected them to be deadly.

They were not there, in the ravine – if they were, they were hiding. He returned almost to the wreckage, crossed to the northern side of the river, to the cliff where it was difficult to climb, being very steep at the bottom, and quite sheer at first. It was the only way out on the northern side for half a mile, and anywhere else led to woodlands and bogs at the top. He listened for a while – to ascend and appear at their feet would be the worst thing he could do – then climbed.

Sheer, with a jump to the first holds – any animal wandering in would have a long, slow and hungry death in the ravine. Nothing was there, but rocks and water, perhaps fish farther down the river – no way out, unless the animal could climb. No animal remains, none that he had seen. None must have come, for even a goat would have trouble on the north cliff – how a bear managed it, he could not imagine, although he had heard that bears could climb trees. In to eat, out to sleep – a frightening creature unseen in the woods. The ox would feed a bear for a week he guessed, and keep it away from his friends. He hated to leave them, bear or no – he hated everything that was behind him in the ravine, the misery, and the men who caused it – and he hated anything ahead that might have had some hand in it.

With that in mind he climbed the northern cliff with a strange mix of anger and care, hauling himself up until it was more of a steep stairway of loose dirt and stone. The northern side was always unpleasant – always in the sun, and so covered in all manner of grasses that held soil, making parts dirty where the cliff was not sheer. The south side was clean, shaded and strong – a different kind of rock from that of the north, and the ravine itself was the same along its length. The north – dirt, or crumbling and sheer, and on the top of the cliff, woodlands. The south – smooth, hard stone and bare, and on the top of the cliff a barren, rocky land, all the way to the mountains that were the same. Two very different lands that once met, then were torn apart to make a rift, filled with the falling waters. The river once was deep, the higher waters had smoothed the lower sides, ravine floor, river stones and rock. A place to play as a boy – a place to explore as a youth – a grave, for his father and his friend. A place of fond memories, torn apart by murder. He did not hate the ravine, nor the lands, only the men he wanted both to fight and to avoid, and as he made it to the top, he peered about the grasses before clambering over the edge, then he dashed at once into the woods.

The woods near the road – the road from the bridge leading north – the way to his home. Miles, and not so far to run. He wanted to run, the faster, the better – but to do so might be a charge into travelling killers, who were looking for him. Or anyone who looked for him and his father, to discover why they were late. He remembered his oaths to escape unseen, and with that in mind he moved carefully, shuffling along the road, peering ahead and to the bushes each side.

If caught or questioned, he would need some story to convince people he was not with the others, that he had seen no wreckage, and that he had come along the road, alone, later, and was of no interest. No story would be believed – what traveller moved with no pack, no food, no water bladder, and just three knives? If he had a spear he could at least claim he went to fish in the lake. Without it, he could think of no story, other than he did fish, but lost his spear and was returning home with neither tools nor catch. A weak story, since he was going by the road that did not lead to the lake, and he was coming from a ravine, claiming not to have seen the waggon, the headless ox and a half dozen barrels of wine. Not to mention the bridge being gone. He could always pretend he was mad – not far from the truth, if he believed he could convince men with such a story when they were likely looking for him.

Two roads led north to his town, one from the lake farther east, and the one from the bridge that he was following. It was newer than the other, but quite old. The "new road" it was called at first, then "the bridge road" – then simply, the road, as none used the other that led past the lake. The bridge road was solid – winding at times, a choice of path through the woods that required many trees to be felled and bushes to be cleared. Chosen for where the soil was shallow and rock underneath meant few trees and bushes – and less effort to clear. So it wound through the woods, only needing clearing in places, the wood removed for the bridge in the south, or taken north to the town, for firewood. Selvorne had done both, helping in all ways to build road and bridge, but it was a very long time ago, and he was just a boy. For the bridge, they should have used stone. He was told that to do so would cost so very much, and the supports would be wooden anyway, and the ground moved at times and rumbled, and stone would crack – and a dozen other reasons were given why it was made in wood. Stone could not be cut with an axe, and made to fall. It should have been made in stone.

Why the bridge was made at all was a mystery until the years of floods – not terrible floods, indeed, they were very mild. A season of especially annoying rain, his father had said, but it took only days to turn the old road into mud. Bad for a waggon, if one wanted to pass by the lake – but a wooden road could be made, and then no bridge was needed, nor a new road of such expense and toil. For years Selvorne had wondered why they did not do that, until he realised it was not the mud they feared, but the bog – and the sickness it might bring. It was after the death of his mother that the plans were made for a new road and bridge, and that was a very long time ago.

All things had a reason, he was told, and that the town of Vaskatohr was there at all had three – the mine, the spring, and the woods themselves. The mine of copper was so important that no matter how bad the lands around might be, even if nothing but stone and dust, a town would be formed. Not that the lands were bad, only that the copper was so precious. Were there no water to drink, no animals to hunt, no wood for fires and no place to sleep other than on cold hard rock, there would be men – harder than stone – who would live there and work the mine. And all other things they might need would be brought from far away – even water.

Fortunately, a spring brought water to the people of the town – the miners, and the pig herders. And the others, though everyone there was one or the other, if not both. The spring alone was not enough reason for a town, he was told, but a fine thing to have where there was no river or mountain stream. The third thing – the woods – Selvorne considered to be as important as either mine or spring, for they gave wood for building or heat, and food for the pigs herded out to forage. Someone long ago was wise enough to clear trees around the town, and plant orchards in their place, so fruit was plentiful for townsfolk and pigs. More for pigs, which outnumbered men, though there were but a few dozen. A small town was Vaskatohr, merely a village, truly, but with copper and pigs it was prosperous. Both were sent north, and all other things needed were brought back. The journey to Tavalehk was an excuse to enjoy a larger town, to meet with friends and family there, and to spend a coin amongst its many stores.

Vaskatohr had one more thing that Selvorne adored, and that was the lake and fish it provided. Not quite in the town, it was miles away along the old road, at the very foot of the mountains, sheer and rising from the still waters. A lake small enough to swim across, yet large enough to wish for a boat – Selvorne had a coracle, which did fine. Delicious fish that he had a mind to spear – peace and silence, away from the noise of townsfolk he knew too well. Streams fed the lake, and it emptied to the river that ran through the ravine, after the tall waterfall. It was a wonder near his home, the lake, a lovely place of many joys. Had he run a little faster, stopped a little more briefly – he would have gone there, found a fish, returned to his home – and wondered where the others were. Then headed south to search – been caught – then killed. On the very road on which he ran, shuffling, cautious, and aware of the danger.

The killers had come that way, he saw their prints at times in the dust, heading south. No care to hide them, and so, no fear – at least when headed south to the bridge. In the dust and slight breeze the marks were already being blown away, but when he came to a part of the road that was slightly muddy, he saw their prints clearly – heading south. And then – at the edge of the mud only, as if made by accident and left with only little care – footprints heading north.

Selvorne froze. Heading north – the mud, quite fresh, very shallow. Perhaps a light rain in the night, which had dried everywhere else – perhaps only dew, or a stream near – no, there was no stream. Just a small patch of mud, and the prints of men who had no care heading south, but a little care headed back north. They were making a weak effort to leave no tracks, and a very poor effort to hide those they could not help. He would take more care to cover his own.

Less speed and more caution. He could not be too far from his home. A mile, perhaps, though he had not seen the dead old tree that marked the mile. Many other dead trees, for the woodlands were thicker at that place, and he remembered the dozens that were felled to clear the way. Deeper soil meant more trees, and they in turn sprouted leaves to shade the road – the damp road, with mud in places. It must have rained, lightly, and the road had not dried in the shade. More footprints – not treading carefully, after a few that seemed to stumble. Not hiding, then, as he had thought, but merely avoiding the mud. Selvorne did hide, and wondered how far ahead they might be – not far, not if they had left the ravine just before himself.

He was not sure if he was in luck or in danger. It occurred to him that men might leave such prints on purpose, making him think they went one way, when they were actually going the other – or hiding, beside the road. He looked less at the road and more at the bushes, and moved slower as he considered what might happen if two men jumped out at once. Likely one at each side, with a signal and a nod – a boy, no more, to be surrounded and captured – questioned, then killed for answers he could not hide.

None would think him a boy, nor think him that young, unless they saw his face. He was not a boy, but youthful. They would see a young man, with two knives at his side and one at his boot – no pack, no purse, no spear. No killers would be reckless, they would either attack or hide, so he searched carefully, anywhere they might be, as he made his way towards his home.

The old, dry, twisted tree – taller than the others, with many branches, one of which had fallen off and caught on another – hanging there, barkless, leafless, bare. It was a bold sign along the road, visible even in moonlight, though its only use was to let travellers know they had a mile to go to Vaskatohr – not far at all. Surely that was not where the killers went? To his town?

Selvorne felt his heart pounding – he would be there soon, gather men and return. Enemies in the town – claiming one thing to his townsfolk, accused of another by himself – and he could appear amongst them all, pretending to have been in town all day, as though he was merely a lazy boy who had slept late, just risen, and had nothing to do with the bridge. None would know he came from the ravine. None would suspect. He could speak with the enemy – offer ale, pretend to be ... not himself. Just one of the townsfolk, who would realise he was hiding, perhaps, and play along with his ruse.

Eagerness and danger – to deceive them, but ... did they know his name? Would some fool say it and give him away – Stara would, the silly girl, even if he told her not to. Especially if he told her not to – but he could command the men to grab the killers. Not, though, if there were more – perhaps a dozen enemies had arrived. His own town was so very small ... a village only, a few dozen people, most were women, girls, boys – helpless. All the men might be away in the mines, and were unskilled in fighting, even if not underground. As he continued and plotted, he noticed the footprints had stopped.

Stopped – not avoiding the mud, they simply were not there, heading neither north nor south. He froze – in the bushes – he saw nothing. Quickly ahead, then,

to the next mud – no prints. Back again – back, farther south to where he had seen
them last – the prints had stopped quite a way back. Just after the old dry tree with
the hanging dead branch – and there, the prints did not stop, but turned and led
straight into the woods.

A camp – it had to be. There was nothing in the woods, no town, not for days
and not by any path. Only forest trails were there, where pigs had roamed. Bushes,
scrub, bogs – many bogs, and not far from the road. Days of travel to the nearest
town, through dangers of mud and sickness and perhaps ... bears. And to find the
town Tawlehk on the other side, many days' journey to the west, it would be
difficult – surely that was not where they went? No, a camp, it had to be – away
from his town. Selvorne winced to think of it.

Only a mile to his town. He should run. A mile, and home – men, from the
mine, women as well – all to come, armed, and to help Girradehn. Only a mile,
but – he could not help himself. The men he had followed were escaping. West –
the woods – Tawlehk. It made sense, they had floated the barrels down river, and
meant to collect them far away. Two men alone had killed two lords and one
guard, all for three barrels. Selvorne had hoped they would go to his town, he had
grown eager to take them, all at once. That hope was gone, they were leaving. He
could not let them get away, so he entered the woods and looked around, as a
strange poem came to mind.

> In to the forest I go with you,
> In to the forest we lose our view,
> In to the forest you go with me,
> In to the forest you will not see.

From his youth – sung by his father, when they played games of hiding in the
woods. May not see – true, he could not be seen. The men would not be looking,
and a forest was a much easier place to hide than a road. It was safer to follow
through the woods, for the sound of footsteps from one man in stealthy pursuit
would be hidden by those being followed, unaware. The careful man would be
unheard, unseen – in a forest. To stand still amongst trees, a man could vanish at
once if he wore no bold clothes, or slipped behind a trunk.

Think like a brigand, that was the advice of Arnlausa. Of course they would not
go to Vaskatohr, that was where they expected the men to go who had just lost
their waggon. His town would be suspicious of two men coming from the south –
so, perhaps they meant to circle the town by way of woods, then come down to it
from the northern road, claim they walked from Tavalehk, and then learn what
they might. Or they simply meant to escape, having done their terrible deed and
stolen what they could without suspicion. Three barrels was quite a lot of wine,
perhaps they saw the waggon days ago, by the sea, puzzled as it headed east, ran
ahead, and cut the bridge. All such thoughts made sense to Selvorne, but
something seemed wrong as he did his best to follow their trail through the woods.

Too Many

The trail led him far from the road, farther than he would usually go with pigs, even when they ran ahead, and it was not the same part of the forest where he would lead them to feed. From his town, it seemed he was one mile south and a little more to the west. It was a place no people should go, yet the path in the woods was too much like a road. Well worn, flattened ground – heavy boots stomping the dirt and crushing bushes that dared cross where men might walk. In places where a branch had fallen, perhaps in a storm, it had been thrown to the side – or more tellingly, snapped in two. A road, then, which was well used, close to the other road, and unknown to any who lived near. Even the son of the Lord of Vaskatohr.

Unexpected enough, but it was also a lush woodland, not the bog that he had thought it would be. The soil was good and must have drained well, and the ground rose and fell in small hills. There were mounds of dirt, covered in bushes or grass – those, he thought, were once trees, long ago. Dead and rotten they fell to collect soil from the wind, until a mound formed as they were overgrown and lost. At times rock could be seen rising from the ground, smooth boulders of granite, or the liming stones. The woodland was not at all what he had expected, and it amazed him that he had not ventured there to explore, though he had no reason to think he would find anything other than unpleasant bogs.

Vines were the most surprising thing, coming from the ground and covering the trunks of trees – strangling them, sometimes to a great height. At times fallen branches remained, hanging from their own tree or propped against its trunk, and there the vines grew as well, making a leafy tent about the base of trees. It was a very strange land, and his astonishment almost made him forget what he was doing.

Two men ahead he saw, and he began to question what he was doing. They were moving slowly, but not with caution. Talking, but he could not hear. He was not sure what would happen if they saw him – by the time they ran to him, they would be exhausted. If he fled, he likely could hide, and in those woods, never be found. Or found as he leapt out at them – he did not know what was best, so he remained distant and followed. It seemed a long time, twice what it should have been to walk so far, for they moved slowly. After perhaps half of an hour he could smell smoke.

His heart sank – ahead, the men were approaching others – so distant, Selvorne could only see dark shapes moving amongst the trees. He froze. He was too far to be seen, perhaps, and unmoving. Yells – shouts, the men were roused, and he looked to hide. Then laughter, and greetings. Not two men alone, returning to a camp they had hidden – two men joining the many, who were preparing lunch by a fire.

Down Selvorne went – down, so slowly. The undergrowth was thick, he could crawl and not be seen. Away – that was where he should have gone. Away for a hundred yards on his belly, then up, to run – back where he had walked, back to the road, back to the town. Then back to the woods, with men. Gathering as many as he could, though ... how many would he need, he had to know their numbers, and also who he would face on return, if they were still there. If he returned and they had left, then at least he would know their faces, should they eat lunch before leaving. Urgency was upon him, for if he left for help, he would not be back before they had finished eating, and they could go west into the woods, and escape. Little time, a great chance, a wise plan, to hurry back to his town and bring help – the best plan, the better choice. Instead he crawled towards the men at camp.

Yards, towards them, on his belly like a snake in long grass. Arnlausa did not know who had been so bold to kill lords – not knowing was a pain worse than injuries. It was also the greatest danger to Selvorne. There, ahead, could be a rival lord, or the man who served such an enemy. Ahead was a clue, if not the answer. A captain of guards, serving an enemy of his father – or a well-known maker of trouble. A man who had argued with Arnlausa, or Girradehn, or even Uhlsko, though that was less likely, for his father rarely stirred conflict. There ahead were the killers – if he could hear a name or see a face, it would be a great victory. Perhaps even ... to tell Arnlausa, before he died. It might be a relief to his angst, a great help to form a plan – either would make him realise he chose well the new Lord of Tavalehk.

Such thoughts were little relief to Selvorne as he crawled. He knew Arnlausa would not approve of what he was doing, which was very dangerous, but he could not leave without learning something. He needed to know who they were. The thought of hiding, and avoiding killers everywhere he went in his life made Selvorne uneasy. Suspecting everyone and having no one he could trust, perhaps for years – what better way to turn things around, than to spy on them? Hiding from an unknown foe would be difficult – but to hide, discover who that enemy was – he could use it to great advantage.

Arnlausa's plan – Girradehn's plan – his own plan. Arnlausa meant for him to hide and flee from unknown foes. Girradehn wanted him to follow and capture what were clearly thieves. Selvorne thought to look, and learn what he could. One cautious, one bold, his own plan a mixture of the two – perhaps in that way he was more like his father. He was not sure which plan was more dangerous. Likely the worse would be jumping out to attack, for he knew not how many men were there. To flee and hide, knowing nothing, to return to the towns, seeking Cienn, when others sought himself – just as dangerous. Not so sudden as charging in to fight. Either was tempting – to charge or flee, at least they would be quick, and not painfully slow as crawling along in the grass. Not as worrying, every yard wondering if a man might see him, and attack when he was at a disadvantage, on his belly. He continued regardless, and found himself quite close – fifty yards, perhaps – as the cover of the long grass and ferns was diminishing.

Facing north, with the sun behind him. He was unsure of the time of day, likely the middle. A camp was ahead. Men were there, it seemed there were only six in all – the two he had followed, and four more, sitting around a fire. They had sounded startled when the other two first arrived, then laughed, and seemed at ease. Welcoming, and all gathered around the fire, which was quite far from Selvorne. One tall, broad man embraced the tall dark man from the ravine – friends, or brothers, Selvorne was not sure. The shorter man was less well received, and the mood was one of bored acquaintances, not good friends. Or perhaps they were great friends, but suffered greater boredom as they prodded the fire and turned some creature roasting there.

Closer he crawled. The men were in a clearing of short grass, alone in a large area that had to be shallow soil. No bush nor shrub, only a single great tree rose from the open spaces of the clearing – near to Selvorne, it had many vines over branches fallen at its base, blocking his view. Annoying for him to spy, safer for him to hide. Another tree had fallen before that, at the very edge of the long grass, and he crawled to it and peered over the top of the trunk. It was old and rotten, with mushrooms and wood turning to soil, and gave him some chance to watch unseen.

A spring – it had to be, with the rocks sticking up near their camp, and the sound of water trickling. Stones they sat upon – large stones, heavy to move, and in a circle – it was a regular camp to be set so well, or they had been there a while, or meant to be. Were they – reeds? Water rushes – a pond, behind. The spring, perhaps, filling it – some low place, and the water must have led to the north, for no stream or damp was near, other than the slight damp of the soil once the dry top was disturbed. A lovely place – a very good place to camp – and it put him ill at ease, for it was clearly used often, and used well by men he did not know in a place too close to his home.

Tents. That suggested they were not there always, but for long enough to bother carrying a tent. It also suggested there could be more men, asleep or hiding – no, not hiding. Hidden inside the tent, but not in fear, they were not expecting an unwelcome visitor. Yet the men did not seem completely at ease.

Where was he – it was a mile north to Vaskatohr when he left the road. Twice that he had headed north through the woods, and perhaps the same to the west. Not too near the town, but a strange location, far from any people or places of worth. Not so distant that it was not part of Vaskatohr, and he almost chuckled to think how bold it would be to step out from hiding, stride up to their camp and request they explain their presence on his lands.

"I am the Lord of Vaskatohr, what are you doing here?" he would demand, and though that might be what he said, it would not be what they heard – "I am the fool you meant to kill, here I am, capture and question me, I have saved you the effort of searching, and I bring a gift of three knives." He almost laughed at the absurdity of it, and remembered what his father once said – a lord without trusted guards, to his foes who mean him harm, is nothing more than a man.

What he should have done was crawl away and leave. He knew that. He had been lucky that day, many times – but luck was chance, not fate. Luck could come and go, unused, with no advantage, if not pressed to appear – seized when it did – noticed, when opportunity arose. What he noticed was a chance, for the tree that blocked his view had many branches fallen about it, covered in vines – it would give him a great position from which to spy. If he dared press his luck.

Between him and them – the tree and its vines. Moved to the side slightly, he was hidden from them, they were unseen, by him – so he dared scramble over the fallen log, walked low, quickly, like a duck waddling as he crouched to his knees. To the tree, to the vines, through a hole there, he hid inside what was much like a leafy cave at the base of its trunk.

Darkness – good. It was well covered, and very large inside. Spacious, almost, and warm. Branches like beams were all around, perhaps it was partly made by men. Long ago, or branches of the great tree had fallen and held, gathering leaves, then vines, then remained like a roof. It smelled of the damp and vines, and of something else ... he waited until he could see, then crept towards the side that would be closest to the men.

Faces and names he wished to know – numbers, the manner of their dress and speech. Anything he could learn was better than nothing. Where was he – facing north. Sun behind, they would not look to see his well–lit face peering out from the vines. He parted leaves and looked, bold and brave, foolish and lucky – close, and a clear view, he saw the men much better than he had before.

The men from the ravine, and another two – six – eight more were there, one a woman, he was certain. Or a very small man wearing a dress, with dark hair and eyes that were too large. She must have had heavy brows, or a constant frown, or darkened around her eyes with paint, as some women did. Perhaps all three – she was the smallest, but she caught his attention first, for she hit another with a stick when he tried to steal whatever she was cooking, in a pot hanging on a spit over the flames.

The man who was hit ran a few paces, and laughed. Then, to Selvorne's amazement – he tumbled into a dive, and sprung up once more, to the laughter of others. Some skill, much jest, and fair hair that also tumbled – to his chin in waves of curls that bounced as he bowed. He was slapped by another man – one who was dark, with hair slicked back by oils or sweat, almost to his shoulders. The two began to fight – Selvorne wondered if it was real – but the laughter of others suggested it was not, and the small woman hit them both with a stick until they stopped.

Selvorne noticed all – a shirt that once was red, faded to almost rose – that was the fair–haired man, the tumbling fool, and a fool he was, taunting the other man, who did not seem pleased. Young, likely, surely older men would not – but they would act so stupid, no matter how old or wise, if they were bored and amongst good friends.

Two more were arguing. They did not laugh and their fight was not with sticks or punches, but words, spoken low, and at times yelled, so others told them to be silent, but they seemed to sneer back at them. One had brown hair, was beardless, and neat. The other had sandy hair, a short beard, and a shirt that was half tucked in, half left out, half unbuttoned, and with one sleeve rolled to the elbow. Selvorne doubted the other man was criticising his appearance, though he did seem to say the word "shave" quite often, and loudly.

What a strange group Selvorne had discovered. Another two men seemed to be talking, not arguing, not comfortable, one of them with tanned skin and hair faded by the sun, and serious, or seemed to be as he sat upright and spoke to the other who laid back, relaxed, laughing. Sometimes at the stern man talking to him – and he was a well–dressed man with dark brown hair, and seemed not to be short of a coin. Or was, but spent them freely on clothes, and had no worries whatsoever, despite being in a camp amongst killers.

Were they, though – they seemed to be nothing more than travellers taking rest and preparing a meal. No waggon could be seen, so, not merchants. There seemed to be a small cart, pushed or pulled by a man, to carry the tents, pots and pans. Where were they going, though, if travellers? And two of the men amongst them – those from the ravine – were anything but innocent. The one man who stood with them, away from all the others, seemed deadly.

Tall – and broad. Not as tall as the dark–haired man from the ravine, but clearly his friend – and clearly not close to the others. He stood with his back to the pond, and around him were poles stuck in the ground – shafts of spears, they would have to be, and he had many. He did not laugh, but looked to the others as though watching them cautiously. He was not unfriendly, but polite, Selvorne thought, and wary. If any of them saw Selvorne spying from the tree, it would be that deadly, cautious man, so Selvorne watched him the most. His head turned to the left, to the right – to the woods, to the others. He was alert, the others were relaxed, bored, mischievous – but that one man was dangerous. Tall, and he seemed to wear a white scarf about his neck, which fell to one side, and it was positioned there with great care, as though worn with honour.

Selvorne was close enough to see them – hear them, if they shouted – but not recognise them, should he see them again. Their clothes, yes – their height and build, perhaps. Most were nothing unusual, save the tall man with the white scarf and many weapons, and the short woman with dark hair and eyes. She moved almost like a crow – yes, he would know her in a moment, he had never seen a woman quite like her before. The man in the rose–coloured shirt, yes, he was a fool and that was plain to see – easier still to recognise, if his darker friend was seen with him, fighting. The others he could not see well, for they faced away, but seemed so ordinary he might never know them, certainly not by face alone. The two from the ravine, however, he would never forget.

He could go no closer. From no place could he creep to watch, the tree where he hid was dozens of yards from their camp, and the closest place he could possibly hide without being seen. Perhaps he could sneak by way of the pond and rushes – the well–armed man would see him, that would be his end. Perhaps he could go to the west and come back behind their tent – yes, that was certainly the stupidest idea. Dangerous, but the only chance to get closer, and he so wanted to ... he almost hungered for it ... to know who they were, and – he hungered.

He had not eaten. Not that day, not well the night before, and he felt weak. Sitting and crouching, the same position for so long – sore, and tired, and hungry, and – cheese? He was certain he could smell cheese. Did cheese grow in trees? No, what nonsense – but mushrooms did, and some smelled of cheese – no, it was true cheese he could smell. And ale, and he was quite sure, meat. He turned back to the darkness behind him, and stared until he could see.

There – where he entered – was that a sack? And that – a jug? With a handle – his eyes grew accustomed to the darkness, and he saw three bladders hanging from a low branch. Only a few feet high, the viney roof – quite a large leafy tent, and warm, yet out of the sun, so not too hot. Selvorne bit his lip as he realised where he was – a larder made of vines, used by all the men.

Quickly he took to the jug – empty, but smelled of ale. Dry as well, not used for a while – but not left there for days, abandoned. The sack – a wheel of hard cheese, wrapped in cloth, a slice was gone. Meat, also wrapped – cooked and cold, but likely cooked that morning, and then – hidden? It had to be, but why would they use the tree and not the tent, or put it in cool water, or otherwise – it had to be hidden there. And the smell of it was agony, for his hunger was terrible.

Thirst was worse than hunger, and he felt the bladder – velvet leather, it was very fine. He opened the stopper – almost spilling it – and sniffed. Veksale, he knew it must be – the finest ale of all the lands. Perhaps ... a good reason to hide it, then, if not wishing to share. Veksale was from the west, from Veksehl town by the sea. The men likely were as well. Sending barrels down the river – hiding in the woods – yes, the west. But ale was a foolish thing to quench his thirst when he had not eaten, and was in such danger.

The second bladder – the stopper fell off and spilt ale all over the meat and cheese. Selvorne struggled to stop it – too late, enough was lost to ensure they would know he had been there. Any who came would smell it, and he hung the bladder back on the branch.

There was no water – why would there be, with a spring so near. Springs everywhere, he assumed, all the way from there to the sea. Or rivers, or streams. And bogs, but even that water could be drunk carefully from the surface – he wished he had something, his mouth was dry and he felt faint. The vapours of ale were not helping. The enemy had water bladders beside them, and jugs and tankards, but their ale was hidden, and that was all he had.

So he drank. Against his fears and more than he should, but he was thirsty and hungry, a danger in itself should he faint, so he ate cheese as well, and meat. He felt as though a thief – so be it, for all he had endured, a thief he would be – and he would be worse, if he had a chance or was forced to fight.

Well fed, slightly drunk, astoundingly stupid – but honest about it – Selvorne returned to his watching position, and spied upon the men. They were settling to eat. Roasted rabbit, he thought – and drinking – ale? It had to be, they were laughing at things not funny. Good. If they had ale there, they would likely not seek it in the tree. It still worried him, and he wondered if, hiding in the dark, he might not be seen if a man entered the leafy cave. Darkness and the tree trunk to hide him – he would need luck as well. His wits were not sharp, dulled by thirst and then by ale, and he realised as he watched that he would have to leave, crawling through the grass then running – and soon.

A tale came to mind, and a warning – of Torlor the unlucky – Molarklod the Foolish – the man made fun of, in so many stories. A young guard who had no end of poor fortune. He was a good man, in all ways but skill – well intended, well trained, he never listened, and tried in vain – so it went. Torlor Kludbo Molarklod rue – rushing in, and something like that, the words were lost to Selvorne as his mind was faltering. But the guard was once real, he had been told, his luck was quite poor, and he did the kind of stupid thing that Selvorne was doing that very moment – hiding badly, killers near, searching for him, and he was drunk. He was instead supposed to be bringing help – no, fleeing – no, killing. What were the orders? Two men had told him differently, then he added his own decision. He had forgotten. How strong was Veksale to addle his mind so?

He shook his head to clear it, and it only made things spin. What to make of the men he watched, they did not seem like killers. Perhaps that made them the worst kind, to be so comfortable with murder – he did not know. They were eating – good. Settling, then, and he would leave. At the latest, when they slept that night. Better when all gathered and not watching – better in the daylight as well. He would not wait for darkness. Soon – then to town, then to return, women to the ravine to help, men to the woods to kill. Enemies were nine men and one woman, against allies that were ... not many more. And the brigands seemed deadly, some at least, and likely all. And likely none of his town could fight well, and would not obey him, or restrain their stupid fury as they rushed in yelling with pick axes or rakes. Miners and pig herders against killers, one with a dozen spears, who alone might end them all. Selvorne would be leading them to their deaths. The wisdom of Arnlausa's advice occurred to him as he watched the foe they would have to face.

Guards were needed, men who could fight. Trusted, also, and he knew no such men. Selvorne fancied that he could wait until night – creep out in the dark, killing one at a time as they slept. It was only a momentary folly of thought. One sound made, all would wake, he would be dead. Could he kill them as they slept – could he do such a terrible thing? Yes, if they were proven to be the killers, without doubt, all hesitation would be gone. They were not proven guilty, indeed they were only considered suspicious for their association with the two from the ravine. And they were only truly friendly with the one dangerous man, he who remained within his circle of spears, rarely speaking to the others. If only those three were guilty, how could he kill the others? And how could he kill such a man of spears, who likely slept with one eye open, if not both – if he slept at all, and was not planning to keep guard all night.

Two men stood – two men came. Towards him directly, too fast, too sudden, too close for him to flee. Impossible, even if they were not near, for looking in his direction, they would see him crawling away. He had only made it to the leafy cave because it had hidden him as he waddled, and his position seemed stupid as the two men approached.

Back he fell, gently – back to the tree, cloaked in the darkness of a tent made of vines. Covered. Hidden – if he did not move, should they look only briefly into shadows. Ready to fight, if they lingered. He knew that could not end well.

He waited – and waited. Nothing. Waiting more, he looked around the trunk of the tree – no man was there, and it seemed none had stopped near. He looked to the camp – eight were there, no, nine, so one was gone.

Selvorne could wait no more and dared crawl around in the shadows – looking out each way, he found the man – he had passed by, and was over away in the woods. Alone. Standing and looking to the forests – Selvorne sighed. Relief, for them both, he from fear and the man from ale. Selvorne returned to his best place of hiding, wondering what it might mean.

Danger was what it meant. Danger he had not seen. If they used that place, farthest from the camp, far from the fresh spring and pond – if they passed by often – his timing would have to be very good, and his crawling swift as he could. Soon. With all the ale they drank, more men would come, and as he thought on his plans, the vines were suddenly parted, and there was movement behind him.

He froze – he was impossible to see. He was not there, hidden behind the wide trunk, unable to be seen. So he told himself. Someone was with him, inside the cave of vines, rummaging, sniffing, fumbling – then gulping.

"So!" came a voice from the entrance. Selvorne's heart thudded – there was a sound of spluttering.

"You startled me!" came a reply that seemed so close, it had to be from inside.

"And you – not shy, but greedy, I see."

"And generous."

"With the ale of another – better not – here, quick," the man said, then Selvorne heard more gulping.

"Better than the other."

"Bog water is better than the other, but ... best not be caught. You go, it will look less suspicious."

"Give me that first, anything but the fruity rot."

"Yes, but – it smells. He will suspect. Wait – I have a plan," the man said. There were whispers, Selvorne heard more gulping and shuffling, footsteps and more gulping, rustling, footfall on soft dirt – then silence.

Back to the camp went the two men – a few words with the others, tankards of ale – then shouting. Selvorne saw them charging towards him, across the open grove, yelling and angry, two men or more – he was found.

He stayed fast and drew his blades – waiting, knives ready, he had some advantage in shadows beside the tree trunk. Waiting for his doom – then the sound of men came crashing past, one falling, the other tripping so they fell over each other, beside the tree. Laughing – his eyes widened, but he could not see – laughter and then, chasing away once more.

Relief for Selvorne, though his heart pounded hard – then the vines moved as a man entered and was there with him on the other side of the tree. Waiting, Selvorne heard shuffling about, as before.

"To my clever friend," the man said. There was gulping before the bladder was hung, the vines rustled again, and the man thudded past.

All men were gone, Selvorne was alone. He had to get out of there. If they did not find him hiding and soon, they would find him later, dead from the fright of a dozen near discoveries. He had to go, so he positioned himself to watch, hoping they would settle and drink.

~

Selvorne watched, waiting for his chance to leave. He wondered at the men there – and the woman – if they were killers, they would have to be cold hearted and cruel to have done such a thing. And yet were jolly at times, not at all as he had thought. Thieves – if so, they were casual robbers of the most modest desires – leaving all kinds of treasures in the wreckage, hardly searching, taking three barrels only, and caring nothing for securing their plunder. Fools – he thought not, but he began to wonder exactly what kind of people they were.

Three men sat apart, one seemed deadly. Seven others, only the woman and one of the men seemed stern. Perhaps some of them were younger, for each sip of ale made them more like children, joking and laughing. The other three joined them –

ale made all men friends, it seemed, though not all drank. And not all laughed or were merry. But what manner of men were they – to kill, to steal, to laugh.

Bold, some of them – yes, they would not care. They would kill and worry not one bit who knew or challenged them, so Selvorne thought as he watched them drink.

Cautious – some of the men there – a little. But it seemed they were wary of the other men at the camp, and Selvorne wondered if, perhaps, afraid. Of the woman, he was sure. She was their leader, or mother – or aunt, he could not guess her age, but she treated them as children the more they misbehaved. They did mischief, she was merciless, though it seemed often with the wrong man. A game, perhaps, to ease the time, Selvorne was sure men were taking stones and dropping them into the bowls of others, and their tankards, and their shirts. No, it was not caution, not fear – they were fearless. And death meant nothing to them, they made merry, with no regrets.

Or perhaps ... they knew nothing of it. Three were grim, softened by ale – seven merry, and it was almost certain they knew nothing. Laughing in the company of killers – they did not know. Surely no men could be so stupid? Though – surely no man could be so cruel, to laugh after such horrors were done, yet the tall dark man and his shorter friend who Selvorne had seen in the ravine – they did laugh. Anger rose in Selvorne until he remembered what they had said amongst the wreckage – perhaps they, too, did not know men had been killed. Laughing in relief, perhaps. His anger eased, then he wondered if perhaps they were such enemies of Arnlausa they all were laughing in celebration at his death – no, they did not know he was wounded, they should have been afraid, and searching. And yet they celebrated something – or were they merely merry?

His mind went in circles and he blamed the ale. And the fact that he truly knew only a little more than he did that morning. Some faces, the manner of their dress – no names, and none were familiar to him. Some relief, perhaps, that they were not treacherous friends or allies. But what he did not know he could not discover, and there was no time to sit and think about what might be true – he had to leave.

As he was to leave, mischief grew in his mind – a moment of inspiration, from the one thing he had learnt from the men – some of them were sneaking ale from the tree where he hid, and likely it would anger others. A plan grew to stir trouble amongst them, cause a fight that might leave a wound – some sign, one clue, perhaps a bruised eye or swollen lip. He thought to steal the precious ale, and – he froze.

All the men at the camp turned. Not to him, not to his tree – they looked to the east. All at once, silent, standing, and the man of spears not only stood, but stood proud and took a spear from the ground to his hands. All were facing east – it was a chance to run – Selvorne should have run – but he waited and saw, from the northeast, men approaching.

Many came, and it was too late. Many men. A distant greeting between those already there and those newly arrived, and eyes were darting all over the woods, as each group seemed not to trust the other. A young man fleeing from the tree would be seen at once, so he sat and barely breathed.

There was the answer to why they camped, why they were bored, why they had waited – for a meeting. Those at the camp formed a line, almost as if to do battle, though they seemed more like drunk men huddling close, not as a formation of guards. The man of spears stood alone, his two friends took positions beside him, and those who were arriving seemed almost to march – not exactly in time, not quite together, but march they did, and all halted at once.

Five more men – all well armed. Standing and assessing the situation, then they approached the others and parted to a group of two and another of three – two tall men, and three of average height. Or short, compared to the others, if they were not tall. Selvorne could not believe his ill fortune. A dozen men, and one woman who alone would be trouble, for she was like a crow, and he had no doubt she would stab or cut, or lie, or otherwise be a danger by herself – alone, she would be deadly. With a dozen beside her – to fight would be stupid. To lie would be impossible, were he caught – his false tale to explain himself would perhaps distract them with laughter, for a moment. To run, he would be chased – and though he thought himself fast on foot, he did not know if he was faster than every one of them. One fast man, one spear or arrow would put an end to his escape. So he sat and watched and hoped for some advantage, and almost forgot to breathe.

He vowed he would live – he swore he would not be so foolish again. It was little comfort as he sat there with his regrets. In silence, watching, learning what he might, though the more he discovered the more they would want him dead for seeing. If they caught him – if he could not flee. And if not, it likely did not matter, so he watched as the groups of men stood, staring at each other, with no greetings.

A man in a cloak, brown or black, and a hood. On a warm spring day – that was strange, and Selvorne wondered if he meant to conceal his face from the other men there. Beside him was a broad, dark–haired man, also tall, with a spear and long knife – looking at the other spearman near. Almost standing square to each other, they stared until both nodded a slight bow, but that did not seem to put either at ease.

Of the newly arrived, the three shorter men were more merry – they laughed, nodded and whispered to each other. But there had been no greeting with the others, they simply stood there waiting. Two in odd clothes – odd, because it seemed their shirts were fine, and leggings rough, as though they had come from the farmyards and only half changed their top, or came from a fine affair and only replaced their trousers for the journey. The third man amongst them wore a fine outfit of green that matched the woodlands well, and so disguised him in the forest. His clothes were both elegant and practical, but he also wore a small green hat – tiny, as though made for a child, and it sat not on top of his head, but to one side somehow, as though pinned there in his hair. A great long goose feather came from it, but instead of to the side as it should be, with the hat at the odd angle, the feather pointed straight up and looked absurd. Selvorne wondered if he realised, and whether the others who seemed to chuckle were keeping it quiet for their own amusement.

The man in the hat seemed no more than a joke until he nodded – then each group in turn nodded back. Selvorne began to shudder as he wondered what it could mean, for no words were spoken, and each man eyed the other as they stood apart.

No movement, just staring, Selvorne waited and hardly breathed. Unknown signals – he hoped not orders to charge – perhaps they spoke in low voices that he could not hear, what they planned, he did not know. What he did know was that the numbers of men meant defeat, for not even his entire town could fight a dozen well trained, armed and desperate men. By the way they stood, held weapons and moved, he was sure they were skilled. Guards, or simply men who were taught to fight. Lords – rivals – armies, invading – a dozen thoughts went through his mind, none of them good. He had to escape, he had to be more cunning than a drunk fool hiding in a tree. His only hope was a chance to run – or perhaps the men might leave soon after their meeting – or none would wish to crawl into the tree where they had hidden cheese and ale. No, there was no chance of that – to run he would be caught. To wait he would be found. The meeting would take a long time or short, either way, the hidden foods were for such important guests, or if not, when they left, the others would claim their ale that had been part drunk, their cheese that had been sliced, and meat half eaten by a man hardly hidden, uninvited, who had seen all in the forest that they meant to be secret.

"So," said one of the men who had been there all afternoon. Selvorne assumed he was the leader – and the owner of the ale. He said no more, just that. All looked to each other for a few moments in silence.

"So ... you ... are ... and it is true? You, in the east?"

The man in the green shirt and tiny hat held up a finger and waved it, then shook his head.

"Very well. We have waited two days – make haste so we may leave," the leader said, and Selvorne assumed he was of men from the west, and the newly arrived men were of the east.

Two of the men from the east advanced, but the man with the small hat held up a hand, and they stopped. And then – he bowed. Elegant and odd, in that rough place in the woods. The man of the west nodded back.

"Apologies," the man in the hat said, "to have left you – so long. However, had you counted correctly, you would realise you arrived early, and us, perfectly on time. As stated in our request, as agreed by your message."

"And who asks to meet at the first half moon?" the sandy–haired man with a short beard demanded, but his darker haired friend seemed to answer him, and for a few moments they argued as before, in low voices and glaring defiance.

"Is the moon different in the west?" one of the new arrivals asked, but the man in the hat seemed to silence him.

"Had we done," the apparent leader of the west said, "it would have been too late. It is done?"

The man in the hat bowed once more, and some of the others nodded. Some agreement seemed to have been reached, and people moved from one place to the other – weapons were never held high as a threat, but held at the ready, and Selvorne was not completely sure they were at ease, but something had changed. In smaller groups, apart, voices were lower – Selvorne could not hear, and he was quite sure neither could the men hear each other, if words were not whispered to them directly.

The two men Selvorne had followed from the ravine were taken aside by the man in the hat, and the two beside him stood as though they had to be guards. Men of arms, in his service, who stayed near wherever he went, obeyed and said little, but protected him as he spoke with the others. That was the group of three newly arrived – and the group of two who had been with them seemed also to be a tall man with a taller guard, for there were signs of orders being passed from one to the other, and none back again.

The man in the hat and his two guards began to leave the others, walking with the two men from the ravine – and, to their apparent annoyance, the spearman who stood alone followed. They all came towards Selvorne, and his heart began to pound. Closer – towards the tree – to get the ale, perhaps, but they stopped near, to the side and away from the rest of the men, and began to speak.

"Report," the man in the hat ordered, and the smaller man from the ravine spoke.

He alone spoke, and in a low voice – the man in the hat listened, and his guards stood back a little, but not so far that they could not keep away the spearman, who was meaning to stand closer. The tall, dark-haired man from the ravine listened as well, but said little unless asked.

The bridge – broken. Said in such a way Selvorne was certain they broke it – and when questioned, it seemed they did. Cut, yes, difficult, indeed – dangerous. Worthy of reward, and yes, reward would come, they were promised. A few words Selvorne could hear, not all, not clear – if he dared move closer, make a sound, be found – he would be dead. He had no doubt of it, for he was hearing the admission of crimes, even had they not meant for anyone to die.

Oddly they made no mention of the men who would have owned the waggon. No questions, no word. They spoke of the ox, but only for its flesh cut away and missing head – the barrels, not all broken, they thought. Signs of a fire, a camp and cooking, no great valuables left that could not be easily carried. But not one word about the men that might have been there, either fallen or fled, injured or unharmed – no question of who they might be – and that, to Selvorne, was proof of their guilt.

But – who were they? He knew they were guilty, but could not see their faces. Nor hear all that was said. He almost dared to move so he could, but sat in silence, peering out of the vines, in shadows of the afternoon sun. At the end of the report, the shorter man from the ravine was dismissed, and the taller, dark haired one was called forwards – not his friend with the spear, however, he was made to stand back.

"The same?" the man in the hat asked in a louder voice.

"That is as it happened."

"Not all, though?"

Silence for a few moments, and Selvorne grew uneasy.

"No," the tall man said.

"And?"

"He floated barrels down the river."

"Did he?"

"Yes, three."

"And why, do you think, he did that?"

The taller man whispered, and the man in the hat stepped back suddenly.

"Coat on?" the man in the hat asked, astonished – it made no sense, but the taller man said nothing, "Thank you, my good man. For this – you shall be rewarded."

The taller man nodded.

"But – not here, where it is clear all are watching, wondering what is said – yes, a reward of great value, I think. Very good. Off with you!"

The taller man nodded again and left, the spearman joined him, and Selvorne was sure another man approached – and as he did, the guards of the man in the hat quickly retreated.

The hatted man and the tall man in a cloak, who had arrived together, stood apart from all others to talk. Both absurdly dressed for the spring, though the tiny hat was useless at any time of year, unless he had long hair pinned up inside it. The cloak was too hot, whoever wore it must have sweated as much as Selvorne, unless they did not feel the heat, or they wore nothing underneath. Either men would be noticed later, so attired – and recognised by Selvorne, though he could not see their faces.

They walked together away from the tree, towards the pool of water and the spring, but others were there, so they turned and headed to the woods. No, that did not seem to do, and they came straight to the tree again, went around its side, then to the back – perhaps to collect cheese, ale, meat – any of which would get Selvorne caught. He held his breath, preparing for the worst, but they did not enter. They went behind the tree, away from the others and unseen, near the entrance to the vine cave, and there stopped.

"They shall not hear us, here, have no fear, of man or spear, I will protect you well my – "

"Say it and you will know fear," the tall man in the cloak said in a rough, deep voice. The silence that followed did seem to be fear.

"By the water," the man in the hat said eventually, in a meek voice, "sound will carry – this is best. I only – thought it best."

"You think little. Your men, less – they are idiots," the taller man said, in such a rough low voice, it was almost as if he had soreness in his throat. It certainly made Selvorne's ears sore to hear it, for it was like broken glass ground by gravel. The smaller man, by contrast, sounded almost delightful, musical, poetic, though at times his voice almost squeaked as though nervous – likely he was, and Selvorne thought that all the men there were either anxious or angry, or unaware of the intentions of the others.

"My men are the very best," the man in the hat replied.

"None of the new."

"Learning."

"And how do we explain their lessons failed?"

Silence – Selvorne listened as best he could. They might have meant the bridge, the killings. He heard a strange sound, and he could hardly believe it – sobbing.

One sob – then another, the smaller man was crying. Tears – sorrow – remorse. Selvorne felt his heart fill with pain. The bridge was an accident, then, some strange task gone wrong, people killed, unintended, and –

"Do you smell cheese?" the man in the hat asked.

"I smell ale. Here, and on their breath. There, spilt on the ground – wasted. Idiots. All of them. Stop sniffing, you sound even more of a fool."

"Be at ease, you must – "

"Explain."

"Do you not feel hot in that cloak?"

"Do you not feel an idiot in that hat?"

"My disguise, no, I feel rather clever," the man in the hat said, then he seemed to bow.

"If disguised as an idiot, it is working. Though I doubt you need the hat, you would be recognised immediately as such – as you have been – I should smack it from your stupid head. Now explain."

"My good – "

"Now!" the taller man said, in a quite high voice, which startled Selvorne.

"All is well, better than well, it is, well, rather – "

"Unplanned. Poorly done. These fools stink of ale and wine and – "

"Sent west – drunk – kept. Clear from where, do you not think? One, implicated with the other. Wine and ale. Not at all difficult to be sure of it, now."

Silence, and Selvorne wondered what was meant. The wine sent west in barrels, he thought.

"Very well," the taller man said, "explain all."

Selvorne sat in anticipation – silence. Movement – silence. The two were walking – away from the tree, perhaps from the smell. Whispering, and he wished he could hear – explain all, the taller man had said. Selvorne only needed to hear the slightest part of it for a clue, for he had none, and knew only that many people seemed to hate each other. Plans were confused, betrayals were likely being plotted. The man in the hat and man in the cloak were walking to the very place where he planned to flee.

Movement was seen near the fire – a man approached – the sandy–haired man with a short beard. Selvorne could see him plainly as he came, wide eyed and gazing, until the two who had guarded the man in the hat came and stopped him approaching the tree. They held him – he stared – and then, with a grin, he spoke.

"No!" was all he said, almost yelled. It was in astonishment, not defiance, then followed by a stare with a wide opened mouth. The two guards dragged him away, one thumping him, and that made him angry, but he did not hit back.

Footsteps came beside Selvorne, and he saw the man in the cloak and the one in the hat return, walking fast.

"Fix it," the cloaked man said, then he turned and headed east, joined his guard and began to leave – the guard snatched a tankard as they passed the others, which seemed to cause a moment of tension between them – he lingered only long enough to drain it and hand it back, and then with the tall man he left along the path to the woods.

Two fewer foes, but danger was near – the man in the hat stopped beside the tree, and was sniffing the air, stooping towards the entrance of the vine cave – Selvorne sat waiting in silence – but then another man came. One of his guards, the smaller one.

"Ahh – there is, my trusted man," began the man in the hat, "and – what do you make of the others? Are they of any use?"

"I am not quite sure," the man replied, and he was almost as well spoken as the man in the hat, "they have made a mess of things already. The tall one seems overly keen to take his payment and leave. From what I hear, he owes all the time, and has some love of a woman in the west. Veksehl, I think – which might work against us. I also hear he has family. If these things are true, he might be more trouble than he is worth, and so far seems worth not so much."

"Disappointing, I did like the look of him. And the other?"

"And he thinks overly keen to join us, very eager, but is he dedicated? Perhaps, he seems to think nothing of the work, perhaps he is ... a little too eager. The taller one, I think he is not so pleased to do what needs to be done. But this shorter fellow, seems overly so – to please. One keen to leave, one to stay. Both overly so. Of course, there is always a way to learn the truth of it."

The man in the hat was silent, but Selvorne thought he was nodding.

"And then there is this third fellow – the tall man of spears. He ... I should wish to ... but who is he?"

"Of the west?"

"And he said no – and not with any of the men."

"Then – why is he here?" the man in the hat asked.

"A good question. He seems a guard to our new men, or friend, and that ... I do not know him. I have not seen him, and he ... has not, he is rather friendly with our new men, I think. Not here to join, not interested in much, but his friend, and he ... thinks we should speak with him more."

"Agreed. He looks fine," the man in the hat said, "take these two to the bridge, there us, determine what has happened. Take one of the west men with you, so they can see it for themselves. Once clear, return. Then we decide which to keep. Back by night, to watch the road. Move fast, prepare now, send him over."

The man, who seemed a guard, bowed – then returned swiftly to the camp. The man in the hat sniffed once more, then turned to face the approaching man of the west – the leader, Selvorne had already assumed, but from what little he had heard, he was not sure what he knew and what he was only guessing.

Or what he was hearing, for at times it seemed as bewildering nonsense. Selvorne listened as best he could, but he was so confused he felt like stepping out from the tree, up to the man in the hat, and asking directly. It was his way, when he could think of no trick – and he was sure, if he stepped out, introduced himself, and asked the man in the hat for an explanation, he would receive one. Then he would be killed. No, he would remain hidden and hope – despite the danger, he was beginning to hope for more than escape – he hoped to hear something useful.

"Harden near," the man in the hat said when the other reached him.

"No names," came the reply from the western leader – and Selvorne bit his lip. A name – had he missed it – or was he ordering not to say any – he was not sure.

"Of course, a far – oh, well – "

"No names," the western leader said, "who are these men with you?"

"And how may I tell you that without names?" the hatted man asked.

"Your men?"

"And yours?"

"You know them."

"Not all – who is the white one?"

"He is not mine. He is not yours?"

The two men looked at each other, then turned towards the camp.

"How can I trust you if – " the western leader began, but the other man waved a finger.

"My, there, good man – trust? How can you trust?"

There was silence, and it lingered for so long Selvorne grew uneasy.

"You can trust me, to do as I do, that – I promise," the man in the hat said very eloquently, "do you trust I would not? Do you think I would not?"

"No," replied the western leader – and meekly, as though threatened, but not quite afraid, for the words of the man in the hat were well said and polite. Firm, though.

"Trust is what a man may think, no, expect, from another – that is what trust is," the man in the hat explained, as though to a child.

"Spare me the speeches, that are – "

"A hurry, then?"

"To return – yes. You are late. Days and – is it done?" he asked, and the man in the hat nodded, "More than I expected."

"And what was requested, as well."

The western leader nodded, and Selvorne wondered what they would do to learn there was a man so close to them, watching.

"Not only by myself," the western leader said.

"Convenient. And wise, you will see – they are to return with you and – "

"I do not trust them."

"Do you trust me?"

"I do not trust them – one has connections there, the other, too eager. Both are simple, more than they pretend. And they do pretend."

"One will go, proven."

"I prefer none."

"None? More than one, loyal?"

"None – than one, proven. None, than one, betrayed."

"My good man, as do I – but none, and I must trust, and one, who I can trust – that is preferred. For me, and shall return with you, and you shall like it."

That was an especially odd thing to say, even amongst the nonsense, and Selvorne watched as the western leader seemed to bow his head a little.

"Or should you prefer both – untested?" the man in the hat asked.

"Send the tall one."

"Perhaps. You think him the better man?"

"No."

There was laughter, but only from the man in the hat. It was very strange laughter, not as though anything funny had been said – or perhaps it seemed odd because what was said should not be considered amusing.

"Done," the hatted man said, "and soon – it will not matter. And back to your beer, or is it ale, or flower wine?"

The western leader nodded – then left, back to the camp. The hatted man sniffed, faced the vines – then quickly turned away and left to join the others.

Much activity – little talk, gathering of things and discussion who should go, and soon the guards to the man in the hat left with the two men from the ravine, and two of the others that Selvorne assumed were from the west. The man of spears wanted to go – he was told not to – there was an argument, and though he remained at first by the fire, after some time he followed alone – south, and east, likely back to the ravine. Selvorne knew he had to escape soon, but time it very well.

Freedom Lost

The men who remained at the camp stayed by the fire and talked amongst themselves. Four of the men who were from the west, and the man in the hat, with the small, dark-haired woman. It seemed odd that the man in the hat trusted them, for his guards had left for the bridge with four others, and the spearman had followed. One small man alone, in an odd little hat, yet he in no way seemed ill at ease.

Unlike Selvorne, who watched carefully from the vines. Six enemies he could see – seven he could not – had they truly gone back to the bridge, or were they watching the road, or waiting in the woods – or worst of all, waiting near his tree for him to emerge. Not likely, not even that they watched the woods, and they were far less of a concern than the six by the fire. He had to go as soon as he thought it safe. He watched until they seemed settled, then began his crawling escape through the tree of vines.

A notion came to him as he reached the food – it had begun before the others had arrived, an idea to do mischief. A bold thought that he hoped was formed not only from ale. A cloth – some cheese – some meat, the finest ale bladder – with another beside it. He gathered all those things in one of their sacks, and took a deep breath before making his escape.

He poked his head outside – no turning back once he had, he was to flee. Waiting, listening, letting his eyes grow accustomed to the light. He dared look towards the camp – none were coming, or even looking. Had they been, they would have seen the head of a man appear at the base of the tree, and would either charge at once or pretend they saw nothing, as they prepared to follow.

Quickly he crawled out, trying to keep as low as he could, crouching. Across the grove, remembering which path had kept the vine covered tree between himself and their eyes. Across the dirt, then grass – mere yards – then, the fallen tree. A problem to get past, it would draw their attention. It was too tall to jump, too wide to go around, so he almost tumbled over it with the bladders of ale and his rough sack of food. Through the grass – crawling, hearing nothing. And then – his plan. He left one of the ale bladders behind – not the fine one, but the other. Spilling a little of the ale, then closing it once more, half hidden by a rock. He continued crawling – for yards – forever – until he dared stand.

To run – that was his wish, but he did not. He needed to move slowly, and cover his tracks. Not that there were any on the wild woodland floor, save the crushed grass. It was agony to move so slowly when he only wanted to run, but he did with all the care he could, making good distance before he thought it safe.

Then he ran – as fast as he dared, not wishing to trip and fall. Not the way he had come, which would take him near the men who had returned to the bridge. Not to the road – that was being watched, he was sure of it. South, not southeast – south and into the deeper woods. At speed until he was safe, for a long time, until he was exhausted, and until the ground became muddy, then boggy, then a maze of wetlands, and he had to stop to avoid their dangers. Panting and resting, he sat upon a large boulder until he caught his breath.

Victory. He felt relief. Success – but it was not great. His triumph was over his own stupidity, not the enemy, and he vowed he would never do anything so foolish again. Though ... he thought his deception was clever – they would discover the missing bladders of ale and wonder what had happened. A man had been there – but who – no, not a stranger, but one of them, who was stealing the ale. Which was true, they had been stealing from each other, but mere swigs of ale, not the entire bladder – what they would make of it, he could only guess. Treachery in their own camp. Or an enemy so bold he had come and heard everything, then dared steal their ale. Either conclusion would start fights and cause fear – either would hurt his enemy, and it was hurt they deserved. Selvorne felt great joy to think they would argue – fight – fear – hit each other, for blame over what he had done. He began to chuckle, and then he dared to laugh.

Only for a while, and only quietly. The danger remained, and as he thought on what he had done, he wondered if it was not a very stupid plan. Eventually, after much fighting, they might conclude another man had been there – why would any of them leave a bladder of ale in the grass – taken away to drink from in secret. They would search for the second missing bladder, and argue and demand to know where it was hidden – Selvorne had it. The greatest ale in the finest bladder. He had never seen its like, and it was a way to identify the men, perhaps, had he left it. Instead, to be seen with it, they would know he had been there. Surely any fight between such men would quickly turn to realisation that none of them would be so stupid to steal an entire bladder from one another. "Yes, I did drink of the Veksale when it was hidden in the tree, but no, why would I leave it in the woods, do you truly think me that stupid?"

So they would soon conclude, and then a search would begin for the stranger who had been in the camp – mistrust, fear, pursuit. Good luck to them, Selvorne was not going to be found. Bold was the stranger. Daring. Terrifying to them, for only two kinds of man would do such a thing – a complete fool, which was the truth of the matter – or the most fearless, frightening foe they could imagine. They would think that, in moments. Arnlausa. Girradehn, or Uhlsko – or all three at once – two lords and a guard, none of them dead, none injured, none found. All avoided harm, then followed the two men from the ravine – who would be punished for their stupidity – and doing so, found the camp, heard everything. Saw everyone. Dared to steal their ale and food from under their very noses, even as they sniffed – dared to leave a trail, dared to leave one spear stuck in the road on the southern side of the ravine. Selvorne bit his lip to think what a warning he had left for them, and a challenge – a threat. How might the enemy react to it – fear, panic, perhaps foolishness to rival Selvorne's own. He felt some victory in it, but he also realised what danger he had brought to himself.

Selvorne rested and grew calm, then found a pond where he might drink. Still water, only from the very top. It must have rained, the surface was fresh, and the depths – they were quite clear, not at all like a bog. A strange land he had found, so close to his own home. Granite boulders appeared from shallow soil, but in places, between them, there were great depths, for their cracks and hollows were sometimes filled with water, and other times with soil – and then, with plants. Trees, in places, twisted to grow roots around the boulders beneath them, the trunks bent and wandering above. In other places were pools where water could not escape. Not a bog, not a marsh, not a wet woodland – he was not sure what it was, but it was not at all safe to travel there without care, for a wrong step might lead a man to a plunging fall, be it watery or stony, it would be likely deep.

He drank and wondered at the men – what were the brigands trying to do? They had killed, but Selvorne was not sure it was their intention. And he was not sure that made them any less dangerous. Perhaps more. There was no good man who could hear of a fallen waggon and not ask at once if any people were harmed. Good men would organise the others to search, to help, to assist in any way that they could. To care so little, to think nothing of it – they were the worst of men. At best, opportunistic thieves, at worst, cunning killers, and either way a danger to other people, not only himself.

And they were too many to fight. Not even if he armed his entire town, he would not lead a dozen miners to fight half a dozen killers. Nor would he lead them, for once he had told them all that had happened, they would charge like fools. Arnlausa knew. Girradehn must have known as well, but did not care – to seek help from the town would bring many to danger. Arnlausa, as Lord of Tavalehk, and, Selvorne guessed, Lord of Vaskatohr since his father had died – his first duty was to the people there, not to himself. Not to Girradehn, his guard. To protect them – administer law, collect tolls, keep accounts of grain and all such mundane matters – but defend the people above all other things. To send Selvorne into danger violated that sworn oath, and to send him to bring more men of the town to danger – perhaps their deaths – it was far nobler for a lord to die, alone, in a cave.

Yes. The answer came to him even before he finished pondering the question – yes, Selvorne would do the same. Given the choice, he would choose the same. A horrible thought, and it was bad enough to think his beloved Arnlausa had made the choice ... it was perhaps not worse that he would make the same. In a choice between dying, alone, unassisted, in the dark – or leading those he loved into danger – even those of the town he did not love – he would choose the least horror. To die, knowing they were safe, was better than to die knowing he had led them to their doom.

With that he grew determined to honour the promises he had made to Arnlausa, to live, escape, and avoid the enemy. To learn to fight, but not to do battle until he could – to put the bodies in barrels, hidden in the ravine until it was safe to remove them, when enemies were gone and allies were by his side. There was wisdom in his advice, and folly in Selvorne's actions. He had almost broken all three promises that day – only one man was in a barrel, and Selvorne had left the others in the ravine. He had followed the enemy, instead of escaping – true, he had escaped again, but he could have been caught, fought – died. Having learnt little other than the numbers of men, their involvement and what they wore. No faces clearer than the two he saw in the ravine. Some hope to recognise them, something to report, but he was grim with the thought of how close it had been, and the realisation that he was far from safe as he began walking south, through the woods headed back to the ravine.

He soon realised the lands were as dangerous as the brigands when he stumbled for the first time, into an unseen crack. A boulder, round and smooth, with a little dirt on the top – so it seemed, it had a small crack once, which had split and been widened by water, made to ice on cold nights. Expanding the crack to be big enough to take a foot. Not comfortably, and not a boot entirely. He praised his strong quarry boots and swore more care – once, twice, three times more he stumbled, and he began to see why all were warned not to wander into that part of the woods.

Poor pigs – taken to forage, at times were lost. There was the reason – not mud, not bogs. Pigs could swim and enjoyed such bathing in bogs. But a pig with a trotter caught in rocks, twisted or broken – away from the swineherd, lost to the woods. That was the reason for being told not to go – was he southwest of his town? Yes, he was sure of it. The poor pigs – there was where they ended, at times, where men had searched to no avail, for their feet were caught and squeals grown weak with struggle. The same could happen to a man, if he wandered away from friends – and for one man alone, it was almost certain.

An idea came to him – dull, at first, but the details sharpened as he walked. A story, a lie. Should anyone ask – he was a pig farmer of Vaskatohr. A pig was lost, he would curse it for its curious wanderings – the spotted one, yes, it was always running away, the defiant beast. Why are you here – to find that cursed pig.

Where are you from – and all the details of Vaskatohr, perfectly given, and a false name, and enemies would not suspect he was the son of the lord. It was, however, only the beginning of his cunning.

Why are you carrying our ale bladder, stolen? That was the question they surely would ask, and that would lead to the trap – denial of the theft, and the story he had bought it from a man – Girradehn – met on the road, heading north. At speed, to Tavalehk. Thank you, my good man, now hand it over – I paid well for it, it is mine – stolen from us – oh, well ... it seems wrong to have what is yours, let us share it.

It was not a great story, not a very clever ruse, but if he could convince them, it would either mislead them northwards in haste, or cause them to flee, or otherwise not kill him at once, if he was found on his way to the ravine. It might, at best, make them friendly, sharing ale and talking of ... no, they would not trust a strange man in the woods. It would be a distraction only, a slight chance to fool them or if not, a delay allowing him to strike, or run. He did not know how to fight, nor did he know what else he could do if they caught him, but he hoped it was enough of a lie to survive, should he meet them on the way to the ravine.

Though he could not fight, he could push – and to push them off the cliff was another plan. He was strong. The quarry men may have proved otherwise, compared to them he was perhaps not as strong, but compared to many men, he was – strong enough to push, anyway. Who are you – pig herder, and I have lost my – push! Over they go, one or two. Not likely three. Not impossible, nor would it be to defeat a man who climbed back up, presenting his head at the top of the cliff.

He realised of course that he faced the same danger, and that he was outnumbered, and that they were well armed. But it gave him some courage as he neared the ravine.

Or so he thought – he walked for hours. It was a slow return, at first expected, for all the boulders and ponds. Then, when the land turned flat once more, and there were forests with slight hills and open paths between the trees – it could not have been so far. He walked by guidance of the sun, and he should have been headed south, but as the day went on, and even adjusting for changing shadows, he seemed to be headed west. He had to be, or he would have fallen into the ravine. After hours, when the sun was becoming quite low, he wondered if he had not travelled west only, making his way towards the sea.

A week, to the sea, through such difficult woods – or many months if he was going in circles. No, that was not possible, but it was the most winding way he could have taken. He had enough, made a sharp turn left and was determined to continue straight to the ... south. He hoped. And he also hoped he would not have to wait for moonrise to determine his direction ... though, it was so late, the moon might have already risen.

Woodlands – bushes. Thick and thorned, and he had to go around, then through. It took a long time and many scratches, but he found himself on rocky ground again with easier paths. The light was fading as the sun was below tall trees to the west.

Selvorne ran. The first chance in a quarter of a mile to run – and he did, for the sun was likely to set if he took much longer. Never had it taken so long to walk from ravine to his town and back, he had gone much farther and by difficult paths. To be stuck in the night, on the top of the cliffs, with no tinder box and so no fire, no warmth, no food – to think of it he could not bear.

So he ran. Careful not to trip, to break a leg ... that could end him as well. Such a slight wound and he would not be able to walk – no one would know where he was – he would slowly starve. Careful not to fall over the cliff, if he happened suddenly upon it. Surely the sun was not setting already – he could not have taken that long, but it was, and he had, and he was tired, hungry and thirsty. And desperate – to be stuck in the woods at night, it was not for himself that he feared, but for his friends in the ravine. So he ran, as fast as he could with care, and the world around him grew dim.

He stopped. Sunset – the skies in the west glowed red. The clouds, pink, the sky, grey – then all the world was dull, fading, and dark. The moon had risen. He waited for his eyes to adjust to the twilight, then, with greatest care, he continued at a much slower pace.

He would not stop. In the cave, in the dark, the tinder box would be found, a fire started if one had not burnt all day. The entrance – he would find it by smell, and perhaps by calling out to Girradehn. No, likely only smell, and the distance was well known along the ravine floor. Moonlight should be enough to see by, to walk in a grey ravine with pale rocks, and it was clear of all bushes where the water was, so it could be done. His way down the cliff, perhaps lit by the moon behind him, perhaps ... possible. Feeling carefully for each hold, he had climbed it many times ... in the day. The way to the road – once the cliff was found in twilight, turn east. Easy to do. The moon was there, and east was left, the only other choices were west, clearly wrong, or back the way he had come – obvious even in the dark – or over the cliff itself. He needed care as he approached, but ... night would not stop him, not darkness nor hunger nor thirst. It must not, for to stop would be to leave his friends alone, and too much pain to bear.

Thoughts of bears – they took the head of an ox. Plenty more ox below, but no longer fresh, and Selvorne might save them a climb in the dark. He tried not to think of them, and then, tried to reason that they had never been seen near the ravine or town. Clearly they were there, only shy, living within miles of his town. Some thought they took the pigs in the woods, but after that day he was quite sure pigs were lost to cracks between boulders. A troubling thought, though, that bears might come.

He hurried, not for fear, though it hardly made him easy to think of bears. Nor was he worried for wolves, they also had not been seen for longer than his life, nor heard, and that was better proof there were none. Danger of animals was not what made him hurry – it was the thought that he would never speak with Arnlausa again, that he would find his good friend dead, and it made him feel desperate.

Advice was what he needed, though he was not sure what Arnlausa would make of his stupidity that day. He had learnt much, it could not be denied. Girradehn would be angrier – and more likely alive. But he could do nothing from where he sat on the cave floor, only yell – and his advice was stupider than what Selvorne had done, and following it, he would already be dead. Girradehn would not see it that way, and – it was so very dark.

Selvorne stumbled at times, and made his way to where the ravine had to be – dark, the ground ahead, then grey – dark, then paler grey – dark – very dark – impossibly dark, and he realised he was nearing the edge of the cliff.

The far side of the ravine was in shadow of the moon, and as black as could be – the road above it was well lit. Odd, Selvorne never thought that the northern side was higher than the southern, though – then he saw a great boulder. Lit by the moon, on one side only – an enormous round rock, larger than a house, on the southern road, at the foot of the mountains, where it had rolled long ago. Half lit, it seemed to be another moon – and seeing it, he knew exactly where he was, and at once grew sad.

Over the ravine, the far side – the southern side, where the road was – where he had travelled not days before, with his father, still living, Arnlausa and Girradehn. And the waggon and the ox – there they had camped. By the boulder, the best windbreak if one was needed, and should the wind blow east or west, camp could be made on either side for shelter.

Two nights ago. It felt like a year. Two nights ago, a fire, and laughter, and jokes – many he did not understand. Some secret humour the others brought from the south, and would not explain. They had returned with grins and wine from MidWaehter, headed north through the Vechransehl pass beside the sea, where mountains ended and waves began. There they joined Selvorne at the quarry, loaded the stones, and all together headed home. It was usually two long days of travel, and at times three, with a stubborn ox. The great boulder was perhaps half the way along that road from west to east, and to see it across the ravine, he knew he was miles from where the bridge had collapsed.

How he had ended there, he did not know. It was as much a mystery as the boulder, which seemed as though it had rolled down the mountain, despite being a different kind of stone to any there, and it had left no path as it fell. Some thought it had rolled all the way from the east, along the very top of the ravine. That was not likely, for the road was not so steep to make it roll. If anything, it seemed that someone had just placed it there – a mystery no one could solve. But how he found himself there, he realised he had travelled west, unknowing, and though he could not believe it, he could not deny the moonlit boulder across the way – there was no other, not anywhere on that road all the way to the sea. He was going to spend the night alone.

The cliff – impossible to climb down there, for it was smooth. He knew that, for he had tried. The river – shallow in recent days, perhaps he could ... no, never had a man ever thought to jump from cliff to water. Ever. Not even the boldest, most drunken man – even he would know it to be a deadly leap. The ravine was much deeper there, and even if he made it down, he was not sure he could walk up the river, for there were waterfalls and sheer parts of the ravine he would have to climb – and it was night.

He headed east as best he could, but gave up after the third crevice – sheer gaps in the ground that he could barely see until too late. Instead, he turned north again, and found a place that seemed safe, sheltered, soft ground on which to sleep – no cloak, no fire, no tinderbox, no kindling, though that was likely to be found if he bothered, but useless without a flame. No water, but he had ale. And meat, and cheese, and so he sat himself in the dark to eat, alone, hungry, but not too cold – it would be an unpleasant night.

Worse for the others in the cave. He hoped Girradehn could push wood to the fire and they would not be so cold. Or thirsty. Or without fire ... he did not wish to think of it, but could not help himself, so turned his mind to two nights before, when all were together without woe. Laughter and drink, and – oddly, all were in a great mood. More than good – truly great, more than pleased with their southern journey that year, though it had not gone as planned. Late in returning, and a bad deal for the wine. Each man had slight wounds they would not speak of – Selvorne suspected they had argued and fought, punching each other – a very rare thing for the three, but the bruises could not be denied, and seemed already a week old, so perhaps some disagreement settled by blows, recovery, and wine. And laughter. And the oddest jokes. Poems that made no sense, recited to giggles – from Girradehn, no less.

No more. One dead, likely two, soon all three. A mere two nights ago – Selvorne might follow. He could have joined them that very day, for all the foolish things he had done. He could yet, that night, or the next. And in so dying, be outlived by Girradehn, perhaps Arnlausa, as they waited their turn in the cave.

In that thought he found misery. To know he would not see them again, to fear it was too late, to realise he had disappointed Arnlausa and would never suffer his silent scorn ... or Girradehn's abuse. Or their forgiveness and understanding, in realising he was young and did not know what to do, and only meant to help, to learn what he could, to ... get revenge for those who had done them harm. They would never know his folly, and he knew it was himself, alone, that had to restrain the urge to climb down to them in the night, a desire that grew with each sip of ale and every thought of his beloved old friend. To climb would lead to death, certain, but the realisation of that did not ease his desperation, and with such thoughts he fell asleep.

Waking – uncomfortable, he turned and found softer ground, and curled himself after stretching, finding peace and contentment where he lay. Rest, at ease, and – no – misery. He remembered, and was troubled as he fell back into a dream.

Again, he woke, and it was the same. Peace, remembrance, pain, exhaustion, then sleep. Many times that restless night, but each waking was only for a while. Moments of wondering if he should try to climb. Then sleep. The moon was becoming full, just a few more days, he could see enough to walk – then sleep. A few times woken to darkness – the moon had set, he was no longer tempted to climb. A few times woken by a noise, perhaps dreamt, then he slept.

~

Dawn. It was grey, the sun was to rise soon, he was to rise first. So thirsty – only ale. His head hurt just a little. It would go. A pond or stream would quench his pain, he gathered what few things he had, and began to move with speed.

No ox, no waggon – nothing to slow him as he made his way. No fear of men wanting him dead. Their order was to move quickly, check the ravine and return. They would not linger, but he would not be a fool. He made his way, with miles to travel to where he might be able to descend.

Fast, with good light and only short scrub to avoid – safe, being able to see the crevices before he stepped into them. He still had to wind one way around them, then back to the cliff, to find another way down. The ravine itself was deep, but waterfalls every so often made it less so with each mile, and he knew he would have to choose his descent carefully, for too soon and he would find himself by the river, climbing one small cliff after another, and from his experience they were always either sheer or overhung.

Two hours, he thought, by the height of the sun – two hours of scrub and he had enough, the bushes scratching him, the crevices too many, and the sun in his face as he made his way east. He found the best descent – into a crack, a wide one that would not be too dark. He scrambled down with dirt falling upon him until he was covered, battered and annoyed, but not truly hurt.

The river he crossed by removing his boots, throwing them over the water, then swimming. He would dry, but his boots, he could not risk them getting wet, not in the depths. Not soaked. He would then develop blisters, and though a minor pain, they would slow him. He had no time to be slow. The water was cold, he did not care. Fresh – he cared for that, and drank well, but not too much. At the far side he prepared to continue, tying trouser legs to his knee, glad he had the tasselled cuffs for such a purpose, and ran along the dry ravine floor.

Carefully, for there he might be seen, though he doubted he would, for he stayed close to the cliffs on the southern side, in the shadows, and went slowly at every rise, always looking ahead. Debris was there from the bridge, washed down and caught on rocks. A few waterfalls that were small, fewer still that were a climb, and then – one he recognised, the first of all he had seen that he knew – the long drop to a fine pool that filled most of the ravine. There he had swum in the past, there he had climbed, and though the way up was difficult, he knew it well enough. Half up the ledge, half up the cliff, at that place where two walls joined, a foot on each at times. It was not too high, a mere twenty feet he thought, not too far to leap off the top into the deep pool, and no problem at all for a quarry man to climb.

It was also not far from the cave, and that must have been as far as the men had gone, where they kicked the barrels over the falls and then turned back. It made sense, for it seemed there that the river flowed well, and few would fancy scrambling down then up again over the cliff where the water fell. There they turned, and it was a short way back – they passed him, when he was in the cave arguing with Girradehn, then they returned to the bridge, the road, and he caught them later in the woods. Not very far to cave or bridge, so he became cautious.

There were no men ahead in the ravine that he could see, though he could not see very far. The ravine was familiar, the entrance to the cave found – no sign of men, no sound other than flowing waters of the river, and he had no reason to think any men were there, either waiting or searching, but he drew knives in both hands and entered the cave.

Silence. The fire was out, it was dark. It was – the wrong cave? A faint smell of smoke, and wine. It had to be right.

"Girradehn?" Selvorne asked in a low voice. Nothing. Louder. No reply, and no sound of breathing, save his own. With no light, it was very dark, so he sheathed both knives and began to crawl.

Dirt, stone, rock, pebbles – wood. Ash. To the right, feeling for the foot of Girradehn – nothing. Farther, to the – mud? Damp, and then the wall. Girradehn was not there.

"Arnlausa!" Selvorne called loudly, but there was no reply. Silence – his breath was heard, then held. Silence – save for his heart, pounding.

At speed he moved, crouched low, almost walking on hands as well as feet, feeling his way – a foot. A leg – cold, and unmoving. Selvorne crept closer, and felt the body of his dear friend – Arnlausa, Lord of Tavalehk, friend of Uhlsko, as good as brother, and so an uncle to himself – family. Cold. Selvorne tried to shut the eyes of his friend, but found them already closed. Perhaps he died as he slept, perhaps ... in no pain.

There was no time to mourn – Girradehn had gone. Impatient as always, he must have crawled out, and could have been found. Selvorne scrambled back to the entrance and carefully left – men might have seen the fool, and be waiting for the return of ... himself. No sign of them, though, and the ravine was still. A one-legged man would have trouble moving without a crutch. There was wood in the cave that was left for fire, and it would do, but he would not get far if he had left that morning, and ... Selvorne had to stop him. Quickly he moved through the ravine, towards the bridge – in the shadows, boulder to stone – hoping to catch Girradehn before he was caught by another. No sign of him, not all along the ravine – and there was the wreckage, there was the waggon, and there was no sign of any man. Not limping, crawling, waiting, watching. No man, no creature, no ... ox?

Selvorne stared and blinked – it was far, but surely he should see the ox. And the waggon – had it not fallen on its side? Landing almost upside down, upon the beast, which had gone, and the waggon had been righted.

Some barrels were still tied to it, but they were broken – yes, he remembered, they had hit the ground and split. Broken and remained, bound to the waggon that was on its side, more upside down than the right way. Yet, that morning, there it stood. The proper way around. Three wheels good, one smashed. A few broken barrels, a few unbroken near – some blood. No ox.

Selvorne dared not approach. He remained hidden, and watched the line of cliffs. What had he done – walked into a trap? Not quite a trap, but the enemy must be there, watching to learn what they could. He could almost hear the order – stay hidden and wait until they come for the waggon, the barrels and the bodies. They will search for anything of value they have hidden, see who lives, learn what they know.

Selvorne did the same – waited and watched, and wondered where men might hide to best see what unfolded at the wreckage. Likely on the top of cliffs, in the woods, hidden by bushes and with an easy escape – on the northern side, where the only woods were found. He waited and hoped he was not already seen, and he searched for any movement along the top of the cliff.

A long time it seemed as the sun climbed, and too long a time for men to wait. How long would that be in all – the afternoon of the day before, through the night and then the morning. Who would wait so long? Enemies, perhaps, but he grew unsettled and could not stand to not know more, for the thought of the seals was troubling him, so he went with greatest care to a crevice. It was exactly what the men would wait for, watching – for him to lead them to the hidden treasures of the waggon. It was the wrong crevice he entered, and Selvorne waited there to see if men might come – none did. No movement, no sound, only the river and his own breathing.

Again, another smaller crevice – no men came. He pretended to find something – nothing. They were either very patient, could not see him, or were not there – or planned to catch him anyway on the road, and make him talk. Tired of waiting, hungry and annoyed, he went to where he had hidden the seals and checked – safe – he opened their case, and removed the small tinder box and large candle. Closing it all again, he pretended he found nothing, left – then checked another crevice, with the thought that he would fool them, had they seen.

Back to the cave where he had left his friends, and soon he had a fire going – a candle, then kindling, then a torch, and what the light revealed made him gasp.

Girradehn was gone – as were their things. All he had brought there, the clothes and the broken sword. Knives, left for Girradehn to use if he needed, and tinder boxes from before. Pots and pans, the oats that were in a small pouch – coins, too.

Fast he went to the back of the cave – the barrel remained. The three small stones he left upon it were unmoved, as best he could tell. If they had been removed, or if they had fallen when the lid was opened, someone had taken great care to arrange them once more just as Selvorne had left them – they were untouched. The wooden tomb of his father, left there, perhaps unseen – not likely, though, unless dark when they came ... but it was always dark in a cave. Men would have needed torches, and with them would have searched its dark depths. Merely left, then, like the barrel for Arnlausa – and Arnlausa himself. Dead, cold, and become stiff, despite the coolness of the cave.

It was not relief Selvorne felt to find his father had been left in his barrel tomb, the thought of it made him miserable. Nor was it to realise Arnlausa must have died in the middle of the day before – left sitting there, with Girradehn pondering his own fate, and wondering where Selvorne was with the men. No relief, though Selvorne realised he could not have run fast enough to speak with Arnlausa one last time. Even as he slept on the cliff in the night, it was too late – even as he was trapped in the vines of the tree, watching the enemy, Arnlausa had passed away. No relief for the sorrow of it all, but worse angst, for the fear of what must have happened.

Girradehn could not have walked. His injury was severe. He did not take a stick and make a crutch – did not amble out, angry and searching for Selvorne, stumbling back to town. He would not, for he was not as much of a fool as he was annoying – and no anger would make him leave. Where could he go? Not climb the cliffs. Not walk to the sea. Perhaps he went for water, having spilt all that was left for him – perhaps he could not suffer to sit in the dark with the dead. Perhaps he went outside, or, more likely, he did not – he might have lived, but he could not have left, not even crawling, and especially not without leaving some trail. He could, however, have been carried. That was what must have happened.

Rescued? Possible. If townsfolk came, by chance, found him – hidden in the cave – carried him back to the town. They would also take anything of value, if there were enough men to carry ... some hope that he was rescued, but Selvorne knew it was vain, for the one thing they had left behind that no man would, especially no man of Vaskatohr – the body of Arnlausa. At least two must have come, one for Girradehn, one for the pots and pans, broken swords and odd things left that no longer were there – no good man would take them and leave a dead lord. Or even a dead stranger.

Perhaps it was a man and boy – some hope remained, of rescue. Or, a man and a woman who was too weak to carry a lord, yet strong enough ... it was possible. A woman might take pots, tinder boxes and knives. More likely. But why the ... waggon ... righted. No, not the waggon, any strong men could topple it with skill. It was the ox that disturbed him.

Selvorne wished he had the pot and oats to cook, and think as he did, then eat and gather his wits. Instead he had ale of the finest quality, stolen from likely killers, and a fire. And a cave, and the silent company of his two great friends. He sat, drank a sip of ale, and thought.

To take the ox – it would have to be cut to pieces. Not even a bear could lift such a beast. Butchered, then, and that took at least one man with a great knife, and perhaps many to carry the meat. It could have been that such men took it and did not find Girradehn, and left for town with their almost fresh feast. Very well, the ox was explained.

Girradehn was gone – did he gather the things and crawl? Hear the men outside the cave, men who had taken the meat, wandering along the river – and decided they were friendly – or no longer cared? A challenge to battle – no, unlikely. Perhaps he heard boys playing by the river – he followed, calling, then collapsed. They carried him away, and no man had entered the cave, or learnt of the lord lying dead there. Girradehn would take his sword, broken or not – but not the pot. Certainly not the oats, unless he meant to cook a meal on his long crawling journey east. No, he would not take cooking things, even if his leg was completely unhurt, and hurt or no, he would not leave Arnlausa outside of the barrel. Or indeed, at all.

Two ideas came to mind, both unpleasant, and only one likely. The first was that animals had come – bears – taken the ox and taken Girradehn. That made no sense at all, for all the missing things that bears could not possibly hold in their paws, let alone use or care to collect.

The second – and only thing that made sense – was that the brigands had found him – and taken all things of value. Six men or more, they had reason and numbers to do it. Butchered the ox, taken that too – left the wine in barrels, too heavy, too hard – or spilt, the barrels broken. Taken Girradehn – dead, as a prize, alive, as a man of much information. Left the others, though they might not have realised the barrel at the back held a man. Or not cared, or not seen it, or saw it, and him, and closed it again.

That made sense, and Selvorne's only relief was that the seals were safe. As he thought on it he realised that if others had come, they must have reasoned that neither Girradehn nor Arnlausa could have arranged the cave as it was, and so suspected a fourth man. He wondered if they were watching, and knew he was there, and waited at some place to surprise him – perhaps the road, where they knew he must go.

Except that he did not have to go there at all, and though he had just travelled through woods that he knew nothing of, most of the lands near his town he knew very well. He would not be caught, unless they came to the cave, and should they see him and give chase, he would head west down the river and disappear where they could not find him.

Girradehn – he felt for the man, taken alive, he would be forced to talk. Knowing Girradehn, instead he would spit. Or bite. Or talk, to mislead them – then admit it, in spite, once they were convinced. Then mislead them more, and spit, and bite. Likely they would end him in anger, and he would likely die with a strange bitter vengeance, taking his secrets and leaving them furious. He would have to be alive, they would not take the dead – unless it was he who was their hated enemy, and they meant to display his body as a prize.

To pursue them would be stupid, and Selvorne had done enough stupid things. As much as he wanted them all dead – as much as he ached for Girradehn's fate – to pursue would lead him to the same. He had seen the enemy, their numbers were too great. The hardest thing, his father had said, was to want to do one thing and yet know it was not wise – to restrain such anger, hate and fury. Arnlausa said the same, though he was rarely a man of restraint. And yet ... had lied to Selvorne that they might live, to keep him safe in the cave, to restrain his stupidity, to prevent him rushing to the town for help.

Selvorne would honour that noble lie, and his promises, and the wisdom of Arnlausa. Lord, and once a guard, he knew more of the dangers that might be faced. Selvorne should have listened and obeyed, not chased after the brigands. He did listen – he would obey.

To the barrel he went, rolling it to the back of the cave beside the other, then opened it and took a drink of the wine. To honour his friend, who he prepared to place within it. A man of fine clothes and few jewels – for travel, anyway, and neither so fine as to suggest he was a wealthy man, willing to pay a high price for wine. His travelling clothes, perhaps fitting that he wear them for the final journey. Travels south with Uhlsko were his favourite time of year. So he said, and Selvorne did not doubt it was true. He heaved him up, carried him to the back of the cave, and lowered him as gently as he could into the wine. Some spilt. He would not miss it. The rest embraced him in death, red like blood, fine and sweet. Selvorne looked on the face of his old friend one last time before closing the barrel, pulling the levers to lock it shut – filled to the brim, and for any who meant to drink of it, a grim discovery if ever it was opened.

For Arnlausa and Uhlsko – two wooden tombs. Selvorne would return one day and take them with many men to their resting place. Father beside mother, and friend near, to guard them both. He asked them to be patient, promised he would be back in a few weeks, ordered them to behave – he wanted to laugh at it, but could not, nor could he weep, or feel anything but ill. So he bowed his head and turned from them both, taking his torch to empty the cave. He doused the fire, scattered the ash, and made the cave as barren as he could.

~

With great care and much sadness Selvorne left the cave, taking the torch some way before dousing it, and farther still before tossing it to a crevice. He then began what he planned to be several tedious, careful, essential journeys back and forth where the bridge once stood.

First, to be sure no men were there – none waiting, hidden, perhaps in a barrel as he had done, amongst the wreckage. He examined the area – the ox was certainly gone, and though a flood might have taken it and turned the waggon, the same flood would have washed barrels away as well, or at least toppled them. A heavy rain would have washed away the blood from butchering the ox, and the flood would explain some things – but there had been no rain, no flood, and yet there was no ox. Nor blood where it was butchered.

The waggon was not too heavy for a strong couple of men to turn over, even with the few barrels that remained roped to it. Why they had done so – to get the ox – not a mystery, but it seemed very odd sitting there at the bottom of the ravine. Stranger still to discover the ropes were gone – all the ropes – anything used to tie it, taken, and the barrels left.

The swords were also gone, if they ever made it to the river. He could not see them, though the waters were clear – he had no desire to dive in and search the depths. Precious, expensive, deadly – not a great loss, despite the cost, for they were one hundred times more valuable if the enemy had taken them – in their hands, or in the hands of those who bought them, they would be clues. Selvorne fancied he would recognise even the fittings of such blades, should any wish to disguise them – taking them was folly, and he was bitterly glad. He would not have minded one, as a weapon for himself, though he did not know well how to use it.

There was no sign of men watching, and he climbed the southern cliff – no men were there, but his spear was gone. He had left it without thinking of it as anything but a nuisance for the climb. Arnlausa had said to leave it, as a warning to enemies – that it was gone was a warning to himself.

Back down he climbed. If any were watching they must have thought him mad or very clever – or he thought himself clever, and they knew that he was not. Back he went, past the cave, to where he had hidden the seals – as cautious as before, but there was no sign of men. The middle of the day, he thought – perhaps they meant to come back every so often and look. He hurried, and with the box of seals hidden as best he could, wrapped in the cloth that once held the cheese and meat he stole – whatever good that would do to disguise the importance of what he carried – he went back to the cliff and climbed up once more.

The southern side of the ravine was quite barren on the top near the edge, other than the lone oak, there were few trees and fewer bushes. Selvorne could see there were no men, not even in the tree, so he ran at speed – no time to waste, no walking slowly, if they were there waiting, hidden somehow, they would find him rushing past. He knew the way better than any man, and he ran along the paths towards the old road that led to the lake.

Into the first woods he passed, and then to wait – no sound. Just the woods. No men. No prints from their boots, he noticed, though it was not wet enough to leave any – then out, along the path once more, and into the trees again, to hide. He left the seals, quickly hidden, and continued with only the cloth and a small branch to seem as though he carried them – no men. Farther, until the lake was near – back, to retrieve the seals. Towards the lake again, and hiding them – onwards, and then all the way to where the waters of the lake began, without the seals that he had hidden again, and taking the greatest of care.

There were two roads from the south to his home town of Vaskatohr, the bridge was where they split from one good road from the west. Over the bridge was the new road, and the only one used for years by anyone other than Selvorne. The old road passed by the lake, quite some way before it found the easiest river crossing for a waggon. Not a bad road, but muddy as it approached the town. It was not a good path in the rain, and annoying enough for Arnlausa and Uhlsko to build the bridge and make the new road, which was neither annoying nor boggy, led more directly, and was terribly expensive, both for the cost of materials and the toil.

The old road was fine for Selvorne, who ran back and forth from town to lake, to fish and feast. A fine lake, and there he found both peace and silence, not bothered by the few dozen townsfolk who knew him his whole life, yet still found things to say whenever he was near. He loved them all, but ... silence by the lake was a great relief. It was silent that day, with no sign of men, and that was a greater relief.

The lake itself was not large, but deep enough to fear dropping anything of value that might sink. He looked over it and determined his plan, nodding, and searching for foes hidden by its waters. The least likely place of all, no one would think he would go there, unless they knew him well. Even so, there were few places to hide men, and many to hide seals – fewer places still to watch him do so, and he wondered where he might.

Of a poor marble and liming stone, the lake seemed in many ways as a quarry that had filled with water. Such a thing was impossible, as no man had ever worked there – and yet it was quite squared and neat, and only the fact that there were no marks of chisels convinced him it had never been a quarry. To the east it was a sheer wall, from water to cliff to tops that had never been explored, for no one could climb the smooth, steep side. Mountains continued above the cliff, up to the sky, but there was no way to climb them either, not on either side of the waters, nor for many miles in either direction. To the east no man could hide, for to the east no man could go.

Nor to the south, for there were reeds and marshes, and though it might be true a man could swim there, hidden, watching for him – Selvorne doubted any would. He also spied geese, and they would not tolerate a stranger amongst the reeds, indeed if any man had hidden there, he would be floating, dead, slain by the beastly creatures, torn by their deadly beaks, choked or dragged under the waters to their doom. Or the birds would make a noise, to alert him, scaring strangers away. More likely, but they could kill a man, he knew it, and they would do so, he was certain.

To the north there were woodlands and streams, ponds and open groves – it was true men could hide there, and watch, but they would see nothing other than more woods, and the lake itself. Not Selvorne, not from so far away. It was the perfect place to avoid men, he thought, and the only other place enemies might be was in the west – from where he had come – and he had seen none. To the west the lake emptied by way of the river that ran to the ravine, shallow and wide, over pebbles where the road crossed it, then deep and narrow, then the falls and the ravine. No one knew how such a small river from the lake could form such a larger one in the ravine, but all suspected some second flow, under the ground, coming from the mountains and joining after the falls. Or a spring was hidden somewhere, or the many streams that trickled to the ravine were more numerous than counted.

Whatever was the truth, no men could hide on any side of the lake, and the waters were still. The one place they might be was the small island in the middle, almost entirely rock, save for one gnarled tree, and Selvorne took to a position at the water's edge from where he knew he could see all. Nothing. Silence. Stillness and calm, no men could be there, and, as he looked over the lake he knew so well, he realised he was completely alone.

Only in the woods could men be hidden, and if there then they were too far to see, or for him to be seen. Perhaps they were. Perhaps they hid by the northern edge of the lake, in the grass, silent and still. For hours, not knowing when to expect him – why would they? They were many, he was one, and he was tired of guessing what they might do or where they could be, so he made his decision. With no spear, the fish would taunt him – he would go without food for a while longer. Not much longer, so he went at once to fetch the seals.

From woods to lake with the box, and no more running in circles. He found his coracle boat, turned upside down in the long grass, beat the dirt and bugs from it, and put it to the water. Carefully he crept into it, wondering how it had shrunk, and began paddling his way to the island.

If unseen, it was the best place to hide things, the rocky island in the middle of the lake. Never flooded, rarely visited by anyone other than himself, and it had many deep cracks that could be used to conceal something of such value. The coracle sat low in the water and his paddling was very slow. Out he rowed, watching – yes, the box of seals would be proof against water. He hoped. Out to the island, on a beautiful day of spring – he should be fishing, laughing, cursing, feasting. He was silent and grim, determined and cautious. He landed the coracle where he knew best, found a good place to hide the box of seals, indeed, buried it deep amongst the rocks. Concealed, completely – the lordship of two towns, the seals and the Will of Arnlausa. All things required to take power and issue orders, including charcoal, parchments and wax. It would not likely be found by a man casually looking, but certainly would for any who had seen where they were buried. Selvorne gazed for only moments, then made a hasty return, hoping they were safe, trusting in stealth, confusion, and the belief that no man was watching.

Back to the place where the coracle must be hidden – covered in grasses, sheltered from the sun, unseen by any who might pass. His alone. How many times he ... had hidden it. A sorrow filled him as he remembered when he made his first simple boat, how his father had helped. Well, taught him, and did most of the making. Then the second small vessel was made without so much help. The third, after the second had sunk, because he was too big – no, Uhlsko did not help then, but the fourth – that one – his father had offered to lend a hand. Selvorne was not too proud to accept help by that age, for the coracle was made by stretching leather over a frame, and that was difficult, especially with only two hands. Of course the hand his father offered was a great wooden fork used for baling hay, not actual help, and he thought himself most amusing. Selvorne frowned and thought Uhlsko an idiot, as he stood there with one hand a fist, the other hidden inside a shirt with long sleeves, and in its place a great wooden fork.

Uhlsko did help, he never teased or joked to be mean. They built a fine coracle, big enough for a man, yet somehow ... no longer. Selvorne was too heavy, and would replace it with a boat. He had no time to build a new one every few years, one boat to last forever, and he – he had no time for fishing, either, likely. Or boats. Not anymore. That only made him sadder still, and he looked over the lake, as though looking for enemies, but he was truly looking at all that had been lost.

There where he learnt to swim. There where he learnt to dive. There where he learnt to climb from the water up the cliff, as high as any man had, until he and all others could not continue – not when it was sheer, wet, slippery, and marbled. Not from the Falling Crack – the last hold high over the water, where all grew tired and dropped with a splash, not even half the way to the top.

There where he had slept – once only, and never again, for no cloak of any thickness made rocks comfortable, or saved the neck of a man from aching mischief, done in the night by cruel stone. There, where his father taught him to spear fish – why, he never knew, Uhlsko never enjoyed it, he preferred using a rod, line and bait. Selvorne was terrible at first with the spear, his eventual success was a great victory – followed by many. He had become fast, and fished alone, often returning with a delicious meal to the town. Sometimes, with good supplies of fish, a great sack, a little luck, and no mercy – a meal for the entire town.

There, where, oddly, his father had caught one of the first fish Selvorne could remember – Uhlsko was not fond of fishing by spear. Selvorne was young, and Uhlsko made him guard the fish against flies and ants. A strange task, impossible to achieve, and pointless, as countless bugs came for their meal – eventually they made a box for the fish together, where their catch could be kept safe against tiny, relentless enemies from the grass. It was a joyful task to build the box, time together cherished. A victory over the ants, and laughter at his father's joke that they should train the ants to guard the fish. It was silly, Selvorne was young – it was wonderful, and he grew sad.

Never again would any of that he do – or he would, again, but it would never be the same.

Had he left earlier, there he would have fished – he never would have seen his friend and father die, and would have returned home to find them missing. Had he never returned to home – had he fled, for any reason, for temper or defiance or folly, abandoned his life and left – he never would have known. He had no mind to flee, two days ago, but had he done, he would have lived his life far away, in another town, thinking his father and friend would mourn him, and perhaps he would never learn the truth that they had died. It was a strange thought. He wondered at once what he might not know, and what else might have been, if things ... had gone differently.

Had they all gone to fish, crossed the river at the ford and returned home by way of the old road – all would have lived. The weather had been good, the old road not muddy – all would have lived, never knowing the danger set for them at the ravine. Some other poor traveller would fall, but that might be unlikely as well – perhaps none would come that way for a year. Few ever did. Selvorne would have checked the bridge for their next journey south, or a storm might have taken it during the summer. The slightest change to their plans would have saved them all – one decision, a different path, all to live. Though, he admitted it was not likely they would have chosen the old road over the new, but that hardly made him feel better.

Regret was what he felt, despite it being for a choice that would not have been chosen. The unlikely other way – the better thing they would not have done. For that he felt regret. Anger also, for the men who knew which road would be taken, and at himself for not knowing such men might plot against his father. Or was that anger at his father ... or his enemy ... he did not know. Anger, and no one to be angry at, not until they were named. He had to calm himself and think. The lake, so peaceful, and there he stood, so unaware of all dangers, by a lake before the waters with depths he did not know. Dangers he did not know – no better than did the island in the middle, made of rock, alone, unknowing, as was he, as ignorant as stone.

His home was the same. Vaskatohr town was also an island, surrounded by woods instead of water. To stand there he also would know nothing. Tavalehk town was vast, yet no better than a village, if it was knowledge he sought. No safer, if men sought him there – they knowing him, he not knowing them. Safer to be with no one, than to be surrounded by strangers. For a moment he wondered if he should head to the wilds, away from all people. All the dangers he did not know, threats he could not see, enemies who sought him – flee to safety. Considered only for a moment, before anger came, from unease.

Anger that had to be contained. Unnoticed, not shown. Wherever he went, he would have to be that island of unmoving stone. Calm, silent, serene. Wherever he went, even to his home, he would be surrounded by unknown dangers and enemies, to a depth he had never suspected. He took a deep breath, preparing to turn his back to the one place he had loved the most – the quiet lake, his place, the same as ever, but he was changed, and the danger ... perhaps was the same as ever, but knowing of it, he was not the same.

The fish – the great fish. It was there, he could see it staring, mere yards away near the edge. Stopped, as it did – looking straight at him, from just below the surface. He had neither spear nor inclination to try – not appetite, or ... odd, he had lost the desire to catch it. Two days before, he wanted little more. It did not taunt, as it usually would – did not spit, splash or snarl. It gazed at him for moments, then seemed to bow its head as it fell into the depths. Gone. He guessed it, too, had changed. With an odd smile, he shrugged and turned away from the lake.

Selvorne took to the road, which led where the lake narrowed to a shallow river. He crossed by jumping on dry stones he had placed, long ago. Walking the road, he left the lake behind, continuing until he knew he could leave the obvious path, then headed to the woods to make his way in secret, back to his home. To Vaskatohr town, where he would find friends to whom he must lie, enemies from who he must hide, and one man, named, who he could trust, but not completely.

For the Day when I am Dead

Vaskatohr town – the home of Selvorne, where his father was lord. No longer lord, that title was meant to pass to Arnlausa, and he had passed it to Selvorne. One piece of parchment, few words, one seal – the town was his, his home was ... his, though, it could no longer be his home. Not if he was to rule Tavalehk as well, he would have to live there as lord. He was sure he would be sad to leave Vaskatohr, but he knew he would feel sorrow to stay. As he did to return, knowing all that had happened.

Fear as well, but for the townsfolk, not himself. Too few to fight his foes, he might be bringing danger to them, and as lord, that was the last thing he should do. A very small place – not truly a town, not in size, his home was only a small village of a few dozen. Called a town only by name, by title, by law – and the name itself was perhaps wrongly given.

It should have been Vaskatohm, for it was in the woods, and that was what "tohm" meant, at least it did with regards to towns. He was not sure who Vaska was, he had never heard mention of such a man, but he did know what a tohr was, and he had to admit that the outcrop of rocks – the tohr – the place where men mined – it was the reason for the town. Not the spring, the woods, the stream, the road, though that at first was reason for the inn, which became his house. Vaskatohr made some sense, then, but he was sure it was once called Vaskatohm, long ago when he was a young boy. Arnlausa had joked that they had not changed the name at all, but that a second town was declared on the same spot, and so Uhlsko was the lord of two towns. A strange joke, to make him laugh and his father smile, and Selvorne frown in confusion. True, it was odd to think such a small place would be one town, let alone two, but the thought was hardly amusing to make a man smile, let alone laugh.

Better tohr than lehk, such a name would make no sense at all, for the only lake near was where he fished, and it was not so grand as the one at Tavalehk – that was a mighty sea, by comparison to a pond – and the size of the town similarly huge. Dozens lived at Vaskatohr, mining copper, tending pigs to the woods – thousands lived at Tavalehk, a true town, Selvorne hardly knew all the trades they did, let alone the people there. Strangers, yet they were his people, and he was equally unknown to them, yet newly made their lord.

Vaskatohr was small, and all there knew him, all of his life, or all of their own. The mine was the reason for the town. Made a town by law – not a village – for reasons of the mine. It was never the number of people living in a place that made it a town, his father had explained, but the law that mattered. A town had a lord, and he made the laws. Other lords could not interfere with his rules. Uhlsko was lord, and so could make laws, and be sure they were obeyed. He could collect tolls from the road and markets, though with a few dozen people, there were no markets, just one street and friends with baskets of fruit, or fresh meat from a pig, quickly divided. The mine was what mattered – control of it, watching it, guarding it against any who might come from the south, being thieves, or from the north, being merchants trying to strike some deal with the miners. Also thieves, but with wider smiles and finer clothes, paying poorly to sell later, richly, at a profit that required only travel and timing, not digging and dirt.

Very few came from either direction, in recent years, almost none. No travellers from the south, and only family from the north. It used to be a well–travelled road, but it was more than ten years since people came regularly from MidWaehter in the south, through Vaskatohr, and then continuing farther north. Ten years, and longer still since they travelled in large numbers.

When the first people built there, it was not a town, not even named, but merely an inn. A place to stay between the great town of Tavalehk in the north, and the very long journey south. It took over a week to reach the first towns of the south – the MidWaehter people, and their many great towns. For men coming from there, Vaskatohr was not the first stop on their journey, or only place to stay the night – many times they would sleep under the stars – but it was the last stop before Tavalehk, and the first building they would have seen for a week. There they enjoyed the comforts of an inn, fresh stream water that trickled from a spring, and, most importantly for people headed from wilds to towns – a bath, and washing of clothes.

An inn – it was a fine building that housed those who came. A barn was built for their oxen, and hunting was done for food. Wild boars, usually, until they were few, then pigs were kept, so there would be food when the hunts failed. Then a patch of vegetables, to feed men and pigs, but that was many years ago – it did not take long for the inn to become a village. Small but fine, and to have a fresh spring so near was a treasure. Trees were felled to build houses, and replaced by orchards – more people came. Then, one day in the woods, chasing bold pigs that had fled – the discovery of the copper in the rock changed everything.

Men settled soon and were answerable to the Lord of Tavalehk, however, being a day's travel from that town – and having their own stream – it caused unforeseen problems within Waehdric law. Lords were to control only one body of water, be it lake or river or stream from a spring. Not two, which never met. That law was not strictly obeyed, usually, but it caused arguments, because other lords wanted the mine. Tavalehk could not claim it, people said, since the stream of Vaskatohr flowed south to Selvorne's fishing lake, joining the river there, instead of flowing north to join with Tavalehk – so, to silence them all, a new town was founded by Arnrok, Lord of Tavalehk, before any of the other lords or miners had the idea to do the same.

Why he named it Vaskatohm was a mystery, the tohm, perhaps, to suggest he meant to control the entire woodlands around it – Vaska was the name of a man not known. Perhaps he was too modest to call it Arntohm, or thought Roktohr was too absurd – most would agree, as it meant "rock rock." Arntohm was a good name, though, and the Lord Arnrok was anything but modest or shy. He was quite ruthless, vengeful and feared – and yet he founded Vaskatohm, and did not make himself lord – or, in fact, anyone. He simply set the laws and left the townsfolk to ensure they were obeyed.

Uhlsko was the first lord of that small town, and long after it was founded. Selvorne wondered if perhaps making it a town in name was not enough – with no lord, people might try to claim it. Or perhaps the miners were unruly, as such men often were. Selvorne did not know. Perhaps they changed the name to secure the mine, which was proving prosperous. Again, Selvorne did not know, and if his father knew, he never said – one thing of many secrets it seemed, and things Selvorne truly needed to know, if he was to be lord of both towns. Especially so, for it seemed likely that other lords would not be pleased.

Selvorne stopped almost beside the road, still in the woods, and watched. To be cautious, he reasoned, though that was not the entire truth. Careful, for men watching – no more careful than he had been the entire day. He leant on a tree and stood close to it so he would not be seen, and breathed as calmly as he could.

Uhlsko had been a wise lord. A small town, but ruled with a love for the people there, who were like family – and were to Selvorne as well. Love, but he was firm – more with Selvorne than the townsfolk, perhaps, though Selvorne had no doubt that his father tolerated no nonsense from any people there. To replace him would be difficult enough, without also having ... to replace another.

Arnlausa was mighty. So Selvorne thought. A large man, younger than his father, not feared, but ... never challenged. And were he confronted, he would eagerly accept – indeed, taunt – and he was not a man to challenge lightly, by duel, by argument, or by jest. Taunt, and he would taunt back without mercy – laugh, and he would laugh harder, so his belly would shake and likely, so would the floor beneath his boots. Selvorne knew men of Tavalehk might wish to push their lord a little, he had seen such desire in their eyes, but none dared push Arnlausa. Selvorne, however, was likely to be a merry joke to them all.

Relok, uncle to Arnlausa, was a very stern man from what Selvorne had heard, and his father, Arnrok – was ferocious. Vicious in his revenge against killers at the time, and ... Selvorne bit his lip to realise that time was upon them once more. He could not walk into Tavalehk and claim to be its heir – not as the simple fishing boy of Vaskatohr, as the young man who worked the quarry, or even the son of a lord – of a minor town, just a village, truly. All would laugh. What was Arnlausa thinking – what was Selvorne thinking, to have accepted it? At that admission of being overwhelmed, he took a deep breath, and continued towards the town.

He knew well what Arnlausa was thinking. He had no sons, he had no heir – he had never named one, for he simply had none to name. Uhlsko as heir, in the unlikely event of the older man outliving him – otherwise, no plan for it. Perhaps, despite his age, he still hoped to find love and have a son, who Uhlsko would name as heir in turn. The two great friends would look after the interests of each other, and the towns. A failed plan, and the suspicions for the killing began to grow in Selvorne's mind.

Some thought Arnlausa might have a son already – in the south. Arnlausa was from MidWaehter, his mother, Rokeli, had wed a man there and when his uncle, Relok, Lord of Tavalehk, died without heir, Arnlausa was summoned to rule the town. Well, not quite summoned, but he came as soon as he heard. And went back each year. Some thought his journey south was not only for wine, but for love – Selvorne doubted that. Arnlausa showed no greater merriment either before or after going south than he usually did, if he was sneaking away to visit hidden children and wife, Selvorne never believed it. Others did, however, but never spoke of it openly.

It saddened Selvorne to think of it. Arnlausa was not very old, he had many good years left, could have found love, had a son, and perhaps many daughters first, as he tried for an heir. He could have had joy in his later years. Old, not as old as his father – perhaps not even as old as his father was, when he met Selvorne's mother Vorlisi – that was a great love, his father said, his greatest joy to find her, his deepest sorrow when she was lost. To think Arnlausa had missed that chance – to think his father had that joy, and lost it – to think of them both in barrels in a cave, it made Selvorne feel ill. And though his loss of his father hurt him more deeply, to think that Arnlausa had his life ended before love, before a child, and ... at a younger ... age ...

Selvorne stopped on the road, and made no pretence of being cautious. He breathed in suddenly then clenched his teeth. Girradehn was much younger – had lost much more of his life than either of the old lords. Lost the chance for love, despite his many interests in it – lost everything ahead of him. Uhlsko at least had a son. Arnlausa at least had a chance. Girradehn did not even have a chance to grow out of his youthful arrogance. He was likely taken by the enemy, without the strength to fight – his life spared, his great skills destroyed, by wounds made useless. He was either captured and dying in pain, or already slain. To think of it, after his own pitiful woes, Selvorne felt ashamed.

A strange shame, which felt more like fury. Cold, in his blood, and rising from the deepest anger – though it was not hot, like anger. It was not reckless and it was not quite fury, but it was strong, so he walked with a deadly purpose towards his town. There was the determination of Relok the Ruthless – there was the mighty strength of Arnlausa – there was the calm will of Uhlsko. The life of a lord was danger – the task of a lord was to take all threats upon himself, so others would not suffer. He would not seize the rule of those towns as a fishing boy, as a pig herder, as a quarry man, but as Selvorne the Vengeful, lord of two towns, sworn to two lords, with a cold, quiet fury, until he found who he sought.

Selvorne neared the town. The first of the plum trees, which had grown from plums fallen or thrown, alone in the wilds. Then another, closer to the path, and then more, lining the way, as travellers long ago had left seeds or overripe fruit by the old road. He ate some, they were not quite ripe, but he was too hungry to care. Farther he went, where the orchards were planted deliberately in rows, and he knew he was very close.

Cautiously he went, or he would not be taking lordship of any towns, but would rule only a hole in the ground. His promises to Arnlausa came to mind. Fight – live – hide. He stopped, and frowned – an odd choice of words, and a strange order. Hide, first – live, then learn to fight. Uhlsko, Arnlausa, Relok – Vaskatohr, Tavalehk, Senylehk town, greatest in all the north. The beginnings of a plan, a progression from hiding to conquering, in a way, for Uhlsko was modest, Arnlausa mighty, and Relok had been indomitable amongst lords. At Senylehk town, greatest in all the north, Selvorne would claim lordship – of Tavalehk, and Vaskatohr. In doing so, he would be just as strong as the men before him. Not that day, but soon. He continued, hiding beside the road, even as he approached his home.

The first of the buildings sighted, and he felt hungry at once. He had not eaten properly for so long, and had pushed the thought of it away, but the plum had drawn it back – there was home, friends, food, and – no people.

His heart thudded – caution grew – no people at the east of town. Understandable, he reasoned, though the town was only one road with houses on each side. No people. It was the middle of the day, perhaps they slept, but surely someone must be awake?

None to the south near the road – none between the buildings. No smell of smoke, and no sign of movement, apart from pigs in pens. They should be out foraging, it was late. The house of his father, on the western side of the road, had its shutters closed. That was to be expected, but so were the other houses, and that was very odd.

A sense of dread as he thought they all were slain – his town, his people, his friends, like family – killed. And the killers waiting, for him, for his father – waiting and watching, and – there was the sound of a whistle.

Selvorne felt his heart pounding – a signal, he was seen – the whistle again. He knew that call, and let go of his breath. That was not his enemy – it was not for him – that was the whistle to the pigs, to be brought from their pens, and the beasts began to leap about in the dirt.

~

One man, alone it seemed, the man he sought. Rerleden, an old man, thin and tanned, wiry and not as tall as he looked. His hair was grey and always kept short – for convenience, he said, not vanity. Years ago short for him meant almost a shaven head, but each year it seemed to be an inch longer, until he settled for enough hair on his head that it seemed he wore a grey fur hat over baldness – practical and warm, rather than for style, he insisted.

Alone – and as merry as Rerleden ever was, whistling to the pigs that knew they were to be let out and taken to the woods. Not laughing, though there was nothing there to make a man laugh. Not wary, or afraid. Selvorne was not sure if that was good or bad, if his old friend was grim or bored, but he was sure he was alone, quite sure he was not an enemy, and certain that if Selvorne did not hurry, the pigs would be loose and the two of them would have to chase them back, unwilling, to the pens.

A whistle from Selvorne – Rerleden froze. Standing still, he was almost lost in the shadows beside the barn. Selvorne made his way towards him, cautiously. Not afraid, but carefully, and perhaps ... just maybe, the town had discovered what had happened, had gone all together to collect the barrels and wreckage, had saved Girradehn – one look from Rerleden ended that hope, for he shook his head as Selvorne appeared, causing his heart to sink.

"No fish?" Rerleden asked, looking Selvorne up and down as he approached.

"What?"

"Fish – no fish. No spear, either – broken? Another?"

"Lost," Selvorne said, and Rerleden sighed.

"How many is that?"

"All of them. Where is the town?"

Rerleden raised an eyebrow, and tilted his head slightly.

"Where do you think?"

Selvorne frowned – a bold answer, or a taunt, or – a fool of a question. He had forgotten, and sighed. None had gone to help Girradehn, none had gone to the ravine, none were there to help, and that was, perhaps, a good thing, for none would be in danger – all had gone to the Festival of Tavalehk.

"You forgot?" Rerleden asked, and Selvorne nodded.

At that, Rerleden frowned and looked Selvorne over once more, completely, seeming to notice all. He shrugged, raised a hand – a signal to wait – then disappeared around the barn, into the town. Selvorne waited for him to return. He did quite quickly, leaving his whipping stick and returning with a stout staff. He approached Selvorne – who backed away a step, then stopped.

"What is wrong?" Rerleden asked in a low voice. Selvorne took a deep breath.

"Have there been any strange travellers, lately?"

130

"No," Rerleden answered, "and there are none here now – nor townsfolk. Where is Uhlsko?"

At that, Selvorne bit his lip, and to his surprise Rerleden nodded once, then beckoned for him to follow into the barn. They went quickly, and he closed the door behind them.

"Your house is better than the barn, though, perhaps not," Rerleden said, "now – tell me what has happened."

A barn – the door shut. A way out, if needed, it was not locked. A place where they could not be seen, nor heard, nor easily attacked. Unless the building was set to fire, which was not an easy thing to do. Not quickly, anyway, and there were ways to escape made just for such a danger, through hatches in the roof, shutters on the walls – even under the walls, in places, by means of covered holes. The fact that there were ways out of the barn to escape fire – and that Rerleden thought to take him there – and that his own house was in every way better for any such danger – it had never before seemed unusual. Selvorne looked around the large barn, and wondered for the first time why such precautions had been taken.

"You do not feel safe – in your own barn," Rerleden said.

"Have I cause to be fearful?"

"Yes – that is clear, even in the shadows. What happened?"

What danger was an old man, trusted by his father, even by Arnlausa, who seemed wary of everyone. Selvorne had been tested, by Arnlausa. He thought to do the same to Rerleden, as best he could, and so took a deep breath.

"On our return, the bridge over the ravine broke – the waggon fell, with ox, and father, and – "

"No names," Rerleden said. Selvorne frowned – then nodded.

"All dead, but the younger man – missing. His injury was severe, and – "

"Dead?" Rerleden asked, and Selvorne nodded, but he thought the old man did not seem very upset to hear it. Not in his voice, nor in his face, from what could be seen of it in the shadows.

"You do not seem surprised?" Selvorne asked.

"I am that you live?"

"I was not on the waggon."

Rerleden nodded, and Selvorne frowned – then, in a moment of inspiration, and though it hurt to do so, he forced himself to grin.

"Ha! I thought you would fall for it," Selvorne said.

"What?" Rerleden asked in a low voice.

"I merely jest. They are on their way, as for the fish – the spear broke in half as I used it as a staff, then, too short, I dropped the stupid thing, and it sank."

"It sank?"

"Too little wood, and too much iron."

"Steel."

"What?"

"The end is steel. Selvorne – that was not at all an amusing jest. You should know better, even if Arnlausa does not – and Uhlsko certainly should."

"He should, and I am sure if he could, he would have stopped such a jest," Selvorne said, "but I wonder why you were not so upset to hear of his death?"

Rerleden took a deep breath, then let it out, slowly, almost laughing.

"Because, my boy, it is not the worst thing I have heard, nor the most grim, nor even the first time I have heard he was dead – and Arnlausa, and believed it. Though I ... wonder that ... you would ... "

Rerleden stopped talking as Selvorne began to nod, then he took another deep breath.

"With no jest, tell me all that you can. I suspect that is not all that happened, if ... tell me what you can."

"Why are you unmoved?" Selvorne asked.

"That your father is dead?"

"And that I do not jest?"

"I told you – it is not the first time I have heard it."

"The first time sworn true, though," Selvorne said.

"No – not even that," Rerleden said, "not the first time, not the second, not the third time sworn true, and though I believe you – for your face is grim – mine is not, because I am not surprised. And it is for just this time that I am here – now tell me what you can, and make no jest, and say no more than you must, and keep your voice low, your mind calm and thoughts clear – no men are in the town, that I know, and I doubt any are here in the barn, listening – but speak low. Now."

Selvorne nodded – unsure if it was comforting or disturbing to think Rerleden considered himself there for just such a time.

"The older men – dead. The younger, wounded, later to disappear."

"Bodies?"

"Away from water, and ... in barrels. Hidden. Is – are there bears?"

"The ox? Was it taken?" Rerleden asked.

"How did you know?"

"Just tell me the tale, boy, I am not so young as you and may not live to hear it if you dally in the telling."

"You are not that old."

"But the danger may be that great?" Rerleden asked, and Selvorne winced – at that, a sigh, and he continued.

The bridge was cut – Rerleden nodded, and Selvorne felt uneasy. Death quick, then, prolonged – more nodding. Men came the next day – again, nodding, and Selvorne was not sure what to make of his old friend, who he had thought nothing more than a pig herder. Selvorne told of how he followed the men into the woods and discovered their camp, hid close to them and listened, but learnt little – at that, he could see Rerleden's wide eyes in the shadows. Astonishment, not fear at being caught, Selvorne thought. He concluded his tale of return and what he discovered, the missing ox, and he made no mention of the seals of lords, his unexpected inheritance, or anything else that might not be for Rerleden's ears, including Arnlausa's reluctance to trust the man who had served Uhlsko so well.

"I wonder that you live."

"I was not on the waggon, I said, for the fishing I – "

"I mean – that you live after such stupid things you have done. You followed them? Into the woods?"

"And unexpected, so I was not found."

"Unexpected – seen – killed. That is most usual. Not at once, only after questioning. Then you walked along the top of the cliffs in the dark?"

"There was a moon."

"Your last, with a fall down a hollow that looks solid by moonlight. It has happened, I have seen it."

"Yet I live – no strange men have been seen? It seems odd that they did not pass through the town?"

Rerleden nodded, then shook his head.

"I saw no footprints just now, not anywhere in the town – if they came this way, they covered their tracks. I have not seen them – no others since the town left, and before that, the only men here were guards from Tavalehk who announced the festival was to begin."

"That is rather odd, though, is it not?"

"Not this year, my boy – not this year. And that is why all the town has gone – a special guest, it might be a middling year, or a grand one, I think."

Selvorne stared blankly at Rerleden, who nodded – almost a bow – then left the barn. He was in the town, Selvorne thought, or the one street that was called a town, and when he looked through the door he saw Rerleden was wandering about as though checking on the buildings, but glancing into the woods and at the dirt of the road as he went. He took his time, disappeared, then returned quite suddenly, coming from the side of the door, and closing it once he entered.

"I see no men here."

"Would you, if there were?" Selvorne asked, noticing Rerleden had brought a large butchering knife from the slaughtering house.

"Perhaps. Perhaps not. You are eyeing my blade?"

Rerleden grinned as Selvorne nodded, and it did not make him feel at ease.

"Good. So you should. You might wish to wear this, when you are here," Rerleden said, handing Selvorne an apron. Selvorne nodded, and put it on – the slaughter apron of Heithris or Thienris, he thought – Thienris, for it was not too large.

"You are disguising me," Selvorne said.

"And you must mean to fool them, by acting stupid? Practising, by saying such obvious things?" Rerleden asked.

"Clearly. Rerl – " Selvorne began to say, but Rerleden raised a hand, and Selvorne was silent – it was a signal he knew, his father had used it often, but he felt a little cheated that any other man would dare order him so.

"Names – usually would not be said," Rerleden said, "but – keep voices low. You must realise this is serious?"

"And you suggest I am acting a fool?"

"It was you, not I, who followed enemies to their camp – alone? Should I yell your name a few times to teach you a lesson, if they search for you, then they might hear it? If they are here, listening?"

Selvorne bit his lip, and Rerleden nodded.

"Good. Some sense. You know I was a runner?"

"I do."

"Good. Loyal, to your father – sworn, and serving with him then, and here, waiting for his orders, if he might have any more for me. Though ... duties now are to the pigs – more obedient than guards. Smarter, too, until led to slaughter, to which they obediently go. Much the same, I guess."

"That is a cruel thing to say."

"For guards or pigs?"

"Either. Men, especially."

"Indeed – a crueller thing to see, my boy, than say – and guards are more than men, and at times must be less than pigs. If duty requires it. Now, let us think on this, and sit, my legs are not what they once were, having run as far as any man might, in his life."

The two of them sat on the best stools they could find, the barn was not used for much, but storage of tools. The one ox remaining in the town had travelled north, likely, the other ... disappeared in the ravine. Some hay, but not much, for a barn that once could house two dozen oxen. They thought to keep the pigs inside, at first, but they dug their way out, or tried, and left holes in the ground where none should be, so they were all sent to the pens where a roof was built, and for most of the year were happier there.

"I am no great thinker on thieves," Rerleden said, "but I do know this – they steal. From what you have said, those men were not thieves?"

"Brigands," Selvorne said.

"Yes. Perhaps. Whatever they may be called – you know of Rigan? Rigan's men?"

Selvorne nodded.

"Perhaps – perhaps not. Men, though, and killers," Rerleden said.

"Intended?"

"The bridge – that is nothing new. It is ... your father knew of such deceits, from long ago. Bridges are good places to stop travellers, so they might be robbed on one side, unable to flee. A few missing planks, a fallen log, small enough to move, not large enough to pass. Blocked only, at first – later, broken, with men upon it – a trap. To kill. Not always, though – if you had many waggons instead of one, perhaps one would fall, the rest would stop, and the men you call brigands would have come out to seize those remaining, leading them south."

"What do you mean, the men I call brigands?"

"Nothing is certain."

"They were – "

"Up to no good? True. Likely. Uncertain. Do not assume they were Rigan's men, do not call them brigands so hastily. Doing so only fools yourself. From what you said, it does not seem they all were aware – or wanted the bridge broken. It seems odd they did not all go to search, even two more would have been wise. Added to that, you said some of them called others of the west? Different men, then, and there is likely much more that we do not know."

"I understand. Do you think the bridge was cut to kill ... those who died?"

"I do not know. Perhaps. It is likely, perhaps. If not, they did not seem too concerned for the waggon, did they? And none have come here, asking of men injured or waggons missing – innocent men would. Guilty men might, also. It is most odd."

"And the ox?" Selvorne asked.

"Also odd."

"I thought someone from the town might have ... come by and taken it, for meat."

"Or for the law, to keep the river clean. That seems likely, but it did not happen. Nor did any travel from the north to the south, who might have taken the ox – and if they had, the chance that they did so at the very time you were not there ... though, I guess if you were in a cave, you might not hear."

"I fear for ... Girradehn," Selvorne said, almost whispering the name.

"I fear for you," Rerleden said, "and for me – and for all men who know what happened, that the bridge was cut. But it is not time for fear, nor to dwell on worries, but to think. Why do this and not steal – there was much to take. Why kill and not be certain the killing was done – why take the ox – why not take the wine? Why avoid this town, that is strange in itself, and suggests – was it a dozen men?"

"Ten and four, and one woman."

"Also odd. A woman who cooks – odd that there was one, odd that there were not many women. Just one. To me that suggests a meeting."

"Clearly it was a meeting," Selvorne said, but Rerleden raised a hand.

"A meeting of different men, perhaps the most feared of each and limited in numbers, restricted by arrangement in advance – and a woman allowed as a mere cook, but likely she was either dangerous, or their leader – and so one group of men increased their numbers to an advantage. Just to be safe."

Rerleden was quiet, and Selvorne waited, but he did not speak.

"Well – what does it mean?" Selvorne asked.

"I do not know. Perhaps they are Rigan's men – perhaps they remain in the lands. Or have returned. I do not know. What we do know is little – the bridge broken. Men dead. Deliberate, or unintended, but with no regret. I do not know – we should not guess. There is nothing for it, but to hide."

Rerleden was quiet once more, and seemed to be thinking, but as he did Selvorne grew restless – to hide was not the plan, it was to find Cienn, and then find the killers. Neither said anything, but Rerleden began to stare at Selvorne.

"You look troubled?" Rerleden asked.

"Should I not be?"

"No – yes, you should. You disagree?"

"I prefer to ... what do you mean, hide?"

"You prefer to hunt them?"

"If I could."

"How? Back into the woods – alone? Or with me? Or perhaps with the swine?"

"No. Though, Krogarve herded swine through a camp of brigands, so they gave chase, then finished them one at a time."

Rerleden nodded, and Selvorne frowned.

"You think that a wise strategy?" Rerleden asked.

"No, I think that brilliant – if I was a skilled killer, and if the pigs would go where I herded them, which, as a man used to herding pigs, I know they would not. It was a story, nothing more – that plan would end with the brigands eating the pigs and questioning me, I think, if not killing me for fun."

"Good."

"And how is that good?"

"It is not. You could join them, perhaps? Share the pigs?"

"Perhaps. Rerl – what are you getting at?"

"Nothing," Rerleden said, "it is nothing. And it is good – that you are not a complete fool. What you did ... was very bold, very reckless, very stupid. Very useful – some clue, perhaps. It might not be so wise to walk around with the stolen ale bladder, though."

"Or it might help me find them," Selvorne said, handing the bladder to Rerleden, who examined it, nodding, and tasted the ale.

"Or them find you – Veksale. Not so common in the east, but plentiful in many places. You bought this in Senylehk, you should say – or some other lie. I did not mean to ... you thought I mean to run, hide, and disappear?"

"Did you not?"

"No. Do you think that is what runners do?"

"Not at all. I thought they took messages, at speed, to those who need to know."

"That, they do – you are calm. Is it because you are angry?" Rerleden asked, and Selvorne took a deep breath, and frowned.

"No. Nor is it that enough days have passed, but ... "

"You have buried it – the anger, the hurt, the hate – in a box?"

Selvorne nodded.

"As your father did. Good. That is what must be hidden first of all, and you have done it well – but your face ... shows too much. A moment, if you will – I must think."

At that, Rerleden stood, and began walking around the barn, into the shadows, into the light that came through cracks in the walls – through hay and dirt, and even seemed to want to climb to the loft at one moment, but thought better of it. After some time, he returned to sit on his stool.

"You must take word to Cienn," Rerleden said in a low voice.

"I know – I told you as much before."

"Yes. Do you know why?"

"Because Arnlausa trusted no other," Selvorne said, and Rerleden frowned.

"No names!"

"Yet you just said Cienn?"

"Selvorne, this is no time for – "

"And now – mine. Rerleden – what are you trying to say?"

Rerleden winced – and Selvorne knew there was something he was not telling, but would not reveal, and he shook his head.

"Selvorne," Rerleden said in a very low voice, "listen carefully. You must take word to Cienn. Word of what has happened. You, yourself – and I, myself. And by another means I must send word, though, I am not yet sure how."

"Because she is the only person that can be trusted, and – "

"Because if you take word – and fail – and die – then I will be going by another means – to take word of this, and if I fall, a third way, perhaps, or more. He who sent you has no great love or trust of me – but I am the only man he has to send, other than you, that he might trust. That I am old, and in a way, dying, that – "

"You are dying?"

"No – but old enough to likely not ... trusted a little, for it ... my age, and that I have had so many chances, and waited so long ... and so am proven. Not trusted, not loved, but your father did. You realise Cienn is not easy to find – not lately?"

"Not ever, from what I have heard."

"Not always, but true for most of your life."

"How do I find her, then?"

"You will not. She will find you. It may take weeks, but if you are – "

"Sorry – what?" Selvorne asked.

"It may take weeks, I am not sure ... if months, perhaps, but – "

Selvorne held up a hand – a signal to halt, he knew it well, his father taught him, Rerleden had used it already – and to his delight, Rerleden obeyed, and was silent.

"I wish to see her now – what is the fastest way to do so?" Selvorne asked.

"Now?"

"Yes – now. You were a runner – you must know how. All runners served her at some time, you must have done, if she is that old?"

"She is. I did. And so I know you will not find her," Rerleden said, and Selvorne was about to speak, but obeyed a signal to be silent, "and runners are sent from one man to another, with directions of where to go and where to find them. What makes you think I know where she is now? Or that anyone does?"

"I had hoped," Selvorne said.

"Wrongly. Taffoanan is the acting leader of Waehdric – he is easy to find, from what I hear, he never leaves the island."

"Then ... would he know?"

"I am glad you did not suggest we speak with him, though, what do you know of him?"

"Nothing."

"More than nothing, I suspect. And more of Cienn than you admit – you know very well she is not easy to find."

"I was warned."

"Are you testing me?" Rerleden asked, though he did not seem upset by it.

"No – only hoping. Is she – hiding? What do you know?"

Rerleden took a deep breath, then sighed.

"What do I know of Cienn – nothing recent. Much of before – she is cautious, more, in her age, and not for fear of threat, but fear of ... being involved."

"With lords?"

"With any she might love, who then might die. She retired from all duties, and yet wields power – she acts, at times, and things are done in her name. Some think she is dead, and nothing was said of it – this is not true, I believe."

"Will she help? If I find her?"

"If you, or I, or any bring word to her of what has happened – she will march with the armies of the north to find these killers – and she will find them."

Rerleden spoke in a very low voice, and Selvorne felt his spirits lift – Arnlausa had suggested the same, but somehow Rerleden was more convincing. Perhaps Arnlausa was only hopeful – Rerleden was certain.

"And now you seem eager to find her," Rerleden said.

"Am I ... that easy to read?"

"Yes. And only ... most would not say read, Selvorne. You are eager, you must be careful. If it takes many weeks to find her – safely – is that too long?"

Selvorne thought on the distances north – days of travel to where she might be. Days to return. Too long or not, he had no choice.

"It cannot be helped."

"No – it cannot. And it does not need be – as soon as can be, no sooner. Do not rush – it is the message that she needs, from your lips speaking, not your dead body found."

"I know. A shame ... we do not have a runner."

"Is that meant to be a jest?"

"No. I did not mean – "

"To insult my age? No insult taken – a runner, that would be good. One from her, to send back – but they do not always run, and so will take weeks, regardless. Also, we do not know where she is – though she could be at the festival."

"Do you think she is?"

"I do not know – perhaps. If she is – I hope she is – then you may find a way to speak with her alone. Tell her what you have told me – and more?"

"And more, that I – "

"Cannot say – you do not have to tell me. I was a runner, I know ... I am not to know all. If she is at the festival, all is well. If not – you must take care. I certainly will. Should you fall, should I fall, the message ... will be left here, in the town. Hidden, where they will find it."

"Is that wise?" Selvorne asked, and Rerleden raised an eyebrow.

"Should the town be burnt to the ground, perhaps the message would not reach her – but that would be a message in itself, I think. You must trust me on this, it is my duty, my advice, my ... it is what I know best."

Selvorne nodded, but he did not like the idea of it taking weeks.

"If Cienn is at Lodlehk – how long? At best?" Selvorne asked.

"Five. Seven. Ten days."

"Ten? Five? What – how can – "

"I be so sure?"

"You be so unsure?"

"Five days at speed," Rerleden said, "running, and you will not run. Seven days if all goes well, and you do not have to hide, and the weather is not the best, nor terrible. Ten days – that is more likely. I suggest ten, for you – then longer back."

Selvorne stared at the ground, and could sense Rerleden looking at him with a frown.

"And you still think it too long?" Rerleden asked, but Selvorne said nothing, "It is that far, it cannot be done faster. If you try to run it – certainly, along the road, you may have a chance. If they watch for you, or for any suspicious messenger, they will stop you – or worse, follow. You must go slowly, or you may lead them to – "

"It is not that," Selvorne said, looking up, "I know it is far. Five days – ten – there is no chance for Girradehn."

Rerleden began to nod, and Selvorne frowned at him.

"So – that is the reason for your haste."

"We cannot leave him to ... them."

"And we cannot save him, if we found him – Selvorne, I will search for Girradehn. I fear he is lost – already lost, should we find him this day or the next, or in five or ten or twenty."

"You do not know that."

"No – but Arnlausa would have," Rerleden said in a low voice, "and would not have let him die if there was a chance he might live."

"Could you have helped him?"

"No. Again, Arnlausa knew I was here, and knows what I know, and knows more himself – if the bone was out, the skin split, the delay too long – the break too messy – at the best of times, a lost leg. Delay, and the blood poison spreads from the air. Both men knew that."

"We cannot leave him," Selvorne said quietly.

"You must. I will not – I will do my best to find him. But ... I doubt I can save him, I will try. You realise they knew this when they ... kept you there?"

Selvorne nodded.

"And you feel guilt for it – that they died to save you?" Rerleden asked, but Selvorne frowned, then shook his head. It was not guilt – not for that. Remorse, and misery, and anger – but not guilt.

"Sorrow."

"Yes, sorrow. They did not die to save you – they died because men cut the bridge, and – "

"I know."

"And they died for the message – not for you. For you, a little, perhaps – for the message, more. I doubt these men in the woods are thieves – they have not stolen. And to kill that way is not the work of a man who enjoys killing, nor one in anger at those who were slain. If so, it seems odd they did not take delight in revenge, unless it was against ... the missing one, and that is quite possible. But the bridge, alone, is a message that needs to be passed on – to cut it so, Cienn must know. And what you saw and heard in the woods ... you must tell only her."

Selvorne knew that already – Arnlausa had explained it thoroughly, or well enough that Selvorne would not question it. But he found it odd that Rerleden would come to the same conclusion, and felt there was something he did not say. Nor would he, for Rerleden was stubborn, and not easily tricked, which only made Selvorne want to know more.

"Arnlausa said I should tell Taffoanan, acting Leader of the Waehdric, if I cannot find Cienn in – "

"No he did not."

"Yes, he did, he said – "

"No," Rerleden said, leaning forward, "he did not. He would not, and you are trying to trick me into saying more than you need to know. Your trick is obvious, but I will tell you all you need to know, and more. Why did he tell you to only trust Cienn?"

Selvorne narrowed his eyes – a trick in turn, that he would not fall for – and Rerleden smiled.

"Not so foolish anymore, then," Rerleden said, "nor so young. Cienn only – for reasons you cannot know, but surely must guess."

"I do not know who the enemy is."

"No – that is obvious. Any person you might tell does not know who the enemy is – Taffoanan least of all, his mind has wandered, you might tell him in secrecy then discover he has made a song of it the next day, singing it to all. With your name in every verse. All your names, and at the end, where you were last seen. His skill with song has not gone, likely it will be a catchy tune that others sing, and spread until all the people of every town know it."

Selvorne winced when Rerleden looked at him with his head slightly down – his serious stare, he was not making some jest.

"The same is true for all others, though, less obvious will be their slip – the guards of Tavalehk, from one to the other word would spread, and fast. Their lord dead – how long do you think that would be a secret? I believe, less than one quarter of an hour – with the horns, and assembly of men – then all the town will know. Soon after, all who know of the town. Then all the lands."

"Surely that is a good thing? Would they not – "

"What? March – on the woods? And the enemy will disappear. It is bad enough I am going to search for Girradehn, at that they might flee. Or that you stole their ale bladder. Do you want them cautious and fleeing – or confident and careless?"

At that, Selvorne began to nod, and Rerleden smiled.

"I doubt they look for you – they might. If they mean you to die – you cannot be reckless. We cannot chance it. Revenge against your father – continued against yourself. Heartless men, to do such a thing, to make you also suffer, they would not hesitate. It may be, though, that they do not know who you are."

"I find that unlikely if they wanted my father dead."

"And if they wanted either of the others dead, and not he? If they did not see you there? If they are men of the south, and – you did not go there, this year?"

"I never have."

"The merchants of wine of the south, following the waggon, to steal back their barrels – or men who saw the deal done there, who followed to steal the wine, perhaps after killing the sellers and taking their coin. An enemy lord, here, or a man with an unfaithful wife, who – "

"My father would not – oh," Selvorne said, and Rerleden raised an eyebrow.

"Were it only he on the waggon, then perhaps we might have a chance to guess. Any three of the men could have an enemy we do not know – or all three. Or two, or no enemy at all, but a mistake, others meant to die – we do not know. And if we do not know, we must be unknown. You must hide, you must find Cienn or allow her to find you, and you must think on this every day that the danger is unknown. Do you agree?"

Selvorne nodded.

"Good. I dread to think what might have happened, had all three died at once."

"Or had I been seen at the camp."

"True – had Arnlausa not lived to warn you, you likely would have done nothing more stupid than you did. Never do anything so foolish again. My boy, if you wish to do something that would make your father proud, then listen carefully to the advice of a man who served him for a long time – beside him, under him, and for him, as a friend – I will advise you as best he would, had he lived."

Selvorne nodded, but then a thought came to him.

"What would he have done – had I died and he lived?"

It was a simple question – Selvorne meant nothing by it, apart from learning what clever thing Uhlsko might do, other than blunder around knowing nothing.

Rerleden seemed to know his father well – better than Selvorne did, for some things, and he had to admit, he knew him for far longer. An honest question, but the look on Rerleden's face was one of almost horror. He stared past Selvorne into the darkness of the barn – for so long and with such a grim stare that Selvorne turned and expected to see some danger lurking there.

"Rerleden?" Selvorne asked in a whisper, and the old man woke from his dream.

"He would take revenge," Rerleden said, "having lost you, and his closest friend – revenge. I am not sure how."

"I did not mean – I only wondered what he would … if it was something I should do."

"It is not. He would advise you to do what I am about to advise – for himself, he might … I suspect he would have done what you did – follow them to their camp."

"Foolish, then, as was I."

"And he would have killed them all, there, as they slept – later, as they travelled – fast or slow, one at a time, or all at once, by some means most terrible, and learnt all he needed to know, as he did."

"I find that unlikely," Selvorne said, and Rerleden laughed.

"Indeed. Do you? He might have come here first, told me, then taken the swine."

"And charged them through the camp, like Krogarve?"

"And poisoned one to feed the men – or set it loose to draw them out – or capture the men in the ravine, and use one against the other – I do not know. Other men may do this, later – you must find Cienn so she may release such men, or march an army, or – you realise the danger this puts on you, and myself?"

Selvorne bit his lip and nodded, as Rerleden continued.

"All who know what happened … any who might bring her out – no man would want her as an enemy. They likely thought themselves undetected. They likely hoped they would pass, unknown. Now … I am not sure of the ale you stole … perhaps they might think your father is loose, and … I do not know. Not if they went to the cave. Perhaps they thought Arnlausa put your father in the barrel, dragged Girradehn to the cave, then died. Who, then, went to their camp and stole their ale? Someone to fear – tell your tale to the wrong man, and both you, and he, are in danger. No man wants the wrath of Cienn upon them, and I think this killing was meant to be done quietly, seen as an accident, not even a theft, and the killers would disappear, untroubled and unknown."

"I need to disappear," Selvorne said, and Rerleden nodded.

"You think well for a young man who has seen horrors so recently – and in that praise, I am not mocking. A little slow, that is to be expected – in days you will realise the truth of it. I am not sure for time, if you wait here, you are in danger. An hour, a day … for now, it is better that it is just us two in town. If asked by strangers, I will say you were here all the time – if you are asked, your face will tell them that you were not, so … you should disappear. If, instead, the rest of the town was here, one of them would say your name, ask a question, reveal too much to strange men who visit. This town is too small for you to hide, and staying here does not make it easier to find Cienn.”

“I should go to Tavalehk, then.”

“Yes – for the festival. Keep away from those who know you, if you cannot, be brief with acquaintances, and hurried with friends. Will this be a problem?”

“No, I have few left in Tavalehk,” Selvorne said, thinking his greatest friend was gone, and those who were close to Arnlausa would be easy to avoid, if Selvorne did not spend much time at his house. Others he knew in the town had left, for other towns, and his friends from Vaskatohr, though close, were so close at home that they did not want to waste their time at the festival with a man they saw almost every other day of the year. If anything, it was hard to find people he knew at the festival, for all were rushing around in wonder at the markets, and enjoying the entertainment.

“With luck,” Rerleden said in a very low voice, “Cienn is there. If not – Hartlehk is not where she would be, nor is it an easy place to hide. Guards ask questions of strangers. At Senylehk, though – there, you will disappear. With coins, completely – a man may live there an entire life with coins and be known to no others, not even where he spends his fortune.”

“That seems unlikely.”

“Have you been there? No? Only as a child. Go there, you will disappear into the Gathering Cloak, and be gone.”

“And – what?”

“What?”

“The – what? Gathering Cloak?”

“The ... crowd. The crowd that gathers – at the festival. Young men from all over the lands, enjoying the festival – and you must enjoy it – and disappear.”

“I doubt I will ... enjoy ... oh,” Selvorne said, then nodded as Rerleden grinned.

“None of the enemy will suspect a happy young man amongst the other hundred there, who all seem the same – go in despair, you will be noticed in a moment. Go with a grin, though you stand beside your enemy, he will not know – unless he knows your face. Sometimes, not even then. A friend unsuspected is an enemy unseen, though expected.”

“What?”

“Even the men searching for you will not think to find you laughing, even if you joke with them – but do not press your luck in such a way.”

“I understand ... and Cienn may be there.”

“She may – or some clue to ... or if dead, perhaps an announcement. I do not know what happens in the lands so much, anymore. It occurs to me your enemies might be there as well – a festival tends to draw thieves, killers, and enemies of lords. Especially lords they have just slain.”

“To do mischief?”

"No – to enjoy the festival. Perhaps to gloat, perhaps to steal, or simply to meet – the Gathering Cloak, in which they hide, the same as for you – to meet, and not be noticed. You have an advantage, though."

"I know some of their faces, and I am looking for them."

"Exactly. And you have coins, and can easily hide amongst people, and as long as you truly enjoy yourself, you will look truly happy – but your face gives away your sorrow. You know how to bury it?"

Selvorne nodded – he did know how to bury sorrow, his father had taught him how to lock it away, as though in a box, and bury it as though in the dirt. Selvorne was not good at it. He always found a thought that distracted him, and also considered it quite a cruel thing to do, to forget such woes. So instead he learnt to simply quieten sorrows so they could be ignored. Remembered and honoured, and wept over at a later time. It was when his mother died that he had been taught such things, and though only a child, he found it helped to mourn gently. Though he had hoped, as a child, that somehow it would bring her back again. Memories of her, it did – happy memories, instead of sorrow and loss – but not his mother, not to life, and not to his side.

"And now you look very grim," Rerleden said.

"And will change the moment I need to – thank you, my friend. Do you have more advice?"

"Prepare – hurry. If men come, you have always been here – behave as though it were not today, but months ago, and so, the lie would then be true. I will come to you and abuse you for not tending the pigs, for being lazy – and threaten that you might not go to the festival at all, if you do not do your chores. If you feel anger – direct it at me. If you feel sorrow – curse the cruelty of your life, that you are denied the festival and all its joys. If you feel afraid – shun my mighty stick, that I will wave. You must lead, for you hide your feelings poorly – I will make them believe our lie, whatever you show on your face. If they come. I hope they do not."

"I hope they do."

"Do you? Then you are a fool who has heard nothing."

"We will fool them, see their faces, know who we seek."

Rerleden took a deep breath, then sighed.

"We will not fool them – but distract them. See their faces – and be doomed for it. Two men alone in a town. A ruse not entirely believed. Our movements watched. Our faces, known. Our play is a distraction long enough only that I might kill them, Selvorne, with this," Rerleden said, holding up the long, broad, terribly sharp slaughtering knife, "and at that, you will follow my lead and do the same – then flee. If they come, it is distraction, battle, death, and chase. Do not say you hope for that as well – it cannot end with me alive."

Selvorne winced as Rerleden nodded, and he began to realise the danger they were in.

"I did not think."

"And some would laugh at you for it, and so try to make you think – you have had no time to think. No clarity, no peace – just horrors, new to you. Today I did not think, either – I have had no time to, there is no time. This plan I did not devise now, I merely remembered what was done before. I know what may happen here, I have seen it before, heard of it – not only in the stories."

"Were they true? Was it ... that bad?"

"Yes. And no, not all true, the stories, and ... worse, at times. Your house is barred and locked, you know how to get inside. Gather coins, smaller are better, but take many. Purses for them, at least one hidden – a sack to pack your things, a change of clothes – present yourself as a young man going to a festival, after a journey of many days from the far north."

"Weapons?"

"Knives that are your best, and a staff. A spear ... is, well, you know as well as I, people do not walk around with spears at the festival. Or swords."

"It is ... lost. In the river, I think. Or taken."

"You said. I might retrieve it, if it is not too deep, though I doubt it is still there, I ... might yet retrieve it, we shall see. If they have it, though – that is good."

"Why is – oh, of course. We will know who they are."

"Now you are thinking."

"No, I considered it before. My friend, if ... the men come, and it comes to ... do not strike in haste, they might be fooled."

"More likely they will pretend to be – you do not know what men we might be facing, my boy, so take great caution to move about your house, and then, if seen, appear careless and angry, sorrowed or impatient. I wish you luck, I will make preparations of my own."

Both men stood, and Selvorne bowed – to his surprise, Rerleden bowed back. Two brief bows, respectful and almost formal, then Selvorne prepared to return to his house.

~

The House of Uhlsko – truly, the House of Skelorne, the name of his father's family, though it was rarely spoken, mentioned or used. Nor was it called The House of Uhlsko, but simply, The House, or The Hall, for it had a hall where the town could all gather and eat.

Small, for a grand house of a lord – large for any other house, for it was once an inn. Quite unlike so many houses that once were inns, for many inns often once were barns. The House of Uhlsko was built from the first as an inn, to house travellers, not their beasts. One large room, with a great fire, common to all as a place to cook and eat. The chimney, in stone, used by the entire house, it ran through almost the middle up to the roof. Not one, but two, and the second chimney was hidden, secret, and built there for the escape of men, not smoke. Made of bricks with double walls, at great expense, with a ladder running all the way inside, to make an exit through the roof, if needed. Proof against fire, should the house be burning. Unknown to any who did not live there – a joyous secret for a young boy, but a curious thing to consider, for a young man who had just learnt what enemies might be all around him that he did not know.

It was a useful way in and out of the house, if a man did not mind climbing a tree to the roof, then making his way down a narrow passage. Selvorne had no need for it that day, and instead moved quickly across the road to unbolt the front door. It was not locked. There was no need for it usually, and there was no lock that day – odd, until he remembered it was left inside, the day they hurried to leave. Perhaps Rerleden should close the house properly once he left – otherwise, the two bolts keeping it shut slid with little encouragement, and Selvorne was inside.

Sorrow was upon him immediately. What should have been his return to life as usual, was instead the realisation it would never be the same as it was. He closed the door to darkness, and the smell of the place made him remember when he was there last – "hurry or run after, the ox is eager, your delay is worse than the beast" – that day when they left, and Arnlausa taunted him. His last spear that was not broken, the chanting of "moo" from outside, calling to him, as if he were an ox. A joke was as good as haste, so he took his second last spear, which was broken already, one piece in each hand, he stepped out of the house holding them to his head, like horns – to laughter of the town that had gathered there to wish them well. A small sack of oats Girradehn hurled at him from the waggon – it almost hit him, almost split. Girradehn's head was almost bruised when Arnlausa slapped him for being an idiot. Anger at the near loss of oats, not for nearly hitting Selvorne in the head. Then they were off, over a month ago, and Selvorne could still smell the fire where they cooked porridge that morning, and the porridge, and the bowls he had left unwashed, as he had hurried and forgotten to check.

A sigh, then in darkness he went up the stairs. Not a bump, no stumble, he knew the house too well. Up to his room, and there he needed to open a shutter to see, if only to choose clothes that matched. Nothing appropriate for hiding, just one shirt of green, most were grey or blue. Nothing dark, all were faded. Coins could buy more, lightly coloured things would not hide him well on his way through woods, only in the town. He had no change of boots, every pair needed mending, none at Vaskatohr knew how, and he was not going to haul them to the festival to have them fixed that year. Not as planned. New boots, and new clothes would be bought. Suited to the task, and the eagerness for the festival that grew in him made him feel shame.

Eagerness was to be his cloak – but he needed an actual cloak. For rain, for ... he would have to sleep outside at the festival, not in the House of Laehtene, Arnlausa's fine home. Not at an inn, they all would be taken. Never before had he thought for accommodation, it always was provided – he likely would have to sleep in a field. A cloak, then, his most comfortable for such a task, and a sack to carry it during the hot days – and a bowl, and a plate, and a mug, of wood or bronze, he weighed each in the kitchen and decided on wood, bronze and tin, as light as he could find.

His house had many rooms, for, being an inn, it once housed many people. His own room was quite large, and had its own secret exit to the chimney, which his father should have either blocked long ago, or not told him about until he was older, wiser, and not likely to sneak out at night and fall off the roof. Unhurt – lucky, to catch a branch as he tumbled. Stupid to try. Painful to remember, but not for the wound.

His father's room – he did not wish to enter. His mother's room – left, as it was, when it once was shared with Uhlsko. He had moved from it after she died, and kept it as it was. Selvorne did not go there, for the memory was too strange. It was locked, and he did not know where the key was kept, nor had he ever seen his father go there, but he knew it was dusted at times, for a bucket appeared in the hall with all the dirt. He was not sure where the dirt came from, for it appeared all over the house, even in unused rooms, but he was quite sure if it was not swept away, his house would, in time, be buried. His father had said it was only dust on the wind, settling, but that did not explain the rooms that were always closed.

Preparation was slow, for most of what he would usually take on a journey had already been taken a month ago, and lost. Some to the river, sinking or washing away. Some to the ravine, with its many dark holes between rocks. Some was stolen by the brigands, or whatever they were to be called. He managed to put together a new collection of things, then took a deep breath – and went to where the coins were hidden.

A corner of the hall, in a wall, where kitchen met the main room – hidden behind a piece of stone that could be moved. He was not sure it was the best place to hide coins, but none had ever gone missing, not even by his own hand, not since he was a child. It seemed an odd place to hide things, though, for any who came to the house could have noticed the crack and wondered what was inside it – but his father said it was best. Selvorne felt some hesitation to take what he usually should not touch, so, with the fear of a thief, he removed the stone and took the purse, then bit his lip in sorrow to realise he was not stealing. They were his – it all was his. The coins, the house, the rooms – all that once belonged to his father. Including the grief and memory of his mother.

And the duty – of a lord, and as a son. He looked into the purse by the light of an open shutter, seeing few coins, and a note.

"If you are not my son," the note read, "then know this – terrible vengeance will be had on you, thief!"

Selvorne raised an eyebrow – that was not in the purse when last he looked. He was a very young boy at the time, though, so he continued to read.

"Look where you burnt your hand."

A strange note, he thought, but for himself – a message. He had burnt his hand many times in the kitchen, though never seriously – a few times in the main hall fire, and it was never something worthy of a note. It was a message – for himself alone – and Selvorne began to grin.

To the fireplace he went, searched a little and found another purse – a few more coins. Nodding, he went to the kitchen which was behind, he searched the other side of the fireplace, and found another purse with a few coins.

There was some joy in his father's cleverness – dead, and unjustly so, but to think that he thought ahead so cunningly, it was almost as if he lived. Selvorne was not surprised. Not by the trick, not by the message, not by his father's ruse – it was what he would expect of his father, and it made him proud. Few would know what was meant by the note – his hand, burnt – but neither of those at the end of his arms. His "hand" was the carved branch he used to throw hay, long ago when they had bales of it to feed oxen – a branch, forked, carved – and burnt. Charred to keep the points firm and strong, length so he had the reach of a man. He had made it as a boy in the corner of the barn – a mighty hand, made by his own hand, and to last.

It had not worked, it did not last – it broke, and Selvorne was furious. He was proud of his carving, shaping and burning – angry and betrayed by the stupid wood that had snapped. Too eager to lift a heavy bale, too sudden and too swift, it snapped. He made a fire of it and burnt it on the very spot where he had made it, despite his father's protests that a large fire inside the hay barn was a very bad idea. He was only seven, and would not listen – his father was patient, and silent, and merely watched. With buckets of water, for he was not as foolish as his son. When it was made to ash, they spoke of it no more. Never did he call a hay fork a hand, again – a spike, a fork, a branch – not a hand. Never was it mentioned, and no other living man knew of it.

"Are you ready? You must hurry!" Rerleden called from the doorway. Selvorne gathered his things in the sack, half expecting enemies to be in the street.

Five Warnings

Rerleden was growing impatient. Whatever he had been doing was finished, and he was eager to begin his search for Girradehn. Selvorne, however, wanted to investigate what might be left for him where he burnt his hand, and he insisted Rerleden lock the house and leave him to be – something that he unexpectedly obeyed without question.

Back to the barn, and Selvorne looked to the corner where the tools were kept in boxes on shelves – a table to work upon, and a stool. Things being mended, being made, tools being dismantled to save their iron once they had been worn or broken. A hole, near, where grain was once stored – a better, deeper hole had been made outside and covered, safe from mice or whatever creatures came to eat it uninvited. And where he had lit the fire to burn his hand, a cabinet stood, roughly made and housing the most important tools. There he began to search.

Nothing but tools, though, and Rerleden called for him to hurry, whatever he was doing. He continued to search, through all the drawers and shelves and boxes, and as he did so, he noticed that as he rummaged in the cabinet, the ground around it seemed to move. He dragged it to one side, scratched at the dirt, and found a small wooden door in the ground – opening it, he discovered a hole, and in it, a flat wooden chest, only a few inches tall.

He recognised it immediately – it was the small box he made as a young boy, given to his father as a present. Absurd in its size and shape, being one foot wide, three quarters of a foot long, half a foot deep – the size of the wood at hand, rather than any usual shape for a box. His father used it for parchments, to humour him, but eventually the corner broke and he stopped using it. Then it disappeared from the house.

Unlocked. Indeed, unlockable, for it was almost dismantling itself as he shook it. Inside, under a woollen cloth was a small sack, and a gathering of parchments rolled up in a glass jar. A hairbrush, a large wallet that opened to reveal many scissors, and a smaller box that had tied to it a leather pouch that he knew held a grooming kit, for he had a similar one of his own. An odd assortment of things, Selvorne thought, and a strange familiar smell to them all. He wondered at the glass jar, which was possibly the most valuable thing in the box, for glass was expensive, and it was finely made. He opened it and removed the parchments, and discovered that one, wrapped around many of the others, was a note to himself.

"My dear boy," the letter said at the start, and it was all he could read, as it was folded around the other parchments. Written in a bold hand, but elegant and careful – strong parchment, and though not sealed with wax, it was bound with linen cord that Selvorne immediately untied, so he might read the rest.

"If you are reading this from where it was placed, it can mean only one of two things – you have either poked your nose where it does not belong, as you usually do, and discovered this secret hidden here. If so, replace the box and all its belongings at once, and fetch me with great haste – tell no person, read no more."

Selvorne winced, and continued to read.

"And I mean it – stop reading, if you can fetch me."

Selvorne sighed, then continued to read.

"Indeed, you continue, and so a third warning, which you need at times, often ignoring two – replace the box, fetch me."

A short pause in the writing, and Selvorne wished more than anything that he could.

"And so – defiant three times, or worse. If you have continued to read, I assume that something has happened to me – assume, and have considered it, and also that you have found my note amongst the coins, hidden by fireplace and kitchen and candleholders. Consider my cleverness! Some joy in the preparation, to think a thief would be so fooled – and hopefully, find the coins, and leave. The treasure here is worth far more – the cunning of my plan, worthy of Krogarve himself, you could say. If I have come to harm, and that is why you are reading now, continue – otherwise, if you have defied me even to this point – three times disobeyed – then I will be very harsh with you, my son – and more than cruel to any other man."

Elegantly written – a stern warning from the Lord of Vaskatohr – politely put, but the wording was firm. And Selvorne was completely sure that any thief who had found it would have ignored the warnings completely, either for the desire of the treasure, apparently in the box, or the simple fact that they could not read. Not so clever, that part of the ruse, but quite likely no man would find it without knowing the secret of Selvorne's burnt hand – Selvorne, however, would be trembling to read it if his father lived, and would have read the entire thing, pretended he had not, and buried the box once more, aching to know what was in it. A few days he might last before digging it up again, or admitting it all to his father, who would neither yell nor hit, but raise an eyebrow that would make his heart sink.

Perhaps Selvorne would have stopped at the first note, but not that day – he immediately opened the smaller box to see what treasure it contained – coins. Nothing special, though they were gold and silver, a great find for a thief, but the other things – and then he bit his lip.

The other things belonged to his mother. Her brush, scissors, a grooming kit for her nails. A scarf, as well, which he thought was a cloth to wrap the other things, and the brush had hair upon it still – fair and few, but hers, and all of her that remained. Carefully he set the box on the table, and placed the things within it, then took the next letter to read.

"So you read, and so I am come to harm. Passed away from this world – and though saddened, you must remember I had a good life, long and rich. For many years I have missed your mother, now I am returned to her, in the great Sea of the Dead. Mourn me not – not so it brings grief. Remember me well, and know that I have ventured out to see many places, made good friends, survived more than my share of dangers, and the only regret I know is pain that could not be changed – even had I the chance to do so. Few could wish for a life as mine, as rich, as long as it has been to this day. And if you are my son reading this, then I have been survived by a boy who is good – clever, kind, and not so reckless that he has yet met his doom."

Selvorne was astonished – never in his life had his father been so ... free from woe. Not that he had seen, though with Arnlausa he was merry, he more often was sad, it seemed, when alone. His last words, free of pain – but they were not his last, they were written long before. A boy – not for years did his father call him a boy, even in jest. Arnlausa did, others did, if they were very old. But his father, who was older still, did not. Young man – even before he should be called such a thing. The only other clue to when it was written was that his mother had already perished – it could have been years before. He continued reading.

"So – who could wish for more? Truly, who could – only that your mother had lived longer with me, and, I hope, that my passing was swift and painless. My other hope is that I consider all things here that you might need to know, as best I can, as completely that I might guess. And take note, my son, the first thing you must do is prepare a similar letter, to be found by those who follow you, be they wife or children or great friends – declare your will, and lodge it with the council. For if you perish without doing so, those who administer the affairs of lords and Waehdric will come – and take much that was yours. Indeed, often without seeing your body."

Selvorne winced – his father was right. Not so for ordinary men, quite true for lords and their sons, and something that he had not considered seriously, despite being told many times it was a danger. Despite having done just that already – years ago Selvorne wrote his will, for all his few possessions to go to his father. Should that fail, to Arnlausa. Years ago, and he was tempted to name a third –

Cassini Cassub, who he then adored – but his father advised against it, and it was left at that. A grim task, an important one – but the council would not know what to do if presented with the bodies of all three men at once. And much had changed since years ago. Or even days.

"What are you doing?" Rerleden called through the door.

"Wait," Selvorne said, and nothing more – he yelled it through the crack of the door, and saw Rerleden nod, then obey.

"I should say at this point," the letter continued, "I would prefer to be buried than burnt, in a tight wooden box, away from the waters. Where no animal may find me, safe from worms in the ground. Beside your mother – there I shall rest. The ground is not so hard, once dug well and deep, and it is dry. However, should I have died of horrible disease, then burn me first in a terrible fire, and collect the ash to an urn and place it in the ground. Take great care, wash often and stay warm, if the sickness has returned. Take no chance for yourself or others, if another, worse sickness has come. Do not let death spread. Swear this to me now."

"I swear," Selvorne said, though he had already sworn the same to Arnlausa. He was not sure a barrel was the appropriate form of wooden box, and inside was anything but dry. The stony grove where his mother was buried was away from Vaskatohr, nearer the mine, poor, shallow rock for a quarry, but solid ground and safe – many were taken there and burnt, those who had died of the bog sickness. Many more in other towns where it had come, and with less elegance or care for the dead. A frightening illness even the Waehdric did not understand, and they knew more of such things than anyone. Few dared visit the places where the people had been burnt, let alone where some were buried. There he would dig, through the rocky soil to make a hole for his father, and another near for Arnlausa, as was his wish. A stone he would cut in granite, and another, a Lordstone for the town, to place beside the road, and that would be used to remember them all. When it was safe to do so.

The letter had finished, but he had read only two of many – the warning, which had bound them, and the first of a pile of parchments that differed in colour greatly. Aged by years, and made by different means, some in leather, others were cloth, even linen – he found what seemed to be the oldest, and began to read.

"Oh, my boy, my greatest joy – to you I am sworn, this day, you are born."

Selvorne gasped – a poem. A dreadful poem – written in his father's hand, and with none of the elegance he usually had with a quill or a finely crafted pencil. When he was born – the very day? Could the parchment be so old – it might, for where it was not yellow, it was brown with age.

"Uhlvorsk we shall call you, and that is for my father, and for the two fathers before him, born of strength, the strength of our love, for each other, for our family before, for you, and for yours to follow. I wish you great joy, as great as you have brought to me, my son."

Selvorne winced. He could not name the oddness that he felt. Love, pain – not only for his loss. Uhlvorsk was a name he did not want, though he knew why it was chosen. It sounded like something a fat marsh frog might say, and though to think such a thing was a terrible disrespect – to himself, as well as his fathers before – he could not help it. Selvorne was an elegant name, and the one he had always used through all his life with friends, in the town, in his home – with his parents. Never Uhlvorsk, except …

Selvorne sat back and blinked. Never Uhlvorsk, except amongst strangers. Never Uhlvorsk, which sounded like a croaking frog, except before those who might not be trusted. It had not occurred to him before, for he had never had a reason to distrust any man for fear – always the name was switched even by his father, Arnlausa, and Girradehn. Who did not even tease him with it, about it, nor make the mistake of saying one name when all were saying the other. The letter said no more, so he quickly turned to another.

"Proud I am to see you so healthy, proud and glad, and I could not be happier. Bold – good, but not too silly, even for a child. Afraid of what can hurt, cautious of what might hurt – good. Though, oddly, unafraid to jump to deep, dangerous water, yet terrified of geese and woodland ducks of the ponds. The folly of a child, a joy to see, no doubt it will change one day to the way it should be. And a happy child, as you should be, for it is a happy life here amongst the woods. All who see you agree, and it makes me very proud."

Selvorne shuddered to think of the geese – no, that fear had not changed. Water was not more dangerous for its depth, when both man and boy could float – geese were every bit as deadly, to a taller boy, even a man – for they could jump, and fly, and peck out the eye. Men were fools not to … fear them … Selvorne bit his lip. He had never seen it done, by a goose, and only heard such warnings said by two men ever – Girradehn, when he was young, and Arnlausa, when he was old. And he was sure Arnlausa was making a joke for his own amusement. And as he sat there in the barn, he knew Girradehn was not – he was just being cruel to a child.

He had no proof of it either way, and geese seemed confident enough that they were dangerous, for they charged and pecked, fearless in their attack. Most birds were, and everyone knew an eagle could take a small lamb, let alone the eyes of a man. He took up the next letter, and began to read.

"A sickness has come – we hope it is gone. It took my beloved Vorlisi, your mother – and others, though I can only think of her, and you, who remains. I wish it were me – we do not know how it came, or if it might return, and though I should send you with the other children to the town, it may be no safer there, and I cannot bear to part with you. I have failed as lord, as husband, and perhaps now as father. This is an enemy I cannot fight, nor flee nor defeat, but only hope. I do not know if it will take me also, and so write this as a farewell."

The letter was brief, and Selvorne felt ill. The sickness had passed – he remembered it, though did not dwell upon it since those years. The bog sickness, the Waehdric decided it should be called. It was from the bogs, but knowing that was little help. Naming it did not make it go away. It affected only towns that were near where waters did not flow, and was absent from those beside the sea, or in mountains where fresh streams ran fast. Tawlehk town, far to the west, was near both sea and lake, but in the woods, not on the coast – it was surrounded by bogs, and suffered terribly. Vaskatohm – not yet changed in name to Vaskatohr, he could remember, and after the illness men were forbidden to the deeper woods of the west. The nearest bogs were drained, and many channels were cut to keep water flowing well away from the town. A new road was made, and a bridge to avoid the wetter lands by the old road that passed the lake. It was a miserable time when the sickness came, more for Selvorne than many others, for, as a child of only a few years, he had lost his mother, his father fell to gloom, and where there once was happiness in the town, there was death and grief.

All who did not die recovered, regaining strength, but were grim for it, to think of it, to remember those they had lost. Himself included. His father did not wail nor grieve so terribly, but he never truly was the same after the death of Vorlisi. Nothing could be done for it.

The letter – a message to Selvorne, from the grave of his father, about the death of his mother. Uhlsko kept grief to himself, and would often say that to mourn those lost was vain. Especially when a man might soon follow. It never stopped him mourning, quietly, when alone. Perhaps at times he wished to follow, and see his wife again. Grief shared by way of a message written in pain, included in the box not to make Selvorne weep, but to give him strength – he knew that much of his father.

To Selvorne's surprise, the following letter said just that – an apology for grief in the letter before, and the warning that a man must always prepare against enemies, illness, and accidents. That he might not be able to, that death would find a man, in the end – always – but never to give up on hope, nor trust in it, but to prepare. Selvorne agreed. He could hardly argue against what he had been told his entire life, and there was no better time to realise it than when he had seen what lack of preparation had done. A bridge unchecked, an enemy unknown, death undeserved – mourning, wasted, and dangerous if he did not hurry to prepare.

There was one more letter, and it was very long. Selvorne made his way to the door, and called to Rerleden, who came at once.

"Ready?" Rerleden asked.

"Almost. I will leave as soon as I am – give me a moment."

"A long way to Tavalehk, you know – not by the road, and – "

"I know. It is late, I might not make it. I must ... give me a moment."

Rerleden nodded slightly, then returned to the street – keeping watch, Selvorne thought, though pretending to tend the pigs. They could not be happy to be penned in all day when the woods had springtime things to eat. More grain for feed, that bored them terribly. A simple life, for the pigs, few woes, and death was usually swift and as gentle as it could be – not so for men, who had to tend and feed them, rake the muck and clean their homes, work to keep them happy, until the last. Rewarded with a meal, and later, a death often not as pleasant as a pig might have. Selvorne returned to his stool and began to read.

"My son. Bold and foolish, as young boys are, though I may hardly call you a boy anymore. And I think, for that, to blame your mother, who was the same. Foolish and sincere, bold and honest, and good. Outspoken – a prank of Arnlausa, who thinks it most amusing, and a joy to hear someone speak their mind, instead of only praise. You anger, at times, for that I blame myself – hidden anger, perhaps too much. You must let it go – in rage or laughter, do not keep it, do not brood."

A strange letter, and though he was not sure when it was written, it seemed newer than the others, and had to be if he considered Selvorne anything but a boy. A few years, then, written and hidden in the barn. He hoped it gave him some clue to his enemy, and was not only full of insults – Selvorne did not brood, he simply liked quiet times alone, away from noisy townsfolk.

"None are faults, though – of that I am glad. A hatred, perhaps – for that fish you can never catch. But you have used it to grow fierce with the spear – good. Let the great fish go, it is your ally, though you do not see it as such. Its taunts are its nature, not intended for you – that is how fish are. It cannot help it, though you like it not one bit. By teasing you so, it has made you calm – by trying to anger you, made you controlled. By defeat, made you less proud, by its own glory, less vain, and by being there always, reminded you that you must choose your fights, live not in anger or hate, and avoid with dignity that which might bring shame."

Selvorne widened his eyes – nonsense, yet he understood it completely. His father did not mean the great fish, not in the least – well, perhaps a little. That huge, taunting trout – desire to catch it had saved his very life, but long ago he had ceased thinking it a foe, and agreed that his pursuit of it made him great with the spear. In doing so he caught many of the other fish. It had become a friend, a foe, and a challenge – and he was not sure if he could ever bear to kill it. Not after that day.

But Uhlsko did not mean the fish. He was writing about Girradehn.

"Now, my son, you must know I am proud of you, but I have left the Lordship of Vaskatohr to Arnlausa. This is not because I think you would make a poor lord – but because I think to be a lord would be a poor choice for you. Many lives are greater than lord – to settle here, in this small town, to remain here all your life – you have never ventured out, shown little desire to do so, and yet know nothing of what is there to see. Wonders, and good friends. How will you make a life here, as lord? Who would you wed? To be a lord is to be wed to the town, first, and to abandon the joy of many things you do not yet realise.

"Do you doubt the wonders you might see? You never joined us on our journey south, never saw the festivals there, or the strange beasts. You yearn to fish in the lake near home – you have never seen the great lakes of the north, larger than at Tavalehk, with the mighty fish – some as big as a pig. No, I will not condemn you to a life led here, but tempt you to see the lands and the people, and then to choose another life.

"Wealth is yours. I have collected some – coins, here, and notes of promise to pay, should you or I present ourselves to those who administer the treasury of Senylehk. Do not lose the notes – without them you may make the request, it will be honoured, but they will dawdle for months to present you with coins. They also may argue to leave you not with coins, but with animals or grain, or iron or copper, or stone. Or whatever they have in abundance, have more than they need, and worth less than they claim. Usually grain.

"Avoid animals. Keslan of the Guild will deliver the old, the sick, the ones that may not breed – unless you have become a great herder, you will never get them away from the town they know. Do not accept the grain – though tempting, it is heavy and awkward to move, and when it goes bad, it does so all at once, and your fortune will be lost, soured by rain, damp or dew. They would not part with grain except in times of surplus, and stored, it might not last for times of need. Coins are best, but iron is almost as good, or copper, or tin or bronze. If you have no hurry to sell it and can wait for a good price, as you know. Whichever you choose – especially coins – prepare a large guard of armed men, and think of which road you might take on your return with this wealth. You may start a life doing anything you wish, even to purchase the mine here at Vaskatohr, if you like."

Selvorne rummaged through the box – notes of promise, sealed by wax, and likely signed in ways he could not determine, but no amounts written. Three notes, only his name and that of his father – notes of different ages, he thought, and over the years he must have sent either copper or coins from their home town to Senylehk, and so accumulated hidden wealth. No amounts – that was very odd. Possibly the tally was kept at Senylehk also, Selvorne was not sure, but to require armed guards and planning, and to secure any life he desired – it would have to be a good amount. The thought of it made him want to weep.

All that effort – all for nothing. Wealth collected, no doubt so much less than the Lord of Tavalehk would enjoy – freedom to make a new life for himself – but he had already taken on the tasks of a lord. Whatever travel Selvorne might wish, or life he wanted to lead, or hopes his father had – his future was duty, danger, and revenge. He would trade all the wealth of both towns and more for it to be as it was, but it could not be, and perhaps his father did not know him very well if he thought he would walk away from the town, if it had no lord he could trust to replace him.

Although, that lord would have been Arnlausa, and Uhlsko trusted him very well. It did not make Selvorne any less angry to read what was written. The mere suggestion he might prefer to run away and enjoy some other life, leaving ... but he would not be leaving his father, Uhlsko would be dead. Selvorne was not sure what he felt. His father should have known him better than that – in anger, he continued to read, but it soon turned back to sorrow.

"In this box are the things your mother left – they are dear to me, and I imagine to you also – her most treasured things, other than you, and me, and those whom she loved. I took them from the house and buried them, because I could not stand to have them near me – the pain was too great. Please take care of them, perhaps ... if you do not wish to have them, bury them with me. I would prefer you keep them, and give them to a lady you might love, or a daughter you might have, or keep them safe and speak of Vorlisi well. Find yourself a woman as wife who could be considered worthy to be her daughter – as good, as noble, as kind."

Selvorne had to agree. Though his mother died long ago, he only remembered her as kind, and good, and – mischievous. She taunted and teased, and joked and laughed, sometimes with a face plain and eyes twinkling. A simple lady. Not born a lady, but truly noble. None had ever spoken ill of her, or much at all, for it pained them to remember the loss of her ... and of others, also lost to the sickness. It made him sad, but when he read what was written next, he was astonished.

"It is a poor secret that the family of your mother still live. At Veksehl, by the sea – I doubt you will refrain from seeking them, so be warned – they are not the nicest of people. When I see you – I see her, and all that I loved. When they look upon your face, and hear your name – they will see me, and all my wealth, and opportunity – and they will smile as if your friends, even as they plan some deceit. Do not be fooled. They may welcome you with wide arms and tears – consider, my son, there is a reason they are neither spoken of nor visited, have not come to our town, or us gone to theirs – and for why your mother did not mention them in your youth. Nevertheless, curious and defiant as you are, you likely will seek them, regardless of warnings. Be cautious – be warned."

His father might have considered it a poor secret that the family of his mother still lived, but it was a kept secret, from him. Selvorne had assumed they all died, long ago. They would have had to be twice as old as his parents, he thought, and his father was quite old. Warned – cautious – and curious, his father was right, he did want to seek them out, and would not be able to stop himself. But finding them, especially if they were to be trouble – or reveal who he was – it would be many months before he gave it a second thought, and as he began to read what followed, in the words of his father, though not stated with terrible menace, he knew there was danger that was not being told.

"There are few you can trust, I fear, few that I do completely – few, but powerful, not many, but true friends and allies of mine, who will be yours. My enemies also will be yours – such is the life for the son of a lord. Even were you to become a merchant and leave the north, even in other lands, there you may find men of grievances against you, for me, undeserved by anything you have done. Remember this, and forgive me for it."

It was the last line that made Selvorne tremble. His father rarely asked for forgiveness. He rarely needed to, and if he did, it was for some minor thing for which he assumed forgiveness was given for the asking. An apology, for drinking all the ale, for letting the fire grow low, for eating all the meat and leaving none for Selvorne's return. Minor, forgotten, overlooked – never requested. In the earlier letter he had apologised, but not asked for forgiveness. Only twice before had

Uhlsko asked such a thing – once, as a joke, and once, when terribly sad, and it was forgiveness for failing Selvorne, for letting the bog sickness come to their town. To ask it in writing – for bringing enemies with their grievances – it was almost enough to make Selvorne shake, even if he had not already seen the death those enemies brought.

"Arnlausa is trusted. My greatest living friend, he saved my life once, in turn I saved him often – neither man has the greater debt to the other, without either, we would both be dead. Go to him – he will treat you as his own son. Or, worse for you, as my son – I dread to think what mischief you both might make. He has cursed me by teaching you his wicked tongue, which he finds so amusing, and I think perhaps you do not fully know what you say, at times. Be careful, though, what you do say to some – not all people speak plainly, nor truthfully. Arnlausa will know this, and may teach you to behave, now I am gone. He can answer many questions you might have, advise you – protect you, and guide you. Go to him before all others, he is as kin. Stronger than family, perhaps, being chosen, and proven true."

Selvorne nodded – though it was odd that his father would think he would need convincing to seek Arnlausa, who was a friend to him as well. He had gone to him first, and felt some relief that he had time to speak with him before he died.

"Girradehn – I trust him, though he is young, brash, annoying and proud. I realise he is no friend of yours. Nevertheless, he is trusted by Arnlausa, and raised by Arnlausa, and honoured by Arnlausa, and loved by him as you are by me. Should I die and Arnlausa be gone, seek Girradehn as an ally, if not as a friend. Trust him – much of what makes him annoying is the frustration of youth, that will pass, and his heart is good."

Selvorne felt a need to hurry – Girradehn's heart might be good, but his leg was bad, and, taken away by enemies, his life in peril. Certain to die, saved or not – but he should not die in pain, questioned with force, or abandoned. To be praised by his father ... Girradehn was more than just a guard, and as a new suspicion rose, Selvorne kept reading at once.

"As I write this, the Leader of the Waehdric is Cienn Reganai Doethmoud. If Arnlausa has passed on, seek her out, but quietly. Even if you are allied with Girradehn – seek Cienn. He might not encourage it, she is a greater ally than he, but seek him first if he is close at Tavalehk – then Cienn. Tell her who you are, tell her when you are alone. She will remember me, if she still lives. However, I do not see how she could live, for she is already very old. If she does, if she is still of a clear mind, she will do anything to help you, and is your greatest ally, other than Arnlausa. She is very old, though, and some wonder if she has already died – for she rarely comes forth to meet the people anymore. Her heir and descendant – Taffoanan – he might replace her, but he is not to be trusted – not for lack of a good heart, but for lack of a clear mind. You may not trust him for that, and I think he might be replaced. However, if Our Lady Cienn is dead, and Taffoanan made Leader of the Waehdric – look to meet with him, intending to say nothing of great importance – then wait. I am known to Cienn and her men, and a man who is trusted – the father of many – will find you. But do not trust Taffoanan, and be quiet as you search for Cienn.”

Selvorne nodded – much of what Arnlausa had said, and nothing more of Girradehn.

“Another, Tordrum in the north, is Lord of Lodlehk. I must admit I do not trust him as well as Arnlausa, but for all his flaws and recent behaviour, he is a good man. Powerful, and should be a strong ally, if no others may be found.

“A guard of good rank and family is Ruollan – I would say you can trust him, and if all others I have named are dead, there must be war in the lands, or terrible illness, or worse.”

Selvorne frowned as he saw, scribbled in small writing to the side, a note that Ruollan had been promoted to captain, and the thought seemed amusing to Uhlsko.

“He is, I am afraid, the last man I might name who I would trust with you, and if he is also dead, then you are alone, and must make your own allies. Be very careful in doing so, allies must be proven. A wealthy son of a lord may attract all manner of smiling friends – and grinning enemies. Friends can be worse, if they are false. Wives worst of all, if they have come to you for title, wealth, or some fanciful ideas of what it is to be a lady – beware, my son.

“Rerleden can be trusted – to help, assist, send messages. Listen to his advice, but do not trust him completely. I do not warn you for any particular suspicion, but only for the reason that he is a runner, not a guard, not a lord, and thinks as a runner does. A servant, more than an ally – a loyal man, not a friend. Sometimes that is the greater. In years you may understand what I mean, and it is no insult to him or to those who run – but the man who delivers the orders is not the man to make them, and he who brings the message should not always know its meaning.”

Nor does he who reads it, apparently, but Selvorne had some idea of what his father meant – Arnlausa had told him things that were only to be repeated to Cienn, not least of which was that Selvorne had been made the heir to two towns.

“Trust no others. Whatever the means of my death – accident, it might seem – be careful who you trust, and I advise you trust no one. This is more than advice. This is by immediate high command – my order to you is silent advance.”

Selvorne bit his lip – immediate high command. Never to be questioned, he was not to argue, to be silent and advance. It was an order taught to him and to be strictly obeyed – if their home was attacked, if there was fire, danger – bears, though he did not see the wisdom in leaving the house, if bears were outside. Fire he could understand, though he would prefer to fight it than flee – his father said not always could fire be fought. But, since a child, they had played such a game of silent fleeing from the house. He never disobeyed such an order. No matter how tired or surprised at the timing. Nor did his father, being ordered to cook a meal, by immediate high command – his father obliged. A few times, but then made it clear it was not to be made in jest or taken lightly. It was his most serious command, and though it seemed a little too strong in the past, reading it in a letter from the dead, after what had happened – he knew that was the reason he had been taught as a child to obey so completely.

"Very well. For now, I must go. A cheerful letter, written when alive, but I suspect you are not so cheerful, reading it after my death. On that matter, I have two things to say.

"First – do not mourn me. To do so is an insult to me, if it ruins the joy of your life. Mourn the loss of wife or child, not father, who writes this in the hope that you will outlive him – and live, as he taught you to do. Or make me proud by living more wisely still.

"Secondly – and, no, I will not soften it – if I have been killed, or there is any suspicion of murder – be careful. Be as careful as I taught you to be, when there is danger – those who may have killed me, likely wish to kill you. Fear more if it seemed as an accident, than if it was done in anger – planned murder is more dangerous to you than drunken rage. Disappear – watch for your enemy. Return to your name of youth, if it has changed already – do not say mine, or yours, or that of our family. Ever. Avoid those who know you, remember who I said to trust. I give you this warning in the hope that you never need it, and that I have died at a great age, quietly in my sleep, or laughing with my friends.

"To you, my son – I wish you all the best. I hope you grow to be a great man. Remember me with fondness, honour me with wisdom, and joy, and kindness, and love."

And revenge. Bloody vengeance, delivered swiftly or carefully – yes, he would disappear. Advance in silence, and watch. Wait and discover who did such a crime – and to them, do the same. He swore it as he began to fold the letters, but then, he paused, and read them through again.

A calmer mind. Clearer thoughts. His father knew there was danger – more terrible than he had warned, perhaps, as was his way. Selvorne folded the letters and replaced them to the box, examined the belongings – they were his mother's, he remembered some of them, but did not find the strange glass cow she once had. Not a toy, he was told, though it was much like one. Too delicate for him to hold, but beautiful in the light, making small rainbows from the sun by the sharp cut of its glass hair. He was told it was crystal, not glass, and a mane, not hair. Not a cow, but something else, a beast from the south. Still he called it the glass cow, and he saddened to wonder where it was – gone, likely broken.

His mind was wandering. Grim words to read, of a man he loved, who was with him laughing not days before – over a silly joke, an absurd poem, giggling, even, and drunk by the great boulder beside the road where they camped. Even then, he knew of danger – then, and before, and years before it seemed, perhaps for all of Selvorne's life. Longer, perhaps twice as long, when he was a guard. And in all those years without incident, Uhlsko had grown careless, and did not think to check the bridge.

Selvorne sat in silence, pondering the message. A warning, and not one mention of him by name, other than when he was first born – and the name given there was wrong. One of many considered, one of many he did not like – Uhlvorsk, as he was called when in the presence of men untrusted. He was being protected, in the letter, and in his life.

His father had enemies. That was clear. His name was a danger. Uhlvorsk and Uhlsko were too similar, too easily connecting one to the other, for often fathers named their sons so. Selvorne was a name not like his father's – like his mother's, true, but Vorlisi had been gone for a long time, and the descendants of Vor were so numerous that any such name was almost common. Not Uhl – that was rare and would soon be noticed. Uhlvorsk, Uhlvorne, Uhlvor, even, which could only be worsened by adding Skolisi at the end – his name of Selvorne was a deception, and had been from the start.

His father had always seemed quiet, patient and sad. At least since losing his wife – Uhlsko did not seem a man with enemies. Not a man who would think ahead to his death, almost expecting it to be anything but injury, old age or sickness. The message was clear, and Selvorne realised far more than it plainly said. Taking another deep breath, the enormity of it began to occur to him.

Very well – danger. He would do as he was told, for a change, and his father, if watching from the Sea of the Dead, would be amazed to see such a change to obedience. He would do what he must. But – as he buried the pain of the loss and sense of danger at his situation, the rest of the letter began to intrigue him.

He had always known his father to be saddened, sometimes he would find him weeping quietly alone, and he hardly lost himself in merriment, except on journeys away from the town. Selvorne wondered if the town itself was a burden to him, always reminding him of what he had lost – his wife, and their life together. It never occurred to Selvorne that his father was stuck in the town through obligations of duty, rather than choice, although that did explain why he dismissed any ideas of moving. However, whenever they returned to the town, his father had often said it was as if, "returning home to her", so perhaps he was caught in the memory of Vorlisi, and could not leave for that reason. Either way, he seemed to think Selvorne would prefer to take what wealth they had and leave – or if not leave, then live the life of a different kind of man. A merchant, a farmer, a miner – or a quarry man. Selvorne had never given any indication he wanted to do any such thing, but he was beginning to wonder if it was a better idea than becoming lord of two towns, with enemies seeking his death.

Selvorne buried the box and its contents, taking the coins and the small wallet of scissors and tools for his nails. As a youth who worked with stones, he knew very well the importance of keeping his nails trimmed so they would not break. It was a magnificent set, similar to his own that was lost in the ravine, but higher quality and kept more carefully. He considered taking the hairbrush, but when he caught the scent of it, he realised it was the smell of his mother, and if he took it with him, that would fade, so he wrapped it again. There were still hairs on it, he took one and folded it into the scissor wallet. Then he buried the box in the ground, covered the hole, shifted the tall furnishings back over it, and spread the dirt to disguise what he had done.

Greatness would have to wait. Greatness, as his father knew it – not yet. Kindness made men great. Noble actions, not entitled birth. Consideration, not inheritance, not conquest, not luck – good or bad. Consideration of all things – that made a lord great. Of the people, the dangers, their problems, the prosperity of others. Greatness must wait. It would not be before vengeance. Not before uncovering of enemies, and that would not be before fleeing – and not before he had his many new questions answered, by a man who said little and thought himself so very clever at keeping secrets. As a plan began to form, Selvorne summoned Rerleden to the barn.

Sixth Way Unexpected

Selvorne had only the slightest idea of how to trick Rerleden, and he knew there was something he would not reveal. To ask, directly, he would not say it. Not if Selvorne tried to argue that knowing would help protect him, he realised Rerleden would think ignorance would help Selvorne more. Better to know a danger, making it easier to avoid, Selvorne reasoned, no matter what it was. The proof of that was the fact they had not checked the bridge before crossing. Had he known any of what he had learnt that day, he would not have left the bridge to chance. What he needed to know, Rerleden likely would not agree to tell him, and trickery was the only chance – he approached, and Selvorne's face was as grim as he could make it.

"What troubles you?" Rerleden asked.

"Letters – from my father," Selvorne said as solemnly as he could. Not a difficult ruse, for it was not far from how he felt.

"Oh?"

"And you seem unsurprised."

"It was to be expected. It was his way – messages clearly written. Rarely spoken. They were hidden here? In the barn?"

"Do you think I would tell you where?"

"I wonder that you would tell me at all. What did he say?"

"That you could be trusted," Selvorne said, and Rerleden chuckled, almost snorting. Selvorne realised he was not going to be any less stubborn. A servant – not a true ally, not a friend. Not exactly, but Selvorne felt an urge to grin, and fought it as an idea came to him.

"I know now why you are so keen to find Girradehn," Selvorne said, "I will help."

"What?"

"Rerleden," Selvorne said in a very low voice, "I know. I shall go, not you – I am better, younger, faster – I will search for him."

Rerleden raised an eyebrow and stared at Selvorne – then narrowed his eyes. "Indeed."

"Yes. It is ... I cannot blame you. No man would leave his son."

At that, Rerleden grunted in the strangest way, and Selvorne nodded solemnly.

"I do believe you are trying to deceive me," Rerleden said.

"No. I know now what was suspected before – the name, obvious. The deceit – clear, revealed by pride. Girradehn and Rerleden – not so similar to be noticed, at first, but your fondness for him, and eagerness to find – "

To Selvorne's hidden astonishment, Rerleden nodded.

"Jarradehn was a good man," Rerleden said, "but could not have children. Girradehn was my gift to them both. It was not for love – you understand – but a debt of a strangest kind, and Girdyni – well, who could not adore such a woman. He was so named in honour of me, but – tell no one, Selvorne. No one."

Selvorne stared with wide eyes, then nodded – and Rerleden burst into laughter.

"You are a complete idiot," Rerleden said.

"What?"

"Truly? You try to deceive me? Fool me – trick me?"

"I know the truth of it," Selvorne found himself saying, and Rerleden laughed all the more.

"Yes – that you are an idiot."

Selvorne ... had to agree. But he was not an idiot, he had just failed at the first – and it was intended. There was one thing Arnlausa had taught him in such pranks, and that was failure at the first could be turned to a greater victory at the second, and so he grinned until Rerleden stopped laughing.

"Some joy, then, to make you laugh – he would be glad."

"Who?" Rerleden asked.

"Arnlausa. His last joke – not the best, but it gave him some delight as he lay dying."

Rerleden nodded, then shook his head before speaking in a strange tone of sorrow and fondness.

"A fool, like you – and not dead, but living on, I see. Perhaps some mischievous spirit went from him to you – how long have you known?"

Selvorne gave a wider grin – a smile, a nod – and not the slightest hint of the astonishment he felt to have guessed correctly.

"Not long," Selvorne said, as though it were nothing.

"And I hope you are not stupid enough to tell others?"

"Do you think me that stupid?"

"No," Rerleden said, "but I think you that silly – you, and he, both find amusement in things at times not appropriate. Especially at this time – and if there is a chance for him, perhaps ... if they think him just a guard, I might find him, release him, if he is bound at the camp you saw in the woods – I must go quietly, and now. To save an heir – it would be well rewarded. Even if ... he did not live. You must not go, nor speak of it, or ... I guess the hurry is not great. Arnlausa would not leave his son to suffer and die, if he thought there was a chance he might recover, but we ... must ... ”

Selvorne was staring, biting his lip. Rerleden stopped talking, narrowed his eyes – and shook his head.

“And you did not know.”

“I suspected,” Selvorne said, “there was something odd about – ”

“No, you did not. Not even slightly, and you dared – Selvorne, be careful. That was ... a well–played trick. To fool me – but be careful who you fool. There are likely men who, knowing you know, might end you.”

“More men to fear, then.”

“No more if you keep it quiet,” Rerleden said, and Selvorne nodded.

“How – has such a thing been kept quiet?”

“Easily, when one man has a huge nose, and one is ... well, handsome. When one is fair, and one dark – one merry, the other sour. One unwed, childless – the other with both father and mother, once, known to all, and pride in his name. That alone would do it.”

“And Jarradehn?”

“Hero of Tavalehk, a woodsman unknown – who killed many brigands to the north, near Hartlehk, actually – who loved Girdyni dearly, despite that she had a child, and years later, all the more for it, when he discovered he could have none.”

“Did Girradehn know?”

Rerleden nodded.

“And did Arnlausa?” Selvorne asked, and at that, Rerleden shrugged – nodded, and sighed.

Many things began to grow clear for Selvorne – affection of a lord for an annoying young man, unearned – promotion, undeserved. Wealth, unexplained – then horror, to think what had happened in the cave.

There Arnlausa lay, dying – there his son, also to die, nothing to be done. Condemned to a slow death, alone, to prevent an attempt to get help, to save Selvorne from danger. The most noble sacrifice, which Selvorne stupidly risked by pursuing the killers, putting himself in danger. He should have been more careful. He should have been told, long ago. Though ... then he would have carried Girradehn out of the ravine at once – moments after the fall. South, by the lake, and ... Selvorne would never have spoken with Arnlausa, never have known of the danger. Not if he left at once. The seals abandoned, perhaps hidden – but the brigands would have found them both as they went for help. Likely those who came late to the camp had been watching the road. Perhaps there were more. Many more.

“Now you realise,” Rerleden said.

“Each man died knowing the last things said to each other were in anger and fear, and – ”

"I doubt that. Each died as guards, as they were in life. Guard before lord – more noble, truly. Guards that failed in one caution – which ended them. It is not the first time it has happened. It is, sadly, most of the time – that is how guards meet their death. Usually not with time to consider their mistake. But usually from a moment of neglect."

"It is very grim, then, to be a guard. And more to realise that father lost son, and son lost his father."

"Indeed. And yet your own father was there dead, and you feel nothing for it?"

Selvorne winced, and Rerleden nodded.

"Good – some pain. Too much to think upon, and no time to think, though you seem eager to waste the day here."

"I am eager for only one thing," Selvorne said, and Rerleden shook his head.

"Indeed. Now, my boy, no more jests, no jokes – no deceits. Did you know before what I have just told you?"

Selvorne shook his head.

"Then ... dangerously unobservant. And unwittingly clever to make me talk. I thought you knew – your face shows your feelings so easily, I did not expect what it showed was deceit. I am not sure it is better that you know. Are you ready to leave?"

"No – yes, for things packed, no, for what I must face."

"Good. We leave together, now, gather all things you need and meet me at the pens."

At that, Rerleden went fast outside of the barn, and when Selvorne followed with his sack and staff, he did not see him again until he reached the pens, waited, and the old man approached with two reed baskets – one full, one empty, which he gave to Selvorne.

"Your sack, in here – your staff, casually held. Come – to the east, to gather fruit. Say nothing. Pretend to be ... bored."

Selvorne did not nod, but placed his things in the large basket and walked as though it weighed nothing. The two left the town, straight to the woods, by meandering paths worn well by a thousand trips to gather fruit. Orchards were around the town, but not so close that fallen fruit might be too near the pigs, teasing them by the smell, or draw creatures to the town, such as mice, or rats, or worse. Into the woods, where the orchards had become rather wild, and deep, until far from the town, where the regular trees planted in neat rows, with few bushes between them, made it easy to see no men were near.

"I wish to prove something to you, Selvorne, and that is this – enemies could be here, even here, where we can see – and you would not know."

"Are there?"

"No – I would know. You would not. Swear to me you will cover your eyes, and wait a moment until I whistle?"

"No."

"Humour me, if you would? I promise no danger."

"And I – "

"Must obey. My request, and a debt I will repay. Obey?"

Selvorne winced, then nodded. He closed his eyes – he felt a breeze upon his face, and was sure it was the waving hand of Rerleden, testing his sight.

Then – footsteps – pounding, bushes, and nothing. A whistle, in the distance – and he opened his eyes.

Nothing. Not a sign of Rerleden, who must have been able to run much faster than anyone would guess. Selvorne moved about the trees – swiftly, left and right, wondering if the thin old man was hiding behind a tree not quite as slender as himself. No movement. No way to hide in the ground, unless in a hole. Perhaps some prepared place, a hole dug and covered – Selvorne was impressed. He called out that he was defeated.

To his astonishment, Rerleden called out from above. He was quite a way up the tree – hidden, by half, in the leaves – not completely, but Selvorne did not think to look above. To climb a branchless trunk so high was impossible – until he saw the old man climb down by way of a rope, its ends in each hand, wrapped around the tree in a tight embrace. Shuffling down then dropping, he landed near, stood, and grinned.

"That was a stupid place to hide," Selvorne said.

"I agree. And a stupid boy searching."

"Not at all amusing. Why bother with such a joke?"

"It was not for a joke, my boy – hiding there worked, against you. I would not do that with others. Did you not hear me whistle?"

Selvorne nodded.

"And yet searched over there?"

"Where the sound seemed to ... come from."

"Indeed. For you, it worked – against those who might be the enemy, it would not. Too close, too exposed, too dangerous. Once seen, ended. A poor trick – and you have no such skill as that."

Selvorne was not pleased to be taunted, and narrowed his eyes.

"And yet I hid closer," Selvorne said, "in their camp. So close that ... they ... did not see me. Oh – "

"Yes, indeed – did not see you. Not so exposed, I guess, and very lucky. As I was, just now. You cannot trust to luck, and had you looked up – by chance – and seen me, there would be your lesson."

"Not needed, I would not – "

"Do it again? Not so long ago, you suggested it wise that you search for Girradehn. Faster, younger, cleverer?"

"I did not say that last ... part. And it was – "

"Not truly your plan, but your trick, to make me talk. Not a boast, a deceit. Also stupid. And quite insulting, though I am not so proud. Nor so old, slow, or unable to hide and hunt."

"I know," Selvorne said.

"Nor am I so foolish I do not realise the danger at their camp – a hungry man may have come to the vines for meat or cheese. A snake, an ant, one yelp from you – a sudden movement. A keen sense of smell, or hearing, or simply common sense of the men there to check all places of hiding – their hidden food saved you, for they wanted that place unchecked by others, and likely kept the curious away. It could have exposed you, if they meant to share it. Now you have stolen some, they would not make the same mistake again. Or any mistake – not now."

"Nor would I."

"I doubt that. I am going alone and searching for him – for, finding me, they find an old man, harmless, a herder of pigs. Finding you, they find a boy of a different name than they might expect, of a description fitting who they seek, or who they saw leaving the camp, or in the ravine, or heard described – I do not know. Finding you, they destroy the entire message – finding me, only the part of it. I am your second messenger, the man to ensure some of it is delivered. And I am not the last, for I have left messages in the town that would be found by others, and passed on at once."

"Letters?"

"Would I tell you that? Or what, and where, so that, when caught, you can tell the enemy?"

"No."

"Finding me – just a man. Finding you – I doubt you could convince them of much other than your desire to kill them – you do not hide anger well. Or hide well. Hiding, you will be found, and questioned – lying, you would be found out, and killed. Or worse."

"I can help – you search," Selvorne said, but he did not believe it himself, and Rerleden simply shook his head.

"And to suggest such a stupid thing – and you never liked him much?"

"Girradehn, no. Arnlausa, very much, and if – "

"Shh! Two names and a secret all at once? Are you mad?"

"You often – "

"Need to say your name, because I wonder if you are otherwise listening. Two men – both guards. I seek him not for love of him, but for any man in danger – and to ensure he does not speak. But rescue, if I can – so he may die in peace. As a guard, he knows danger and death comes to him – serving the guards, once, as a runner proud, I must search and save him. Not you – not a boy."

"I am not a boy."

"No? A girl, then, and it would explain much. Certainly not a guard, and hardly a man. I wonder if a girl might be cleverer, sometimes."

Selvorne felt insulted – he was hardly a girl, in any way, even hair, though grown quite long and fair, to his shoulder. As a girl he would be the strongest ever known in the lands – the most bearded also, though his face was only a few days unshaven, and could be mistaken for dirty. Insulted, but it was not intended as such – a warning, and he had to accept the truth of it.

"Less clever than Stara, sometimes," Selvorne said, and Rerleden, after raising an eyebrow, began to chuckle.

"Indeed. We all are, at times, more foolish than her. She is, however, always as foolish as her. I think she would have a better chance than you, my boy – a pretty girl, witless at times, but stubborn. I am quite sure she would choose a lie and defend it with such vigour they would not dare question it – it would not be death, but other dangers, for her, if found searching for ... him. You know I mean no insult?"

Selvorne nodded.

"You are untrained – you should have been. To be a guard was not the life your father wanted for you, but the skills of a guard – I am quite sure he would have sent you to be trained. All ... men such as he, do, for their sons."

Selvorne nodded again – Girradehn, for one, if he was the son of Arnlausa. And he had heard the same for the son of the Lord of Hartlehk, sent not long ago, there was much talk of it at the festival the previous year. Likely all lords sent their sons to be trained as guards.

"He thought I should be a merchant," Selvorne said.

"I doubt that."

"He said so."

"I do not doubt that – what he said and what he meant were likely two different things, such was his way."

"You are ... a very odd man," Selvorne said, not quite believing what was said of his father.

"Though you have known me your whole life, you thought?"

Selvorne nodded.

"And not the only man you thought you knew well?" Rerleden asked, and Selvorne frowned – but then realised he meant Girradehn.

"I – yes," Selvorne said, "now I can see it. Only the eyes of Arnlausa."

"And temper, though not controlled, like ... his mother's hair, nose, face – and so, hard to tell, even when one man stands next to the other. Indeed, especially then, for he is not as tall, either. Stern like Jarradehn, and rough, not gentle, though his father was as well, when young. Quite a rough young man, coming from the woodlands. Violent, you could say – love, age, a home – all softened him. Love the most, as is usual for rough men with tender wives."

Selvorne wondered at how odd Girradehn's life must have been – both parents dead, long ago, both parents living a lie – one parent remained, his father, truly, a lord, and he could not speak of it. For the arrogant, boasting, proud young guard, it must have been agony to conceal. If he knew – how long, Selvorne could not guess. Or perhaps it gave him some secret pride, and so was the cause of his arrogance. He must not have been told when young, he would have boasted to all his friends. Selvorne felt upset to learn such a secret had been kept from him as well, but then, as he thought on it, he realised something far more terrible.

"Was he the reason for the killings?"

"My – that did not take long," Rerleden said with a smirk.

"Very funny – my mind is occupied today."

"Not with what it should be – yes, it may have been. Kill the lord and his heir – or, if not heir, then his son. Why, I do not know, it is not the only secret being kept. How many sons do you think he had?"

Selvorne bit his lip – one, hidden, but ... Arnlausa the Unwed, Arnlausa Without Heir – he dared not think of it.

"Indeed – none know," Rerleden said, "many guess. It is likely most of the sons would have guessed, at some time in their lives. If there are others. It is not the only reason to hate ... Girradehn ... but a very good reason to kill him."

"To inherit the town?"

"Hard to do, if not named, even for the son of a lord, who must then prove he was not named heir for a good reason, no longer relevant, and convince others he was intended. But without a named heir – "

"My father was named, and he named ... oh – "

Selvorne bit his lip to hold his mouth shut, but it was too late – none were to know that, even after it did not matter. Rerleden seemed to realise at once, and stared at Selvorne with wide eyes, then shook his head slowly.

"And he named his friend," Rerleden said, still shaking his head, "and I did not know that, and was not to know it, nor were you to say it, and you realise this just now."

"I ... yes."

"And speak before thinking, at times. Once told, it was your secret to tell, perhaps – or to keep. I can be trusted, but ... it is better not to know, than to know what should not be said."

"You are ... very strange to advise me such a thing. Have you no curiosity at all?"

"I have discretion instead, and wisdom. I was a runner, my boy, and we are strange folk, for our duties are dangerous in ways unlike guards. To know ... when questioned, when asked by those most persistent – I might say what I should not know, and, once said, I am of no further use, and then ... might be slain. Otherwise I might have lasted through terrible pains, long enough to be rescued. Ignorance to save me where strength of will cannot. No man can be forced to say what he does not know, and for a man taken, delay might be his only hope. Delay long enough to be saved. Or death, with dignity, not betraying men to whom he is loyal. Do not tell me what you should not – I know too little to guess at meanings, plots and enemies. I only know they are there, you saw them, we do not know them, and they kill with little regret and much planning, and likely, no hesitation."

"I ... know."

"I think you do not. Perhaps you realise a little, but not the all – you are a boy, not yet a man. Tell me, do you think perhaps they were too stupid to see you hidden at their camp, or saw you, and let you lead them to who they truly seek?"

"If they did, they managed to get there before me, and unseen, unheard."

"Possible, if they had lamps and made their way to the ravine, then spent the night moving down river and found the cave. Possible, but unlikely. I did not mean that, though."

Selvorne frowned, and Rerleden raised an eyebrow.

"To you?" Selvorne asked, and Rerleden laughed.

"A man of no importance, unless I was the one who wanted you dead."

Selvorne was shocked for only a moment, then shook his head.

"You have taken your time, then, having known me all my life."

"Or was waiting for you to tell me the heir to the two towns?" Rerleden asked, and at that, he drew his knife – Selvorne stepped back, and the old man laughed, "Silly boy, first for saying it, then for believing me – no, not I, but perhaps they mean to follow you to ... Our Lady. Have you forgotten I said she was hard to find?"

"I am not sure what I have forgotten, or have been told, just now," Selvorne said, "nor who to trust."

"Trust her – and me. There are none watching us here, I think, in the woods, none can see or hear. Follow you – I doubt it. Not impossible. They could. Through woods, or towns, a very hard thing to do, even were they a trusted friend at your side. Cienn is not easy to find, and once found, would likely have doubts of you, let alone someone following, or a friend. But ... you may be enough to draw her out – all this might be only to get to her – but I doubt that. It would take great patience and care – and risk, for Cienn is ... not likely."

Rerleden stared to the distance and seemed disturbed. Selvorne looked to where he gazed, but there was nothing, and Rerleden was only thinking to himself for a few moments before he continued.

"Another guess is anger at Girradehn, or a chance to replace him – anger at Arnlausa, or your father, or you. I do not know. I cannot guess. Or I can, all day. It hardly helps. Not if I knew all you did, and all who you did it to – and I dare not ask – your task, to deliver a message to Cienn, and mine ... I have two, and they are now at war with each other."

"Dare I ask?"

"There is no need, since I offer to tell – two orders were given to me, standing, which must be obeyed until released by he who gave them, and now that is impossible, for he is dead. I am sworn, until my death, not his – the first, to serve you well, upon the death of your father. And so I knew as I swore it, I could never be released from it. Heir or not, son of a lord, or not – I am sworn to do so, were you truly a pig herder or quarryman."

"As I am."

"As you are. And as I am, though also a runner, who knows something ... not only of what to do. Something I am sworn not to tell, my second order, conflicting with the first, and ... not even now do you mention it. And I cannot decide if you were also sworn, or do not know, or think the matter so trivial, or silly, or ... and yet you show no signs of it."

"Perhaps I know, and hide the fact well?"

"Unlike everything else you know, or think, or feel, which shows on your face as plain as if written on parchment, and presented to one who can read – no, you do not know, and I find it more than odd to think I should tell you, but I am not sure who else could. And if you do not know, then ... there may be danger."

"Deadly danger, if you delay any longer."

"I am not so easily harmed, my boy."

"I meant to me, dying of waiting."

"Spoken with all the mischief of a man ... who will be missed. Tell me, boy, what is your favourite tale – the most enjoyed story for the fireside?"

"The Killer Duck," Selvorne said, and Rerleden raised both eyebrows.

"The – what? That is nonsense, for children."

"Nevertheless, my favourite."

"I thought you did not ... like ducks?"

"Or geese. But in that story – "

"Which is complete childish nonsense," Rerleden said, "the only way a duck could kill a bear would be if it choked after eating it."

"Do ducks ... eat bears?"

"Now you are being ... childish. And defiant. Your favourite story – of guards."

Selvorne had found himself amused, for a moment, a relief from the danger, from the woe. A taunt of an old man. The Rerleden he knew was stern, and easily made fun of, and with, at times. He had chuckled at the mention of Stara, the silliest girl of the town – he had smiled, he had joked with his eyes, and for moments Selvorne felt at ease. The Killer Duck was a serious tale ... he had no doubt a duck could hurt a bear, if not kill it. A goose certainly could. The eyes, the throat – the flapping wings. But to ask for a story of guards, tales from the fireside, it could only mean one thing.

"Krogarve?" Selvorne asked, not daring say Torlor, even as a joke, lest it bring bad luck.

"Is known to you," Rerleden said.

"Yes, I know the stories well enough, and – " Selvorne began, but Rerleden was shaking his head, "I ... know ... him?"

Rerleden nodded, and Selvorne bit his lip – Krogarve was a feared man amongst the guards. Stories, said to be true – a man long ago, who was formidable. As was Arnlausa – if so, he must have many, many enemies.

"I thought ... it was the Lord of Veksehl?" Selvorne asked, remembering something he had heard of that town, and a duel fought there, long ago.

"It was ... and it was not questioned. Yes ... that rumour lives. No, it was not. And yes, he ... was real, and the stories ... not exactly as things happened."

"Were any true?"

"All were true, simply not ... truly told."

"That is not the same."

"No, not the same. Little said of past happenings is accurate or complete, even if meant to be so. Even if not made to stories. You realise this means there may be many enemies, with nothing to do with ... the man I seek to find."

"Girradehn?"

"Yes."

"Why do you ... sometimes say names, and other times not?" Selvorne asked.

"Habit to not say them, the wariness of an old runner – opposed to the realisation that no man can hear us in these woods, and if they can, they already know everything anyway, having killed the three men who by habit I do not name, and likely mean to kill us both as well, if only by habit of their own. You do not sound surprised?"

"I am not sure I believe it. But I guess it could be true, he certainly boasted often of his time as a guard, and how he enjoyed it, despite the danger and – "

"What?" Rerleden asked.

"You did not find him boastful?"

"Not – no, never. Truly? I – never would have thought it, perhaps I did not know him so well."

"But – everyone should know that of ... Arnlausa," Selvorne said, and as he said it, and as Rerleden raised an eyebrow, he realised he had guessed wrongly – it was not his friend who was Krogarve, feared – it was someone much closer.

"Not – " Selvorne began, but Rerleden nodded, and then there was silence as he considered what it meant.

"It seems silly to speak of it, almost," Rerleden said, "the stories are not ... what happened, and what happened was very grim."

"More, or less?"

"Both – more at times, less at others. Truly, he did not tell you?"

"No. Nor many things, it seems."

"Indeed. You realise there is a reason for that?"

"Yes. What I did not know, I could not say. He was hidden?"

"In a way," Rerleden said, "not only I knew, but few others did. Very few. Hiding, but not from them – from those who might find out. Some of whom we do not know."

"Enemies ... unknown?" Selvorne asked, and Rerleden nodded, "We have a reason for the killing, then, as well."

"Perhaps. Likely. Suspected by Arnlausa, I am sure of it – but uncertain. Old enemies who found him – but it has been a very long time since they fought the men of Rigan."

"Long enough for a son of Rigan to grow to a man, discover the truth, and take revenge."

"Yes," Rerleden said, "it is not only long enough, but just about the right time for it – and yet, strange, is it not, that someone would seek such vengeance their whole life, and not be there at the end?"

"Arnlausa thought the same. And now I know why he considered it at all."

"And why he was as bewildered as I am, though I must admit, and he must realise – to kill in such a way and not be there, that is a very clean revenge. An accident, perhaps blamed on others if discovered, and the quiet satisfaction of bringing it about. It is the best way – it is what I would recommend."

"And it is not what I would – oh, but you are right," Selvorne said, "it is ... clean. I would want to face them. The killers who did this."

"And it might be your undoing. The best revenge is done in silence, unsuspected – then to live, unknown, unpursued, unthreatened. This is what your father did, living here. With you, safe."

"Until now."

"Until now. And I am telling you only to make you more cautious."

Selvorne nodded, but it was curiosity he felt, not caution – the stories were fanciful, for children. But to have some truth in them ... and then he gasped.

"Was my mother Rulisia? From the stories?" Selvorne asked, and Rerleden chuckled.

"No. Yes. Sort of – no, not intended. Yes, by chance only, the names are so similar. Amusing, dangerous, annoying, but what could be done? Vorlisi – Rulisia. Similar enough to raise eyebrows of an already curious man, different enough to be unconsidered by most. Made worse as he called her Lissi, as did Krogarve call Rulisia, in the stories. That were told before he had even met your mother."

"I – am not sure I remember."

"You were young."

"And fooled, and lied to."

"And protected and still live, where others are all dead. Make no mistake, all your father did was intended, and none were better at devising such intentions. Even your name was a ruse."

"For all the good it would do me, had I been on the bridge as it fell. He should have told me."

"I have no doubt he meant to – when would have been best? Last year? The year before?"

"Yes."

"And yet a boy who knows that he is the son of Krogarve might wish to tell friends – boast – say it, when drunk. And you do talk, when drunk, so it is a good thing you know little," Rerleden said, then chuckled.

Selvorne clenched his jaw, knowing Rerleden was right for saying it, but not for laughing at him. Rerleden must have agreed, for he stopped chuckling and took a deep breath before speaking in a low, solemn tone.

"One name, one word, one rumour spread – under stood, over heard, forever dead."

"A nice poem. Yours?" Selvorne asked.

"A grim reminder. Ours – the guards. The runners say it, more than the guards. And the reason you were not told, and the danger that I tell you now, though, I doubt you would tell any others, having seen the danger for yourself. Be cautious, like Krogarve – not reckless, like Torlor.”

“Was he also real?”

“Yes. Not so ... well, yes, and reckless. Do not be as he was. The lesson is not to be an idiot, the stories are for children, and for men ... to make them fear Krogarve, a man who was worthy of fear, if you were his enemy. Worthy of revenge, too, for the same – twice the lesson, then, for you.”

“It seems ... he was more timid than in the stories, though.”

“Do you think that of your father?”

“I – no. But Krogarve – ”

“Was bold? Three times the lesson, then, for you – bold and cunning, a dangerous man. Usually such men end up dead, if they are not at least a little timid. Do not think it an insult, do not say it as if it was – he was not afraid, if that is what you mean. Enemies might think he was, to their regret – or that he was foolish, or easily fooled. He was many things, but afraid was not one of them – not for himself, anyway.”

Selvorne nodded – that, he could believe.

“And not always for others, sadly,” Rerleden said, “and you do not seem very surprised?”

“I am not sure what would surprise me anymore. In days my life has changed, and today I learn perhaps it has not at all, it merely was always a way I did not know.”

“And dangers there that you did not know, and now, no one to protect you from them, so be careful.”

“I will.”

“Indeed, so you say – be careful, going through the wilds, also – east, then north, then by the foot of the mountains and I fear, not to the villages across the lake until the night. There are things in the woods that are dangerous – worse than bears.”

Selvorne widened his eyes, and Rerleden watched him for a few moments, then nodded.

“What – what is worse than a bear?”

“A hungry bear,” Rerleden said, and though he did not laugh, Selvorne almost did.

“Very funny.”

“Not if you met one. Wolves are worse still, but from them at least you might climb a tree, for safety.”

“Can ... bears climb?”

“Yes – very well. Trees or cliffs.”

“So ... it could have been a bear?”

“In the ravine – yes, it could. Not a wolf, it would never get out again, the base is too smooth, there is no way out for miles to the west. But a bear would.”

“And would it take an ox?”

“Apparently it would. Delicious to a bear, I think.”

Selvorne was horrified – in the ravine, it was one thing to meet a bear – in a cave, with a knife, with a fire. But in the woods, if they were there – he dreaded to think of the times he had spent alone, with no fire, sleeping in the open. The very night before – and possibly the night to come, and near the mountains where bears were more likely.

"Is it safe to go this way?"

"Through the woods, where may be bears, hungry, perhaps, but uncertain – or by the road, where killers lurk, well fed, well rested – and watching. Quite certain. No, neither way is safe."

"I need a spear."

"So you could break it, or lose it? Here is your greatest weapon," Rerleden said, and then he pulled back a cloth from the basket he carried, and Selvorne expected to see a small sword or a bow, but instead saw the remains of a leg of ham.

"Against hunger?" Selvorne asked.

"Against a hungry bear – or a curious one. Drop this, and run – it will stop to sniff it. If that fails, drop your cloak, it will stop for that as well, men say. And so you may have time."

"To escape?"

"Yes. The bear may lose interest, especially with a delicious ham left to eat."

"And a wolf?"

"The ham, yes, the cloak – no. That will make them follow you forever, once they know your smell. Drop the ham, run for a tree."

"And then?"

"With knife, fashion a branch to a spear, at your own convenience as they growl from below – then try to kill them from above."

"Had I a spear already, I could – "

"No. You could not – not even you, who spears fish so well. One man, one spear, two wolves – perhaps you may escape with mere scratches, or a bite. Not against a dozen, or more, as they tend to be in large groups. Run for the tree, you cannot fight them on the ground."

"And a bear?"

"Usually alone, slow, easily distracted – deadly, even against a man with a spear, if you are alone. Drop the ham and run – even a boar might stop a charge, for that. And a wolf, I hope, it is said that a man offering such a thing might tame them, keep them as a pet – though some argue it is the other way around, and the man must work and toil to feed the beast."

Selvorne was not listening – the thoughts of bears and wolves disturbed him more than brigands.

"How likely will I see a bear or wolf?"

"There is no chance of it," Rerleden said, then laughed.

"What?"

"No chance – they will be upon you before you see them."

Selvorne frowned as the old man laughed harder, and he realised he was making some twisted joke.

"Rerleden – you are sworn to serve me, answer me, honestly."

"Honestly," Rerleden said, and he stopped laughing, "very well. Chances – low. Even if they do attack. None have been seen for a long time near, and that is a concern in itself."

"Why?"

"I think because they are so very cunning, now, being hunted so often in the past. Both bear and wolf make a fine coat. Perhaps there always were timid ones, the bold ones being all slain – those unseen before, remain. But behold – your fear – so great for things never seen, so small for men you have seen, and seen what they might do."

"And plan to avoid."

"Yet would take greater caution against a bear, it seems. Selvorne, I prefer you to walk in fear of bears than walk fearlessly into another camp of enemies. You want honesty – you are not cautious enough. And in truth, though unseen, it does not mean bears are not in the woods."

"You could have simply said that at the start."

"I doubt that. You ignore me, and I must let you go, alone, and I fear for you. I could keep you here for a week and tell you all the dangers – bears, wolves, and worse – men, most likely, worst of all. To avoid enemies, through the woods is the least likely path to go – is it then, the most likely watched? I do not know, but it is the widest, with care you should avoid all dangers. On the road you cannot. By road, to Tavalehk town before dark – by woods, you have no chance, and will need to camp."

"Knowing there are bears."

"Yes. Can you sleep in a tree?"

"No – can any man?"

"Yes."

"And does it make a difference to a bear that can climb?"

"Yes, plenty, it makes a sleeping man a very easy meal, when in the trees already. But it is safety against wolves."

Selvorne felt grim, and Rerleden smiled.

"Good. Now you are afraid. Be careful – take care. You have seen the death of two lords, and one son of a lord – and you are likely wanted dead as well. If not before, then certainly now, after seeing the faces of the killers, and stealing their fine ale."

"I know."

"Good. Seek ... you know who to seek. But how, be careful – quietly, and cautious. Be someone else – be no man of importance, not of this town, not of any interest. Just a boy, enjoying the festival. And you must enjoy it, to disappear, not walk around grim."

"I shall."

"Good. I would take care with those coins, also, that jingle so – if the noise does not bring thieves, the bulging purse might. Split them, hide one elsewhere ... show some sense."

"I ... yes, I meant to."

"I would not expect to hear from you for ... a long time. Good luck, my boy."

"And if she is there?"

"The same – she would send spies, runners, scouts, guards back to here. Not you, at first – not back to danger. Then an army. I believe – actually, I think you should ask of the guards. Such a thing could be planned already."

"Guards to march? Here?"

"Men to come, south, it may be so, your father ... he thought it might be soon. Yes, seek the guards, but not as ... yourself. Beware friends of Girradehn, men of Arnlausa, folk who – know who you are, and knew where you were, and when you might return."

"That is the entire town."

"For Arnlausa, yes, not for ... you."

"Most would expect my father to be with him."

"And not know who he was – some might, perhaps. Do I truly need to keep warning you?"

"No. If I seem eager, it is because you have drawn attention to the dangers I wish to avoid. That I shall eagerly avoid."

"Good. Then, farewell, and ... remember all."

Selvorne nodded, but was about to leave when he realised where Rerleden was to go – into danger, searching for Girradehn and brigands. He embraced his friend, who seemed surprised.

"You are an odd boy."

"And you are a brave old man."

"Indeed – and today I do nothing I have not done before, many times. A pig herder, a reason to be in the woods, a lost pig – the spotted one – that I shall let loose. Well, not that one, it might then truly be lost. But a pig is a promise – a reason for the killers to keep me alive, for invitation to dine on pigs, and hope to learn more of our town. I have more than a few tricks besides. Fear not for me – fear much for yourself. Do not try and solve this all in a day – a week – a month. Only try to solve it well, quietly, with caution. I cannot give you any better advice. To remain here is madness, when here is where they expect you to be."

Selvorne nodded a bow, and Rerleden returned it – short, formal, brief bows, acknowledgement of orders, of duty, and of departure. At that, Selvorne took his sack, the ham, his staff, and headed along the paths into the woods, and when he turned to look, Rerleden was already unseen.

Mist Past

The journey from Vaskatohr to Tavalehk was an easy one for any man with waggon or cart, for the very young, or for those who were no longer sturdy on their feet. A road as good as any in the land, it followed firm ground along a ridge of rock, winding its way through forests, and never overgrown. Miles to the east were higher lands, where mountains began, steep and hilly. Not so many miles to the west, the lands dropped away in a cliff, and those lower lands were woods and swamps. The road leading north was between the two, on hard ground where differing lands met, and it ran the way from Vaskatohr to Tavalehk, then continued to the next town. A ridge along the tops of cliffs, for some of the way, and a good solid road for the rest.

That was an easy way to travel. Unfortunately for Selvorne, it was also the road most likely watched by his enemy – or if not watched, then used, and he would be discovered wandering past them. If they looked for him, and if they waited. He had every reason to think they did, and whatever their intentions towards travellers met along the road, he did not wish to be seen.

For Selvorne the journey was east, not north. East, into the woods near his town, where paths were many and winding, sometimes leading into thick bushes or bogs. Never too terrible or boggy in the east, and he knew enough of the land to make his way safely, but it was a difficult journey compared to the road. Slow, safe, no enemy would find him, and at times he wondered if he could find himself, or his way. There were two distant mountain peaks he could use as a guide – "try to keep the distance between them the same" – that was Rerleden's advice. Selvorne was not quite sure what he had meant, but he did know that it was impossible to get lost, even if he did not take the most direct path. The town of Tavalehk was on a great lake below the mountain slopes, and to the east of that were three great rivers, coming from the mountains. None of those rivers could he cross without knowing, for they were deep and fast. All he had to do was find the southernmost river, then turn west, and continue to a village beside the lake. There he would find a boat and pay for passage across the waters, and he would be at the town and its festival. Even if terribly lost, at worst he would add half a day to his journey.

Unless injured. A trip, a fall, a broken leg – he would perish, crawling through the woods alone. Only Rerleden knew where he was, and did not expect to hear from him again for days, even weeks. It would be impossible to search for him in the woods, his body might never be found. His plan to evade capture could lead him to a disappearing death, and so Selvorne walked carefully, paid attention to his direction and footing, listened and looked for enemies, and travelling that way, with his mind so occupied, gave him some peace.

Until he realised the day was ending, and his journey had taken him miles. Hopefully not in circles, but certainly not to the mountains, the streams, the rivers, or Tavalehk lake. He was not lost – it was impossible, he was assured, he was certain – how could any man be lost, heading east towards mountains that did not move? At worst he would reach the rocky ground of such mountains, realise his mistake, turn north once more and find his way. If he somehow continued south without reaching the mountains, he would end up at the lake where he hid the seals – his lake – and he knew his way from there. That was absurdly far, though, and completely in the wrong direction. With that in mind, and watching the distant peaks when they appeared between the trees, he continued east as the sun headed west, and it was a long, tiring walk before he realised he needed to camp.

Wood for a fire – thankfully, no recent rains, and branches in abundance to collect. A fire would attract brigands, frighten bears and wolves – none of which he wanted there, but brigands he could lie to, at least, and the others he could chase away with waving flames. Who would see him, anyway, so far from any town, in the woods – and why was he there, when he could have walked near the road instead?

To be safe, he told himself as his tiny fire grew. To be away from enemies, he reasoned, as he cut himself the last of the ham – a large meatless bone might tempt a bear, he hoped, if needed the next day. Or he could return to Vaskatohr and club Rerleden over the head with it, for sending him on such a stupid journey.

Despite his anger, his fear, his worries – he ate well and drank ale, rested and soon fell asleep. A cloak and flame for comfort. Much more wood, to ease his mind, he was determined to keep that flame burning well. Knives and a staff, and the bone near, to throw at the creatures that might come for it. He hoped the smell of smoke was stronger than that of ham to eat – or than himself. He hoped the fear of flame greater than hunger, and he drifted to sleep, wanting nothing more than to wake refreshed, alive, safe, and ready to continue.

~

The morning was quiet, save for the birds. No sounds of danger, a good rest, fresh air, and his woes returned to him as he lay there in the early dawn. The sky went rapidly from dim to grey to blue – he knew he must be near the mountains, for such a sudden dawn.

Rough sleep out of a house, it had been weeks since he last slept in a bed. On the journey south he had slept outside, near the waggon. At the quarry, in a fine tent with a sheepskin bed, which was quite comfortable, despite the hard ground beneath. That was for over a month, and the return was much less comfortable that year, with the unexpected inconveniences of murder and danger. He groaned at his own thoughts, trying to make light of his grief, but he felt cold, and more than slightly sore. He wished he was home, but he was not, and if he was, he was not sure he would be happy in that house alone. He rose, stretched to make his joints crack, and thought to eat. Undesired oats were heated to give him some joy, but it was not a hearty breakfast, and a long hungry day was ahead of him.

With dirt he buried the last of the fire, and made sure flames would not return to burn the woods. With silent resignation he gathered his things – his coins gave him some amusement, how useless they were in the woods. His staff gave him little relief, it was no spear, and he wondered if he should whittle one end to a point, to use if a bear came – he should have done so the night before, it only occurred to him in a dream. He was not suited to such dangers, and, though he fancied he could fight such a creature, Rerleden seemed quite sure he could not. Inexperienced, untrained, he thought of his promise to Arnlausa – learn to fight – and nodded to himself in silence as he continued on his way.

Annoyance, to be sent on such a journey. Far from the road, very slow, a night spent in the woods that could have been at the festival. Frustration, as he did not seem to be making any progress – it turned to anger as he decided to head north, for, although he was not as far east as he had planned, he was surely far enough from the road to not be seen. Miles, as many as ten, and for men to search so far – no man could find him. There was some relief in that, but little in the journey. The woodlands never seemed to end, and if roads and rivers wound through such forests, Vaskatohr would be a wealthy town. Logs could be floated or dragged to where people would need them. He felt anger at that as well, for there were neither roads nor rivers nor streams, just wetlands in lower places, and slight hills that led nowhere and offered no view. Thankfully, there were no thick bushes with thorns.

Until the latter part of the day, and their rough branches had thorns and no berries. Or any value of beauty or flower or good wood, or any use other than to hinder his journey – it should have made him angrier than the morning, and yet he was not. He was calm, growing patient as he slowed his pace, walking with care.

Rerleden might have been more cunning than Selvorne had realised. Likely, he was – likely, everyone was, for they all had hidden much from him. The walk in the woods, the delays, the long journey and sleeping alone, in fear – but exhaustion – it was enough to calm him, ease his anger and eagerness to fight. It made him think on his situation.

There were no bears. No wolves. Not seen for many years, and when seen –
killed and skinned for coats or rugs. It was no wonder they were never seen, they
likely fled from any sign of man. No, there was no danger in the woods, unless he
fell and broke a leg.

The danger was the town. The road, perhaps, if watched – but the town,
certainly. To go there angry, confused, frustrated – Selvorne would be noticed,
and ended. Or followed. He had been warned, he promised he would be calm –
but he knew, as he walked, it was a promise in vain when it was made.

Selvorne was no longer angry. He was not afraid. The frustrating walk had made
him calm. He would, judging by the mountains to the east, reach the far side of the
Tavalehk lake by the end of day. Villages were there, he would pay to cross on a
boat, and so approach the town from the most unexpected direction, arrive in the
night, and be unseen by enemies. Unnoticed, and safe. And calm – Rerleden was
not a fool.

Selvorne had been, though, and the long walk of many miles made him realise
just how dangerous his situation was, and how lucky he was to live. If his father
was Krogarve – if half the stories were true, and then, only partly – his enemies
would be the worst men the north had ever known, since the early time of
Tromvos, when war was fought between families and towns. Were all the enemies
of Krogarve killed, as told in the tales? Or did some survive – or sons, or brothers
– it only took one angry man to seek such revenge. Those were the words of
Arnlausa – one man who hated Girradehn, to kill them all. He did not mean
Girradehn, for though many likely hated him, none did enough to kill – he meant
Uhlsko, and he meant the danger was to Selvorne.

A cruel revenge if it was unsatisfied by dead father, and turned to living son.
And yet ... if Selvorne had a son, and he had been killed – but that was not the
same. He wanted the killers brought to justice, not their sons. That would be
unjust, that would be cruel, that would be ... wise.

And there was the reason for the danger to Selvorne – the enemy needed him
dead. To let him live was foolish. Not for vengeance, but their own safety, to
prevent Selvorne taking revenge. To stop him doing just what he was, searching
for them. The death of Uhlsko could have been thought an accident, but not if
Selvorne lived, they had to fear not only himself, but any friend of Uhlsko who he
might tell. Stealing their ale only gave them reason to fear. They knew someone
lived, it would not take long for them to determine who it might be – he had been
a fool.

With that in mind, and with much time to think on all he had discovered, it was
in silence and calm that he continued his journey. Twenty miles by road from
town to town – he could not guess how far, by way of woodlands, wandering lost,
too far one way, then back again, but he came to the first stream that he knew
must come from the mountains through the forest, and then would lead eventually
to either the lake of Tavalehk, or the wetlands to the south of it. Not wanting to

walk to those wetlands, with their deep mud, tall reeds and vicious geese, he crossed the stream and continued heading north.

After many hours, several streams and one odd wide path heading to the mountains that almost tempted him, though it went completely the wrong way, Selvorne came to the first river of Tavalehk. The lands opened to meadows and gentle hills, and he could see some way in all directions. Relieved that he had not walked too close to the mountains, he turned west and followed the river. He came to a gentle slope that looked down upon the great lake, which seemed small in the distance down the hill, and he saw a village at the waterside. Taking a deep breath, he sighed as he prepared himself for all manner of casual lies to explain why a lone young man was appearing out of the wilds.

The village was small, although by his guess, much larger than Vaskatohr town. No lord there, though, it was under the control of Arnlausa ... or of himself, soon. Much larger than Vaskatohr, and the fact that it remained a village seemed somehow unfair. It was in other ways much like his home, he thought, apart from the great lake behind it – and like his home, there were no people about.

Strange and silent, Selvorne felt some relief to come to the first building on the slope, where he saw an elderly couple in a pen beside a house, laughing and scattering feed to chickens. It was the first pleasant laughter he had heard in a long time, and though they stopped and stared as he approached, his spirits lifted and he smiled – and they smiled back.

"Greetings there, young fellow!" called the elderly man as he moved to stand before a woman, who was likely his wife.

"A good day to you," Selvorne replied, "could you point me the way to the festival, if you please?"

The old man looked back at Selvorne as though puzzled, yet seemed reassured by his friendly tone. He and his wife had moved, however, with their bucket of feed, to stand nearer the house, and the old man had taken up a stick, pretending to use it as a crutch, though he clearly did not need it.

"Aye, the festival is farther down the river, come to the pier, there may be a boat to take you across the lake, there may be not."

"Thank you kindly, I shall be on my way," Selvorne said, nodding a bow as he left.

They stared at him as he passed by – certainly wondering who the strange boy out of the wild could be, and where he might have come from to their village. Not afraid, but concerned enough to be distracted, and not ask. Selvorne was not sure if he should have explained himself or not – the unlikely story would be from the north, which would mean he had become very lost, and the true story was ... just as difficult to explain, if he made no mention of brigands and fear for his life. No man would come from Vaskatohr that way. The third explanation – that he had come from the mountains in the east – was absurd. No man went there, it was almost forbidden, warned against and avoided, and even woodsmen did not go into the rocky heights. A woodsman – perhaps he could claim to be, but he had no axe, and such a small village would likely know any young woodsman working near. Especially a house so alone on the hill – likely their sons were all such men. Selvorne continued towards the village by the lake, and wondered what story he might devise for any others he might meet.

The slope became gentle and woods became thick for a short while, then thinned again. Selvorne could see over cleared meadows where the river flowed faster down a hill, and there he saw the great lake of Tavalehk in all directions before him. The town of Tavalehk was on the other side, and he had never realised how wide the lake was, for he had only been on the other side, and never given it much thought. From the town, low down and looking across the waters, it seemed very wide, low and flat – but from the village where he stood, on the edge of a hill, high above the lands, he was looking down upon the lake – and it was vast. Only a mile or so wide to the south, perhaps, to his left – but miles to the north. Miles, and he could not see the end of it. Why he had not explored it – taken a boat, rowed across it – fished in it, for surely there would be good fish to spear somewhere in its shallows – though, whenever he went there, he was occupied with festivals or other matters that seemed more important. He never knew it was so vast, and how that had escaped him, despite the townsfolk boasting of it at all times, was a mystery.

Lack of wood in the town, however, was not. A growing problem, he was assured by Arnlausa, which had never made sense until he stood on that slope and saw, all the way near the river, the trees had been felled, dragged to the waters and floated down to the lake. It was not trees they were lacking, forests were plentiful in the distance – it was the easy drag to a nearby river they needed. Meadows had grown amongst the stumps of where there once were woods, and Selvorne took to a firm, well–worn path beside the river, heading to the village below.

From a distance the village had seemed empty, but Selvorne was surprised to discover there were quite a few people about, mostly at the pier, some waving out to the lake. He could see a boat in the distance, rowing and headed to the town. There were no other boats in sight, not on the lake and not at the pier. To his dismay, when he asked about it, he learnt that he had missed the last boat of the day – and that it was not even full. The boats had all left, with all the things the village meant to sell at the festival. All boats would return in the morning, and then the village folk were to travel, all together, across the lake – all at once. That night would be a small celebration of their own in the village, a feast before the festival truly began – it sounded lovely, but Selvorne's heart was sinking as he listened to the Pehrnohc – the master of the pier – explain a situation that could not be changed. There were no boats. He was too late.

In those last leaving boats, young men and maidens of the village had gone ahead to town – with the excitement of the festival, and hope of meeting others from afar, perhaps finding love. Some meant to find lodging, others to pitch tents. Many wished to be there early, changing clothes to be more presentable in the town. Such thoughts gave Selvorne no joy – not the hope for love, or the fact he missed the boat, or the realisation that the only people left in the village were the very old, the mothers and fathers, and the children they had. Many of whom were screaming because they wanted to go to the festival that very night, some even threatening to swim. That Selvorne was young and not of the town turned the Pehrnohc's mood to suspicion, and Selvorne gave a gruff explanation of coming from the north, lost, and ending up at their empty village, not at all impressed by the lack of boats, planning or welcome.

Gruff – it had worked. His unplanned short temper ruined their festive mood, and no one seemed to want to speak with such an unpleasant fellow, even those who began to ask of the north. Hartlehk, he said he was from, and there was nothing to tell, but it was the same as ever, and he complained of the poor signs posted on the road to the south. It was the kind of behaviour they expected of people from Hartlehk, and though he gave them no news, they would arrive at the festival the next day with much talk of how rude people were from that northern town.

Arnlausa NohcLehk Laehtene. Lord of Tavalehk, and all villages near. In such a small village, across the lake from the town, Selvorne did not expect to hear news of him, but the people were aware that their lord had not yet returned. It was not so unusual they would know, for the boatmen must have brought news and taken passengers – not unusual that people would care, for it was often the cause of wagers over when Arnlausa might arrive. Every year he went south – every year his return could not be guessed, yet people tried, and placed coins on the guessing. Best returns were for those who thought he would be there early – he rarely was, and the promise of good returns usually ended in lost coins. Selvorne was certain such coins were changing hands at the pier, and new wagers were being made, despite the losses. All would lose, that year, and Selvorne, despite his advantage, had lost more than any. He turned his thoughts from grief, and grew curious about the wagers – many were worried more for their loss of coins than loss of lord. Not for lack of love, but because they likely did not fear for him.

The Late Arnlausa, as he was known – many years before, he, Uhlsko, Girradehn and Selvorne had missed the festival completely, earning him the second title of Arnlausa And Later – the townsfolk celebrated first at the festival, and then again later. None worried for him, save the men who meant to sell his wine for profit, and those with wagers – a strange situation, every year, that meant the wine sellers, despite being desperate to learn when he might return, were not permitted to wait for him in the south, nor hasten his journey – or they would face the wrath of the wager makers. No townsfolk went south, lest any might see Arnlausa's approach, running ahead to place wagers. Only guards might, if trusted, and then on their return they were watched with suspicion, or hope. The guards, if they did go south, went to inform the people of Vaskatohr that the festival was starting early, or late, or otherwise changing its arrangements. Sometimes they sent a waggon with a request for pigs, and more than once a cart, in need of copper to make coins. Usually no guard was sent, the people of Vaskatohr knew when to leave, by looking at the moon, and they arrived to be greeted by dozens of people with just as many questions. Where was Arnlausa, when would he arrive – for which day should I make my wager, how much wine has he brought? Selvorne's townsfolk rarely knew the answers, for they usually arrived without seeing his approach, or with Arnlausa himself, hidden amongst them, making some kind of mischief, disguised and giving terrible advice for any wager they might make.

Selvorne was soon ignored by the village, for word of where he was from and how rude he could be had spread quickly, faster than he could walk, so he found himself glared at until he took lodging that looked over the lake. Inside there was peace, and the lake was beautiful to see, from his small wooden room. Magnificent, but impassible. There was no way to Tavalehk – he could not walk through miles of muddy river banks. He could not swim across the lake, he could not pass around it, he could not ... think of any way there, except by boat. Perhaps floating on a log, though he would not be there before morning, when the boats would return. Possibly one might return earlier in the night, and he could pay his way. An expensive journey, to be the only man in the boat, other than the rowers – but he no longer cared to hurry. The village avoided him and was in a merry enough mood, food was plentiful, if he paid, he could eat alone and sleep early. No enemy would seek him there, and his day had been so very long. After a quiet, pleasant night of eating and avoiding others, he took to his lodging and watched the moonlit lake.

His lake. His town. His village, and his people. His task, to find Cienn – Leader of the Waehdric, the wisest of them all, independent of lords and towns. From her he would receive good advice, but more importantly she was the High Commander of the Waehdric Guards – those who served neither town nor lord, but would, on request of either, assist in any great task. Cienn would join with Selvorne – his vengeance would be taken to her heart, her men to his side. Their sweep of the woods, seeking enemies who dared do what they had done. His justice, his law, his lands. And his bed, which was soon all he cared for, as he put himself to sleep.

~

Selvorne woke early and could no longer sleep. All weariness was gone, his body well rested, but his mind stirred from peaceful dreams to uneasy realisations. Anger – fury – no longer fear, after a night of safety. He sat, he stood, he opened the shutters and looked out to the lake in the dim morning light – mist and fog, with drizzling grey rain.

Anger, but no enemy, would make a man ... weak? Was that what his father had said? Yes, something like that. Selvorne did not feel weak, he felt ... strong, furious and frustrated. He was sure his father said something about that, also, but trying to remember made him grim, angrier, sadder and ... yes, his father had said something about that, as well.

Selvorne knew his father had been a guard, but did not know the all of it. He must have been more than a guard, if he inspired the tales of Krogarve. If he was

Krogarve. And, if he was, it was likely he said such absurd things to his son for a reason. Anger made him weak – no, he had said that anger unrestrained, in time, would weary a man – then his enemy might strike. Weariness would bring mistakes. Selvorne was only that morning beginning to realise what his father had truly meant. He needed to calm himself, keep his mind clear and wait until it was time to strike. Rerleden had said the same, as had Arnlausa – enjoy the festival – hide in the Gathering Cloak of the crowd, disguise himself with merriment, and a smile. Selvorne rubbed the stubble on his chin, and a thought came to him, so he looked through his things.

A knife. So very sharp – it needed to be sharper. There, the stone, and there – the small bronze mirror polished so he might see his own face. Selvorne set it on a table and began to hone the blade, thinking on what he had been told.

Hone the blade before it is used – clear the mind before the day. Calm the anger and remove all thought – deadly is the morning shave. Care, and focus – no blade will cut. Not pass the skin and draw the blood. Not even the sharpest, in a hand with skill. To shave the skin, not cut, not kill.

No other thoughts mattered, just the scraping of hair, the steadiness of his hand. Selvorne began to nod as he remembered. Then, when the blade was to his satisfaction, he began to shave.

Not much of a beard, the short stubble of days. Not much of a beard, if he left it for weeks – not yet, though he was not so young. Others his age were bearded. His father had said it took him a while as well, for his first beard, and his mother, well, from what he had heard of her family, Selvorne wondered if his first beard might be white. Still, he felt some joy as he cleaned his face – he was presentable, and would seem a young man fresh for the festival, not some wild man fleeing from the woods for his life. His mind was clear, he packed away his things, then looked out the window once more.

Clear the mind, clear the face – wash the eyes, look to the day. His plans – the festival, go there unseen, unnoticed, and search for Cienn, Leader of the Waehdric. She might be there. Or her second, or who she trusted. Speak only to those most trusted, enemies might be any man amongst any men. Two lords were killed – though horrific to him as son and friend, there was no place for such misery. Such thoughts would have made his hand shake, the knife cut as he shaved – his voice tremble as he spoke, his secret revealed to those who might want him dead. They would kill him – or, perhaps worse, they would flee and hide, and he would never know who they were. No misery would he show, no sign of who he was – truly to be Lord of Tavalehk, unknown to the town. One day he would be introduced and well received. Lord of Vaskatohr – well known by the people of that town, and loved. Not yet. Not that day. He was Lord of Vengeance, cold and clear. Calm and ... cruel. Well shaved, well dressed, welcoming with his smile – unnoticed amongst the crowd.

From the mists of the lake Selvorne saw boats appear. A tiny bell outside began to ring, and the villagers stirred from their homes.

The men who rowed the boats were keen to return to the festival, though it was so early in the morning Selvorne was not sure the sun had even risen – perhaps they were in the shadow of the mountain, for the light was quite grey. It could have been the drizzling rain, the mist or the clouds, but it seemed odd that anyone awake so early could be keen for anything. Yet the men in boats and the entire village were eager to go, and soon all the boats were loaded.

Payment – three bits for passage, and the boatmen would make a tidy sum. Eager for the festival – no, those who rowed, Selvorne decided, were keen to return to their sleep. A promise had been made to gather the village and children early – a regret, after little rest. He offered to row, which only earned him angry stares, as if he meant to take part of their toll. He shrugged as though he had, and they ignored him as he sat himself at the head of the boat.

If those who were older were eager, it did not show – they were sleepy, despite being used to such early mornings on farms, they were not used to late nights of feasting. The children were excited, the young boys and girls had to be ordered to behave in the boats. Selvorne was soon surrounded by children, and when he asked if he should move, the rowers said he should stay at the front to balance the boat. Perhaps it was true, though it was also clear that the parents wished to remain at the back, and curl up on cushions to sleep.

Selvorne was ordered to ensure no children fell over the side, and to keep them quiet, if he could. It was not a request, for in the boats the rowers were as lords – or commanders of men, anyway, and on the pier it was the Pehrnohc who was lord. Not even Arnlausa would argue with such men, more for wisdom than fear, for a Pehrnohc could organise boats to annoying disadvantage, and rowers could, by way of splashes, make a journey miserable and wet. By accident, of course. Selvorne obeyed, he would have watched for the children regardless. It did not escape him that passengers in a boat could disappear over the side, and never be found. By accident, of course.

It was early morning when they left, the light was low, mist more than rain, and fog over the lake. He could not see far, and the boats left the pier, heading into the hidden waters. Peaceful, silent, serene – it should have been, crossing that magnificent lake.

But it was not. Selvorne was at the front of the boat, staring into the mists, enjoying watching them parted by the breeze of the boat's approach, but he was surrounded by children who were doing the same. When they were not trying to reach down and touch the water, or splash each other, or fight over positions on the seats.

Tiring of the waters, they crowded on his seat until he was jammed against the nose of the boat. Tired from the early rise, they grew unpleasant, snapping at each other and at times, punching with small fists – both boys and girls alike. One had brought many small pebbles in a sack, and had a mind to throw them into the mist at times, hoping to hit the shore – each time he threw, he listened, then clenched his fist in anger that the journey was not over. Each flew past Selvorne's head – the first, he thought a bird, swooping for a fish. The second was also unexpected, but the third gave away that it was someone in the boat throwing stones. The fourth he almost halted with a raised fist, and the boy looked only a little afraid.

Apart from the children, the oarsmen were almost exhausted from the start – little sleep, already a long row, and the same journey repeated with many people in the boat, their strokes were rough and the boat lurched. The mist which had seemed so lovely made everything damp, Selvorne decided it was drizzling rain after all. The crossing was far from pleasant. Selvorne tried to sit calmly, and thought if he could survive such an ordeal with his mind clear, he could face anything – although he began to wish he was instead back in the woods, hiding in a vine–covered tree, watching enemies who meant to kill him.

After half of the longest hour he had known, the drizzling rain stopped, the mist cleared and the fog gathered into patches over the water that the boat entered and left, as though gliding through clouds. The day was bright and blue. The sun had risen over the mountains – it was in the eyes of the rowers, another reason they had wanted to hurry. Broad hats appeared from under seats to shield their faces, and for a moment the boat was wandering in the lake as they tied lacings under their chins. Any children with a mind to sleep suddenly sat up, staring about the broad waters of the lake – any parents with a hope for silence pulled cushions from where they sat, and put them over their ears.

Selvorne marvelled at the lake. It had seemed so vast from the hills, but even greater once he was upon it. In all directions, water, with the only interesting things to see being the mountains and the distant haze ahead, where the town should be. And other boats – one, with well–behaved children, singing a low song, their families sleeping in the back. How he wished he was there with them, their passing was enchanting. Another boat had the children jumping up and down, joyful at the clearing mists, and in danger of tipping. On a third boat, worst of all, all sat sulking, and they seemed to be soaking wet. All noticed as it passed them by, and things settled in their own boat. For a while there was some peace – until the town could be seen, then many began to cheer. Only for a while, as the town was still far across the waters.

Selvorne had never seen it from there before – never seen Tavalehk from a distance. Always he entered from the southern road, it was a farm, then a house, then more houses and pavings, wide streets with gutters and the town itself was arranged along one long, lakeside road. Very long, for a town, for most people wished to be living near the water. It was not possible to see it all at once, not from the woods and hills in the west, and not from the northern or southern end of the main street. From the lake, the entire town appeared before him, from left to right, so long, so vast, it was all he could see, and it was the greatest thing he had ever seen. More houses than he could count – more people than he knew – more accounts, affairs, business and deals between townsfolk than he could possibly guess. Daunting. Fifty times as many people as Vaskatohr, he was sure – if not a hundred – and two hundred times as complicated. The words his father had written came back to him – take the coins, become a merchant, it is easier, more profitable, and free. Did his father say free? Selvorne was unsure, but as the boat lurched forwards he began to feel he was being taken against his will or wishes – to be a captive servant – and a thought came to him to jump over the side.

Possibly the same thought came to the children, who were eager and chanted for the rowers to hurry. The rowers would not, and they began to turn the oars a little to splash the children, dousing their demands, until Selvorne ordered them to stop it, with no more authority than a low tone and a harsh glare. The children's eagerness was not dampened, and they began to speak of contests and toys, prizes and games – childish things that Selvorne cared for only long ago. Although ... he had meant that year to buy a new fishing spear of quality, and that was ... not a toy, he thought. Necessary to replace the one that was breaking, which had replaced the one he had broken, to ... an eagerness, though, like a child wanting a toy. The men were no different, even the ones resting at the back of the boat – the men, and their wives. Toys, spears, dresses, food – the boat was becoming a merry place of chattering folk. Even the rowers seemed to grow eager to return to the excitement, and Selvorne remembered a rhyme.

"Some dreamt of toys, others of boys. Hair set in curls, some dreamt of girls. Some thought to game, others of fame. Strangers once met, in search of a name."

Strange, Selvorne thought, to remember that old poem – from some story of adventure, told to him as a boy. It went on for a while, listing all things desired at the festival – love was often in the verse, for love was, as Arnlausa said, most important. Uhlsko had never agreed – not with words. But Uhlsko had loved his lost wife for a very long time, and Arnlausa ... he was never wed. He must have known love, at least once. Selvorne wondered only briefly at his lost friend, returning his mind to calm, and ... then he was distracted.

Cassini ... Selvorne's silly adoration came to mind, and he bit his lip to think of it. That was where the other boys – men – his age were, already at the festival, a day before it truly began, looking for maidens – who were looking for men. Or boys. Hair set in curls – not a very popular style in Tavalehk, though. Long and straight was the usual, perhaps with ribbons or bows. Weighted at the ends, if the hair was defiantly curly, against the wishes of the girl. He chuckled to remember that one year, giant bows were the Festival Folly – the absurd fashion that was chosen for the year, for all to follow. Great bows a foot wide, tied atop the heads of maidens – two feet wide, for men who liked to jest, or not so large for the very bold, who dared attach them to the front of their trousers, then strode proudly through the crowds, to much laughter.

Another year, and it was ribbons, which trailed all the way to the ground. That was an expensive year for the young men, who bought ribbons to give to maidens they adored. Costly to men, and painful to some women, for one ribbon from each admirer meant that for the prettiest their hair was all ribbons, and to the delight of those with fewer, the weight of so many pulling their hair to break it.

"Some dream of vengeance, terrible and cold. On men without mercy, for crimes yet untold."

Selvorne grinned at his clumsy addition to the poem, though the thought of it was grim, and that year would not be so festive for him, though he was told he should –

Something hard smacked Selvorne in the back of the head. Stunned, he turned and saw some children trying to pretend nothing had happened, though it was clear who had thrown a stone, and doing so had hit Selvorne. He glared until some of the children pointed at the one who he already knew was guilty.

"Look," Selvorne said, making a fist with one raised knuckle, "see this? If you do that again, this knuckle is going to crack down on your head. Understand? No more stones. I mean it. Stone thrown – knuckle – head."

The boy nodded fearfully. Selvorne wondered at his stupidity, to even try to try to hit the land with a stone when they were so far from shore. When his head was so much nearer, and in the way.

Selvorne rubbed his sore and thought about what he would do at the festival. He determined that he should be able to move through the town and few would know him – he would be safe enough. Those of Tavalehk who only saw him a few times in the year were not as close as friends, only some might recognise him, half of them would care to speak with him. His own townsfolk, despite being as close as family, and having been gone for over a month, usually only wanted to hear of his journey when back at Vaskatohr, saving such stories as entertainment for their quiet town. Often Uhlsko would insist, so Selvorne was left to enjoy his time at Tavalehk alone. Many of his town met with their own distant families, or were consumed by the excitement of the festival. All such people he should be able to casually avoid.

The most important thing would be to determine what powerful people were visiting there, especially guard captains, or lords. They could lead him to Cienn. The other thing, which he was more eager to do, was to move through the crowds and see if he recognised any of the brigands. Dangerous, but they would not notice him, one young man amongst so many.

The boats were approaching the lakeside, and it was clear they were all going to land at once, pulling up beside many small piers. Selvorne had a thought, and turned to the boy who had hit him with the rock, beckoning him to the front of the boat.

"Here, now, wait a bit, then throw your stone," Selvorne said, and the boy waited as they were approaching, then threw his rock – badly, but very far to the shore, hitting the pebbled beach.

"First on shore!" the boy exclaimed, very pleased with himself for such an absurd victory. Selvorne smiled at him, and messed up his hair.

"Nice work – first on shore."

The final mists parted and the boats glided in silence to the piers. Oars were planted to make waves, and the journey halted. They rocked sideways to bump the wood – silence – then cheers, and thanks to the rowers for bringing everyone safely across the lake. Some smiled, others grinned, most began yelling orders to leave the boats carefully, as people tried to hurry. Selvorne did not, he waited, as did the mischievous boy, already pleased that he was the first to hit the shore. Selvorne left him there grinning, his parents calling to him, and he was certain the boy meant to be the last to leave the boat.

Festival Folly

Tavalehk was a proper town, unlike Vaskatohr or so many smaller towns, which truly were only called towns for they had lords. Tavalehk was huge – it had surrounding villages, several quite distant, a few quite large. Hundreds of families, some with dozens of people in each. So large that one family might take it upon themselves to learn just one trade, and pass all the skills of it to their children, and to theirs, and had done for a long time before, until the craft was a mystery to any others who might wish to compete.

That one family could dominate an entire trade – such as clothing, or wine, or working in iron – was the reason that in great towns, it was the people who truly ruled. Selvorne's father had explained it several times. A lord made the law, gave the settlement the name of town, answered to those other lords of the land, and the Waehdric had some influence, but none of those truly controlled the people. They made the town – the people, more than law, or custom, or even the number of people who lived there. That confused Selvorne greatly, so his father explained more clearly.

A small village will have a woodsman, Uhlsko had said, perhaps a family of such men. They cut the tree, clean it, dry it – shape it to beams, or tiles for the roof, or even make it to furnishings, which then may be sold. But a town – that was quite a different place. True, such families of woodsmen were there at Tavalehk, but unlike Vaskatohr, or any small village, there could be one man who cut the tree, one who cleaned it, one who dried it – another to shape it. A dozen to make furnishings, and yet more who would sell such things in the market. Half a dozen families in a town, to do the work of one, in a village – and do it so very well. In a village, one man must do all things – in a town, he must do just one thing with great skill, and that would make his fortune. But he may have no other skills, and depend on the people around him for his food, his clothes, repairs to his tools, perhaps. Most things, and so he was friendly to his neighbours, but it was a strange friendship of need, as well as joy. Uhlsko thought that men of villages were more independent, able to do many things, perhaps not so well, but well enough to get by. They also needed their neighbours, but it was need that came from isolation and danger, usually, in the wilder lands – not a need for trade and profit. A slight change in mood from village to town. His father explained that neither was necessarily better – a man should be able to do most things, and a man should find what he is best at, and do it well.

The same he said for towns, for one town might do just one thing well, and so make its fortune. Selling to other towns, of course, with a similar friendship bound to need. Vaskatohr mined copper and herded pigs, but would not even try to grow grains, there simply were no fields, and grain came easily in sacks on waggons from Tavalehk, which had fields, but was known for its fine clothing, for its leather and for its boots. And for its festival, once per year, the first full moon of early spring. Tavalehk was known for wine, which was good, but also for its ale – for it was very, very bad. Some poor folk coming to the town for the first time, who had not been warned, were sure to warn all friends on their return home. Avoid the Tavalehk ale. Or offer it to enemies in spite, or to good friends, as a joke. Wine, however, was sought after, but in poor supply – one cup of wine to dull the taste of three tankards of ale, that was the usual. Not mixed, except in the stomachs of the drunk. Tavalehk usually did not have many drunk folk, with such poor ale and the rare supply of wine, but at festival time, any who visited the town must have thought it filled with people who did little but drink. As did Selvorne that morning, climbing off the boat to find many were sleeping by the lake where they had collapsed. Selvorne stepped around them, shaking his head – the festival had not even properly begun.

A true town was also large, far greater than a village. A man could walk around a strange town for a month and not see everyone there – meet a dozen new people each day – be noticed and remembered by only half of them. Even at Tavalehk, a town Selvorne visited more than once a year. He looked around – not one person near knew him – none on the boats, none at the village across the lake, none who greeted their arrival. None of the drunk, none of the passersby, though he must have seen them before. Who was he – no one. Even if he seemed familiar, he might be thought the servant of Uhlsko, who was a friend of Arnlausa. Some would know him at once, and likely not care, but most passed by and gave him not a second glance.

It was the Gathering Cloak – it was to be hidden in the crowd. Selvorne was not angry, sad or afraid. He did not cheer, sing or shout, run nor weep, threaten nor laugh, and so he was unseen. A change of clothes, a hat, a beard – perhaps he should not have shaved – but such a disguise was nothing if he walked around furious, like a man who had seen murder. Undisguised – he had no hat, no beard, his clothes were little different to before, but he was just one man of many, and it made him almost laugh to think of it. Rerleden was right, he had completely disappeared.

Selvorne looked back on the lake. He had a new fondness for it, after making the crossing. Such a different place on the other side, and the village folk were disappearing into the crowd as well. The boats left piers to be dragged to the pebbles, some of the oarsmen collapsed on the grass by the water, their pay was a bag of bits cradled as a pillow, for keeping, not comfort. They would sleep half the day, rise to eat and drink, then enjoy excitements through the night. It was likely that all people from the different villages across the lake had arrived – the rowers would do little work during the festival, they rarely did, and Selvorne wondered why they did not compete to race the boats, for entertainment. Perhaps for exhaustion, having made so many trips, and having to do them all again in days to come. Still, they remained by the waters, in case anyone needed to be rowed, and would pay well for it.

The lake was the boundary of the town, the place where all houses ended. It was the most desirable place to live, so few streets were away from the waters. It never flooded, nor did it rise, for at the southernmost part of the town, the entire lake emptied into a great river, which flowed fast or slow, depending on the rain or melt of snow. Three mountain rivers to make the lake, one woodland river to take its waters away – west from the town – miles, then over waterfalls, dropping to the low forests, then perhaps a hundred miles to the sea. Winding its way through woodlands, wildlands, and bogs – to a town called Veksehl, on a cliff by the sea. There to tumble over great falls – too high for a man to jump down, and sadly, too high for fish to jump up, so no salmon came to Tavalehk from the sea. Trout were there, but it was a shame.

Few streets in the town, and only one main road passing through. The lake was a road in itself, boats could carry things easily across to the eastern villages, or indeed, merely along the length of the town. Many houses had long wooden piers, and boats of their own. Looking along the row of houses, made of wood, with great long piers supported by trunk beams, Selvorne began to realise where all the forests had gone.

There was something odd about entering the town from the lake, and Selvorne could hardly believe he was there. He usually arrived from the south, by way of a low stone bridge over the woodland river. That road came to the crossing roads where the Lordstone was set – that stone which named the lords of the town, as far back as the first. To enter that way, a man knew he was at Tavalehk – to jump off a boat, it was unlike anything Selvorne had ever known. No long walk half a day in the sun, no river, no bridge, just sit and be rowed, and then – in the town. In the middle of it. He was not sure he preferred it, if anything it made him feel confused, so he walked to the south to be sure he was at Tavalehk, and not in some strange village that looked exactly the same.

Tavalehk, he knew it. More familiar with every dozen paces. Houses of wood, houses of lake clay, some of both. Some of brick, fired and hardened – and expensive – and far more such houses than he remembered. More reason for the loss of wood, burnt to fire brick – colourful, cheerful bricks – but he preferred the bright white of the clay houses, with their bold wooden beams, and thicker walls with deep windows. Yes, it was Tavalehk, and it was the festival. At first he was determined to enter as though from the south, but he found himself drawn towards the many stalls, some still being prepared, and – what was he doing?

To enter from the south – to walk there, and pretend he was arriving as usual ... a stupid thing to do. If people were looking for him, they would be there – if people looked for his father, be they killers or merchants of wine – they would be there, and recognise him. He did not stop walking, but turned, and did not continue south – he saw the bridge, that would have to do. Low and stone, and a tower on the north side with a man as a lookout watching the south ... looking out for him, no doubt. Well, for Arnlausa, anyway, perhaps eagerly awaiting, with wagers placed for that day. Selvorne could not enter that way, not the same as the year before, and before that, and ... it would never be the same again.

Not the same, not for him. Perhaps for the people, for the festival itself had not changed. Every year it had been held, for longer than any knew – roughly the same time, on the full moon of the fifth month. Easy enough to determine in advance, though some arrived early, and others were late. Most could guess the time it would take to make the journey, setting out a week before. Some only left when the moon was almost full. Some when it was full the month before – but such folk were from far away, or slow travellers, and usually loud tellers of their journey's tale – so Arnlausa made them feel welcome. Very welcome, for he knew that a four–week journey back, in any direction, telling of the wonders of the festival and warmth of the lord there – it could only make the following year all the better.

In a popular year, the size of the town could double during the festival, or even – as once had happened – be four times its usual size. Then the festival would struggle to cope as people ate everything on offer, and plenty that was not. Then the festival would end abruptly, with no food, no drink, plenty of coins profit and nothing left to buy, and many townsfolk needing to make an unplanned journey to Hartlehk in the north to spend their earnings there. Such a year of successful disaster was usually followed by a quiet year, with an oversupply of food, as many prepared hoping for the same crowds, but instead found those from afar reluctant to come again. Then, the following year would be filled with all who had heard of the bargains of the previous year, the plentiful food and things bought at wonderful prices. Crowds would again begin to swell. Selvorne expected that it was to be such a year – a middling year – busy, but not overly so, with bargains for both sellers and buyers, depending on timing, desires, and luck.

Selvorne found it a little sad that few came from the south anymore. Those who were not of Tavalehk came from the north. Perhaps as few as one in fifty were from the south, and of them, most were from Vaskatohr, people who could hardly be considered from another town. At least regarding interesting tales of travel.

From Veksehl, which was by the sea, by way of the very long road – very few, if any in recent years. A shame, for they used to bring the very best ale, better than wine, selling for great profits – and in turn they purchased wine, for they claimed they were so sick of ale they would drink anything else. They must have grown sick of the wine, or were taking their ale somewhere else to sell.

From MidWaehter, a land in the far south – very few came. Perhaps none. None that Selvorne knew. They would have to pass through Vaskatohr, and if they did, it must have been in silence as Selvorne slept, and so they were unseen. Long ago, trade from the south was common, but the north had little to do with their distant southern folk. It was disappointing, for the south was the reason for the festival in the first place, to buy and sell things that each land did not have. The only rare thing coming north for a long time was the wine that Arnlausa brought each year. Great profit for Arnlausa and Uhlsko, but no new southern people to meet for Selvorne.

From the north those who came were also not in great numbers – it was the many villages of Tavalehk itself that swelled the town. From the north, it was mostly merchants with valuable things, expecting great profits. Rarely did important lords or ladies come. Often annoying administrators arrived, serving the Waehdric and poking their noses into Arnlausa's affairs. Selvorne chuckled – he always laughed when Arnlausa said such a thing, for he had himself quite a large nose that was hooked, and if he poked it into any affairs, he would likely pull it out with a fine catch. Selvorne joked that he might fish with it, and his father laughed – a rare thing for him, but not for Arnlausa. He agreed his nose had served him well, for he always smelled fine, unlike others, and though it might be ugly, it was not something he had to see – unlike others.

Towards the administrators, Uhlsko was not exactly kind, but considerate. Meddling men who wanted to be sure that whatever share of the lord's tolls that was due to them, went to them – and to be sure of it, they wanted to know everything. One meeting, once a year, at the festival – early, for Uhlsko, presenting his accounts. They could find no fault, ever. Twice they would meet with Arnlausa, who disagreed they were necessary, welcome or wanted – loudly, in their faces, just behind their back, making them uncomfortable wherever they stood. Uhlsko argued they were needed to be sure things were tallied well, and welcomed by some lords who had made a mess of things – Arnlausa argued the opposite, shouting his view and at times, pounding his fist to the strong walls of his house. As a child, Selvorne had been frightened – as a young boy, thought his friend bold, and his father weak. As a young man, curious – and as he thought about it that day, wandering the streets of the festival, he realised the two of them were working together to make the administrators uneasy. One man almost friendly, the other almost violent. Unsettled, the administrators would cause no trouble, make no demands, and perhaps not return the next year. At least, not the same men, and so, would not have a good memory of the accounts.

Dampening the mood of the festival – that was the accusation of Arnlausa. He said it was a great annoyance, and complained bitterly of all the wonderful things he was missing – bitter words of complaint, and speaking eagerly of the festival joys, smiling even as he yelled. Selvorne began to suspect that was also deliberate. The unwanted men were quick to finish accounts, and soon to join the festivity. And there he saw a new deception – that was why the administrators were there at that time, and not during the year when they might stay weeks, lingering over all the profits Tavalehk made. They had come to enjoy themselves.

And collect their share of the town's wealth. A share to the Waehdric – a tiny share, for a town, but a large portion of Arnlausa's coin, which could ruin him – although Selvorne suspected that wailing lament was also a ruse. He had not given it much thought before, but as he looked upon the stalls being set, he realised Tavalehk was to him no longer a festival town, a place of fun and frolics, free of care and woe. It was his town, his worry, his concern for a hundred things. Should he welcome the administrators, let them do the work for him? Or force them out as Arnlausa had done ... he was not sure, and the thought of it dulled his enjoyment.

Guards. Waehdric guards, who served the lands, not the town. There were many – though they did not wear the same clothes as each other, nor display any sign that they were guards, Selvorne knew that they were – and not of Tavalehk. Weapons were the main clue, no man walked around with a sword, let alone a spear, at a festival. Some guards had neither, just knives – as many men would carry, but longer and hung to be drawn and used, not simply carried to cut a lunch. Others carried no weapons that he saw, but walked together in groups that seemed suspiciously confident, powerful and strong – not in a boastful way, like young men might do to catch the eye of maidens. One group of a dozen seemed especially comfortable, unafraid and dangerous. Selvorne was not sure why, it must have been how they moved, without clumsiness or doubt. They smiled, rather than laughed, and noticed everything – including himself – he grinned back, to seem a silly boy, then looked away, feigning interest in a stall.

Were they at ease or alert – at ease, he thought. Alert, a little – no, astonished, more likely. That group of a dozen were calm, but others he noticed had gaping mouths and wide eyes, and were prone to sudden excitement when some wonderful thing caught their gaze. Enjoying the festival, as everyone else – but guards, from afar, and the reason for their presence could only mean one thing – important guests. Selvorne nodded to himself, one guard noticed and nodded back, and he smiled simply before averting his eyes.

Find Cienn – find the killers. Gather men, such guards as the man who nodded – have revenge. The day ahead, and he would do all that – he knew he could, if he remained hidden, and watched carefully. Victory within a day, with luck and speed. Mourning the next, grim celebration of vengeance, and memory of the lives lost. A new lord, and no time to waste.

Selvorne raised his eyes from the ground to the crowd – from the stalls of the festival to the people gathered there. It was men he sought, not stalls. Killers he looked for, not bargains. Brigands, not guards, so he turned his attention to the strangers around. He was safely hidden in the crowd, but began to realise just how vast it was, and how little he had to go on other than the height of the brigands, and some of their clothes. He had seen little of their faces, and even if he had, so many people looked similar that they might not be recognised. After a while he began to regret not attacking the brigands when he had the chance – although, he never truly had the chance. Not to win.

Then he saw – a hat in the crowd – unmistakeable, bright and tiny, sitting on a man's head at a funny angle. It was the hat from the forest. Pushing his way through the crowd, Selvorne approached the man in the hat and jumped in front of him – staring into his face. Height – yes – but ... fat. Very fat, with a large beard, tiny eyes and a bewildered expression as Selvorne stared at him. Angry, too, or frightened, Selvorne was not sure as the man excused himself and pushed past, lumbering off, looking absurd with his tiny green hat.

Selvorne was bewildered. It was the hat, he was certain – but not the man. He would have noticed an enormously overweight, heavily bearded man amongst the brigands. His heart sank as he looked around, and noticed that quite a few people were wearing tiny hats. Tiny hats – the Festival Folly. Selvorne sighed. There was no hope in it, they were the absurd thing to wear that year. Coming in all colours, that was some advantage, for he sought a man wearing one that was green. Too small to fit on the head, they were pinned in people's hair, or strapped under the chin if a man was bald, having no hair in which to pin it, and with a good sense of fun. Selvorne fancied that the fat man was bald, and he vaguely remembered noticing a bow tied amongst his thick beard.

To the hat stall he went, the Festival Folly was usually sold from the same place each year. It was a large cart – the size of a waggon, but truly a cart, for it had only two great wheels. Itself a folly, to move it took a dozen men to lift its great arms, more for awkwardness than weight. It was like a barrow more than a cart, but a huge one, for a very large – and strong – man. A small shed had been built upon it years before, and from inside two small women could work, tossing the follies out to the men selling at the front. They did not seem to be selling many, the prices were too high, Selvorne thought – for a folly. A hat was a complicated thing to make, even if it was tiny, and it could not be sold for less. The hat merchants might have made a mistake that year, negotiating to provide the Folly – a costly one, if they returned home with a cartload of hats, of many colours and no use at all except for tiny men.

The year before, the Festival Folly had been an absurd scarf. Overly long, brightly coloured, easily stained, neither warm nor proof against water – but the essential item of the festival, worn with pride. Or vanity. Anyone with the wealth to buy such a useless oddity would be at once displaying both their good fortune, and support for the prosperity of the town. So the sellers usually explained,

Selvorne thought all the Festival Follies were a ruse to part folk with coins, and buying such things only said one thing to all who saw it – I am wealthy.

No, that was too cruel. None of the things cost so much, and jewels were a greater sign of wealth. If the Folly said anything, it was that the wearer had good humour, and was excited by the spirit of the festivities. Often the things sold could be turned to something else, afterwards – something useful. The hats, he learnt, could be folded upon themselves to make felt socks, which might not fit perfectly, but could be tied to keep feet warm in the coming winter, when lying around in the house, or when asleep. Not such a bad idea, not so useless after all, and it seemed some were buying two, and arranging both to look ten times as absurd. One elderly man even ordered two of the red, and people gasped, for the red hats were the most expensive. He handed one each to children who were near, a boy and a girl in green tunics who had been watching the stall. They seemed to thank him – some who were near clapped – then the children ran away, delighted. If Selvorne guessed rightly from their faces, the children were not known to him, and it was a very generous gift to strangers. For those children, the festival that year would never be forgotten.

Selvorne's spirits lifted, and he realised that, although the hat would not distinguish the enemy from so many others, it did mean that the man had been at the town in the days before, and likely would return, for the festival had only truly started that day. And Selvorne knew his hat would be green, and perhaps, if he saw the man, it would be a way to speak with him, and seem innocently interested in the hat. When did you buy it, I cannot find any of that colour – that was his plan. A few days ago, the man would say – aha, I have found you – so Selvorne would think, if met on the road or in the woods. At the festival he would seem to be just an interested young man, unrecognised, unsuspected – perhaps. Or not, and he wondered if it was wise to speak with a man who likely wanted him dead, whatever lovely hat he might be wearing.

Backing away from the crowds, Selvorne leant against a fence post beside stairs that led away from him, down a small slope. It was a vantage point where the street side dipped, and he could see over the heads of people, and across the crowd. He also could examine their faces as they passed by on the stairs, without getting in their way or drawing attention to himself. It was quite a busy part of the town, and Selvorne thought he would arrange for new pavings at the top and bottom of the stairs, for the old ones were wearing badly, and some people almost tripped in holes.

Then he saw someone near – familiar – tall – long dark hair, tied back, a slight hook to his nose. The taller of the two brigands from the ravine, who he had followed back to the camp. Selvorne moved closer to look him over, to study his face, to ... but he was too happy. The dark-haired man had a gleam in his eye, and was much too young – just a young man, like himself. He did look like the brigand, and wore a similar dark outfit of faded black shirt and dark grey trousers. Nothing about him was unusual ... apart from the way ... he stared into the crowds.

The dark stranger was standing beside the path, much the same way Selvorne had been, across from him and watching someone amongst the stalls. He did not seem to notice Selvorne approaching, even though to do so he was battling across the crowds on the path to the stairs. As he grew close, the stranger looked straight at Selvorne – grinned broadly – then dashed off into the stalls.

Astonished, Selvorne blinked a few times and peered after him – did he just flee? Why did he smile – was that a taunt? The dark youth was moving quite swiftly, not running, not pushing his way, but – then Selvorne smiled. He was chasing a tall young lady, who seemed not to notice, and the two of them disappeared into the crowd. Selvorne sighed, then grinned – he envied the young man's folly, and wished it was his own. He returned to his position at the fence post to watch the crowd, and realised several other young men there were doing the same – looking for maidens, not killers, at the highest place, with the best view of the crowd. At least he would not seem suspicious. He stepped a bit away from the stairs and took a quieter position near some tents, and watched.

~

Selvorne jumped back as a man burst out of a tent with a sudden mighty "Ha–ha!" – a dark–haired man, who stood tall, whisked a scarf from around his neck, then tossed it back into the tent. He brushed off his shirt then stood proudly, as if all the crowd were there to admire him – only Selvorne was staring, with wide eyes. Broad and elegant, a wonderful outfit of well–cut trousers and shirt, his face a bit rough, but his hair was groomed to magnificence, and he had been well shaved. Around his neck hung by a chain was a medallion that signified he was a guard of some importance, for such tokens were rare, and rarer still to be displayed so casually, most men kept them concealed. He certainly was not dressed as was usual for a guard, but stood proud as one.

"Ladies, beware! Shaven and groomed, ready for battle! To arms! To neck! To head! To bed!"

"Do you want the hair?" came a voice from inside the tent.

"Keep it, I am sure it will grow back!" the guard replied, then he winked at Selvorne, who grinned, "Take my advice – get your hair cut, and here. The best cutters of any town, anywhere in all the lands. I wait all year for this. You will go in a boy, and come out a man!"

He then gave a slight bow, winked again, looked over the crowd and seemed to pick some lucky maiden – then left swiftly, as pleased as could be.

Selvorne thought – he was startled. Almost delighted. He had no time for such nonsense, though ... the idea of changing his appearance seemed a wise idea. A trim of his hair that had grown a little long, and ... no, it was more than that. Change. And enjoyment. He stepped into the tent, and there an elderly man was collecting hair and carefully putting it into a box, likely to sell it for a wig. He was pleased to see another customer, and quickly led Selvorne to a chair before he could change his mind.

Hair trimmed, Selvorne was astonished that it had grown to fall around his shoulders – he had not been paying attention. He thought to take it up to a very neat trim, but kept some length to give it life, the old man advised. He was surprised that he agreed to purchase a shave as well, though he had already not hours before – and as he sat there, a strange old man with a knife at his throat, he wondered at how easily he had given such trust. That was it, though – that was what he needed, more than a shave, or a trim, or a disguise. To trust just one man, unknown – even with his life, with a knife to his neck. A stranger who did not want him dead, and the relief that not all men in the lands were enemies.

He paid and thanked the man, who bowed, and Selvorne left his hair – some strange wig it would make, mixed with all the others. Perhaps for a play, or a puppet, or a false beard. An odd beard, though, of different colours. Selvorne stepped out of the tent, chuckling to think he was supposed to remain ordinary and unnoticed, not appear dashing and strikingly handsome. He laughed, strangers frowned, some seemed impressed, though, and some of them were maidens passing by, more slowly than uninterested strangers should walk.

Back at the stairs, not many yards from the cutter's tent, Selvorne noted the tall dark youth had returned and was watching the crowd once more. Selvorne went to him, thinking he would be friendly – he was sure not all strangers wanted him dead, after trusting the cutter with his life.

"I see that she has strong, muscular arms," the dark youth said without turning to face Selvorne, "and my father says it is a bad idea to fall for a woman with strong arms. One day, she will use them against you. By blows, or by gathering all that is yours, and carrying it away as she leaves. Regardless ... she is quite a vision."

Thinking it a very strange greeting, Selvorne looked into the crowd. No attractive woman caught his attention, although there was a tall one with bare arms in a long dress – very precisely dressed, he noted, with hair firmly drawn back in rigid braids, and a stern expression on her face as she looked over a stall. Next to her was the dashing guard who had burst out of the tent with freshly cut hair, and he was joking with her – chatting, teasing, smiling – at passing ladies, as well, and for some he gave a slight bow.

"Does your father say anything about falling for a woman who is with another man?" Selvorne asked.

The dark stranger looked him up and down, then began staring at the woman again.

"You have had your hair cut. It looks good. I might consider that myself. It has taken so long to grow it, perhaps ... a shame to change it now. Although ... no, she does not seem to be too keen for that fellow – I think he is having no luck."

Selvorne looked over at the lady again – it was true, she did not seem to pay the man any attention, despite his newly cut hair. It did not seem to bother him at all.

"Or, he is her brother," Selvorne suggested.

The youth squinted at them, then frowned.

"If so, he has a different father. And a different mother. They look nothing alike," the youth said, then he turned to Selvorne, "my name is Rohy. Who are you?"

"Selvorne," he replied, immediately regretting it, though it was the name he would use, it was his name – his preferred name – but he had not thought he would say it to a stranger. Somehow he imagined the only person he would speak with would be Cienn. Perhaps her guards, he guessed, but only in passing. Certainly not some strange youth with an odd name, which sounded like, "Rroi–heh," and seemed shortened from something longer. As "Selv" might be from Selvorne. An odd manner to him, but friendly, almost familiar to have given his shortened name.

Rohy nodded once and turned back to the crowd – some might consider that a bit rude, but Selvorne could see he had a gleam in his eye, and he was quite enchanted by the young lady as she moved amongst the others at the stalls. Rohy began to explain in a dreamy voice that she moved with such grace and elegance, and had a strength and intensity to her, and it was something he had never before seen, and she was captivating, and so very ... alluring.

Selvorne, however, thought she was quite rigid in her movement, a bit plain in her sense of dress, rather square in her build, despite being slender, and almost could be mistaken for a man – a handsome man – but not a pretty girl, and certainly not a great beauty worth adoring from afar. Rohy, however, seemed delightfully enchanted, lifting Selvorne's mood and moving him to mischief as he spoke.

"Methinks, perhaps, your eyes are not so good. Have you seen this lady up close? Sometimes the longing from afar becomes the longing to be afar, once you have been close," Selvorne said, quite pleased with his witty remark, which he had only half remembered from a story told by Arnlausa. Rohy, however, did not seem pleased.

"I have seen her close. She is handsome, not a great beauty. But strong, I can see that in her – and fine. Besides, I do not think someone like me would have much chance with a great beauty. We cannot all be striking, handsome fellows, to choose from maidens the same."

At that moment the young lady looked up in their direction – straight at them both, Selvorne was sure of it – and she seemed shocked. She then quickly looked away, and disappeared into the crowd. Rohy nodded once at Selvorne, then took off after her. An odd fellow, briefly met, likely never to be seen again, but he had made Selvorne smile and his eagerness warmed his heart. For that, at such a time, Selvorne was very glad, and missed him a little, almost as a friend.

Selvorne remained at the top of the short stairway, looking out over the crowd. It was becoming very busy at the top of the stairs, for it was such a good vantage point that many people who were looking for others were stopping and searching below. The task was beginning to feel impossible as Selvorne was overwhelmed by the numbers of people, below him and about him, and he wondered if he should think of another approach. An elderly man who walked with a stick made his way to the bottom of the stairs, then began a rather long battle with the first step.

Nobody seemed to notice him – those at the top were watching the crowd, those at the bottom were pushing past, some almost knocking him over. Selvorne frowned and quickly shoved his way down to help the fellow, who at first thought he was about to be robbed. Selvorne took his arm to steady him as he climbed each step in turn – there were only six – but it was a challenge for his old legs, the left one especially wobbled. He thanked Selvorne at the top, claimed his legs were not what they used to be, swore that the stairs never were so steep in the past, they must have been made anew, and Selvorne agreed, though he knew it was not true. The old man recommended a place where the best food was to be found, then he went on his way.

As Selvorne began looking out to the crowd once more, a tall, elegantly dressed man, who had been watching the people for some time, came over to stand next to him.

"Few do as they should," the man said. Selvorne frowned as he almost nodded – a strange thing to say. The tall man had piercing eyes, fixed upon him as he peered down, and a slight smile.

"What?"

"A considerate thing to do, helping that old man up the stairs. Not many young men are so thoughtful. Not these days."

The tall man gestured to a group of young boys on the other side of the path, who were pointing to girls in the crowd and laughing at comments made, not quite softly enough to be kept amongst themselves.

Selvorne broke the spell of bewilderment, and looked the man up and down – he was well dressed, and must have been someone of importance. He was tall, but stooped a little. Not quite old, but past his best years. His dark black hair was short and well presented, but needing a trim, and a few white hairs were appearing, very striking amongst the black. Well shaved, with a long thin face, and dark, striking eyes that showed a bright cleverness, but also suggested weariness with tedium. His clothes were not the most stylish, but very well cut, simple and elegant – a buttoned shirt, not laced, each button bright, white and polished, very bold against the dark black shirt.

In moments Selvorne found himself doing what he had been trained to do – bow, with all the best manners as though he was before a lord. Elegant as he could manage, from what he had learnt, but rarely practised, and he gave a flourish of his hand that was not quite clumsy.

"Selvorne, at your service."

Astonishment – the man was greatly impressed. He stood upright, bowed slightly and presented himself.

"Temnere Nohc Rindaber, pleased to make your acquaintance."

Such formalities were usually a greeting, or a polite farewell – a brief acknowledgement of each other, before each would return to their business.

However, the "Nohc" grabbed Selvorne's attention, for it was the official title of either a powerful administrator, or a lord's relation. Selvorne decided to initiate conversation, which was not difficult to do, for the gentleman seemed quite interested in such an unusually well–mannered youth.

Their talk was brief, though, and as one sided as Selvorne could make it, for he did not wish to reveal anything of himself. It was easier than he expected, for Temnere was keen to speak of his own interests, and he seemed to think he knew Selvorne completely from only a few things said – a farmer boy, with some graces, learnt from guards, perhaps, with a neatness of presentation, pride in appearance – but he was not overly dressed, nor proud. A grain farmer boy who also tallied the sacks of grain, and dealt with the lord, and was, perhaps, a young man of intelligence and ambition. Strange, Selvorne thought, that Temnere would conclude such things from the little that was said – stranger still that he would say what he thought back to Selvorne, who did not care to correct him, for it saved him devising his own lie, but especially when he heard more of Temnere, for it filled his heart with hope.

Temnere was not only an administrator of the lands – he was The Administrator – of all the lands. The Head, as he was known, or the One. He was in charge of all other administrators in all towns, responsible for tariffs and tolls of the roads – and the roads – and all the accounts of the towns. He was likely there to annoy Arnlausa, but that was not what interested Selvorne – the administrators also controlled and coordinated the guards, those who served across towns and lordships, answering to one central command. To Cienn, their Leader – to Taffoanan, who was acting in her place. To any lord who requested their services. Guards were at the festival in great numbers, and when Selvorne mentioned it, he was told that they were looking for new recruits, building their numbers to do a sweep of the entire area to – in Temnere's words – "Eradicate all brigands, everywhere, once and for all."

At that, Selvorne showed much pleasure, and at his smile, Temnere seemed to show great approval. He was especially frustrated when he spoke of the brigands, explaining they were ruining the accounts of many towns, smuggling goods without tolls, stealing coins, stealing goods, selling goods in secret, for coins that avoided tolls, and so were just the same as stealing. Then most likely stealing back again what was sold or what was paid. Temnere shook his fist, or perhaps he made a fist so tight that it shook itself – and his eyes turned to the stalls of the markets, narrow and glaring, as if every vendor was at fault.

"They could even be here now under our noses, and we would not know," Temnere said, and Selvorne found himself nodding.

It was a little odd that someone would reveal so much, Selvorne thought, not only of his concerns, but also the plans to sweep the lands – surely that should be kept secret from the enemy? But, Temnere seemed to genuinely like him, and on parting, he even recommended Selvorne should contact the guards in the next few days to join them – perhaps after their usual recruitment speech, which would be timed to happen in the afternoon, when people were not too tired to attend, and not yet too drunk to listen.

Just as Selvorne was about to ask of Cienn, though, Temnere saw someone in the crowd and quickly nodded once, then left, hobbling down the stairs – an abrupt way to leave, but Selvorne noted he seemed to have a slight limp, and was in a great hurry. He ambled down to the stalls, pushed through the crowd and headed straight to the young lady that Rohy had been watching. Rohy was quite near her, and seemed to have unsuccessfully tried to talk. He stood as though in the middle of a difficult silence, uncomfortable, the lady was ignoring him, rummaging through a stall. When Temnere reached her, she looked down, bowing her head, and after a few brief words the two of them walked away, leaving Rohy looking dumbfounded – for a moment, before he followed them, at a distance.

Selvorne shook his head – that pursuit was doomed. Then he began to feel at ease – his heart lightened – as he realised there may be hope to solve all his problems. The horrific events of past days, the terrible people he had encountered – they were just a few amongst thousands, and he had the misfortune of meeting their malice. It was a great festival. There were thousands of good people there, and some, truly noble, brave and determined to keep the peace and safety of the land. Most of the people were good. Few were killers or thieves. A united force of guards would sweep through the forests and find the brigands, bringing them to justice. It would be done – it would be done, even without him making it be done. And he could help them, lead them – identify the enemy. A witness to their crimes – he could even help in such a way in secret, speaking with their captured leaders, and perhaps learn more than they would otherwise reveal, thinking him an unimportant youth, contradicting happenings that Selvorne had seen for himself. He took a deep breath, then sighed with relief.

Amongst the crowd, he was safe, unknown, unnoticed, and could relax. Apart from that, he was at a great festival with coins in his purse, and when things were over, he would take on the lordship of the entire town, which would be a difficult job – but, surely administrators such as Temnere could handle the tedious tasks, and leave him with the coins? Selvorne had every reason to be filled with joy – apart from the terrible deaths, which still made him furious to think of them. Calm, let it simmer, not boil – anger was not needed, not yet. Perhaps a week. Then his father and Arnlausa could rest peacefully, beside his mother. Soon.

Eagerness

The festival had a different feel to it once Selvorne had relaxed. He kept his eyes open for brigands, but his hope of seeing them by chance was fading. He noticed any men who looked like guards, and there were many. Good for the sweep of the woods, bad for any chance to see brigands amongst the crowd, for they would notice the guards as well, and likely hide. Such worries became less important, and he wandered amongst the stalls, turning his mind to the excitement, to the things for sale ... to the ... food.

Selvorne stopped, astounded by his own stupidity. He turned at once and took himself to where he knew he had to go, for he had forgotten the First Rule of the Fair – change coins early.

Food was what he wanted, he was hungry and though early in the day, he had not eaten since the fine meal the night before. But he could not eat – could not buy – he only had coins, and coins were not well liked by those who sold food. First Rule of the Fair – to get a fair exchange, square bits for coins, one must be first to the Changing Cart. He was far from the first, but the longer he left it the worse it would be – thoughts came to him, crawling to a stall of food, starving and weak, weighed by a bag of coins that no one would accept – he laughed, it was absurd, but he hurried until – he stopped.

A fair exchange? Coins for bits? He could not help laugh to himself. Others heard him and thought him odd as he chuckled, so he continued quietly, at a leisurely pace. At the Festival of Tavalehk, square bits of copper were used to make purchases, instead of coins, when purchasing food. He wanted to eat, and soon, and so must change coins to squares – but there was no hurry. It did not matter if he was given a poor exchange. It did not matter if one of his coins bought ten square bits or twelve. Little mattered, for the whole town – the lordship – had changed.

Strange problems, Selvorne thought as he headed to where he knew the coin changers would be – odd thoughts for a lord, and considerations no ordinary men would have. Arnlausa had explained them many times, as had his father – were they preparing him? To be lord? He was not sure, but he understood such things as well as many merchants.

Long ago, the biggest problem the festival had was not crowds, not thieves, not poor weather or few attending – it was coins. There simply never were enough coins for people to use to purchase and sell so many things at once. Twenty times not enough. Arnlausa put it simply – if a man came at a usual time of year with ten chickens, wishing to sell them all and then buy clothes, that was not a problem. Even if he swapped chickens for clothes. Someone would want chickens – someone would have clothes. But if one hundred men came with a thousand chickens – that was a terrible problem. All at once, all on the same day – not even from the same town, and all wishing to spend and sell.

Ten men with ten chickens, perhaps enough coins for them all – but not for one hundred men. Not for one thousand. For most of the year, so many coins were never needed – but for the festival, they were desperately in short supply, and the frantic selling of, say, chickens – for coins – made a mess of everything. And so they began the making of bits.

Bits – also the name of a bronze coin used throughout the lands – square bits at the festival, to be more accurate. Different to any other coin in the lands. Copper melted, spread, then pounded flat to a sheet of even thickness – rolled, in recent years, to be certain of that. Very neatly. Then cut to squares measured to a size that meant, by weight, their value was worth slightly more than the copper of which they were made. Each with a stamped picture on it, different each year. Once it was Arnlausa's nose – that was Selvorne's favourite. People were supposed to bring their true coins and exchange them for such square bits, and then spend them at the festival. Anything unspent was changed back at the end.

Simple – and essential. Value of each square bit had to be greater than the weight of copper, for the second year they were used, long ago, that was not the case – someone managed to gather many and melt them down, then sell them back as copper, at a great profit. Made all the greater by the sudden lack of copper in the town. When the value was made more than the copper by weight, though, people started bringing copper to the festival and making their own square bits. So, then they stamped them the following year. Then the stamp was copied. It was a delicate balance, an ongoing battle, and changed each year by Arnlausa – the stamp, the shape, the weight and value. But, despite all his efforts, someone – likely children – were snipping off the sharp corners of the square bits, and melting them down to copper balls, then selling them for a pathetic profit.

Arnlausa cursed at that, but Uhlsko explained that he always won – so what, if people brought copper and copied the square bits. If stores were low, it made Arnlausa wealthy in copper – it all came back to him, and he could trade it elsewhere during the year for a profit, at his convenience, when the demand was high. Some advantage, then, but delicate decisions had to be made at each festival to ensure he always came out ahead. As for the forging of the stamp – usually, only by the second day after the picture was revealed was it copied, and that was why people were wise to change coins early for a fair rate. Arnlausa preferred to call it a festive rate than a fair one, perhaps because he knew it was not completely fair, or he wanted people to feel festive.

He was a cunning lord, Selvorne realised. He spoke of the value he gave to the weight of copper, well in advance – it might have attracted copper merchants from afar. Or kept them away. But a favourable value brought them all the way from Vorletohm in the far north, Selvorne heard. They would get a good price, true, but how much could they possibly bring, with the intention to forge the fake square bits – and they would need lodging of fine quality, and food, and entertainment. Such men of wealth would not usually come so far to a festival – and so Arnlausa encouraged profit for his town. No, he did not mind any who might make their own square bits – but he often spoke against those who cut the corners off, explaining it was a waste of time and effort, that youths doing so could earn far more for far less, doing almost any other kind of work. It did not stop people, and many bits that once were square came back to the changers almost round.

Round were the bits that were true coins – long ago, after the success of the square bits of the festival, round bits were made. Well made, of bronze, not copper, with deep stamps, and used throughout the lands. They were just about exactly the value of their weight, for people were melting them down and using them to make other things – if they needed. There was little point to it, when the same coin could be taken to buy bronze of the same weight, saving the effort of melting it. Such true coins could be used at the festival, if a vendor was desperate, but it was almost frowned upon, for the square ones were easier to handle, tally and store, and caused less fuss when the lines were long and customers impatient, for all prices were measured exactly to numbers of square bits, and irritatingly not to exact counts of the round.

Selvorne reached the coin changers and watched them – not too busy. It was neither early nor late in the day. A stall beside them collected all manner of things, items brought by those who had no coins – farmers, herders, craftsmen. Some rightly should be setting stalls to sell their wares, but had no patience for it, so the square bits were given in exchange for chickens, tables, sacks of grain, baskets of eggs, or simply baskets. Pigs – that was the most annoying thing to bring, for pigs tended to smash eggs, chase chickens and gnaw baskets, and men would have to remove them quickly from the pens and hand over a vast amount of square bits to any swineherd who dared bring a pig. Selvorne often wondered if he should, as a joke, perhaps dressing it in feathers and claiming it was the greatest chicken in all the lands. He was not sure his father would approve. Arnlausa might. Selvorne would not, perhaps, as he thought on it – if he were lord, and someone did the same. Not if it harmed the other animals, or broke the eggs, or hurt the pig to be disguised in such a way.

The animal pen had no pigs, and a crowd of men at the front were quick to buy anything that came along at a good price. Beside the bit changers, it could be either the most profitable stall, or the least, depending on the day. The men looked glum, so Selvorne assumed it was a poor day for trade in animals. Was that better or worse for Selvorne? He did not know, but he felt for the men who were stuck there, bored and waiting, with a great festival around them and small profit from trade.

He felt no sympathy for the coin changers, for they made good profits always, and were so cunning that Arnlausa had to change them every few years to prevent them growing too clever and sending him broke. Trusted ... not quite the right word. Proven consistent, that was how they were described – predictable. They were likely keeping some of the coins, likely collecting pieces of copper, likely giving fair exchanges to their friends and less fair ones to others, and neither matched the tally. Bits returned never added to the sum of bits sent out. But Arnlausa was always ahead and ... Selvorne had an idea.

He took his coins to change, and waited for his turn – not many, he did not plan to eat so much, though he did make sure he had more than enough for the few days ahead. The last thing he wanted was to argue over food and coins, to be recognised during such a fight ... back to his plan. He paid too much, and dropped one coin too many, seemingly unnoticed by himself, to see what the changers would do – and to his astonishment, they not only corrected his payment, but returned his dropped coin.

Did they recognise him? Friend to Arnlausa, sent there to test them – no, he thought not. They paid him little attention, and turned to the next in line. And he thanked them, and, the significance lost on them, he declared that he looked forward to seeing them the next year. Were they honest, were they fair? Perhaps one coin or two was not worth the risk of deceit, if noticed by another in the line, or if it was detected by Selvorne after he left. Or if Arnlausa always sent men to test them. Whatever the case, Selvorne felt pleased, and took his square bits away, wincing in pain, the corners digging into his fingers as he put them in his purse.

How he wished he had a bit purse – small square boxes, to take small square bits. The edges were not so much sharp as rough, and the points – many encouraged their children to snip off the corners, not for profit, but for their own safety. To clench his bits – that was what was said of those who were unwilling to spend. A sharp bargain, a cutting deal. Or, an unhurt hand, for those who were quick to part with them. And those men with the most elegant, most fashionable box purses, finely made, fancy and jewelled and on display for all to see as they hung from their belts – a handy dandy. Selvorne wished he was such a dandy, or at least had a purse handy – or gloves. Or a coin purse not made of cloth that would not allow the corners to poke into his leg, as they were when it bounced. Arnlausa's cunning, no doubt – hard to hold, quick to spend, all returned by festival end.

Selvorne looked back to the changers – each change made Arnlausa ... no, not Arnlausa. Not anymore. But it had made Arnlausa profit – he was a fair man, though. So he always said, and Uhlsko laughed – a fair man? Or a Fair Man ... his hair was fair, once, faded by age before he coloured it back again to black. That was not what they had meant, and Selvorne wondered how much of the wealth of Arnlausa was coming from the festival itself – the sale of wine, the changing of coins, and whatever else he controlled, with cunning beyond Selvorne's knowledge, or understanding.

He wandered towards where food might be, and thought it strange he had never looked at the festival that way before – his festival? No, not truly. He did not own it. He did not understand it as well as Arnlausa, and would have to learn much before the year was over. Would the next one be grand? The timing was right. With a new lord – would other lords come? Make him rich, or would it send him broke, badly managed, make him seem a fool. Or would it run itself, a thousand people with their own desires. Arnlausa was not there, and it continued regardless. Selvorne was unknown to them, and not one person cared. Law? No lord, and yet there was still law – any crime would be quickly punished by townsfolk or guards. Selvorne began to feel unnecessary, even ... unwanted. Who was he, to them? Never presented to the town, never named as Uhlsko's son, never put forward as the heir, never ... needed ... or known.

He stopped walking and looked over the crowd – the lord was not needed. Not usually. Not him, and not Arnlausa. Not a long day's walk away, their lord lay dead in a barrel, put there ... well, by Selvorne, but murdered by enemies in the woods. Arnlausa was needed – Selvorne was needed. A lord was needed. A town might continue without one, but without a lord and men to fight, without command and courage – other men would come, and they would fight, and soon that town would have a new lord, new laws, and a very different way of life. Selvorne took a deep breath, and continued, not feeling so useless, but beginning to feel alone.

Almost lonely, despite the crowds. There were many people. Perhaps it was going to be a huge festival that year, for Selvorne had never seen so many before, and especially ... girls. Maidens. Ladies. He had to admit he was noticing them, and ... they even noticed him. A glance, a smile, a nod – even a bow, and a curtsey, or a giggle. Had there ever been so many maidens before? Young ladies of his age – no, not that he could recall. There seemed to be just as many young men chasing them – the town could not possibly have grown so fast. Yet, few of the people there seemed from far away. Not that he could tell, though most of the maidens had straight hair, which was fashionable at Tavalehk. It could have been fashionable everywhere. Hats, too – small ones, sometimes several at once, and some of the youths soon realised that having one pinned to each shoulder made them look broader than without, and they perhaps looked the most foolish of all, with their tall walk and wide grins. None of the young men seemed to like it when Selvorne laughed at them – none of them dared challenge him over it, though.

Maidens – hmm ... lunch. Food was what he craved, and the festival was known for fine foods. Strange things that people would not usually bother to cook for themselves, and would not on an ordinary day be able to afford. It was said that the enormous town to the north – Senylehk, largest in all the lands – always had such strange foods, from stalls that were always open, festival or not, and that the whole town was as if in a constant celebration, where the wealthy and idle could find anything they desired to eat. So said those from Senylehk – their town was a great wonder. Selvorne wondered greatly why they bothered coming to Tavalehk, then, to eat their simple food. Perhaps just to boast. No, it was the food, which was far from simple, and well worth the journey.

For the morning, for his hunger, there were many things he should have chosen – hearty meals for a strong young man. What he chose instead were honey sticks – grains of many kinds, stuck together by honey like tiny hives on the end of a stick. He had not seen them before, and was impressed with the other foods in that part of town where he usually did not go – or went, but never noticed. Delicious, he ate it as he walked around the stalls, planning his meals for the day. When he finished, he returned for another. And finishing that, a third – of which he could eat only half, and the seller laughed when he tried to sell the rest back. Instead he gave it to a young boy who was eyeing the stall longingly, but seemed to have no square bits.

At the back of the food stalls, on the woodland side of the main road, away from the lake, in a place he almost did not go, save for wandering with no aim, where only a few interested folk were browsing – was a stall that seemed to spring from a small, four wheeled turning waggon. A cart, truly, despite the two small front wheels, it had two much larger ones which bore most of the weight. Not always well, he guessed, noting that one wheel had been recently replaced, and the older, more ornate one had taken damage. The sides of the cart folded out and down, and cloth was propped up with neat, straight sticks, so it seemed an open tent with wheels. A large goat was sitting in the shade near the waggon, chewing on the grass, and a strange little man was tending to the stall. Slightly shorter than most men, and dressed flamboyantly in many colours, what was odd about him was his long, yellow–grey beard, which hung past his chest and was separated into seemingly endless golden braids. Selvorne had not seen such a beard before, and stared until the little man began staring back. Quickly, he turned his attention to the wares.

There were all sorts of well–made metal items, and a few well–built boxes of wood. Everything seemed to be either unusual wood, or bronze, or both. There were scissors, files, small knives, and boxes of so many kinds – a tiny cabinet for jewellery, and what looked like an impractical wooden satchel, which Selvorne thought could not be comfortable to carry in any way at all. One wooden bowl sat alone, it was undecorated, yet stood out for its plain appearance. Simply made, but elegant and pleasing to the eye. Selvorne gazed at it for moments until he began to yearn, then frowned to wonder why, and looked to the other things for sale.

What caught his attention was a four foot long, elegant wooden spear – for it had a golden polished bronze head of two prongs. Along its length, at each third were bronze rings, and on the very end a small bronze loop for attaching a fine rope. The wood was a deep orange–red, almost brown, the grain flowing gently in a pattern, and very elegant. Selvorne's eyes were already wide, but his jaw began to drop in speechless awe as he realised it was a fishing spear of the very best quality – the two prongs were finely barbed – it was for spearing fish from a boat, or a coracle, or from a rock ledge beside a lake, or even when wading in a stream. As his excitement rose, he realised his foolishness for seeming eager, so looked at other items and tried to feign disinterest.

"How much for this wooden bag?" Selvorne asked, but the little man was looking at him with a sly eye.

"Eleven silver coins," came the blunt reply.

"Eleven!" Selvorne said, shocked, "That is more than a gold coin!"

"I will also accept a gold coin, with another silver as well."

"It does not look very practical."

"You are correct," the little man said, leaning forwards, "it is, perhaps, the most impractical satchel possible, for someone who has longing in their heart for spearing fish. Why, only this morning, a man came to the stall, and asked me for the worst possible satchel, for carrying soaking wet, freshly caught, still wriggling fish – and I recommended this one here. As you can see, the wood will be damaged by the water, and the velvet lining will take all the odours of the fish, and keep them always as both the years and crowds pass by in haste."

Selvorne stared at the little man – struck by his taunting candour, his bold attitude and his twinkling eyes. He was doing mischief. He was teasing. And he had likely seen a hundred customers try and feign disinterest in an attempt for a bargain, with far more skill than Selvorne.

"Very well then, how much is the fishing spear?" Selvorne asked.

The seller's eyes lit up, and he began to speak as though well rehearsed – a little flat, his voice, though his eyes were bright. He no doubt had said it so many times that the sound of it was making him numb, as it was Selvorne, though he only had to say a fair price and it would be sold at once. That, of course, was what Selvorne began to fear – that he might not hear the price, and had already decided it was fair.

"Let me introduce myself – I am Hramullo, merchant of the finest items crafted by the most skilled hands in all the lands. I choose only the best – and choose from the best – and bring what is bestest to sell, far away, to distant peoples, and only to the most discerning, of finest taste."

"Indeed," Selvorne said, and Hramullo frowned.

"You doubt your tastes?"

"No."

"The quality of my wares?"

"No, not that either – but I am starting to doubt the size of my purse."

"Only the finest woods," Hramullo continued, ignoring Selvorne, "best metals, and greatest craftsmen are found – and then their wares bought, after ferocious negotiation of price – to be passed to you, the best deal possible."

"You sound keen for this ferocious negotiation of price – good," Selvorne said, "I shall hold nothing back, then, and all others shall seem tame."

"Consider the cost to yourself," Hramullo continued, still ignoring him, "if you had to endure the months of travel, through dangerous places, on unfriendly roads – to seek out the greatest craftsmen of all the lands. What would it cost, then, for this box? For this dagger? If you take the price at first, then add the cost of the journey, and the unmeasured dangers to your life?"

Selvorne could not help being entranced by his speech, despite his attempts to tease Hramullo – he found himself agreeing that it would cost a great deal to journey far, to find such items, although he was beginning to be more interested in the dangerous travels than in anything for sale. Of all the lands – is that what the little man had said?

"Here, I see you have a good eye for this spear. Feel how light and fast it is – but sturdy, strong," Hramullo said, then he handed it to Selvorne for a moment – and just as quickly snatched it back. Selvorne felt a pain of loss – and gasped as Hramullo bashed it against the side of the waggon. The goat jumped up and let out a bleat, then started pulling at its harness until he settled it down with a single snap of his fingers. Selvorne stared at the spear, greatly distressed it had almost been broken – but it was unhurt.

"The tip is hardened bronze, it will not bend, it will not rust – it is polished to a finish like a mirror, and will clean away the smell of fish, to shine like new."

Hramullo pointed the spearhead so it was close to Selvorne's face, and as he stared at it he agreed it had not a scratch upon it. When it was removed, he wondered how he had let a strange man put such a deadly thing so near his throat.

"The wood is Osgevoud from the land of the magnificent Osge, far to the east – feel how smooth – the pores are closed, and so this wood will not take water, neither swell nor stain, and if it scratches – unlikely – you can polish it smooth once more, and it will be the same as new."

Selvorne's eyes were wide as he examined the wood – it was true, the pores were closed. Better than oak – better than ash. Such a thing would be a pleasure to hold, and he wanted it back in his hand.

"The end has a small loop to attach a fine rope, this means you will never lose the spear in deep waters – dropped, thrown, or if a fish proves too strong, and swims away with your spear. Such a great fish you will pull back by rope, and all will be amazed at your catch. Also, it allows you to hang the spear on a wall, allowing it to drip itself dry, or merely leave it by the door to impress visitors, or be at the ready, if an enemy arrives."

Selvorne was astonished at all that was said – not only of the spear, but of lands and people and woods he did not know. A young man spoke beside him, and Selvorne almost jumped in surprise.

"Move it along Hramullo, this poor fellow might fall asleep, and you have not even begun with the best bit of it yet."

A boisterous fellow – how long had he been there, Selvorne was not sure. He seemed young, similar in height and build to Selvorne, with light brown, shoulder length hair. Neatly groomed and simply dressed, he wore a few delicate ornaments such as rings, bracelets, and a necklace of fine silver – he had some wealth, but more modesty. He was a handsome and happy young fellow, his fine appearance spoilt only by the strange arrangement of several tiny, coloured hats upon his head, all pinned at odd angles. Selvorne counted four, but suspected six, and though unusual to have so many, he had to admit they were almost like one great colourful hat, rather than six tiny ones, and so were quite stylish. He had a glint in his eye, suggesting he was teasing Hramullo – fond of him, but also fond of mischief.

"Show him how it comes apart!" the young man said, and Selvorne frowned.

Comes apart – that did not sound too good. The last thing he wanted was a spear that came apart, he had enough trouble keeping them together as it was, but – to his amazement – Hramullo began to unscrew the spear in the middle, dismantling it to three sections of short staves, and the bronze, double–pronged head came free. He then lifted up a wooden case from inside the waggon, opened it, and removed another two sections of spear, and two different spearheads – one was straight and sharp, the other was shorter, with a guard to stop the point piercing too far. Both of those ends Selvorne noted were steel, not bronze, and he began to appreciate the spear was far more than it had seemed.

"With this spear, you get not only one for fishing, but one for birds, and even small boar. You can make it longer, and throw it, or stab with it, or shorter, and cut with it like a long knife, which is excellent for carving. Indeed, two–handed carving of logs, if that is your desire. If you use the blunt end instead of the spearhead, you can use it as a walking staff, and it will serve you well into your great years, though I doubt one strong like you shall limp, but may look most eloquent taking strides with a fine staff. Another thing, more useful now, should you camp the night – you may hang a lantern from the eyelet at one end. The shaft is wood – for decoration, and feel – but the core is the greatest steel, and will not break. Like a – do they have them here?" he asked, and the other man nodded, "Like a pencil. The trim in bronze to never rust, and the whole spear may be taken apart as I have shown, placed in this box, that comes with it, no added charge, and can be thus carried conveniently to either the woods or lake, in your hand, or on the side of a goat, or as some might do, hidden by straps underneath a waggon, away from the eyes of thieves."

Selvorne was completely astounded by the sophistication of the spear – the likes of which he had never seen – and the elegance of which he had not only never seen in a spear, but not in any thing of any kind. He reached for his purse to purchase it, and as he did, realised he had not asked the price.

"And the price?"

"For such an elegant item, what price would you think fair?" Hramullo began, "Considering how far we travelled to bring you this, it has come all the way from the land of – "

"Three gold coins," the teasing youth said, "expensive, or a bargain, depending on your wealth."

Selvorne was stunned. That was ... quite a lot. And although he had the coins, it was more than he had ever spent on anything – or seen anyone spend, on any one thing. He had seen more coins change hands when his father sold the barrels of wine, but that was very different, and those buying the wine were many men with the aim to sell to many more, one cup at a time. The spear was a single item, Selvorne was one man alone, and his heart began to sink.

The youth pushed his way between them, and looked to each in turn.

"Come along then, Hramullo, he is not going to pay that much for it without having a go first," the youth said, and he reached over, snatched the spear staves, and quickly began to assemble it to its maximum length. Before Hramullo could argue, the youth had gathered the spare pieces into a sack. Then he unpinned three of his tiny hats, handed them to Hramullo – who looked repulsed – at which the youth shook his finger at him.

"Come along!" he said as he dragged Selvorne away from the stall to a quieter place in the woods. He still had three hats on his head, which, if anything, looked more absurd than six.

It was easy to find a clearing since the town had felled many of the nearest trees, leaving the grounds to meadow with small saplings rising up. The youth introduced himself as Ulfwyd, a name he felt the need to spell as well, for it was to be pronounced Ulff–widd, and not as it was spelt. An odd thing to feel the need to make it clear, Selvorne thought, firstly because it sounded exactly like the way Ulfwyd pronounced it, and secondly because, even if they saw it written, few people could read. Selvorne looked carefully at the man's clothes, wondering if his name was written somewhere, and Ulfwyd watched him, smiling.

A smile was returned, that was sincere. It broadened – that was usual, when meeting someone pleasant. Warmth, friendship, fun – warnings, enemies, danger. Others were near, none near enough to help, and the stranger before him was armed, and deadly – yet casual, and friendly. Ulfwyd's eyes narrowed – there it was, a sign of danger – no it was not, for Selvorne's stare had grown wary first. Six hats he had before, one of them was green – about the right height as an enemy he had seen. Clothes were wrong. Clothes could change. His stance was wrong – most everything seemed wrong, for Ulfwyd to have been one of the men at the camp. He could not have been there, he simply did not seem ... the right kind of man. Dangerous, the way he held the spear, and he was only holding it as if about to drop it to the ground, not strike with it – and he could end Selvorne in moments, there away from the crowd. Instead, he laughed. Selvorne had to smile again, but he was a little more wary than at first. Of two things he was certain –

that Ulfwyd, if he wanted him dead, had not recognised him – and that if he did, Selvorne would be dead, for Ulfwyd was deadly.

Nevertheless, he was a friendly fellow, and he explained that though he was not the owner of the spear, he was responsible for it. He encouraged Selvorne to swing it and throw it, and on seeing how badly he threw it, encouraged him to find time to learn. But for Selvorne's handling of it, he had some praise – especially his fishing skill of stabbing it down with fast and accurate strikes. Selvorne impressed him by thrusting the point to the dirt between two stones, placed barely a spear's width apart, and he felt pride to be so skilled. Until Ulfwyd did the same, easily, thrusting the blade between the stones, several times in a row. Selvorne shrugged and guessed he was good, but not great, despite his years of spearing apples from the trees. At least his strike had been powerful, Ulfwyd seemed to have only flicked the dirt between rocks – but in staring, Selvorne thought that the stones had changed position, the dark one moved to where the light one had been, and the reverse. He blinked several times, then shrugged – it could not have been.

It certainly was a fine spear, and Selvorne reasoned that if it lasted a long time it would be worth the cost – well treated, he could leave it for those who followed him – his sons, perhaps theirs. If he did not break it, something he had a habit of doing. Ulfwyd assured him it would withstand most use, in fact that he had been practising with it for many months, causing Hramullo great angst – and it had taken no damage, even thrown by accident into stones.

After some time, Selvorne said he would think about it, which seemed to cause Ulfwyd some confusion, as if he thought the purchase had already been made. Returning to the stall, Hramullo said it was a terribly cruel torture, to lead a vendor along like that, who had hoped to feed his wife, and children, and theirs with the sale, only to learn they would suffer and starve for the night. Ulfwyd said not to mind him, he was doing very well indeed, and clearly was not starving. Besides, being so far away, he could not possibly feed wife or family, and likely would use the profits to buy more stock to sell.

Hramullo then tried to convince Selvorne it would be sold to another as he thought about it, but Selvorne was so confused by the two of them he hardly heard anything that was said – the sale would be made in his own mind, and the arguments for and against it there were too loud to hear much else. Ulfwyd assured him it would not be sold, having been held already so long, why would they sell it at the last. If another came to buy it, he promised he would search the festival for Selvorne – Hramullo seemed pleased to hear that, perhaps thinking rival bids might increase the price, though ... something seemed quite odd to Selvorne as he packed the spear away. Ulfwyd whispered to him that another had already shown an interest in it that morning, and another for his son, but it would continue to be held until he was certain, he owed that to him at least. It was just the sort of thing a merchant might say to make a sale, yet he seemed sincere. More than sincere – loyal. He also seemed to wait for an answer, but the only answer

Selvorne could give was gratitude and farewell. As he left the stall, he could not help think that it was all very, very odd.

~

Selvorne spent much of the day wandering the festival, almost aimless. Nothing took his fancy as much as the spear, everything else seemed ordinary and of no use. True, he had little use for anything – clothes perhaps, boots certainly, but his strong quarry pair were still good. He was never a boy who wanted for much, just to do his work and fish the lake near his home, and as a young man he wanted little more. His house itself was good, well fitted with furnishings, and ... it made him sad to think of it without his father, so he turned his attention back to the festival.

Arnlausa's house – was that, then, his? It was a Great House, or so such large houses of lords were titled, usually for their fathers before. The Great House of Laehtene, home to Arnlausa, Lord of Tavalehk. Or Arnlausa's house, as he preferred it to be called. Square in shape, on the hill away from most of the town, at the south western corner. The river was near, and there was a small spring to supply the house, which was much better than fetching water up and down the hill. Inside were more furnishings and things than Selvorne could imagine – no, he did not need anything more. Clothes – yes, to look the part of lord, the last thing he needed to do when people were searching for him. He needed boots, but to fit them would take much time, and his would last some while longer. What he truly needed could not be bought at market stalls. He needed men, and information.

Guards – they were at the festival. Waehdric too, and administrators. Should he approach them ... no, he decided to wait until their speech, when they would request men to join. He was told to trust Cienn, no others. Not the guards, not even Temnere, even if he was the head administrator. No, he could do nothing, and searching – asking for Cienn – might sound suspicious. If she was there, she would appear. Perhaps give that speech, to encourage men to join the guards.

The spear – he wanted it. He had the coins, and for such a purchase coins were needed, not square bits. No man would accept hundreds of bits. Thousands, actually. Selvorne was not sure anyone could carry so many, not without a large box or small cart. But would he need his coins for other things? Would Vaskatohr have trouble that year? With the broken bridge, they had lost all the barrels and many of the stones – and the bridge itself, that would be costly to replace. Perhaps that year he would have to buy sacks of flour for bread, paid for by himself – for they did not harvest their own grain at Vaskatohr, and without bread for the townsfolk, he would not be much of a lord. There were many pigs, so the town was not poor, but pigs could all die at once from illness, should one come, and then what would the miners eat?

For the first time he found himself worrying about things that usually were little concern, and he realised why Girradehn had accused him of being a careless boy, not a man, and certainly not a lord. Coins to keep for Vaskatohr, and then ... he realised, the few coins he had in his purse were nothing compared to the wealth of

Tavalehk. The small town of Vaskatohr could lose all its pigs to illness or woods, spoil all the grain, burn the houses down and flood the mine, and in half a year he would have it all back again, better and stronger and proof against disaster. Pigs bred, grain stocked, mines drained – he even knew how to do that, and floods would only bring delays, not ruin. Suffering of only a single day, should all things happen at once, the people could walk to Tavalehk. And, if needed, sleep in the House of Laehtene.

The spear, then, was something he could buy. But ... if he was to join the guards, would he need his own spear – or would one be provided? Would the other guards laugh at him for having such a ... not flimsy, it was strong, but it looked quite delicate. Lady Spear – that would be what Girradehn would have called him. But ... fishing was a good way to eat, and ... he would use it after being a guard, at his home, or perhaps in that very lake at Tavalehk. The Fishing Lord.

He walked past the place where his father used to sell the quarry stones. Merchants, who bought them all, then took them north to Senylehk. No stones for them that year, and they were not in a pleasant mood. He usually would not speak with them – that business was done by his father on his behalf – but he was sure they would recognise him, so he quickly moved away.

Wine merchants at their stall – no wine, though, and many buyers who were not happy to be stalled. The sellers were good men, not merchants of wine, not usually. Friends of Arnlausa who held the stall on his behalf, both buying and selling at a good price. They had no stores of their own, they kept no supply of wine, and with the absence of Arnlausa, their stall was only stocked with ale. Elderly men, with little other trade or craft, who likely needed the profits. They would be sorely disappointed that year. Selvorne wondered if he took over the town, if he would somehow be obliged to continue the tradition of bringing wine for them to sell. He felt sorry for them, even though they seemed quite cranky in turning customers away – each demanding a taste of exotic wine, and receiving instead only bad Tavalehk ale. One seller seemed especially angry, at the customers and at Arnlausa – Selvorne knew him, and Pachure was his name. A rounded man, of short breath and brief temper that came in shouts between gasping pants. Selvorne thought he might be recognised, so he watched and listened, but hid his face by keeping his head turned.

Rumours were being told that Arnlausa would miss the festival that year, but Selvorne doubted such rumours were based on any fact. The same rumours spread every year about their Lord Arnlausa And Later – even when he was already at the festival. Wagers were made, odds were being thrown, Selvorne was sure of it – wagers and rumours. He did not think people would be concerned for Arnlausa until weeks after the festival had ended. If anything, the town would be excited that he would come back late, bringing plenty of wine that they could enjoy cheaply, for many months after the crowds had left. And if sensible, those who usually sold the wine would have been wise to make a small wager that Arnlausa would be late – their profits lost would be gained again from winnings.

They seemed rather upset, though, so perhaps they did not place wagers that year. Or they did, but the amount was too small – or too large, and wrongly placed – they were growing desperate, even though it was the early days of the festival.

The tall, dark–haired youth Selvorne had met was there – Rohy, and he was one of the customers. Selvorne was near enough to hear him ask for a cup of wine, but instead he received a cup of ale. At first he was overjoyed at the cheaper price, and paid eagerly – but then spat it out and cursed with the first taste, before arguing with the vendors, and being shoved away from the stall. Selvorne followed, and the two met where there was no crowd.

"Would you like to buy some ale? It is quite good, only one bit?" Rohy asked as he offered the cup to Selvorne, who refused it, though he was thirsty.

"No, thank you, I have my own already," Selvorne replied, and at that, he let his bag fall from his shoulder, then took out his elegant ale bladder – some of the fine ale was remaining, and he took a good swig.

Rohy's eyes widened at the sight of the bladder.

"That is one of the finest I have seen, where did you get it?"

Selvorne suddenly realised the stupidity of taking out that bladder – and quickly made up a story of it being a gift from his father years ago, bought at that very festival. After Rohy had a look at it, Selvorne put it back into his bag.

"I like to protect it from the sun, and the prying eyes of thieves," Selvorne explained, and Rohy nodded.

Rohy tried to finish his ale, the taste was not improving even as the effects took hold. Tavalehk was not known for its ale. Or, more accurately, was well known for its bad ale – but it did not stop people trying their luck, hoping in vain that somehow the brewers had done well, for once. The town was known for its wine, though none in the town knew how it was made or what grain it was from – those who made it kept it all very secret. Selvorne once heard it came from raisins, explained to be dried grapes, and so he and many others thought wine was from raisins – not that it made any difference, since no one knew what raisins were, nor grapes. But many who believed they did, tried all kinds of fruit and grains to make it – they failed. And so the few wine merchants who could produce the fine red ale known as wine – they enjoyed good profits, and complete control. As did Arnlausa, who made none, but brought much up from the south. Quietly, so others would not try to do the same. Though everyone knew he did, very few others tried, and none of them could pass Vaskatohr in waggons without it being known, reported, and then a toll charged that made the lord laugh. The whole business seemed unnecessarily secretive, and the prices were annoyingly high – for those who wished to drink – but many others lamented that supplies were never as great, not as they were, long ago.

That year supplies were nothing, and the drink was ale. Rohy, who said he was not particularly fond of either, complained for the lack of wine. Mead was there for all to buy – made of honey, for any who could afford it. Very few could, fewer still to drink it in festive amounts, so it hardly mattered. Other brews also, worse than the ale, made of all manner of things, including grass, and Selvorne thought it would be a very sober festival that year, until he remembered the tavern to the north.

"I know a place that should have wine," Selvorne said.

Rohy's eyes widened as Selvorne began to describe an inn, converted from a barn, to the very north of the town that had a large, open space inside, many tables, and an old grain store under the ground that they had cleaned before filling with barrels of wine. Kept there, especially for such times – when there was a shortage in the town. At festivals. To supply the hundreds who desired to drink. Then, they could demand the most terrible prices, something that made Rohy uneasy, but Selvorne assured him it would be not be so bad as it sounded.

The most northern part of town – the last place travellers would stop when leaving, or the first on arrival – on a slight hill, looking down upon both town and lake. Like the House of Arnlausa, it had its own trickling spring, and the waters were collected in barrels and sold as a healing drink. It did not likely work, unless they meant to heal men of being sober, for the barrels filled with water of the spring once contained wine, and Selvorne was sure they put a little in for added measure – to give customers a taste for it, moments before offering it pure, and praising the healing powers of wine.

The inn was expensive, perhaps justified for being so fine. Well appointed, despite having once been a barn, in some rooms the decorations were done with no fear for the cost. Even glass was used for the cups in the common hall, at quiet times when no one would smash them – rarely during the festival. It was in no way an inexpensive place, so it was no wonder that Rohy had not been there, for he did not seem a youth with coins in abundance. Prices would be excessive that day, when there was a shortage of wine in the town – it would be costly to drink at The Winer's Inn. A strange name – perhaps the owners thought it read much like The Winner's Inn, as it was written over the door. Certainly they must have felt they were winning, to make such a fortune, but they had overlooked the way it sounded. The Whiner's Inn was what folk called it, for those who whined about the price of wine, and the owners who whined that customers were not always happy to pay. Still paying, just not overly happy about it.

Selvorne cared nothing for wine, or whiners or winnings or wagers, not for ale and not for all the noise of a tavern – he had another reason to go there, but as he thought on it, and when he mentioned the name of the inn, Rohy's eyes lit up at once to distraction.

"Aha! Yes! Yes, I am headed there tonight! The Winer's Inn!" Rohy said, overly eager, and quite loudly – Selvorne thought the ale was either very bad or rather strong to have made Rohy so suddenly excited, "Demni will be there, oh yes – I am happy for that – let us go!"

"Who?" Selvorne asked.

"Demni, the lady I saw in the markets – the elegant one."

"Was that a lady? I thought it was a handsome lad in a dress?" Selvorne asked boldly, which was ... not quite unusual for him, though a little more mischief than he would expect of himself. He hardly knew Rohy, he knew the lady not at all, and yet had insulted them both – perhaps, after throwing the spear for so long, Ulfwyd's mischief and many jests had worn off onto him, for it was not quite like the Curse of Arnlausa.

Rohy was stern for a moment, frowning down at Selvorne, but seemed to decide he was joking – perhaps the kind of jest that meant the opposite, that Selvorne thought Demni was quite a beauty.

"Demni Nohc Seseasel, that is her," Rohy said, "and I saw her first. And I did, in fact, speak to her, though she was called away to business. She was quite noble in her manner, and short on time, but she told me she was headed to The Winer's Inn to hear someone sing. It is not cheap ... I have learnt that since, for to hear the singer, there is a fee. However, she will be in the town tomorrow night, for all to hear, for free. But tonight I plan to meet with her and speak with her for longer, alone, and then, perhaps, longer still."

"The singer?"

"No – the noble Demni," Rohy replied, frowning.

Selvorne had half seen that conversation with Demni, and from his observation, she did not seem very interested in Rohy. He assumed that perhaps Rohy was blinded by his adoration, and decided he should go along to ensure his new friend did not make a fool of himself. Or if he did, was amusing about it, made the lady laugh, and then was not too hurt. The significance of Demni's title was not lost on Selvorne, nor the fact that she seemed to know Temnere and be under his command. She might be someone worthwhile to speak with, especially if she had a little wine to loosen her tongue, and knew more of the plans against brigands that had been mentioned.

Rohy seemed to notice Selvorne's new eagerness, and narrowed his eyes – and Selvorne laughed at the signs of jealousy, for a lady he hardly knew, so he frowned sternly back at Rohy. In jest, to tease, but only for a few moments as the mischief in that gave way to the sincere joy for his new friend. So happy he might find love, the world seemed delightful, everything bright, his mood cheerful, despite his dark clothes and stern frown. His eyes were gleaming, and a smile came soon to them both. It cheered Selvorne immensely to think of anything other than murder, vengeance, and the tallies of accounts.

"It is settled, then," Selvorne said, "we shall both go to this Winer's Inn and enjoy a night of singing, and perhaps learn more of this Demni. And who knows, find love – a little wine and a crowded room, the best manners, and ... I think you should smile more, Rohy, but – no – not like that, very well, just your eyes, unless you mean to scare her – no, that is a frown. Very well, I shall teach you, and Demni will have no chance to avert her eyes from the mystery of a solemn face with smiling eyes."

Selvorne laughed to see the odd face Rohy made, how he made it, he could not guess. A frown, a smile, a grin – a snarl? All at once, through confusion and ale. Passionate delight – yes, and terrible nerves. Selvorne was a new friend to help him – with the costs, by coin, and for his nerves – by firm encouragement. It would be a memorable night for them both.

Lady of Old

It was already late afternoon as they approached The Winer's Inn, Selvorne did not remember it being so far away from the town, indeed it was at the end of the main street, which was over a mile long, and he started to regret that they were leaving the greater festival behind, with all its nighttime merriment. Dances, music, games, and a great gathering of laughing folk – some they passed, rushing the other way. A few more in costumes, dressed as animals or trees. A show? It could have been a themed dance, people in disguise, or a parade – such was the variety of entertainment, often not told in advance. Selvorne was not sure what it was that people hurried to, and it was not long before the road was quiet and the only people near were headed their way, or already gathered at the inn at the top of the hill. A good crowd, and Selvorne eased to think that the singing was at least popular, so it must be good. Asking those headed towards it, nobody knew what time the singing would begin, and Selvorne was sure that was deliberate, to make people arrive early, and hopefully, sell them much food and wine before the entertainment would start, end, then crowds leave.

As they left the main road and climbed up the hill, Selvorne's heart gave a good thump in his chest – hard, and strong, and unexpected, for it had been two years since he had last been there. It was strangely exciting. Not as before, and though he thought he might feel something, he did not expect to tingle as well.

The Winer's Inn was owned and run by a very old man with a young daughter – a lovely daughter, warm and friendly, pretty and ... Cassini. Selvorne's Cassini, his childish betrothed – Cassini Cassub. His heart pounded hard to think of her name. Many, many years ago, they were friends. Not so many years ago – captivated. He was just a young boy, and pledged his adoration of her, and she ... laughed. Again, two years ago – an older boy, old enough to be considered a youth, and bold enough to think himself a man. More serious, so solemn – so taken by her maidenly charms. He was harshly teased, both by her and Arnlausa. Then one year ago – he was still angry and did not visit her, not at the festival and not during the year, indeed ... not for two years, since he learnt what was thought to be tease was taunt.

Had it been the wine, too strong for a youth, or was it her smile, her eyes, or the warmth of her ways? Selvorne could not recall what captivated him, or he could, but it was mixed with pain. Looks she gave, so alluring – once rejected, he thought they were given in jest. Her warmth was false, not lovely – done in mocking, done to hurt. No, he did not believe that, even when he was truly hurt. Cassini was kind, not cruel – and she simply was not interested in Selvorne. He knew that, and was not sure it hurt less.

It was her age, he thought, or his lack of age that made her laugh. They were friends, he believed that even for the years he was angry – and he had promised Arnlausa – what had he promised? To look after her? Selvorne's heart pounded as he walked, as he thought – not only of her lovely, smiling eyes, but her closeness to him, her friendly warmth, and her love of Arnlausa. Almost family. And he had no family. And he was almost there, at the inn – and he needed a well–planned lie to meet someone so familiar and so close.

At the inn, Selvorne would have liked to stay outside for as long as he could to think, but Rohy, once he determined that Demni was not outside, wanted to go in. There was a payment to enter, and once paid, if a man left then tried to return – the same payment again. Also, they would not allow any baggage inside, nor any weapon larger than a small cutting knife, which was less for safety and fear of fighting than it was to stop people knocking things over with sticks, or spears, or long knives – or even, once, a farmer had bought a new rake at the festival, and would not leave it outside. Bringing it in, he knocked over a large wooden jug of someone's wine, and started a brawl. Selvorne and Rohy left their things where they would be safely watched, paid their fee and entered, free of all they carried, and Selvorne with no lie.

Inside was not pleasant. It would have been lovely, if half the people left, but people were crammed in, would not leave, more were coming and many were forced to stand or share six to a bench where there should only be four. Some sat on tables, as others tried to eat and drink around them. At one end of the room was a railing, and behind it a long table at the height of a man's chest. A table to serve drinks, and a bar to keep men back from it at safe distance and good order. At the other end of the room there was a small raised stage, with one tall, broad man keeping people off it – which did not please the crowd being crushed, but none dared challenge him, despite his friendly smile.

The mood was mostly good, for the people there had resigned themselves to the absurd expense and crammed conditions – and they were drunk, on wine, happy and going to enjoy the show whatever they had to endure. Some, especially the wealthy and spoiled, had come expecting their coin could buy them comforts and consideration, and perhaps privacy. Not so at The Winer's Inn – it could only purchase disappointment. Even that melted with more wine, which could be bought, and was known to be very good.

Rohy disappeared soon to buy some wine, and after a while returned with a small, single wooden mug of it, and lamented that Demni was not yet there. Selvorne looked at him in disbelief, then looked at the tankard.

"Where is my wine?" Selvorne demanded. Rohy looked dumbfounded. Selvorne shook his head before pushing his way through to the bar and serving table.

It was unusual to serve from one table at the end of a tavern, let alone from behind a bar which forced people into a line. More usually a maid would bring drinks to the tables where men sat. But The Winer's Inn was busy, and some sort of order was required to keep the patrons under control. The layout of the room did not help. A converted barn for oxen, well located to the north of the town, but since replaced by bigger barns that might hold more beasts. In the main area for customers, they had knocked down the dividing walls of the stalls to make a great open space. In the back of the barn the stalls remained, and it was an area for storage and kitchens, and also a retreat for those who worked there, allowing them to breathe and have space to move before pushing their way back into the crowds. Unusually for an inn, they also served drinks in glass, if people were willing to pay, otherwise all had to make do with wooden tankards or clay jugs. Never cups of leather and tar, for it spoilt the wine. All the glass was locked away that night, safely at the back of the stalls – cups of glass were very expensive, and easily smashed. People swore that it tasted better from glass, though Selvorne suspected it was just a trick to make people pay more for use of the glass cups, and a way for the wealthy to display refined tastes.

Selvorne had a fistful of bits and made his way to the front to be served, and found himself looking into the stunned face of a robust woman who was almost exhausted. Despite that, she was beamingly happy, but her forehead was dotted with sweat, and her thick, curly dark hair was beginning to sag. She had a lovely face, and Selvorne thought she would have been very pretty in her youth.

"A large jug of wine, medium quality, and two of your best vessels, thank you," Selvorne ordered, knowing well that medium quality was ordinary, yet good wine – he wanted that which had not been watered down, as the wine usually was. High quality was very expensive and not much better than the medium. Old wine was the most expensive, and the mystery of why something older would cost more was lost on him. For a few years, long ago, Arnlausa had been tricked in the south to pay more for new wine, the sellers claiming it was better, and he was not at all happy to eventually discover the deceit. Or his anger might have been because he learnt he was being mocked. Arnlausa swore by the difference in taste, once he had both to compare, and ... why was the woman not fetching his drinks?

"Selvorne?" asked the woman, still staring at him in disbelief.

"Ahhh .... Cassini?" Selvorne asked, looking into her eyes – surely that was not Cassini? He remembered her as a young maiden, slightly older than himself – her hair was fair, not dark. Blonde, even, though curly, and ... it was her.

Laughing, she came around from behind the table, kissed him on the cheek, took him by the hand and led him back into the stalls, much to the amusement and cheers of those waiting to be served, who all turned to the next maiden taking orders. At the back of the stalls it was quieter, Cassini led him to a dark room of tables that had been stacked out of the way, where cups of glass were safely arranged in wooden crates, placed carefully against the walls. She closed the door, and it was quiet – she opened a second shutter, and the room grew softly bright. In that warm light of the late sun she stared, and smiled, and looked him slowly up and down.

"Well, you have grown into a fine young man," Cassini said in her sweet, delightful voice, "perhaps I had better hold you to that offer, which you made all those years ago?"

Selvorne could not believe she was the same ... girl ... not quite the same, and he felt foolish for feeling romantic so many years ago. Someone who he thought was a young maiden – but standing there, he realised she was a young woman – once, years ago – she had looked, then, much younger than her years. He had never bothered asking her age. He was embarrassed to guess it as she smiled at him – the teasing, it began to make sense. Two years ... three ... as many as six years ago she had first caught his eye, and then he knew she was older than he, but ... she had never aged. Not in all those years. Many years ago, a boy alone at the tavern of wine – she had likely been told to keep an eye on him, keep him out of trouble – because he was just a child. Regardless, they had fun that day, playing hide and go seek, and other childish games – talking, but of what? Childish things. He was fond of her then, proposed to be wed, at which she laughed – and then, he promptly forgot her, as the months went by and he went back to Vaskatohr.

But years later ... he had returned, he had changed. She had not. He was older, she was the same. No longer a boy, and she – a maiden? Still? Was she to be wed, he had asked – why do you ask, she asked back, lashes fluttering, as was his young heart – teasing. Like Arnlausa, she liked mischief, she liked to tease – as did Arnlausa tease, to hear of it. Relentlessly. Without mercy. She was not wed then, was she ... yet?

"You are not wed, then?" Selvorne asked, and she smiled.

"No. You?"

"I ... am too young," Selvorne said, though he felt an idiot saying it, and wondered if she might take offence – for she was anything but too young to be wed. No insult was taken, and she laughed delightfully, as though it was a joke between them.

"Too young?" she asked, "It seems two years ago you were not, are you, then, ageing backwards?"

"I – no," Selvorne replied, and she smiled.

"No – growing wise, though, no matter. Many years until you are childish again – too young? Half the tavern there is filled with younger men than you, already wed, already preferring wine to wives, who in turn prefer markets to men. And men who have come for the singing lady – have you?"

"I ... yes, but also with a friend," Selvorne said.

"A friend? A ... lady friend?"

"No, a man I met at the festival," Selvorne said, though he was not quite sure whether to call Rohy a boy, a youth, or a man – or himself, for that matter. Not boy, but youth sounded absurd, and man was not quite right. He had never given much thought to any such things, but with Cassini standing before him, taunting – no longer unchanged, but clearly older, and with hair of a different colour – age seemed suddenly to be a very important thing to notice. Perhaps the need to do so was the difference between boys and men. Or maidens, and ... once young women, who tended the tavern.

They talked a little, she had remembered him far more than he would have expected, and he guessed his absurd proposal had stuck in her head. Tending the guests, she had such proposals many times, but "never so eloquently put, nor so sincerely hopeful", and she laughed as she teased to speak of it. She was not so old as she looked, but the recent years were harder on her, she said, since her father aged and was too old to work, and the running of the inn fell to her alone. Rich, young, pretty, and popular in a place of crowds with many travellers, she truly had no shortage of suitors from all around the town, and even distant, northern lands. But, for the same reasons, she had no time nor mind to settle for just anyone who came along. So was unwed, but Selvorne thought she needed a good husband who did not drink, who worked hard and could give her many children. Or if not, then a few stern maidens to tend to the guests and tavern.

Selvorne liked and trusted Cassini, but not enough to tell her what had happened, despite Arnlausa's fondness for her – he instead explained that he wished to remain unnoticed, and was enjoying the festival quietly. He dared to mention there had been trouble with brigands, without elaborating, instead saying there were suspicious men. He described who he was searching for, though the descriptions were not very good and either no persons came to mind, or many did – she promised she would keep an eye out. Cassini was unexpectedly understanding, although he reasoned that in such a tavern, she might be exposed to such intrigues often. Mostly husbands avoiding wives – or men seeking them, either husband or wife. But even brigands in the wild needed to come to the towns to eat and drink, at times, and perhaps meet – and smugglers also, who were merely evading tolls, rather than robbing and killing. No, she was not shocked by the mention of such men, nor afraid for what it might mean.

He did not say his father was dead, only unwell, which was kind of true, though he said he was unwell only mildly and weeks ago – and let her conclude that the two lords were moving slowly from the south. Selvorne said nothing of Arnlausa, though they were at the back of the inn, away from any who could hear. He let her come to her own conclusions, which must have been very far from the truth. The name meant too much to her for Selvorne to hint at anything, and he was glad he said little enough that she did not pry – better left unsaid, and perhaps she was wise enough to realise that. Not only for fear of murder, but for other reasons.

He felt bad. His oaths to Arnlausa were conflicting with his promise, of a sort, to the same man – that he would care for Cassini, but that he would only speak to Cienn. The lord was fond of the tavern maiden, despite being rivals in trade, of a sort, they were quite similar in mood and mirth, enough to make Selvorne even more miserable as he missed his good friend. Cassini would very much want to know if anything had happened to Arnlausa, but could not be told – worse than not saying, Selvorne had to tell a lie. He convinced her that he had left the stragglers behind, going ahead, alone to the festival, not wishing to miss even a day of it, let alone it all. A lie told as briefly as he could, in a way that she would not pry, in a tone that she thought serious, not sorrow. She nodded, knowing what he meant, and not suspecting what he hid.

Cassini was wise, working in a tavern, as was Selvorne, for even if Arnlausa lived and was on his way, what he had told her was almost as deadly – he had hinted at the time of their arrival. Between such friends it was not a danger, but he could only imagine what would happen if he made casual mention of the name Arnlausa. If he announced that Arnlausa was dead – in the middle of an inn, full of drunken townsfolk – if he spoke it plainly, swore what had happened, declaring himself as the new heir – it would be instant suspicion. Conclusion of guilt without evidence, punishment without trial, possibly his half–accidental death, in a tavern brawl with angry drunken men. If he said what had happened – but even to mention his name – to let any man there know he knew anything at all – half the men there likely had wagers on when Arnlausa would arrive, and all the men there were drunk. Say the name, the questioning would begin, and it could not end well, whatever was said. How long before someone recognised him as that boy who was close to the friend of Arnlausa, what was his name, who knows – where is he – how long – what wager should I place? Another fight, or worse.

So he realised in moments as he spoke with a woman he thought he once loved. True, he did, a little, but not in the way he had thought. She made him smile, she was as warm and lovely as ever she was, and he found himself wishing he was several years older. Perhaps ten. No, perhaps more ... he was either blind in his youth or blinded, or she had held her youthful looks far longer than other women, though, he had not known many, and so could not truly judge. So he thought, his mind wandering as she spoke, from beauty to danger to lies and his loss – and then she laughed, and he was sure he was gazing at her in a dream.

A slight laugh and there was no mocking to it. Cassini was considerate for his wishes to have a quiet time at the inn, and she showed fondness for him, and promised a jug of the old wine – but no glass cups, for they would likely be broken, so she gave him their best tankards, made of oak, which were much like drinking straight from the barrel. The supply of wine was not bad that year, not at their inn – though she complained they had to open barrels they had meant to leave ageing, for they were taking record of the taste and age, and trying to determine what was best, and would have to start again with a fresh supply. Selvorne said they should grow twice as much wine for such a test, but his suggestion only made Cassini frown awkwardly for a few moments. She surprisingly kissed him on the forehead, as she might do to a child, and prepared his drink.

~

Selvorne returned with the large jug and two great tankards dangling from his fingers, and found Rohy was nervously nursing his empty wooden cup. Demni had arrived and was at the back of the room, as far as possible from the serving table and close to the stage, in what was perhaps the quietest part of the hall. The tall, well–groomed guard was with her, he who had leapt out of the hair cutter's tent. He was paying her little attention, watching the crowd and grinning proudly as he showed his new cut of hair by means of posing whenever women were near. If possible, he was even more pleased with himself than before, and more elegantly dressed. He did not fail to catch the subtle eye of many women, who no doubt felt intimidated by the stern presence of Demni at his side. But they glanced at him, nonetheless, whenever he was not watching, as was the way of women, or so Selvorne had heard.

Rohy had found a high table at which to stand, and whether it was his glum mood or pointy elbows sticking out to the sides that kept others away, he sat alone. He stared into his empty cup and would not look up – or down, as Selvorne determined when he stood beside him. His eyes seemed to be staring into nothing, and his long fingers tapped at the sides of the cup, as though it were a flute of sorts that he meant to play, but had forgotten how. Selvorne frowned – shook his head at his hopeless friend, but was glad for the table, and set the tankards down before filling one to the half and one to the brim. He pushed the half full one to Rohy, who looked at it, clearly disappointed.

"Half empty?"

Selvorne raised the large jug, grinning.

"Mostly full!"

At that, Rohy grinned, and they both took a large gulping drink of the wine.

It was very good. Never having the old wine before, Selvorne realised why it had the greater price. Rohy was also surprised, and thankful, wondering what it was, and when he found out, swore he would never touch the cheaper new wine again. They finished their first tankards before realising how strong it was, and worry grew with the first slurring of their words – stronger than ale, they both agreed, and more than twice as strong as the watered wine, which perhaps was more than half water – they had unwittingly both drunk more than they had planned.

The crowd of the room, though crammed in, became tolerable – even amusing, once they were slightly drunk. They began to wish they had a seat, but were glad for the table, which kept their drinks and themselves off the floor. Wine without food, but no room to eat easily. More wine – not wise. Or did it make a man wise? Wise in eyes? No, wide of eyes, wise of tongue, Selvorne argued.

"You have it wrong," Rohy insisted.

"I – yes, I remember," Selvorne slurred, then he gathered his thoughts and took a deep breath, "Wide of eyes, wise in mind – not by morning, most will find. Fists are thrown, for what is said – the drunk lie down, in any bed."

Rohy spluttered as he laughed, and Selvorne felt proud of his perfect rendition.

"That is nort it," Rohy slurred, "kisses thrown for what is said."

"Kisses? How is that a fight?"

Rohy grunted, then almost laughed – he leant over to whisper.

"It is nort arbout fight," Rohy said, then, shaking his head, he turned to look where Demni was standing, "for luck!" Rohy said, then he began to fill his tankard again, but changed his mind – putting it down clumsily, he picked up Selvorne's tankard and filled it from the jug. When finished, Selvorne reached for his tankard, expecting it to be handed to him, but Rohy put the jug down instead, picked up his own tankard, then began to leave the table with both.

"What are you doing?" Selvorne asked.

"Taking are drink to Demni, she has nort one, and I thinks she might like it," Rohy replied.

Then, pausing for a moment, realised he was taking Selvorne's tankard.

"If that is all right with you, here, use my cup," Rohy said, nodding to the first cup that he had used. It was near their table, still sitting on the shallow wall–railing table, where it had been left to be collected.

Selvorne was slightly annoyed, though looking in the jug, it was still rather full, and he thought if he drank much more he might collapse on the floor – or in any bed – so he let Rohy go and allowed his wits to return. He watched Rohy cross the room and hoped that Demni was not as sober as she seemed.

The guard with Demni was busy flirting with Cassini, at least Selvorne thought he was, for he flitted his hair as he spoke and she seemed at once flattered and annoyed, for she was carrying many empty jugs and tankards, and likely was keen to take them away and put them all down. Perhaps she acted flattered, and nothing more – few men there were bothering her except for wine, and she truly needed more help. Why she had so few was a mystery, it was her inn to run, and she was far from too poor to hire more maidens. Perhaps none would come to work, instead preferring the festival in the town. No matter, she knew her business, and Selvorne had to watch for his friend.

Rohy, once nervous, walked straight to Demni, greeted her, offered her the tankard and stood there holding it as she glared back at him. Selvorne could not hear what she said, but it did not seem to go well. Those nearest burst into laughter – not at Rohy, though he must have thought it was for him – but for some poor fool who had been nudged off the end of a bench onto the floor. It was obvious Demni did not want the wine or the company, and Rohy continued to stand there, looking foolish. Her guard turned around, spoke a few words to Rohy, stern at first, but then took the tankard himself, clinked it with Rohy's and took a big swig of it. Then he was all happiness and cheer, though Demni seemed to have a disapproving look as she excused herself to leave. Instead of leaving, she stepped out and around Rohy, only a few paces before she stood with her back to him, facing the stage.

There could be no clearer sign of disinterest than that – she had almost danced around Rohy, and were it a dance, it was not done for love. Delightful steps of teasing mischief, had she then turned back to look at him, tossing her hair and laughing – no, she did not, she stared at the empty stage. The cold, harsh rejection of – dare he think it – he was not sure why he did, but it seemed as though Rohy faced a judge, at trial, the punishment to be death, and the one lady who could have spared him merely turned from him and left. As seen in a play, as seen – Selvorne was sure he had seen the same before, somewhere, and whether Rohy had seen the same performance, or realised what she had done – he must have felt terrible.

The guard, however, was most cheerful, as any man would be to be given such wine. It was not long before he was beckoning Selvorne to join them, and motioning as if to fill his tankard with more wine from an imaginary jug. Such a jug was on the table before Selvorne – annoyed, and a bit dazed, he shook his head clear, then remembered that he had planned to speak with just such people as themselves – high guards, administrators, nobles. Such powerful people, when drunk, might say more of brigands and plans for a sweeping march of the guards – and Selvorne might discover if Cienn was there at the festival, perhaps – so he picked up the jug, and the cup, and stumbled his way across the room. It was only moments before his table was taken, and there was no going back.

The name of her guard was Savak, and the wine made him an immediate friend. He was the same guard who had recommended the hair cutter to Selvorne, and he noticed immediately Selvorne's fresh style, and was pleased to have been of some service. He was also rather quick to reason that the wine was payment for his recommendation, well earned and for it, Selvorne was not in the least bit owed.

"Demni never drinks," Savak said, speaking well for a guard who seemed to drink for them both, "never, ever, ever, never, not a drop, never. And that is why she is so hard."

Apparently she was not hard of hearing though, for she turned around and glared at him, to which he gave a slight drunken bow before she turned her back once more.

"And she will not drink out of wooden mugs," Savak said, "for she is fussy. And she would rather stand there sweating in the heat, and blaming the crowd, than see sense in it or lose her position."

Savak spoke well enough, but seemed a little too drunk to speak with on important matters, or indeed, on trivial matters, for he made little sense. Demni was sober, and Selvorne had an idea, so he dashed off at once to the serving table. Cassini smiled at him, though was astonished he had finished all the wine. With a quick word between them, she sent him to the back rooms, from where he returned with a large clay vessel filled with fresh spring water. He showed Cassini, she nodded whilst continuing to serve others, and Selvorne rejoined his friends – but stepped in front of Demni.

At first she raised her nose at him, but he quickly began to speak.

"Selvorne, at your service, with a clay cup of sweet spring water," Selvorne said, as best he could, considering he was having a little trouble walking properly, and he might have slurred his words a little. She took the drink and was thankful for it. And if she was even a little well mannered, she would be obliged to make some conversation – for a while, at least, for he had presented himself not as a worker in the tavern, but as an equal.

"Demni Nohc Seseasil," she began, slightly emphasising the Nohc, and he knew well enough that implied he was not entirely considered her equal, "thank you for your kindness. Have you come here for the wine, the women, or the song? For either, you have come to the right place, although if it is women you are after, you are facing the wrong way."

Selvorne stared and blinked – she had said only three things to him, and asked one question, and already he wished himself far, far away. A rasping voice, and a gruff tone. Insulting, as well. He wondered what Rohy saw in her, she was handsome, he guessed – a plain, long face – striking dark eyes, if a little small for his liking. There was no kindness in her eyes, nor humour in her gaze, nor gratitude, he thought, despite her words of thanks for the water. She was tall – taller than him, and very slender, almost snakelike, for he could not determine where her waist ended and hips began in her dress, which seemed to simply hang from her shoulders – exposing her arms, which were more like those of a strong boy, than a slender young lady. Long fingers, but with short nails, practical rather than vain. Her hair might have been long, but it was forced back into braids that sat tightly on her head. Selvorne believed that it would only take a small beard and she would look like a young man. Handsome, slender – but not a woman. Not to his liking, not even in looks.

He finished examining her, and when his eyes met hers once more, he realised he had taken quite some time, and she had been watching all the while. He remembered her question, and thought he had better say something polite before he said something insulting.

"I am here for my friend, though the wine is good, I rarely drink. And the women seem friendly, and not as rowdy nor drunk as these men. I should like to hear a song, but I know nothing of the singer. The best part of my night so far, I would say, would be the honour of meeting a noble administrator. Earlier today I met and spoke with Temnere, who was most friendly and kind."

With that she looked almost horrified – even afraid – nodding quickly, she turned away from Selvorne, but found herself facing Savak and Rohy. Clearly she did not wish to speak with them either, so she stared across the noisy room, almost facing Selvorne, almost politely, but with no sense of an invitation to talk.

He tried to read her responses, but found her very difficult. She had seemed bored at first, then a bit relieved. Her eyes seemed to light up briefly when he mentioned the singer, but then turned dark and narrow when he spoke of Temnere. He was her superior, and likely a cause for distress. She did not drink, she did not wish to speak – she was there for the singer, and nothing else.

As much as Selvorne wanted to learn what was going on with the guards and their sweep of the forests, he was not going to waste the night by talking to a drunken guard who likely would collapse, or struggle to speak with a woman who seemed about as pleasant as cutting fingernails with a broken rock.

"Tell me about the singer, if you know anything, if you would?" Selvorne asked, and his guess was right, for her face changed immediately. That was why she was there, and what she was interested in – if he could not get information out of her, or friendship, then at least he would make an acquaintance that was slightly agreeable.

"Ah, the singer, you know nothing, truly?" Demni asked – and she was a different person. The tone to her voice, almost pleasant – nearly sweet. Her voice, which was a bit gruff and almost hoarse, took on a nicer, lower tone to it. The change was unexpected, almost enchanting, almost ... beguiling ... and she almost touched his arm when she said "truly" – making him jerk back a little, for he thought she was about to hit him, "The singer is Dyneti, she is a dear friend of mine, greater than a friend, closer than a ... she is very dear to me indeed ..."

For a moment she drifted into a dream, as Selvorne wondered if fumes of wine in a room could affect a person who never drank.

"Tonight she will give a performance so wonderful, so magnificent, you will see, she is quite something," Demni said after a brief silence, then she fell back into her dream, gazing at the empty stage. Selvorne asked again of the singer, and Demni blinked several times as though waking – she did not mind telling him anything of her, however, and she answered more than he asked.

Dyneti was the name of the singer, and she was a wonder with song, more than a wonder, as were the ways Demni described her – a rising star, a shining moon, the glorious sun, a magnificent bird, and many other comparisons that made him wonder if Demni was not truly an administer of town accounts, but made profit somehow from the singer as they travelled across the lands.

The facts of Dyneti he learnt were brief – she was not merely a singer, but Waehdric – a spiritual leader of the people. Such men and women who were Waehdric usually only spoke of wisdom to children, advised elders and lords, gave peace to troubled hearts or stirred passions in those who had none. They healed any who were sick, as best they could if no healing men were near, and they collected all the knowledge of all the people, kept safe and taught to all who needed to know how to do most anything in the lands. Keepers of knowledge – givers of wisdom. So Uhlsko said. Takers of coin – givers of grief. So Arnlausa said, but he joked, Selvorne was sure, and he had no dislike of them. Cienn was their leader, and for her he had greatest respect. Their singers – dancers –

performers of plays – those Waehdric who did such shows were fondly welcomed, for it was by such means they taught wisdom to any who had no wish to have lessons put upon them by solemn words alone.

A Waehdric singer, then, that was unexpected, and Selvorne found it odd that a fee was charged to hear. It did explain why she would sing for free the next night, though, so all would have a chance to hear Waehdric wisdom – that meant the songs were likely to be noble ballads of spiritual inspiration, rather than the bawdy, humorous or boisterous singing he was expecting in a room full of wealthy folk, drunk on wine. Rich men did not want wisdom. Drunk men did not seek lessons. He was a little disappointed, he was hoping for some instruments of music and stomping of feet, clamouring of tankards and people falling over – to be lost in laughter, to be swept along, to ... forget.

Indeed, he wondered how a ballad would be received by such a crowd, unless it was a particularly daring one, about battles and dancing girls, and the drunken celebration of victory ending in all kinds of unwise mischief. The lesson might be hidden amongst much bold amusement, so he expected, but he dared not mention that to Demni.

Demni was leaning against the wall, cradling her water cup, dreaming as she looked out to the stage. Selvorne was quite sure the wine fumes were affecting her, she was certainly drunk on something. Savak was worse, far worse, he had his arm around Rohy. The two of them had almost finished the jug, and were pointing at every woman in the inn, loudly discussing the merits of each. Luckily, half the men in the room were doing the same, and a third of the women as well. Selvorne remembered his father saying once that such a thing was to be expected, when the stronger wine was served to those used to drinking ale.

Strange – Selvorne felt ... almost moved. When he looked to Demni – a gleam in her eye, a change in her voice, handsome her face, and ... perhaps it was the wine. Yet Selvorne had been more drunk when he first spoke to her, not less. He thought he began to see what Rohy had seen. True, she was not quite shapely, as a woman perhaps should be – but she was slender, elegant, and leant on the wall with an attractive, casual strength. Her strong arms seemed slight, girlish – bare, and her skin delicate. Her steady gaze was alluring, though she did not gaze at him, and the lips of her wide mouth were drawn to almost a pout. Though ... he had heard nearly nothing nice from them. He began to imagine a smile to match her dark, twinkling eyes, and that she might say something –

"What are you staring at?" Demni asked suddenly, not moving her head, but her eyes turned and fixed upon his own.

"You are ... very handsome," Selvorne replied.

"Is that supposed to be a compliment?

"Could it ... be taken any other way?"

Demni frowned, stood up straight and looked at him – down at him, for she was taller, though not by much – and then, to his surprise, she shrugged and shook her head.

"Is that the wine talking?" Demni asked.

Mischief within him, so barely restrained – what was he doing, Selvorne did not know, his thoughts too slow to chase where habits led. He raised the cup to his ear, listened, nodded, then looked straight into Demni's eyes.

"The wine agrees – you are very handsome," Selvorne said, "and also it praises your choice of water, recommends the same for me, and declares that it is most unpleasant being drunk. For man, for woman, and for wine – worst of all."

Demni stared, Selvorne stared back – and she laughed. She leant forward and touched his shoulder with her hand – he felt a shudder run through him, and she quickly took it away.

"You are fast, I will give you that," Demni said, "and mean neither taunt nor mocking. I see in your eyes – you are a sweet one. And quite pretty, like a girl."

Selvorne frowned, Demni stared – then laughed again, and touched his arm once more.

"And as delicate, perhaps, if so easily slighted," Demni said, "but if it is love you seek, then you are facing the wrong way."

"So you said before, but I am not here for love, only to hear the song, and mind my friend, as I said, before."

"Your drunk friend? Who can barely stand? Not well minded, I think."

Selvorne looked to Rohy, who was stumbling a little and laughing with Savak.

"Your man is no better."

"My man is not mine – needs no minding – and minds his own ... Selvorne, be silent. You speak too much, too loudly, and may spoil the show."

Selvorne felt – he did not know what. She was not angry, but firm – not impolite, though not very warm, and yet ... strangely delightful. She leant back on the wall and ignored him. Savak did the same, but eyed him, and Rohy was wondering where to look, his eyes going from one to the other. He must have noticed Demni touching Selvorne's arm – a gesture that meant nothing, for most people, but from a woman so oddly cold, it might have meant quite a lot to a drunken, jealous ... rival?

Cassini came near, looked at Selvorne and the almost empty jug, said something about him drinking too much, having few friends for such a jug of wine, and that she thought earlier he was with many men – but Selvorne heard little over the crowd and merely shrugged before she left him.

Any enchantment Demni had for him disappeared when she suddenly yelled out to the room for all to remove their hats – loud, bold, commanding – not at all like a lady. Except, perhaps, if she was The Lady of the town, and they were all in her house. Few wore hats, for it was a warm night at a hot inn – only the small hats, the Festival Follies – but she did not want them blocking her view. Few obliged her request, most ignored her – none ignored Savak, however, when he repeated the command more loudly and surprisingly, he yelled in the clearest voice, without seeming drunk. Then he waited until all hats were gone, and slumped back against the wall near Rohy, laughing.

Demni must have known it was to begin – realised, or been told by way of a sign from the guard at the stage – for moments after, there was a loud clanging sound as someone pounded some bronze instrument of music. Very loud, completely surprising, and everyone went silent, turning to the front. Then there were whispers, some began to speak eagerly with friends – a round of "Hush!" as those less drunk tried to quieten the others – then "Shhh!" – and louder, as the drunken folk tried to silence them back.

Clang! Clang! More clangs and more instruments, the players came forth and took positions around the stage. Others came and moved about the room, closing shutters on the windows – slightly, to reduce the late light of day that was filtering through, then they positioned lamps about the room as safely as they could, upon the wall–railing table to create a very gentle glow. The room was dimmed, few people dared make a sound. A small surge of people came through the door from outside, squeezing in at the last moment before it was shut, then all were still. It seemed not unbearably crowded without people moving about, but it was very warm and tense.

Two men entered from behind the stage, holding poles that quickly unfolded to reveal a canvas of a painted background. Beautiful mountains, waterfalls and rolling hills. Everyone gasped as the stage was transformed into a wonderful mountain view. Smaller screens were positioned before the backing – paintings of trees. Also a bench was arranged, and a string instrument placed. Someone clapped in delight and was immediately silenced – the entire crowd was both delighted and tense, the excitement growing as the sounds of the instruments was rising, from soft to strong.

Vooom! One of the trees disappeared – there standing – appearing behind at once – a tall lady. A powerful note – her voice – it could not be, but it was – so strong it sent shudders through Selvorne's body and likely every person in the room. Some opened their mouths to gasp, but their pathetic breath was drowned by the sound of her voice. Magnificently attired, striking and – she could not possibly still be singing? Some started to clap, but could not be heard, and quickly stopped. Her voice continued – instead of fading – grew more powerful. The note stronger, it went on until Selvorne thought she would have to lose her breath – she did not. Looking around, he noticed everyone was staring at her, Rohy's jaw had dropped, Savak was beaming, and Demni had a strong gleam in her eye, and was clawing her nails into the railing against the wall.

The note finally ended and there was a moment of silence. Then the music and the song changed to something less powerful – a sweet rendition about a dark–haired youth, his journey from the rising seas and into the mountains, founding a town and most of the lands of the north. Many were familiar with the story, Selvorne knew it was about Tromvos, from the far north, long ago – but he was too astounded by the singer to care about the song.

Selvorne thought she was the most beautiful lady he had ever seen. He was quite sure she was also the most beautiful lady he ever would see. Dressed in a long, flowing white gown, with subtle frills, shining from the darkness of the inn – striking against the painted background. Her skin was beyond pale, impossibly white, whiter than the gown, and her hair was the deepest, brightest red – blood and fire, perfectly straight, falling down the front of both shoulders. She was very tall, especially on the stage that was raised only a foot, and elegant in all her movements. Her lips were red, her eyes were bright and sparkling and deep – and her voice was an enchantment, more musical than the harp, more powerful than the drum, more magnificent than was possible and more beautiful than he had ever known.

The first song finished, everyone clapped and called out. They stood, they cheered, they had a few moments to talk frantically with their friends. Astonishment and wonder – the applause did not stop until she raised one hand, signalling all to silence – and they were, almost at once. Then she began another song.

Cassini was standing next to Selvorne, watching the performance. She seemed amused at Selvorne's interest, although she was enjoying the show herself. At the end of the second song, where there was a longer break, she spoke.

"Beautiful, is she not?" Cassini remarked. Selvorne nodded without turning his head, "Worth a proposal, do you think?"

"Oh, oh no ..." Selvorne replied, "no, she is far too beautiful for me."

He only glanced at Cassini, so did not realise her hurt until after she had taken herself away, back to the serving table. An insult. Unintended. But a thoughtless thing to say, even if ... clearly the woman on the stage was far more beautiful than any other, so why should any woman be jealous? Women were like that – gentle, his father said, easily hurt, and tender. To tend to, Arnlausa had said, agreeing, though Uhlsko argued they should be treated gently. Tricked, though kindly, with the wisdom of a man and the mischief of a boy – that was Arnlausa, not Uhlsko. Selvorne bit his lip – Cassini, if feelings had been hurt, they had healed, for she was soon back to her duties, serving, and smiling. Not as hurt, perhaps, as Selvorne had been years ago, by her rejection. Savak was winking at him – that was most odd. Rohy was staring in astonishment to the front, then to Selvorne, then to the front once more. Demni did not take her eyes off the singer, whether singing or resting – she was smiling – and as he looked, every head of every person he saw turned, all at once, to the front for the next song.

A third song, just as beautiful, all were well behaved, apart from some trouble at the door. It was becoming distracting, so Selvorne went over to see what was happening. Someone apparently wanted to come in without paying, and when he looked to see who – it was Temnere. He claimed he should not have to pay, for he was not there to drink or listen, and he was raising his voice with each insistence – even pushing the doorman, who was easily holding him back. Selvorne took the doorman aside, gave him a dozen bits – which was quite a sum – and asked him to let the man in, anything as long as they would all be quiet. Temnere then pushed his way in, oblivious to both the song and the crowd near the door, who were glaring at him as he looked around. He strode straight over to Demni, almost knocking people's drinks out of their hands – then, a few brief words later, the two of them quickly strode back outside. Demni had an infuriated look on her face, turned neither left nor right, except once – back to the stage, as she passed through the door.

Selvorne rejoined Rohy and Savak just as the song was ending, and there was a break with a chance to speak. Rohy was entranced by the show, just as everyone was, and although he was a bit puzzled by Demni's sudden departure, he seemed glad she was no longer blocking his view. Selvorne reasoned that he must have shifted his affections to the singer – as most of the room had done. Savak was leaning against the wall, humming along to the music that continued softly even after the song, and he sipped the last of his wine.

Another song, and the singer Dyneti began to move through the crowd – not at all an easy thing to do, and she could only make it halfway across the hall. Too many people and not enough room, less room as all wanted to be near, and some shoved and cursed as she had to retreat from paths blocked. To even think of walking amongst so many drunk men was not a good idea, perhaps – Selvorne gasped as she approached his table, stopping at the one behind.

Words were sung – to Savak, almost certainly. To Rohy, perhaps, one or two. Her glance was landing on the eyes of every person there, not only men – and then Selvorne, who stared back blankly, his mouth open, his heart pounding.

Their eyes met and – was that silence? A moment, no more. A surprising break, what she was singing had missed a few words. She quickly turned away, then continued. Had his heart stopped – no, just skipped a beat, or two. It was pounding again, and he longed to have her back before him.

The song ended with her return to the stage – terribly loud applause, shouting as well, and the shuffling of people trying to be closer to the front, in case she did it again. She spoke for the first time, and said she would do another tour of the crowd, not that night, but perhaps the next, on the great open meadow of the town, should any wish to hear her sing again. More applause, and then there was the shouting of requests.

"Ahhh, ahhh – you are enchanted by Dyneti," Savak said to Selvorne, though he might have said it to Rohy, as well.

"She is wonderful," Selvorne said, and Savak grunted. Rohy said nothing, but stared ahead.

"Not all who have a heart, can sing – not all who can sing, have a heart – she has a bit of both," Savak explained, and the two of them nodded.

Savak seemed to have a thought, for he frowned most curiously – what it was, Selvorne could only guess, for he put his hand under Selvorne's chin and turned his head to face himself – then let go. Selvorne stared in astonishment, and Savak burst into laughter. Drunk – but not unfriendly. Selvorne shrugged and smiled, and Savak nodded. A tough man and his hand was strong. A guard of some importance, and though drunk, he seemed quite steady on his feet. And not too foolish, considering how much wine he had taken.

A call for songs, but the singer Dyneti only looked out on the crowd – reading their minds, perhaps, their desires, their dreams. To weave them to a song. To choose one from many – not their suggestions, however. Certainly not the Crazy Cow, the Leaping Goat or the Rowdy Sow – the last earned a man a slap over the head from another beside him. Those were farmer songs for farmer boys, Dyneti was singing great songs of the past – Tromvos the Conquering KroiNohc, the Golden Eagle of Vorletohm, and of the Witch Voneri, Locked in War. After many poor suggestions, she began a song that seemed to be of love, though it soon turned to loss and sorrow, and made Selvorne's heart ache to hear of it.

The singing continued for a few more songs, all were enjoyed, each was different to the last. If any thought at the start the price was too high or room too crowded, by the end of the night all were glad they had come. Likely they would speak of it the next day with praise, and all the town would gather on the meadow to hear Dyneti sing.

The singing and music ended quite suddenly, and behind a rising cloth, Dyneti vanished as quickly as she had appeared. How, Selvorne was not sure, but all stared and wondered if she might return. She did not, though the music did, and the room changed moods to one of talking, and enjoying of wine by the light of candle lamps. Many left, headed back to the town – half at least stayed. Perhaps hoping Dyneti might return, even join them. That was Selvorne's hope, but after some time, and after asking Savak, he discovered she would not. Demni was also unlikely to return, and there was no reason for any of them to remain at the inn. Apart from Savak, indeed with a town lacking in wine, there was no reason for him to leave.

Rohy was drunk and not drinking. Selvorne was sobering and wondered if he should drink. Savak had found more wine and offered it to the both of them, but they took only a little. As the night was late, it occurred to Selvorne that he had not considered where he might sleep. All rooms in the town that had been available were taken, many homes were also filled with guests. The Winer's Inn itself had no rooms, for it was a tavern, no longer an inn, and they had not bothered changing the name. Perhaps on purpose, so travellers looking for a room would find wine instead. Selvorne had little doubt he could find room to sleep there, though, but he did not think he would be comfortable imposing on Cassini after insulting her, even if it was unintended.

Rohy said that many others were headed to a field in the town, behind the houses where he had slept the night before. It was unsheltered, but safe, with a large fire so it was warm enough, if needed, and the ground was soft. Rain was unlikely, so Selvorne agreed to join him.

Being sure to say farewell to Cassini, and to gather their things from outside – which Rohy nearly forgot – they left The Winer's Inn and headed back to the town, stumbling in the dark. Some people walking the road had bright burning torches, but that only made it more difficult for those who did not, who were trying to adjust to the moonlight, but kept having flames spoil their sight as others passed them by.

The field was within the town, near the road, but back a way, with few houses near. Hundreds of people were gathering there, and had started three huge fires, growing larger as people threw more wood to the piles – it seemed as if they were competing with each other. Dancing and drinking took place around the great fires, but farther away smaller ones kept people warm as they slept, or tried to sleep, with all the noise. Every so often someone had passed out, usually in an inconvenient location, blocking a path, or atop a firewood pile. Rarely were such people left sleeping where they had fallen, and some would wake to find themselves propped up with buckets for hats and long sticks within their clothing, as though to scare crows away from the field.

It was not cold enough to need a fire, so Selvorne chose a place where he would least likely be kicked or tripped over in his sleep – away from the people, and near a foot–tall rock, but not too near, in case someone decided to sit upon it and rest their feet upon his head. The ground was soft enough for no bedding, and Rohy lay down, and was asleep in a moment.

Selvorne lay back for a while, pondering the full moon, then covered his eyes and thought over the strangeness of the day. Joy – and not even guilt at the joy, though he was quite drunk, and his memories were vague. He should have felt guilt, or fear, or sorrow – but he did not. Anger was buried, vengeance delayed, his plan followed – hidden, in the cloak of the crowd. Hundreds sleeping near him, none of them he knew, save one – who he had only just met. And yet, safe. He would not be slain that night, nor suspected, nor found. And though there would be vengeance and anger so very soon – there was hope. Delight, and ... he began to drift to sleep, closing his eyes to the moon, and remembering a smile, wide eyes, and magnificent red hair.

Maiden of New

Selvorne woke late in the morning, and what woke him was not the noise of those around him, the groaning or laughter, complaining or excited shouts. Nor was it the accidental kick from a passerby, though that made him turn to his other side, and in so doing the sun hit his face, making him turn back. What woke him and made him rise was the growing heat – unpleasant, and unusual for so early in the spring – he could not continue sleeping as all thoughts turned to the lake.

He sat up, and looked around. The meadow grasses had been flattened by a hundred bodies, most of whom had risen and left. The ground was soaked by dew, or rain, or ale and sweat and drool, he did not know, but all moisture was rising in a hazy mist of heat. His head was just as foggy, and he needed a wash. One leg was a bit numb. A bright, cloudless day, and just as he had been gazing up at the moon the night before, he found himself shielding his eyes from the sun – quite high in the sky, for half the morning had gone.

It seemed Rohy had already left, without saying farewell, which annoyed him a little because he assumed they would look out for each other when asleep. So he thought when lying down drunk – how that might be possible, when both were sleeping, was anyone's guess. In a sudden panic he checked his belongings were there – they were, none taken, none lost, including the coins in his purse beside him, sitting there in a lump for all to see.

He could hear people splashing in the lake, and thought a swim would be a good idea. He dragged his things over to the lakeside, removed his boots and placed them on the pile, then waded through shallow waters in his trousers and shirt, which he meant to wash. The shore was gravel, good pebbles, in places, and it seemed someone had strewn such rocks all along it, to make it easier to drag boats to and from the lake without feet sinking in the mud. All the boats had been moved to one end of the beach where they had landed, piled almost on top of each other. The lake was cold – too cold to swim for long, but it quickly cured his drowsiness. When he came out he shivered a little, but lying on the hot gravel lakeside he soon warmed himself, and dried.

A wash of his face and he realised he needed to shave – needed, if he wanted to look his best, but also because he felt his grief returning. Grief and overwhelm, anger and ... he prepared his things. The sharpest knife, only for shaving, never blunted by ordinary use. His tiny mirror of bronze, but he would only need it to check he had missed no hairs. All preparations, as he always did, with his mind on arrangements and nothing else. The knife, so sharp, the cut so smooth – careful, with a mind focussed, no blade could pass his skin ... no pain could come to him ... no thought nor fear could enter his mind. He shaved, washed, then checked the mirror to see all was to his satisfaction. His shave was complete, and he sat back on the gravel.

Shaving at the lake was not unusual at the festival, nor so very odd at any time of the year. Nor was washing, though people who lived beside the water were often not too happy to have others bathing before their house – fathers of daughters especially, if the bathers were young men or bold boys. Arnlausa had made it law not to, but that was only enforced when people complained – fathers of maidens, and the like, after one especially bold incident. Arnlausa had found it amusing, he admitted in private, the brothers involved were daring, the maidens more so, perhaps – but the father was unbearable. So he banned swimming near the houses at all times, except during the festival.

During the festival, the only thing frowned upon was late night, drunken swimming – not to protect the modest, but because it was too dangerous. There were times when people swam the wrong way, grew desperate and swam farther, ending in the middle of the lake. Usually dead, after falling asleep in the water. Guards did not enforce such a law nor stand by the waters at night, but anyone near who was not so drunk would ensure no others were foolish, and during the night the lake and its shore was almost a forbidden place to go.

Not in the day, especially such a very hot day. Dozens who had bathed left the waters, to be replaced by dozens more, and Selvorne watched the people there, refreshed, groomed, happy – shivering, laughing, wet – relaxing, drying, and eager for the day. A festive day – a day of joy. He sighed once before straightening up – and at that moment, he decided he would buy the spear.

The night before, he was glad he did not have it with him at The Winer's Inn. He would have been made to leave it outside, then would have worried about it all the time inside, for it was terribly expensive. However, he could see the sense of it, especially if it could be used to hold a small candle lamp in the dark. He wondered if he could stick the sharp end in the ground, and hang such a lamp from the other end when setting camp – he could see no reason why not, and as he thought on it, other uses came to mind, just as practical, just as ... justifying of the price, so he set off with some urgency to Hramullo's waggon.

The festival was a different place that day. More people had arrived, especially children, who were running around excitedly. It was the Games Day, where they could compete in races and throwing competitions to win prizes. The games were to be held in the late afternoon, so, naturally, the children rose early and spent all morning wearing themselves to exhaustion before they needed to compete.

Hramullo's waggon was there, but it was shut and he was nowhere to be seen. The goat was stretching its tether, trying to eat juicy grass just out of its reach, for it had chewed to dirt the ground around the cart. Beside the waggon, a young, dark-haired girl had taken one of the elegant boxes, turned it on its side and sat upon it, leaning against the cart in the shade of a large tree. At first Selvorne thought she was asleep, but then decided she was merely bored, and somewhat flippant to sit on a box so, which surely would scratch from a stone on the ground. She must have known what he thought, for she sat up properly and stared with a blank expression of guilt.

"Good morning, my lady," Selvorne said, "is Hramullo here today?"

She looked at him and shook her head, but said nothing.

"Is he likely to return anytime soon? Perhaps in the late of the day?"

Again, she shook her head, then looked away.

"Tomorrow?"

More head shaking, and she only briefly glanced at him.

"Is he ever coming back?"

She shook her head and had an uncomfortable look on her face – quite aghast. Was Hramullo dead? No, she was not grim ... indeed, she had only winced a little, but her eyes seemed almost afraid. Selvorne wondered what it could mean, and then a thought came to him.

"Was Hramullo here yesterday?"

She shook her head again, stood up, then shrugged her shoulders. She raised one finger, pointed at the waggon, turned her hand and moved two of her fingers as though they were the legs of a tiny man walking. She then pressed her hands together, and put them against one ear, tilting her head as though – sleeping on a pillow. She said something – quite a lot, none of which Selvorne understood except "Hramullo" and "sleeping", then she repeated the hand gestures.

"Aha," replied Selvorne, "he has gone away to sleep. I see ..."

Again, she shook her head.

Selvorne thought she must have been odd in some way that made her unable to speak. But she must have been able to hear, and she said two words at least that were quite well pronounced. He looked her up and down, once, twice – and it seemed to distress her, so he bowed. But he did not leave – apart from her quite strange behaviour, she was an elegant young lady. Well dressed, in soft pale blue, with long, straight black hair. Dark eyes of deepest blue, very fair skin, and was in every way slender. She had an expression on her face that seemed to suggest boredom, but her eyes looked pained, frustrated and annoyed. Selvorne thought if he spent any more time trying to talk to her, he would feel the same, so he bowed again and headed away.

The spear ... it meant more to him than a useful tool, or beautifully crafted ... toy. It was for fishing, and fishing was ... his past. And perhaps his future, if he could go back to ... no, not quite to how things were. A sorrow began to grow in him, but he steadied himself against a tree and looked to the festival around him – happy people, and fun. Merriment and delight, excitement and ... none of them knew their lord had been killed. Only Selvorne knew. In that, he was alone.

But they would. In time they would mourn and want revenge. Soon. He had to clear his mind of nonsense such as grief, for it would not bring vengeance, and a spear would not ... put things back as they were. It could, however, bring vengeance. A bigger one, perhaps, not a fine one meant for fishing. A mighty spear, driven into – no, he had no time for anger, either, nor any form of fury or sorrow. He wandered the back streets of the town where fewer stalls were set, and looked carefully at who was there.

~

In the back area, away from the main road and most houses, in a grove not quite a field, a few large tents had appeared since the day before. Arranged in a circle around a fire, most were plain, all were nice, but one in particular was very elegant and well decorated, though only half raised. They were the kind of tents people would sleep in, though they were very large – tall enough to stand in, if people wished, large enough to hold a merchant's wares, but there were no stalls selling things at the front.

Selvorne asked a man passing by, and he said it was the Waehdric camp – a few had arrived early that morning and established it.

He wondered – had he heard correctly, or was he drunk – he had spoken with Demni, the administrator, the night before at the singing. Did she say that the singer was ... Waehdric? She was, was she not – songs of old, of great men and battles, of love and ... yes, Waehdric. He bit his lip and went closer to see if she could possibly be there. Such a tall, redheaded beauty would surely be easy to find.

Few people were at the camp. Some were guards who served the Waehdric, cooking something over the fire, otherwise not doing very much guarding. Others were young boys and girls, he assumed taken by the Waehdric at a young age to learn – they were well behaved and tidying around the encampment. A few older men seemed to be wanting to go out to the festival, but as they tried to leave their tent, each in turn forgot something, then went back to retrieve it as the others waited. They seemed quite jovial about it and laughed, especially when one cursed and ran back inside for his hat – that was already on his head. He emerged, annoyed he could not find it, and another tried to snatch it from his head, but was too slow, and to Selvorne's delight the three old men began to chase each other away from the camp, slapping at each other and laughing. He smiled and shook his head as he watched after them, and was noticed by the one person other than the children who seemed to be doing anything useful – a young, dark–haired maiden who was beside the nicest tent, struggling to pull a peg from the ground that appeared to be stuck. She glanced at Selvorne only briefly, then quickly returned to her task.

"Allow me," Selvorne said as he stepped close to her and grabbed the peg – he meant to pull it out of the ground with an impressive heave, but he, too, found it stuck – and she laughed. Insulted and angry – no, he was neither. He almost laughed with her, for the sound of her voice was delightful.

"Well, that is odd," Selvorne said, staring at the stuck peg as she meant to try again, "wait, let me try this."

He took the pack from his back, used the strap from the sack, ran it through the peg eye and began to heave at it. The girl grabbed the strap as well, and the two of them managed to pull it out, stumbling backwards and almost falling over. As did the tent, with Selvorne hopelessly snatching at its ropes as it fell – half of it crumpled, half still standing, and that was mainly with help from Selvorne as he held one rope.

"Wait!" she commanded with a wonderful voice. She disappeared to the front of the tent and reappeared with a wooden mallet, pulled the tent out as far as it would go, much farther than it was before, and began hammering the peg back into the ground. Pleased, she stood up tall – she was not very tall, though – and smiled at Selvorne.

"Perfect!"

Perfect – he bit his lip. She was a pretty young girl, about Selvorne's age, with darkest hair falling in large curls past her shoulders. Her face was rounded with a pointed chin, her eyes were bright – sparkling – long lashes, and dark – and her smile was friendly. She was shorter than Selvorne, both slender and well curved at once. She was wearing a light brown dress that was far from elegant, looking rather like sackcloth, with dust down the front and mud over her knees. Hard, he bit his lip – perfect.

"Selvorne," he stated, offering his hand to shake hers, as if she were a boy. She shook it, laughing.

"Is that your name?" she asked, and Selvorne was stunned. What ... did she mean?

"What?"

"Is that your name, or the name of your family? Or title?"

"It is ... my name."

"Very well, you may call me Adyleh."

He was a bit bewildered by her, but she was friendly, and in good spirits, a welcome change from many of the people he had recently met. He assumed she was some kind of assistant or maid to the elderly Waehdric, or to the guards. Perhaps a cook.

"Adyleh, can you tell me, is this a Waehdric camp?"

"Of course, can you not see the signs?" she replied, waving at various signs, such as a gathering of flowers, the symbols on the tents, and a few other things that were completely unknown to Selvorne, for Waehdric did not often visit Tavalehk, and never Vaskatohr.

"Is this, then, the camp where Dyneti, the magnificent singer is staying?" Selvorne asked, and at that she spluttered and began to cough. Selvorne thought she was choking, so he moved quickly to her, but she held up one hand.

"Yes, it is," Adyleh replied.

"Oh, is – are you all right?"

"Yes, quite fine. Some might say – a cough, nothing more – a drink will fix it."

"Oh – could I get you one, I have some ale, I think," Selvorne said, then he bent to search in his pack, and she looked at him and raised an eyebrow.

"Ale?"

"I, yes," Selvorne said, wondering if perhaps Waehdric did not drink ale. He looked up at her from the ground, and she shook her head – but was smiling.

"Wait here," she said, then she disappeared into a small tent.

Selvorne felt his heart pound as he quickly stood – and almost fainted. Had she – gone to bring Dyneti? No – she had not, she returned with a jug and two wooden cups, set them on the ground, poured one and drank from it, then waved her hand to the other, and looked at him with large eyes.

"Oh," Selvorne said, "I do not need a drink. Is ... is Dyneti here now?"

Adyleh looked around, took another sip, then looked around again.

"Perhaps – can you see her?" she asked. Selvorne looked – he saw no one with red hair, no tall lady, no others apart from the guards, some of whom were watching, and the children – all of whom were watching. He poked his head around the door of the tent, perhaps to see her hiding inside, but all he saw was a mess of sleeping arrangements and bags that had been dumped there, even though the tent was not completely raised.

"No, she is not there. Unless she is in another tent?"

"I promise you, she is not in tents," Adyleh continued, "why are you looking for her?"

Selvorne did not know how to reply. Why was he looking for her? What would he say to such an elegant and powerful lady? Beautiful, talented, one of the spiritual leaders of Waehdric, of whom he knew little – and a singer most likely adored by hundreds of men. And, if she was anything like Demni, who claimed to be her friend, she likely terrified hundreds of men. The thought of meeting her made him shake, the idea of speaking to her made him nervous – but the lovely maiden before him put him at ease, and so he smiled.

"I have to admit," Selvorne began, "I honestly do not know why I was looking for her. Perhaps to tell her that last night was a wonderful performance, she sang very well, stirred my spirit and warmed my heart. Although, I think if I had the chance to say it, I would most likely instead be lost for words."

"Well, you are not lost for words now, you speak most eloquently for a young man."

Selvorne thought she was teasing, and perhaps she was – her eyes were gleaming, with mischief, he was sure.

"Yes, but it is easy to tell you – I think I would be nervous if I was talking to her – such a beautiful, powerful lady."

"Well, that may be true," Adyleh said, "but you are not nervous with me, so I think you would not be nervous with her – yes, I am sure of it. She is not as scary as you would think. Unless you cross her, and then – she is a terror! But away from the stage, she is quite a different person. Bright, cheerful, intelligent, a delightful sense of humour. She enjoys a good joke, be it clever, or witty, or of the practical sort – well prepared, or unplanned. She is most approachable, as long as you watch out for pranks. All things considered, a lovely person, if I do say so myself, and I think I have known her longer than most everyone, save for her dear parents. And I might add, she is no lady – not in title, and not by age, being not much older than you are, I think."

Selvorne gazed at Adyleh with wide eyes and an open mouth, and she blinked back at him – many times, as if astonished – then began to laugh. He was encouraged by all she had said, and decided he would like to meet Dyneti – not so old as he had thought, nor so scary, indeed she sounded lovely in every way. He grinned widely, until he grew embarrassed, then bit his lip. And at that, Adyleh raised an eyebrow.

"I ... I must stay with the guards," Adyleh said, "and they are about to eat. Unfortunately, I must eat whatever they cook, and I do not think it will be good, despite the best preparations. I would very much like to taste some unusual food from the festival – could you perhaps bring me something?"

"I ... you want me to bring you lunch?"

"Lunch? Is it lunch, already? Yes, if you would. I – you are welcome to wait here, if you wish, with me and the men – until Dyneti returns. If you bring food."

Selvorne grinned, and Adyleh widened her eyes – yes, he would very much like to do that. To meet Dyneti, he could hardly do worse than by pleasing her ... assistant? Selvorne was not sure what she was.

"Certainly, I shall bring an assortment of whatever you like. Or whatever you might wish to try, if you trust me – I am wondering, though, are you Dyneti's assistant?"

Adyleh laughed again, and he thought she certainly laughed a lot – it was lovely to hear, and made him feel warm.

"Yes, I guess you could say that. Certainly, if there is anything Dyneti needs doing, it is always me who does it. As for food ... surprise me."

Selvorne bowed and left her, eager to return – eager to meet Dyneti – eager to ... join Adyleh again. He found himself amongst the best food stalls he had discovered the day before, with his collection of square bits, his vast wealth in coins besides, and his knowledge of what was good to eat, he returned with an assortment of foods, sparing no expense, and at first he had difficulty carrying it all. So much food that he had to purchase a basket halfway through the task, and though he only meant to make it easier to carry, by the end he had filled it. Honey sticks were the last things he bought, and he was considerate enough to think that perhaps the guards and others at the camp would want some as well.

Adyleh was sitting with the guards on his return, but all had moved away from the dying fire where they had cooked, for it was too warm to be near on such a hot day. They were eating some kind of meaty gruel they had boiled up in a pot and slopped onto wooden plates, and it smelled terrible. It was a simple meal, and Selvorne wondered how they had ruined it, perhaps by overcooking, too long or too many times. It did not look good, smell good, nor even sound good as they chewed – and, by the expression on their faces, it did not taste good. He found it strange, then, that they smiled as they ate it ... as though eager. Not always, only when they noticed they were being watched by others. They all looked to Selvorne when he returned – hopeful, perhaps, or protective – but ignored him as he sat by Adyleh, who had spread a cloth for all the food.

As he laid it out, the guards paid more interest, and he was sure to tell them that he had purchased enough honey sticks for them all, much to their approval spoken with mouths full of gruel.

For Adyleh, he did not know what she wanted, so he brought samples of everything that was best – each of which she tried, and he marvelled that one so slender at the waist could have such an appetite. Even so, there was food to spare, which the guards longingly gazed upon and willingly took at the end, thumping Selvorne on the back in gratitude that he would prefer was given in words. Nevertheless, he felt he was almost part of their group, and they seemed a good lot of men, if a bit rough.

~

At the end of the meal, a strange man ran up to them – flustered, he began looking about the tents. He was neither short nor tall, but he was slight, and so seemed small. He also seemed a little nervous, especially when he saw Adyleh. He wore delicate, finely cut clothes with tall boots, and was obviously wealthy with coins to spare, for he wore one of the tiny hats in bright red, the most expensive colour, pinned awkwardly to his thin hair.

"What do you want?" Adyleh demanded in a tone that was almost stern.

"Ahh ... nothing. Is she here?"

"No."

"Do you ... know where she is?" the strange man asked, and Selvorne thought he seemed very timid.

"No. I have not seen her today."

He did not leave, but stood there awkwardly, looking about the tents and also out to the crowd. Selvorne had the impression that he was definitely nervous around Adyleh, for he avoided her, and she seemed quite abrupt with him – he also could not help wondering why the guards had not stepped in, if anything,

250

they were avoiding him and trying to keep to themselves. After some time, and to Selvorne's complete surprise, instead of leaving he sat himself down at their informal meal, uninvited, certainly not wanted, and began to take some of their food.

"Ahh – honey sticks, very tasty," the little man said, snatching one from those that had been set aside for the guards.

Selvorne thought that was very rude, especially since he did not ask, and he was intruding on their conversation.

"Nice hat," Selvorne found himself saying – a cutting remark that he regretted even as he said it, but did not stop himself.

The little man's mood changed immediately – from anxious oddness, to a strange kind of smile – and he blinked at Selvorne with beady eyes, grinning and tilting his head.

"Do you think so? Does it suit me?" he asked before he began pulling at his hat to make it sit straight. Selvorne said nothing, but gave a slight nod, "This is my third, you know," the small man said, "she knocked the other two off in the mud. I am not sure about the colour, but now only red remains. I thought it was too bold. You cannot clean them, once muddy – that is it. No more, felt, you see – also, if you tread on them, they lose their shape, and it does not return."

Two guards near were chuckling to themselves, but Adyleh sat there, rolling her eyes.

"Taahr, I do believe she was looking for you earlier, with Temnere. If you wait here, they may be back soon," Adyleh said, "or, you could go look for them by the lake, perhaps."

The little man, who was apparently called Taahr, stood at once, and without a farewell or a bow, set off into the crowds.

"What a strange little man," Selvorne said, though he realised he was being disrespectful, "I mean, what odd behaviour. Does he not realise those hats are meant to be a joke? They are not a fashion item, no one wears them seriously, or cares how they sit."

"That was Taahr. Answer me quickly – did you like him, yes or no?" Adyleh asked.

"No," Selvorne answered after giving it a moment of thought, "no, not at all. He seemed rude. I am sure he cannot help being odd, but there is no excusing such manners. He did not even say hello or farewell, and he took a honey stick, chewed half of it, then put it back. So, no – though, perhaps he improves with time?"

"No, he does not. He is odd. He has odd ways, and does not obey the rules of good manners, whether taught, told, written, or unspoken. He cannot help that, perhaps, and I like to see the good in all people, and though I cannot find anything truly bad about him, I must admit I generally do not like him. Something feels wrong about him. And I think I am a good judge of character, if I need to be."

Adyleh smiled at Selvorne, and his heart fluttered.

"But, despite that, would you believe that he is Taahr, Captain of the Northern Guards?" Adyleh asked, and Selvorne felt his eyebrows raise, "And of all the guards, those under him seem to be the most successful. Against brigands, and thieves. So ... perhaps he is some brilliant tactician, with an odd mind. Or something. But not at all pleasant to be with – and now he has ruined a honey stick."

"Perhaps he is so annoying he drives them out of the north?" Selvorne suggested, and Adyleh giggled. Some of the guards also coughed, and Selvorne was not sure if he had insulted them, or almost choked them with laughter they dared not release – the latter, from their glistening eyes.

It was becoming late in the afternoon, and Adyleh said she had to return to her duties, but that night she would be at the singing, and that it would be free for everyone to listen, in the Festival Field, with many shows besides. Until then, she had as much to do as Dyneti to prepare. Selvorne looked over the camp hoping to see her, but did not – then remembered he was supposed to be looking for Cienn, but there was no sign of an old woman, either.

Adyleh warned Selvorne that he would have to arrive early to find a good place to sit, but at that, one of the guards – the tall, fair-haired man who had been at The Winer's Inn, guarding the stage – jumped up and declared it was nonsense – that Selvorne would be welcome to join the guards and sit at the front. Selvorne was not sure if he should accept. Adyleh seemed a little hesitant, but the guards were all eager, and claimed that they owed him for the meal, and they insisted.

Welcoming, but oddly – he did not know their names, and when he thought to learn them, Adyleh stood before him, took both of his hands in hers, and promised she would see him there – that made him smile and nod, and unable to speak.

Did he promise, did he thank her – did he thank the guards – he was not sure as he left the camp in a daze, half hurried away as the men became busy and Adyleh returned to setting the tent. He would see her that night – that was something wonderful – he could hardly contain his joy, but ... he was not sure for who.

Wandering for a while, he decided he would see if Hramullo was back from his sleep. He wanted the spear, but other things were also coming to mind, and a plan was forming.

~

Hramullo's waggon seemed to have expanded, and though Hramullo had returned, he was not done with his sleep, for he leant back in a folding chair, snoring. Ulfwyd was talking to the odd, dark-haired girl, and also a similar looking young boy, who seemed tall for he was quite narrow. The odd girl did not seem to have any trouble speaking with them, and the three of them seemed quite cheerful. Or Ulfwyd did, the others did not smile. The waggon itself seemed to have moved ten feet to the left, much to the happiness of the goat that was eagerly chewing lush grass, and when Selvorne approached they all, including the goat, nodded – but let him be.

252

New items covered the waggon stall – brushes for hair, simple jewellery, large steel scissors, and quite a few mirrors. Selvorne was not sure if Hramullo had been purchasing things at Tavalehk to sell, or if he kept many items hidden in the waggon, taking them out or putting them away depending on the festival mood. He hoped so, for the spear was nowhere to be seen. Many other items were gone as well, including the wooden satchel bag, and Selvorne could only assume that Hramullo had a very good day that morning and had sold most everything – at that Selvorne's mood began to fall.

Ulfwyd seemed to notice and headed over, saying nothing, but he reached under the waggon and took out a cloth roll, which he unfolded to reveal the spear, completely dismantled.

"I will take it," Selvorne said, and Ulfwyd signalled the girl to join them. She stood before Selvorne and took a slight breath.

"That will is five gold coin," she stated.

"What!?!" Selvorne asked, astonished. Her face was unmoved, and his heart sank. The price had almost doubled. Ulfwyd leant over and whispered something to the girl.

"That is three gold coins," she said, sounding certain, but she looked at Ulfwyd, and he nodded.

"Sorry, she is just learning," Ulfwyd said.

"And she is a bit slow," the other boy said, "my sister be have trouble crushing words."

The girl frowned, Ulfwyd shrugged, and the boy seemed pleased with himself, with a wry smile. Selvorne thought the boy was just as bad, if not worse, being more dangerous if he thought he spoke well. Selvorne handed over the three gold coins – painfully, in disbelief that he would part with so much – but he was filled with joy to receive the spear rolled up in a cloth.

Hramullo jumped up at once.

"Aha! Back again, for the spear perhaps?" he asked, then, seeing Selvorne had already paid for it, "Perhaps something else? You could use one of these brushes, and a mirror as well."

Usually Selvorne would not have cared for a mirror, but on hearing that, he picked one up and looked himself over. The day before his hair was cut and looked perfect, so he did not expect to see it sticking out at odd angles on one side, with the other side flat. Perhaps it had dried badly from the swim, or perhaps he had slept on it strangely – had he been like that all day? He began to feel quite foolish – perhaps that was why some of the younger boys at the festival were poking fun at him. His bit his lip in angst – then, sighed in relief – glad he had not met Dyneti like that, he would have looked a fool. He began brushing his hair down with his hands, and Hramullo started to explain the various qualities of the brushes, which he insisted helped one's hair to grow longer and faster, claiming his beard was such an example.

But Hramullo was not a pushy man as he showed his wares, not once Selvorne had bought the spear, and he felt they had formed some bond of friendship. Merchant and customer, an alliance of sorts, and the presentation of his goods felt as though it was delivered for Selvorne's benefit. Perhaps genuine, or perhaps he was a truly masterful seller – Selvorne had parted with a great sum. And he found himself wanting to purchase more – and it was not long before an idea that was in the back of his mind had been drawn to the front, and was growing, until it became all he could think of – to buy a present for Dyneti.

A mirror – yes, Hramullo agreed, most important for a person of the stage. Strange, did Selvorne mention he meant it as a present for the singer – he must have done. A box – what for? Jewels, of course, to store, and the hundred things a singer might need to prepare her face for the stage. A grooming kit, of finest quality, to –

Selvorne froze as he stared at the grooming kit. Small scissors, a bronze mirror, files and stones to sharpen, and ... the same as his own. The same as his mother's, exactly, and that had not been bought at Tavalehk.

Could Hramullo detect a change of mood – yes, he would have to be that skilled. Could Selvorne hide his astonishment – no, but he thought he managed to make it seem for the quality of the items, not suspicions. He was not even sure what those suspicions were, but he needed to know – where Hramullo sold his goods, whether such a grooming kit was new to him, or an item he had sold for many years. If Selvorne was not quite suspicious, Hramullo quickly grew very much so, and Ulfwyd stepped between them.

"You have seen this before?" Ulfwyd asked, waving his hand at the small grooming kit.

"My mother had one just like it," Selvorne said.

"Hramullo?" Ulfwyd asked.

"It is new, and not at all used."

"That is not what – "

"Aha!" Ulfwyd said, interrupting Selvorne, "See, now he is relieved. None of these things are old, none used, all tested, all the best. Mirror and a box? A gift?"

Selvorne nodded, and before he could argue, he found himself handing over coins, and being presented with the wooden box and a mirror, also in a wooden box, as well as the brush in a leather box, and the wooden box for his spear – so his arms were laden with boxes. He saw his coins disappear into yet another box, in the waggon, but it contained surprisingly few coins. Beside it in the waggon was a sack, loaded with what looked like strange gnarled nuts. Selvorne found the whole thing very odd, even more when he saw Hramullo staring at him with a raised eyebrow, the boy and girl gazing at him blankly, and Ulfwyd grinning, before leading him away from the waggon.

"A mirror and a box should be well received," Ulfwyd said, "though, be sure to say the mirror is the finest you could find, unworthy of the lady's beauty, or she may be insulted."

Selvorne nodded, it seemed wise enough.

"The same for the brush, though I suspect that is for you?"

Selvorne nodded.

"And the box ... for a lady you admire, a gift of a practical nature. For a lady you desire – to be filled with delightful gifts."

"Not ... now?" Selvorne asked.

"Now? Oh – no, not necessarily now. Not at the start, that might seem a little too much – a promise of gifts to come, empty at first, as was your life, before you met her – desire, then?"

Selvorne frowned, and Ulfwyd laughed.

"Uncertainty, then – all the more reason not to fill it with gifts at the start. You are wondering about the grooming kit?"

"Yes," Selvorne said.

"The same as your mother's, bought at MidWaehter."

"How – did you know that?"

"You said."

"I mean – MidWaehter?"

Ulfwyd raised an eyebrow, and Selvorne felt foolish – of course he knew where it had been bought, if he was the seller, or there at the time. Although he did not seem quite old enough to have sold it to Vorlisi – unless Ulfwyd had been there as a boy.

"That was a long time ago," Selvorne said.

"My guess is, not as long as Hramullo has been selling."

At that Selvorne laughed – very likely true, for the little man seemed quite old. Ulfwyd seemed ... he was not sure. Not a youth, perhaps not a young man. And the other two, brother and sister, although – not his children, surely? Certainly not Hramullo's, they could hardly look any different. Selvorne looked back at them, and at once they all turned towards him and stared.

"Will you be here for the whole festival?" Selvorne asked.

"Likely, although – when does it end?"

"I – actually, I am not quite sure. A few days more, I think."

"Oh, good. A chance to sell and lighten the waggon, then – do you have a sister?"

Selvorne frowned – it was an odd question.

"No. Why?"

"Well, your father perhaps might have been interested in the grooming kit, if – "

"My father?" Selvorne asked in astonishment, but Ulfwyd merely frowned.

"Who – bought one for your mother? Surely? A gift?"

Selvorne bit his lip – yes, he had. Long ago – a sister – a daughter – another gift would be required. The question was innocent, from a merchant, not a foe. Selvorne had no father, though, no mother either, and no sister – just himself, alone. And one grooming kit already, which once was hers, and was now his – pain and unease, and Ulfwyd seemed to notice.

"No matter," Ulfwyd said, "and for the spear – do not sharpen the bronze prongs. It is not necessary, and the bronze will wear fast if you do, and a sharp spear for fishing tends to slice the fish in two, both halves lost to the lake. If you find the shaft too narrow for your hand, wrap it in leather for ordinary use, and wind a cord around it for fishing, the grip is better and if the cord ... begins to smell of fish, you can easily remove it. And always tie a rope to the end in deep water – it will sink. It is made of steel, not wood, all metal through the core and will go straight to the bottom, lost until the lake is dry, and no lake may dry when filled forever with your tears for the missing spear."

"I am not one to cry over a lost spear," Selvorne said.

"No – but sorrow for a grooming kit?"

Selvorne frowned, and Ulfwyd nodded.

"Rope attached to spear, rope attached to belt, or a heavy stone if you prefer. There is only one other like it, lose it, and it is lost. You may find yourself attached to it by more than rope – I am, and I am only the seller, and I own the other spear – and yet know already I shall miss this one, as you carry it away. Please do not lose it – keep it, for a long life, and pass it to your children, and theirs, and perhaps one day they shall meet mine, and be amazed at the two spears reunited."

"I – well, if you put it like that, I promise. I have no intention of losing something that cost – how much was it?"

Ulfwyd smiled.

"A price forgotten in moments, not remembered for a lifetime, and likely exaggerated for the next," Ulfwyd said.

"Says the seller to the buyer."

"Says he who owns the other spear," Ulfwyd said, and Selvorne nodded.

Friendly, and ... somehow odd. All of them. The boxes were growing heavy, and though Selvorne could have put them down and talked all through the day with the strange sellers, he was keen to practise with his new spear – and he had much to prepare for the night ahead. A farewell, and he stumbled away with his gifts, thinking he needed some small cart or a large sack. He took himself to a quiet part of the woods at the edge of town, and began assembling the spear in different ways to test it.

Throwing – he needed much practise. He was doing something wrong and did not know what, for the spear never travelled straight. He used it like a staff, but was not sure it would last long if he began smashing it into a tree. For thrusts it was excellent, and at that he excelled – fish would have no chance. Nor would apples on a tree, nor pears nor ... enemies. He wished he could throw it, and he wished he had more – with many spears and a good arm, he could kill more than a few men. With two dozen he might kill twelve, kill all those at the ... camp ... if he had many ... stuck in the ground, ready to throw. As he had seen. That was the purpose of the poles around the brigand at the camp – spears, ready to throw. Not quite a dozen, but likely that man would not miss. Selvorne took a deep breath, then practised more.

He needed training. He did not know what to do in a fight. He could punch and wrestle, but do nothing with skill. Stab, swing a blade – no style, no knowledge of what to do or when. And fighting was more than one man against another – he did not know what to do if confronted by several men, even if he was hiding and watching them, waiting.

The guards did. His father did – Arnlausa did. Girradehn did as well, for what good it did them all when ... killed the way they were. And it made sense to kill them that way, though grim to think of it. The same way, Selvorne could kill many of his enemies at once. Half a day of cutting with an axe, waiting for them to come – watching them fall. But he would have watched them and finished them, were they enemies he caused to fall. Some things made sense, others did not, but the one thing he realised every time he thought about it was that he was completely unprepared to be a lord – to be in such danger – to face such men – and to avoid such plots. He did not even know who he could trust. Not guards, even those of Arnlausa – for none of them were named worthy of trust, so all must be suspected. Only Cienn, or who she may have made her successor. Perhaps Lord Tordrum, from the north. Or Ruollan, the guard – no others were mentioned by his father – and only Cienn, truly.

Selvorne planted the spear and looked around the grove – there was one more person who he could trust completely, but not yet rely upon – himself. A strange realisation came to him, and he sat upon a large rock.

His father trusted himself – and Arnlausa. Arnlausa trusted himself – and his father. The two of them, closer than any – a lifetime of danger and friendship. Arnlausa also trusted Girradehn, though Selvorne wondered if perhaps Uhlsko did not, so much. Did they all trust Selvorne? Trust, yes, but not rely upon him, that was clear, for they had told him little.

Whoever killed them must have known – and might have meant to kill just one, but knew very well that to do so would incur the wrath of the other. Two men dead, by accident unquestioned, accepted by others and no fear of pursuit. Perhaps Girradehn needed to be silenced, and Selvorne – was either unknown to them, which was possible, or was thought to be of no consequence. Also possible. But even a hopeless boy was a threat if he knew what had happened, and it was one thing that explained why no enemies were there to gloat, and why none had come for him, at the ravine. For if they knew he lived, they might let him live, and follow him to who he might tell. If they knew that much of his father and Arnlausa, they would know Cienn would not believe it was an accident – if his father was hated for things he had done so many years ago, Cienn would be hated a hundred times more – and hidden, far more than his father – and found, if a hopeless boy was followed.

Perhaps. He did not know. All he could do was guess, and try to think as a brigand might, but he did not know what manner of brigand it was who had done such a thing. Uhlsko had mentioned a few people he might trust, but Arnlausa had said only Cienn – he must have known the danger. Not only to Selvorne, but what he might bring to her – tell her, alone. Tell others along the way, and he would surely be followed, noticed – fooled. Tell none, and go in hiding – that was his oath to Arnlausa, and things seemed more complicated than before.

Selvorne stood, paced around, then was unsure if he should sit or scream – frustration, anger, fear perhaps. Enemies he did not know. A better warning would have been appreciated – an explanation, thorough and ... but Arnlausa was dying, and what he said made little sense at the end. Selvorne looked back to the town – his town – he should be able to blow the horns and gather the men, and march on the woods. Blow the horn – gather the ... enemies, unknown to him amongst the men, a march through the woods, a knife in his back, some story of brigands jumping from bushes and fleeing, all would be fooled and give chase to shadows. Selvorne would be dead, for being such a fool.

He did not scream, nor continue to pace, nor shake his spear and throw it angrily. He sat, and put his head in his hands. Breathed and rested, thought ... of shaving, to calm his mind. He became quiet, then looked back on the woods.

Hidden – in the crowd. Safe – unknown to enemies there, though it was not wise to be alone at the edge of town. Cienn might be hundreds of yards away, or a few days' journey. Join the guards and he might meet her soon, as a new guard introduced, not as a fool being followed. Or see her that night at the singing. Care would keep him alive, lack of care had killed his father. That was one thing he could do – be calm, and take care. He was not entirely unprepared, then, not completely without skill. He spoke well, and could pretend to be a man of no consequence.

He wished his father had told him more. Letters hidden were not enough. He might have hidden more – Selvorne hoped so, for he needed to know. Not a hundred yards away was a waggon with a grooming kit just like that bought for his mother – sold by the same man, who had met his father, how long ago? Twenty years, perhaps? Longer? In MidWaehter – it made sense. Hramullo and his friends had strange voices, the girl and boy were both dark haired, as was common in the south, he had heard. As was curled hair, though, not straight – and how had they come to the north without passing him on the road? Not by the quarry, though he laughed to think how many men could slip by the quarry along the road near, and be neither seen nor heard with all the pounding of the rocks.

A pretty girl, too – every one of the quarry men would notice her, even those already wed. Even Selvorne, who had to admit she was oddly alluring. Her face said little, her eyes not much more, and her words said nothing that made any sense. Not the sort of girl who usually would catch his eye, and being unable to speak with him, she likely would drive him mad – but pretty, if a man wanted a silent, pretty wife. And she was elegant and clever, he was sure of it, and had heard her speak with the others, and – not words of the Waehter. A different people? How had he not noticed, they –

Selvorne stood quickly, and meant to gather his things and return to the waggon, but then stopped himself. Care, it was only moments ago he swore to be careful.

Danger? No, he did not think so – they seemed to be sincere merchants. If looking for him, they did not know his face, and if they did, they were giving away many opportunities to kill him, having taken him to the woods once already, with spear, and knowing he was there that very moment, alone. Perhaps they meant to follow him – he would be careful. If they came from the south – they would need to be questioned. No hurry to leave, there was time for that later. Was it suspicion he felt, or a rush of excitement? Different people, different words, such visitors had not been in the lands for a very long time. Not in the north, anyway, but often in the south, his father had said, though it never interested him much before.

Sitting again, he began to think on his plan, and his mind was racing. The singing, for all the town to hear. Eat first. Groom himself before that, and perhaps ... a fresh change of clothes, if he could purchase some. To meet the singer Dyneti – Waehdric, and if she liked him, she might introduce him to Cienn. Or perhaps Cienn would appear, being at the festival all along. She liked to do that, he had heard, in disguise – perhaps that was just a story for children, to make them behave, for fear she spied on them, and might catch them doing mischief. She could be anyone – though, she was old, and quite short, so perhaps not truly anyone. Hramullo? Selvorne laughed – that would be amusing, and a feat of astounding skill in disguise. Not impossible, though, and not entirely unexpected.

A plan, and care, and eagerness awakening within him – Cienn, vengeance. Dyneti – adoration. But ... Adyleh ... he bit his lip. Warmth and laughter, he began to yearn to be with her again. Sitting and watching the show, laughing and sharing and ... he longed to see her eyes.

Guarded Welcome

Selvorne made his preparations, finding a sack to hold all his boxes, buying a new shirt and washing himself once more, he felt prepared to meet – well, he felt quite unprepared to meet the most beautiful woman he had ever seen, but it was the best he could do, and at least he had presents for her, and the acquaintance of her assistant, friendship of her guards, and – he was a lord, after all. She was only a singer.

No, not just a singer, a Waehdric – well versed in the history of their people, their laws and customs, all their beliefs and secret knowledge. Far more than just a singer, she would be amongst the smartest people in the lands. And what a singer – a gift, honed by training – but a gift, beyond the abilities of any other. He was sure all the Waehdric learnt some kind of instrument to play, and he had heard that many of them were terrible. Some were good, others brilliant – but to sing, that was something else, a talent that practise alone could not create.

Word of Dyneti was known in the town, even before the festival, and after the performance he had seen, all people of the town knew they would be at a show greater than anything ever before seen at Tavalehk. And that was why, as the day grew late, great crowds of people moved south and west, to the Festival Field.

Selvorne made his way, but in no hurry – he never was, not for the night of the great show. That night his seat was being held by a dozen guards who had invited him. And ... he sighed to think of it – his seat was always being held for him. Whether the town knew who he was or not, they must have seen him sitting near Arnlausa at the show. A few seats apart, in not a bad location. He usually did not spend much time with his father and friend at the festival, for they arrived each year after spending days together on the road – but at the great show he sat to the side of them, on a comfortable stool with a good view.

Not the best view, for it was not directly in front of the stage – once he took himself to the centre, but he was young then, and found it uncomfortable sitting on the grass. He knew the guards of the Waehdric would sit to the right somewhere, a good position not too far to the side, and so he walked slowly. People rushed past him, and he felt some guilt to think that they, not he, would be struggling to find a good place on the Field. Even if it was his meadow, his town, and if he wanted to be strict about it, part of his house.

The Festival Field was a large, open space of wild grasses almost at the main part of town, the southern end, near the river that came from the lake. It was away from the road, out of the way and yet, close to everything. It was large enough to easily hold the entire people of the town, even were their numbers doubled – which was a good thing, for that year their numbers might have done just that, and some years, double again.

From the Field to the east was the town, only a hundred feet or so from the meadow end to the first house, then a hundred yards to the road. To the north it was not quite woodlands. Small trees, trying to grow large, to replace those long since cut. To the south it was much the same, but then there was the river, and Arnlausa was caring enough to build a wooden fence beside it to stop people wandering from festival to their watery death, in the dark, or when very drunk. Some had fallen, none had died, and no one did either since the fence was made – at his expense, for which folk were grateful. Thanks soon forgotten when he banned them from sitting on it – an obvious seat to watch the show, but somehow they had overlooked the more obvious danger of falling backwards into the fast flowing waters behind.

To the west of the Field – headed away from the town, up a slight slope, then a gentle hill – on the top of that – the House of Arnlausa.

No, not the House of Arnlausa – the House of Laehtene. Of Arnlausa NohcLehk Laehtene – Selvorne never called him by his full name, let alone title. He sighed – not his house, either, it was to be the House of Skolerne. It felt wrong. That was the name of his father's house, at Vaskatohr, the warm stone home he knew his whole life, not the cool white house of painted clay on the hill. He stared across the field at it, and wished those he loved still lived.

Grim grew his mood, and it was not the time to be so. It was a good house, quiet, as Arnlausa preferred, away from the town – also preferred. He let others handle town affairs and he did whatever lords did on his hill. A spring was there – saving everyone from carting water up the hill all day, for many lived there, not only Arnlausa. Guards and maids and boys to do odd jobs about the place, men to tally accounts – in many ways it was a village of its own. Cooks and butchers, animals kept – herdsmen, and vegetables grown.

And the meadow – the Festival Field. Wild grasses that were always harvested before the full moon of the fifth month. Too early, usually, not making the best hay – but it made grass short to sit upon, and the meadow was for the townsfolk, not the hay. The second harvest of the year would be fine. Although, as Selvorne looked on the vast crowd gathered, he wondered how any grasses could recover from being so trampled.

That meadow had been used all day. Few stalls were there, only for food, and mainly to feed the parents of children who had been competing that afternoon in games of running, races, chases, throwing – for prizes. Wrestling, some of the older ones. Climbing of poles – the poles were still there, men were struggling to remove them from the holes. Children were sleeping – Selvorne laughed, that was himself not so very long ago. He wondered who won the Sudden Race – where all the children were in the middle, and when signalled, they had to be first to the man with the flag. However, the man with the flag was hidden in the crowd that encircled the children, and for quite some time they desperately peered into the crowd, not knowing where to run, or when. Not daring cross the line early, bunching up in a group in the centre, and not sure whether it was worse to be at the starting line of the circle, perhaps to find themselves on the wrong side of everyone when the flag appeared – or to wait in the centre, surrounded by others who would be in the way.

Selvorne had won it once, through luck alone. One boy ran, all followed, except himself and a few others – for they had all raced the wrong way. He easily beat those others who hesitated, and all the others who had run as fast as they could in the opposite direction. His father was proud, and when Selvorne reluctantly admitted it was hesitation, and not cleverness that made him win – he was praised for modesty. Undeserved, and ... he was so terribly missed. Selvorne took a deep breath, and looked over the meadows.

The eastern end of the Festival Field had a low platform set, which was the stage where the show would be performed. A large cloth had been arranged like a roof to cover it against rain, but there would be no rain – it was a very hot, sticky night, with a clear sky and sadly, no breeze. Puppets were on the stage, small and easily seen only by the children who crammed up at the front. The first of many shows, not only Dyneti would appear that night, and the eager crowds stretched all the way from stage to hill, then up the hill and to the sides, into the woods and – Selvorne was sure people were sitting on the river fence. He shook his head with disapproval.

It was early, and yet very crowded. Selvorne saw where the guards were to sit, it was a good position, facing the stage, but to the right. Not the best place to be seated, that was on the ground before the stage, but the guards had actual seats – great long benches – and it would be comfortable. No people dared sit there, knowing who it was for, apart from a few mischievous children who claimed the ends of the benches for themselves.

Selvorne found food and ate alone, away from the Field, but where he could watch it filling with what had to be the entire town. The puppets ended, the children cheered, then cried, then ran as they were chased back to their parents by a man dressed as a bull, with great horns – two on his head, and more blown by men who followed him, making sounds as though the roar of a bull. Musicians appeared on the stage and played – some people danced, most sat and chatted and ate. Guards began to arrive, and when they took their places on the benches, Selvorne realized they had tankards of ale, and sang along. The seats rocked as they swayed and danced where they sat, almost tipping seats over at times, which caused a panic to save their ale, then great laughter if none was spilt.

He would be glad to join them, and not only for the view, or seat, or jolly company of drunken men, but for the position, which was far from a place of memories. Across the Field, to the left of the stage, set aside from all people, was a small platform only half a foot high, a wooden place off the grass, and upon it were three chairs. Proper chairs, with arms and backing, tall and strong, wide and comfortable, with cushions. Well positioned, though a little to the side – to see the stage, but not block the view of others behind, Arnlausa had said. No persons sat there. Any children who dared were quickly scolded and made to climb down from either chair or platform.

Arnlausa sat there. Uhlsko sat there. In his mind, Selvorne could see them – that was where they sat, usually. Not that year. Not ... not any year, again. He sighed, and took a deep breath as sorrows blended in his heart.

Three chairs – and the third was another memory. It was not for him, he sat on a stool, behind the others, or sometimes on the platform itself, with cushions. The third chair was for his mother – and had been empty for many years. Was it ten ... ten, at least. Always empty, always honoured. What should he do with it – keep it, still? Three empty chairs sitting there each year, and his own in front. No, it was not there for her, it was for his father, and his father was also gone. Perhaps he would have new chairs built and keep the three aside, in the house, safe for ... memories.

It hurt him to look at them, so he turned away, and wondered what the townsfolk must have thought. Arnlausa And Later, that year, rather than The Late Arnlausa. More than late, he was missing the entire festival. Was he missed, though? Selvorne thought he was, and wondered if he should go to the chairs and see who looked on with sorrow, sadness or concern. Or watched in silent menace – no, he should not go near the chairs. No killer would be so foolish to watch without themselves being hidden. Care, and caution. He took himself to the benches of the guards, and looked on who was there.

Many guards had arrived, and Temnere, Demni, Savak as well. The mood had changed. Administrators also, not only guards. To be expected. Guards were removing themselves from the first bench where they had sat, for Temnere was glaring at them – they did not move to the second, but back quite a few rows. Well behaved, behind his back, apart from one who was still standing, shaking his finger at the others, indicating for them to – move back farther? And then they laughed, and were quickly silent when Temnere turned.

Demni sat beside Temnere, and the only look on her face close to joy was a slight smile at the laughing guards. Then she was grim, and turned away to face the front. Beside her was Savak, who might have been happier at the back, drinking ale with the others. Selvorne thought he had better greet them, for good manners, so he walked around the benches and stood before them all.

Three sat tall and stern, though Temnere seemed restless at first – they all stared at Selvorne, who bowed, and only Savak stood and gave a short bow back.

"A good night to you all," Selvorne said, but Temnere and Demni just glared back at him.

"Hello, what are you doing here?" Savak asked.

"I was invited to sit with the guards," Selvorne replied, "by Adyleh."

"Who?" Savak asked.

"Adyleh, Dyneti's assistant."

"Who? Dyneti?" Savak asked, and he turned to Temnere and Demni. Temnere was glaring at him, shaking his head, and seemed almost furious. Demni raised an eyebrow, and Savak moved quite close to Selvorne.

"Look, I would not want to sit here, if I had a choice," Savak whispered, "why not go to the centre, there, and sit on the ground – it is better viewing."

"Nonsense!" came a booming voice from behind – one of the guards had quietly approached, unseen by Selvorne, who turned – a man who had shared lunch with Selvorne that very day. He was tall, broad and fair haired, and quite merry. As was Savak to see him, and he grinned back.

"He is sitting here with us," called the guards from the rows behind – many stood, beckoning eagerly, but with a shake from the tall, fair man's head, they instead came forward – and to Selvorne's surprise, a signal to Savak made him nod once and be silent.

Selvorne was greeted by thumps on his back, and made to sit on the very first bench, on the right of it, and was soon amongst guards who sat everywhere else – to his left, behind him, and in the row behind that. His pack was taken by one and placed with others – near where they sat, but not so near that a fast thief could not heave it up and run. Who, though, would be so bold with many deadly men so close – not Selvorne, he dared not even argue against where he was being sat.

"Sit down, Savak!" one man ordered, for his view was blocked. The tall fair man went straight to Temnere, knelt beside him, spoke a few words, rose up and returned to Selvorne, taking a place beside him.

"Are you sure it is all right?" Selvorne asked the guard, who assured him it was.

"Temnere is just ... an old stick, in the mud. He will not bend, he will not move, and if you push him too much, he will flick mud at you, and fall down. Or break."

Selvorne felt a little better, but was surprised at Temnere – that someone who had been so friendly the day before could be so rude, and for no reason. Temnere sat, staring ahead, and seemed quite angry. Selvorne did not like being so close to him, even with several men sitting between them. It was not seeming to be the night he had expected it to be.

After a while, Demni excused herself, left the area for some time, and came back with a large jug of what Selvorne assumed was water. She took it to the men behind, some accepted it, with empty tankards, others did not wish to water their ale, others said it would be an improvement, even if it was mud. As she passed behind Selvorne, she knelt down and handed him a wooden cup, then filled it as she spoke in a voice that would have been a whisper, if it was not so deep.

"Do not mind Temnere. He is stuck on codes of custom ... and the rule, as long as it is one he agrees with, and especially if it is one he devised. It was his idea to have an area for guards and administrators. Having you here ... is making him quite angry, but he will not challenge Dyneti. Hopefully now he will be annoyed enough by you to leave soon."

Selvorne took the water, nodded, and she left him. He wondered if she was not as bad as he had first thought – perhaps she was before in a bad mood, with good reason to be. Kindness, to offer water – consideration, to think to ease his concerns for Temnere. Selvorne wondered if he saw a bit of the sparkle that Rohy was so keen for – her eyes, twinkling as she spoke. Or something, he was not sure what – perhaps her gentleness, which seemed so unusual for her, and whenever she was pleased, Selvorne yearned she would be again, and he smiled as he thought of it.

Despite that, it was little comfort to learn that Temnere was angry at Selvorne. He was not feeling at ease sitting there, and wished Adyleh would soon join them.

"When will Adyleh be here?" he asked the tall fair guard beside him, who chuckled, as did several sitting behind, who were at once very quiet. Selvorne thought one of them groaned, and the fair–haired guard waved his hand back at them, as though a dismissal.

"Oh, she will be here just when the show begins, I assure you. Always perfectly on time."

"Yes, you could say, exactly on time, for the show cannot go on without her," a guard added from behind, and it earned him an elbow from one and a slap across the head from another. The tall, fair–haired man beside Selvorne looked at them, and they were silent, then he shrugged at Selvorne who thought that, if Adyleh was Dyneti's assistant, she was likely preparing her for the performance, and of course could not join the crowd until the show had begun.

More guards appeared to take their seats, each of them stared at Selvorne before shuffling along a bench behind him. Few greeted him, except with a nod. They were all different ages, some he thought no older than himself – some much older. The three quite old Waehdric appeared, each one wearing a novelty hat of a different colour, and the one with a green hat wearing it upside down, sitting tall and straight, and apparently using it as a bowl for nuts atop his head.

It occurred to Selvorne that he hardly knew anyone around him – only a few names, nothing of the people. If they were all killers of his father, it would have been a very strange tale if he survived. But they were guards, and not so drunk as they behaved. Merry, and dangerous, and good men. Not what he had imagined, not of guards and not for the night. He had expected, though it seemed absurd to think of it, that somehow he would have sat on the platform as usual, in a chair, guards standing around him, laughing, drinking – the show magnificent, the singing delightful, and the lovely ...

He blinked and bit his lip. The lovely ... Adyleh? Sitting beside him – his heart pounded. He meant to ... think of the singer. He meant to think of Dyneti – he was there for her, with a present and a new shirt. But his waking dream was to sit with Adyleh and laugh, and it was an unexpected idle thought.

"Will Adyleh sit with us?" Selvorne asked the tall fair man, and he smiled.

"You are quite taken with her?" the guard asked in a low voice.

"I – she is lovely," Selvorne replied, and the man nodded.

"And Dyneti?" the guard asked.

"Is ... impossibly beautiful," Selvorne found himself saying, and the guard laughed. Several others were leaning forward, and the guard threw his hand back over his head in a sweeping blow, which would have slapped them if they were nearer, so they all moved back.

"That, she is, though I assure you – quite possible. And truly. Tell me, Selvorne, are you always so rude?"

Selvorne frowned – what had he done – nothing rude, or was he bold, to speak of her that way.

"What?"

"Do you always sit amongst those you do not know, and neither introduce yourself, nor ask their name?"

Selvorne blinked – and winced. That was very rude, and he could not believe he had ... but he had not forgotten. It was rude, and it was almost ... deliberate. No, he had not introduced himself – he wanted to remain hidden. But that was not it, not then, not at lunch, not when he preferred to be alone with Adyleh, instead of starting a conversation amongst a dozen guards ... selfish, not rude.

"Kalgevun," the guard said in a low voice, "I am Dyneti's guard. Usually. Fear not, the men care nothing for formality. Or manners, at times. Nor do I, and it is half expected from ... but look, now things are beginning."

Some people appeared from behind the stage, and drove all the children way back from its edge – sternly, with no costumes of bulls and horns, just harsh words and angry waving hands. Men placed two large clay pans on stands, roughly five feet high, at either side of the stage – then poured sand into them from small barrels. The entire crowd watched with great curiosity. There was movement on the stage, not as well concealed as the night before – people were obviously doing things behind sheets held high. Being slightly to the side, Selvorne had a better view than most of what was going on, but had no idea what that was, and like everyone else, he stared in wonder until all the people disappeared from the stage.

Then, suddenly, voom! Mighty flames flaring from the clay pans – many people screamed, jumped back – even the guards were astonished, several rising and preparing to run. Away? No, likely for water, before sitting back down, shaking, with wide eyes. Selvorne felt his heart pounding – the flames were furious, tall and terrible – then settled to low flickers. Then, and only then when it seemed safe, the crowd burst into applause and cheers. Thousands of people screaming with delight

– the sound of it was as extraordinary as the sudden fire, and Selvorne knew it was going to be a night he would never forget.

That the guards were as surprised as he suggested it was something new, they stared with childlike wonder at the stage. All of them, even Kalgevun and Savak, who Selvorne assumed were the highest in rank, for they were in the first row. Demni – mildly amused. Perhaps that slight smile was her look of astonished awe. Temnere was stroking his chin and staring – he had not seen it before, either. The guards behind were so funny to see that Selvorne chuckled – and the old Waehdric men were giggling like children, and one gestured to the others as though explaining something complicated. They had some hand in it, he was sure, and delighted in the mischief, looking over the crowd and chuckling, with sly grins. They saw Selvorne, and all three at once touched hands to their hats, so he nodded a bow back at them, before facing the front and frowning to himself at their unexpected show of respect.

When the crowd had settled from the shock, and silence was threatened only by murmurs, the music began softly and then it grew – louder by the moment, from musicians who had appeared around the stage. It was a festive song, rather than a ballad, and an old tune that everyone but Selvorne seemed to know – they were humming and swaying along with the words. The guards, perhaps a little too eagerly, the bench behind rocking forwards and backwards, and Kalgevun almost knocked Selvorne off the edge. Children were clapping as loudly as they could, right near Temnere, who was neither swaying, clapping nor humming. Perhaps fuming in time to the song. Demni was staring at the stage eagerly, sitting at the very edge of the seat on her hands, swaying ever so slightly, like a tall fine tree in a breeze.

A few performers ran out onto the stage and began to sway and dance, all together, joined in a line. From amongst them one figure emerged, to cheers and shouts from the crowd. Selvorne stared – a bright blue outfit, of trousers, and a tunic for a shirt, like a forester boy might wear when such things were in fashion, but with all the elegance of a noble lord addressing the council. He was holding a large staff, and began to sing – Selvorne knew the words, then, if not the tune – the first verse of a comedy song, entitled The Silly Brigand. It was a story of a simple-minded thief who patrolled the roads, and with clever plans he managed to rob all the other thieves without realising it, then returned all the goods to the town, to be sold back to the children of the original owners, at half the price they were worth. The story was a favourite for children, for he was a hero in strange kind of way, thought to once have been real – although, as children grew older, they were assured no such person had ever been, and that it was only a story.

But a story for children, and the night was early, the time of puppets, music and songs for the young. Selvorne wondered how long it would be for Dyneti to appear, perhaps quite some time. The singer on the stage was popular, and Selvorne knew nothing of him – he might sing for hours. Golden skin, and dark hair under a bright blue cap, and a rather high voice for even a young boy. Selvorne turned and realised many of the guards were staring at him.

"Will Dyneti appear for this song?" Selvorne asked, thinking she might sing later verses – they all laughed – all but one large man, who groaned as though in pain.

"Well, looks like you won this one," the large guard said, which earned him an elbow from another that he ignored, "double by the end of the song!"

The man who had elbowed him nodded, as did several others, though Kalgevun frowned – and Selvorne was very confused.

The song ended with much cheering and bows. Kalgevun watched Selvorne and seemed amused by his confused clapping.

"How about – double by show's end?" one of the guards behind asked, but another, rather ordinary looking man snatched the wrists of the first, clenching them until he yelped. And then oddly, the guard was silent and sat nicely – as though he had surrendered. Several of the men looked to Selvorne.

Odd men, strange behaviour, most of all Kalgevun who was making the weirdest face as he stared ahead – but it was Temnere who caught Selvorne's eye, for he was complaining bitterly about something, stood up suddenly, rubbed his back, then stormed off across the field, passing in front of the crowd who jeered, and demanded he should get out of the way. That only angered him more, and did not make him hurry, but slow his pace and glare at the crowd as he passed by, annoying each in turn.

The singing forester on stage waved farewell to all, then turned to the side and pretended to walk on the spot, as assistants clumsily dragged painted trees and shrubs past. Not the best illusion of walking, and some people laughed at the jerky movement of the trees, some of which almost toppled. Great gaps, and the obvious dark forms of those who carried them, at first – then more trees, bushes, shrubs, and none of the assistants could be seen. It truly looked as though the forester walked through the woods. Each tree nearing the end of the stage disappeared as it was turned to show its dark side, then moved fast as a black shape lost against the dark curtains, only to reappear on the other side as a tree once more. Selvorne was entranced, and gazed on in amazement, then appreciation, then boredom as it went on for such a long time. One very large bush passed by, and as it did, the forester disappeared behind it – only for a moment – to appear on the other side, transformed. From a young man in blue to a lady in white – a flowing dress, magnificent and bright, and with dark curly hair falling about her shoulders.

The crowd let out a gasp. It was not possible – but of course, it was, they had all seen it – a change so swift and unexpected it was almost missed. The trees were turned around and folded and arranged to reveal paintings – the wonders of the skies at night – stars, the moon, black silhouettes of trees against the dark blue sky. The music was sweeter, and a song began about the wonders of life, the mysteries of the dark, and the importance of being a good boy or girl. Another song for the children, but all people stared in wonder, for the sound was so beautiful no one could tell what was instrument or voice. The singer descended into the crowd, approached those at the front, and sung to the children for a verse, before returning to the stage and singing to all.

Selvorne stared – he was stunned. It was Adyleh. It had to be – he could not mistake her, even at that distance. But it was also Dyneti, he knew her voice. But – she was neither tall, nor pale, nor with red hair – nor as old as he had imagined. Unless the two ladies were playing some joke on him.

"Who is that singing?" Selvorne asked Kalgevun, "Dyneti – or Adyleh?"

Kalgevun grinned, raised one hand, clicked his fingers twice, and many guards behind groaned.

"Both, you silly boy," called an angry guard from the row behind.

"Do not mind him, he is just sore," Kalgevun said in a low voice as Selvorne stared at the stage, "Dyneti is Adyleh. Dyneti Dric Adyleh. Nobody calls her Adyleh, though, anymore – apart from her family."

"She – what?"

"We had a wager, to see when you would determine the truth, which I have happily won, and I look forward to claiming my winnings tonight. Most thought sooner, and he thought you would work it out as soon as the show started. Dyneti thought you would determine – or at least find out – before the show. I, however, had little faith in your keen eye, after watching you spend hours with her all day and still not realise – and I was willing to risk that it would take at least a song or two."

"Stupid tunic dressed as a boy," the large man behind mumbled.

"You can hear us?" Kalgevun asked, turning to the men behind, who nodded.

"You are hardly whispering," the smaller man replied.

"And hardly poor, now," Kalgevun said, "so sort the coins, if you would. Wine for all – my treat. You know from where."

They nodded and grinned, but Demni leant back – very far back, so that she was between the two rows, and glared at them all.

"Will you all be silent – you are ruining the song – and stop drinking," she ordered. They all bowed their heads, and she leant forward again to stare at the stage.

"I also knew what the first song would be," Kalgevun whispered to Selvorne, "but do not tell the others. Unfair, I guess, but winnings fairly shared. No harm done, no insult meant. Rucarik thought you the dumbest, but I would not challenge him on it."

So ... Selvorne, apparently, was the target of their jest – their wager, a deceit. Perhaps not so warmly welcomed, not so liked, merely ... to be there amongst them so they might guard the outcome of a wager. Entertainment ... part of the show. And Adyleh – or Dyneti – was part of such deceit. He was not sure if he should be angry, or pleased. Part of him felt betrayed – he had been made a fool of – or had been a fool, and ... he remembered she did laugh a lot, it must have been at him. And his hair had looked absurd, so perhaps, to her, he was no more than a joke. Was it anger he felt or something else ... a crushing feeling was upon his chest.

She had seemed so sincere, so ... approachable. That was Dyneti? The singer? How many men had approached her – thousands. What was he – special, perhaps, as a joke. It would have to be a rare thing for a man to come to her and not know her face – every person in town would know her, after the show. He felt an idiot, and did not know if she was a cold–hearted beauty, or a sincere young lady, who enjoyed laughing and did not care if he was a fool.

He was not sure he cared if he was. A fool, he could accept, but betrayed – mocked – no, he was not sure he was hurt by that, either. Arnlausa mocked him all the time, and was loved for it. So did Girradehn, in a very different way. Which way, then, did she mock him – if the latter, he was not sure he wanted to know.

Part of him also felt lacking. He was supposed to be trying to determine who the killers were, to find Cienn and make an alliance, to gather men and hunt enemies. Instead he was enjoying himself at the festival, chatting to maidens, tasting the foods, spoiling himself with presents. Distractions from his duty – and he was so caught by them, that he had been fooled easily by a bunch of drunken guards, and a girl playing a silly joke at his expense. If he did not recognise a maiden he ... had spent so much time with, how could he possibly recognise his enemy, who he had hardly seen?

He looked over to the three chairs set aside for Arnlausa, his father, his long lost mother – and he felt pain at how he had let them down. Sitting there, watching a show, as their bodies were crammed into barrels, hidden in the crevice of a ravine. In the darkness of a cave. He felt ashamed of himself, and sat with his head in his hands.

"Cheer up, good fellow, it was only a joke," Kalgevun said, putting a hand to Selvorne's shoulder, "when you know her, you will discover she is full of them. She did not mean anything by it – if anything, it shows she is quite fond of you, for she has little time for fools, or those she does not like. Beware, though, she is more fond of tricks than of singing, and better at them – and you can hear how well she sings."

Selvorne felt a little better – perhaps he was being too grim. He had every reason to be, but ... no, he was being a fool then, not before. A sulking fool. Mistaken appearance – of course, from tall to short, red haired to dark, a change of names. A sackcloth dress. How could he not be confused? She gave neither clue nor correction, that ... mischievous ... deceitful, and – he grinned. There she was, on the stage – that was Adyleh? That was the charming girl from lunch? She was magnificent, and ... he began to wonder what the rules were for Waehdric to be wed.

The song ended, many clapped, and Kalgevun turned quickly to the men behind.

"Men!" Kalgevun said, "Dyneti – her worst prank played upon you. Quickly!!"

Confused stares, until all looked at Selvorne – and nodded.

"The raising of one heel of my boots," the smallest man said, "to make me think I had a limp. It hurt, too, and the next day I did have a limp."

"A strange man, if Dyneti made you – " a large man began, but then stopped himself, just before being hit with several thumps, then he continued, "she raised her own boots, hers, and those of everyone that day. And made them stand tall – convinced me I had shrunk. Changed my trousers, too, with larger ones. It was a most baffling day."

None laughed, and another large man leant forward from the row behind. He had been listening and nodding as the others spoke.

"Mine were smaller," the second large man said, "she said I had grown fat. Do you think she swapped our trousers?"

"Are you sure you did not simply get fat?" the other large man asked, and then several laughed, but the one farthest back winced, and then shrugged. He was a little fat.

"She would not have said it, if you had," Kalgevun said, and the large man grinned, "but – you have."

"True," the large man said, "but a few more lunches like that and I fear I shall be thin again, if not dead."

Several laughed, and Selvorne wondered what a strange woman Dyneti must be.

"Sand witch," said the large, fair–haired man behind him, and Selvorne frowned – the others seemed to breathe in all at once – and were silent.

Savak, who was not participating in their stories, turned to them all and glared.

"Oh – I – she put sand on the meat between bread," the fair–haired man said quickly, "which was ... rather crunchy."

"Are you sure that was a prank? She might have thought she was doing you a favour, preparing lunch?" the smallest man asked, and all laughed again.

"I hate to admit it, but that is the worst prank of all," Kalgevun said, "and I have endured it longest, and the most."

"You are a brave man," the small man said.

"How you live is impossible to reason," the large man added.

"What has sand on meat in bread got to do with a witch?" Selvorne asked, and some of the men gasped.

All were silent, many sat back on their bench and pretended they were not involved. Demni leant back in her seat, glaring at them all before fixing her eyes on Selvorne. Kalgevun leant back as well, and blocked her gaze.

"You heard that?" Kalgevun asked.

Demni nodded.

"Nothing intended."

"I know," Demni said.

"Worst prank – you must have had the worst, surely?"

All eyes fixed on Demni, but few heads turned her way. She was leaning back impossibly far, and Selvorne could tell her arms were straining – no, not straining, but strong. He imagined, if she wanted, she could have lifted herself off the seat –

or flipped backwards, tumbling in reverse to her feet. Easily. Those who sat behind her moved, but also seemed interested in what she might say.

"A snake, in my dress," Demni said, and the men gasped.

"What?" Kalgevun asked.

"You heard."

"In your – dress?"

She gave one nod, and then was silent.

"I am not sure if that is less believable than that you had a dress," the smallest man said, and Demni glared at him.

"All Waehdric wore dresses."

"That long ago?" the large, fair–haired man asked, and Demni nodded.

"A snake, alive, in my dress," Demni said, "moving as it laid on our bed – once I had disturbed it. You can imagine – "

"Ohh ... " many of the men said at once, and others said "Aha!"

"Not wearing it, then?" one of the large men asked, and Demni glared at him immediately, "I meant – not that – but – a snake?"

Demni nodded.

"How is this even possible? Or sensible – or funny?" the smallest man asked, astonished, as though he had not believed any of it until then.

"It was neither," Demni said, "and I screamed. You asked the worst – that was but one of the worst. She thought it amusing – at first. The other is more pain – the other we all know."

Silence, and then there were nods from the men. One, then another. Most of the men – not Savak, and not Kalgevun, who both shook their heads.

"What ... did you do?" Kalgevun asked, and Demni just grinned – then frowned.

"Silence – she is to sing," Demni said, and at that she snapped herself straight and disappeared into the row, half hidden by Savak, who had kept quietly to himself.

Selvorne was ... confused? Astounded? Delighted – or afraid. Whatever he felt, he no longer felt a fool, or mocked or ... he was one of them, in a strange way, and no longer begrudged their wager. He thought he might buy them all some wine. What kind of woman ... he winced, he clenched his jaw, he knew what kind of woman would do such terrible mischief as that. His kind. That gleam he had seen in her eye was not the simple adoration of a plain lovely girl – it was wicked mischievous delight.

And that simple gazing idiot she had fooled could continue to look a fool even as vengeance was his – one thing he could do, and do easily, was convince others he was dumb. Plenty of practise, and all the evidence men would ever need to believe it, Arnlausa had said. And the fact that it was true, Girradehn had added. And the secret that it was not, his father had said, though Selvorne usually thought that was to lift his spirits, in recent years he had discovered it was true.

A song was to begin, the break had been long, and the crowd became restless, but were being hushed by each other when the music began to grow loud.

Kalgevun was disturbed – at something said, realised or observed, Selvorne was not sure.

"Why are you grim?" Selvorne dared whisper, and Kalgevun nodded.

"It is nothing."

"I doubt that."

Kalgevun looked at Selvorne, and nodded again.

"Demni is usually not so friendly," Kalgevun said – an odd thing to say, even stranger to whisper, and then he leant back to look at her, before turning to Selvorne again.

"Not so friendly," Kalgevun whispered close to Selvorne's ear, "nor did I think so cruel. She pretended the snake in her dress had bitten her, she feigned she was to die – perhaps wise, for our lady never played a prank so foolish since. I did not know she placed it there, though."

"That seems ... cruel," Selvorne said.

"The snake? Or the bite?"

"Either – both."

"Yes. One was done first, unwise, and dangerous to handle a snake. For both of them. Children, though, and neither harmed. Silence, she sings – speak of this to no one, not even ... either of them."

~

Dyneti had started a new song – of love found, and lost, and longing, and found again – then lost again, then found, but not wanted. All the follies of love and romance, jealousy and hate, longing and despair. Each verse about a different couple – or so Selvorne hoped, and not one couple with such erratic lives. As she sang she walked down to the crowd, and all were completely silent so they could hear. She sang a line to men and women alike, many of whom blushed or giggled, some stared dreamily, and not only men. It was an enchantment, an honour and a wonder, and though her voice did not carry so well from amongst the crowd, those who had her sing when near gazed with eyes of wonder.

Demni was leaning forward, sitting on both her hands and grinning. Dyneti came up to her and sang her a few lines about love for learning, for study, for books – and touched her cheek as she left her friend to stand before the guards. Frozen, silent guards – she sang a few lines about the love of duty, brotherhood and alliance, a love as great as any – a devotion of muscle and heart. At the end they cheered and pounded their chests, once only, all together with fists.

She did not look at Selvorne. She did not look in his direction, and he felt cheated somehow. But as she walked briskly past him, she touched his shoulder briefly – and his spirits lifted as his heart pounded hard. Then she quickly ran her way around the benches, back into the crowd – halfway across the field – and delicately tried to step between where people sat, to reach as many people as she could, often repeating her lines from before – but allowing them all to hear her best.

"Ahh, do not be disappointed. I am sure she would have sung you a few lines if she could. It was not you she feared, it was this," Kalgevun said, and Selvorne looked up at him – he stuck his tongue out one side of his mouth, opened his eyes wide and tilted his head in the most absurd expression, then returned to normal. Selvorne shook his head and blinked in confusion, "you see, I have another wager – with her alone. That I could make her laugh in the middle of a song. So, I think she is likely more scared of me than of any man in all the lands, at the moment. And I think I will lose this wager, for I have pulled faces all night to no avail. I am beginning to wonder if it is not some prank she is playing on me."

As Dyneti continued her rounds of the crowd, Taahr ran up from behind the stage – straight to the guard's benches before stopping to stare at them all. He looked over everyone there before fixing his eyes on Demni, then moved to her at once. She was turned in her seat to watch Dyneti, and startled by Taahr's breath in her ear as he whispered something. She scowled at him, turned back to Dyneti, but he insisted and she angrily stood and strode off with him. Every guard noticed and watched as they disappeared, then let out a cheer and began singing along, swaying back and forth – as they were before Demni had appeared. They almost rocked the bench over, and some also drew out flasks to begin drinking.

The song ended, Dyneti returned to the stage, and the show continued well until it grew dark. When it came to the end, the last brief song was called "Hush" and it was about being quiet and falling asleep. The music softly died down, and the assistants ignited the flaming display again, but it was a quiet, gentle fire – bright and powerful. When the flames died down, the stage was empty. People knew that was the end for the night, and most also knew not to applaud or wake the children, so the crowd began a slow walk back to their homes, tents, or other festival areas where the night was considered young. All in a strange silence, with perhaps some sorrow that such a wonderful show had ended.

Which

It was not late, and that was not unusual for the end of such a show. Arnlausa liked an early night – he usually would move quickly back to his home on the hill for a good sleep, and, wanting to discourage merry making in front of his house, organised the "Hush" song at the end of each show. Hush – be quiet – and go away, if you please. Early to bed, easier to rise, he said, and often that would make men chuckle. He was not there that year, but the town did what was expected, perhaps not thinking of it, perhaps with plans already made. Revelry that would be far from his home and meadow – the Festival Field would be left that night, little used in the next days, cleaned at the end then left to grow. One hay harvest before winter, then bare silence until ... the next year. The next festival. And never again would their lord sit on his chair, make them laugh, then leave early after the song of Hush. Selvorne decided that moment Arnlausa would be remembered by that song – always, and every year.

He did not feel grim, he felt strengthened. Around him were strong men, likely worthy of trust, once proven. And he had met and befriended a great ally without realising it – and at that he felt elated.

To meet the magnificent Dyneti – how he had trembled that morning at the thought of it. Selvorne was no longer nervous. He boldly stood, gave farewell to the guards, gathered his pack and sack of presents, then headed straight for the back of the stage. Not to meet – to confront. Not to tremble – but oh, how he would make her tremble. Dyneti. Adyleh. Mischief maker. Mischief taker – delightful prank, was it? Then delight was what he would give her – with a prank so clever she would shake. No, he was not angry. Not hurt, not a boy, but his eagerness for mischief might have betrayed him, so he took a deep breath and tried to seem glum.

As the stage was set in a field, not a tavern, there was neither hall nor room to which she could retreat. An area behind had been arranged from the painted wooden scenery and great dark cloths on poles, allowing Dyneti to change, unseen. All the town was walking past, so her assistants – some of whom were guards – ensured no one came too close. Well, they tried to – Selvorne was close enough to see Dyneti had already changed back into her brown dress, and when made to halt he said he wanted to speak with Adyleh, at which they laughed and let him through.

It was not the best light in the oddly walled area. A few torches burnt, their flames making the painted trees seem strangely real, and it was as though all her boxes and clothing and tables and seats were set in the middle of an enchanted wood. The sound of people passing by, though they spoke only quietly, seemed stranger still – as though spirits moved through the trees, unseen, unseeing – they were, of course, just behind the wooden walls and cloth sheets on poles. But it was the oddest place to be, and before him, ignoring him, packing her finest dresses – the strangest young lady he had ever met.

"Did you enjoy the show?" Dyneti asked without turning.

"I did, it was quite a good performance," Selvorne said quietly, "although – I was very much looking forward to hearing Dyneti sing."

Dyneti stopped packing, stood up and looked at him, tilting her head slightly. He stared back at her, straight at her, but through her eyes – vaguely, like a fool gripped in sorrow – it was difficult, for her eyes were peering into his, and they were piercing, and most distracting. And she was silent.

"You sang well. But ... I am sorry, I think I prefer her singing – last night, she was much more ... powerful. Clearer. She was one of the best singers I have ever heard – easily amongst the best five. Certainly the best this month. I hope – she is not ill?"

"No," Dyneti said, still staring into his eyes.

"And also – so very, very beautiful. Is she here?"

Silence.

"Her long red hair – I have not seen its like. Splendid. Not like ... well, I guess, uncommon. There is ... nothing wrong with dark hair, though, some prefer it, I am told. I mean, I – I like it."

Selvorne could hardly make out her face in the light of torches – she was partly in his shadow, as he was in hers.

"Well," Dyneti said, "your redheaded beauty could not sing for you tonight. And if she could, I think you might find her voice a little harsh if she tried to sing like that, two nights in a row. Perhaps then you might find she is not the perfect singer that you imagine."

"Oh – well, I do not think her perfect, just – she was good. A pity, though, I brought her this lovely present," Selvorne said, and at that he held up the sack that contained the box and mirror, as well as his spear and change of clothes.

She frowned.

"A sack?"

Selvorne laughed, and dared touch her shoulder with one hand as though she had made the funniest joke – she raised an eyebrow, and ... though she did not remove his hand, he quickly did, for to touch her was making him tremble. Quickly he put the sack to the ground, knelt and opened it, and removed his old shirt.

"A shirt?" Dyneti asked.

He ignored her, and took out one of the sharp ends of the spear.

She stepped back suddenly, but he had already put it down. Slowly she returned to him, and he removed the box and the mirror, and stood, holding them out.

Her eyes lit up – her face, too, which was odd – no, not odd, he was holding the mirror so the light reflected upon her, and she narrowed her eyes. Just for a moment, for she reached – and he pulled the presents away.

"No, I would prefer to give them to Dyneti myself," Selvorne said.

"That is Dyneti, you fool," came a gruff voice from just outside the wall, "just give her the presents and be off with you, some of us need to change clothes."

Dyneti clicked her fingers and the man disappeared.

"No ... it cannot be? Adyleh? Dyneti? You ... truly? One and the same?" Selvorne asked with as much astonishment as he could feign – and he knew even as he spoke that it was not enough, for her eyes narrowed and head tilted. Angry – no, she was embarrassed.

"Very funny. Well – now we are almost even," she said. Selvorne smiled, and she seemed thoughtful, "when did you find out?"

"Ah, yes, when did I find out. Well – I know about your little wager. I did not find out until the second song. Kalgevun is the winner, and as winner offered to buy all the men wine."

"The second song! Are you blind? I was looking straight at you during the first!" Dyneti said, and Selvorne shrugged.

"Dressed as a boy."

"Dressed as ... ugh! And despite Kalgy's absurd faces – I – am I truly that little known?"

"I have only seen you the once, and – "

"I told you my name!"

"You – what?"

"You did not know me? By name? Not one of your friends – or are you their fool?"

Selvorne bit his lip – he had no friends. None that he sought out, just townsfolk and ... but no friends. And if he had, he was not sure they would know ... but they would. Arnlausa would, his father would, Girradehn certainly would have known her, likely ... quite well. And that was a danger he had not paid enough attention to, so he was silent and she seemed – too upset at being unknown. Selvorne could not help notice the strangeness of it, since he was trying to remain unknown.

He explained that he had not spoken to anyone that entire day, sleeping late and making purchases at the festival, and much of the day was taken up with her – perhaps everyone knew her, but he did not. And he had no reason to expect deceit – by which he meant her prank – but saying it like that made her uneasy.

He offered her the present, although he felt quite silly about it – it was meant to be a formal offering to an intimidating, noble lady. The custom for which was an elegant bow, a statement of the offer, explaining that his intentions were not necessarily romantic, then the polite or eager acceptance on her part, making the gift easier to give. As Waehdric she was, after all, almost a lady in status – and he was a lord. Things were meant to be done properly, but ... she had fooled him, with a wager. He had taunted her, even teased. He presented the gift from a sack, and handing it to her so casually – it was the sort of thing a farm boy swineherd might do as a betrothal to a milk maiden.

"I was buying a spear, and the seller liked me so ... he gave me these at a good price," Selvorne began to explain, "and I thought, I have no use for this, but what a practical thing it would be, to hold all manner of things, for ... someone to prepare themselves, for a show, so ... here, it is yours."

Dyneti looked the box over and was very pleased. She looked in the mirror, raising it to her face, a hand on either side, elbows out and wide – a strange way to hold it, and her head disappeared behind it, so he could not see her face. The rest of her was unhidden, but he stared at the wooden back of the mirror and wished that she would – then, quite quickly, she moved it aside and was staring straight at Selvorne. He felt – almost – caught? And she smiled and gazed at his face.

Her assistant waiting outside must have been listening, for he came quickly from the entrance to stare at the box, picking it up and looking it over, opening the compartments and nodding.

"You are right, this will be useful. Well done!" he said, nodding at Selvorne, glancing at Dyneti, who was frowning – he took the box and put it on a table, to Selvorne's dismay – next to others quite similar. Then he left the enclosure without saying a word.

"Better than all the others," Dyneti said.

"I – yes, I hope so."

"I think so. So far, proven so."

Selvorne nodded, stared – and she laughed.

"Are you sure you want to?" Dyneti asked.

"Want to ... what?"

Dyneti laughed again.

"Give me the box – the mirror – the presents? Even now? Now you know my hair is black? Some prefer it, I am told."

"I was teasing," Selvorne said.

"I know. Quite bold, for a man with no shoes."

Selvorne frowned, then looked down – he had boots – and she laughed.

"Now we are even."

"We – what?" he asked.

"Now even, a new beginning. I am – "

"How is that even? Your two to my one, though, that was a rather ... pitiable prank," Selvorne said, and it was – a hopeless jest, and most odd she thought it amusing, and ... she was more than odd, she was delightfully pleasant, and he stared at her in astonishment, for she was unlike any maiden he had known.

She stared back at him, then laughed. Then frowned – stared – and gasped so suddenly that he was startled.

"Oh – oh my," she said, once she regained composure, "very well. You owe me one – a small joke, and I should prefer something witty said than ... not as before. Not a trick. Are we agreed?"

Selvorne shrugged, and she held out her hand. He took it – shook it – and she laughed.

"My word – you are not going to kiss it?" Dyneti asked.

"I am not sure what I should do," Selvorne said, which was true – he was quite confused, overwhelmed and – he had met not one person like her – no man, no woman, certainly not anyone so pretty. But to call her so was ... almost absurd. Kiss her hand? He almost wanted to kneel. And not for her rank or her status or her affection – but because he was completely astounded by her ... spell?

He stared, and she laughed again, but only a slight laugh and she touched his shoulder. It did not help him clear his mind.

"You are quite an odd young man."

"It has been a rather odd day."

"Ahh – he speaks!"

"I ... yes. Kiss your hand? You truly are Dyneti Dric ... Adyleh?"

Dyneti nodded.

"Waehdric, then – I am not sure if we are meant to kiss your hands?" he asked.

"Not the men – though I think they might find it amusing."

"And find me amusing every time they see me after, as might most people who hear of it – the whole town, I think, soon enough."

"Indeed. Well, then, what of Adyleh the singer?"

"Who is that?"

Dyneti raised an eyebrow.

"I mean – what do you mean?" Selvorne asked.

"If I were not Waehdric, would you kneel and kiss my hand?"

"I dare not."

"Oh? And why?"

"For I know Adyleh is lurking in there, no doubt with some prank, and, once kneeling, I might be vulnerable to who knows what."

Dyneti laughed, and Selvorne grinned – and dared continue.

"And, kissing, I may be in danger of who knows what else."

One step back – her arms folded across her, one slender hand raised to her chin, and she cradled it, stroking it as though stroking a beard – eyes narrow, peering back at him. He did not move, except to smile.

"Dyneti – or Adyleh?" she asked, and Selvorne frowned.

"What?"

"Which – choose."

"Is there a choice? Are you not one and the same?"

She held out one fist, and he frowned.

"Choose – I will count to five. One, two – " she said, and at that, she began to count, a finger raised from her fist with each number spoken.

"Adyleh," Selvorne said, and she stopped.

"Truly? Why?"

Narrow eyes – suspicion and a silent stare. Selvorne, not her – he was being tested. The demands, the counting, the fist, the pressure to make him reveal what he might not otherwise – it was their way. Of Waehdric. He knew something of it, and did not like it ... though ... she was not being malicious, cunning at worst, perhaps merely careful. His mind calmed – then sharpened. He stepped back half a pace, and began to stroke his own chin, and she tilted her head as she watched him.

"You think me a fool, for I did not realise you were Dyneti, today?"

Dyneti said nothing.

"And you think that is an insult, of sorts," he continued, "the magnificent Dyneti, great singer of the Waehdric – and oh, she is great. And magnificent, and beautiful."

"And modest."

"And likes to joke," Selvorne said, "but perhaps does not like to be thought of as a joke. And perhaps is not so certain that she is as beautiful as people say – for that is surely impossible. Perhaps, now with a mirror, she might know the truth of it."

Dyneti waved her hand back to the tables, and Selvorne saw several mirrors.

"They must be broken," Selvorne said.

"Like so many hearts," Dyneti replied.

"And promises?" Selvorne asked in reply, and she frowned. Why he said it, he did not know – had it hurt her, he was not sure. Perhaps it was a poem they both knew, but he only half remembered.

"Broken or not, they clearly do not work," Selvorne said.

"They are mirrors – clear or clouded, they tell no lies."

"But as mirrors, cannot see."

"Says the young man so blinded by beauty, he cannot see who is who."

"Says the young lady so blinding in beauty, she thinks that is all men may see. Yes?"

Dyneti shook her head, but he thought she was not disagreeing.

"You are very bold," she said.

"As bold as I dare. Which is rather quite a lot, I fear."

"And foolish."

"Quite foolish. And you think me a fool for being so easily fooled."

"No," Dyneti said, and then she sighed, slumped, and turned away from him a little, "I think you are a fool for thinking me so simply flattered, my favour cheaply bought, my affection easily won, my – "

"You fooled me," Selvorne said, and she turned back to him.

"I told you my name, one could argue I did not. You fooled yourself – blinded, by Dyneti. And did not think – "

Selvorne smiled and shook his head – he stepped closer, but she stepped back. He held up a hand – just as he had seen her do, to stop others. And she stopped. A habit, a signal known to Waehdric and guards. Halted by command, she obeyed with a puzzled look on her face.

"My lady, you do not understand," Selvorne said, "even though you have tested me and asked me already. You think I was fooled – confused – blinded by the beauty of the lady I saw on stage? So that I could not see the simple girl before me was the same?"

Dyneti blinked – she seemed curious, as best he could tell in the light of the torches, so he continued.

"I was blinded – but by the maiden, Adyleh, lovely and warm. Her laugh, her smile, her eyes, her – you, Adyleh. I could not see Dyneti, because I could not see past you."

Whatever was the look she gave, he had never seen it before – not in any face, not in any eyes, not in any silent gaze. Her mouth open – it slowly closed. To a pout. Then one lip folded back and was bitten, and she said nothing.

"I came to hear you sing – not you, though, I did not realise – I came to hear you sing, with you sitting by my side. Or any to sing – as long as you were at my side. Laughing – when allowed, of course, not to ruin the song. Joking, and ... perhaps a meal or drink, later? And a dance?"

"No," Dyneti said, and his heart sank, but she nodded, "no – I mean, it is not ... appropriate. You are a strange boy."

"I am thinking just about the same of you."

At that, she took a deep breath, and laughed slightly as she moved closer. A hand to his shoulder – a thrill through his body.

"That, I assure you, is not true," Dyneti said, "despite my performance earlier, as a forester youth – were these gifts for me, or Dyneti?"

"Are you not one and the same?"

"You know what I mean."

"Dyneti."

"Honest, then. She will – no, I thank you for them. The mirror is very clear, I can see that even in this dim light. The container for it – very excellent, for travels, I noticed the silver backing was covered in glass, easy to keep clear. The box for – jewellery, I assume most would use it for – yes, I have some. Is it from the south?"

Selvorne nodded – he assumed it was.

"Bought here?"

Selvorne nodded again.

"Tomorrow, you must show me from who – as a gift, I appreciate it. But – if they have more, do not take offence if I purchase them all. I cannot have enough such things, and this one has linings that may be removed, and is designed for paint and brushes."

"I ... take no offence. If anything, to want more is proof it was a good choice – paint? Brushes?"

"For the face, for ladies. As is done in the south. Selvorne, that is truly your name?"

"Of course," he said, frowning at the odd accusation, "why would I give you ... oh."

Dyneti smiled slightly, and he smiled, feeling awkward to realise she had given him a name that was almost false.

"Selvorne – I have much to do, tonight. The end of a show is often as long as the show itself, and the time before, as long again. Tomorrow?"

"Yes?"

"Meet with me?"

"Do you think I would not?"

"Hard to know what to think, in this light – tomorrow, then, and you perhaps should call me Dyneti. Unless you wish to be thought of as my brother?"

Selvorne bit his lip, and she laughed.

"I am not sure what he would make of you. Like you, or hit you."

"Like me, I hope."

"Most likely. That tends to mean he would hit you many times over many years, rather than once on first meeting. Otherwise, I think he might like you quite well – you are roughly his age, I hope."

"I ... why would you hope that?"

Dyneti smiled and Selvorne forgot his confusion and gazed back. For a few moments, forgetting he was meant to leave.

"Thank you again," Dyneti said, "and I promise I will not ... fool you again. Not like that, anyway."

He stared, and did not leave – she jerked her head to the exit, and he frowned. Shaking her head, she held out one hand for him to – and then he realised – she wanted him to leave.

A bow – formal, as he was trained to do. He took her hand, and kissed it lightly. She curtseyed – also formal. Did he impress her with his skill in such matters – he did not care. He wished he knew nothing of them, none of the customs of bowing a farewell, for such an exchange meant he had to leave. He nodded once, turned and left – but wished instead he had seized her in his arms, held her in an embrace, and kissed her lips, not her hand. He wished, he thought, he wondered – he was not sure. Something of the sort – he did not want to leave. But he left, and left her there, and glanced back only as much as he dared, to see her placing the

box gently upon the table. She did not look back at him, and he wished she had –
but in a moment he was gone, on the other side of the cloth, away from the
enchanted woods, walking, wandering, and found himself away from the stage, the
people, and the light.

Revealed

Selvorne rose early and washed quickly, for the lake was cold. The day was not as warm as the previous, and a bleak chill was in the air, with thin grey clouds spread across the sky. He shaved by the lake, but was not grim, even at the start – and that was enough to make him uneasy. To be lost in enjoyment and delight was not ... no, his thoughts were clouded. He settled his mind, calmed himself and prepared properly to shave – clear thoughts, just the task, only the knife. At the end of it, he washed his face and sat.

It was the third proper day of the festival. Things would begin to return to normal for the town. Some might leave that night, if they had far to go or chores to do at home. The previous day was the most festive – games, prizes, children exhausted and delighted. Food might be running low, some of the stalls set for the festival were already out of things to sell. All animals, grains, even ale was usually sold by the third day. Fewer boats were at the lake, as people left, and the pile of them was a nuisance to any who were unlucky to find their boat at the bottom.

That day – later, though – would be the usual recruitment of the guards. Every year they did the same, a speech saying how wonderful it was to be a guard, serving the Waehdric, travelling the lands. See how respected they are as men, watch them fight – impressive? Why not join? Selvorne had enjoyed a position of honour the previous night at the singing, at the front – that was rather a new thing, he thought, for only for a few years did guards sit there, and he was sure Girradehn had something to do with it, even if Demni had suggested it was Temnere's idea.

Thousands of people were in the town, and such a speech was usually lucky to get one new guard. Certainly many showed interest, but few truly desired – or were allowed – to leave their families and serve, far away. Of those who were, not all were accepted – some even returned from a journey north, disappointed, and would not speak of it. Those who were accepted usually found themselves years later back at Tavalehk, serving Arnlausa and being commanded by Girradehn – not a pleasant end for many, who thought he was a bit of a ... an unpleasant fellow, at times. Disliked, but he did not deserve ... not that ... not what he got. Selvorne wondered how many would join if they knew what had happened. Some, perhaps to avenge him, and others ... knowing they would not have him as commander, or captain, or whatever it was that he called himself, which seemed to change depending on his mood and who was listening.

Selvorne would join. Or at least be there to listen, perhaps they would mention the sweep of the woods. That would be stupid, if they hoped to surprise the brigands hiding there – when, that was the question. Afternoon – but of course, he did not have to know when they would speak, for they would announce it with a horn. As long as he was not asleep, or took off to the woods, or swimming in the lake – he would not be, not that day, the waters were freezing and he wondered that there was no ice.

Fresh, washed, shaved, at ease – alert. Calm. Careful. His hair brushed and checked with a mirror to be sitting well, not absurdly as before. He had another reason to rise early, other than vengeance, fury and hate – quite the opposite, though he was not sure what the opposite of vengeance was, and fury ... he was hardly feeling relaxed. Up he stood and gathered his things, and made his way through the town.

~

Tavalehk was much quieter than the day before, being so early on such a cool morning. Many had stayed up late, he fancied that half those awake had not yet slept. Night of the main festival day was the greatest night for some. Songs and drink, dancing, and he had avoided all of that – early to bed, easy to rise, Arnlausa had said. Early to bed – hard to sleep – powerful dreams – soon to rise, perhaps not easy.

The Waehdric were awake. Selvorne doubted they spent the night drinking, perhaps dancing. They seemed rather fond of feasting, also, and had made another stew with freshly baked bread. Unlike before, it smelled delicious, and was eagerly being eaten by all.

Guards of the Waehdric – yes, they were there as usual, not doing much guarding, as usual, though whether they stood still and defiant with weapons at the ready, or sat relaxed – with weapons near – he did not think it made much difference if a battle began. They raised tankards to him when he appeared – it was a round of wine provided for them, at the expense of his pride. Good. Cheaply bought goodwill. He would dance with a dead fish on his head if it won them all to his side – such pride he had in plenty to spend.

Many guards – far more than before – where had they all appeared from, he did not know. Though, at the singing, the bench seats were quite full, but there were more at the Waehdric camp than the day before. The three large men were sitting together and eating, and the smaller one was near, wrestling with a boy. Savak,

288

Kalgevun – more men, and girls he had not seen. Girls, not maidens, young and – ahh, he remembered they had been tidying in the camp. Well behaved, for such young ... ladies. Waehdric. So strange he could walk into their encampment as if he was one of them – perhaps they liked him so much that he was, and – two new girls, laughing with their backs to him, one sitting behind the other, braiding her hair. A sweet laugh, a rough one, and voices too rich for girls.

Selvorne raised an eyebrow – Adyleh – no, he meant ... Dyneti, sitting before the other, who was braiding her hair, and had herself a single long plait falling down her back, which swung like a tail every time she moved. Terribly long, almost to her waist, and Selvorne knew it would be longer still if released from the knots. Slender, and she moved with ... such fine swaying – it was Demni. And her rough laughter was delightful.

He walked straight to them. A few men almost rose to stop him, but he noticed nods from Savak and Kalgevun eased their fears. He placed his pack out of the way, and stood beside them until they both looked up.

Demni seemed a different – girl. Her hair let down changed her look – no, it was her dress, no longer a shirt and trousers, but a light plain dress with a small shawl over her shoulders. No – not her dress – her laugh, that was it. Was that a smile? She seemed as though she had not slept in a week – her eyes dark, her face tired, but despite that she was only happiness and delight.

And Dyneti – was frowning when he finally looked to her – then an eyebrow raised. Was that ... jealousy? Selvorne grinned, and the other eyebrow went up. And then she laughed. Demni whispered something to her, and the two of them ... giggled.

He wished he had checked the mirror one more time, and began to stroke his hair with one hand. That only made them laugh more, and his unease grew.

"I have a mirror, if you need one?" Dyneti asked.

"Oh, thank you," Selvorne replied without thinking. Both ladies, and several of the men, laughed. As did he – he was so concerned for his hair, he had forgotten where he was – to his surprise, Dyneti was not joking, and she leant over to pick up a mirror that she held out to him – the one he had bought for her – and though he was pleased, he was not sure it was a good idea to leave it lying in the dirt, where anyone might tread upon it.

Selvorne took it – looked at himself carefully – his hair was fine. His face was fine. His – pride was gone. The men were laughing, some almost choked on stew. No one thought he might actually use it. The ladies were – he was not sure. Astounded? As was he – and then he grew bold.

"Magnificent!" Selvorne declared, holding the mirror at arm's length and striking the most victorious pose he could. Spluttering, coughing, roaring laughter from the men, giggles from the ladies. Pride lost, regained – pride spent, to purchase their goodwill. He could not have planned it better, and he grinned at his own inspiration that was – he truly believed – magnificent. And it must have shown on his face.

Dyneti stood and went to him, took the mirror and looked into it carefully.

"Strange, I only see a fool," she said – that also made some laugh. She handed it back and Selvorne looked into it, and saw himself grinning. Clever, but he was as well.

"That is odd," Selvorne said, "I see only beauty."

"I meant you, you realise," Dyneti said.

"I know. I see just what you see."

"A fool?"

"Beauty," Selvorne said.

Coughs, splutters – not laughter. The men had become silent, were listening, and ... restrained.

"Oh, please," Demni said as she stood, dusting her dress before standing before them both.

"And what do you see?" Selvorne asked, handing her the mirror.

Silence. More than before – more than he could have thought ... possible. Only the dull sounds of the festival in the distance. He did not look back at the men – he looked to Demni, who was ... pale. Dyneti shook her head ever so slightly, but it was too late – slowly Demni took the mirror, held it up and looked into it. Silent, and staring, for moments until she spoke.

"Sorrow, and loss."

The silence returned, until a young girl ran up to them.

"That is very grim," the girl said. Demni looked at her, nodded, then smiled.

"Of your age," Demni said.

"Demni – " Dyneti began, but Demni looked at her, and nodded just the once.

"Broken mirrors, broken dreams, broken – " Demni began, but Dyneti held up a hand.

"No."

"It is – "

"Not today," Dyneti said. At that she took the mirror, held it out to Selvorne, who took it, then she took both Demni's hands in hers – the two ladies faced each other and stared.

"Now what do you see?" Dyneti asked.

Demni smiled, nodded, then let go and left. Where she went, Selvorne was not sure – around the tent. Perhaps to hide there, perhaps to wander into the festival.

"Savak!" Dyneti snapped, and Savak, who had been sitting on a low stool, put down his plate, his tankard, and threw his hands in the air.

"This is not very pleasant for me either, you know," Savak said.

"I know. Please?" Dyneti asked.

Savak stood, nodded as if a bow, then smiled.

"You did not have to ask," he said, then ran after Demni.

The mood was grim. Selvorne was not sure what had happened, and was less sure he should ask. Dyneti sighed, and the young girl beside her shook her head in disapproval. Selvorne looked at Dyneti, who tilted her head, took a deep breath and gently took the mirror from him.

"Mirrors show not what is real – clouded, clear, they cannot feel. The heart alone is our true eyes – opened once the vision dies. For beauty is not what we truly see – that seen in you, is true in me."

The voice of Dyneti was truly magnificent, and all the men there put down what they held, and clapped. The young boy most eagerly, the young girl less willingly, and many of the men were gazing longingly at Dyneti – what they saw, they clearly adored.

"That is not even half of it," the young girl said.

"And yet is the most true half, here, what do you see, Ceolirn?" Dyneti asked, handing the mirror to the young girl.

She looked – like a girl. Dark brown hair, slightly wavy, quite thick and rich – not a maiden. Not yet, or just that year, perhaps. She looked like a girl, and looked at herself in the mirror – like a girl – until she seemed to realise something, then she narrowed her eyes.

"Cleverness, that detects a test," Ceolirn said, and Dyneti nodded.

"Not bad," Dyneti said, then took the mirror and moved quickly to Kalgevun, thrusting it out so he took it. He looked into it, then seemed sad.

"Sorrow," Kalgevun said.

"Not you as well? What is this, the Festival of Glum?" Dyneti asked, and Kalgevun grinned.

"Now – that I should like to attend," Kalgevun declared, "I think such a festival might have many fine ladies, feeling glum, in need of cheering. What say you, men?"

Some cheers, some laughter, and Dyneti was tricked. By her guard, who was anything but glum. Selvorne laughed as well. At that she turned to him – furious – frightening – and Selvorne grimaced, wondering what he had done wrong.

"Ha! Got you!" she said, and Selvorne knew she had fooled him – with just a look. She cared little for it, and none of the men laughed. A private prank, then? He was unsure, and she took the mirror from Kalgevun.

"You seek women to cheer?" Dyneti asked.

"You know I do," Kalgevun replied.

"If it is love you seek," came the voice of the smaller man amongst them, though, as Selvorne saw him in the daylight, he did not seem so small at all. Short, but rather frighteningly muscular, "you will not find it here."

Kalgevun bent down and picked up his plate and his tankard, holding them high.

"Found it!" he declared, and many men laughed. Dyneti nodded, then smiled.

"Not bad. Certainly that would cheer – is that the stew I made?" Dyneti asked.

"It – ahh, yes," Kalgevun said.

Dyneti looked over at all the men, smiling, and they were ... quiet.

"I shall make you all another tomorrow!" she said.

Selvorne was sure the cheers were not sincere, but he was not sure if they were believed – Dyneti did not seem to notice. She took the mirror to another man, held it out, he took it and looked confused.

"Well? What do you see?" Dyneti asked.

He looked at it without looking into it, then handed it back.

"Silver. Wealth. For some, more desired than beauty. A gift?"

"True, a gift," Dyneti said, speaking to all the men, "a thing given. Silver – given or taken. Often desired. Beauty – also desired. Given to some by birth, by luck – made by others, through craft, and care. By their own desire to make beauty, rather than have it. Remember that, my men."

"Desire to make them wealthy so they can buy – " the guard began to say, but Dyneti looked at him and he was silent.

"Yes?"

"Gifts," the man said.

"You are not a very cheerful man, are you Rugel?"

"You ask, I answer. I did not ask to be asked."

"And I did not ask to be questioned. Rurev?" Dyneti asked, holding the mirror out to a man beside the other. Both seemed similar, perhaps brothers, though Rurev had fairer hair and seemed less glum. He took the mirror, looked into it, and shook his head.

"Doom," Rurev said.

"And – why?"

"I see a man with neither wealth nor good looks."

"That is just stupid."

"Who is also, apparently, stupid. As I said, doom."

Dyneti looked appalled – the mood was grim, and she clearly had meant to cheer them, or teach them some kind of lesson. It was not working as she had expected. The young Waehdric Ceolirn walked quickly up behind the two guards and slapped them both at once across the back of their heads. They spun and cursed, and she glared at them.

"You two are idiots," Ceolirn said, "this is a test – use your heads."

"Deceit," Rugel said.

"Despair," Rurev added.

"Fist," said the shorter man, clenching both fists and holding them up as if he might strike the other two.

"Where did I find such grim men?" Dyneti asked, and Kalgevun stood beside her.

"They are guards, my lady," Kalgevun said, "their work is often grim. You two – is it a run you desire? You both look rather soft."

"No," they both replied.

Dyneti took the mirror and handed it to the young boy who had been wrestling – a Waehdric, who stared into it for a moment before grinning.

"Krivan?" Dyneti asked.

"The future," the boy replied, and Dyneti nodded with a broad smile.

"Not bad. Take note, you two – Krivan will likely be your commander before you know it. Or Ceolirn there – a few years, not long."

"I want no idiots for men," Ceolirn said.

"Neither man is wrong," Krivan said, to their astonishment, "there is wisdom in their words. You know that, and only tease. Ceolirn does as well, but is rather cruel today. Men – cheer yourselves for the festival, who knows what the future will bring!"

Selvorne was as surprised as they at the young boy who seemed so wise – how young, years younger than a young man would be – but only years. Was Dyneti teasing them? Testing them? Was Ceolirn – was that how the Waehdric taught? Selvorne knew their ways were cunning, at times. There was no malice – except in what the two guards had said, an almost bitter harshness. That was gone, instead both sat there grinning. Two commanders to be before them – a young girl, who was falsely harsh, perhaps clever, perhaps worthy to follow. And a young boy – who thought them smart. Selvorne knew they were not clever men. He also knew that those who were not, rarely knew it, let alone admitted it, and thought those who were clever were either odd or deceitful.

He also knew that was a weakness he could not afford, and his father had told him many times – never assume anyone is stupid, for it can be a ruse to fool you – that was what he warned. Uhlsko also said never to assume that he was more clever than another, and – and many other things that swam around in Selvorne's head. Silly things that were beginning to make some sense, and he was not sure what he had started with the mirror, but he did realise it was Dyneti who mentioned it first, not himself.

Krivan handed the mirror to the short, strong man, who took it, but shook his head.

"You will not like it," the short man said.

"Rucarik?" Dyneti asked.

"I see Resa," he replied, and many nodded.

"We all see that, in your fists," Kalgevun said.

"And I see it in my face. You realise that is why she – "

"I know," Dyneti said, "we all know. Are you sad?"

Rucarik frowned, then smiled.

"No. Proud."

"And that is why it is called a vanity," Kalgevun said, and a few laughed.

"For him," Rucarik said, but then grinned, "and for me. Yes – vanity, why not."

At that, he stood, held the mirror at arm's length, and looked proud.

"Magnificent!" Rucarik declared, and all laughed at him, but glanced at Selvorne. Rucarik bowed, then handed the mirror to the large, fair–haired man that had sat behind Selvorne and lost the wager the night before.

The man stared into the mirror, and did not seem pleased. Larger than he should be, hair thinner than it once was, face too round, but he did not seem weak or ill, he just seemed a little sad. Dyneti stood before him, and it only seemed to make him feel worse.

"Kuoren?" Dyneti asked.

"Lies," Kuoren replied.

"Explain?"

"That beauty is in the heart, not the face. So say the ugly, never to be believed. So say the beautiful, so pleasantly, before they seek others of pretty faces, who look like girls."

"Indeed," Dyneti said, and then was silent for a few moments. Kuoren said no more, and seemed to grow more glum, "you would have them, instead, find beauty in one who is ugly of face?"

"It is your lesson, not mine."

"And so my lie?"

Kuoren was silent.

"Perhaps, Kuoren, some might search for the beauty within another, be they pretty or not, instead of complaining that others – who are pretty – should do the same to them? The lesson is to look inside yourself, as with a mirror, not judge others for not doing what you want. Or worse, for not looking as you want."

"The lesson said is not the lesson shown," Kuoren said.

Kalgevun strode over to the large round Kuoren, held out his hand, and the mirror was given to him. Kalgevun said nothing, but turned to Dyneti.

"That is one man who should never be allowed to have a mirror," Kalgevun said, "for he has a big heart and an ugly head. Though, if we punch both his eyes, perhaps they will swell, and he might see things differently?"

Dyneti shook her head and looked down at the man.

"Kuoren," she said, "you are an idiot. This is a festival – what are you even doing here? Your men are not on duty. Get out and have some fun – there may be a dance later, and there are many women here – some not so ugly – who might find you worth a dance."

"Is that an order?"

"Yes. Go."

Kuoren stood, bowed, then left the camp.

"His brother will find him," Kalgevun said, handing the mirror to Dyneti, "and soon they will be drunk."

"Suggestions?"

"What can I suggest? Convince Guroukane to let him go, make him patrol the roads. He is too fat, too idle, too hard to find a woman in a town he has lived in his whole life. That is why he is here – men, are you all listening?"

"Not only men," Ceolirn said. Kalgevun bowed to her, and she curtseyed back.

Dyneti sighed, then handed the mirror to a very large man – tall and likely strong, with blond hair to his neck and the most astonished, nearly frightened look on his face as he took the mirror.

"Akfe?" Dyneti asked as he stared at it in silence.

"Yes?"

"What do you see?"

A frown at first, then a grin.

"A mirror?"

Laughter, from all. Akfe seemed pleased. Selvorne was convinced Akfe had no idea what he had just done – stated a perfect truth. Perhaps some of the men did not, some seemed to be laughing at him, but Selvorne did, Dyneti did – the young Waehdric did – Kalgevun, and – Savak was back. As was Demni, who nodded to Dyneti.

It was Kalgevun who took the mirror from Akfe, who had begun to admire himself – the mirror disappeared inside a tent. Men returned to their meals – cold, but they ate eagerly. Some returned it to a pot, then the fire.

Dyneti returned to Demni, spoke in whispers, then sat and had her hair untangled before beginning the braiding once more. Selvorne did not interrupt, he felt he should not. Something had happened, and it was partly his fault. They were not so cheerful as before, and as they braided hair they were quite silent, and quite grim.

As for the men. Not silent, but quieter, and he did not like them all as much as he once had. The message of the mirror was clear to him from the start, a few lines of a poem he half remembered, spoken so sweetly by Dyneti. What was seen in others was usually what was in oneself. Not always, not with all people seen – but often, especially when in love.

But not always was it a reflection on himself, he knew, and he did not like what he saw in some of the men. Grim, glum, bitter – spiteful, perhaps. Not jolly men he had thought at first. That he at first thought them good – that was what he expected, for good was what he was. But not what they were, and to see them properly he needed to remove the mirror of his mind. And if he did, he thought he might see the reason Arnlausa warned him to trust no one except Cienn.

Selvorne sat with Kalgevun, but found he had not much to say. Nor did Savak, and he wondered if he should be there at all – he was neither guard nor Waehdric, and though not unfriendly, it was Dyneti that he was there for, and she was with Demni. Her hair was going to take a very long time, and though the two ladies were seeming much happier, and he might have been welcome to sit and talk – he did not like the idea of making conversation with Demni listening. He stared over at them – they noticed, and Demni started to laugh. Whispers, and Selvorne felt he was not being encouraged to join them.

From a tent came the three old Waehdric – had they been asleep, or listening the whole time, Selvorne did not know. They left together laughing, at him, perhaps, a glance suggested it was possible. It seemed they headed to the lake to swim. Selvorne was sure he had met one of them before, long ago, but was not recognised. Such men must have met thousands of people. Such men – could one be Cienn? He watched them walk away – no, surely not. Men, not old women. Not old enough, anyway.

The young Waehdric Krivan, who had started wrestling again with Rucarik, seemed to consider joining them for a swim, but then was snatched from his feet and lifted before being collapsed to the ground. He did not laugh, but struggled and almost was free. Savak and Kalgevun were relaxing, almost napping, and the others had moved away from the fire into groups and spoke amongst themselves. There were many more guards than those who had been given the mirror – some had listened, others from as far away as they could be without leaving the camp. Selvorne looked around at them all, and thought that, though it was not an unfriendly group, he was beginning to feel quite alone, and his thoughts turned to leaving.

Discovered

A strange, powerful sound of music in the distance – something exciting, and Selvorne sat up. A dance, perhaps, and that would –

Another sound, the same, and the guards all stopped what they were doing. Dyneti laughed – and was hushed by Demni.

Again – the same. Selvorne jumped up, and they all looked at him – he stared back, wondering what they were waiting for – three horns was a summons.

A horn – closer, or louder, or both – clearly a horn, and some guards jumped to their feet. Another horn, and those few who had not moved, did – and listened to know the sequence. The third was sounded, and everyone moved fast.

"Ugh!" Savak said, "Someone had better be dead or dying."

Dyneti glared at him, but he did not notice – he was fast, and already armed with a long knife, he ran to the tent behind the guards, which had been thrown open to reveal a rack of weapons. Spear and sword and a helm in one hand, he was amongst the first to be armed, but moved to Demni, where others snatched weapons and were running at speed towards the horns.

Any who were annoyed at first showed no sign of it as they gathered their things and ran. A dozen guards went ahead, he counted, many others were circling the camp, as though to protect it. One boy running fast stopped outside the camp, blew a horn three times – yelled out the Crossing Roads Square – then continued into the town, headed north. Selvorne knew he would do that until the end of town, to be certain everyone heard the call.

Three horns, that was – everyone important. All the guards, all the ... nobles, or powerful people of the town. The lord – that was him, though he could hardly believe either his position or the summons. He knew the Horns of Tavalehk, and he knew they were similar in all the lands.

A single loud, long blow – everyone in the town was to assemble immediately. Usually such a calling involved a runner yelling out where to go. Selvorne had only heard it once, when a house caught on fire, and by the time he had reached it, the fire had been put out by a hundred people with buckets. It was not a very large fire, and he was amazed at the thousand buckets that appeared from every house in the town.

Two blows of the horn, of a medium length – that meant able–bodied people must hurry, but only if they wanted to help. Not an emergency, no danger, but people were needed. Not many people responded to two blows, because it usually meant someone wanted a lot of work done, for example, draining a ditch, moving hay, turning a waggon over, or catching the rogue ox that toppled it. Sometimes people came anyway, just to see what was going on – but it was never meant to call the curious, nor, at first, to summon men to work. Two blows of the horn was supposed to call the men to defend the town – but it had never needed defending, and so the message had changed.

Three strong blows, with a pause between them – that signal never changed. It was a call to guards, lords, administrators – Waehdric. Everyone of rank. It was meant to be a call for only those people, but to blow the horn three times would always summon the entire town, for nothing was more important, and everyone wanted to discover what was happening.

Sometimes, runners would be sent to blow the horn many times, in short, musical bursts – that was to inform the whole town there was an announcement to be made. Perhaps a betrothal to declare, or a meeting of council, or something quite interesting was happening. Such a thing also attracted most of the town, but usually not running – they would wander along the roads, spreading rumours along the way.

That was how the horns were meant to be used. It was not always how they were used. Years ago, three blows of the horn made everyone run to the main square of the town, to learn it was just a ruse of the guards. The recruitment to join the guards – the speech given, by Girradehn that year. Selvorne remembered it well, how Girradehn explained that all the town had come, thinking there was danger – all the town, despite not being guards, or administrators, or nobles or trained to fight – all came when needed. Join the guards, be ready, when needed – and so on he went. Selvorne was not sure anyone joined that year, he thought more people were annoyed at being called so early for what was nothing but deceit. And they did not let the guards forget it – some even wondered if Girradehn called them just to taunt them for not being ready to fight, or coming when not summoned. Nobody enjoyed being tricked, not when danger was suggested, and not to serve the purpose of the guards.

That fear was in Dyneti's voice, Selvorne thought, for he heard her ask advice of Kalgevun and Savak – what to do if the signal had been given falsely for their own purposes. Some of the men argued that it was another ruse, others that they could not take the chance – either way, Kalgevun and Savak agreed – the damage was done. All the town was moving, and to not be there when summoned would be the worst embarrassment, whatever the reason for the call.

Something more was going on amongst them that Selvorne could not determine. They had forgotten him, sitting quietly in their camp, and the minds of the men were on something other than rapidly running to where the horns had been blown. Many had left – many more seemed to have left, but instead they formed a circle around the camp. Many had stayed, many had come from the festival and taken up weapons. And with so many men all around, Selvorne could not help but think that Dyneti was in the middle of them all, and he thought if she moved, they would as well.

Frantic discussion – again, about whether it was a ruse, but they had already decided to go if it was, or not. Dyneti had not approved it – that meant something was wrong. Or someone had done wrong, or – Savak said they must go. At once. Kalgevun agreed. Whatever it was, discover later, argue after – and at that, Dyneti nodded, clapped her hands three times, and all the men began to march.

Without Selvorne. They paid little attention to him as they left, and he found himself alone in the camp, the others fifty feet ahead of him, moving steadily. Those in the greater circle ran ahead and cleared the road before her – Demni stayed at her side, Savak and Kalgevun as well. The three old Waehdric stumbled back into the camp, in various stages of undress, grabbed shoes and followed. And outside of the camp – closer to the road of the town – hundreds of people were running to the south.

But it was quiet in the camp. The fire doused, it smelled of smoke and ash. Selvorne stood, alone, and took a deep breath.

Knife – yes. Spear – no. Not wise, with all the guards running around, to carry such a weapon. Quite trusting to leave so many things unguarded at the camp. Stalls likely had been left unguarded as well – thieves would have easy choices during such a calling. That was most likely why it was punishable to summon everyone without need – and for the reason that doing so, often, would make them less likely come when needed most.

A drink of water, he left what he did not need and began to walk. He knew what it must be – he was not in a hurry to run there. It was no ruse, no trick to recruit new guards. The killings must have been discovered, and soon – within an hour – he would be revealed, guarded, unsure who to trust ... but maybe, perhaps ... he might soon be leading those guards through the woods.

~

The town centre – the crossing roads – the square, though it was hardly a square – that was where the main road of the town entered and met the only other street that could possibly be called a road. The main road ran from south to north, and the other – east to west. Only called roads for they were both paved and had gutters – but the main one led from Vaskatohr in the south, twenty miles or more, then through the town of Tavalehk and to the north – double that distance again, or more, to Hartlehk town. That was a true road, which some said continued the whole distance of the northern lands in a great circle, through every town.

But the second road – the crossing road – that was nothing by comparison. From the lake in the east, through the town, past Arnlausa's house, but not close enough to be very convenient, and into the woods of the west. There it ended, for it was mainly built to bring timber in from the woods, and the square where roads met was made only to allow waggons to turn more easily on a good paved surface. Selvorne wondered if Arnlausa had meant for people to live in the woods, and had built the road to tempt them, but that would not make much sense. The waters of the lake were a better road than any made of stone, and at its edge was where everyone lived.

The crossroads, though, or the Crossing Square – that was a large square of paved ground where the two roads met. It was a nice place if the weather was neither too hot nor cold, and it did not rain. Unlike most towns that he had only heard of, the square was not surrounded by houses, and not used for much except for waggons to come and go, making great circles as they came from the north, turned around, then headed north once more. Rarely did they go south, on to Vaskatohr – but Selvorne did, and he had forced the ox many times to make that turn. Oxen were stubborn, especially his, and sometimes it would sit in the lovely square, enjoying the sun as other waggons made the turn and merchants laughed at him – his father and Arnlausa doing the same, no doubt, from chairs at the side of the square. Stubborn oxen – the real reason for the wide paved roads. On a fine day the square might be full of them resting in the sun, well fed on hay, and conspiring to halt all trade.

And perhaps it was vanity that built the square, though it did not seem so proud to Selvorne anymore. In the centre was a large stone, part natural, sticking up from the ground, and partly carved to smooth sides. The Lordstone, for upon it were cut the names of all the Lords of Tavalehk, from the time it was first founded, until ... Arnlausa. Selvorne had wanted such a stone at Vaskatohr, but his father said it would be absurd to have such a thing with just one name on it – almost like a stone to mark his grave. And it would be vain. Selvorne said it would not, and he knew the reason for it was – from the start – a great stone in the middle of the square to prevent oxen marching themselves there and sitting, blocking the road in all directions. It was to force them one way or the other, to left or right, usually to the right, but ... Selvorne took a deep breath as he reached the square.

He was, he knew, distracting his mind from the task at hand. Memories of Arnlausa – of his father – to think of them made him feel as though they lived. They did not. There was the Lordstone – a new name was to be added. He would put one at Vaskatohr as well. And there was a large crowd – a vast crowd – the entire crowd, perhaps, gathering at the square. One youth was on the Lordstone, blowing a horn, as if anyone there needed to hear the summons repeated. Nothing but people, on every foot of the square. Taahr, the annoying Captain of the Northern Guards, was standing near the boy with the horn, searching the crowd.

And the only thing in the square that was not a person seemed to be a cart. It was surrounded by people, shoving their way to look at it.

Dyneti was not there – nor were her guards, save those who had run ahead. Selvorne could not have beaten them at a walking pace, so he searched to see where they might have gone.

"Attention!" Taahr yelled to the crowd – several times before people calmed enough to listen. People were still arriving, and every new arrival asked the same question – what was going on – and many people replied by saying they did not know, then asking those who arrived what they knew – and so on went a thousand murmurs.

"Attention! There has been a killing!" Taahr yelled – that had everybody talking. It was suddenly so loud and people pushed so hard that the crowd seemed to sway like waves on a lake, and the boy with the horn started blowing it in short bursts.

A killing – the cart. It must have been a body – Selvorne breathed in hard. Into the crowd he pushed – and though others were keen to see, he was almost furious – to take ... to place ... on display, for all to stare – he was quite strong for a young man, and cared little for the comfort of those who were pushing ahead to gawk. Three men it could be, and any of them would not be pleased to be displayed so, for all to see. As he neared the cart, he realised he was doing something terribly stupid, and he stopped, waited – and looked.

Any faces he recognised – no. Brigands, killers, enemies – none that he had seen. People were looking at him, when he pushed – not when he stood there, apart from those behind, who he had recently shoved aside. He ignored them. He needed to see the body, and needed to do it in such a way to be seen as only one of the crowd. He continued pushing his way ahead, trying to seem not too eager.

Close – he clenched his teeth. He was not sure he could stand to see ... not his father, not again. Though he wanted to very much – not like that. Nor his good friend Arnlausa, nor Girradehn, though at least he might be only dead and not ... he cleared his mind. He had to look like any other man in the crowd, and with a final push of another aside, Selvorne looked down on the cart.

And stared.

He was not sure if he looked like the other people there, perhaps he did, if they were astonished. It was not his father – not Arnlausa – not Girradehn. And thankfully, not Rerleden, who he also feared for – it was the body of the tall, dark-haired brigand, who Selvorne had followed from the ravine to their camp. Laid upon the cart, on his back, staring at the sky – looking several days dead.

People shoved Selvorne, he would not move aside. Fast eyes – no sign of wounds. Still, lifeless – it was him. One of the few faces he knew, which he would never forget. Dead. Selvorne felt ... sorrow. Not five days ago, he wanted to put the man there, but seeing him there, on the cart, people staring at him – he wanted to put him to rest. Dead, for his crime, paid. Justice was done. No – not entirely. He looked to the faces around the cart. Two men, who seemed as guards, were watching all the faces of all who came, including Selvorne, who turned and allowed the crowd to move him away from the cart, away to the edge of the square, where fewer people stood wondering who had died.

Some fuss was going on at the Lordstone, and Taahr climbed upon it and called out to the crowd.

"Pachure has found a body – on the road south of here! Come! Listen! Hear his tale!"

It was a very strange way to announce things, and Selvorne thought Taahr was enjoying the excitement of it all – an inappropriate response to a very serious situation. Taahr repeated his announcement, then urged a man of the middle age to climb up. He was a rather portly, nervous man when called upon to speak – usually he was not so, for Selvorne knew him as one of the wine merchants. He usually was quite brash. Pachure began to speak, but was too quiet, and after much urging from the crowd, he started to shout his tale.

"I am Pachure, as you know, seller of wine," Pachure yelled as loudly as he could, "and I headed south – late – yesterday – to see if I could gain any news of Arnlausa, who everyone knows, is late again."

A few people chuckled, but were quickly hushed. Others called out that he was a cheat – men with wagers, Selvorne thought.

"I did not get far, a mile or so, before I saw a man lying on the road, face down."

All hushed. They were already listening, but – a mile away, that was too close to the town. Close enough to have been killed in the town, and left on the road.

"At first I thought he might have been drunk, and wandered into the night – along the road until he collapsed, asleep in the dirt."

Possible – but everyone knew that the man was dead, and if they did not wonder who it was before, they suddenly realised it could have been any one of them who had not been seen since the day before. A new surge of worried folk shoved their way towards the cart.

"But then I saw he hardly stirred, and did not seem to breathe, and I wondered, who could have been so drunk or tired to have slept the whole day long, especially in that heat?"

A few people nodded, thinking that was quite a sensible conclusion.

"And then – horror, I thought, this might be a trap. For was this not the kind of trick a brigand used in the days before? Pretending to be dead or wounded on the road, and then, when you approach, a dozen jump out of the bushes and attack. So, I moved to the side of the road, and looked every way for people hiding, and I thought it only wise to throw a small stone at the body, to see if they stirred. And he did not. And so I approached, cautiously ... "

People listened with wide eyes – for a man at first so reluctant to speak, he was beginning to enjoy the attention of the town.

Selvorne looked the crowd over. Most were listening keenly – all were silent. He reasoned that if anyone was standing there bored, half interested, or even better – very interested in observing the crowd, as he was – then they might be suspicious.

But as he looked, the only people watching the crowd were guards – he recognised many, and saw at last Demni and Dyneti. Some of the guards looked not quite bored, but less interested than they should be, though Selvorne guessed they had heard the story already.

There was one tall, broad man of fair hair at the back of the crowd – it was difficult to see what he was looking at, but he was not staring at Pachure. Selvorne was unsure if he was suspicious, though he seemed to gaze towards the cart. Rohy also was there, near the cart and staring, as were a few others.

"As I approached the body," Pachure continued to yell, "he did not jump up. I shook him, but could see there was blood on the ground, and stained on his shirt, so I turned him over, and could see that the poor man had been stabbed to death on the road, and left there, to die. And was dead."

"So, who is he?" Taahr asked, jumping up to the stone and waving Pachure aside, "Does anyone know him?"

Murmurs ran through the crowd. All those who had not yet seen the body, which included many who did not realise there was a body to be seen, began to push their way towards the cart. Although a terrible thing to see, everyone was curious, even more so when they realised it was nobody yet named. The crowd thickened near the cart, until it became impossible to get close to it, and then people shoved hard.

Selvorne had to think clearly, and it was difficult in the crowd. Dead – left on the road. Guards would not do that, but would brigands? Their own man – why – failure, or betrayal. Surely they would not ... perhaps they might. Selvorne took a deep breath, and looked over the crowd.

No obvious enemies. Why would there be – they were not stupid. If he saw them, he would unlikely recognise them – one of the men he knew, was dead. How clever were they – how ruthless were they – he could not be certain, but he could not risk ... anything. He dared think like a brigand, as Arnlausa had told him to do, and what he thought, he did not like, so he moved to the edge of the crowded square and took himself away where he could breathe.

It was foolish of him to have taken the brigand's ale. To start a fight, to anger them – they worked it out. Someone had been there, in their camp, but who? A survivor. Perhaps they only suspected, perhaps they knew. Perhaps they had asked Girradehn, and not accepted silence. Footprints on the road, not hidden well by Selvorne – followed. Ale bladder taken – someone so cunning, so bold, had seen them all and knew their faces, taken ale as a warning – left their spear, stuck in the ground of the road, as a warning.

At that thought, Selvorne grew uneasy – for he was thinking like the brigands, and what he thought was ... unthinkable for himself.

Very well, they would think – a man knows who we are, we know not who he is – or we do, and now we must find him. One of us was followed, one of us must die. And so they killed their own – and left him to be found.

And Selvorne, like a fool, went to look at the body – did they see him? Of course, they would not be so stupid to kill a man and not have another waiting near, watching. Did Selvorne hide his reactions well? Unlikely. He had been seen. Selvorne was the one man of a thousand who stared not with horror, but with recognition. He was likely being watched that moment, as he stood alone. Being alone was suspicious enough, he had taken time to breathe, and in so doing had thrown off the Gathering Cloak. Every other young man wanted to see the dead body. Only Selvorne stood alone, acting oddly.

A whistle – a very loud whistle, and great movement nearer the road. The crowd pushed hard. Odd, they moved aside, not towards the cart. Guards were marching, and would not stop. Every few paces they slammed the ends of their spears to the pavings, all at once to make a terrible sound, and people moved aside. A road through the crowd was being made, from one side of the square to the cart – guards lining it, keeping townsfolk aside, and Dyneti was walking through them all.

Selvorne climbed upon a large rock and looked over people's heads. Dyneti reached the body, looked at it – said a few words, then with one hand closed the eyes of the dead.

Then, each guard in turn marched past the body. Many were shaking their heads, then returning to positions to keep the crowd away. One after another – they were trying to recognise the man. Selvorne was astounded by how many guards were there, and almost all of them remained, forcing back the crowds until they were made to stand where the pavings turned to dirt, so Selvorne found himself crowded once more.

"All people," Dyneti yelled – though it did not sound as a yell, but a strong, powerful voice heard by all, "are to pass by this poor fellow, and any who recognise him – or think they know of him – they are to remain here."

She waited to be sure the people understood.

"Every other person – who sees the body and does not know him – you are to assemble at the Festival Field before the House of Laehtene. Any who do not assemble there will be captured by guards and questioned – all are required to obey."

Murmurs, then silence as she continued.

"At the poor dead man – you are to look only long enough to remember him, and whether you know him or not, whether you liked him or not, you will speak a word for his passing, and bow your head as you leave. For this man met a terrible end, and someone must have love for him – and will suffer their most terrible day, to discover their husband, their father, their son was killed – by murder. Remember the dead – passing to the Sea, to all those gone before."

Many people bowed their head and repeated the same – to the Sea, to all those gone before.

Others said nothing, but were silent, and Selvorne wondered if they were ashamed at their behaviour, coming to stare at a poor dead man as though he was part of the festive entertainment.

Selvorne was not ashamed, and was not sure the man did not deserve death, but he was not angry, either. He was impressed at how Dyneti saved the situation, for he knew just what she was doing – and why she stood by the body of the dead man. She was reading their faces as they passed, looking for anything hidden. As the brigands likely had done already, but if they were there before, they were not since she made guards move people aside. But ... would brigands pass by? Or would they go straight to the Festival Field, and wait ... Selvorne was not sure, but if they passed by he wanted to see them, and he hoped the guards considered him familiar enough to allow him to stand with them, so he jumped off his rock and made his way to the start of the guard path that had been forced through the crowd.

There at the start was Demni, though she did not notice Selvorne, for she was glaring at Taahr – and he ignored her, for quite a while, but when finally she caught his eye, she pointed straight at him, and then to a tree. Reluctantly he made his way from the crowd, and the last Selvorne saw of him he was being spoken to sternly by Demni.

Those ahead seemed to half recognise the dead man, they had seen him around the town, but ... some thought just that day. He seemed a tall man, some said, with dark hair and a hooked nose. Surely – yes, such a man was there, and ... no, actually, there was the man, in the crowd and alive – I do not know this one, and have never seen him before.

The guards seemed to realise at once, for they stopped everyone, then walked along the line – passing Selvorne, they took a man aside. He was tall, dark haired, and in a bright green shirt – he looked otherwise like the dead man, but with a nose hooked enough to be ugly, and dark eyes. And then, another. The guards began collecting such men, and brought them to the front where Dyneti watched them study the man in the cart. When finished, the guards did not let them go, but instead they led such men to the side, and the line began to move once more.

It was clear what the guards were doing, even before Selvorne reached the cart. Many people thought they had seen the dead man, but most, after looking over the gathering of tall, dark men at the side, realised they had instead seen one of them. Men from afar – from Hartlehk, from Senylehk for the most – one from Tromtohr, farthest town to the north. One even from Tavalehk, who was astounded that men he knew in the town would be so stupid to mistake the dead man for himself. Most of the tall, dark-haired men were uneasy to be there – forced, politely, by guards, with no say in the matter. But that was not it, they each seemed aghast, and as Selvorne approached them and saw their faces clearly – they did look like the dead man. Tall and thin, dark hair to the shoulders, a long nose, almost straight – dead, and laid to rest. It was not because they knew the man, not because the guards were intimidating, not because the crowd all stared at them – it was because they saw before them a glimpse of their own doom. Their death, their fragile life. Or that of their father before them, as they were made to stand beside a dead man of their own appearance.

Selvorne stood before the body. He was not interested in looking. He knew who the man was – he was not keen to reveal it, not to the guards, if others were watching. The man seemed peaceful, with his eyes closed. Asleep, not dead. Selvorne wanted to turn him over and examine the wounds – search his clothes – do anything to learn more, but he dared not, and did his best instead to look confused.

He examined the faces of those who were also tall and dark – none seemed dangerous, only disturbed, so either they were very good at pretending, or innocent. Yet any could be the first – any could have been there, at the brigand camp, and he was sure there was at least one other man in the woods who was tall and dark. Those townsfolk passing by, once finished, were meant to bow their heads and move to the left, but Selvorne realised some were claiming to have an idea who the man was – and Selvorne dared join them, waiting with the guards.

He waited and said nothing. Two men were held there, some of the guards frowned at Selvorne. More came – saw the body – most shrugged or simply shook their head. It was a strange procession of the entire town, one at a time, very well behaved and grim. Not a festival that would be soon forgotten, and Selvorne wondered what the people would think to see the magnificent singer from the night before had become the solemn Waehdric standing by the dead – silent, and watching.

Only a few came who were quite sure who the man was – half a dozen, though more swore they saw him at The Winer's Inn, not two nights ago. They stayed as well, and waited with Selvorne, who realised what their mistake must have been, but said nothing.

Rohy approached the body for a second time, but looked only at the man's face. Rohy was quite similar in appearance, and he had a ghastly expression that made him seem almost as pale as the dead man. He bowed his head, muttered something to himself that sounded like a sigh, then moved to the side, waved by the guards to join the others who looked similar. He stayed, and several men near Selvorne left, nodding as they realised that in the town they had seen Rohy.

It was a long time before the town had passed by, an unpleasant morning for a festive day, and not very useful to Selvorne. Having remained was a daring thing to do, but he had hoped to see the other man from the ravine, or at least something in the faces of people coming to look. He doubted he would. He also had hoped that he would draw the attention of those looking for him – a bold plan, but he assumed they had already seen him, and it was his one chance to make them look twice. Surely they would watch him, surely they would wait and stare to see what he might do ... and hopefully he would notice them in the crowd.

He also wanted to hear what the others who knew the man would say. Some who stood near him remained, and spoke amongst themselves. The dead man was not of Tavalehk, but from the north, or outside the town, or the woods – he would do work about the town, go to the taverns and inns, at times – buy things. A quiet man when sober, and not a very hard worker – most knew him as a man to seek only when desperate for men. Farmers, Selvorne decided from the look of most of those who knew him – farmers in need of men to harvest fruit or grains, to dig ditches or clear stumps of trees from the field. Not one knew his name, and the dead man had not been working in their fields for quite a few years. Some said he was a braggart, and styled himself as a lord, once paid, with fine clothes and absurd generosity at the tavern. Selvorne looked to the man's clothes, and had to agree they were quite fine, if not too old and worn. And at the sides – made dark with blood.

Selvorne agreed with the others when asked, repeating what he had heard, or said he thought he agreed, but was not sure. He said less than they, and nodded or shook his head, acted puzzled and said it was a very long time ago when he might have seen the man – but anything he could add was better than nothing, so he remained to tell the guards all he knew. He was not sure if they appreciated it or found it all the more frustrating, but when the guards had decided which men knew the dead man best, they led them away in the direction of the Festival Field. Selvorne was not one of them.

Fewer people were near the cart, fewer guards as well. All were meant to go to the Festival Field, and Selvorne knew it was to keep all the town in one place as the guards would sweep the town, looking for anyone suspicious. Those who looked like the dead man were questioned – away from Selvorne, though, and he was not sure what was being asked. He could guess. Dyneti was asking them, with Kalgevun – they were looking for hidden relations, friends, cousins – anything.

But – Selvorne had to do the same. His eyes glanced from face to face of those who remained. Who was watching him? As far as he could see, in the entire square, no one. None paid him any attention. Part of their deception? Sidelong glances at him as he turned away? No, he thought not. Some stared at the cart, from a distance – some in groups, whispering. Some guards as well. Some looked to the group of tall dark men, also whispering. Few were alone – one man, tall and with long fair hair – at first Selvorne thought it was Kalgevun. He watched and was silent, and seemed grim. He was staring at the group of tall dark men, and Selvorne wondered if he was also a guard, from the way he stood, for he seemed ready to do battle.

None of the men there he recognised as brigands, that was odd in itself. There had been all manner of men at the camp, men of all appearances, be they short or tall or slender or wide. Yet none of the town seemed to resemble any of them – perhaps a little, but not enough to make him think twice. Perhaps it was the way the townsfolk walked, sombre, heads down, grim in the presence of death. The camp of brigands was filled with lively men, laughing and joking – or deadly stern. Perhaps it was their clothes, worn differently at the festival than in the woods. There, shades of green and brown and black – at the festival, the brightest colours, usually. The silly hat in the woods – common at the festival, yet none dared wear one to view the dead man, and few kept wearing them on the third day. Those who wore cloaks in the woods – cloaks were common on a cool day, and it was quite cool, so a few in the town wore cloaks. Not with hoods over their heads to hide themselves, but if they did, it would hardly help matters. Selvorne felt it was hopeless, and he nodded at a guard who was waving for him to move along. He left the Crossing Square, and saw the guards lay a blanket over the dead man on the cart.

~

At the edge of the Festival Field, where the crowd was thinner and the woods of saplings began, Selvorne found Rohy waiting alone. Some of the others who were tall and dark were near, but none were held – they had been allowed to go where they wished, as long as that wish was to go to the field, of course. Selvorne approached his friend, who stared and was quite pale and shaken, as was most of the town.

Rohy looked up at him from where he sat on a stone. He had a very different mood to the young man who, days earlier, had eagerly chased Demni through the crowds. His face had gone from pale, to grey – and his eyes were distant and staring. He said nothing, but looked at Selvorne briefly, then continued to stare, half at the ground, half to the distance.

Selvorne ... was not sure what to say. He looked to Rohy – perhaps he had not seen death before. He looked to the others – many were doing the same. Was that how Selvorne had been, to see his father dead? He was not sure. Perhaps, for a while, but the sounds of Girradehn in pain, the realisation Arnlausa lived – he had no time to stand and stare in horror. Nor did he see in his father's death his own demise. His father looked only a little like himself, thankfully, though Uhlsko was considered roughly handsome, despite being old. Selvorne clenched his teeth to think he could be so vain at such a time – but it was not vanity that made him think such things, it was that he looked on his father and saw the death of Uhlsko. Selvorne was quite sure that Rohy, and all the others who looked like him, had just looked upon their own death.

"A terrible thing," Rohy said, nodding to the crowd. Selvorne looked – true, most of the crowd must have thought the same. They were also shaken, but many in the field were angry, some afraid, some had forgotten already they were meant to be solemn.

"Yes," Selvorne agreed.

"She said that there was our own death before us," Rohy said.

"What?"

"She – the Waehdric – she said there, in the cart – there was our death. Before us. All of us are dying, all of us to die – one day soon, before we know, as that man perished – before he expected. Not too old. Untimely, and ... it was not pleasant."

Selvorne frowned – it seemed a very odd thing to have said.

"A threat?" Selvorne asked.

"I am not sure ... yes, I think it was a threat. Or a warning."

"Did anyone ... speak?"

Rohy looked at Selvorne, then shook his head.

"None knew him," Rohy said, "we were there because we looked like him."

"I ... realise that ... some of the townsfolk were confused."

"You knew him?" Rohy asked suddenly, and Selvorne shrugged.

"I might have seen him once, I was not sure. I thought it would be better to say what little I knew. I could be mistaken."

Rohy nodded, then stared out to the field.

"I am quite sure," Rohy began in a low voice, "that my father was killed by brigands."

Slowly Selvorne's heart thudded in his chest ... one ... two ... three slow thumps, as though limping. Rohy stared – he was distant, and then turned to face Selvorne. Pain, and –

"Years ago," Rohy said, "I am sure of it. He disappeared on the roads north of here, and – "

"North?" Selvorne asked.

"North," Rohy continued, "and was found, also by the road. It was said he was drunk and fell asleep, and choked where he lay, but he had no purse. He was killed, and robbed, I was sure of it – now I am certain."

"You must tell the guards, they – "

"Already know. Told then, and again now – his purse was empty, for he spent it on ale, they said. Then. But it was gone, not empty, and ... now I am sure of it."

Murder – unpunished. Horror – sorrow – shared. Selvorne felt shame at his own ... failings. And Rohy had suffered ... the same as he ... different, though. Years – years, without justice? Worse, years of ... almost mocked, to say his father choked to death on drink. Possible, though, Selvorne had to admit – but a missing purse was surely a sign of malice. Though, to think like a brigand, who would be so stupid to take the purse as well as the coin, surely it would be better to make it seem to be ... an ... accident.

Selvorne breathed in deeply – Arnlausa had said to trust not one person, except Cienn. Not his guards, not the men of his town – none of them were named as men to trust. When Rohy's father had been found dead, no guard could be so stupid to not realise what Selvorne had in moments, and perhaps ... some of the guards were not quite doing their work the way they were meant to be doing it. Some might have been involved.

Rohy was not a lord. He was not wealthy, Selvorne knew that by the way he measured each purchase, and by the quality of his clothes. His father murdered, no justice done – there was a second crime, and he had neither power nor coin to pursue revenge. Selvorne felt a fury rise within him, and he clenched his teeth.

"You are angry?" Rohy asked with a frown when he looked at Selvorne.

"To not pursue the killers of your father is a crime."

"And now this man is dead – perhaps the same killers. There was no mention whether he was robbed."

"There was little mention of anything. Could they be the same ... killers?"

"I hope so," Rohy said in a quiet voice, and Selvorne frowned.

"What?"

Rohy took a deep breath and seemed to clear his thoughts, but still seemed disturbed.

"I hope so – for if they are the same who robbed and killed my father, then they will surely be caught. A man dead with no wound, called a drunk and forgotten – that is one thing. But all the town now will want revenge – and all the guard will act. The same killers – I hope so. And also," Rohy said, and then he took another breath, "if the killers are not the same – then there are two killers loose."

"Oh," Selvorne said, for he had not considered that. He also had not entirely realised the pain Rohy must have felt – he had seen not only a dead man, not only a murder that reminded him of his father's – not only a reminder of the injustice, but then had Dyneti make him aware of his own unstoppable doom. And yet, despite all that – Rohy had just emptied his mind of all the anger and pain, and was thinking clearly. Selvorne was impressed.

"I only know," Rohy said, "the face of the man he was last with."

Selvorne blinked several times – the man from the ravine – no, he must not speak. Think. Wait. Rohy continued to stare at the crowd. Hurt, for his father – Selvorne meant to ask ... but no, he did not mean the dead man in the cart. Rohy meant the man his father had been with before being robbed – Selvorne had meant to ask if he had told the guards. Of course he had, and everything he possibly knew about the man, the suspicions and fears. And had been ignored. Selvorne also thought to ask if Rohy had seen the man in the crowd – but he was glad to be silent. His grim mood had, for once, kept him quiet for a few moments, long enough to realise it was a stupid question. It would make Selvorne seem dumb and perhaps hurt Rohy, somehow. Had Rohy seen the man, he would have said. Or acted at once, or told the guards. He was watching the crowd intently, and Selvorne knew, without asking, that he searched for his only clue – one face he knew – one man who might have been there long ago, recently returned – involved in his father's death. As did Selvorne.

"This is to assemble the people," Rohy said, waving his hand at the field, and the growing crowd.

"They mean to sweep the woods – they are recruiting new guards to do so," Selvorne said casually, and Rohy widened his eyes.

"Guards?"

"Yes – new guards. Today."

"They – yes, they do that, at the festival. A ... sweep? What is that?"

"I ... imagine it is like sweeping a floor?" Selvorne asked, "Many men, to march through the woods. Nothing missed, all ground covered, like a broom. I am quite sure I will join them."

"When?" Rohy asked.

"Today."

"They are sweeping the woods today?"

"No, I mean – today, people will be asked to join."

Rohy was quiet as he thought and watched the crowds gathering about the stage. It had no siding, no sheltering roof of cloth, all decorations were removed, and it was nothing more than a wooden platform raised a foot above the ground.

"Will they be paid?" Rohy asked.

"New guards?"

Rohy nodded, then waited.

"I think so – I am quite sure. Guards will, some might ... offer to help without pay?"

"Not all can afford to, especially now."

"Now? That one man is dead?" Selvorne asked.

"Now that the festival is on – most have spent all they have, or close to all. Few can afford to spend weeks without pay, although, on the farm, it is a quiet time of the year, for some."

Selvorne nodded – he had not given much thought to pay, to coins – he never had to, for his father took care of such matters. He never wanted for food or shelter, except when caught on the road in the rain, and then no coins mattered. There were cave houses in the quarry, crude, but made comfortable if his tent was not enough. His own house was always lovely, if he kept it clean. Perhaps not so much after holding a feast for the entire town inside, but usually a very comfortable place to live.

Rohy was right, on many things. Few would join without pay, and it would take at least a week to sweep the woods. Unless they marched that very day with an angry town and found the brigands – no, that would be impossible. It was a day south and a day return at the least – food, shelter, wood for fires and torches. Impossible, since the festival had just used all of those. A thousand angry men would storm south along the road – a dozen clever killers would flee. Half a thousand, the angriest men, would continue more than a day – the wrong way, no doubt, into the woods of Tavalehk, not the ones at Vaskatohr – five hundred becomes three, at night. Two by morning. One hundred by lunch, as hungry men march home. Anger becomes annoyance, inconvenience and a desire to return to comfort. To protect their homes, that might be the excuse – and in a day most would be gone. Much sooner, with rain or lack of food. Without planning, it would not last two days, let alone a week, not even for fifty poorly organised men, the noise of which would drive away animals that could be hunted ... enemies pursued ... few would persist, until the only men left would be Rohy, pursuing vengeance for his father, and Selvorne – doing the same.

"They must be careful who they take," Rohy said, and Selvorne nodded. But that made Rohy look at him oddly, raising an eyebrow, "You see it, then?"

"I – what?"

"No, you do not," Rohy said, and Selvorne frowned.

"See what?"

"How do you know there is to be a sweep? Nothing has been said?"

It was true, nothing had been said – to the town. It was Temnere who had said there would be a sweep – to eradicate all brigands, everywhere, once and for all – his exact words. He was Head of Administrators, who controlled the detailed affairs of Waehdric, and the guards. He should know. Perhaps he was not meant to tell people – but – to have such a plan before the man was found dead, it must have been planned already, perhaps as long ago as the discovery of Rohy's dead father. That made sense – that was why they had not pursued it, and said he was drunk – and the guards were cunning, not deceitful. All such thoughts occurred to Selvorne at once, but he still did not know what Rohy had meant, or what he had realised.

"I heard it from one of the guards," Selvorne said, "what is it you see?"

"I see nothing," Rohy replied, and then was silent as Selvorne frowned, "Selvorne, I–"

"What?"

"I fear this is all more ... than a robbery – or even a murder."

Rohy looked grim, and Selvorne was growing impatient.

"And ... why?"

"Because," Rohy said slowly, "if you were a robber – stole on the roads, killed a man, by accident, or for ... cruel anger – would you leave their body there to be found?"

Once again Selvorne felt foolish – no, he would not. Nor would he as a brigand, unless he wanted it found – he had concluded that already. And not questioned it. The body found, to draw Selvorne out – but to do such a thing would make the guards realise something other than theft and murder was happening.

"A message," Selvorne said, and Rohy nodded.

"To the guards. You are planning to join?"

Selvorne nodded.

"I think the killers will as well," Rohy said, and Selvorne gasped.

"What?"

"Or watch – closely – those who join. They would join if they could. Selvorne, I think I will join the guards."

"You – "

"Want to find the men. And I am not sure the guards are thinking things through."

"And I am quite sure they are, but are perhaps not telling us everything they think or plan to do."

"Perhaps. But consider – someone told you of a sweep? A secret plan, that needs surprise. Why did the guards present the body of the murdered man to the town? Now? Whoever did this, be they clever killer or dumb, now knows the entire town is looking for them. They may flee, and – "

"That is why we are made to assemble here in the Festival Field."

"Made to assemble? To prevent an escape? Please – any man could wander off, there by the river, there to the woods. A dozen ways to leave. Those here first could have wandered to the woods in the west. Those here last – might never arrive."

"And be found in the town, or the woods," Selvorne suggested, but Rohy shook his head.

"Found? In the woods? Fleeing? If the killers are already there, hiding, perhaps if they know nothing of this. Surprised as they sleep. But fleeing, a man can cross the entire lands, pursued by a thousand noisy townsfolk – or simply leave along the road, to other towns. Never to be found. Showing the body was a stupid thing to do."

Selvorne bit his lip – it was stupid. Very stupid. If anything, the guards had done exactly what the brigands wanted them to do, and made it easier to escape.

"I think," Rohy said, "the guards do not know what they are doing. I think they do not care to find a killer, if they claim one dead man was drunk. And not choked. I think they are fools, and ... and I am going to join them, and make sure they do nothing foolish."

Selvorne nodded, but he disagreed – the guards did want to find a killer, but ... it made no sense, if they had kept quiet about the murder years ago, with the intention of planning – why had it taken so long, and why, after so many years planning, would they ruin everything by losing the advantage of surprise?

"And I think it is time I did something for my revenge," Rohy said, and at that, Selvorne nodded.

"And me," Selvorne said, immediately regretting it.

"What?"

"I am also joining," Selvorne said, "for revenge. For you – and that poor man who was killed."

Rohy nodded, and looked just briefly at Selvorne – his eyes gleamed, and he turned away to stare at the people gathered on the field. Selvorne took a deep breath and did the same. Both were likely looking for killers in the crowd, both realised it would be hopeless. Both had lost a father, though Selvorne could not let anyone know. Not yet. Especially not then – when it was almost certain killers were searching for him. He had an ally, unexpected, and surprisingly – friendly. Happy, the day before, or was it two – friends and allies, with a grim task. United in grief. And vengeance.

Yet he dared not trust Rohy with more, and he was sure Rohy did not entirely trust – anyone. Not that morning, though he freely shared his thoughts on matters. Rohy explained what had happened at the cart – those who looked like the dead man were gathered, some of those were from the very far north, and not at all pleased to be detained, threatened, questioned – they had nothing to do with the murder and were only there for the festival. Of course that only made them seem more suspicious, so they were questioned more and grew angrier at it.

The guards did not mention a sweep, but suggested something would be done. And that men would pay for what had been done.

Rohy also explained to Selvorne the need for care – for caution – to trust no one. The killers likely had spies, and Rohy made it clear that no mention of his murdered father should be made. Such a thing might draw their attention to him, and that was the last thing he wanted. Selvorne agreed, thinking the same thing for himself, though he was not completely sure why Rohy would not want them to come for him, if he meant to kill them, but when he looked Rohy over he realised he was a tall, thin young man – not a man who would likely fight in a deadly brawl of vengeful anger. He would be quiet, watching, waiting – and be certain of his attack. Give no advantage, no matter how slight. Selvorne felt glad to have him as an ally.

Overwhelmed was what Selvorne felt. Though he expected things would be complicated, he had hoped they might be simple – come to town, watch the crowd. Drunken brigands enjoying their plunder. Recognised easily, and captured, perhaps not too easily. Taken and punished. Or so he had hoped – he knew it would not be that simple. Every day made him realise it all the more, and the appearance of one of them dead – one of the very men he sought – it worried him.

Not to think like the victim, not to be angry as the man who was hurt – to think like the brigand, what would he do? But ... more than that, he had to think like the brigand, who was thinking like his victim – his pursuers – his enemy. And then again, to think as they might think, in pursuit. It was too complicated, there were too many things unknown and so, unconsidered. And the danger was too great. Rohy stood and stared – determined, and confident. Selvorne stood and gazed – frustrated and confused.

Once, when very young, he made his first attempt at herding the pigs back to their pens. From the woods it was difficult. Through the town – not so hard, they knew where the pens were. Into the pens – no, they would have nothing of it. Chasing them, hitting them with sticks only made them run and squeal. He was sure they were laughing, not screaming, those defiant pigs. Smarter than he – no, but stronger and faster, and used to evading the stick.

Young Stara came out – younger than he, and, as he had seen her do many times before, she whistled and shook the buckets of feed. All the pigs ran – ran to her will, into the pen, into their place, trapped by their own desire. She knew them well – no, she knew only how to summon them, where Selvorne did not. Outdone by a young girl who was in so many other ways foolish. That day he felt a fool – then, long ago.

But not standing there, watching the crowd. Overwhelmed, but not a fool. He knew when he needed help, and the guards were the help he needed. They would know what to do. He would listen, and learn how to whistle with feed. How to draw out the enemy, and how to trap them in a pen.

Broken and Accepted

On the Festival Field it seemed the entire town had gathered, but not the guards. Few were there, and many besides Rohy grew restless. Selvorne included, and the two of them wandered away from the field to search for the guards, taking to the road and hoping to learn what they could.

Guards were assembled away from the crowds. A gathering of them all – many dozens – some from the town, who served Arnlausa. Strangers were not welcome, and as they approached, a guard came to them and glared at Rohy. Selvorne seemed to be recognised a little, and when he explained he was bringing Rohy as a new recruit, the guard nodded – he must have assumed Selvorne was a guard already. And, for that matter, Rohy was as well.

They dared not enter the meeting, but stayed at the edge and watched. Rohy was nervous, and Selvorne knew that stepping into that group of men would have him recognised in moments by the guards of Arnlausa – their lord, who was missing. And that was likely suspicious, since the discovery of murder, and it was not the time for Selvorne to be revealed.

Taahr, Demni, some of the Waehdric, some of the town guards. Not Dyneti, not Kalgevun. Selvorne was not sure who was in charge – there was much arguing between Taahr and some of the other guards, and anger at the way he had handled things. Some yelled that he should have assembled all the guards quietly, before blowing the horns to gather the whole town. Demni seemed especially annoyed with him, though she argued the least – but when she did, she glared at him and made cutting remarks about his stupidity, so all the men could hear.

So ... administrator was a higher rank than captain, Selvorne thought. Or perhaps it was that she was a woman, or ... was right. It was a stupid thing to do. Many agreed. The men of the town who served Arnlausa wanted to march immediately, to find the killers and their lord, and one even tried to blow a horn before Demni slapped it out of his hand.

Dyneti was there, he discovered. She was sitting, and he only saw her when she stood, her head barely appearing amongst the shoulders of all the men. He knew her voice, as soon as she spoke – loud and clear, commanding, though she seemed unsure what command to give.

Taahr, however, seemed to know exactly what commands to give. He ignored accusations, criticism and abuse, and to all things posed as problems, he had a solution. Or an answer, to questions. Or a report that it was already done, to suggestions of action. He kept saying, "I have already thought of that," and though impressive for a while, Selvorne soon grew annoyed. That seemed unfair, though, for Taahr appeared to be just the man of action required to be Captain of the Guards.

Taahr said that as soon as he heard of the discovery of the body, he informed all his guards that were with him, and left immediately, leaving one man in the town to "watch for suspicious activity." They had journeyed all night, quietly on the roads, alone, to see if any brigands were about – all the way south to the river. They had found evidence of a large number of people in the woods, which is what the guards had suspected for some time – and all the more reason to prepare with caution, and proceed only with large numbers of men. Not to rush out foolishly with a few trying to hunt them down, "for then, they would soon be hunting us," or, alternatively, "they might slip through our net of men."

Selvorne was impressed, despite Taahr's constant grin, as he seemed so pleased with himself. Taahr assured the men of Arnlausa that runners had been sent ahead – all the way to MidWaehter – to search for Arnlausa. It would be better if the town guard remained in the town, to ensure the people were safe – their lord would agree, and if anyone could take care of himself, it was he – and if anyone would be furious to think the town was unguarded, it would also be he – for there was also the possibility that the killing took place in Tavalehk, and the body was left on the road as a ruse. Arnlausa would not take kindly to another death in the town.

The Waehdric and guards were also assured that hasty actions that day would drive the brigands into hiding – and then he added, quite casually and to Selvorne's astonishment, that doing so would ruin many months of planning. That seemed to silence many men, who nodded or looked to the ground, and Selvorne was quite sure he and Rohy should not have been there to hear such things said.

Temnere arrived at that moment. He strode straight to the centre of the group, stopped Taahr talking with a glare, then began to address Demni, before Dyneti interrupted him.

"Did you not hear the horns?" Dyneti demanded.

"Yes," Temnere replied, not facing her, making a dismissive wave of his hand before continuing to speak with Demni – as though no others were there. She gave him a quiet summary, which must have been very brief, for he spoke a few words back, turned to face all the others, and announced that Demni was in charge. At that, he strode out of the gathering of guards, back the way he had come.

Demni seemed pleased and pushed Taahr aside – who was not at all happy. Oddly, she then issued the same orders he had just outlined – none were to leave the town searching for the brigands, few details would be told to the people, the town would be protected, none would look for Arnlausa, either. As many new guards would be recruited as possible, and then what had been prepared would be enacted. The first task was to announce what was happening to the town.

The men seemed pleased. They also seemed used to having Demni order them around, which she immediately began to do, sending them in all directions. Selvorne suspected most preferred the idea of planning and thinking and going out in numbers – very few still seemed restless, wishing to go out at once in small groups. None said as much then, but had done so before, shouting their desire to act immediately – they had become silent, but were still shuffling their feet as though uneasy, and eager to charge. To do so was madness – what they might hope to do, if they ran to the road and stumbled upon dozens of the enemy – they may as well send Selvorne out, at least he knew where to look, and he alone would be just as useless as three, alone.

A very strange lot of men, Selvorne thought, quite diverse. Not at all the big, strong men from the Waehdric camp, some were quite ordinary in their appearance. Some were runners, messengers. Others he was sure were nothing more than assistants, perhaps they cooked or carried packs and tents. Perhaps they merely helped set the stage for Dyneti's show. Girradehn was the guard he had known best, and he seemed – quite different to most. More like Savak, and like Kalgevun. More ... intimidating. They needed more such men, and as Selvorne looked on them all, he realised he could be such a man. He was at least as strong as some of the others, from heavy work at the quarry – it was no wonder they wanted to recruit more guards before setting out to find their enemy.

The meeting ended, the guards ran to their duties. The old Waehdric men, who had been seated, left and walked slowly away, with the young Krivan and Ceolim beside them – it soon was only a few guards who stood in the clearing. Dyneti also left and did not see him – but Taahr and Demni remained, as did Savak, and they were arguing quietly.

Rohy watched – stared – and Selvorne sighed to think he was still enchanted by her beauty – perhaps more so, after watching her order all the men about. Some men found such boldness appealing, he had been told. Something seemed odd, though, in what he had heard, and – Demni and Taahr stopped talking, then left, going different ways. Savak followed Demni, and Rohy's eyes – they followed Taahr.

“A good plan, I think,” Selvorne said as the two of them began to leave as well – not wanting to be the last few in the area, not as guards were starting to frown at them.

“Interesting developments,” Rohy said in a low voice, “and likely the best plan.”

It likely was, Selvorne agreed. There was far more to the plan than had been said – and it would not be said. Not to them, not to the town. Not to the new recruits. Not even to the old guards, the town guards, or their commanders, though – perhaps some of them knew already. Taahr said he had been all the way south – to the river. There was only one river south, and only one crossing, for the main road, and that was a bridge that had been collapsed to ruin. Taahr said nothing of it. And to keep it quiet – to lie about it, by saying nothing – it could only mean that it was more than the death of one man that the guards feared.

~

That day the Festival Field did not feel very festive. As before, guards and their assistants made preparations for the stage, which involved making people leave it, rather than bringing painted trees or clay pans to contain fires. The crowd was as large as the night of singing, for they were the same people – but not the same. Not in mood. Just as much anticipation at first, as Dyneti took to the stage, perhaps some hoped she might say something to comfort them, or sing, or anything other than leave them not knowing what was happening. Demni stood beside her, but seemed nervous as the two of them talked, and Selvorne noted her voice was quite rough from arguing with Taahr, so she had trouble speaking.

All looked to the stage, but Selvorne looked to the House of Laehtene – of Arnlausa – of his. All the town must have noticed it that morning, bright and seemingly cold white on that cool day. All must have wondered where he was – it would not be simple to put them at ease. The day before, that he was late was a joke. That morning, that he was late was a grave concern. Selvorne fancied he heard people mumbling of it, but the voice of Dyneti made them all silent.

Dyneti spoke, the people listened. She suggested – he thought they would obey. Commands, gently put. Firmly delivered. Stay in the town. Do not go hunting for brigands. Watch for each other, young and old and of any age between. The guards would find the killer – the guards would keep them safe. No man must attack any other, even if they think he did the murder – no man must be harmed without proof, and then, not harmed, but taken to the guards. Those who meant to travel home, away to other towns and villages – they must travel in large groups, with the guards, who would leave the next day. To protect them from brigands, but also to prevent them doing harm. To travel alone, a man might be considered suspicious by the townsfolk – and then attacked.

Who would disobey such advice? No sane man. But who would make the mistake of attacking a lone traveller, a man walking from Tavalehk to, say, Hartlehk in the north – such a man would not be suspicious just because he was alone, surely – it made ... no ... sense. And then it did. Selvorne thought about it, and it made perfect sense – it was what she meant, but not what she said, and likely not all the town would realise. One man alone – innocent, returning home. Ambushed by the brigands, and killed in the struggle – he pulled a knife! A sword! He meant to rob me, I fought him and won – here is the killer, or so the killer would say, of the innocent man he had just killed. Or convinced others to kill – a few lies carefully spread, a drunken lot of men might kill a man alone. Walking alone, leaving the town, could be thought suspicious by itself. Killed – all suspicion diverted from the truly guilty.

The guards knew. They knew far more than Selvorne, and he felt he was constantly trying to keep up with what must be for them standard practise. One killer certain, an entire town of killers, perhaps, if they were left to avenge the death of a man they did not know. Panic and fear, suspicion and – during a festival, the worst possible time, when many were drunk and strangers were amongst them.

It had to end. She was ending it. Warnings and orders, and the festival mood was dying. That night would not be drunken dancing as planned, it would be quiet gatherings around fires, and the suspicious watch of all strangers. The next morning – the guards were to leave – all visitors were to leave the town. That was her order, presented as protection. A strange end to the festival, and a great change in Dyneti, to handle something so grim. She was a stern lady of great power and command. It was only the night before that Selvorne stood near that very spot, and spoke with a pounding heart to Adyleh – a pretty, delightful, mischievous girl.

Those who lived in villages across the lake – were they annoyed, or relieved to live away from the town? Or afraid, he was not sure. In small villages, would they be safe, or in danger? They likely thought the murderer was one man alone, who might flee across the lake to their homes. Not easy to hide in a small village, though, for those who lived away from towns tended to be wary, sturdy and capable – against one man. Selvorne feared for the old couple he had seen, feeding chickens on the slope of the mountains where they lived, alone. They had been wary of him, for what good it might do.

Those from the northern towns, some were standing near him, and spoke of how the festival was turning sour. They had come so far, and were not yet done. Back to Senylehk they would go – from Senylehk, by way of Senylehk, near Senylehk – the name of that town was said many times. It was as if a festival there every night of the year, and with one hundred of us and coins to spend – a merry time of it, they said, almost eager to leave and find joy, without the inconvenience of killings.

Hunters were also annoyed, perhaps more than any other men. They were forbidden to go hunting – unwise, Dyneti said – banned was what she meant. After the festival they were often needed to bring meat from the wilds, they likely had spent most of their saved coins and would need to earn more, somehow. Hunters would be the least at risk in the wild – also, perhaps, the most suspicious, and that must have been what was thought in keeping them in the town, though claiming it was for their protection. It could also have been a ploy – no hunting, join the guards. Your skills appreciated, your pay certain. Selvorne narrowed his eyes as he wondered how clever the Waehdric might be to use the situation in such a way, to their advantage. Perhaps not planned, but they must have realised it.

Vaskatohr – people of his home town would not be pleased. The festival ended too soon, they would return back to – not the same, dull life in their town. Back to chores, but not the same. Their lord was gone, none yet knew, and fear would be with them – but danger? He had to do something, he could not let them walk the road alone.

"What is it you see that I do not?" Rohy asked, and Selvorne frowned. He looked to the stage – nothing unusual, there was a break as guards were preparing something.

"Nothing – why?"

"You keep nodding."

"I – oh, do I?"

Rohy nodded, and Selvorne explained his fears – he did not wish to speak of his home town, so he explained how he thought travellers would be suspected and attacked, if walking alone, mistaken as fleeing or escaping. Rohy nodded in agreement.

"I had not considered that – yes, a danger, to townsfolk. To killers ... "

"No, I mean people who are not, just – anyone, travelling alone."

"I know – I meant," Rohy said, "that the ordinary people of the town would be turned to ... killers. In anger, or fear. You are not as foolish as you look."

Selvorne shook his head in astonishment, then narrowed his eyes – and Rohy smiled.

"But easily teased. No, you do not look a fool – you look confused, as does everyone here – listen – some are already wondering what kind of killer leaves his victim to be found."

Selvorne listened, but heard no such thing – people had heard Rohy, though, and repeated what he said to others beside them – and a rumour had begun.

"Now they do," Selvorne said.

"And before, I heard. Now – the guards will speak."

~

The guards on the stage had formed a line, and looked most impressive, tall, being raised above the ground, and of course many were quite tall to begin with. Oddly, Dyneti was just as tall as the men. She spoke, as did Kalgevun, and Selvorne thought that not in any year before did so many people listen.

Of Arnlausa, once a guard – honoured and strong, a lord to be proud of – but he was missing, and that made many keen to do something, for fear he was in danger. Keen, and that was when the barrel bucket was presented – half a barrel, cut in two at the middle to make great buckets. One empty, the other was filled with wooden tokens, made from flat tiny planks, each of which would also be split in two. Recruitment sticks they were called, and the barrel bucket that was filled with them was placed before the stage. Men would come to join – also boys, and the old – and be viewed by guards there, who either waved their hand sharply away, or nodded. One solemn nod – that was the signal to take a token, which was snapped in two – half for the guards to keep, half for the new recruit. That half token was proof of acceptance, and, being broken from a half that the guards kept, could not be forged, faked or copied. The half token itself was something to be proud of, for it meant – for all to see – that the man carrying it was considered strong enough, tough enough, good enough to be a guard. Boys proven men, men proven brave. Half tokens were shown to maidens of the fair, to impress.

That was how it began – take a half token. Think it over. By the next day, return with it, show it – match it to the half kept by the guards, as proof. Accept the duties of guards, and have your name added to the list. The half token given was acceptance, the half token returned was agreement. Not all men came back, but kept the tokens, with pride. Some might have collected one each year – never to truly join. That was frowned upon, though the more men seen to take tokens, the more encouraging it was for those who might actually join.

Usually it took some convincing to get people to take a token. Usually the crowd was shy to begin. But the crowd surged forwards, and many took to the bucket even before it was properly manned. Dyneti raced to the front of the stage, seemed to snatch some young man from the crowd, and dragged him up with her – to the centre, amongst the line of guards. The man seemed unusually tall, rather slender, for his height, but strong, and – dare Selvorne think it – quite handsome. He was astonished to be dragged to the stage, but quickly warmed to the idea of the attention of the crowd, and the touch of Dyneti's hand – something Selvorne did not like at all, nor did he enjoy seeing her put her mouth to the young man's ear as she whispered, or he put his to hers in turn.

"Good Aigel!" Dyneti called to the crowd, who all looked at once, "A brave young man, strong and true. He is to join the guards! See – we can use men such as he!"

The young man – called Aigel – bowed and waved. And blew kisses to the crowd – Selvorne chuckled, and thought Dyneti did not entirely approve, though she left Aigel there, towering over the other guards.

"He is on a box," Rohy said.

"What?"

"He is standing on a box – so is she," Rohy explained, and Selvorne frowned – he hoped not the box he had given as a present.

"Why?"

"To make him look – taller, striking, important. Better than the guards they have. Who look quite intimidating – look now, how many are rushing to join. Strange, though, I think on seeing him so tall I would be less inclined to try, thinking myself too short."

Rohy was anything other than short, but Selvorne watched – he was right. Guards were yelling for those who had tokens to back away – each man wanted to be brought to the stage, to be seen by all the crowd. Some were, most were not. Those who stood idle at the front, staring at the stage as if it was a show – they were urged to leave, and that included Selvorne and Rohy, who shook their heads at the request, then nodded towards the barrel.

The yelling voice of Kalgevun, the sweet loud voice of Dyneti – the joys of being a guard, the travel, honour, pay, danger – adventure. Pay, again. The company of strong men on the road, alone, to protect her – when Dyneti said that, two dozen eager men charged to the barrel. Selvorne chuckled to think they might end up alone on the road with Demni instead. Rohy would not mind that at all, and he noticed his friend was watching her at the side of the stage, and wondered if that was why he led Selvorne to stand where they did.

"Are you joining for Demni?" Selvorne asked.

"Yes," Rohy replied.

"That is rather – "

"Silly? Childish? I agree. Today it is, but I have been giving this some thought since The Winer's Inn, and ... yes, it is silly."

"You still fancy her, after that night?"

"I do not know what to think of her – that only makes me wish to know more. Yes, I think I do – Savak speaks highly of her, very."

"Love?"

"Yes, but like a brother. He said never to say that, she is rather ... complicated."

"I know."

"Yes I know you do – she was quite friendly to you."

"I would hate to have her as an enemy, then, if that was friendly," Selvorne said, and Rohy grinned. Fearing Rohy was jealous, Selvorne had not said much of the night – not on the night. Besides, both had been drunk and exhausted. But Rohy had clearly seen past gestures she made to Selvorne, which might have been mistaken for affection – Demni was complicated. And to Rohy – not Selvorne – alluring.

The line to the bucket was long, and as Dyneti continued to speak, it bent around in a half circle, then back the other way, so all had a good view of her on the stage instead of the man's head before them in the line. It was a festival of its own, of sorts – how tankards of ale had appeared amongst those who were waiting, Selvorne could only guess. They laughed, joked – taunted each other, claiming some had no chance to be accepted. It was an army forming before his very eyes – an army of idiots, but men nonetheless.

At times, women would come, not to join the line, but to remove men from it. No, no and no – the orders of women. Wives, lady friends, loves. Sisters. Mothers – most embarrassing of all, to be dragged away by their mother, no matter what age they might be. Men who were already sworn to serve another, knowingly or not. Howling laughter from the rest of the line, then all the louder as some who laughed the hardest soon were dragged away by women of their own.

By far the funniest was when a very elderly fellow was dragged away by an equally elderly woman. He had, as everyone heard – for both old woman and man shouted loudly – only understood the part about free food, and thought he was joining the yards. Whatever that meant – it took some convincing and a surprisingly strong grip of the old woman to remove him, and the sudden appearance of another woman to explain – shouting – that he was going the wrong way for free food. The old man at once ambled away with what had to be wife and daughter. Selvorne laughed, and Rohy chuckled, though he was still quite grim in his stare.

Some returned from the stage looking almost as grim – rejected. Their faces said it, even as they laughed and claimed it was all a joke to try. Those in the line must have wondered if they would be accepted. Not all would be, not all could be, yet it seemed to be one in every ten men of the town trying.

"We must hurry or they will run out of places," Rohy said, grasping Selvorne's arm. His fingers were long and firm, and it almost hurt before Selvorne shrugged him off.

"That is stupid, they never run out of tokens."

"But – all these men?"

"No. All will have tokens. Wait, you will see. I am not standing in the line, I ... you know why," Selvorne said, and Rohy frowned – thought – then nodded. Odd, Selvorne thought he was doing the same, watching the line for suspicious men, but ... surely Rohy had not been watching Demni, when he should have been looking for killers?

Too young, too old – no, most were being accepted, and that was strange. Men who seemed too casual, perhaps – or sickly, or known to be a man of trouble. For the first time tokens might have been running out, for one guard was cutting at a slat of wood trying to make more. That he had one, ready to cut – it even had symbols burnt into it – to think that they were so well prepared – Selvorne knew they must have expected large numbers to wish to join. But not as many as those who were waiting. It was a very different year to those of the past.

"There are too many," Rohy said.

"More is good, the more, the better."

"I mean – too many men to watch them all. Can you? I cannot."

"Nor can I – and I doubt we will see much from here, or even if we were the men at the bucket asking questions."

"No – perhaps. What do you think they are asking?"

Selvorne shrugged – but then grew uneasy. What were they asking – name, family, where he was from – nothing he wanted to answer.

"I think they would accept you," Rohy said, and Selvorne frowned – accept him, of course, but ... the questions were the problem. Did his fear show on his face? Rohy's certainly was, but why would he fear?

"And you," Selvorne said.

"I – am not sure. They are turning quite a few away."

Selvorne looked at the men returning – no, they were not turning many men away.

"One in thirty are denied, no more."

"One in twenty – and there, another, that is two in twelve."

Two annoyed young men – annoying, too, Selvorne thought. Perhaps annoyed at being rejected, he was not sure, certainly not small men, and – Rohy was straight off to approach them. Selvorne waited and watched. A strange greeting, Rohy was almost pushed aside. Why did he wave his hand so – and off they went, Rohy with two angry men rejected, away from those waiting to join, passing them as they walked, and Rohy was ... sneering? So were the men. Selvorne watched and wondered as they left – then waited, until Rohy returned, which was quite a lot longer than he expected.

"Well?" Selvorne asked as Rohy stood before him with an awkward grin.

"A good thing I asked – they are turning men away," Rohy said, "for various reasons. Sick, weak, old, young – thin."

"Those two were neither, and everyone knows all that already."

"Yes – they were neither. And so were insulted, and had few answers – at least, did not fully understand why they were not accepted. I asked others as well, those rejected are gathering and drinking, to the side of the field."

"Did you drink?"

"No – I do not think they would like the smell of it. On the breath or on the shirt."

"Oh – that is something, I guess. Though hardly fair, at a festival."

"True – Selvorne, they are turning men away who claim to join for ... revenge."

"What?"

"Revenge – for the dead man."

"Friends? Of the dead man?" Selvorne asked in astonishment, looking over the faces of the men in the line once more.

"No – just angry men."

Selvorne frowned, it made little sense, yet Rohy nodded.

"I thought the same – odd, that they would ... you would think that was what they wanted – angry young men. Vengeful – but they do not. They are looking for ... those with a grim, serious sense of duty."

"That is hardly true of half these men – and certainly not of the one they put on the stage," Selvorne said, remembering the youth who had been blowing kisses to the crowd.

"Again, I thought the same – the reasons of the guards, perhaps not entirely true. That is what they say they seek – I think what they are trying to do is turn away any who seem ... well, angry."

Selvorne nodded – that made more sense. Although – it also made less sense. Never before had they turned away such men, half of Girradehn's guard friends were angry young men, and – where were they? Not at the recruitment, none of the Tavalehk guards were. They must have been in the town. Rohy seemed oddly concerned.

"So?" Selvorne asked, "You hardly seem angry."

"I was going to sound very angry – in the hope it would help my chances. Do you think – they would take me?"

Selvorne nodded, but he thought he understood Rohy's concern – he was not a big man, but tall. Not narrow, not broad. He had no doubt Rohy could swing a large axe, but not for long, and likely took a hatchet to the woods, and chopped away for hours at branches of trees already felled, or scraped the bark, or tied the ropes – but did not drag the logs. Hay cutter, not baler, who lifted great bales to stacks. Ox feeder, not wrestler, though why men wrestled the beasts was beyond Selvorne, and more likely done to impress the women on a farm, who in turn more usually carried the feed. Rohy was not the usual man to be a guard – he looked similar to, and rather quite a lot like, Temnere the administrator. He also seemed quite smart. Perhaps that would be a better role for him than to be a ... fighting man.

"You have guessed," Rohy said, and Selvorne nodded, though he had no idea what he was talking about, "I would not mention ... Dyneti, either."

"What?"

"I have noticed you looking at her – do not say you join for her, they are ... it is strange, is it not? First they put her on the stage, asking men to join, then they turn them away, if they wish to join for her – hardly fair."

"No doubt some ploy of the Waehdric – are they truly turning men away who say that?"

"Her, or Demni. Yes, they are – and they do not admit it. They find other reasons, but all the men are sure of it."

That was unfair. To him, or to others – it simply was not fair. Something snapped inside him and Selvorne felt – angry. Perhaps ... that was it, that was what they were turning away. Not anger for the dead man, or revenge, as Rohy had said – who in that entire town could care so much to feel furious vengeance for a man no one knew? Nor was it adoration for Dyneti, all the men must feel something for her – Demni, far fewer men, but some. No, it was neither – he knew what it was, and he was quite surprised Rohy had not realised the same, and that it had eluded himself.

"They are turning away braggarts," Selvorne said, "rough men, and the very angry, or drunk. They do not want such men as guards. Those who do what you were about to do, Rohy – those who pretend to be angry, to impress."

"I am angry, I – "

"Yes, but they do not know that, nor why. You are worried? For Demni? Because you think that if they suspect you are joining for her, they will reject you?"

Rohy nodded.

"I doubt they care about that, either – but do not go there staring at her as though enchanted, she is at the bucket now, you see."

Rohy turned and saw her at the bucket – stared with dreamy eyes, then turned back and took a deep breath.

"I do not know what you see in her," Selvorne said, chuckling.

"I am not sure how you cannot."

"Talk to her a while and perhaps you may – you are worried they will not accept you? Take my hand," Selvorne said, holding out his hand.

"I doubt that will help matters."

Selvorne frowned, then snatched for Rohy's hand – he moved it back too fast, and Selvorne was quite impressed – but caught it on the second try. Perhaps Rohy let him – and then he crushed. Rohy squeezed back – at first to protect his hand from being squashed, but then he seemed to realise what Selvorne was doing. Eventually he yielded.

"Your hands are strong," Rohy said.

"Yours are not bad. You – what do you do?"

"Odd work on farms. You?"

"Pigs and stones. You do not look strong – you look like you spend all day inside, for you are pale and slight – but you are used to work, they will want you as a guard."

"I work hard, but wear a hat in the fields. There is some sense to it, you know, the sun can be more tiring than half a day of chopping – "

"Roll up your sleeves," Selvorne said.

"It is cool."

Selvorne frowned at him, and Rohy rolled up his sleeves – better. Less like administrator, more like a farmer.

"Follow me," Selvorne said, "stay behind – do not talk as we wait our turn. Look solemn, make no boast. Silent and stern – yes, that is it."

"What? I am not doing anything?"

"Well, just look yourself. Make your arms hard when you stand there, but like this," Selvorne said, and he flexed his forearms every so often, which was quite noticeable. Rohy did the same – not quite the same, but it looked less ... foolish.

"Good, good," Selvorne said, and he grinned, "and they cannot refuse you. Or should not, once they see me – and whatever you do, do not look at Demni. Or they will think you have not come to join the guards, but to ask for her hand – and do not ask for her hand, indeed, do not take it, but if offered then bow over it instead, a short bow, like this."

At that, Selvorne did a short half bow, and did not let his eyes meet Rohy's – the safest and most polite refusal of the hand of a lady.

"You seem to know quite a lot," Rohy said.

"Yes, perhaps."

"And you are sure this will work?"

Selvorne was sure – he nodded. Confident, because he knew much more than how to behave amongst the guards, he knew many things he would not say. What they looked for, what they would do, how they ... and of course, he was Lord Heir of Tavalehk. He was, at that time, the highest authority in the town. He could not help but be confident, even if revealing that secret would mean hours of uneasy explanations, danger to his life and suspicion for murder – he laughed, and Rohy raised an eyebrow. Confident – bold – hopefully not a braggart, to be rejected.

And ... he hoped he was not becoming like Girradehn. Dangerously close to it ... and the stirrings of the Curse of Arnlausa must be ... controlled. With all that in mind, he led Rohy to the end of the line to join the guards, to become a guard – not like Girradehn.

Serious in the line of guards, well, Rohy was – Selvorne was closer to grim. They waited in silence, not talking, and his mind turned back to his task. To join – he would meet Cienn. He would have to do, surely she greeted all the new men – was she there, or back at Senylehk town, waiting? That was more likely. Had she been there, a murder would have drawn her out, in the absence of the lord. Dyneti, then, was her most trusted in that town. Not the old Waehdric men – perhaps Dyneti was to replace her when she ... died. Could she have died – no, news of the death of Cienn would have been everywhere. Rumours of it often were, every few years – she was the oldest of all the Waehter, of all their people, in all the north and likely in all the south as well. One hundred years of age – and that was announced not the last year, or the one before. Hard to travel, easy to recognise, likely to meet – as a guard.

Selvorne also wanted to train. He wanted to know how to fight. More, he wanted to know how to outsmart the brigands. Despite his successes, he felt a failure. Had he died on the bridge instead of any of the other three, he was sure all the brigands would be caught already. Or killed. He felt ... not useless, but almost like a sword, unfinished. A sword that was not a sword, but a great bar of steel, clumsy and strong, but slow – not sharpened, not shaped, not honed to allow skills of a trained man to use. Just a point would be enough, to run the enemy through – instead of charging through like a fool. Or walking into their camp, hiding amongst vines of a tree.

What was the sweep of the woods? He imagined a hundred men with sticks, bashing at such viny trees – brigands wailing and running in all directions. It made him chuckle, and made him grim. He wanted to be part of it, whatever it would be. He was beginning to think it would be a lot more careful, quiet and cunning than bashing at bushes. He hoped it would also be soon.

He had another reason to join – he feared being alone, though if he said that, he was sure people would take the wrong meaning. It was not loneliness that disturbed him, nor truly fear of danger. It was the fact that alone, he could do only little. Not fight, perhaps not flee. Not hide too well, and clearly not spy very well, since he saw none of the faces of the men except a few, and one of them was already dead. How had he missed it, that the tall dark man was not truly part of the brigands – or had Selvorne started some fight by stealing the ale? Stealing the ale itself was stupid. That was his true fear, not being alone, but being allowed to do such stupid things that might bring trouble. He needed allies, training, and friends – and protection, from himself.

"I hope you do not plan to stare at the lady when we are there," Rohy said in a low voice, almost in Selvorne's ear.

"As I said, I do not fancy her – and did I mention we should not talk in the line?" Selvorne asked – but Rohy nodded, then tilted his head towards the front of the line.

Dyneti had appeared at the barrel – and Selvorne felt his heart thump hard. A warning from Rohy. Good, it was just the kind of protection he needed, from himself. Better warned before he arrived than to unexpectedly look up and see her – he would stare and look a fool. And there were not many men ahead of them, for the process of choosing seemed to have sped up greatly since Demni had arrived.

The man before them was slightly short, rather quiet, alone and had said nothing to them, but Selvorne thought he listened whenever anyone spoke, and all the time until it was his turn in line, he seemed nervous. But then he stepped up boldly to the bucket, bowed to Demni, then to Dyneti – and to Selvorne's surprise, they both nodded. He took a token, tilted his head in a bow once more, then left.

Selvorne was astounded. He did not look the type to be accepted, and though it bode well for Selvorne, who never thought he might be rejected, he had expected some kind of discussion, and ... he looked at Dyneti, and his heart pounded. Amongst his jumbled thoughts he realised he had been secretly looking forward to speaking with her, spending more than a few moments, and convincing her to let him join.

Dyneti was not quite smiling, not with her lips, anyway, for her eyes were very bright. Demni stared at him, and the man at the bucket was Kuoren, the grumpiest of the guards Selvorne had met. Kalgevun was behind Dyneti, and he nodded. Savak was behind Demni, and he grinned.

"Name?" Kuoren asked.

"Kuoren," Selvorne replied, and Kuoren frowned.

"No it is not."

"Who are you, then?"

Only Savak chuckled, but Dyneti raised an eyebrow and Selvorne suspected she found it amusing.

"You are Selvorne," Kuoren said.

"Yes, you know. So why did you ask?"

"My," Savak said, "he is bold. I say, make him a guard."

"He is annoying," Kuoren said.

"Perhaps make him captain, then?" Savak suggested – and to Selvorne's surprise, all of them chuckled, including Kuoren. Even Demni tried not to smile.

"Reasons for joining the guards?" Kuoren asked, trying to sound grim, but he who laughed the least seemed to be struggling the most to contain it.

"To defend justice, and the people," Selvorne said, "and also – see the lands, in the company of good men."

"I see," Kuoren said.

"And I wish to bring bloody revenge on those killers out there who did murder," he said terrifyingly, "they will suffer my fury, when I – "

"You do not," Demni said.

"Oh, yes I do, I – "

"Selvorne, this is no time for jests," Dyneti said, and for a moment, her sweet voice distracted him – but only for a moment.

"I also wish to be made guard to such sweet ladies as these," Selvorne said, then smiled.

"You are an idiot," Kuoren said, and Selvorne – a little hurt – looked down at him.

"It seems that does not stop men becoming guards."

Kuoren began to stand, but thought better of it, and just glared. But Selvorne smiled so kindly, the angry guard had to laugh.

Selvorne was not serious, not with his insults, anyway. Kuoren was not smart, but not an idiot. And Selvorne was, at times. Most people were – he had to say such things, he had to act a fool – act angry, or so they would think, for there were things he could hide as a joke, but not in silence. He did want bloody vengeance – better thought a jest, than truth. He did want to be with, well, Dyneti at least – and he did think some of the guards were idiots. He knew enough guards to know it was true, for some.

"A bit short, I think," Kalgevun said, "also, too well groomed, he looks like he lives the indoor life – the son of a rich merchant? Spends like it, as well."

Selvorne had never been called short before, and he was quite surprised – until he realised Kalgevun was teasing.

"Hands of a lady, I will wager," Savak said, and at that he stepped around Demni and took Selvorne's hand, then turned it about. Selvorne's nails were well groomed – trim, clean, filed smooth and neat. The back of his hand was also fine, and his palm was smooth, apart from where he had gripped the stones, the chisel, the mallet and leather straps, wooden carts and a dozen other tools. Weeks of stonework at the quarry, rough work, but he always took great care of his hands, knowing that any injury, uneven wearing or break would ruin his work. Even a slight flaw in his hands might create problems of nuisance, which led to distraction – that led to accidents, which, in a quarry, could cause death. Even his hair was always kept neat, or it might catch in ropes. His trousers tucked into strong boots, or tied high at the knee – his shirt sleeves often rolled back a bit, to keep cuffs clear of a dozen deadly tools or riggings. Neat, and safe. He did look like an indoors fancy man, with fine quality clothes, but his hands, they were not those of such a man. Not even calluses were left, but smooth, sturdy and gentle. And strong.

Savak was astonished, gasped – he squeezed Selvorne's hand, and Selvorne began to crush his, until Savak broke away with a sudden twist – and laughed. Kalgevun peered over, and nodded. Demni stared, and Dyneti – she seemed as though in a dream.

"Well – seems we had you wrong," Savak said, "what can you do?"

"Wrestle, a little, I am good with a spear, quite strong, too, and – "

"What – work – can – you – do," Savak asked slowly.

"Am I here to be a guard, or to work?"

"Answer the question," Demni said.

"Well, I herd pigs to woods for feed, and back to slaughter and butcher," Selvorne said.

"Dangerous to pigs, then," Savak said.

"Some men are pigs," Selvorne said, "neither as smart, handsome or tough."

"Most," Demni said.

"I – also work with stone, and – "

"What?" Demni asked – suddenly, and her eyes were wide.

"I work with stone, and – "

"Cut? Carry? Lay?"

"Yes."

"Which?" she asked, and people were silent. Selvorne felt almost as if accused, as if he had admitted to a crime, yet he was the only person there who seemed uncomfortable.

"All," he dared reply, which was true, "and more. All."

Demni moved closer, reached for his hand and took it, pulled it close and looked at it, then turned it over. Selvorne, without thinking, as soon as his palm was raised, with her hand in his, bowed – and kissed her hand.

He did not mean to. He certainly did not plan to, it came to him so suddenly he was as astonished as the others. All stared with wide eyes – then Demni giggled.

One giggle, then silence. More astonishing than what he had done, she pulled back her hand at once, turned to the others and nodded.

"Take him," Demni said. Then she quickly left.

Savak followed, but not before his stare became an astonished laugh. Kalgevun and Dyneti were looking at each other – disbelief. Kuoren seemed he could hardly be more surprised if the two of them had embraced. Whether it was the kiss or the giggle, Selvorne was not sure, but the kiss was good manners, and the giggle – he thought that was most unexpected from Demni.

"Well," Dyneti said, "you are taking longer than all the others. Are you truly joining the guards?"

"That is why I am here," Selvorne said.

Dyneti leant to reach into the barrel, took a token, held it up and broke it in two – for a moment he thought she had just rejected him – but then she handed one piece to him, and kept the other for herself.

"Decide by dawn. If you change your mind, return your token to that empty barrel there," Dyneti said, waving her hand to somewhere that Selvorne did not look, for he could not stop staring at her eyes.

"I will not."

"You – are not to join?"

"I will not change my mind."

"You know, then?"

"What?"

"Your mind," Dyneti said, but he was not sure what she meant, and nodded, "we will travel together, then – north, in the morning."

There was only one thing she could have said he would have wanted to hear more, and that would have been ... impossibly bold to think of, but he thought of it nonetheless – that they would have travelled together, alone. He said nothing, but knew he must have looked a fool.

"Next!" Kuoren commanded, but Selvorne only moved aside when Dyneti led him by the hand.

"I have work to do here," Dyneti said, "and will see you tomorrow, yes?"

Selvorne nodded.

"Then, a good day to you for the rest, and ... I am sorry I may not join you for lunch."

Selvorne nodded, grinned – then realised she was sending him away. A bow, a slight curtsey, and he left. Wandering, alone, dazed and entranced, and – oh, he had forgotten Rohy. He looked back – he seemed to be doing well. Kalgevun was testing the strength of his hands, and nodded. Demni was not there to distract him, his friend would be fine, they would meet away from the line, as planned.

As Selvorne walked, he realised Taahr was near, away from the bucket, congratulating the new recruits – eyeing each of them up and down. He took Selvorne's hand to shake it, which felt as awkward and clumsy as if Taahr had instead clasped his elbow. Taahr had a wide grin on his face that made Selvorne uneasy, but he remembered what Dyneti had said – that he was hopeless in all usual manners, and so was almost rude – but, as a guard, he had great achievements. That very day he had shown himself capable of taking rapid action against the enemy – indeed, he went with few men into danger at once, and during the night.

"Welcome!" Taahr said.

"Thank you, and well done, Nohc Taahr, Captain of the North – on your quick, decisive action against the enemy in the south."

Taahr's jaw dropped. His grasp of Selvorne's hand softened, and their hands fell apart. Insulted? No – astonished at the honour, and it was not that much of an honour to give. Nor was it false, nor entirely planned – Selvorne had, almost by instinct, just named Taahr as Captain, as high as a lord. He knew he was Captain, but to move that to the last and put Nohc to the first was ... no one did it.

From astonishment to pride, amazement and a bow. Taahr said nothing – Selvorne suspected he could say nothing. For a man so keen to praise himself, perhaps he was not used to it from others. Selvorne bowed in turn before walking away without saying another word – smiling, also, for Taahr was not a person he wished to speak with at length.

A dozen yards or more, and Selvorne looked back – Rohy was approaching Taahr, who did not offer his hand, he just stared. The two looked at each other, then Rohy nodded a bow – Taahr seemed so distracted, he shook his head, shook

Rohy's hand, welcomed him and allowed him to move on – watching Rohy leave, staring, but then seeing Selvorne again, Taahr grinned.

"A very odd little man," Selvorne said in a low voice when they were too far to be heard. Rohy grunted, looked back, and shook his head, but seemed to agree.

All Gone to Grim

The townsfolk had been allowed to leave the Festival Field halfway through the recruitment. Whatever it was that the guards were doing in the town that required none of the people to be there, Selvorne could only guess. Most likely look for anyone who was not in the field, trying to leave – by boat would be the best. A boat across the lake could reach villages that knew nothing, and a killer could escape to the north by a mountain trail rarely used.

Hours, then, since the townsfolk were uneasy, thinking there was a killer amongst them – on the field, it was not long before they found friends. And courage. And almost wanted to find the killer – the guards were right in trying to subdue them. Weapons were discouraged in the town, and at festival times, seized – a crowd carrying axes over their shoulders, or spears or rakes or shovels, or any ordinary tool from a farm – accidents alone were a danger. But even without their weapons, in large groups, and with the assurances of the guards, the people were no longer afraid. They began to revive what they could of the festival spirit, and many were already cheerful.

Selvorne was not so happy, or not so relieved. He wished he could finish things that day. He wished Cienn was there. He was not in a hurry to become lord, he only thought the plans lacked urgency. But there were plans, and so much more was happening than he realised. The lie about reaching the river in the south – the hiding of the discovery of the broken bridge. A lie to the people, a hiding of the fact – the guards must have realised something had happened to Arnlausa. And they must have known there was danger – perhaps they all were marching back north to find Cienn, to report and determine what to do next.

But many had said things, done things – suggested that there had been a planned sweep for a long time. No, Selvorne was not at ease, not relieved, not as unafraid as he had been before, despite knowing he was to be a guard heading north to join an army of allies. The guards were many, and they were armed – and they were not at ease. Only one thing could make so many guards nervous – secretive, cautious – lie. Another army.

What had he seen, in the woods – a few dozen men? Not similar men – some from here, others from there. From east and west. Meeting. A bridge ... armies needed bridges. Men could climb in and out of ravines, but armies – they had waggons, and oxen, and sometimes herds of goats and sheep to eat. It was one thing he had considered before, but thought nonsense. Yet it was one of the few things that made sense, and it was all the more reason to join the guards and find Cienn.

Oddly, the fears of the guards gave him some relief for his own town. If they suspected the same things as him, they would post spies in the woods and warn the people of an advancing enemy. Vaskatohr would be protected by such means, and all would be ready to flee. That may have been the reason for escorting people on the road, as well – to be sure they did not walk into danger. Taahr had said he saw a camp once used by many people – he must have known the dangers. It was some relief to think they were preparing, but not a great easing of his fears.

Rohy was more agitated, and had lesser concerns. His mood seem to fall with each step he took after joining the guards. Perhaps before, he was consumed by fear he would not be accepted, and once accepted, had to face new fears of actually going to danger. No, he did not seem afraid. Grief, then, over the death of his father, and frustration for the delays – that did not seem it, either. But he was silent, stared at the ground as he walked, and was not pleasant company. He seemed to like having Selvorne walk beside him, and thanked him for his generosity when he purchased them both a meal for lunch.

They sat by the lake and ate. It was quiet, for a festival, other than the occasional rush of people running past – laughing, not fleeing in danger – they only made things seem stranger. It was worse when such laughing folk were recognised as men from the line who wanted to become guards, accepted or rejected, it seemed to make mockery of serious duty, on a day when grim murder had been discovered. The worst of all was the dark–haired youth named Aigel, who Dyneti had brought to the stage. He strolled along beside the lake in the company of several maidens, some of whom were pleading for him to reconsider and stay in the town, as they almost hung from his arms on either side. He smiled, he made them giggle and wail and laugh and beg. Selvorne narrowed his eyes in disapproval, in disgust, in ... envy. The youth disappeared along the road, and it seemed more maidens joined him as he strolled.

Selvorne and Rohy did not speak of vengeance, guards, brigands or death – only shirts, boots, the taste of their food and unusual coolness of the day. Selvorne did mention that the half token they had was meant to be returned. They had been accepted, but they had not yet accepted. Think it over, return the half – be added to the list. Then it was final. Rohy was glad he mentioned it, but otherwise had no desire to speak of the guards, or anything ahead of them.

In silence there was a closeness between them – both had lost fathers to killers. Perhaps the same killers. Though Rohy did not know Selvorne's loss, he appreciated his compassion. And help, and it was an alliance, of sorts. They ate, and drank very watered ale, and watched the lake for the afternoon.

~

Despite their closeness, Rohy wished to be alone after a while. Selvorne said he understood, though he did not completely, and he left Rohy by the lake. He wandered back to the festival – stalls were closed or closing, things had all been sold, or no one was keen to buy. The following afternoon, the town would be almost as normal, and Selvorne was not sure if there would be any revelry that night.

He laughed – where was his attention, distracted and vague. He had left his pack and all his things at the Waehdric camp, taking only a knife and his purse of coins. He was not used to carrying a pack – not in the town, he always left his things at Arnlausa's house. He wondered if he should simply leave them with the Waehdric, they could hardly be safer – no, it was not quite right. And he thought he might see Dyneti, though ... she said she would be too busy.

Busy or not, Dyneti was not at her camp. Kuoren was, resting, and another man who looked similar, also resting, but more friendly when Selvorne appeared. Each recognised the other, but did not know names – Bluoren, the large man said, and Selvorne introduced himself. Cheerful, friendly – welcoming, to the guards, though Bluoren was a guard of Vonersehl town, far to the west, by the sea, and was not serving Dyneti or the Waehdric. Helping, though, at such a time. A good festival, otherwise. He offered to mind Selvorne's pack if he wished, he was, after all, a guard. Selvorne thanked him, but took his things, not for lack of trust, and certainly not for the desire to lug them around, but because he wished to find a quiet place and think over all the things he might need for the journey. Bluoren said farewell, Kuoren nodded a bow, as though ... Selvorne was captain ... and then he chuckled.

Dyneti was busy, he had learnt, organising the men, and then to spend the early night reading poems to children, at various places in the town. Children and their parents, and likely many others who could attend. Waehdric poems, to inspire and uplift, especially important at such a time when the very young were afraid. Or worse, unafraid, with a mind to catch killers. Selvorne passed by one such place where she was to read, and he knew he would not be able to get inside the shelter of the hay barn where it would be – not when all the children came. It was no matter, he would see her the next day.

Back he went to the Festival Field, which was very quiet. A few guards lingered, but seemed tired. One guarded the bucket for tokens returned, watching him as he peered inside. Selvorne was disappointed to see only half a dozen tokens had been returned. More would be during the night, some in the morning, he expected, but so few – not many must have been serious. Six, of perhaps two hundred men, boys, youths – who only wanted the token to keep, perhaps, or to show maidens

335

and boast. Or taunt maidens – yes, I am joining – no, do not leave – oh, but I must – please, stay, do not join, I will do anything to keep you here with me. Or some such nonsense. Six men only of strong will – six men, he would prefer, to a hundred boys. Perhaps not. Perhaps more would join. He took out his token half, and tossed it into the barrel.

"Ahh ... what are you doing?" the large guard asked.

"Joining," Selvorne replied.

"You are Selvorne?"

Selvorne nodded, and the man shook his head, then reached into the barrel and found the token he had just thrown in – and took it out, handing it back. Selvorne's heart sank, but the man nodded at him.

"You are meant to keep half."

"And put half in."

"Yes – well, Our Lady has taken that half, it seems. Throw that in and you will only confuse the count."

Selvorne frowned, but – the guard was right. All other men had half kept by the guards, and half taken, to be returned when they were listed. Dyneti had kept his other half. He guessed that he had already confirmed his acceptance.

"You are keen?" the guard asked, and Selvorne nodded, "Good. Better six keen than sixty forced."

Selvorne nodded again.

"And better sixty forced than one hundred fools," the guard added, "though we may have that as well, soon enough."

"What is happening?" Selvorne asked, and the large man raised an eyebrow.

"True, then, you have no manners."

Selvorne frowned in confusion for a moment – then grinned.

"It seems you know my name and I do not know yours?" Selvorne asked.

The guard stood – large, not quite tall. Rounded – but not fat. His chest and belly seemed shaped like a barrel, and his arms were quite strong, and though also large, seemed thin compared to his body. He had a big head and sandy fair hair, but his eyes were kind. And when he dipped to a short bow then up again, Selvorne thought it was almost meant to be funny – but he was sure not to laugh.

"Liogur," the man said, "of Vonersehl. You are keen to join, not only the guards?"

Selvorne frowned.

"Our Lady?" Liogur asked.

"Oh – she is lovely," Selvorne said, and Liogur did neither laugh nor joke, but nodded.

"Most think so – all should. She is. These are difficult times for her, but – I have watched you, and think you seem a good lad."

"And you are warning me, in a way," Selvorne said, "are you her brother?"

Liogur widened his eyes, then burst into laughter – loud, and it was quite embarrassing in the almost empty Festival Field, most who were near must have heard. He rumbled as he laughed, and Selvorne was sure the ground shook, though it might have only been himself.

"My guess is, no?" Selvorne asked when the man grew calm.

"No – do I look like her? I hope not!"

"Well, no, and ... brothers may look quite different?"

"Rarely. And then only with great suspicion of the mother – so, now you are a guard, though I guess when she took your token you had already accepted. Not completely, though – a new recruit. Selvorne, you seem a jolly fellow – but we are not to speak with new recruits. Certainly not treat them as guards. Not until – later. I must bid you a good – is it after noon, or later?"

Selvorne shrugged – later, but not yet night.

"I could use the company, sitting here is dull, but the rule is strict – I would warn you, though," Liogur said in a low voice, and Selvorne moved closer, "at such a trying time, do not expect a lady to behave quite as usual, even when usually, ladies tend to behave quite oddly."

That was the warning – mysterious and strange, but Selvorne nodded and thought he had some idea what Liogur meant as he smiled and thumped Selvorne on the back. Guards tended to do a lot of back thumping, Selvorne wondered if a thick coat or a wide pack might be a good idea. He left Liogur to work himself back into his small chair, and crossed the Festival Field wondering where he should go.

The platform had girls dancing on it at one end, and young boys watching, when they were not climbing up and jumping off as far as they could land. Not exactly what the guards had in mind for staying together and keeping safe, but the group of children was watched by Liogur, otherwise the field was quite empty. Where the grasses ended and sapling woods began, Selvorne fancied that he saw Rohy.

He thought to approach him, but he was not alone – Rohy was arguing in a low voice with a tall – taller than Rohy, perhaps – man. Rarely did Rohy raise his voice – never did the other man – yet both seemed angry. Selvorne thought he should not interfere, for Rohy even kicked his foot and stubbed his toe, and seemed furious over some personal matter.

Quietly Selvorne walked away from them, and took a path that led beside the river that ran west. The path there was good beside the water, peaceful and quiet. And safe. One side of the river was town, the other was impossible to cross without a bridge. All the lake flowed through the river there, and though it was wide, shallow and slow in appearance, Selvorne knew it was truly deep and fast flowing.

Safe to walk there, for the path was not only well maintained, but the river edge kept good – every so often was a short pole with a bucket on the top, turned upside down and left there so it would not blow away or fall into the waters. The fire trail – and on call to a fire, a hundred men could make a line along the path, and move twenty buckets along the line at speed, into the town, shifting the line once they had all the buckets, directing it to where it was needed. The town had grown so long, and stretched so far from the river that a similar arrangement had to be made along the lake – all homes were protected. Arnlausa had a tendency to think ahead on such matters. Not always, but usually.

His path of peace led away from the water and joined the second road of Tavalehk, and that led him back to the crossing roads. And the Lordstone, and the square.

The cart with the body was gone – where, Selvorne was not sure, but it could not be left there. The square was quiet, and stalls had moved from its paved edges. Packed to leave, or taken away to a place less grim. No people were there, not even guards, but he could see the bridge to the south had two guards standing watch, chatting on stools. They should be in the tower, but perhaps there was a man up there as well.

That was his way home to Vaskatohr, but he could not go. Not home, not south – not without suspicion, and to go alone would serve no purpose, but to walk into danger. Perhaps save Rerleden, no, more likely get caught, and Rerleden would save him – perhaps learn what happened to Girradehn. Perhaps suffer what happened to Girradehn ... but there was no chance to destroy the Tavalehk bridge. It was stone, not wood. Low sides, easy enough to push a man over. A short fall to a fast river. Selvorne turned away from the south and found himself walking to the Lordstone.

A great list of lords – well, not too long. Tavalehk was not as old a town as some. The cut stone was a square pillar, the names carved on the side facing the town, but only filling to halfway down, and it had three blank sides left to carve – to fill it might take a thousand years. Selvorne took a deep breath to think that one day – even, say, five hundred years from then – someone might read through the names and come across his own. So he pondered, but only for moments, as he glanced over the other names, until he found Arnlausa. The last name, and under it ... his own would be cut.

Not the sorrow, nor honour, nor astonishment of it came to mind, but a poem he recalled that would require a new verse, for himself. A recital of the Lords of Tavalehk, not all, but those most recent. He thought hard on what it had said.

Tarvorna, Tavana, Radehna, Laehtene.
First man as lord with laws made to mean
in rule of the towns only men could.
Before all were ladies, in all ways were good.
Boys to make men, and men to make law
to sever the ties with the houses of Vor.
Mocked with no sons, but daughters had two
the lordship was lost to the best man he knew.
Siniavor Lady wed to a man
Lauserelerok Lord of the MidWaehter land.
Relarn and Roksini, twins gentle and sweet
loved by the town and all they did meet

mourned by the people, in fury once learnt
they died in the fires deliberately burnt.
Arnrok the Avenger to foes he brought war
united in battle the houses of Vor.
Rokeli his daughter and Relok his son
Ruled Lord and Lady, ruled both as one.
Hand of forgiveness, hand with a sword
Never again would death take a lord.
One son – our Arnlausa – unloved and unwed
lay late Arnlausa, not often his bed
early to rise so he makes the men wait
early to bed and he makes ladies late.
Arnlausa Arnlausa, late all the time
off with your friend, it is said to buy wine.
Not just for wine the merchants do say
a dozen Arnlausa's may rule here one day.

Selvorne must have heard the poem a hundred times. The last of it was not ...
officially part of the poem. Rarely did a lord have more than a few lines about
him, and rarer still would they approve of such verses – Arnlausa did not.
Selvorne's father also was not so fond of it. Yet he chuckled to hear it, then shook
his head.

The grim truth of it struck Selvorne – Arnlausa had no heir. Uhlsko, certainly,
but he was older, unlikely to have outlived him, and that was not known to people.
Clearly whoever wrote the poem wished he had a son – wished he might get
drunk and fall in love. He did get drunk, and was friendly with many women, but
never for love. As for being late, he was only late to the festival each year, and not
even every year – never for meetings with important folk. He did keep people
waiting at times, but that was because they had no appointment beforehand to see
him, and –

Selvorne took a deep breath. His mind was wandering, and though he did not
usually feel grim during the day, there was pain deep within him that was only
barely subdued. When he thought of Arnlausa – or his father – it was as if they
lived. It was relief, it was ... the way it was before. He hid the pain as he
remembered they did not. He unclenched his fist, and touched the Lordstone.

No heir. It was a problem. He was heir – problem solved. Son of his closest most
trusted friend – the best Arnlausa could do, when there were no men he trusted.
When his only son – who may or may not have been considered as heir – was
dying. Selvorne had not killed him. The one thing Arnlausa knew for certain. Any
other man may have done. If proven not the killer, if there at the end, in the cave.
All others were suspected. All the men entrusted to guard him, serve him – laugh
with him. Any friend. Any foe – any stranger, also, or man well known. Selvorne

could not imagine how that must be, for Arnlausa to think that all people he knew could not ... be ... trusted.

No, Selvorne could not imagine it. He did not have to. It was the same for him as well.

At that he took a deep breath. So – all were untrusted, but not hated, and Arnlausa was not friendless. It was not the fact that his men were suspected, but that the importance of matters were too great to take any risk. Selvorne was in the same position – yes, he had friends, but no, he had no idea what was going on. Arnlausa might have had a few ideas, but was just as confused. Cienn was his only ... rock.

Odd, she had been called that – an old woman he imagined her, but not frail. As hard as stone. As the Lordstone, and all lords of the land, mere names cut upon her strength. Arnlausa and Uhlsko agreed on that, but Selvorne had imagined her not as the Lordstone, which was carved smooth, but as the uncut rock beneath it from where it rose – rough, harsh, strong – unmoving. As unlike water as could be, which was an odd thing for the leader of Waehdric, who said that people were as water, at least in spirit.

He felt quite eager to meet her – eager, and anxious. Perhaps afraid. He had no doubt she was like the rock, nor did he doubt that when she found the killers she might tie them there, and pelt them with stones until there was nothing left of them but water and dust. Killed against the very Lordstone bearing the name of Arnlausa, who had suggested in the past she had done much worse – or much better.

As many lords had. Many who were listed on that very stone. A long list of ruthless men. Selvorne felt it was unfair that all those lords who fought for the town, defended it, lost it – lost those they loved in doing so – and then Arnlausa was forced to give it to him at the end. No choice, no chance – one last chance, though, but Selvorne did not deserve it. Selvorne owed him – he owed them, all of them – and he wondered what would be his verse in the song.

Selvorne Skolerne, there by luck.
With a brigand's knife was stuck.
Made a lord, then soon to mourn.
Though to care he once was sworn.

Standing at the Lordstone, musing over its list of lords – that was just about exactly what the next heir would be doing, and the square was likely where enemies of the heir would be watching. Selvorne turned and walked away, heading back into the town. No one was watching. Or ... he saw no one watching, and that made him uneasy.

The poem said that never again would death take a lord, but it had. It always would. Sudden or expected, and he needed – no, he would not think of it, not there so close to the square. He took himself away along the road headed east.

The eastern road, which was so very short, for it soon came to the lake and followed its edge only briefly before it ended between the lake, and the start of the river that ran west.

No houses were there, it was too dangerous. It was the only part of the lakeside that flooded, for there the river began and swelled with rains or the spring melt from the mountains, but the surge of water was less than a foot, and made mud at best, and a larger lake at worst. A strong wind could blow waters over that flat land – it was no place for a house, for not even on stilts could anyone rest easily at night. No houses, no piers, no boats and few people, it was one of the quietest parts of town.

Selvorne sat on the gravelled shore and looked at the lake. It was vast, and with his head so low and close to the waters, it seemed larger still. Sunset was not quite soon, but with the woods to the west the shadows were long. A strange cool day for the spring, and the waters were very still, like a mirror. The full moon had risen over the mountains – not quite full, it was beginning to wane. Not quite risen, it was just over the distant peaks. Not so distant, either – he had wandered near the feet of those mountains, only – three days before? It seemed so much longer. Five days before that ... he had watched that same moon rise, over ... not quite the same mountain, but near enough.

Just over a week. There on the southern side of the ravine, a happy camp by a great boulder that had fallen from the mountainside. With his father, Arnlausa, Girradehn – yes, he was happy as well, oddly. He had giggled. Oh, what a mistake to laugh so, like a girl – with Arnlausa and Uhlsko near, the teasing went for hours as the two old men giggled during the night, in mockery of the youth. Why had he giggled, it seemed ... a strange joke.

Selvorne frowned – it was quite a strange joke, not even a joke, and Selvorne tried to remember what it was exactly that had been said ... and how.

"Hey – you on the – stone, cold, staring – warm yourself, by the flame, by the bed. This stone looks cold, I assure you it is not. Try it – the coldest stare, the hottest, bare."

That was Arnlausa – slurring his words, at times, though not drunk, and he spoke as though timing his words to a song. And Girradehn ... giggled. Uhlsko raised an eyebrow, Arnlausa shrugged – but continued to taunt Girradehn, and though it was amusing, and though Girradehn was ... blushing? None of it made sense. You on the stone, you on the log, you on the – standing there, you on the bed. That was the worst, to make Girradehn laugh, but also ... seemed to make Uhlsko annoyed, and he turned to Selvorne and said the strangest thing.

"You will on the festival square – you will on the beauty may stare. You will on the love may feel ill – you will on the choose as they will."

Uhlsko was also not quite drunk, but slurred his words – it was not quite a joke. You – ull – on – the. Not exactly amusing, except to see them behave so oddly to think it was. Selvorne was confused, and assumed it was a joke from the south, so he raised his eyebrows and laughed politely. Arnlausa shrugged and Girradehn – to hear Uhlsko's remark – his mood became grim.

Nonsense. All of it. A joke between themselves, insults, taunts, laughter. They would never explain it, and none of it Selvorne would ever understand, were he to think of it for days.

But to think of it, Selvorne felt they still lived. Seven days ago. The sun was setting, the festival ... ending, though some would make merry at night, perhaps. People were distant. The town, the piers, the past – all distant. Selvorne sat by the lake for a long time, and watched its still water grow dark, and thought that he had never felt so alone.

First Report

Selvorne woke in the sleeping field, early to the noise of others rising, gathering their things, talking as they prepared to eat before leaving. Not so many had been festive the night before, and not so late as previous nights, for it had been cold and the mood was quiet. Instead of three large fires, dozens of small ones had been lit and people slept near them for warmth, and close to each other, for safety. Selvorne had kept to himself, trusting no one very well, though those sleeping nearest seemed to want to do no harm.

He had a cloak, a plain one, which was more of a blanket. It would be useful on the journey, as it was likely that guards often slept outside. The day before, when stalls were closing, he purchased a small bronze pot with a clasping handle and wire hanger, at a good price, for cooking on a fire if he must. Such a thing he had at home, but he was not going home, and he knew the journey might not be as well supplied as some men might expect. Dozens of men sharing one pot would be very friendly to one man with a second – and he needed men to be friendly.

That had been his last return to the festival. He had sat by the lake for some time before realising he should prepare. Alone, and likely, the last time he would be alone. Perhaps for a very long time. He settled to sleep away from the others with his own small fire, and woke during the night to find it had grown larger, and attracted others near. No matter, but he was not in the mood to speak with anyone, so he moved farther away. What had begun as a cool night turned cold ... then a breeze came, and by morning it was very warm once more. His cloak was pushed aside to become a pillow, and he wondered if it would be unnecessary for the next few days.

Early – it was too early to assemble for the guards, so he took himself and all his things to the lake. To wash, one more time before marching. There would be no other chance – to shave, and clear his mind.

His mind was already clear. It was the first day the shaving was not a matter of will, of settling his mind, of calming his fury. One enemy was already dead. And ... there was an unexpected sorrow at the man's death. Had he been brought to Selvorne alive – proven the killer – Selvorne would have killed him. Any man would – every lord must. Some might not do it quickly.

But not proven, and the death of the man he had suspected only made things more complicated. Was it a sign that the man was innocent, or incompetent? Or expendable. Or none of those, but merely convenient to others, who thought nothing of killing a man to achieve their ambitions. What kind of men were those, who laughed and seemed so friendly at the camp, warm to their brigand friends, wary of their brigand allies? To kill one of their own – and it had to have been done by them, for no guard would have left a man on the road after doing battle. Dangerous, cunning, ruthless – hidden. And watching. Selvorne had to be all that, and more.

No, it was not sorrow, or grief, or pity for himself – or for those who had died. None of that he felt. He only felt silence. With his mind so quiet and still, he washed and shaved.

~

To the place where guards were to assemble, at the north of the town, near the field where he had slept – they were far from leaving. Some had just risen and were not hurrying, and those who had were waiting. Leaving at dawn, a man could walk all the way from Tavalehk to Hartlehk – forty miles or so, a very long day. To walk in the dark during the winter, or arrive when it was dark in summer. Or if very slow, to arrive the next dawn. That was for a strong man, a good walker – guards rarely meant to walk so far or so fast without reason, and that day they were to go with Temnere, who was neither strong nor fast.

Selvorne went to the Waehdric camp to learn what he might, and Dyneti was brief in speaking with him that morning, but generous to do so, when she was busy. Most of her tasks seemed to involve a grumpy goat and a small cart that could only contain her things if packed precisely. She was not to walk with the new recruits, which she stated almost as an apology – she would leave the next day, and join them before Hartlehk. The new recruits had to travel with Temnere, it was his wish, his will, his order. Although Selvorne did not like the idea, he did not want to argue and draw attention to himself, so he agreed to do so – which surprised her, for she did not think she was asking his approval.

A warning she dared give him – and she was not supposed to, she said – that he should bring food, for the first night as a new recruit was very rough. Deliberately so, to discourage those of low resolve. A test of the men, but such a thing was unwise at a time when there may be killers on the roads, and also, unfair. Take food that would keep, but not ale – water, though there would be streams. At that, she returned to her duties, and Selvorne left the Waehdric camp.

Selvorne was a little sad she was not to travel with him, for he had hoped to walk with her, to talk along the road, to ... spend the night beside her, by the fire, sharing a meal. Not alone, with so many guards near, though he did imagine that ... he knew to be alone with her would be impossible. Or – it would be less often than he might like. He had grown fond of her, and – no, not grown fond – he was from the start. When he first ... saw her, though – not when he first saw her, he realised.

He stopped on the road and people rushed past in both directions. The ending of the festival, they had many things to do. He took himself to the side of the road, out of the way, and thought – he had much to do as well. Many things to prepare, but memories of her were clouding his thoughts, and they needed to be cleared.

Stage was where he saw her first. Dyneti, not Adyleh. She had been a vision of elegant perfection. A lady. No, greater still – she was then as the ladies of old, those who had fought with Tromvos, both with him or against him – impossibly beautiful, powerful and strong. Striking to behold, her red hair was as fire. When she first appeared on the stage.

Adyleh he adored, from that first glance and smile as she struggled with the tent. Warm, laughing, mischievously cheeky, and with cheeks that had dimples as she smiled, and eyes that twinkled when her lips were ... pouting.

Powerful lady, delightful girl. Wonderful singer, adored by all. Kind, spiritual leader, who led the town as she spoke for the dead. Cunning. Clever – commanding, no, not quite commanding, though she spoke and others obeyed. Still a girl – that was unfair, she was clearly a maiden, or perhaps that was also an insult, of sorts. A young woman, but in some ways, a girl. He was enchanted, and despite all other things that had happened that were ... terrible ... in that one matter of meeting her, his luck was very good.

He hoped. Possibly she was merely playing with him, though fond of his good nature, and amused by his clever wit. Perhaps he was merely enchanted by her beauty – or, by her clever wit. He did not know, but he liked being with her, and when he was not, his thoughts turned to her – and all of that was stupid, dangerous and distracting, at a time when the two of them had much to do.

Demni moved past along the road at speed. She walked very fast, almost skipping her step, but without any of the childish joy of a girl at play. Selvorne cringed – she was almost pretty, and handsome, and lithe – if ever he wondered if it was beauty that enchanted him, there was his answer – it was not. Rohy, yes, he could see it as she passed. Other men as well, he suspected. Trousers, like a man – shirt, like a man. Dark clothing, like an administrator man. Her hair out, though – like a woman, and he had not seen it unbraided and untamed – long as any he had ever seen, past her shoulders, to her waist, and thick, billowing out behind her as she walked at a pace that for some might be a shuffling run. She almost charged into guards ahead, snapping orders at them to make them scatter, and Selvorne felt pity for them – then angst, to realise it might soon be himself.

But it would not be him as guard just yet – not until he had done one last thing, and it had to be that morning. Before he left, but no sooner, lest word spread amongst those he knew that he was there – how he had managed to avoid them, he did not know. Luck and attention. Only a few times had he seen familiar faces, and immediately he lowered his gaze, concealed his face – in the Gathering Cloak – they had not seen him in turn. Had they done, things would have changed in a moment, and he had to take care choosing who he would approach.

A message he had written on parchment and sealed – a letter to Rerleden, to be taken to Vaskatohr, and done so in secret. A runner? He could afford one, easily. But to send one would raise suspicions. The only people who could take such a letter would be his townsfolk, and not all of them could he ... trust, yes, but not rely upon.

"My friend, I looked everywhere for good wine, and found none that were great, a few that were promising, none that were terrible. One on a cart, known to be bad, already spoilt. Heading north to Hartlehk and Senylehk to find the strongest wine known. Roads are dangerous, so I have joined the guards on this journey. Hope to return with the guards soon, and the most potent wine I can find. Watch the grain, I hear there are rats about, and mice, and it is hard to tell them apart, or know which ones to trust. It may be safer in Tavalehk. Your S."

A letter that seemed harmless, and only Rerleden would guess the message. He hoped. Few others could read, anyway, and if they could they would discover nothing other than the lack of wine, which was hardly news. But it had to be delivered to Rerleden alone, and done so quietly.

Most of the people from Vaskatohr were good, some better than others, none of them bad. Selvorne felt he could trust them all to stand behind him if needed. Rerleden he trusted for many reasons, not only for his father's friendship, but because, despite being cranky at times, he never did wrong, and seemed he never would.

As for the others in the town – trust was a delicate thing. Friends. Almost family. But a child was family, and he would not let a child drive the ox and waggon unattended. Nor would he let them tend the fire, and hope they obeyed when ordered not to play with burning sticks. Nor would he ask just anyone of his town to take such a message – a letter – sealed so they could not read it, though most could not read, and those who could, not very well. Some might open it, to look – drop it, by the fire. Spill ale on it, or sit on it and crush the seal – anything could happen on a long walk, and nothing must happen to his only word sent south.

Hurlich – trusted, liked. Unreliable. Once he left the pen gate open and the pigs escaped into the night. A man whose mind wandered too often. His wife as well – Oeilie, a good woman, but ... perhaps their daughter had driven them both to distraction. Stara – trust? Yes. He could trust her to squeal in delight to see Selvorne, then yell to all around how good it was to see you, my lord, so impressing anyone who might hear – she was a girl he must not see. Or ... she must not see him.

Even if he managed to meet with her quietly, she would tear open the letter in moments – by accident or defiance, wondering if it was a secret proposal to herself. No, not wondering, just taunting him, and too curious about everything.

Pretty – once he thought so – wild, and rough. A pig herding girl with a piggish nose that he once thought dainty and – no, that was unfair. It was many years ago that he learnt not all girls were so tough, unrestrained and ... rather scary. Not a lady, and not one to whom he would hand such an important, secret message.

But ... if harm came to Stara, he would find the men who hurt her, and pound them to pieces. So would she, as he thought of it. If any men hurt her, or those she loved, she would be merciless, even though she was a young maiden. If she knew what had happened ... yes, Stara he could trust, but not rely upon, and the thought of it only made his position more delicate, and task more important. He loved her and all his town, and had to protect them from enemies – and themselves.

Dasol was honest and reliable, but Selvorne did not like him much, and not for any reason other than he was annoying. Loved, yes, liked, no – most odd, and so he would not be sought. Besides, Selvorne had no idea where he might find him at the festival – in a house, sleeping late, with his relations in the town, perhaps.

Kren the miner, turned pig farmer, and his wife Stinci were the ones he wanted to find. He had a good idea where they would be, especially at the end of the festival. They would be staying with family at the lakeside in a dark red wooden house, sitting on the wooden deck that went out to the waters – yes, especially so early in the morning – trying to catch a fish on a line for lunch, and chatting amongst themselves. The advantage to Selvorne was that, at the early time of day, their children would be running around the town playing, and the house itself was in a quiet part of town, easily accessible from the lakeside without attracting attention.

Selvorne found the House of Inci, made his way around the side of it to the lake and managed to draw the attention of Stinci, and she came over to see what he wanted. At first she walked slowly towards him, disturbed from being idle, but then she stopped – as if realising something – and ran over to him.

"Oh Selvorne! You are all right? How is your father?" Stinci asked – and after a moment of confusion, Selvorne smiled, embraced her briefly, then grinned and shrugged, "So – late again, as usual?" Stinci asked, and Selvorne – though he did not know how – chuckled.

Selvorne felt a tear well in his eye, and he stifled it. A chuckling tear, she would have thought. It occurred to him that she would assume that, if Selvorne was there, Uhlsko must be as well. He bit his lip, and forced a smile as he thought of a way to explain.

"Oh, he is not even here now," Selvorne said, "and so will not make it this year – last I heard, they were on the southern road, dawdling – I came back ahead."

A lie. A necessary lie – poorly conceived, explaining little, and desperate to prevent any questions, he continued.

"I am in a bit of a hurry, and I have a favour to ask – could you take a letter to Rerleden? It is important. I am going north for a while. Looking for wine in the north."

Stinci nodded – she did not think it too odd, since Selvorne was always going off on his own at the festival. If anything was odd, it was the fact that he was telling anyone at all. She took the letter, which she could not read if she wanted to, and promised to deliver it to Rerleden. He explained also that it was to be done with no others knowing. She must have thought he meant his father, for she frowned, but Selvorne explained she should definitely show his father if she saw him first, or Arnlausa – but otherwise, only Rerleden. And not to let any others know.

"Also," Selvorne added, "take care on the roads. Travel with the guards, or at least with the others from the town back to Vaskatohr. They are organising groups today, and with all the guards around, it should be safe for a while, but please promise me you will do this, and take care – the killing of that man is very grim."

She laughed again – and that was rather grim. Touched by his concern, rather than laughing at the dead, he hoped. She promised, they parted, and she returned to her sister. Selvorne watched and wondered – as the two women began to gossip – did she even bother mentioning him? A young man she saw just about every day of every week of every month for every year of his life. What was there to say – oh, Selvorne is here, he seems to have cut his hair, being a fool as usual, we might meet his father on our return. No, she did not speak of him – they went straight back to whatever fascinating discussion was keeping them away from their husbands, sitting on the decking for hours at a time, chatting and having some peace.

Likely recipes – alternatives to fish that would not be caught. Selvorne was sure the men were doing the same at the end of the pier, and as he watched them he put words to their moving lips. Fish – blergh – roasted spring lamb if we are lucky. Brother by wedlock, how I tire of pigs. Live by the lake my friend, I would take pigs over fish any day. Lamb it is, but how to sway the coins from dresses and fine furnishings. Last of the lamb, today is the day, first lambs of spring, for those willing to pay.

Kren stood, and seemed to try and creep along the pier, as if sneaking past the women – Selvorne took himself quickly away, back into the town, and avoided where the lambs might be sold, and though only guessing at the conversation, he knew his townsfolk well. One hundred men could clear a field from the woods, forests made to meadows, trees made to fences, and a dozen sheep could be brought to his town. The next year, they might have lambs of their own. But he did not have a hundred men to clear the woods, there were no sheep and would be no lambs, and likely all such plans would end with more pens and pigs for the woods. A hundred men would come and mine, and there was the wealth of Vaskatohr, not in pigs or pens or lambs of spring, but copper and rock. Yes, Kren was sick of both, and sick of pigs, and off to find his last lamb for many months, for a lunch he would remember for the rest of the year.

As was Selvorne – but for ham, not lamb, and he remembered what Dyneti warned him – salted ham, then, wrapped to keep for the night. He made haste and avoided all who might see him who would know his face, bought the best he could find, then packed, prepared – and at the last, almost forgetting, changed his remaining square bits back to coins – he returned to the guards.

~

Departure would be soon. Gathering was at the north of the town, and the barrel bucket was moved there, huge and so very empty. Selvorne's heart sank to see how few tokens were inside, but spirits lifted a little when he realised each token that had been inside as a tally was being removed as each new recruit arrived. Guards checked one half against the other – why, he did not know, he could not imagine anyone so bold to try and trick their way into the guards – and then it was returned to the man who presented himself. Young men – all of them. None were old, none were boys. All seemed proud, and they gathered to total a dozen.

Liogur, Kuoren and his brother Bluoren – to Selvorne, a nod, a half bow, and a grin, also with a nod. Three large men, all quite similar, and all from Vonersehl, he had learnt – and none of them truly guards in the service of Dyneti, or the Waehdric, but of another lord who was not there. Why they had been chosen to check the new recruits, Selvorne did not know, but it had been a strange few days. And there was an odd collection of new recruits.

Rohy was there, and Selvorne was glad of that. The others were men he did not know, some he had seen around the town, but nobody he thought who would recognise him. They were all roughly of the same age as himself, and did not seem to know each other, apart from two, who looked like brothers, if not twins, and were wrestling to the ground or tripping each other over. Two young men were twirling sticks, one with sandy–brown hair, one with dark – aha, Selvorne knew him – Aigel, the young man dragged to the stage. He was impressing maidens who were near, with his twirling stick – no, with his glances and smiling eyes. The maidens giggled when he dropped his stick and had to bend, fetching it from the ground, something he did so often that it almost seemed deliberate. He was at one moment skilled, then clumsy, and those who watched were captivated – as was Dyneti, when she passed them all, stopping to gaze upon the performance for a moment.

Selvorne felt ... jealous. There was no other word for it, to see her standing there, gazing on a man who had all her attention. No, not all, Selvorne noticed she watched both young men, where the other maidens were only looking to the one with dark hair. And then, as Dyneti walked past Selvorne, she glanced at him and rolled her eyes – and Selvorne almost laughed.

Three other young men were absurdly overdressed – did they think they joined the guards, or were on their way to a grand feast? A fourth amongst them was scruffy, wearing what looked to have been once a sack for grain, cut to be a tunic, and worn untucked over trousers, with a cord for a belt. Was that for practicality or poorness, Selvorne did not know, nor could he guess if the other three were dressed for pride or lack of sensible clothes, though such a lack could only come from so much pride, it had completely filled their wardrobe.

349

One of the other youths who stood alone approached Selvorne and Rohy, he had short, sandy–brown hair, an average build, and Selvorne thought he looked a little delicate in features to be serving as a guard. His clothes were simple – plain – but tough, and he seemed like a well–travelled young man, with a good pack and strong walking boots. Selvorne was sure he had been the man before them in the line to join the guards.

"Good morning to you both, I am Bitier, son of Ritien, the Tinker," the man said, then he did a short polite bow, which Selvorne returned and introduced himself. Rohy, who was near, clumsily copied Selvorne, "I am sure I have seen you both around the town, here at Tavalehk," Bitier said, looking at Selvorne, then at Rohy, "and at Hartlehk? Where are you from?"

Where are you from – four words, one question, and it suddenly occurred to Selvorne that joining the guards would mean meeting quite a lot of new people, and having to explain himself to every one of them. There was no way he could avoid it, not as he did at the festival – dismissing them, saying little – being rude. Not on the road. Not as they walked, not if they camped together. Such journeys were new to him – not the journeys, just the company of strangers. His father, usually, Arnlausa, mostly, friends and townsfolk – always. Not strangers, and the timing could not have been worse.

He had to think fast. He could not say he was from Vaskatohr, people would either have heard of it or not, neither would be good. Brigands certainly would – and their spies. Everyone would have questions. The honest answers to which would inevitably be, "Yes, Vaskatohr, the town of my father, disappeared with Arnlausa, Lord of Tavalehk. Indeed, both men are lords, and both are missing – no, I do not know where they are, should I be concerned?"

Word would spread faster than the wind, until everyone knew who he was and what had happened. Or wondered what had happened. Men with wagers, men with ears for a story or rumour, followed by uncomfortable questions from those who were mildly interested – and danger, from any who actually cared. How could he have been so stupid to not consider it before?

"I am from the north, around Hartlehk," Rohy began to say, and he did not seem too pleased to be asked, either, "I travel a lot, doing odd jobs. I do not come from any one town, truly. I know you, Bitier – tinker's son – are you not from Hartlehk? If so, what brings you here?"

Rohy was ... stalling. For Selvorne? He frowned. Perhaps, or ... distracting? No, he was turning the talk back to Bitier, and doing it rather clumsily. Rohy was suspicious, but not as good as Selvorne at hiding it. And Bitier grinned – he was better, but not quite so clever, or perhaps not quite as suspicious, but very curious – what a day it was going to be, their first new friend, and nothing but wariness from all.

"Indeed, my family are from Hartlehk, and I am here for the festival, of course," Bitier said – he had a twinkle in his eyes, which suggested mischief, not suspicion, "and to join the guards – why not. There is a good coin in mending things, but – "

Bitier stopped talking – odd, in the middle of a sentence like that, but he looked at them both with a grin, and jingled a small pouch on his belt. Why would any man do that, Selvorne thought, drawing attention to his coins hanging so easily within reach of a thief?

"But – steady pay, as a guard, very good compared to even a happy tinker. Sitting around all day, for a guard – mending things all hours, for a tinker – and none have yet said you cannot do both at once. Double the coin, perhaps? For me – and you?"

Selvorne could not say he was from Tavalehk, because every man there was from some part of Tavalehk, and would know people in any village or part of town he could name, and he was embarrassed to think he could not name that many. He did not know the town well enough to describe every village, let alone name the townsfolk. It would only take moments for people to suspect something was wrong, and it could only end in the truth.

He knew the names of many other towns around the lands, but he did not know them well enough to pretend they were his home. He had visited few, and only as a child – the other problem was that many were so far away he could not possibly explain how he found himself as far south as Tavalehk. He could pretend he was from the southern lands of MidWaehter, he even knew something of that place – but doing so would make him an outsider, from distant lands, and draw more attention to himself than if he said he lived under the sea with the fishes, perhaps ... even if he could prove it. All would wish to hear of MidWaehter, likely few would, of the sea.

Then it occurred to him – Veksehl. The seaside town his mother was from – he had never been there, but then, who had? Likely none of them. Selvorne knew something of that town, enough to pretend he lived there, and he could invent the rest. It was far away enough that nobody would have likely visited it, and boring enough that nobody would be interested in hearing about it. And if they were, he could talk endlessly of the wonderful sea, until boredom drove them away. The sea, at least, he was familiar with, for the quarry of Vechransehl, where he worked, was by the sea. Sand, rocks, waves and crabs – for hours, if needed.

"I am from Veksehl, but I have not been there for quite a long time. I came by way of Tawlehk, then Vechransehl, south along the sea road, then east across the old road to Tavalehk. I, too, am a wandering worker, a traveller, and I thought, why not be paid to wander with the guards? Do you think we could earn a coin on the side, perhaps, if work was needed where we go?"

It was enough – Bitier was curious, and began asking questions, to which Selvorne began talking about the beauty of the sun setting on the sea, and how the waters can change their colours and moods – until Bitier was bored. Rohy listened and was silent, and Selvorne wondered if he was a man more pleased to listen than to speak.

"Attention!" called out Temnere suddenly, with a surprisingly commanding voice for an ageing man, "All new recruits – form a line here. All other guards, prepare to leave. Those who are neither – go away."

The guards were already preparing to leave, or ready and waiting. The new recruits lined up clumsily, twelve in total. Of all the men considered and given a chance, only a dozen had committed. Temnere looked them over, each in turn. Some were nervous, others were indifferent, perhaps hiding their unease as arrogance. Selvorne had already decided Temnere was a man to treat with the best of official manners, so as he passed by, Selvorne snapped his feet together and straightened his back, staring directly ahead.

"Ahh, very good!" Temnere said, also standing tall from his usual stoop, to a surprisingly good height, looking down on Selvorne. "I know you, yes, I remember."

Selvorne felt ... concern. Remember from – no, not before. Perhaps the Festival Field, when he dared sit with the guards – but Temnere, was he angry or delighted?

"Aha, yes – you helped that elderly man, on the stairs. Very good!"

With that, Temnere continued along the line, although he remained standing tall and was even more intimidating to the young men he studied.

"Some of you will leave," Temnere said, "because you are no good. Some of you will be thrown out for the same reason. All of you must obey orders, as ordered. We are heading north, now, to Senylehk, by way of Hartlehk. There you will be trained – if you are accepted. You are not guards – not yet – so you must provide your own food. Shelter. Lodging. You are not to be paid for any such things on this journey, and you must obey. We leave in a few moments. Be ready."

Temnere's address was short and as abrupt as if he was reading a letter to himself – he gave no further explanation, and when some tried to ask questions, he ignored them. Some of the new recruits were unhappy, especially at the mention of providing their own food. Selvorne had already stuffed his sack with anything good he could find, as much as he could carry. He had his travelling items with him – the pot, cups, a store of oats which he did not prefer, but would fill his belly if needed, and his brand new spear carefully packed away. He was used to walking for days and sleeping rough, foraging if need be – but, as he looked to the men around him, he realised some of them had never been away from their homes.

When Temnere said they were leaving in moments, they discovered he truly meant moments – and they found themselves marching north as soon as they had lifted their bags, moving immediately along the main road of town. The new recruits, some of the guards, Temnere ambling along with his slight limp, keeping them at a slow pace. Some of the townsfolk waved, some seemed to be families of the new men – mothers blew embarrassing kisses their way, and some of the men were mocked by friends.

A tall, fair–haired man in grey was watching from the side of the road – it was the man Rohy had been arguing with the day before. He watched the men march past, taking great interest in each of them – especially Selvorne. When Rohy passed they exchanged a gaze and a brief, polite nod.

"Family?" Selvorne asked.

"Distant family friend," Rohy said, "and he thinks this is a waste of time, and a bad choice. It is, however, my choice. I will miss him, though."

There was nobody there for Selvorne. Nobody waved or blew an embarrassing kiss. No family to miss him, or talk him out of it. There was no guard of honour, no gathering for the parade of the departing lord. If things went well, he would be their new Lord of Tavalehk, and any future departure from the town would be met with a warm, or at least polite, wave from every person along the road. But that day, he was unknown. And though it felt a little lonely, he knew it had to be that way.

Ahead, the rising slopes that led to The Winer's Inn – the end of town. Beyond that, all the lands of the north. Allies, and the unknown. Behind him, the only life he had ever known. All that was familiar, but perhaps not known as well as he thought. His home, his lands and people, friends and ... no, no longer. Family – in a ravine, in a cave, in a barrel, in the wine – the only family he knew. Only as he headed north, only as he saw the end did he truly feel he was leaving them behind, abandoned to their fate. Hidden well, he hoped. Safe. Lost ... and though he had new friends, some of the men eager, cheerful and keen – Rohy, with a similar grim stare, the same loss ... Dyneti, behind, but soon to join him – despite them all, he felt alone.

Then he saw a small boy on the side of the road, watching the procession. The boy looked at him – there was something familiar in his grin – he stood up straight and proud, grinning wide, back at Selvorne. The boy from the boat, who had hit Selvorne with a rock. Selvorne felt a huge smile grow across his face, and he nodded back as a bow, as he passed. His spirits lifted, and he left Tavalehk knowing there was at least one friend amongst the people of the town.

No Man Worth Knowing

The road from Tavalehk led to the northeast for most of its way, though it was a winding journey at times. One or two days north to Hartlehk, depending on the pace – not a great distance for anyone keen to travel there, but few who lived in Tavalehk were keen, because Hartlehk was not a nice town to visit. Perhaps more would have done, if it was merely a one day journey – if closer, and easier – people would venture back and forth, and the two towns would be united in customs, friendships – perhaps families. But it was not, it was two days' travel for most people, and that meant spending a night at camp in the wild, so few went and fewer came, and the two towns had become very different places.

Only one road led from Tavalehk to the north. The same road led south, to Vaskatohr, but even fewer went there – north was the only way to leave the town for most, and Arnlausa swore that, if Hartlehk was the only other town in all the lands, no one would ever leave Tavalehk. He was not fond of it, or its lord, and so was exaggerating a little – it hardly mattered, for Hartlehk was not the only town north. It was, however, the first town to the north, and unavoidable for anyone wishing to go anywhere else. There was the reason for his dislike, for its presence on the road and control of the river crossing meant it held power over Tavalehk and all its trade.

Power undeserved. Isolation which could not be changed. Tavalehk and all its villages was a realm of its own, but the entire northern lands combined were perhaps ten times as vast in people, lands and wealth. Ten times the opportunities for prosperity and joy – for knowledge shared, for excitement – for love. Perhaps one hundred times, Arnlausa claimed, explaining such opportunities rarely expanded directly, but branched out, like a tree, to yield a thousand fruits, ripe and delicious. Unusual also, unlike any at Tavalehk. Selvorne wondered if such rare trees could be brought back and tended, which made Arnlausa laugh, and his father pat him softly on the head.

Perhaps. Selvorne had since learnt not all trees enjoyed growing in all lands, and only by trade and travel could Tavalehk enjoy such unusual fruits. Mines could not be moved. The crafts made by skilled men could – the men themselves might not. Or the women, even for love, if leaving their other loves – their family and friends – far behind. Only travel and trade, and though travel was free for all the North Waehter people, trade was tolled, restricted and robbed, Arnlausa said – all profits taken until it was no longer worth the journey. That was not completely true, Uhlsko had explained, but it was one of the few things that truly angered Arnlausa, being so helpless to avoid that town. Anger briefly shown, held, and turned to mocking spite, in a song Arnlausa enjoyed hearing, but Selvorne doubted he had composed it himself.

Hartlehk town, sneer and frown, the people on us there look down
Hartlehk town, knock it down, a push to the river and let it drown
Take from the lord his toll and power
Take from the folk their droll mood sour
Build a new road, a good go–around
Journey in joy, a northward–bound
Until then you must
Go through and trust
Of there a few
They will not you
Do ...
Hartlehk town ...

The song continued, growing ever more insulting, but less violent, as the second line was suggesting the entire town be destroyed. Latter verses merely made fun of the women's sense of dress. Arnlausa argued it was better to start hard and finish soft, at which many chuckled, but Selvorne never thought the mockery of another town was fair, and neither did his father. Uhlsko did agree that Hartlehk was a difficult place, and not at all like Tavalehk.

Suffer the customs, Arnlausa had said – it did not sound pleasant, though Selvorne could not recall anyone from Hartlehk who was too unpleasant, despite everyone at Tavalehk saying they were. The new recruit Bitier seemed quite cheerful, mischievous perhaps, but sincere. Rohy agreed, noting that when Bitier was in the line of recruitment, both Dyneti and Demni had accepted him at once – likely knowing him, and likely he was worth knowing. Selvorne agreed that both ladies were likely a good judge of a man, and that Bitier seemed a friendly fellow, but he chuckled to think that Rohy was perhaps hoping Bitier might help him get close to Demni. Rohy was, for the most part, silent on that morning walk, almost solemn, but his eyes were bright whenever he made mention of her.

Senylehk town – that was where they were headed. Not Hartlehk, it was, as for all travellers, merely the town along the way. Senylehk was the largest town in all the North Waehter Lands. It was positioned roughly in the middle of the lands, though it was not the same distance to all the borders, not by road, or river, or by flight of bird.

They were unusual lands in the north, Selvorne had been told, though the north was quite usual for him, as he had lived there his whole life. Arnlausa thought them odd, having come from the southern lands of MidWaehter, and Uhlsko had to agree there were differences between there and the North. As both men had been far south to the MidWaehter lands, perhaps they knew better than Selvorne what should be considered usual or not.

The lands of the North Waehter – their lands, contained by mountains on three borders, and the sea on the fourth. Rarely visited by anyone from afar. Selvorne had seen maps, the shape was roughly an oval, narrower than tall, with mountains on three sides – the south, the east, the north. And to the west was the sea.

Beyond the southern mountains were the lands of MidWaehter – beyond them, farther south – the South Waehter. Beyond them were other lands and other people, but that was a very long way, and then was the southern sea. No more lands, and no more people – but the Waehter people, almost all the way south. They spoke the same, but were different in many ways, Selvorne had been told, but he could not imagine them to be too different, as Arnlausa was from the south. He guessed they were larger, laughed a lot, and were friendly.

Farther east, beyond the mountains – more mountains. So he had been told. People may have been there, or on the other side, he did not know. None had crossed the eastern mountains, and it was discouraged to try. Bears were there, he was certain. The far north was much the same, almost endless mountains, but a people on the other side were known – the Vog. They were wild, rough and cruel, and did not come to the lands of Waehter.

So the lands of North Waehter were encircled by mountains, and in the west – the sea. Nothing was beyond that, other than the dead. Whether a man believed in the Sea of the Dead or not, none could argue that heading west, and never finding land, a man was making a journey to death. Swimming, or in a boat – with food and water, travelling until all was eaten and drunk. The lands ended at the sea, and life could go no farther. Or not much farther, without coming back. Certainly not to find the setting sun, or the place where water touched the sky.

That the lands were surrounded by mountains was not strange. Most usual, he was told, for mountains were in all the lands, and the sea bordered everywhere at the west. The mountains also were always in the east, but not the north and south as well, at least there was no such range of mountains between South and MidWaehter. A great ravine, with cliffs, but not mountains. The opposite of mountains, being a great crack in the lands. What was strange in the North was the cliff at the feet of the mountains – the ground dropped away, down to a plateau of woods and bogs – all the way around, encircling the lands. That, Arnlausa had said, was rather strange for any land.

Selvorne knew the cliff, he knew it well. Mountains, ending in slopes – then usually a flat ground, sometimes for miles, sometimes for mere yards – and then a cliff. The drop was sometimes a long way, sometimes, again, merely yards. In some places what once was a cliff of stone had crumbled to steep slopes. For mountains to end in cliffs, then fall to woodlands below was considered strange, and yet that was the way of things in the entire North, all along the southern range, the eastern and the most northern slopes, he was told – a land encircled by cliffs and mountains. And the sea, to the west, where there was often another cliff falling to the water below. It was as if the entire northern lands had suddenly dropped, long ago, breaking the ground, leaving cracks at its edges, one long cliff, like a wall made of stone.

The northern road they walked upon followed the top of that cliff. Not on the very edge, of course, but near enough to look over to the forests below. The tree tops loomed above them or fell below them, depending on the rise and fall of the lands, but on their road there were no trees, just good solid ground. That was the great fortune of the north, for the cliff top was often bare and good for a road. A natural road requiring little care, and Selvorne realised just how valuable it was when he noticed wheel marks in the stone – for wheels to make such marks meant they were rimmed with iron, which was costly, and that meant they must have been making very many journeys. Unlike his own wooden-wheeled waggon ... broken ... he turned his mind to the road. Well worn. A natural road that required no paving, no clearing of trees or bushes, or fallen logs. He looked on it, and frowned.

It was the same road he had often travelled. It led from the sea, from the Vechransehl quarry, all the way to ... the bridge, which was also broken. He would not think of it – the ravine, that was an oddity. The land there was torn apart. One side slightly higher than the other, he knew that when he built the ... bridge. And Vaskatohr was on the lower side of the cliff, down where the woodlands were, and from there it was a slight rise – nothing steep nor sudden – to reach Tavalehk. Though he had not come that way that year, he had instead hidden in the mountains.

It was unpleasant to think of his journeys, but the road intrigued him, so he kept his mind on the cliff. It did not end – all the way from the sea to Tavalehk, though there it was west of the town, in the woods – the river that left the lake poured over a lovely waterfall in the forest. That same cliff was to his left as he walked, and though he was leaving his homelands, he felt somehow connected to them, to think that it continued all the way back to his home.

As he walked, grateful for the solid road, he began to wish there were more shady trees. Just over the cliff was a lovely woodland, a nice place to be on that warm day. But after rain it could be boggy and dangerous, or at least annoying. Woodlands, sometimes wet – bogs, sometimes swamps. Moors – he had not seen them, they were far away and hidden. Wild lands where no men went, except, he discovered, brigands with their camps. Perhaps the lands were more unusual than he had thought.

~

Walking beside Rohy was growing dull. He was silent, and did not even wish to speak of Demni, perhaps sulking that she was not with them. Selvorne seemed surrounded by cheerful fellows and stuck with one who was glum, and he was sick of amusing himself with thoughts on the lay of the land. The view, though lovely, was the same most of the way, and not even rabbits or hares were there to entertain them, likely because the excitement of the guards far ahead made them flee, dashing off into the grass to hide. Most of the older guards were ahead or behind, Temnere at the lead – setting the pace, or restricting it with his limp. Perhaps if they walked at a more usual speed, Selvorne would be catching his breath instead of wishing to talk, but as they went slowly, the journey was growing tedious. He felt trapped beside Rohy, for he knew that approaching the others, he would have to talk about himself.

Despite Rohy's reluctance to speak, Selvorne learnt something of his friend, even if it took an hour to learn what he could have said in moments. His father ... lost. He certainly did not want to speak of that. His mother as well, to sickness when he was young – of that, Selvorne also did not wish to speak, or be reminded. The Bog Sickness, most likely. Rohy had no home – he wandered and worked, foraged or hunted, helped on many farms, settled on none. He did not mind such a life, his only regret – apart from his loss of family – was that he had no home to leave all his things, for he was growing weary of carrying them wherever he went. Selvorne looked at his pack – it was not very large, and if that was all he owned, he was not a wealthy man, unless it was full of gold. Nor was Rohy generous with good cheer that morning, so Selvorne thought he would discover what he might learn of the others, and went to each in turn, preparing to practise his lie.

Bitier was a pleasant fellow – friendly, inquisitive, the most outgoing of them all. Selvorne interrupted him joking with three other youths – Rhede, Toavel and Aigel, who were reserved at first, but quickly warmed to Selvorne.

Rhede was quite young, almost of an average height, slender – no, thin – and walked with a slight shuffling gait, as if he was not picking his feet up high enough. Every so often he kicked a rock across the road, unintended and barely noticed. He was also very talkative, and never seemed out of breath. His hair was dark brown, to his shoulders in rough waves, and Selvorne noticed he was not sweating, despite the day being warm. He came from a small, unlanded family, which Selvorne took as meaning poor, and he wanted to earn a steady pay, save it, and bring it home. Unlike most young men, he made no pretence of wanting to be a guard – he only wanted to be a runner, taking messages from town to town. None of the others said it was likely for the best – none of the others suggested he would not do well if he fought – for politeness, for Selvorne was sure they all thought it.

359

Toavel seemed a friendly fellow of few words, for he was often catching his breath, though not for lack of stamina or strength. Indeed, he was quite broad, despite being slender, with wiry muscles, delicate features, and short sharp sandy hair. He was out of breath because he had spent the first hour racing Rhede along the roads, getting ahead of all the guards, then returning, until stern words were spoken. Then they began dropping back behind everyone, and racing up again to join the others. A vigorous game, and he had been paying the price for such folly ever since. Doubly, when he laughed about it, then had to recover his breath once more. The stick he had been twirling so elegantly in the morning had become a crutch as he ambled along, and he would have been left behind if Temnere was not doing the same in the lead. Despite his fatigue, he was obviously excited, in good spirits and keen for adventure, and said as much when he could. Perhaps not as serious as he should be, but Selvorne thought him amiable enough to make a good guard.

Aigel – the dark–haired youth from the stage – was surprisingly quiet, reserved, almost shy. At first. Wary? Perhaps, though why he would be wary of Selvorne ... he was not a weak young man. He seemed quite strong. And, though Selvorne hated to admit it, quite striking in appearance – if not handsome. He was, but ... that was for maidens to decide, not Selvorne, though he thought it, and he had already seen several maidens who must have decided the same. Aigel had dark hair, slightly past his neckline, and it tumbled down the back of his neck in bold curls that seemed as lush as if he had just bathed. Many men would envy him for that, and not only those who were bald. Many maidens would also. A strong build – yes, strong, but different to Selvorne, in a way he could not quite guess. There was a spring in his step, and an elegance in how he moved – like the flourish of a bow well performed, but with each and every movement of his hands. And a constant, beaming smile. Despite all that, Selvorne thought he liked the man, and the others clearly did as well.

Aigel carried a stick to walk with, just as Toavel did, but instead of limping along using it as a crutch, he had it over his shoulders, both arms hanging from it as if he was about to snap it in two about his neck. His family did quite well, thank you very much – raising chickens and selling their eggs, but he was sick of chasing them around the yard, sick of the mess, the noise, and their sharp, wicked stares. He wanted a life of adventure, or at least to get away from the smell. He did not say much, for he was shy even after some while, but he did say he believed that good luck would only come to those who sought it out, where bad luck may find a man wherever he was. And so he sought it out. Selvorne admitted it was a jolly attitude, but argued that venturing out might bring more bad luck as well as good. True, but fewer chickens, less smell, and a more restful sleep without their haunting cries, and dreams of their cold, cruel stares.

He was teasing – and they laughed. And then he assured them he was not – and they laughed harder. Shy, but only a little, there was a sense of boldness desperate to burst forth. There was something about him that angered Selvorne, and though he hated to admit it ... he knew it was jealousy. Aigel had no reason to be shy, or wary, or worried – or a guard, for that matter, if his life was as good as he said, and Selvorne had no reason to think he was boasting. Fine clothes, but well made, not fancy – as were Selvorne's. A fine face – and hair – and both better, Selvorne had never had maidens giggling at him, all in a row, their attentions so obvious, their intentions so clear. Jealous – but something more – he had the same boots. Just the same – but blackened. The same maker, they had to be – and yet each step was as though they weighed nothing. As though made of ... feathers ... and he stood – no, strode – like a rooster.

Selvorne blinked, and almost laughed – just like a rooster. Strutting – but shy. Cautious, but ... magnificent, and bursting to announce it to the world, to crow to all the hens. Even his arms hanging high were like wings. Was it on purpose – or was it from a life amongst the chickens, copying them without realising? Did he smell, though – yes, magnificent. He had some sweet scented oil dabbed to make him even more – aha, and Selvorne bit his lip. That was it. Shy – he was not shy. He was sly. A scent for the ladies, and clever enough to be quiet, to lure them in. All the fine things of a fancy man, played down, and played well – and all the good fortune of a man born to fine looks. What vengeance could Selvorne have on such a man ... Chicken Boy, if once called, would be always remembered. No, the man had no malice, he did not deserve such a ... but Selvorne saw the eyes of Bitier were lit with mischief, and when they met with his own, he was sure they both had the very same thought.

But also the same restraint. No one called Aigel the Chicken Boy, and all taunts were done in good spirits. He was friendly and strong, had reason to be proud, and was not overly so. Selvorne noted that, should he let go of the stick with one hand, he would be very likely able to swing it with the other, and in a moment whack someone in the head. A strong ally, and perhaps a good friend. Terrible envy, though, and Selvorne had not forgotten how Dyneti chose him above all others, and had whispered so close to his ear.

A group of six others were walking ahead, and two of them dropped back to join Selvorne's group. They were obviously brothers, for they looked very much alike, and it was easy to see why they were accepted into the guards, for they were two tough, hardened boys of a farm – no longer boys, but young men. Big young men. Raised on a farm doing all manner of men's chores, likely from the time they were just children. Obviously strong, bulky in build, and making light work of the walk, with energy in abundance, so they would at times leap upon each other, or one might try to trip the other as he walked. A few times that morning they had knocked each other to the ground, but after a stern warning from Temnere, subdued their eagerness for violence, if not fun.

"Nakla!" said one, "Reklo!" said the other. They shook everyone by the hand, Nakla with a sturdy, formal handshake – Reklo with a rather wild, two handed grasp. They were the sons of wealthy farmer merchants, who harvested apples from the northeast of Tavalehk, across the lake where the mountains began. Bored of that boring life of boring apples and boring cores – they certainly said boring a lot – they wanted to see the lands. And so, with family to spare, and likely leaving unnoticed amongst so many other brothers, they joined the guards.

Nakla was the more serious one, with a chiselled face and squared head, and dark brown, short straight hair. Reklo had a sense of humour, although his pranks might not be so funny to those who found themselves suddenly tripping, the ground rushing towards their face. He had longer, less dark, but still brown hair, a more rounded face, and bright eyes. They both had heavy dark eyebrows that exaggerated their moods. Oddly untanned for farmers, though Selvorne thought that if they worked orchards and woods they likely were out of the sun for much of the day. Or wore great hats made from straw, with wide brims, chewing on long stalks of grass as they sat against an orchard fence – bored, and planning their escape.

They were a bit older than Selvorne, but would not reveal their age, nor who was older, which no one had asked. It was then that they revealed they were twins – born together, but not the same, exactly, apart from their manners and mood. A year ago Selvorne would have avoided them, for they seemed quite rough, but he was glad to meet them as recruits, for they would be good allies. He could not help wondering what might have happened if they were with him when he hid in the forest, watching his enemy – he fancied he might have had a chance to kill them all, even with just those two men. He certainly would not restrain them if they charged – even if he could. But no, that was folly – still, they were promising.

"Those four are sour," Reklo said, waving a hand at the four youths ahead, "they have no sense of humour. They dress like fancy men, and find it neither amusing nor helpful to be told so."

"Traglan is a good fellow," Nakla added, "but slow, and they have him trapped in witty conversation, jokes made at his expense. Someone save Traglan!"

Reklo looked at Rohy and commanded, "Save Traglan! Bring him here!" but Rohy just glared at him silently. So Nakla turned to Selvorne, "You – bring him back here. Any excuse! Go!"

Selvorne was not keen to be ordered around, but he was intrigued by their comments, and felt more than a little unable to resist. They were overly cheerful fellows, and likely it was some strange prank, but he was curious, so he trotted up ahead to the other four.

"Greetings! I am Selvorne. I am wondering, which of you is Traglan?"

The four looked at him, some sniggered. Selvorne looked them over and thought they were a very odd bunch. Three of them were dressed to impress, and yet it was the fourth who stood out, for he was tall, lanky, had a mop of messy brown hair, and was wearing what was, when seen close, an actual sack cut to make a tunic, and badly done at that. He approached Selvorne, but the others interrupted.

"Traglan? Who is he? I think he is nobody," said one of them – a youth with long blond hair, tied back with many silver clasps. He had a fine blue tunic with far too many buttons, also made of silver, and such a thing was rarely worn outside of formal meetings of noble – or wealthy – people, for it was absurd.

Selvorne thought a man could hardly wear a more inappropriate outfit for the task at hand – joining the guards, to train, to battle. Until he looked more closely at the second and third youths. One was wearing fancy soft boots, which obviously hurt his feet to walk on rough roads, for the sole was as soft as a glove. He also wore a short cape. Yes, a cape, Selvorne was not seeing things, nor had he gone mad, nor was it some fancy collar or the hood of a cloak, the other half hidden or removed to his bag. It was a cape. It draped from his shoulders halfway down his back, serving no purpose other than to announce his vanity to the world. Guards would never wear such a silly thing. Apart from that, Selvorne guessed he was not poorly dressed, though the shoes alone were a stupid thing to wear.

The third youth was worse – far worse. He was wearing trousers so tight, the only way he could make them tighter would be to wrap cords around his legs and tie them hard – which he had done. All the way from tiny stiff shoes to his tiny thin waist. Over that, an enormous jacket – short, it just passed his waist, where it was also drawn in tight – but bulky – puffed out at the shoulders and arms. Done to make him look enormous, perhaps intimidating, yet it only looked absurd.

Selvorne looked at the four and thought they might be some assemblage of performers, who had done a show at the festival, and were returning with the guards for safety on the roads. They would not need protection, for any brigands attacking would collapse with the pain of laughter – perhaps they were a good choice for guards, after all.

"I am Ragval, son of Varrag the Merchant," said the youth in the huge jacket and tights, "and who are you?"

He was handsome, Selvorne had to admit that, and well spoken. An average build, of a young man who had done only easy work, if any – but a striking face, with pale skin and deep dark hair in curly locks. He was not so proud that he would neglect an opportunity to tell people how great he was, though.

"Selvorne," Selvorne replied, thinking that he had already told them that.

"No, he means who are you," the other youth said, "what are you, not your name. I am Franek, son of Ranek, son of Anek, Heir to Nekvil. And this is Igusli, child of Uslia, Cloth Maiden of Tavalehk. Who are you?"

Not many things brought Selvorne to anger – rarely did he feel his blood fill with fury. Before the horrific killings, before the discovery of the murderers hiding. Most of his life, anger was at himself, usually for being an idiot. A stubbed toe, a broken – well, many things. Spears, doors, boxes, even a fingernail, once, not for pride, but for hitting it with the mallet, instead of the chisel. He often met frustration with calm – in his life, there rarely was need for anger or immediate fury. Perhaps with the pigs, but that never worked. Bigger, stronger, faster than men, anger only seemed to make them ... laugh. By squealing. And in their piggish defiance they had broken his mood to anger, taught him patience, and so made him the master of the pen.

But anger was what he felt – anger and fury, cold and hot at once. Dare you, Franek, name your line? No – that was not it. It was what was not said that caused his fury – name your father, show your pride. Selvorne did not care. Not impressed, somewhat interested, actually, of their family, especially if they were important merchants of Tavalehk. But Franek was not saying it to explain the reasons for his pride – he was making clear Traglan's reasons for shame.

And shame to Selvorne, though he had nothing but pride for his father, and the foolish boy could not possibly realise who he was – but he assumed he was nothing, and he was insulting a man he had just met, for things Selvorne could not possibly be responsible for – family. Their past. An inheritance. His name.

Traglan – and all men who were not son of one, son of the other, all the way back to someone long gone. Shame to those who had no line. Shame to those who did not know, to those who wished they did not know – and to those who could never know.

Poor Traglan did not understand, and smiled awkwardly. Selvorne more than understood – enough to anger, and more than enough to suppress it, twisting it to mischief instead of a fist. Love grew for the men walking behind – and astonishment that the two rough brothers had managed to last the morning without punching at least one of the three before him.

Selvorne was silent, only for moments as he considered his plan – long enough to confirm in Franek's small mind that Selvorne was not a man of importance. So be it, there were the beginnings of his revenge.

Igusli ... Selvorne knew that name. The blond–haired youth in the bright blue tunic, who turned his nose up at Selvorne and soon put distance between them. Selvorne had heard of Uslia, she was a wealthy cloth merchant at Tavalehk, and made good fabrics – perhaps his very shirt, which was a fine weave. There were many wealthy merchants of cloth in Tavalehk, but he had never heard of a Cloth Maiden before – he felt an urge to call after the boy, to ask if Igusli was a Cloth Maiden as well, for the name seemed girlish, and he did not know the guards allowed girls to join – but he held his tongue. Perhaps later, at the camp.

Franek was the youth in soft boots and an absurd cape. Perhaps the pain of the boots explained his rudeness, Selvorne certainly would not like to have sore feet, and be made to walk all day. But Selvorne did not like the boy – and he was a boy, if not in years. Franek thought himself important, inheriting pride from his father and his father before, whatever they had achieved, and somehow overlooking the fact that he had not earned it for himself.

He knew the name Anek – a good man, an untitled lord, if such a thing was possible – for Anek looked after the village of Nekvil where he lived, but could pass no laws and collect no tolls. A respected elder, but that village was just a few families settled along the lake, not something anyone could inherit, and not recorded as a town or centre of administration, nor of tolls or markets. Although, Selvorne had to admit, it was not much smaller than Vaskatohr. Perhaps larger.

Three youths, wealthy, soft – surely the guards were not so desperate, yet so few men had returned tokens. No, he would not insult them – they at least were marching to be made guards. He let his anger go, and ignored them, turning to the fourth youth and offered his hand. "You must be Traglan?" the boy nodded eagerly, with wide eyes. "Come then! Reklo would have a word with you!"

The arrogant three sneered as Selvorne dragged Traglan away – stealing their entertainment. They joined the friendly lot behind, and Reklo congratulated Selvorne with a mighty thump on the back – through his pack, which helped soften the blow only a little – then took it upon himself to keep Traglan company.

Traglan was a simple fellow. If the new recruit Rhede was to be considered poor, then Traglan might be considered hopeless. Selvorne wondered if the guards had taken pity on him, for he did not seem robust enough to be a guard, nor – dare he say it – smart enough. He spoke well if plainly, but did not have much to say, and when he spoke he either did not think first or perhaps did not understand what was going on. The others had been poking fun at him for hours and he had not once been suspicious, no matter how obvious their teasing became. It would have been cruel if he did, but – in an odd way, his confusion for so long must have taunted them back. It made Selvorne almost chuckle, almost wince, and he wondered what would have become of them both, if they both were watching brigands in the woods. Traglan might wander out to join them, greet them – serve them, and not realise he was doing harm. Too simple, too obedient – dangerous, and for all the wrong reasons. Selvorne guessed that the guards were giving him a chance.

Warm and Cold

After a long day of walking they came to a beautiful river, which flowed straight from the forest on their right, then off to the left. There it became a magnificent waterfall over the cliff edge, pouring down into a pool below, before continuing west to the wild lands of the lower woods. It was a small river, so no bridge was needed, for people had piled rocks into it at the ford so a waggon could pass through carefully, and men could cross easily – perhaps even without getting wet, if the level was low. But the flow was strong, so everyone had to remove their shoes. Except Temnere, who had guards carry him, much to their annoyance and his distress as he stared down at the waters, only a few inches deep.

"Why does he not ride in a waggon with an ox?" Selvorne asked a guard, "We would make better time, and he could cross the river in style."

The guard laughed so hard he spluttered.

"An ox! My, lad, you do not know him well. Temnere hates oxen. And pigs. And goats. And any creature – or person – that does not obey him, both immediately, and without question," the guard said, and then he looked about to see if anyone was listening, leant down, and whispered, "now ... if we could harness a cart to Demni, perhaps that would suffice. I am quite sure she would do it, if ordered to do so, by him."

He snickered, and Selvorne could not help grin – despite the insult to Demni. Yes, perhaps she would do it, but more likely she would order it done by another. And if she heard the guard – yes, he was well aware what would happen if she heard him say such a thing, and he made Selvorne promise not to repeat it, and did not quite apologise, but ... would be sorry to pay for it. Selvorne obliged and the guard returned to the others, but he could not help think it was rather bold to risk saying such a thing – the guards had taken a liking to Selvorne, perhaps, after their wager and mockery of him at the festival.

The intended camp was on the other side of the river, by the water, and that was the end of their journey for the day. They were meant to establish it immediately, but instead many guards ran off to scramble down the cliff and swim in the pool below, and others, not bothering with the climb, jumped in the shallow river at the top – some in all their clothes – but without their boots. It was a hot day, most were sweaty and tired. A few of the older guards had sore heads from celebrating the last night of the festival, and had not bathed that morning, and they were amongst the first to wash.

The new recruits stared at the other guards – wide eyed and surprised, each responded differently, either amused, confused, or completely astonished. What had been an orderly walk along the road had suddenly turned to madness, and before the new recruits had even crossed at the ford. Was not the order to set camp? Two guards by Temnere were establishing the camp to his satisfaction, and he was not yelling at others. They gathered wood and erected a tent as he sat nursing his feet. Enough obedience to satisfy, then, and all others went wild. Most of the other guards were putting as much distance as possible between Temnere and themselves, and relishing the sudden freedom. Perhaps their walk beside him had been very unpleasant, not the casual chatter of new friends that Selvorne enjoyed, but grim silence or stern criticisms. Down by the pool, some guards began drinking ale from flasks, and Selvorne thought that was not a good idea if they were swimming, and had not yet eaten.

There was a mighty "Hroar!" and everyone near the river turned in amazement to see Reklo had wrestled his brother Nakla, beaten him, then lifted him up above his head. It was a great feat to lift a man so – shakily, and he was stumbling towards the river, but it was impressive to see. The two of them tumbled to the waters, fully dressed, then surfaced laughing and spluttering. They were not stupid enough to go in with their packs, but Selvorne wondered at their boots. Everyone clapped and cheered as the two men climbed out of the waters – but those nearest quickly scattered when they realised they meant to do the same to any who they could catch.

Bitier did not challenge them, he unlaced his boots with uncanny speed, dumped his things and leapt into the river himself. Rhede, Toavel and Aigel did the same, but were too slow, and found themselves darting barefoot around the riverside meadows to avoid being caught. Traglan wanted to be thrown in, but had not removed his shoes, so Reklo did it for him, before hurling him into the deepest part, where he made a great splash and spluttered as he laughed.

Rohy appeared to have no desire to go in the river, and with three astoundingly long leaps, he crossed the river waters on stepping stones, completely dry, and headed over to Temnere. The three arrogant fools tried to follow his lead, but with mixed success, all slipping, and Ragval tripped in his tights because he could only take small steps – he fell face first in the river, grazing his knees.

Selvorne wanted to go into the water, but at a time of his choosing, and at a place where it was best to swim. He was not going to run like a chicken about the yard – which was what Aigel did, exhausting both Reklo and Nakla – he even flapped his arms like wings, making all kinds of noises that were just like a chicken. Selvorne was calm – he removed his boots, stacked his clothes upon his pack, and in long under–trousers prepared to stand his ground – ready to face Nakla, who noticed the challenge and charged at him like a playful goat. Selvorne tried to dodge him, but was never great at wrestling, and found himself firmly grabbed around the legs. To his surprise, Nakla could not lift him, likely from exhaustion, and after three attempts backed away to catch his breath. Selvorne grabbed him around the waist with the intention of lifting him to his shoulder, the way he might heave a quarry stone, but he could not lift him either, and in trying, the two of them fell into the river – which was, incredibly, warm.

Bathing, splashing, laughter and fun – then washing, of clothes and men, as they realised it would be their last chance before another long walk the next day. Parts of the river stream were deep, parts shallow, and it was all much warmer than expected. Every man washed, but some only their faces – and Temnere not at all, except from water fetched in a jug.

After the bathing, the new recruits gathered their things and crossed the river properly. Temnere had nothing to say to them, he was busy in his tent with his own affairs. Selvorne caught a glimpse of a table inside – where that had come from, he could only guess, but the older guards carried far more than most men would on such a journey. They had settled to preparing food and drink, fires and their own tents. Some were showing the trinkets they had bought at the festival, some clearly presents for women, though they laughed as they pretended jewellery and dresses were for themselves.

Water at the camp was coming from a fresh spring on the northern side of the stream, and Selvorne was told to drink only it, and not ever from the river. Not that the water was bad, but it was two springs mixed, and one was warm waters from the mountains, and had a strange taste, and made some people ill. Selvorne thought it might have been a good idea to tell them all before they had jumped in and swallowed it, but the guards argued their orders were to set camp – not jump in the river – and besides, everyone knew not to drink of warm streams. The hot river was the reason no town was there, no village, no inn – the little fresh spring was not enough to provide for even a house. The warm water of the river was good for your skin – bad for your belly, so it was said, and Selvorne realised those who had climbed down the cliff were drinking fresh spring water, not ale, from their flasks.

It might have been too small a spring to found a town, or even an inn, but it was a wonderful place for a camp. A river to wash in, warmer than expected – even in winter. Fresh spring water. A pool to swim in, and a waterfall – magnificent views over the plain lands below, and forested woodlands supplying firewood. Soft grasses to make a bed. Selvorne thought it was ideal. Perhaps, if it was windy, it might be unpleasant, or if it rained – but otherwise, a great place to spend the night.

Some of the others disagreed, having never spent the night out of doors, and they had assumed that when the new recruits were promised food and lodging, it meant cooked food, and some kind of house. Not a handful of oats, firewood which they had to gather themselves, and a space on the grass to lie down. Selvorne thought it was amusing to hear them complain, and he overheard some of the guards say something intriguing – "Three fails already, on the first day, no less. A record! Quick, write it down." It made him wonder if they were all being assessed, or tested somehow.

Even so, it was not just the three proud boys who complained, and of the others, those who were used to rough sleeping were not expecting a handful of oats and a single pot to cook them. They looked longingly at the other guards, who had the foresight to bring their own food of hams, sausages and pies. They would not share with the new recruits, which some thought was mean – but then they would not sell to them either, which they all agreed was cruel. Especially as they so loudly enjoyed their meal.

"They are testing us," Rohy whispered to Selvorne, "look at them. Every so often they glance over at us. Who eats like that? Who waves a leg of ham around, declaring how delicious it is?"

Selvorne nodded – even if a man was to do that, rarely did he say those exact words – I declare this ham is most delicious – they were being taunted.

"Not taunted – tested," Rohy whispered, "they are trying to make us jealous of their meal – to see how we respond."

Selvorne nodded, and patted his pack.

"Look what I have," Selvorne said, then opened the pack to show Rohy his salted ham, wrapped carefully. A treasure. It was a lot of meat, enough for six nights he thought, or six people. He was not sure if he should eat it in front of the older guards, though, especially if there was some kind of test. "Should we eat it?"

Rohy looked thoughtful. The other new recruits were gathered around the pot of oats looking miserable, except Igusli, Ragval and Franek, who wanted to cook theirs separately, and seemed to have some of their own delicious foods as well. And Traglan – well, he alone was stirring the gruel with wide, eager eyes.

"Well, those three are eating their own food, but look how the guards are glaring at them," Rohy explained, "so I think we could hide the ham in the gruel?"

Selvorne was not sure how it would go with the oats, but he cut it into small pieces quietly, signalled silence to all the others, then dumped it into the pot, quickly burying it in oats. When it was ready, they all took a bowl and ate it secretly, at least at first.

"Oh well, nothing but gruel. No matter! We are men!" Reklo said, loudly, so the guards would hear. Selvorne winced, but vengeance had begun, and could not be stopped.

"This gruel is delicious. And so filling, I do not think I can eat it all," Nakla added, also loudly, defiant and yet – they were not breaking any orders by eating their own food.

"Oats! Oats! Water to thicken! Better than goats, and sweeter than chicken!"
piped up Aigel, very pleased with himself.

"Chicken does not rhyme with thicken," Toavel said.

"Yes it does," Rhede said, "it just does not make any sense." Rhede thought for a
while, then added his own, calling out loudly, "Men will eat chicken, men will eat
goats. But the beasts – they know better – they will only eat oats."

"Ohh, that is a good one, very good timing to it all," Aigel said. Rhede did a
slight bow without rising.

"Ahh, you do realise there is ham in this?" Selvorne reminded them, concerned
at the attention they were drawing from the guards.

"Best meal ever!!!!" yelled Traglan, after licking the bowl and jumping up to
wave it around. It was not poetic, but it certainly seemed sincere.

One of the guards came over, greeted them, pretended to stir the fire, and
casually glanced at their bowls. Half the people had finished, the others had half
bowls of oats, having eaten all the ham at the start. He frowned, then left them,
and some chuckled.

Though the new recruits liked Selvorne at the start, he had, through that,
become their hero. In secret he shared out a few other treats, but at the end of the
meal he had nothing left except a ham bone, carefully hidden in his pack, and a
single honey stick he had kept for Dyneti, which he would continue to save until
they next met. It had been, after all, her idea to bring food.

~

Under the stars, by the light of a waning moon, Selvorne had slept very well,
waking rarely, falling back to dreams easily. Neither too cool nor hot, he woke to
see the first light of what would be a bright clear day.

Few others were stirring, no others seemed awake. Temnere, he was told,
enjoyed sleeping late, so all the camp were prepared for a late rise. Many of the
guards had not slept properly in days, that morning was their chance to catch
needed rest. The new recruits seemed very tired, Selvorne was not sure if any of
them had ever walked so far, and they were lying around the meadow as if dead.
Apart from the snoring, it was a very quiet, peaceful dawn.

Selvorne turned to his side and was happy. Despite everything, he was pleased.
There were perhaps three times as many guards with him in that single camp than
there were brigands he had spied at theirs. Within a week, he thought, he would
be part of an army – trained and capable, and the sweep of the south would be a
story to last for ... for many lifetimes to come. Perhaps the brigands would
surrender, faced with doom. Or be captured suddenly by an easy ambush. He
would play some part in it, perhaps a small part, perhaps a large one – either way
would fulfil his obligations of honour by bringing the killers to justice. But – more
importantly to himself – it would be revenge against those who had wronged him.
Then he would announce his titled rights and take control of Tavalehk. True, it
was too much for him alone, but not thirty feet away slept the Head Administrator,
who would appoint people to assist. The festival the next year would be the best

ever held – with plenty of wine at good prices, and statues revealed in memory of Arnlausa and Uhlsko.

Perhaps not statues, they might cost a fortune and take years to complete. But something – perhaps a feasting day, each year at the festival. Where tales were told and the best foods eaten, and ... a song, from the greatest singer of the land. Yes, the townsfolk would approve of that ... as would the beloved dead.

Selvorne smiled and was happy in his private dreams, safe amongst so many men, until he looked over to the river and realised they were not alone. There was someone bathing in the warm waters. Someone not of the guards, someone – oh – he bit his lip and widened his eyes. It was Demni, it had to be – he was sure it was her, for the shallow waters of the river only came to her knees, and she had her hair out. None of the men had hair so long – none of the women he had ever seen, either. Looking around, he saw her tent, and it seemed Savak was before it, lying in an awkward position as if he had fallen and slept where he landed. They must have arrived during the night, a few other tents had appeared as well. Selvorne felt stupid that he had not woken with all the noise, and wondered if anyone had woken – if brigands had come, would they all have been slain? He lay down a little, pretending to be asleep, but watched her with half–closed eyes.

Demni was annoying, and frustrating, and strange – and her voice at times was like choking on inhaled rust. But – from a distance, and in the silence – she was beguiling. Moving with a soothing smoothness, delicately tossing water to her face. Her hair was dry, as was the long white dress she wore – until she dipped down and disappeared beneath the water, where it was deep.

Beautiful, perhaps – a wonderful wife, perhaps. From a distance, Selvorne thought – if she did not speak. And if she did not glare. Or snap orders. Or poison the food, when defied. A strange wife, perhaps. Even so, he could see why Rohy was so keen at the sight of her, for she moved like no person he had ever seen, almost as if she was dancing – an enchantment of dance, even more elegant than Dyneti.

Rohy was curled up asleep and near, so, when Demni was not facing them, Selvorne crawled over and poked his friend. Suddenly, silently, Rohy sprung into a crouch – arm folded over his throat, with a knife in his hand, glaring as his eyes came to focus. Startled, Selvorne jumped back – then put a finger to his lips to be quiet, and pointed over at Demni. Rohy was confused, but soon relaxed to lie back down, and put away his knife. Then he grinned, and put a finger to his lips as well, acknowledging the need for silence.

Without a sound the two of them watched her bathing, until she left the river and threw back her hair. A spray high into the air, across the pale dawn sky – then she moved swiftly on her toes as she crossed the camp to return to her tent. A hundred tiny light steps, as if she danced on the air above the grass.

"Ohh," Rohy whispered, and then was silent for a while, and said the same again.

Selvorne just grinned.

"Thank you for waking me," Rohy whispered after some time, and Selvorne nodded.

"Still?" Selvorne asked, almost in a hush.

"Still – do I like her still? More, now, and perhaps – always. Now – when did she arrive?"

Selvorne shrugged his shoulder.

"I ... ohh, I ... my perfect lady," Rohy said in a very low voice.

"If she was trained properly?" Selvorne dared asked, and Rohy frowned, then winced.

"Do you think she is just ... harsh when first met?"

Selvorne shrugged his shoulders, which was not easy when lying down, but his shoulders alone seemed not enough and he did not know what to say. Perhaps she was, or perhaps she only sometimes was – they hardly knew her – perhaps all women were harsh at times, Selvorne was not the man to ask. He also was not sure if Demni was, perhaps, the only normal person of all the guards and administrators – for the men were jolly in the face of death, casual in their duties, and absurdly unafraid. If anything, she was not harsh enough, considering all that was happening. And bathing in the morning waters, she seemed anything but ... for she was only beautiful. The two of them lay back down, lost in the visions of a dream.

Ruined soon enough – not by dawn, not by waking men, not by the morning duties of preparing for the day. Through all such things they rose and made ready, moving as though in an untainted dream of beauty. Dazed and distracted enough to provoke taunts from Nakla and Reklo, though none of the others were safe from them either, that morning.

No, the dream of Demni lasted through all of that, but no matter how enchanting she had been in the river, how lovely she looked or moved or seemed, it was only moments after she stepped out of her tent that all men there began to regret her arrival.

Demni Nohc Seseasil – as if she needed to be announced, as if anyone did not know who she was already. Savak was the one calling her name, with emphasis on the Nohc – a noble title, almost lordly, granted to administrators of importance. Not so often said, to guards, anyway, and it was clear from their faces that her name alone was enough. They knew who she was, and Selvorne was sure some of the men groaned. It was not long after that the new recruits learnt why.

Where Temnere was happy to blurt out a few clear orders, and expected them followed immediately, without question, and in his absence – Demni liked to fill in every detail of every task, then watch over the men as their duties were performed. Her disapproval was obvious, in her face and her tone, and her approval was disguised as more disapproval, criticism and opportunities to improve. The new recruits, other than Selvorne, Rohy and Bitier, knew only vaguely who she was – letting her know that was a terrible mistake, whether taunted or challenged, or sincerely, through ignorance. Selvorne felt uneasy to realise that even the older guards feared her – there was Rohy's answer – no. It was seen in the faces of the men, and the realisation in the face of his friend. She did not improve with time, did not soften with familiarity. Savak seemed to be the only one unaffected, likely because he had spent so much time with her, he knew what was an idle threat and what was true fury. Or perhaps that part of a man that fears stern words, the tenderness deep within him, she had crushed long ago.

"Why, why, why is such a beauty cursed with such a manner?" Rohy lamented as quietly as he could.

"I think perhaps it is the other way around – why has this monster come, to lure us with its beauty?" Selvorne asked when they were very alone, Rohy nodding slowly, as they gathered their things, "And, unlike you, I am resistant to its curse – although I do not think this is a good thing. It certainly does not make things easier for me."

Rohy sighed, despite Selvorne's grin. Demni was no attraction to him, but he wondered ... if Dyneti was so unpleasant, would he tolerate such a manner? He thought not, even though Dyneti was splendid to look upon – it was her manner that warmed his heart, where Demni seemed almost to rip it out, and that was just with her voice, let alone what she was saying.

~

The journey that day would be easier, for it was not truly a day's distance they had to walk. Rising not long after dawn, they walked slowly at Temnere's pace, stopping often to rest before coming to the outlying lands of Hartlehk town. Quite far from the town, but they were not to walk the entire distance that day. As the road came to a place where the ground was rocky and the cliffs to their left were steep, all talk amongst the new recruits was of Hartlehk and its lands.

Hartlehk was a hard town, hard partly because it was ruled by a hard–headed lord, but mostly because it was filled with hardened, powerful men. So Bitier said, though most thought he was teasing a little. It was his home, and Selvorne was sure he was saying such things not to elevate himself, but in a kind of mockery of the stern folk in powerful positions.

The town itself was in a powerful position, Selvorne knew that quite well without the embellishments of Bitier – Hartlehk was the true gateway between north and south, for all trade from Tavalehk had to pass through there to reach any of the other towns. Once it was a wealthy town, rich in timber – again, for its position, for it had woodlands of oak meeting forests of pines, and a river ran through them all, leading all the way to Senylehk, and to other towns besides. Logs were cut and floated down in great quantity, for vast profits. Easier for other towns to receive logs by the river, stopping at docks right where needed, than to drag the same from forests not so near. Sadly for Hartlehk, few trees remained near the river, forests were cleared and meadows remained. They changed much of their trade to barrels instead, and wooden products, such as furnishings. Mostly barrels, for they used little wood and fetched large prices, and were easier to send down the river than chairs, as Bitier explained.

Ruchten NohcTohm Ultainen – the Lord of Hartlehk. Very unusual for a lord to take the title of NohcTohm instead of NohcLehk, since it was Hartlehk, and not Harttohm. The oddness was not lost on the others, though all agreed Harttohm sounded absurd. However, Bitier explained also that there was no lake – no great lake, anyway, not even in the mountains, and the naming of the town was quite odd from the start. Otherwise he said little of it, and spoke of other things – but Selvorne knew more than the others, for Arnlausa had spoken of his rival northern lord more than once, and rival was the gentlest name he called him.

To title himself so, Ruchten had broken tradition – NohcTohm, not NohcLehk – he showed he considered the vast woodlands of his realm far more important than the lake, which was a mere widening of the river. The woods and woodlands he claimed as his own, and though that was true for any lord of any town, what Ruchten actually meant to claim were the woodlands farther south, and north, and higher into the mountains – and perhaps, if he could, those much farther south – those of Tavalehk, suggesting that they were somehow connected by mountain streams that flowed to the two rivers. Uhlsko had said it was impossible – forty miles was a very long way to make such a claim. Arnlausa said he did not mean to make a claim, he only envied the forests there, and besides, he was already spreading his town to the south, using any stream or rivulet he could to bring timber to the roads. A greedy lord who was too stupid to think of another way to make his town wealthy. On that they were both agreed.

Selvorne thought Ruchten would have to be ignorant at the least, if not stupid – clearly he had not been to Tavalehk recently, or he would not have envied the cleared woodlands, where only stumps remained. And he must never have looked at a map if he thought wood from there could ever be brought to the road, and then to Senylehk – or anywhere of any use. Surely he must have walked the distance south? Selvorne just had, it was two full days – no sane man would try and drive a team of oxen that far, dragging logs. Why would they, when the same trees were right there not hundreds of yards away – why bring them two days along the road? Four days, with bad oxen. None of it made sense, but both his father and Arnlausa were concerned by such ambitious desires on their land – and with recent events, that made Selvorne unsettled.

But Arnlausa was not afraid of his rival to the north. Annoyed, more than anything – he could not stand him or his nagging wife – neither was invited to the festival, even politely. If anything, messengers were sent through Hartlehk, loudly declaring they were passing through to bring invitation to other lords – and Ruchten's control of the road might have been the reason few ever came.

Selvorne had been to Hartlehk, but it was so long ago he did not remember it. Just a child, he did remember riding on a cart, and being incredibly bored all the way. And likely at the town, and then, back again, with no great interest in the place.

He was not bored that day, not as he made his way north knowing there was danger. His head was filling with suspicions. Alert, look, listen – but his task was to quietly find Cienn, not to confront rival lords along the way, even if they might have had reason for murder.

~

A halt in the march, and all the men stopped. They were close to houses, seen in the distance once they topped a rise. A gentle slope down, a river, the town, he thought, in the distance – it all seemed much smaller than Selvorne had expected. Something was announced at the front of the procession, and a guard came back to explain. Savak, who was not at all cheerful.

"We stop tonight at the inn," Savak yelled at them, "best behaviour from you all – or face the worst punishment. None of you have the protection of guards, nor of the Lord of Hartlehk – oh, except ... those from Hartlehk. No others. You will do as you are told, not as you wish, or be immediately dismissed to make your way, as you wish. Understood?"

Eventually all replied that they did, and accepted his warning. Savak nodded, then returned to the front.

Bitier was the one he had meant – as a man of Hartlehk, he could call on the lord for protection – for whatever good it would do. Ruchten would more likely be harsher to him than the others, should any break some law, and Rechtvaar would make an example of him, by hanging in the square, if he could. Or so Bitier explained. Only two days together, but Selvorne knew his new friend was not joking.

Hartlehk the town was still a quarter of a day to the north – miles, only, but not yet seen. What Selvorne had thought a small town was in fact less than a village, and what he thought a river was just a large stream. Large enough to require a bridge – and the waters were fast, for they came from many streams that met farther up the hill. Meadows – no, woodlands cleared, there were stumps of trees everywhere to the right, all alongside the river going up the gentle slope – then up the steeper hill – then up the side of the mountain, which loomed to the very sky. Selvorne could not see the stumps at the top, just the line of dark river water, and the soft green grass. Then far from the water, the bright green of forests, which also turned dark farther up – up, high on the mountain, where oak became pine. Then pine became stone, and at the very top – ice. Behind its peak, more mountains, taller, and some with great caps of snow.

The River Bridge Inn – that was where they would stay. Bitier explained that no one stopped there anymore, if they could help it – but Temnere did. He had always stopped there, when travelling south, and so he always would, no matter how bad it had become. And from what Bitier said, it had become very bad indeed. But, because Temnere stayed there, all the guards, administrators and new recruits had to stay there as well. Whether he was there or not, with them or not, whether they liked it or not – if they meant to have the lodging paid by the administrators. Some guards asked if they could go ahead to Hartlehk, "to gather new recruits from town, and make preparations," though Selvorne suspected they just wanted better lodgings. Bitier agreed it was likely.

All moved ahead, down a slope to woodlands near, over a hill and then another – a mile perhaps, or it seemed as far with the falls and rises. As the road approached the inn, all forests near the road abruptly ended, giving way to a vast expanse of low grass, slight hills, tree stumps and bushes – unkempt lands. Every so often was a deep furrow in the dirt, where hundreds of logs had been dragged to the river, and the woods had been cleared until it was too far to drag logs anymore.

When Selvorne had first looked down upon the inn, and thought it a town, it seemed very small – for a town. But as he approached, knowing it was only an inn and a few houses, he was astounded by the size of it and number of buildings – almost a small village. Perhaps even large enough to be made a town, if a small one, with many houses, huts and – no, very few people. Smoke only from one end, the largest building. The rest was abandoned, with many wooden houses all along the riverside, but those that once were elegant had turned to ruin, and what was once a street was deserted.

Selvorne found himself nodding as they walked closer – he knew the place, he knew the story. The second river of Hartlehk, south, and that meant the Lord of Hartlehk was the only lord who controlled two rivers. Not much of a river, the southern one – but two, as no others did, and not merely two branches of the one, for that rivulet did not run to Senylehk, but to the south, joining with the Tavalehk river, and flowing west to Veksehl, by the sea. That was why Arnlausa considered Ruchten his rival – for Ruchten, and those before him, sold wood from there at Veksehl. Tavalehk could not compete, for Tavalehk needed the wood for itself, and that small village – of only woodsmen – sold much and needed little.

That was long ago. Once it was a busy place, not large, like the river – but wealthy. Until Veksehl town began to build all things in stone, not wood, so very soon after, it was a small village of woodsmen with no market in which to sell. Logs could not be dragged north, nor south, and the west wanted no more. To the east there was nothing but mountains and more woodsmen in camps – their own people – and so they all left. Everything they had built was left behind. Fine houses, small farms, even heavy furnishings, he had heard, such as great beds. There it all was, beginning to rot.

Selvorne thought, remembering what he could of maps – it was a very long way to send wood, all the way to the sea. A hundred miles perhaps, though, floating a log along a river would not be hard to do – one hundred miles floating peacefully, or ten miles dragging the thing with an ox. But ... if that was the river to Veksehl, then they were quite far from Hartlehk. Perhaps Arnlausa was right – perhaps Ruchten had an eye to expand to the south. Once, not anymore – that was a terrible abandoned place before them, and only the great inn with its billowing smoke showed any life. By what he had heard from Bitier, it was not pleasant – indeed, he spoke of it almost as though it was a horrific place to stay.

The River Bridge Inn was once a barn, a gateway, a house for collecting tolls – a grand house for rich merchants, and a storage place for grain. At each change it grew larger, until it was an impressive wooden building of three levels high. Larger than many homes of lords, but a jumbled mess of added rooms, and buildings joined by covered passages, which then were walled, then expanded, then rooms. It was enormous, dark and strange, and stood on the southern side of an equally odd wide wooden bridge, that, instead of being dismantled and rebuilt, simply grew wider and taller with each new addition of fresh wood. The inn was very close to the bridge, and right beside the river, which flowed strongly to the west before crashing over a cliff to the cleared woodlands below. Some thought to somehow cover the bridge as well, and join it to the inn, though that made no sense at all to Selvorne, but when he was about to ask why, Bitier's tone went from a solemn tale to almost a warning.

Bitier said that many years ago, the inn was run by one of the friendliest, most outgoing fellows, who had taken it over from ruin and built it into the preferred place to stay for anyone travelling between Hartlehk and Tavalehk. It was well fitted with anything travellers might need – yards and barns for oxen, which had remained from the days when oxen pulled logs, so anyone with waggons could safely leave their beasts. There were vegetable patches to provide much food for good stews, and forest hunting close enough to provide great game in an enormous banquet hall – that was once the barn. There were many quality rooms available for a good price, for when it had been a wealthy village, rich travelling merchants spared no expense buying and decorating their own permanent rooms – all were since abandoned. Some furnishings taken, but they had been replaced, and the common rooms for those with fewer coins were of great warmth and comfort.

Sadly, though, the owner of the inn died – and the inn had since been run by his unpleasant wife. Some suspected she killed him with a shovel, and buried him in the vegetable patch, after an argument regarding muck for the carrots. Some say it was not a shovel, but "pure, relentless nagging," and though that might have sounded as though a joke, any who met her began to wonder if her sour mood was what killed him. Others said he did it himself, for the same reason.

"For one whole year after his death, excited travellers arrived at the inn – only to be met by the grisly news of his demise," Bitier said to all the new recruits, "but, after giving their initial condolences, they endured disappointing service, complaints, abuse – even threats – they left the inn, vowing never to return. And they never did. One year was all it took, one year and reputation ruined – or, to be more accurate, for a new reputation to be deserved. And all the while the widow woman grew ever more nasty, meaner, and cruel – until only the festivals – or the ignorance of travellers – brought any guests at all. And some of them, it is said, being unfamiliar with the lands – and so, unmissed should they disappear – never continued their travels, and paid their lodging not only in coins, but perhaps with their very flesh – for the inn keeps no animals, yet offers all guests meat."

So said Bitier, and as he told the tale, all of the new recruits – including the three arrogant ones – listened in silence. And walked, slowly, without saying a word – until Bitier grinned.

"You ... liar," Reklo said. Some of them laughed, though it was not very funny.

"That was a tale?" Nakla asked, and the men began to breathe more easily.

"Bitier, are you telling a tale?" Savak called back to them, and Bitier nodded. Savak dropped back to join them, and looked them all over, "The killer innkeeper?"

"Just at the end," Bitier said.

"Men – behave. Do not tell that tale there, and do not let him hear it," Savak said, jerking his head towards the front, where Temnere was far ahead of them, "as for the rest – bad inn? Bad service?"

"Yes," Bitier said, "and suspicion of the wife."

"Well – all quite true. But it is bad enough already without angering her – as for the husband, who can say – with no one to see him die, who knows. He was healthy and not old, and died. Usually that happens with some grisly accident. You will take no drink, do no nonsense, tell no tales and ask no questions of his death – those are orders."

The men nodded and Savak quickened his pace back to Demni, oddly stooping to touch the road as he went.

"Did she kill him?" Reklo whispered – and at that, Savak turned and threw a stone back at them – a small stone, and he missed, but it was meant as a warning.

Bitier whispered that most of what he said was true, even the suspicions. They would likely believe them once they met the woman, but ... the last, that she killed the guests and put them in the stew, that was just a story. Some of the men frowned, and insisted that Bitier had said nothing about putting them in the stew, at which Bitier was astonished – he was certain he had mentioned it – and then he began to list, still whispering, the names of men who had disappeared, along with what was suspected had happened to them, giving details of each dish, which sounded delicious if not for the grim ingredients. It was quite some time before Savak turned again and threw another small stone, and that one hit Bitier in the chest, to silence him.

You Are Kind

To hear such tales, and to have them partly confirmed by others, the men expected the looming great building to be abandoned, silent, filled only with their few dozen men and one mad, murderous woman. It was to all of their surprise instead to round the next gentle slope and see that the inn, its yards, the road before the bridge – the entire village at one end was filled with people, drunk and laughing, shouting and crowding the hall so badly they had to shove to get through the doors. The guards all marched to the yard, stopping in astonishment.

It seemed odd for Temnere to go himself, but he went alone, straight to the door of the inn and pushed his way inside. Demni soon followed, then Savak and several other guards who seemed more curious than devoted. After some time, one guard returned, shaking his head.

"It does not look good," the guard said to the others, "the inn is full, even our rooms were given away – Temnere is furious."

Selvorne thought he could hear yelling coming from inside.

"Great! Let us all to the Bettah Inn!" another guard called out, but the first guard shook his head and looked grim, and then began to explain what he had learnt.

The Bettah Inn – it was named as a joke, and an insult, for it was new, not much farther away, supplied by a small stream instead of a river, and stood alone in a field beside the road. It was also better than the River Bridge Inn. It had good, small lodgings, hearty food and friendly service. It had become the preferred place to stay for all people travelling the roads, since the River Bridge Inn had become so unpleasant – that was until two days ago, when the whole place burnt to the ground. Luckily, no people were hurt, because it was nearly empty – everyone was already at the Festival of Tavalehk. But that meant no people were there to notice, or fight the fire when it started – just the innkeeper and his wife, and it was a battle they lost quickly.

So, everyone who had attended the Festival of Tavalehk and was returning north
– and unusually made to do so on the same day, for safety against the unfound
killer – were lodging at the River Bridge Inn. Merchants, guards, travellers, curious
townsfolk, relatives visiting those in the south. There were not that many people
truly, but it did not take many to completely fill the inn and eat all its food.

"And that is not the worst of it, because there is also nothing here to eat,
apparently," the guard lamented, and all the others groaned.

The surprising surge in guests consumed everything the inn had at hand, and the
crowd was also drinking all the ale, for the Tavalehk festival had little wine and
terrible ale. To make matters worse, one group of rowdy men had quickly assessed
the situation, bought all the food they could, including the livestock, and had then
made roasts to sell the food back at prices to make men rage. Those men were not
returning from the festival, but had been lodged at the inn for over a week and
already had eaten much of its stores – some wondered if those men had put
torches to the Bettah Inn, as a way to make a profit, but such suspicions seemed to
come from anger as people begrudgingly handed over coins for small portions of
food.

Temnere returned to the yard before the inn, and seemed much happier. The
mean woman who ran the inn was smart enough to have kept Temnere's lodging
aside, knowing if she angered him she might lose all the business he brought each
year. Her idiot son, however, was not smart enough to keep food for Temnere,
and was beaten soundly in front of them as he promised to get something at once.

Temnere was happy enough, but the other men had nowhere to sleep, and
Selvorne thought the lodgings expected for some must have been quite good, if
their disappointed faces were a clue. Demni had a room, though she still looked
glum. The guards possibly were more upset by the rapidly depleting stocks of ale,
and were frustrated when ordered to establish a camp farther up the river on a
grassy hill, and to stay there. The new recruits were made to join them, and were
the most disappointed, for they were to have the worst of everything – no tents, no
food but oats, certainly no ale. Selvorne had given away all his stores, and unless
they could find something in the woods, oats and water was their fate. Some of the
new men were already wondering if that was what life would be like on the road,
as a guard, to which the guards replied it was not – it was usually much worse,
being colder, and raining.

Selvorne, however, was excited and happy, for he had seen something the others
had missed – the telling splashes in the river that suggested fish. He dumped his
things at the camp, grabbed the box with his spear inside and took off at once for
the river alone.

He ran a while, and soon found a quiet bend in the river, with gentle water so it
was easier to see a fish unhidden by ripples. They were about, trout, he thought –
big ones. His spear assembled with the two–pronged head, he wanted to make it
full length, but thought better of it, then attached the cord to the end so he would

not lose it – which would be terrible, considering its price, and it was the first time it was to be used. Even for him that would be unbelievable bad luck.

When Rohy arrived a while later, he could scarcely believe what he saw – Selvorne had already caught one good sized fish, and another truly enormous one, and was carefully stalking another. He held his hand up for silence as Rohy's eyes bulged at the sight of the feast. Then, with a quick jab, Selvorne caught a third – another good sized fish, thrashing on the end of the spear.

"Victory!" Selvorne cried out, bringing it over to the pile, "That should be enough, perhaps with some to spare."

Rohy stared at him in disbelief.

"What, have you never seen someone catch a fish before?"

"Not like that, not with a spear," Rohy replied, "only with a net, or a line, or a trap. But not with a spear."

"Well, that is ... odd, I do it all the time," Selvorne said, cleaning his spear and gathering up his catch, "here, can you carry this larger one? I do not think it will fit on the spear."

The smaller fish were as long as his forearm, and he hung them on the end of the spear. The large fish was as long as his arm, almost, and Rohy gingerly held it out by the tail, at least at first – then it grew so heavy that he had to cradle it.

They returned to the group as heroes – even Rohy, who had little to do with it. Rohy had hardly spoken to the other guards, but found himself warmly welcomed by all. Some of the men thought they would go for their own fish, until they realised Selvorne was offering to share it with everyone, which made them cheer.

"On the condition," Selvorne added, "that you clean and dress them, and cook them, I want nothing to do with that messy task."

Few others did either, but Traglan volunteered and claimed he was very good at it. He would also cook the fish through, and there would be no scales or bones remaining, unless wanted. Scales, not bones, he explained, then asked if anyone wanted bones.

Selvorne determined that the large fish by itself might be enough for the twenty of them, but to be sure that it was, he left them one of the smaller fish as well, and took the other to sell at the inn. As he left, he had a thought, and took out the remains of the ham bone from his pack to sell for soup. It would be a profitable evening, he thought, as he waved to the others, who were fussing over the enormous fish and gathering wood for a fire.

As Selvorne approached the inn he felt his heart begin to pound – at the front of the inn was the small goat–drawn cart that belonged to Dyneti, who must have caught up with them as he was fishing. He started to run down, then stopped – he must have smelled terribly of fish, especially as he was carrying one.

He made his way to where the kitchen seemed to be, and though it smelled like a kitchen in use, the door was shut fast and nobody answered when he banged upon it. Around the side, he found a small, barren vegetable patch, and a rat at the edge was gnawing at some dead animal. Something else was thrashing around in the bushes near the rat, which backed away every so often, then crept carefully forwards to have another go at the dead thing there, which did not seem quite dead.

Selvorne winced and left that unpleasant place, and began to feel glad to be camping away on the hill, instead of in an abandoned village. He had meant to sell the fish to the inn, but he soon had another idea, and headed to the road that ran to the river and the bridge.

The roasting men were still roasting what little remained of a pig, turning a spike to make best use of a dying fire. A few people were paying good coins for tiny portions, there was little meat left and each sale turned to an argument, then ended with intimidating stares from the sellers. With no other choices, people had to pay what was asked, and accept what was given. Selvorne thought it was ... well, unfair, but it was as it was – and he had an idea.

"Who wants to buy a fish?" he called out, waving the good sized trout by the tail. "Freshly caught, what price do I hear?"

"That is not cooked!" someone yelled back at him.

"I never said it was cooked, just fresh. Add fire and wait a few minutes, delicious! Enough to feed many people – yes, quite a few meals here, to share, or sell. What price?"

It took only moments before people realised what he was saying – not just a fish, but the chance to profit by selling it cooked to all who were hungry. The men roasting were annoyed – at first – then eager to buy it themselves, and almost did so, but for the fury of the crowd and Selvorne's dislike of their mean ways. He sold it for an embarrassing price to five men who carefully took it away to prepare, with the intention of tenderly dividing it to sell as meals at the inn – much to the displeasure of the roasters.

Selvorne took himself to the river to wash his hands and arms and anything that smelled of fish. As much as he liked eating fish and fishing, he was not fond of the lingering reminder – he would prefer to close his eyes and remember the taste, rather than try to close his nose to block the smell. After much washing, he was satisfied, and he looked out over the river – there were fish even there, though not as many nor as big. How could the people be so lazy, or stupid, or – why did they not catch their own? Was that how townspeople thought – he did not know. It took them quite a while to realise they could cook the dead fish on a fire – were they so used to having food served to them on plates? Perhaps they were, most were merchants of some kind. But not all, some were ordinary families returning from the festival. Traglan – the poorest of the new guards – was the most keen to start cleaning the fish, of all the guards. The whole thing was puzzling to Selvorne, who could hardly be more confused than if they sat with a meal before them and did not know how to use their hands to eat it, sitting there waiting for knife and spoon, or even a fork.

Clean and fresh, and after checking his hair as best he could in his reflection without falling in the river, Selvorne entered the common room of the inn. It was an enormous room that could seat forty people, or cram in one hundred standing. Once a barn, it had a very high roof for hay, and so, although it was bright outside, the barn had few windows and needed a great fireplace for light. Selvorne looked to the walls – it seemed that usually many torches would be lit along them – but instead were a few dim lamps. Why – oh, of course, fear of fire after the Bettah Inn had burnt. All that made the place quite unbearable. Hot, with the one huge fire, and dark, with many people blocking its light. Noisy and crowded, and a dozen unpleasant smells that he was not sure were food.

Selvorne could not see Dyneti, and did not think she would be there if she had a choice. Also, looking at the great many drunken men, he reasoned that if she was there, it would be in the middle of some commotion, either singing, or refusing to sing, declining all manner of offers to dance or share ale.

He moved through the room, squeezing between people, and found a quieter table at one end where Temnere, Demni, and Taahr were seated. None of them looked happy, comfortable or pleased. Taahr looked nervous and small, hunched over the table, arranging his fork and knife this way and that. Demni looked bored, hot, and bothered, but sat upright and proper. Savak was behind her, looking longingly into an empty tankard. Temnere was drumming his fingers on the table, each strike perfectly measured, his brow in a frown and his lips moved in silence as if he was counting the time that had passed since his order should have been fulfilled.

Before Selvorne could disappear into the crowd, Demni glared at him and beckoned him over.

"You are not meant to be in here! Go back to the camp," she said when he was beside her.

"Yes, what are you doing here? Away with you!" chirped Taahr, waving a finger at Selvorne.

"Wait!" Temnere ordered, silencing the other two, "He can stay if he wishes. But first go to the kitchen and find our food. We have been waiting a long time and I am not at all pleased."

Selvorne nodded – he was glad to be treated well by Temnere, especially in front of the other two, who had been put in their place. Though ... he was not supposed to be there, as a guard or a recruit, for they had been told to stay at the camp.

"Yes, at once. What did you order?" Selvorne asked.

Temnere stared at him, and he wondered what he had said wrong, but after a pause Demni spoke.

"You mean, what did we order to eat? You want to know what we asked for, in case they have forgotten?" Demni asked.

"Aha!" Temnere said – and he seemed relieved. He leant back in his chair, stared at the wall and seemed to drift away in his own thoughts.

"I ordered the sausages," Demni continued, "Temnere, the venison steak, well done, not too well done though, but the edge must be very well done, and the inside, slightly pink."

"And myself, my boy," piped up Taahr, "the venison stew. And an extra portion. With bread."

Selvorne was puzzled – venison? Steak? Stew? Sausages? Where was all that food going to come from? He nodded and began to force his way through the crowds towards the door, when Demni stood quickly and caught him by the arm, and politely directed him to the kitchen through a smaller door the other way, instead of through the yard, where he was headed.

"Please hurry them along," Demni said in a low voice, "he is getting restless and the quicker we eat, the sooner we may get out of here."

He looked back at the table, and Temnere certainly looked angry. Taahr was chatting with some maid of the tavern, kissing her hand, waving his, and she seemed flattered.

"How can they have all this food?" Selvorne asked Demni.

"We ordered last week and they were meant to prepare it for us in advance. I do not care what they have, as long as they hurry. So ... hurry!"

Selvorne was about to rush off, but first he asked about Dyneti, and Demni said she was feeling ill, and was asleep in her room.

He went through the small door, but nobody was in the kitchen. The fire was burning and a tiny pot was boiling over it, with a clear broth and a few vegetable ends that perhaps should have instead been returned to the soil. An iron grill near the fire had tiny sausages and a large steak grilling on it, but the smell was not quite like anything Selvorne knew. The door to the yard at the back was open, so he went outside.

There the son of the innswoman was on his hands and knees, trying to get something out of the bushes at the back. He snatched at it, then quickly jumped back – holding in one hand a dead rat by the tail.

"Who are you?" the boy snapped.

"Selvorne," was the reply, along with a polite bow. The youth relaxed, seemed flattered, and did a clumsy bow of his own, still holding the rat, which he then held up proudly.

"Look what I caught!"

Selvorne was not keen on rat. He had never eaten one, being told it was not wise, but he had spoken to those who had – some in desperation, who said they were awful, and some who considered it a tasty delight. It was clear where the meat was coming from, and Selvorne supposed it was hunting, of a sort, and could be called game – but could hardly be presented as venison.

"How did you catch that? With your hands?" Selvorne asked, trying to make conversation, though he was curious that the boy had bleeding bites along one arm.

"Well, no," the boy admitted, "not me. Him. He kills them, I get them."

The boy was gesturing towards the bushes at the edge of the vegetable patch, where something was moving furiously.

Selvorne thought the boy must be simple of mind, by the way he spoke and behaved. But he did not seem completely stupid, though perhaps not as clean as a cook should be, digging around in the dirt of the yard. Selvorne looked into the bushes, expecting to discover a trained weasel, or perhaps a ground hawk – either would be impressive, neither had he ever seen, not a trained weasel, anyway, and he was not sure if such a thing existed, but – what he saw instead sent a shudder down his spine.

A tight snare cut into its leg – held it fast, against the trunk of low bushes. Furious, thrashing in pain – a rabbit. Or a hare. Wild eyed, it glared back at Selvorne for one moment, then chewed at its own leg. It was cruelly held, struggling to get free, and was covered in bites, scratches and blood. Selvorne's first thought was to cut the bond and let it loose, but even as he thought it, as he moved closer, he froze – it seemed so wild it might attack him if he dared.

"Caught this morning, stealing carrot," the boy said, "but it bit me, so let it die. When I came again, it killed a ground rat. And a bear. And now, a rat. Now there is meat to cook!"

"A ... bear?" Selvorne asked. The rabbit looked very mean, but he doubted it could kill a bear, even a small one. A rat, perhaps, if it was lucky, though he had never heard of a rabbit killing anything, except perhaps another rabbit, if they were fighting in the spring. But a bear?

"Yes, a bear, I can show it," the boy said, then he led Selvorne away into the kitchen. The rabbit looked at him glaring, then went back to chewing at its leg.

In the kitchen, on one table was the carcass of some small creature from the woods. It had not been skinned, but a huge piece had been cut from its rear leg, and it looked to have bites all over it, still bleeding. It was black, furry, with two white stripes and a fierce pointed face, and long claws.

"A bear," the boy insisted, so Selvorne humoured him and agreed. He did not know what it was, but it was no bear, not even a baby bear. He reasoned it must have been drawn to the fresh rabbit blood, and then – the rabbit killed it?

"Where is the ground rat?" Selvorne asked, wondering how that was different to an ordinary rat.

The boy pointed – Selvorne did know a weasel when he saw one, even if it had been skinned and its insides removed. The boy also pointed to the sausages cooking, then quickly realised they were burning, so he rushed over to turn them and the steak.

Selvorne thought about everything he saw – it would not do. Rats, weasels and some unknown thing, but – to his surprise, the boy began preparing the rat, and despite the mess of it, and the idea of eating rat, he did so properly, cleanly, and with little fuss. He removed the meat and discarded the waste. The animals, if it was true they had recently been killed by the rabbit, at least were fresh and had not been rotting for days. The boy seemed to know what he was doing, even if he was a bit simple of mind. He added the rat meat to the tiny pot and it bubbled furiously.

"Do you taste your food before serving it?" Selvorne asked, because if something was bad, he would not want it served, not even to Taahr, and especially not to the others.

"Of course, to test it. I know how to cook!" he claimed defiantly.

"You are a clever fellow!" Selvorne replied, smiling, and the boy grinned. Simple, and ... it was no matter.

"Yes! My best, I do, since father died," the boy said, and then looked very sad.

Selvorne felt for him. The death of the innkeeper, years ago – a nuisance for travellers. Fanciful tales of murder, born from complaints and inconvenience. But it must have been a terrible loss to that young boy, younger then by years, worked hard by his mother – beaten, before the crowds, and with profits falling each year since. But to lose his father – Selvorne knew his pain. And the mother – she seemed worse than Demni, and Selvorne shuddered to think what it must be like living there. Almost as a captive servant, unable to leave – as he heard they had in the far south.

Selvorne had a thought, so he unwrapped the ham bone from his shoulder sack, and held it out to the boy. "What do you think of this? What would you do with it?"

The boy smelled it, looked it over and frowned.

"I think it is old, it smells, and I would not use the meat on it, only the bone. I would cook it twice in the pot, once to take the meat off, and away with it – and once to cook the bone, for flavour. But just the bone, or people get sick and will not come back," he said, and then winced and seemingly without realising, moved his arm to protect his head, as if someone was about to hit him.

Selvorne gave him the bone to use if he wanted it, and was satisfied the food was good enough, so he nodded farewell and returned to tell the others their meals would arrive soon.

~

Pushing his way back through the common room to Demni, he only wanted to tell them of the meals, but they made him sit with them until they arrived. Demni was anxious to leave, and Temnere seemed to be watching, judging, and Selvorne could not help wonder what would happen if the meals were much later, or never came – would he be held to blame – if they were not fond of ... what clearly was not venison?

Taahr had turned his chair and was flirting with a fisherman's daughter every time she passed by – a young maiden who was flattered by the attentions of the well–dressed captain of the guards. Each time she came, he took and kissed her hand, and he was not at all shy to tell her of his great deeds, at which she giggled, and Demni shook her head.

388

There were rough people in the large room, though most seemed to keep to themselves, sharing only their noise, not their ale. Savak had taken a seat on a bench against the wall, and somehow managed to fall asleep amidst the crowd.

It was not long before the food arrived, though it seemed a very long time. The innswoman barged her way through the crowd with two wooden plates and a small pot dangling from her arm, placed the plates gently on the table, and stamped the pot down for Taahr. Selvorne was surprised at how good it smelled, and all three inhaled the aroma, complimenting the woman, who smiled and returned to the kitchen.

There was a moment of uncertainty as each looked to the other meals, and Selvorne clenched his teeth – was it wrong – confusion on their faces. But then Temnere looked at Taahr and nodded, and with a few moves of his hand, Temnere swapped a piece of bread beside Taahr's soup with a piece of cheese on his plate – both small, but Taahr's eyes lit up. Demni seemed relieved, though she frowned at the smell of her sausages – Selvorne sniffed, and realised – and hoped she did not – that they were drenched in a sauce made with wine.

They ate – Selvorne held his breath – and to his relief, Demni praised the tiny sausages, and did not mention the wine sauce, even after drinking it from the spoon. Temnere said nothing, but his face gave away his delight as he bit into large pieces of the steak, and Taahr, with the first spoonful of stew, began to compliment the cook, not only between mouthfuls, so juice dripped from his lips. Demni waved her hand at Selvorne to excuse him, then pointed firmly to the door that led outside, in so doing turned even a dismissal into a command. He nodded, and left, thinking they were the oddest three people he had ever met.

As he reached the door to the common room, he defied her order and turned instead to the corridor and stairs leading to the rooms at the back of the inn. Dyneti would be there, somewhere, and if she was able, he would ask her to join him for a meal of fish. He could not bear to think of her eating at the inn, no matter how clean or well cooked the ... meat ... was. If she was already too ill to leave her room, he would perhaps bring her something from the camp.

It must have been a separate building once, for the style of walls changed as he passed from corridor to stairs, and then to another long narrow hall of doors. The rooms behind the doors were filled with noisy people who could find no space in the hall. Listening at each, he heard a few things he should not have heard, though nothing important or useful. At the far end he heard the delightful laughter of Adyleh – Dyneti – and the voice of a man who seemed to be trying to sound like Temnere.

Selvorne knocked and the room was silent, then there was scuffling as people moved about. The door opened to reveal Kalgevun with a stern gaze – he looked at Selvorne, then to the corridor.

"Selvorne – Dyneti is ill, not to be disturbed. I see you are alone. What is it you want?"

Selvorne thought it odd that Kalgevun was speaking so loudly, but then Dyneti jumped up from the bed and came to the door, poking her head out, looking down the corridor and dragged him inside. She then motioned for Kalgevun to stand guard at the door, so he left and almost closed it behind himself. Dyneti took Selvorne's hands in hers.

"You look well!" Selvorne said, and she did, not at all sick.

"I am – why are you surprised?"

"I heard you were – "

"Ahh – that. I needed an excuse to not sit in that noisy place," Dyneti said, then went on to explain that as much as she liked Demni, she could not stand being with the three of them at once, not for hours, shouting at each other over the noise. It would make her ill – so she feigned sickness in advance, and was trying to sleep, but could not, for some animal was making terrible noise in the yard, people were drinking in their rooms, and she was getting very hungry, but there was no food.

"I am also starving," Kalgevun said, poking his head inside the door that he had not completely shut, "if you were wondering."

Both looked expectantly at Selvorne, who explained that the men had a lot of fresh fish at the camp, just caught, likely cooked and ready to eat – if they wanted to join them for a feast.

Dyneti and Kalgevun looked at each other, nodded, and began to prepare. Dyneti was wearing a long loose white robe, and motioned for Selvorne to leave the room and shut the door. He switched places with Kalgevun, and when the two emerged from the room, Dyneti was in trousers and boots, wearing Kalgevun's jacket with a hood over her head, and looked like a short young boy guard. Perhaps a little round, for a boy.

The three of them quickly moved down the corridor, then pushed through the crowded common room as gently as possible and out to the yard. It was not hard to go through unnoticed, Dyneti was especially unnoticeable, for she was short and looked rather absurd, but not enough to attract stares. Selvorne had a feeling they had done such a thing many times before. They moved fast across the yard, but Selvorne's thoughts turned to the snared rabbit.

"Please, go on ahead to the camp, I have to do something first," he explained, and though puzzled, the two of them left at speed before anyone saw them, and Selvorne went to investigate the rabbit.

On the way he saw a pile of wood with a small bronze–headed axe, so he took it, not sure if he would kill the creature or free it. Either way he did not want to get near it, not with only a knife, for he feared being bitten – his hands were not as fast as a rat, or a weasel, and he was likely not as tough as the other thing that it had killed – but he could not bear to think of it trapped there, struggling and in pain.

It was beginning to get dark, the sun was low and soon would set. He could barely see the rabbit in the trap. It was there, at least ... some rabbit was there, yet it looked like a fresh catch. He was sure it was not bleeding, but it had blood on its fur, and its eyes looked more vibrant and alive. Was it the same rabbit? Its leg, which previously had been gnawed and bloody, seemed fine, but was still held fast by the snare, high in the air, almost out of reach of its teeth, holding it firm. The rabbit was calm, and stared at him, snapping as he got too close, but no longer thrashing about.

Strong enough to survive, so he thought he would free it. He took the axe and raised it to cut the cord. The rabbit thrashed about at first, but when he hit the small tree trunk where the cord was attached, the rabbit stopped still. The cord did not cut. Strange, the axe was sharp enough. A few more hits, and instead of cutting, the cord seemed to be driven into the tree as he cut away the wood. Very odd. The rabbit was hanging quietly, the snare had been tied in a strange knot, so he thought he would untie it – then was astonished when it untied itself, with an easy tug of one loose end.

Selvorne jumped back with the axe held high as he realised what he had done – the ferocious rabbit freed before he was ready – but it fell to the ground, shook its bound leg, and pulled at the cord with its teeth. It seemed very well behaved, and unharmed, even though its fur on one side was matted with blood. It looked at him – and for a moment he thought it might pounce – but instead it stared, turning its head each way to examine him with one eye at a time. He blinked and stared back. The rabbit seemed to nod – once – so very odd, it could not have been ... a bow... then it crawled back through the bushes and disappeared.

He was not sure what to make of it – astonishing – but, perhaps he had just freed a trained rabbit, which was once part of a festival act. No, the boy said he had caught it. It was no pet, and who trained rabbits to bow, let alone catch rats? Confused, Selvorne took the cord, but returned the axe, then went to join the others at the campfire.

Death Undeserved

As Selvorne approached the campfire, his mind was already bewildered by what he had seen, and as he neared, he realised everyone was suddenly silent, and turned to face him, all at once. Rohy walked up to him and held out a wooden plate with a small piece of fish on it. It smelled delicious, but it was the tiniest portion – barely one bite.

"I am sorry," Rohy said, "but this is all that is left. We have eaten well, though – it was delicious ... we are all grateful."

Selvorne was horrified. He was starving, and after all he done, they left him with nothing. He looked around, and could see no sign of the fish. Dyneti stared at him with wide unblinking eyes, no smile, and almost seemed to glare.

"Oh Selvorne," Dyneti lamented, "you promised us a feast, and there is nothing here. Shame on you!"

She sounded almost angry, stamped her foot, and Kalgevun looked as though he was getting ready to swing his fists. Selvorne looked Dyneti over – he could not help notice she was perhaps prettier, when angry, for her lips were pouting and her stare intense, her eyes wide, gaze unbroken, eyes delightful, staring – gleaming – a twinkle – a curled lip – that mischievous little –

Suddenly she burst into laughter, and as if they had strained to contain it, all the men did the same. Selvorne thought the prank especially cruel when he was so hungry.

"Very funny – is there fish?" Selvorne asked, and they laughed harder – he narrowed his eyes until Rohy nodded. Then he sighed, Kalgevun grinned and returned to the fire, and Dyneti, eager to eat, followed – but not before touching Selvorne's shoulder and making him tremble, more, perhaps, once she had left his side.

"That was Dyneti's idea," Rohy explained in a low voice, "apparently, she enjoys a cruel joke at your expense."

Selvorne felt a fool – again. But he was starving, and the smell of the tiny portion before him – and the sudden despair that there was no food – only made his hunger worse. And he was beginning to shake.

The guards unwrapped the cooked fish and presented it to him – they had covered it in leaves to keep it warm until Selvorne returned. Not one of them had eaten, all were starving, waiting for him, and were just about to send men to find him, thinking perhaps he had been attacked by the hungry crowd for the other fish.

"No harm done, and we all had fun. Thank you, Selvorne," Dyneti said before they sat to eat, and with that she took one of his hands in hers and clasped it warmly as she led him to sit beside her, something most of the men must have noticed.

Kalgevun made a mighty fist, hunched over the meal where he stood and roared, "TROUT!!!!" – it made the new recruits jump, but the older guards all began to chant the same – "Trout! Trout! Trout!" and stamped their feet in time until they had served themselves a portion. Kalgevun pushed his way to the front, but he returned with a plate for Dyneti and Selvorne, then took a position with the others to wait his turn.

Everyone was happy, and there was plenty of fish. Traglan and Bitier were good cooks, and had wrapped the trout in leaves that added flavour and kept the flesh moist. The smaller fish was tastier, but sadly a little overcooked, the larger fish was more subtle and very tender. Selvorne had never tasted trout cooked in leaves like that before, and asked all the details, which Traglan explained. He might have been a poor, simple lad, but he was not completely simple of mind, and Selvorne thought that when Traglan did eat, he ate very well by taking great care to prepare his meal.

When the feast finished and all had a chance to settle, Dyneti sang a few songs and told a few stories. Many of the new recruits had never seen her so close, and wondered what her connection was with Selvorne, with whom she was so familiar. Even the arrogant three were impressed, for although she was no lady, she was known to be amongst the five highest Waehdric of the lands. Selvorne did not know that, and he only learnt it by first overhearing it, then asking Dyneti directly – all she said was "perhaps," and she was polite, but did not wish to speak of it, likely for modesty.

All was happiness, for a long time until the sun set and the twilight of the night became darkness lit by flame. A lone figure appeared, stepping out of the shadows to join them – it was Demni, and Selvorne thought he could hear the hearts of men sinking around the fire. There was silence as all expected some kind of abuse – for noise, revelry, disorder, ale, not having a man positioned at watch, not seeing her approach, crooked clothing, slouching in their seat ... not sharing the meal. Selvorne hoped she was not fond of trout.

However, she said nothing of the sort. Demni was not there to be a nuisance, nor as a commander of guards, nor as an administrator – she was looking for Dyneti, and happily pushed Kalgevun aside to sit with her quietly, and they spoke in whispers no one could hear. Selvorne thought Demni looked a little sickly. Dyneti gave her some water and cared for her until she fell asleep before the fire, curled up on the ground. It perhaps was not correct to say the guards did not like her much – all were concerned for her health, especially Selvorne, who wondered if she was sick from the food.

"She will be all right," Dyneti assured them, "she is just a bit ill."

Dyneti looked concerned though, and kept checking Demni's forehead, which was one moment hot and the next it was cold, so she draped a cloak over her or removed it accordingly. Demni was fading in and out of sleep, and mumbling.

"You care for her a lot," Selvorne said, handing Dyneti a wet cloth. Dyneti was about to dab it on Demni's forehead, but she had suddenly cooled again.

"Of course, she is my oldest friend," Dyneti said, stroking her head. She continued to speak, recalling fond memories of their time in their youth when they trained together with the Waehdric. Selvorne thought she was speaking more to Demni than to himself, but he listened.

"We had many good years together, learning, playing, singing and dancing – and we would travel to different towns, meeting people. It was a lovely time, until she left to join the administrators."

At that, Demni tensed – rigid, and her eyes opened with a piercing stare into the fire. A few moments, then she closed them and curled up. Selvorne bit his lip, and Dyneti was doing the same.

"We still meet when we can," Dyneti continued, stroking the head of her friend, and she then applied the wet cloth, for Demni seemed very hot, "there, relax, be at ease my darling Demni, you will be all right."

Comforting words for her friend who was ill – but Dyneti raised her free hand and gave a sudden gesture to the men, and in a moment Kalgevun appeared at her side. She whispered something to him. He grabbed a torch and ran back to the inn, and Dyneti turned to Selvorne.

"Can you carry her?"

"I ... think so. Where?"

"Back to the inn. I need my things."

"Some of the others are stronger," Selvorne suggested, wondering if he could lift Demni, for she was quite tall.

"But she trusts you, and so do I."

"She said that?" Selvorne asked.

"No, but I can tell. I assure you, she is very light. Please!"

Selvorne slipped his arms under Demni and lifted her straight up. She was very light as Dyneti said – tall, but slender, he fancied he could almost lift her over his head. Hard, though – she was strong, and tense, but then went soft. Dyneti spoke some parting words to reassure the other guards, suggesting they sleep soon, and keep a watch, and assemble early the next morning. Taking a torch to light the way, she prevented anyone following – except Rohy, who seemed to her to be the most concerned, so he carried a torch as well, as Selvorne carried Demni.

By the time they arrived, Kalgevun had assembled others and erected tents at the front of the inn, started a fire, arranged lamps, laid out a blanket and brought boxes from the cart. Selvorne was amazed he had done so much so soon, though it did take a while to carry Demni back from the camp. Selvorne laid her on the blanket and Dyneti began mixing what he thought were remedies, known only to the Waehdric. The three elder Waehdric were there, examining her and offering ideas on how best to make her well.

Selvorne and Rohy backed out of the way and watched. At one point the innswoman came out began berating them for establishing a camp at the inn grounds, but a few cold words from one of the guards sent her scurrying back to the inn. Selvorne thought Demni might be better inside, but they had tents, and furs, and cold water, and needed to keep her well – and knew far more than he did. Likely about everything. It was a warm night, a few clouds, the moon was no longer full and there was no sign of rain, though he still thought it would be better inside.

When Demni seemed to be finally, peacefully asleep, Dyneti approached Selvorne and Rohy.

"Thank you, both – you had best get some sleep. We will be with her all night. I think she will be all right."

"Are you sure?" Rohy asked, and Dyneti touched his arm.

"I think so. She was sick like this years ago, and I nursed her then. One winter, she had cut all her long hair off, then promptly caught a chill, and was sick for a week. Worse than this, she was coughing, or complaining, or sneezing, and quite tedious."

Dyneti half smiled, but Selvorne thought she was trying to convince herself more than them, so he agreed with her, then he and Rohy returned to the camp for a restless night. Rohy could not sleep, worrying for Demni, and Selvorne could not sleep, worrying that it was his fault.

~

Selvorne was not sure if he woke early, or had not slept as the light of dawn crept over the distant mountains. Sitting, he looked around – everyone was asleep, including the watch. Rohy was missing, and he felt restless, so he decided to head to the inn to see if Demni had recovered.

As Selvorne neared the inn, he saw Rohy's body slumped beside the stump of a tree – motionless – awkward – as though draped across the path. Selvorne froze – then dropped amongst the long grass. Nobody was about. A few birds, no other sounds. Silence ... and then, snoring. Frowning, crawling forwards, he realised Rohy was asleep, not killed. Exhausted, certainly looking dead the way he was crumpled up against the stump. Selvorne took a deep breath, then sighed.

Propped up against the stump, Selvorne had a good view down the gentle hill to the inn. There were bodies around the tents, it looked like the slaughter of a battle, but every so often one would roll over. And there – in the open space of the yard – a figure was dancing silently, spinning, turning, wheeling her arms in great circles, then leaping. It was Demni – he was sure of it – her hair was long and swung wide as she turned.

"Is she still dancing?" Rohy asked, stirring and blinking, "Oww! What ... what is this?"

Rohy rubbed his side – he had slept on an exposed root by the stump that looked very uncomfortable.

"Yes, dancing," Selvorne said, turning back to Demni, "she is ... she is very good at it, too."

"It was much darker when I came down here, I am going back to sleep."

Rohy was about to leave, but on seeing Demni dance, he watched for a little longer. Demni performed a few difficult moves with perfection, which was impressive enough, and then she attempted a few impossible ones – with slight failure, and they stared in awe. At one time she tried to stand – on one hand, legs in the air and pointed, her other arm out to the side – then, tumbling down, she fell into a roll.

"Have you seen anyone so good?" Selvorne asked with wide eyes.

"Yes," Rohy replied in a low voice, "I have seen tumblers do that – but never on one arm, she almost had it. And never so ... eloquently. She should do a show. People would pay to see this – I would. A lot, if I had the coin."

Demni stopped dancing and began looking over the sleeping bodies. She seemed to be searching for something, and poked at the men – after a few, she dashed off towards the river.

"So ends the show," Rohy said, "and it only cost a bruise. I thank you, again – that is the second time you woke me to see her – are you sure you are not enchanted?"

"Quite sure, I am ... well, no, not truly. But the first was luck and this – I was heading down to check she was well. It seems she is more than well."

"More than well ... she is ... " Rohy began, but he could find no words, and gazed after Demni. Selvorne laughed.

"She certainly is something," Selvorne said, "and I am enchanted, perhaps – from a distance. Or when close, when she is silent – and does not glare – nor frown, nor sneer. Now I think of it, at a distance, quite lovely."

"When close, none of that matters," Rohy said.

"When close, she is rarely silent, and always looks like – oh," Selvorne said, for Rohy was grinning, and Selvorne shook his head, "I see. That close – I guess you would not hear her raspy voice or complaints, if kissing?"

Rohy grinned wider.

"Indeed," Selvorne said, "well, perhaps not – but you had better do a good job of it, I cannot imagine how she might complain if you did not – silent, for the kiss, complaining for a week after, perhaps, at how poorly it was performed. Enchanting – to watch, hidden, as we have – but terrifying to think of her as – ”

“Oh, Selvorne, be quiet,” Rohy said, for his mood was growing poor, “you are ruining my dream. And I like her voice.”

“Like an old rusty nail drawn slow from dry wood,” Selvorne said, and Rohy glared at him – Selvorne laughed, “now you seem as disapproving as her – will you dance for me, Rohy?”

Rohy chuckled, and the two of them headed back to the camp, to sleep if they could before all the others woke.

~

Selvorne woke to heavy shaking and sudden bright sunlight in his face.

“You! Wake up! We would not have been so quiet, had we known you sleep so well!” yelled the voice of – was it Nakla?

The others had woken, and quietly packed the camp, but had let Selvorne and Rohy sleep as they did. The guard watching the camp had seen them return late, and they thought it only fair, as they had been helping Demni, and had brought fish to share. The guards had even arranged a shelter made from a cloak and many sticks, to keep the light off their faces as they slept in the morning sun.

Late – not too late, yet all the guards hurried to assemble at the inn, expecting an early start to the day, but those at the inn were disorganised and exhausted. Confused, too, as guards stumbled about trying to pack the camp. Guests of the inn who had slept well poked fun at them, and the Rough Roasters – the name given to those unpleasant men who had sold the pig at terrible prices – they were up early, started roasting, and already serving something that smelled delicious to the growing crowd.

None of those outside at the front of the inn had slept well. They were scattered about the yard, few in tents, and were vague when ordered or asked to tasks. All except Demni, who was standing by a short wall, growing weary of assuring everyone in turn that she was fine, not ill, had never felt better, and her only complaint was having to answer to idiots who asked. Only the first few dared try to feel her forehead.

Dyneti seemed worse than Demni that morning, being unrested and dazed. She was trying to gather her things for the small waggon cart, but kept forgetting what was packed and what was not, what she took and what went to the men, and the goat was missing, which caused her great distress, so when she looked at Selvorne, it was with exhausted eyes.

“Morning, Selvorne – could you find Gruffy for me?”

“Who?” Selvorne asked.

“The goat. Who pulls my cart. He has wandered off.”

Gruffy – very well. A funny name, but – a goat, and important to pull the cart. He was quite big for a goat, likely from years of pulling carts instead of frolics in the fields. Strong, too. Selvorne headed off, wondering where a goat might go. Thinking that they liked to eat all the time with any chance that they had, it might have gone to the vegetable patch. A moment of horror as he thought the poor thing might be trapped there – he ran, but the patch was as barren as usual, no sign of any animals, or vegetables, or goats, or even hoof prints in the dirt.

Heading down to the river, he looked about the grass. Perhaps it was thirsty? Could it fall in the river? Could goats swim? If not, did they know it, or did they leap into the waters and bleat helplessly as they washed away?

"Gruffy! Gruffy!" Selvorne called, wondering if goats came when summoned. Pigs would at times, though usually for feed – goats tended to have a will of their own, if not the cleverness of a pig, they were rather defiant.

The smell of the roasting wafted down to the river – it smelled good. It was not pig, he could tell that much, for he was ... used to pigs, and there were no ... pigs left to cook. Selvorne took a deep breath – his heart sank, and he ran to the beginnings of the bridge, where the Rough Roasters were cooking. A large crowd were eagerly pushing their way to be served. Selvorne was more than eager, he was desperate, so he pushed his way through their bodies and abuse.

"Wait your turn," one of the roasters cheerfully ordered, enjoying the busy morning, with a wide smile – until he saw it was Selvorne, "no – none for you!"

Selvorne stopped and stared – in horror. His mind grew foggy, but were it clear, he could not think of a gentle way to tell Dyneti that her beloved Gruffy was rotating on a spike over a fire to feed a crowd. But he had to tell her, and quickly, so he forced his way out through the jeering crowd, and ran back to her.

He told her plainly. At first – vague disbelief, a shaking head, the tired annoyance that Selvorne would dare play such a prank on her, so cruel, even after – then she sniffed the air, and her face was all horror. For a moment, and Selvorne felt grim – but he saw her take a deep breath and regain her wits, calm herself – faster than he had ever done himself, or seen. Moments, a few breaths – the calmness of a killer – then one deep breath, before she almost yelled for Kalgevun. Stronger, sweeter than a yell, but every bit as loud, and almost as terrifying. He ran to her and when he arrived, she had slumped to sit on the ground beside the cart.

Kalgevun and Dyneti spoke in low voices. Selvorne did not hear the commands, but the guard stood in a way that almost seemed he would draw his sword. Instead he signalled, and a dozen men ran to him, then all marched in formation upon the bridge. There was a lot of shouting and complaints, but Kalgevun returned with six guards, two on each of the roasters, only one of whom dared struggle, and that was no use.

Dyneti had been breathing deeply and her expression, though every few moments it was that of a distressed girl, had fixed itself to that of a fiercely serious woman. She rose before them and stared at each in turn, with a glare so cold and accusing, long enough to change their faces as well – from defiant, to ashamed. Or afraid. When all were silent, she spoke.

"Tell me now, clearly and completely, how you came to have a goat roasting this morning, when there were no animals around this entire village, none in the pens, none roaming free, save for my poor cart goat, which now has gone?"

Her voice was cold, and seemed to give them a chance to explain themselves, but Selvorne detected accusation, pain, anger, and distress. Not fear, however, if anything she was struggling to restrain fury.

"We found it," the first man blurted out.

"You found it? You mean, you took it and killed it?"

"No, it was already dead. We thought it was wild. It was dead, down by the river."

"You found a dead goat by the river, and thought you would take it, and roast it, without finding its owner?"

"We thought it wild! We asked him," the roaster pointed to the inn boy, who had come out to see what the fuss was in the yard – with his mother, who stared at him at once.

"He said it was not his. And it was dead, on his land. So he said we could have it," another roaster explained.

Hearing that, the innswoman turned to the boy and hit him hard across the head. He did not flinch, he just glared at her, she stepped back and stared.

"True, they asked me," the inn boy said, turning away from his mother. It seemed to Selvorne that he was very bold that morning, "it was dead on the grass. They gave me a silver coin for it."

He dug out a coin from a pouch at his belt, and held it out. His mother tried to grab it, but he snatched it back and glared at her. She shrank away, surprised, and he offered it to Dyneti.

"I did not know – it was your goat? I am sorry. Have this. I did not kill it," he looked at the roasters, "I think they did not kill it. It was a mess. I would not have cooked it."

Some of the people who were eating the goat whilst listening to the arguments stopped – looked at the meat, smelled it, then went back to eating quickly, lest their meal was to be taken away.

Dyneti did not take the coin. Doing so would have immediately admitted an agreement that she accepted the sale of the goat. She tried to maintain her authority, but Selvorne thought she was wavering, and unsure what to do, and that all the guards were watching to see exactly what she would do. If she was considered high amongst the Waehdric, she would have to judge well, measure punishment and enforce the law – at times. He thought she was too young for such a role, and he could see the goat meant a lot more to her than a mere beast of burden, or a stolen meal.

As she considered what to do, Temnere stepped out of the inn. It was late in the morning, even for him, and he blinked in the sunlight, dazed as though he had been drinking. Looking over the yard, he strode straight over to Dyneti and the restrained men – if they were anxious being held by guards, they were starting to shake to see Temnere staring down at them – he was known to be harsh, and, in the absence of a lord, he was the highest authority they feared. Dyneti outranked him in many ways, but unlike her, he was not obliged to be considerate or fair. It must have occurred to them that they had cooked and eaten a goat belonging to the Waehdric, and so the beast was under control of the administration – if it had not before, it certainly did as Temnere stared at them in silence, standing to his full height, which was half a foot more than most men.

"What is this?" Temnere demanded.

Kalgevun gave a summary. Temnere thought about it for only a moment.

"Fifty meals from the goat, thirty bits for each man you must pay, as a start. The carcass is yours to cook and sell, but five bits for each meal you sell goes to Dyneti, who owned the goat, and you must pay for that you have already sold. Charge nine at the least to be ahead. The guards must be served first, starting with me, and we will pay no more than ten, with generous portions. So I rule."

The men dared to argue, but Temnere raised one hand and continued, "Failure to comply will result in fingers for bits. For every coin short of my estimates, we will take one finger from each of you, in turn, to a count of no more than four each, and then toes to a count of eight. Men, release them to serve, guard them, collect the coins. I will be inside."

At that, Temnere turned and left – straight back inside, to wait for his meal.

Everyone was shocked – everyone, including the guards. Severe, even for Temnere, even if the second decree was merely a threat to make them comply with the first. Selvorne had to admit that even with a severe threat for the second, the resolution of the first was quite fair, and if Dyneti wished to contest it, she could not argue that it was not generous in her favour. Except ... she cared for the goat dearly, much more than just a goat. She had only nodded once before Temnere left, and Selvorne was not sure that he cared – or that she had meant to agree. Dyneti glanced at the faces of others, briefly at each, and for a few moments at Demni, who was sitting across the yard on a low wall. She turned away from her friend, and Dyneti frowned, then looked to Selvorne, who could think of nothing to say.

Guards gathered around the roasting goat to mind the men and collect their meals – but those who seemed closest to Dyneti did not, and glared at the others who would dare to eat Gruffy, until very few remained near the roast. Dyneti did not take notice of who did or did not eat, but went to Demni for comfort. Demni was quite cold, though, saying it was just a goat, they could buy another, and guards could pull the cart to Hartlehk. At that Dyneti was terribly upset, and to Selvorne's astonishment, Nakla and Reklo pushed their way to stand before her, and both bowed.

"Reklo can pull the cart, for sure, he looks quite like a goat, is easily as strong, and almost as clever," Nakla said loudly, and Reklo made a face, not exactly like a goat, save for his stubble beard, and he bleated.

"Or, Nakla could pull the cart, if he walks backwards," Reklo suggested, "for his face has often been mistaken for the rear of a goat. Though not as pretty, and the conversation will be poorer."

The two started pounding at each other – mocking, rough blows that sounded loud and hurt little, and then wrestled themselves to the ground.

Dyneti laughed, thanked them, then took leave and disappeared behind the inn. The yard became busy once more as guards packed the camp, and ordinary travellers gossiped about what had happened. Demni jumped up, and though she looked after Dyneti, she instead went inside the hall – surely not to wait for a meal?

Selvorne ran after Dyneti and found her alone by the river, standing near a patch of bloodied grass, holding a broken halter. She wiped her eyes as he approached, and tried to look dignified, strong, proud, tough – but he shook his head, patted her shoulder, and let her cry on his chest, for a moment.

When she regained her dignity, she knelt to wash her face in the river. Standing, she watched the waters flowing past, for a few moments in silence before she spoke.

"It is only a goat, I know, but he was my goat, I raised and trained him, I will miss poor old Gruffy. He deserved better than this," she said, waving her hand behind her at the bloodied grass, "and I cannot let something like this upset me."

"Why?" Selvorne asked.

"Because I cannot let Temnere take my authority like that. Even if he is right. I should have added a condition. Administrators serve Waehdric, not the other way around, though he would want it that way, and sometimes acts as though it is."

That was a surprise to Selvorne, he thought the Waehdric were their own authority, the administrators were their own as well, the lords were different, yet again, and each had their own guards. But then, he had almost no experience of Waehdric or administrators in his small town, and in Tavalehk had heard only the moans of Arnlausa and agreements of his men. Arnlausa had said once that the whole thing was, "beyond complicated," and the only thing that truly needed to be known was that a lord ruled in his own lands, but must obey the laws common to all the land. That might have been fine for him, but it was hardly much help to anyone who was not a lord.

"And the Waehdric serve the lords?" Selvorne asked.

"No, the Waehdric serve the people. And so do the lords, unless they serve themselves," Dyneti replied, but then she added, "although, in this case, the Lord of Hartlehk would overrule either of us, on his own lands. And knowing him, someone might soon be hanging from a tree, or losing his head. Any other lord would have a say, were he here, but in his own lands, Ruchten rules. Unless ...." she said, then struggled, as if trying to remember something, "unless it was me who did the crime, or Temnere, or another lord, or someone under the protection of another lord, for example, a man speaking on our behalf, or one of our runners. Any of the guards, commanders. It is complicated, delicate, but essential to get it right. The people need to see it is done right, and I failed, not in the law, not in fairness, but in a show of clarity and strength."

Selvorne thought she was showing a lot more strength as she spoke, and was growing in determination as she explained – and then seemed to have had an idea. He looked on her with wonder – how did she manage, she was only a year or so older than he was, but had such a weight upon her, at times. Since the moment he first had met her, she had almost no rest from many exhausting situations – performances, intrigues of murder and brigands, defiant and annoying men, others who were ... lost in her eyes. Not only himself, many men watched her, wherever she went. And he could not guess what subtle manipulations were going on between herself and others of power. As he watched her look out to the river, she turned to him, and her eyes seemed to be trying to stare through his own.

"Do you like Temnere?" Dyneti asked.

"I – he is an odd fellow," Selvorne replied.

"But – do you like him?

"He was ... he seemed quite kind, when I first met him."

"When?"

"At the festival."

"Just now?"

"Now? No – days ago. He thanked me, for helping someone."

"Who?" Dyneti asked, and Selvorne frowned a little – she was being very ... suspicious.

"I helped an old man climb stairs on the path, if you must know. Temnere noticed, and said it was a kind thing to do."

"Did he ... do you usually help old men climb stairs? Or only when Temnere watches?"

Selvorne, who thought she was being odd, began to wonder if it was another joke.

"Are you ... teasing me?" Selvorne asked. Dyneti continued to stare, and then stifled a laugh as he stared back, "What?" Selvorne asked, a little annoyed, but she put a hand to his shoulder.

"You are a strange man, Selvorne. Most are not fond of Temnere. Smart, clever – too clever, and he thinks everyone else is not. Rarely kind, and it is odd that he likes you."

"He – likes me? He has an odd way of showing it, then. He was very demanding at the inn, when he – "

"That, Selvorne, is liking you – you truly do not know him?"

"No, and I am beginning to wonder if I want to."

Dyneti nodded and was quiet, and Selvorne felt uneasy.

"Cienn likes him," Dyneti said in a low voice.

"Cienn – our leader?"

"Ours?"

"The ... Waehdric, and so ... for all of us ... she is our leader. You do mean her?" Selvorne asked, and Dyneti nodded.

"Yes. There is but one – no, actually, there are a few, but ... yes – Cienn, our leader. She is fond of Temnere."

"Will I meet her?" Selvorne asked, not particularly caring about Temnere. At that, Dyneti tilted her head.

"Why would you want to meet Cienn?"

An odd question – who would not want to meet Cienn, Leader of the Waehdric, oldest lady of the entire lands. Selvorne frowned back at her, and she tilted her head a little more.

"And you have nothing to say," Dyneti said.

"I ... did not know I had to have a reason? Surely anyone would want to meet Cienn?"

At that, Dyneti smiled, and he thought she had been holding her breath, for she breathed out, almost a sigh. She nodded, and kept smiling.

"It is no matter – yes, I think you might meet her, but do not mention it, and I cannot say when, she is fickle in her age – does not like to meet people anymore, and those the least who should have most cause to seek her – do not tell the men, to get their hopes up. That, by the way, is an order – do you accept?"

"Do we accept orders?"

"Oh yes, if you are wise and do not wish to be punished for rejecting them," Dyneti said, "a man might lose quite a few fingers for that."

Selvorne winced, and Dyneti shook her head.

"But all his pride, for challenging me."

An odd thing to say, but the day had been very strange, and her mood had lifted – he could see it in her eyes. She thanked him – and hugged him, her gratitude surprising and unearned, and her embrace – unexpected. Overwhelming, to hold her, he almost collapsed, but then she stepped back and left him to join the others. Selvorne stood, looking at the river, heart pounding, mind spinning, wondering how he would cope with all that was upon him – too many things he did not understand. Not least of all the sudden embrace, and the way it made him almost fall.

Should he have stepped in to the ruling – as Lord Heir of Tavalehk, he had power. But no, not for a goat. Not even Gruffy. Not even for Dyneti's fond affection for a pet, or to save her some sorrow. Three days' journey south, his father lay dead in a barrel, nothing was going to force him to reveal himself before a time of his choosing – before he knew it was safe. Gritting his teeth, he looked at the grass beside the trickling waters, wondering if a rabbit could take down a goat, and if not a rabbit, then what could have made such a mess of the lawn. And what animal could not only tear a leather harness from a cart, but would bother removing it from the goat. And then ... most disturbing of all ... not eat the carcass once it was dead.

One Amongst Us

It seemed the guards were going to wait all morning as some of the men were served and ate the goat. Those doing the cooking could not charge as high a price, for if they did, none would buy – it was a very different day to the one before. All the people who had been trapped at the inn and previously had no choice for a meal, woke that day refreshed, and merely hours away from Hartlehk town. Not so far to walk, even on an empty stomach. So the roasters charged little, much of their earlier profit going to the guards, and they made the servings large to be done with it as soon as possible. For guards unwilling to eat the goat, it was painful to smell something so delicious, and to see servings so generous – and there was no escape as they all remained in the yard, wishing the breeze would blow the other way.

Dyneti had been speaking with some of her closest men and the other Waehdric, away from the others. When they returned they all seemed to have agreed on something of importance, then assembled the men to prepare for travel.

Kalgevun blew a small horn to gain the attention of the crowd, and Dyneti stood on the short wall to address everyone. They all were there – all the guards, new recruits at the back, Temnere and Demni had come out from the hall at the sound of the horn. Savak was holding his head as though sore, but he was there, and even Taahr was good enough to come forth from his room, having risen late. He seemed unwell rather than rude, and was rubbing his stomach.

"As you are all aware," Dyneti began, in her strongest voice, no longer distressed, but forceful and commanding, "this morning, some tragedy befell Gruffy."

Several of the travellers and one of the new recruits sniggered at the name, but was soundly thumped by an older guard.

"Gruffy – yes, an amusing name, he was a pet, and just a goat. But he was also a member of our guards – served with me for many years, and as a member lost, deserves the proper respect that any of you would receive – if any terrible accident befell you," Dyneti said, then paused, letting her words become clear to all, though none knew what she was up to, Selvorne thought that all the guards could see that the goat had been a devoted ally, in a strange kind of way.

"Gruffy was loyal, and deserves our honour, for if any of you fell, you would be so honoured, and others would step forth to take your place, for in the same cause we are all servants, all equal – but servants, nonetheless, regardless of title, status, or rank."

With that she glared directly down from the low wall at Temnere, who stared back at her in silence.

"Some of you have honoured Gruffy, giving him respect in his death. Others have paid him no more honour than a common goat, kept for food. For shame! Gruffy, who carted your heavy loads over steep hills, through the mud and rain with no complaint, for many years saving you toil. He carried your food and ale, and made your travels easy. For shame!"

At that, men were starting to feel ashamed, and bowed their heads.

"Gruffy was not just a goat, he was years of my patience, training and care. He was a noble beast, and a strong ally. His passing must now be replaced. Here, I have many coins of profit from the dishonourable sale of his flesh. This is his inheritance, and it is proven he was rich – I shall distribute it according to his wishes, as I who knew him best, believe he would desire. The Will of Gruffy – a portion to purchase three more goats, one elder and two younger to train. Six new harnesses that are comfortable and strong. Coats for all the goats, for the winter and the rain. And to all my loyal allies, brave and noble guards, there at my death – I leave the rest of my wealth to be distributed equally."

Selvorne had never heard of a goat leaving an inheritance, however his understanding was that it certainly was possible, the biggest problem either being explaining the laws to the goat, or interpreting its will. And that few goats had any wealth to leave. The signing was easy enough, but he was unsure if a goat would willingly put its hoof in ink, and if so, not then everywhere else on the parchment or scroll, or indeed, the table, witnesses and every place where it walked. Nevertheless, it was possible by law – Dyneti would know better than he, and a huge crowd was gathering, all those who had stayed at the inn, and the Rough Roasters, who were regretting ever coming to that place, fearing what might come next.

"And I, as the Commander of Gruffy, now decree that his most important role be filled by his allies. I name those who dishonoured his death to repay this debt, as is standard practise," Dyneti said, and then she stared directly at Temnere.

Everyone stared at Temnere. He had been silent – glaring, angry and restrained – but when she said that, he frowned and looked thoughtful. He stroked his chin, then relaxed and shrugged his shoulders.

"I agree," Temnere said, "you are right. Well argued."

A short bow, and he went to gather his things. A few people were chuckling, others looked quite glum, perhaps ashamed, and hid – others were almost celebrating, with wide smiles and the bumping of elbows to ribs.

"What just happened?" Selvorne asked Rohy, who shrugged his shoulders – in much the same way as Temnere had, but with a look of confusion, not resignation – so they turned to Kalgevun.

"Something very clever," Kalgevun replied, his face full of pride, "a very clever interpretation of the law and customs that put Temnere in his place. She will go far to put things right – I am proud to serve with her today. Every day – but today, especially so."

Still confused, for it was hardly an answer, Selvorne soon discovered for himself what was happening. The coins paid as compensation for the roasting of the goat were substantial, more than enough to purchase a few more goats, harnesses and all the things she had described. From hungry, eager travellers they had taken back more coins than the cost of the goat, and most of the profit from the past few days that the Rough Roasters had earned. That was a lesson in itself, to any who would take such advantages in the future.

The remaining coins were to be split between all the guards who had not eaten the meat, and those who had – and it was the best part of all – were to fill the role of the goat. Selvorne only realised what that meant when the first of them was harnessed to the cart, and began pulling it down the road towards Hartlehk.

The entire guard followed, leaving the River Bridge Inn, crossed the bridge, and headed north on the road to Hartlehk. The new recruits walked together at the rear, and the older guards walked ahead, some solemn, some laughing.

"Ha! That is not punishment! I would have done it for fun!" Reklo said to the others.

But it was punishment of sorts, because it made them ashamed for their actions. They each did not have to pull it far, and it was not difficult, nor heavy, and the group did not walk at a fast pace. Each one at the end of their turn was thanked by Dyneti personally, and patted on the arm – so kindly that soon people were looking forward to the task, and others may have wished they had eaten of the goat. She must have noticed that, for she began wandering from man to man who had not, and thanked him several times, in much the same way, walking with them and remembering times past when they had travelled together, when Gruffy had pulled the cart.

Demni was not impressed with her punishment, as she had eaten the meat, something that horrified Dyneti when she found out – the two of them had known Gruffy as a kid, fed him together and raised him. Demni argued that he was already dead, which hardly helped matters. Unable to spare her the indignity, Demni was harnessed and had to pull the cart along, just as all the men had, during which she spoke not a word. At the end, she turned her back on Dyneti, and strode off ahead of everyone.

Temnere was oddly accepting of his fate. He was a man who believed in doing things by the word of law – to follow the rules as written, as read, as meant, as interpreted. Dyneti had reasoned perfectly. He was not ashamed of eating the meat, and did not care for the goat – indeed, he declared that its death was very profitable, as one goat would become three, and meals, and coins, and harnesses. In an odd way he was almost proud of the beast for having done so, as if it had sacrificed its life to enrich the guards. Or the administrators purse, which supplied the guards.

He felt some shame, however, for his oversight of the law. Selvorne began to wonder if Temnere thought he should have suggested the men pull the cart. It certainly seemed that way, for Temnere not only did not complain, but pulled the cart with vigour. Which was strange in itself, because he usually walked with a stoop and a slight limp, and seemed often tired – but he dragged it both uphill and down with good speed and almost an expression of joy.

Taahr was glad he had none of the goat, though he was very hungry. He had overslept, claimed his head ached as agony, his belly was grumbling and food would make him ill – he declared such woes often and to any unfortunate enough to be near, even those he had already told. He hid his eyes from the sun by walking with one arm folded over his brow, when he was not scratching his body all over. An odd rabble of men had joined him, and suffered the worst of his complaining. Selvorne learnt from Savak that they were his northern guard, and they were all returning to the north. Apparently they had been drinking through the night, and Taahr could not remember anything from then, or even the morning, except that for much of it his head rang like metal pots clanging together. Savak admitted quietly that was actually himself, clanging metal pots together outside Taahr's window – to wake the men, of course.

Temnere ended his turn reluctantly and was unharnessed. He stretched out his arms and declared that pulling the cart had fixed his back. Delighted, he waved his arms over his head. He was tall, six and a half feet, most of the men guessed, with broad shoulders and long limbs. He was not muscular, not by any measure, having spent so many years stooped over a table writing orders, keeping accounts – he was usually hunched, slightly pale of skin, and his dark hair was beginning to whiten. The day before he looked older than he should, but after pulling the cart, he seemed almost young again. Dyneti thanked him as she had the others, and he nodded with solemn respect. Then, with vibrant delight for his newfound vigour, he marched rapidly along the road, passing all the men, many of whom stared in astonishment.

~

It was only a few miles before they passed the ruins of the Bettah Inn – the entire building had been made hastily from wood, so it burnt to cinders and ash. Selvorne wondered how different things would have been had the inn stood. All the travellers would have been there, all the guards would have had the River Bridge Inn to themselves. Perhaps Dyneti would have sung, perhaps ... he took a deep breath. Perhaps it was not such a bad thing that Gruffy died. One of the men, she had said of the goat – better he, than one of the others – one of the actual men. And it could easily have been, for no creature that could do such a thing to a goat, could not instead have done the same to a man.

Dyneti told no one of the blood they had found, but a few knew – the boy at the inn did, having seen it, and was warned. Wolves or a bear – neither of which had been seen for a very long time, but the mountains were near and such creatures might come down during the night. That must have been what she was telling the others, she said nothing to Selvorne, but it was clear something big, silent and … not hungry, perhaps it was frightened away by a noise. Hopefully by fire – the guards had camped away from the inn with a fire through the night. It made him shudder, though, to think something might have been lumbering around in the shadows.

Passing through small settlements, they rounded a hill and looked down on the wide valley of Hartlehk town. A powerful river came from the mountains in the east, through the town, then cascaded down the waterfalls of Hartlehk. Below was the river that widened to form the great lakes of Senylehk. It flowed all the way to the sea in the west, passing three more towns as it did – from Hartlehk to Senylehk, Dartehs, and Vonersehl – then the sea.

The lands were grassy fields of low bushes, tree stumps, and a few small trees, but otherwise quite barren, so it was easy to see across the entire area. Many wooden houses had been built on both sides of the river, most were low, some were tall, few were far from the water and some seemed to be partly in it, sitting on stilts as though built on half bridges. It never flooded in the main river – it merely flowed faster every spring – but someone had cut small channels leading away from it, for watering farmland. Selvorne was sure such canals would flood at times, so the farmhouses were built either on hills, or also on stilts.

It was not the same river as at Tavalehk, and not the same as that at the River Bridge Inn – it was the great river of Senylehk, and Selvorne wondered at the size of it. He had heard that fish swam all the way from the sea, up the river, jumping the falls, determined to reach the mountains, every year in great numbers – so many that if a man held out a pot, they would jump straight in. He did not believe that, but he did know there were great fish there, salmon, in many ways like trout, but larger. It had to be a story – the cascading waterfalls looked impossible for any fish to jump.

They came to the edge of the town and stopped on a slight hill, where a tollman sat in a small hut eating an early lunch. He dared to halt the procession to request their business – perhaps to charge a toll, and immediately regretted it when confronted by Temnere, who reminded him that administrators, guards and messengers were exempt from all tolls, on account of the fact that all tolls ultimately went to them. The tollman then foolishly suggested that, if carrying goods for sale, they might be acting as merchants, and so began the long, painful speech that gave the man an aching head for the day, and some of the guards the same as they listened.

Many of the guards ignored the tollman and walked past to enjoy the view. The hut was on a slight rise in the road, and had sweeping views to the west, with a glimpse of the tumbling waterfalls of the great river, and the huge lakes below that continued almost half the way to the sea, before narrowing back to a river. Dotted with islands, some green and some rocky grey, the water itself was very blue. It was a beautiful sunny day, though a cool breeze descended from the mountains in the east. Too soon they had to continue, though not too soon for the tollman.

By the Hartlehk piers they gathered, at the far west of the town on the southern side of the river, near the top of the cascading waterfalls. The piers were a dangerous place, for woodsmen floated huge logs down from the mountains, then collected them at a barrier of piled stones where they crashed and smashed into each other. Once gathered and stopped, they were released carefully, one at a time down the waterfalls, only to be collected at the bottom once more. Men working the docks had to ensure no boats were in the lake below, or they would be crushed by the logs – and also they had to be certain logs did not miss the barrier, or get stuck, or twist to block the waters of the river. To do so, they had to communicate with other men both upstream and down, and did so by yelling loudly over the crashing waters – and at times, blowing a horn as a warning. From a distance the river had seemed so peaceful, but when Selvorne and the guards stopped on the rise of a hill above the piers, they looked on what seemed to be deadly madness below.

The falls were very wide, which made it possible, if not much easier to send logs down. On narrow falls the logs would be hurled out instead of rolling nicely. Wide, and the fall itself was not too far – a brave man could sit in a strong boat, and perhaps, with luck, crash their way down. Bitier said that some fools had even sealed themselves in barrels for a dare, riding the falls inside, although that was likely not much safer than a boat. Anyone with any sense would leave their boat at the top of the falls, and walk the well–paved stairs to the bottom – taking another boat to continue their journey. Or at least stand aside and let their boat go down on its own. That would require carrying it up again, though, later, and – yes, on the far side of the river, men were doing just that – so people must have braved the cascades at times. Or at least their boats did.

"Barrels, stones, barrels, logs, barrels, rocks, barrels," Bitier said, "that is what is sent to the west. Stones and rocks often in barrels, amongst other things. Barrels are the most fun – a hundred barrels all at once, quite a thing to see, many come to watch, and sometimes place wagers on each as a race."

All the logs were held that day, not released to the river below. Bitier explained there must have been boating planned for later. There were too many logs and the stone barrier was beginning to be overrun. Two very large, wildly hairy men were arguing with the Pehrnohc at the pier, who was an older fellow, much smaller than they, but determined to have his way, shaking a long stick and poking it at the logs. One of the large men was shirtless, but his body was covered in hair so thickly it was like a vest. He wore trousers rolled to his knees and massive boots. The other wore a once elegant shirt that had seen too many years of service, rolled up to his elbows, and his trousers were tied at his knees – he also had massive boots that came half the way to his knee. His beard and hair were braided neatly, where the other man's beard and hair went in all directions at once, his beady eyes gleaming from within. Selvorne thought they both looked very intimidating, being huge in muscles and girth and height, and boots – with frightening, booming voices. But after a few moments he realised, although shouting, it was not in anger, but to be heard over the waterfalls – and they were half joking with the Pehrnohc, trying to get their way, knowing well they had no chance, but trying anyway.

The night before some guards had gone ahead to Hartlehk, having claimed to do so to gather new recruits, and to Selvorne's surprise it was not just an excuse to avoid the unpleasant inn. They had two new men with them, and all were enjoying ale by the pier, waiting for the others to arrive – guards were up quickly when Temnere appeared, and introduced two new youths. Or, rather oddly, they introduced Temnere and the other guards to the new recruits – and then presented them in turn.

"This is Vugecarauk, of the family Arauk," one guard began, as a huge, tall, heavy youth with masses of wild black hair grinned and bowed, then looked embarrassed as the two large men by the piers clapped and cheered.

"And may I present Orrikler Ultainen," the guard said, and the second youth performed an elegant bow. He was average in height and build, but very well groomed, with short, neat sandy hair, a well–trimmed small beard, tailored trousers and a buttoned shirt. His boots were only a medium height, but had no less than seven buckles, and though that seemed a little too many to Selvorne, none of them seemed to be there just to look fine. Temnere returned the bow to Orrikler with great precision, as did all the guards, and Selvorne wondered why his name was so familiar.

"Greetings, young Ultainen," Temnere said, "you need not go with the others, and may ride with us."

"I prefer to be treated as any others," Orrikler insisted, "just as the others, thank you."

"As you wish," Temnere said, then bowed again, though the guards were not sure if they were meant to bow as well. Selvorne thought Temnere was trying very hard to impress the young man, who seemed not to care one bit.

Once introduced, they were expected to join the other new recruits. Vugecarauk began greeting the others, but Orrikler stood there, not exactly being unfriendly, and everyone avoided him.

Except Bitier. He snuck around behind Orrikler, and with a sudden loud crack, smacked his knuckle down hard on the back of his head.

"Oww!! What – " Orrikler yelled, then spun around – saw Bitier, and made a fist of his own, then chased him screaming about the guards until, catching him, he cracked him on the head. Then they both burst into laughter, firmly clasped hands and began to cheer in some chant known only to each other. Selvorne stared in amazement, and thought the only thing that could have been more surprising would be that if he discovered they had only just met.

~

The others began to greet each other, but Kalgevun came to Selvorne and told him to follow, then led him away from the other men, away from the road, down a small passage between buildings near the pier – passing Demni, who quickly stepped aside as she hurried along the other way. They went quite a way, west, past the waterfalls and came to the edge of the cliff, where there was a stone wall. From there, they could look down on the cascades and the lower piers, and the only person there was Dyneti, leaning on the wall, watching the waters below. She saw Selvorne, nodded to Kalgevun, and he returned to guard the path.

Selvorne had been wondering where she had gone, and though pleased to see her, she seemed very solemn.

"Hello!" he said merrily when he was near.

"Selvorne," Dyneti said, turning to him, almost whispering, and looking to see no others were about. He could hardly hear her over the waterfalls, though they were not so loud, "I have a favour to ask of you."

"Of course, what is it?"

"I have to leave you now, and head north, but I have a message I need delivered, and it must be done – and none must know."

Selvorne felt sad that she was leaving, but surprised she would think to send him, of all the men, with a message.

"Why?"

"Because it is a secret, silly," she said, and then laughed.

"No, I mean, why are you leaving?"

"Oh, well that, too, is a secret ..." she said, and she sounded serious – but then laughed, "no, that is not a secret, I have to go to the north to sing. And meet with some of the younger Waehdric – I will not be at Senylehk for a few weeks. But the message ... that needs to go now. And quietly. Yes?"

He nodded, and she explained.

"Dangerous news has reached me, and it must be passed on, but to one person only. By the end of the day, this day, one way or the other, you will meet a man named Tarbo. Do not ask for him, he will introduce himself. You must then ensure you are alone with him – completely alone – even if it takes a week, you must speak to him alone. I would prefer immediately, I hope before the night – but he is a difficult person to see, sometimes."

"And is the message for him?"

"Not ... exactly. When you get him alone, for whatever reason, and you are sure no others can hear, you must look straight at him, and tell him you have a message for Torlor. Then – "

"Torlor?" Selvorne asked, astonished to hear the name.

412

"Yes, Torlor. Then you – "

"Torlor, the unlucky name? From the poem?"

Dyneti looked at him with an odd frown, both eyebrows seeming to want to raise and lower at once. Selvorne took a deep breath, then recited what he knew.

"Torlor Kludbo Molarklod rue – in rushing and unlucky for you. Wishing to hide instead he will shout – stubbing his toe and yelping about. Torlor is – "

"Selvorne, I know the poem."

"And someone so named?"

Dyneti blinked several times, then seemed to grow serious.

"Torlor is who you will ask for – yes, that name – you will ask Tarbo, alone, and not mention the name Torlor to anyone else. Not to anyone else. And now, you must tell me where you heard this poem?"

Selvorne thought she was acting oddly – everyone knew the poem. All the children, anyway, it was a warning about being ... foolish. It did not seem to work for Selvorne, though he had known the verses his whole life. He knew another poem as well.

"Torlor the guard, so full of pluck. Torlor the guard, never in luck. Rode on a goat, fell in the muck. Washed by the pond, bit by a duck. Attacked on the road, his sword it got stuck. Dodging their blows, his leg it was struck. Torlor the name, brings you bad luck."

Dyneti burst into laughter, and struggled to regain her dignity as she leant on the wall.

"I have not heard that in a very long, long time," she said, but then grew serious once more, "nobody has sung it in many years, because they think it is bad luck to do so. How have you heard it? How do you know these poems?"

Selvorne could not think what was strange about either poem, everyone in the town knew it, his father taught it to him, at times they all would sing it. He remembered it very well because he also had a slight ... distrust of ducks. And geese. And Arnlausa said they might look weak, but could take a man's eyes, even his throat, if angered. And they were easily angered. And ... Arnlausa ... and his father – no, he could not say they used to sing it together.

"I read it somewhere," Selvorne said. Dyneti's jaw dropped, and she stared at him.

"You ... can ... read?"

Selvorne immediately realised how stupid a thing that was to say, for he had no way to explain how he had learnt to read.

"Just a little, I was lucky that my family had a collection of parchments with childish poems on them – and I asked everyone I met who could read, to read them to me, until I learnt a few words. Only a little, mind you."

"Truly ... " Dyneti said, but she likely did not believe him, and was already acting as though suspicious, but he could not guess why. She went to her small pack that was lying on the ground, and returned with a few parchments, and a fine charcoal wrapped in linen to write with, but that she put aside.

"What does this say?" she asked, holding out a parchment that was covered in writing – tiny words crammed to make best use of the page. It was a complex list of rules of law, copied in tiny, elegant writing, with notes scrawled in every available blank space. He wondered if that was her own hand, and admired the well–formed letters, if not the almost absurd overuse of the page.

"I cannot read that! Look how small it is, I can hardly make out the letters. It would take me a year to work that out, and likely the person who wrote it would have to explain it a hundred times."

Dyneti was not convinced. She rolled it up and handed him another, with larger letters on a scrap of parchment. It was a numbered list of all the items she was taking on a trip – tents, food, plates of wood, and, sadly, the coat for Gruffy in case of rain. She was determined to see how well he could read, and he was determined to convince her he was very bad at it, no matter how she tricked him.

"This is easier – a list of items," he said, then he proceeded to misidentify several items and numbers. She did not seem convinced, rolled it up, then her pout became a slight, almost wickedly curled grin. She took a scrap of parchment and her charcoal, and wrote something with long, elegant strokes.

With a completely blank expression on her face, she suddenly held it out for him to read.

"I love you."

He felt his heart stop in his chest – for a moment – then pound like a mallet, surging blood to his face. Just as quickly he bit his tongue hard, and looked at her – she was completely blank. No smile, no grin, no frown – nothing. Clever – very clever. Determined not to give anything away, he bit harder on his poor tongue.

"Ahh," he spoke clumsily, "a message, or a tally. It says 'one lost ewe', but the 'one' is written as a number. See, I can read a little, and – oh, oh no – do you mean Gruffy?"

With that he did his best to look horrified, but she stared back at him.

"No, I do not mean Gruffy," Dyneti said, "who was a goat, not a sheep, and whether you can read a little – or not – I would not let Temnere know it. None of the guards can read. Not at first. Anyone who can is taken to be a messenger, a runner, or administration – or rejected. He does not want guards who can read his business when they are running around freely on the island. Ignorant, and obedient. Some learn to read later on. Some of the sons of lords can read when they arrive, but they are exempt ... from many things. If he finds out, it will be a problem for both of us."

Selvorne was only paying half attention, wondering if Dyneti had meant what she wrote, for since the ruse was over, she was beginning to blush.

"When you are alone with Tarbo, tell him you have a message for Torlor – tell him the following message exactly, do not change it, do not let others hear, do not forget it – 'There is a duck amongst the geese, the eggs all look the same. But some may be bad.' That is the message, repeat it now."

Selvorne repeated the message, word for word, exactly the way she had said it.

"I would not talk about Torlor, nor recite that poem to Tarbo, if you know what is good for you. Some people think it is bad luck, they are just being silly. But if you say it to him, or around him, I assure you, bad luck will soon follow."

Kalgevun whistled from the path, and made a sign as if to hurry.

"Ergh, we have to get going, buy new goats and head north before the end of the day. Repeat it again!" Dyneti ordered, and Selvorne did so, exactly, even with the right pauses and tone.

"Tarbo, alone. Message for Torlor. I understand."

"No matter what happens, whether you join the guards or not."

"I swear it will be done. But what – "

She smiled and grabbed his hands.

"Thank you," she said.

"It is – of course, I – "

"I would have asked Demni, but she is not herself ... in one of her gruff moods. She said a lot of nasty things about Waehdric, I fear she is far closer to the administrators than us, now. I thought she was just upset for poor Gruffy, but she did not seem to care. Not at all, and she ... she ate him – which is horrible, since we raised him together, I even ... named him for her," Dyneti said, and seemed to grow furious as she spoke, but then paused and quickly added, "do not tell her that. She does not need to know that."

Then, with a slightly wicked smile, she took out the note she had written.

"When you are alone with Demni, hand her this note. That should cheer her up."

Selvorne looked at it, and thought there was no way he was going to hand over a note to Demni that said he loved her, not even in jest.

"One lost ewe? A strange thing to tell her – very well, and I will be sure to let her know it is from you."

Dyneti laughed, then seemed to grow solemn.

"In that case, I had better sign it," she said, then wrote something at the end of it, and handed it to Selvorne.

"Give it to her when she is truly down, in a poor mood, or acting exceptionally grim. And tell her it is from me. That should cheer her, and make her like you more. And please, could you watch her for me – she has sour moods, but usually is much nicer to be with."

With that she said farewell, told him to look for her in Senylehk in a few weeks, and ran off with her pack to join Kalgevun.

Selvorne opened the note and read, "I love you, your friend, Dyneti."

Stone Water Ale

Selvorne returned to the road near the piers and discovered everyone had gone. Except Rohy, who was waiting anxiously.

"Where have you been?" Rohy demanded.

"Ahh ... it was something personal. Where is everyone? And – where are my things?"

"Gone. Some went on the boats. Others were put in pairs and sent on errands around the town. Temnere was furious you were not here, but I spoke for you, and said I would be your partner and wait for you. He said if we do not make it on time, we are both out."

"I – oh – I did not know," Selvorne said, "sorry, how ... long have we got? To go where?"

"It is all right," Rohy said, easing a little, "we have plenty of time. I just – did not know where you were, and Temnere was quite strict. With everyone. You should have seen him get into the boat, though, he was afraid of falling out, then Demni was rocking it and pretending not to – I think he was more upset by that, than your wandering off."

Selvorne looked at the waterfall, looked at the boats – looked to the terrible whitewater crashing down the cascades, then looked at Rohy with wide eyes.

"Would you not be upset to be riding a boat down that?" Selvorne asked, waving at the falls, and Rohy frowned.

"Down there – they are taking the boats from down there, not up here – all the guards have gone to boats. We have to go in pairs when they come for us, because there are not enough boats for us all. They said it could take all day, so we should wait at the Axeman Inn, wherever that is – actually, they said we must wait at the Axeman Inn, and go there at once. And we have to wear this," Rohy said, then handed him a bright red scarf, and Selvorne noticed he had one himself tied around his left arm, "to signify we are with the guards. Something about the law of Hartlehk."

Rohy explained again that the older guards divided the new recruits into pairs, first asking them who they wanted to be with, and then putting them with someone else. Which was funny for Nakla and Reklo – they ended up together. Selvorne asked who Rohy chose, and he said Bitier, because he seemed to know the town best.

Rohy had Selvorne's pack, he had kept it aside, but more than half of what was in it had disappeared – taken and safe, he was assured, by boat to save it being carried. Selvorne doubted it was done for their convenience, but he had to admit he was relieved not to have to heave around the bronze pot and his wooden plates. The spear was gone – he hoped it was safe, but with his luck of spears it likely was lost. With so much removed, all he had that remained were some clothes and the sack pack itself.

Together they began to wander the streets of Hartlehk on the southern side of the river, looking for the Axeman Inn. Rohy seemed to be leading him away from the centre of houses, towards the forests in the east, though Selvorne found himself heading west at first, even though there was nothing in the west but the cliffs and the wild lands below. His head was filled with thoughts of Dyneti, her secrets, her eyes, and her message – and the one he had to deliver for himself – and so his feet wandered after his mind. Until Rohy led him the other way, and Selvorne was not sure he saw much of the town, for when he closed his eyes he saw Dyneti's mischievous smile and gazing stare, so found himself blinking quite often as he walked.

"She was truly glowing, today, magnificent," Rohy said as they walked.

"Yes, she is ... wonderful ... a very pretty lady, for sure," Selvorne said, as though in a dream.

"Well, I think striking is a better word. Dignified. Noble, and so elegant."

"Yes, striking – strikingly pretty. And very noble, earlier, she handled that very well, very dignified, and yet so ... vulnerable, at times. Still a girl."

"Far from a girl, or a maiden, though vulnerable, yes, she was shaking terribly."

"Oh, I did not see. Nerves, with all that has happened lately, but she is strong."

"Very strong. And tall."

"And ... adorably pretty."

"And – adorable? Pretty?" Rohy asked. He frowned, and stopped walking.

"You disagree?" Selvorne asked, stopping to face his friend, and Rohy shrugged. At that Selvorne frowned, "Did you say she is tall?"

"She is taller than you, my friend, easily. Taller than most women."

"Who are we talking about?" Selvorne asked – and then, as Rohy grinned, he realised – Demni, as usual. He wondered if it would be funny to get Rohy to hand her the note, then remembered it would not be much of a joke since Dyneti had signed it. And he shuddered to think how it could go wrong if she had not. Then it occurred to him they were wandering aimlessly, and were headed away from the town.

"Where did they say the inn was?" Selvorne asked.

"They did not say, they said it was a test to see how good we were at finding things in a strange town."

"Not a very fair test, since at least three of us call this town home."

"True, but they were sent first, and we all had to look the other way."

Rohy thought an inn called the Axeman would be near the forests, where axemen worked. That was why he was leading Selvorne away from the bridge and the main part of town, which was on the other side of the river. The southern side was much quieter, and though it was true that there had been much cutting of trees on that side, Selvorne argued that no woodsman would last long if they were drunk whilst chopping, and likely the Axeman would be near the piers, where they took their lumber at the end of the week – back at the bridge, where they had started. Perhaps on the other side, where the town truly began. After some thought, they both agreed it would more likely be an inn near where woodsmen lived, or near a blacksmith who sharpened and repaired axes, so they could drink as they waited.

"At least if that is true, we could look for the smoke coming from the forge," Rohy suggested.

"Or," Selvorne began, rolling his sleeve up to his shoulder to cover the red band, "we could just ask someone."

He walked straight up to a man with huge woodsmen boots and asked what inns were about, for a good drink and perhaps a meal on such a hot day – saying he was a stranger to Hartlehk, all the way from Senylehk, and wanted to know all the inns of the town, by name, position and offerings, so he might decide. The stranger was happy to oblige, listing all the inns, their advantages and likely prices.

"But stay away from the Axeman today, we were all told this morning that the ale went bad, and everyone was made ill. Otherwise it has great pies, small, sold in pairs, one to eat and one to take for tomorrow. Very good indeed. But they put ale in the pies, so they might be bad, too."

Selvorne asked where it was, so he could easily avoid it, fearing he might go there thinking it was another, and he had no wish to become ill. He thanked the man, then returned to Rohy.

The inn was on the other side of the river, and they crossed not on the main good bridge, but on a rickety narrow and high wooden one – the most direct way, the man had said, but Selvorne did not think it completely safe as they stood upon it. He noticed Rohy was very unsure, and looked disturbed by the fast flowing deep river, ten feet below. Selvorne shook the bridge only once to test it – and doing so, saw the immediate horror on Rohy's face, despite it seeming stronger than it had looked. But he crossed carefully regardless, having good reason to fear a failing bridge, and Rohy followed, every bit as wary.

Winding streets, alleys and passages, few people were in the town to ask directions and all of them seemed unfriendly – almost avoiding them. Selvorne wondered how long it would take to find the inn without knowing the town, they only had a vague idea of its location – perhaps they would never find it, for he was told it had no sign, no name, not even an axe hanging over the door to let people know it. The only directions the stranger had given was that it was roughly in the middle of the northern side of town, in a paved square that had at its centre the old stump of a tree.

They found it, to their surprise. The square was not as small as they expected, and the buildings not so crammed, they were mostly houses and seemed all empty. On each side they surrounded the square, with only narrow paths leading in and out at the corners – a difficult place for a crowd to make an escape, but there was no crowd, or indeed, anyone in the square, other than at one corner building. Quiet, rather than abandoned, the houses were well kept. Perhaps busy on a market day, yes, some of the pavings seemed well worn from excited crowds. On that bright day it seemed quite peaceful, cosy, and a pleasant place to see, for any who lived in a house that looked upon it. The only shame was that what once would have been a mighty tree, standing right in the middle of the square, had been reduced to a stump.

On one corner, the Axeman Inn – it had to be, though it began to sound rowdy, not empty as they would expect if the ale had gone bad. Shouting, the crashing of furniture and yelling – the patrons, or the owner, they were not sure. Otherwise the streets were silent and dead. The courtyard was paved, even to the edge of the stump, which had a smooth flat surface, except for a rounded dent on one side – perhaps left there as a table of sorts, but why they had not dug it up was – Rohy grabbed Selvorne by the arm, and his fingers were almost tight enough to cause pain.

"Do you know what that is?" Rohy asked, staring at the stump.

"From where I come from, we call that a stump," Selvorne joked, but Rohy was distressed. Staring, he let go and walked around it, at a distance – then close, with his hand stretched out, but not daring to touch it. Selvorne noticed there were many deep cuts into the wood across the top.

"A butcher's block?" Selvorne asked, "Perhaps this is the slaughter yard?"

Rohy looked up at him, a ghastly expression on his face.

"No?" Selvorne asked.

"No," Rohy replied, "or ... yes. In a way. This is the old execution square. This is the Hartlehk Horror Square. This is where they cut the heads from brigands in the days before, way back, before they started to hang them, thinking that their bodies dangling was more amusing and cruel. Many have died here, and some say it is haunted by the spirits of the dead, who listen to the living, and pass judgement on them, just as they were judged, and punished, in this very place."

Selvorne was fascinated, and went to touch it, but Rohy stopped him. Selvorne did not believe in spirits of the dead, if there were any, he reasoned they should come back and help the living, doing chores, or at least give wise advice. Rohy, however, seemed to hold some strange mix of fear and reverence towards the execution stump.

Just then a door burst open – both of them jumped – out of the inn stomped Nakla and Reklo. They looked like they had been wrestling, their clothes and hair were a mess, and Reklo had a bruise forming on the side of his face. Without their usual jokes or even a word, they looked at Selvorne and Rohy, then quickly ran out of one corner of the square and were gone, disappearing into the town. Turning to each other, both shrugged at once.

Selvorne and Rohy entered the Axeman Inn, realising it had nothing to do with woodsmen, especially when they saw the enormous executioner axe securely hung over the serving table at one end of the room. It was very busy, considering they were in a quiet part of town, in the middle of the day, near a haunted tree stump, and at an inn which had apparently poisoned all its patrons with bad ale, just that morning. It was full, and also, quiet. Everyone was muttering, and nobody looked at them longer than a brief glance.

"Why are we here again?" Selvorne asked, Rohy replying they were meant to meet someone.

"What do you want?" a burly man almost yelled when he came up to them.

"Nothing," Selvorne replied.

"You want to stay here, you have to have something."

"Oh, all right, what do you have?"

"Ale and pies. Where do you think you are?"

"The Smelly Pig?"

The burly man glared at him, then looked at Selvorne's arms. Both were bare because he had rolled his sleeves up to his shoulders. He turned to Rohy, and noticed the red band tied around his arm.

"That is down the road. This is the Axeman Inn. Ale, or pie, or both?" the large man asked.

"Ale," Rohy answered nervously.

"I will have ale and two pies, provided they are not poisoned, and not bad, as we have heard," Selvorne said.

"Who told you that?" the man demanded.

"That is the word on the streets of Hartlehk," Selvorne replied merrily. He was exceedingly confident and demanding, teasing and insulting at once, and the burly man stormed off.

"What are you doing?" Rohy whispered as they took a place against the wall, away from the other patrons.

"Relax," Selvorne assured him, "we are being set up – for something. Look around, what do you see."

Rohy looked around, but saw only angry looking patrons muttering and giving him a sidelong glance.

"No women," Selvorne began, "not one, even serving. Moments ago a fight, we walked in and not one person was talking of it. I just insulted the – I do not know what he is, not the owner. I see no food. Anywhere. At midday. And everyone has a full tankard – a full tankard, Rohy. And yet everyone is drinking. That fellow by the door has had ten sips already, and his drink is still full."

Rohy looked again, gazing over all who were there, then nodded.

"You are right, I was upset by that tree, and not paying attention."

"They have set us up for something. Perhaps a test. Stay alert ... I think Reklo did not get that bruise from Nakla ... not today."

The burly man returned with two pies and two ales in wooden tankards. Selvorne insisted on paying him immediately, indeed he almost had to force his coins upon him, then took a cloth from his sack and quickly wrapped the pies, stuffing them in the pack as the man left.

Then, to his astonishment, another large man came over to their table and took their two ales. Without a word he returned to his friend across the room, and Rohy looked at him sidelong.

"Well, if it a test of some sort, I do not know what they want us to do. Hit him?" Rohy asked.

Selvorne looked around, half expecting to see Temnere sitting in a corner enjoying some childishly contrived test of the new recruits, but he was nowhere to be seen. He wondered if perhaps Dyneti was playing another joke on him, but no, she was not there, nor anyone he recognised. Anyone there could have been responsible, because they all seemed to be watching him to see what he would do – some slyly, almost unnoticed, others quite obviously, though they tried to hide their stares.

Selvorne stood up, found the most dangerous looking man he could, walked over to him, took his ale and that of his friend, and then walked over to the first man who had taken his own ale. There he put the tankards down on the table before taking a seat.

"Hello, I thought I would join you. Here are two more!"

The entire room was not even trying to conceal their interest – they all stared, and seemed bewildered by such strange behaviour. None more than the dangerous looking man, who had his drinks stolen and just sat there in astonishment, and the large man Selvorne had joined, whose eyes were unblinking.

"Ah, thanks. I mean, what?" the large man asked.

Selvorne began shuffling the tankards around until nobody knew which was which – not hard, since all were full and all were the same. He then stood up again, bowed, thanked the man, and returned to Rohy, with what he thought were the original two tankards, though it hardly mattered. They did not sit where they were before, but Rohy led him to a place where they could easily see the entire room – and it was closer to the door, should they need to flee. Selvorne immediately took a large drink and encouraged Rohy to do the same.

The dangerous man jumped up and headed to Selvorne, then stood over him and Rohy.

"Give me back my drinks," the dangerous looking man demanded.

"Oh no, this is not yours, yours was full. This is half empty," Selvorne said, showing that part of the drink was gone, "yours is over there with that gentle fellow."

"You took mine!"

"Are you sure?" Selvorne asked, feigning confusion, "That fellow said he was going to put my drink on your table and take yours. He said it was a custom of the town. Go ahead, ask him."

The dangerous man shook his head, frustrated and confused. He was clearly completely sober, such a ruse might have made a drunk man fight, or laugh, or fall down trying to fight and laugh – but he was completely bewildered as to what to do next. He went to the other table, took his drinks and sat down again. And then the first man came to Selvorne's table.

"I took your drinks because we have been waiting for ours for longer than have you," he said, then he made a move to take them back, but Selvorne pulled both tankards away.

"Surely you do not want this one? It is nearly empty. Innkeeper! More drinks! Now!"

The burly innkeeper came out with no drinks.

"We are all out of ale, those were the last two we have."

"No ... all out of ale?" Selvorne asked in feigned disbelief, "That is terrible. You took the coin of this man and brought him nothing? Had you paid already? Guards!"

They all stared – Selvorne had them, for if the man had not paid, as seemed usual, he was not entitled to any ale – and if he had, then the guards would have to be called to charge the innkeeper with what was practically theft. Either way, it was nothing to do with Selvorne, who had paid already, and begun to drink, making compliments on the ale between sips.

Just then a young boy entered the inn, asking for Selvorne and Rohy by name. He said he had a message, that they were to go to the boats at the bottom of the hill, immediately. Selvorne drained his tankard, thanked everyone, and as he left, noticed only one person at the inn was shaking his head to himself. Rohy also drank, messed around with his belt beneath the table, then walked out – almost laughing as they left.

"Well, I think we passed, and at least we did not get hit," Selvorne remarked when outside, pleased with himself.

"Yes, but I would not do that in an actual inn, full of drunks who steal your drinks," Rohy said, growing serious, but added lightheartedly, "I wonder what Nakla and Reklo did? My wager is they started the fight before ordering their drinks."

Selvorne chuckled – and accepted the wager, but only for a tankard of ale, and he pointed out to Rohy that he had just purchased two, and pies, and so it was a wager he could not lose.

"That messenger boy," Rohy said, "did you see, he had been sitting at the back of the inn the whole time, then ran out another door, around the outside, and in the door to the front once more."

"I missed that, well done. Did you see the man sitting in the low chair on the left? He was alone, and the only person who was actually drinking, but I think not ale. He also had a half–eaten pie. I think he was watching us."

Rohy agreed, and added, "We will have to be very careful what we do, if they are testing us. I want this very much, and do not want to be excluded by some absurd trick that Temnere thinks is clever. I do not know how we can outsmart him, because he has some stupid ideas, I have heard, and I am not sure I can outsmart stupidity – or should we try to outstupid it?"

Selvorne agreed, though he was not sure how to "outstupid" something, he did think things might become very odd and complicated. The day before, his plan had been simple – if he could not join the guards, if all hope of it failed, he would simply travel to Senylehk alone and search for Cienn. He was safe enough, he thought, to travel alone – surely men would not have been looking for him so far from Tavalehk, if they were looking at all.

But Dyneti's message had changed everything – he had to do his best to join the guards. She might have thought she had concealed her meaning well, with an innocent message of ducks and geese, and bad eggs. And perhaps it would seem innocent to anyone who overheard it, though rather odd. To Selvorne its message was clear – brigand spies had infiltrated the guards, possibly the new recruits as well, and she did not know who they were.

~

Through the town they went and to the bridge, but were on the other side of it than earlier, the north side, and they did not cross, but descended stairs near where the waterfalls cascaded. At the bottom was the wider river, almost a lake, and there were many piers and sheds for boats. And, oddly, many boats, considering they had been told there were none to take all the guards at once.

Selvorne thought it also strange that the two of them were to share a very large boat that could easily take a few more, but the lone boatman was to row them along the river to Senylehk. Selvorne jumped into the boat, rocking it wildly, much to Rohy's distress – he seemed uneasy around the river, which was understandable above the falls, but the lower waters were quite serene, though flowing strongly.

It was an enormous boat compared to Selvorne's coracle, in which many journeys on the lake resulted in it filling with water and sinking, for he had outgrown it years ago, and refused to paddle carefully. Again, Selvorne rocked the boat wildly with glee, praising how stable it was, until both Rohy and the boatman told him to sit down and behave. Rohy was nervous, but the boatman seemed secretly proud of his vessel, so Selvorne gave it a few good thumps, and grinned.

Settling in for a nice relaxing journey, Selvorne brought out the pies, offering to share with the boatman, who had to stop rowing to eat. Selvorne took the oars, clumsily splashing everyone with each stroke. It was cool on the river, and the water still held the wintry cold of the mountains from whence it came. The sun was gentle and warm, so the two of them napped when the boatman took back the oars. Peacefully, until they woke with a sudden thud as the boat beached itself in the dirt.

"All out!" the boatman ordered.

"We are there already?" Selvorne asked, staring around in wonder – the journey was supposed to take hours to reach Senylehk, and there was no town anywhere to be seen. The river was wide, more of a lake, but still flowing strongly.

"All out! Senylehk is that way," the boatman said, pointing to the west, "keep walking, you will get there eventually."

They got out, the boat lifted off the dirt with their weight removed, and the boatman turned it around to begin the hard row back against the current. "Good luck," he called out, almost as an afterthought. Selvorne thought him a bit rude – especially after eating so much of the pie, which was very good. Not very grateful, and surely he had been paid to take them all the way to town, not leave them miles away to walk themselves.

The walk was pleasant beside the lakelike river. The shores were either reeds or short grass, sometimes rocks, and the waters bright blue, shimmering in the breeze. Beautiful, quiet and fresh, but the town was nowhere in sight. Neither man was sure how far they had come, or how far they had to go, but knew they were supposed to get there without dawdling, so they began a shuffling run along in silence.

Every so often they passed a pier extended into the lake, each with a rough path leading to it, and they thought people must fish there, or launch boats, but no people were around. It was a good sign that they must be nearing the town, so they hurried.

After some time they came across one pier that had a commotion, for people seemed to be yelling and a child was crying. Selvorne stopped immediately, looked briefly at Rohy then ran the path to the wooden pier, all the way along it to the end.

"Help! Help!" yelled a young boy half Selvorne's age. There were three young boys yelling and a little girl, crying and pointing out to the lake. There, an old white–haired man was struggling to hold a rock against the current. He was not very far from the shore, but the flow was strong at that narrower part of the river.

Selvorne dropped his pack and tore off his boots, looked carefully at the water, then took a running leap off the end, landing upstream and quickly swimming hard, to the rock. He almost did not make it, to Rohy's horror, for the current was powerful, but he grasped the rock and then began to comfort the old man. Rohy looked around, and realised the pier had a broken handrail with an old rope running along it. He ripped it away easily, tied one end to the pier, then threw it out to Selvorne. He missed and it swept downstream, so he pulled it back in, knotted the end to make it heavy, and threw it again. That time it worked, and Selvorne began pulling them both back, the old man nearly choking him, so most of the way Selvorne was under the water, until they crawled out in the mud beside the pier.

"Are you all right?" Selvorne panted.

"Ouch! Mind my head!" the old man complained, surprisingly not out of breath, and rubbing a large bruise on the top of his head. For a few moments he seemed angry, then seemed ... not quite relieved, "Thank you, both of you. I fell off the end of the pier and was swept out. I think I would have drowned out there."

Selvorne agreed, for it was very deep and the flow was strong. He wondered how the man had bruised the top of his head, and why the little girl kept crying, until one of the boys told her to stop. Some of the young boys thanked them as well, but neither as well or as warmly as Selvorne thought they deserved.

Gathering their things, and not bothering to dry, they continued towards the town, which the old man assured them was not much farther west along the river.

"That was a stupid thing you did," Rohy said after they had walked some way.

"What? Saving the man?"

"Diving into the river. If I had not found that rope, you would have been lost."

"You are being silly. I would have caught my breath then swam with him farther down the river. I know how to swim in a strong river, Rohy."

Rohy was silent, and seemed to be considering it for a while.

"What if you were caught in the reeds?"

Selvorne reached down to his belt, meaning to draw the bronze knife he usually had, when swimming – it was gone. Not gone, but not taken. He always had it when he planned to swim, he usually had it when he travelled – for he often swam whenever he left his home. He had not been carrying it since the festival, and he felt a fool.

"There were no reeds, the water was too deep, which is the purpose of the pier, you realise," he said, quite sure that was true, but not at all sure there were no reeds or vines under the water to catch his foot. It could have been the reason the man was drowning – and to save him, Selvorne might have leapt into danger himself.

Rohy nodded thoughtfully, and seemed impressed that Selvorne had been so alert. Rather than praised, Selvorne felt foolish, and vowed to never rush in like that again, as he had done the last time he was caught in reeds. They walked for a short while, Selvorne leaving a trail of water as he went, and when he had recovered well enough from the swim, they began to run.

~

After a while they came to what they thought was the town, but it was a small village still quite some way from Senylehk. They slowed to a walking pace, thinking it would look suspicious to run fast through the street. It seemed abandoned, until they reached the main square – a dusty area where the entire village had crowded and were jeering, cheering, and yelling.

Everyone had gathered before some unfortunate young boy who had been tied to a pole. Many were cursing him, others were near and seemed to be practising their aim by throwing large river pebbles at a wooden target, which was breaking into pieces with each good hit.

"Please! Please! I am sorry!" the boy pleaded, but the people only jeered, so Selvorne grabbed a man by the arm and demanded to know what was going on.

"Ahh, he is being punished. He threw a rock, and hit a girl in the head. Now we are going to throw rocks at him," the man said.

"That hardly seems ... fair?"

"Of course it is fair. He threw a rock, we throw a rock."

"True," Rohy said, "but it looks like there are many of you, and you are practising. Surely his hit was an accident – just how many rocks are you planning to throw?"

"One good sized rock each," the man said, and held up a rock almost the size of a boy's fist.

Selvorne thought the boy was going to die. He had not heard of such a thing being done in any town, ever, not even Hartlehk – not even if a boy deliberately threw a rock, for he was just a boy. A man, yes, if done to do harm – but not a child.

"Surely, you are just trying to scare him?" Selvorne asked, "You are not truly going to throw these, are you? The girl did not die, did she?"

"No, she is fine, she is over there," the man said, then he pointed at a little blonde girl with a bandage on her head, throwing rocks at the target, in anger, and very badly, "she gets five rocks, as is the custom. Hit by one, throw back five. Hit by ten, throw back fifty. That is our way. Until the timer runs out. So, if we are quick, we can gather another round of rocks and throw again. After all have had a go, you understand."

Selvorne was horrified. Rohy was sickened. The man was laughing, but they thought he was not joking. Selvorne asked about the timer, and the man waved towards a huge wooden water timer. He had seen them before, they were not very accurate, and easily clogged, but useful for timing. A bucket was filled with water, and a small hole opened at the bottom by a lever, so the water would steadily drain out and stop at a certain time. Not always emptying the bucket, although people were assured it was the same amount of time, every time, verified in measure by careful counting. Selvorne guessed the bucket they were using would drain for one quarter of an hour, at most, and half that time – at least.

"When the lever is pulled we start throwing, and when the water stops, we stop. If we use all our rocks, we get another go. That is why I have five ready. He will get what he deserves, we do not like rock throwers in this town," the man said, then pushed his way to the front, ready to throw, leaving them to wonder if the man saw the absurdity in what he had just said.

"He will die," Rohy said, watching the boy, who was pleading and wailing every time someone got a good hit on the target where they practised.

"I know, he will not last a moment if thirty people throw stones at him."

"I knew of someone who was hit just the once in the head, and the next day, he died from it," Rohy added, "do you think it is another test?"

Selvorne thought about it. If it was, he could not see how, if it was not, he could not see why – it made no sense.

"We cannot take that chance. If it is a test, they want us to intervene. If it is not, then this poor boy is about to die, or be very hurt, in my opinion unjustly," Selvorne said, and Rohy nodded.

Selvorne wondered what Dyneti would think of him if he let a boy die for such a minor offence, then he wondered if he should invoke the privilege of a lord, claim protection for the boy, and take him along with them to Senylehk. Doing so would reveal himself, and people might not believe he was a lord or heir – but they would have no choice other than to yield the boy to Selvorne, and then determine if Selvorne was a lord, and the only way to do that would be to go to Senylehk. Revealed, though ... but it was worth it, to save the boy. Selvorne made as if to get the attention of the crowd, when Rohy grabbed his arm.

"I have an idea," Rohy said, and quickly explained his thoughts. At the end of the plan, Selvorne began to smile.

"How good are you at throwing, Rohy?"

"Deadly," Rohy answered with a twinkle in his eye, "when I throw – I throw to kill."

The two of them pushed their way to the target where people were practising, and gathered up many stones. Selvorne threw them with great noise and bragging – he was not the best at throwing stones, sometimes he hit the target, more often he missed. When he hit he was cheered by the others, and when he missed he cheered himself.

Then Rohy had a go. He stood there quietly, staring at the target. Then he let out a cry of "Die!" and threw the stone with such force it hit the target and smashed part of the wooden plank, which was surprising enough, but he then let out a shout, "When I throw, I throw to kill!"

People had cheered his accurate hit, but they were taken aback by his violent victory shout, and began to be unnerved by his cold disposition. They stopped cheering Selvorne, who started yelling "Anyone who throws a rock must die!" and "If anyone throws a rock at me, I will kill them!" like some mad person who had wandered into their town. Some of the children began to cry and stopped stoning the target. Rohy coldly continued with his ritual of shouting "Die!" before smashing the target, then, as if the spell of a curse, "When I throw, I throw to kill!"

Many were disturbed, but some were still eager. The village elder called everyone to attention, and the boy on the pole was still pleading as people lined up to throw stones. Selvorne and Rohy easily made it to the front, people were too scared to get in their way, or even look at them.

"An unpleasant business," the elder began as he addressed the crowd, "but it is our custom, and must be done. No stones to be thrown until I give the signal to start. All must stop when I signal the end."

There was a tense moment as he prepared, and it was silent except for the crying of some children, and the boy, whimpering as he crouched at the base of the pole, trying to cover his head.

"Start!" yelled the leader, pulling the lever that caused a steady trickle of water from the bucket to the ground.

Immediately Selvorne and Rohy ran out to the boy and took positions directly in front of him. Nobody had thrown a stone, they seemed to be waiting to see what would happen when Selvorne and Rohy threw theirs – and they were bewildered.

"Move!" someone shouted, eager to throw.

"If anyone hits me," Selvorne yelled as loudly as he could, "I will claim the attack in complaint, here seen by all, and you will be tied to the pole next, by your own custom."

Silence – even from those who had been crying.

"When I throw, I throw to kill!" Rohy yelled in his cold, flat way, holding a rock as if to throw it at the crowd.

None spoke. None threw. All stared, and the boy, who was hiding near their legs, dared to peek out to see what might happen next. Parents pulled their children back before they threw any rocks. The water was steadily trickling away. Some men moved around to the side, trying to get a clear angle to hit the boy, but could find none – then they went away, laughing. A few people began to clap, but were silenced by angry others. It seemed a very long time before the elder called "Stop!"

"Will the boy be all right?" Selvorne asked the elder.

"Yes, of course ... he has learnt his lesson. I think we all have. Best stoning yet! Well done," he said, then untied the boy.

"Thank you, you are very brave doing that," the boy said, then, once freed, he ran across the square through a gap between houses, as if to hide.

"I think you had better leave, now," said the elder, pointing firmly to the west, "Senylehk is that way."

Selvorne and Rohy left, Selvorne trying to make haste, but Rohy was striding through the crowd, glaring at any who dared get in his way, and seemed to enjoy it. When they were safely away from the village, they fell down, shaking, and not only from laughter.

"That could have gone badly," Selvorne said once he had calmed.

"But it worked. Their unjust laws used against them. Dyneti would be proud of you," Rohy said, a twinkle in his eye and grin on his face.

"It was your idea. What if it failed?"

"We would have been pelted with rocks, and then, the second plan, cut the rope, free the boy, we all run away," Rohy said proudly.

Selvorne wondered what Rohy would cut the rope with, he never seemed to have a knife except when it was needed, and he remembered that when he woke him nights before, a knife had appeared from nowhere. No matter, he thought, and they continued towards Hartlehk.

"Strange," Selvorne mused, "that elder said this is the way to Senylehk."

"So?" Rohy asked.

"Well, how did he know we were not going to Hartlehk?"

The two of them mused on whether they had just experienced a very elaborate test, or wandered into a land of strange harsh customs and crazed village folk. No matter, it was done, and they made good speed headed west along the riverside road.

Tested and Betrayed

They continued until they came to gentle sloping sides of the river, covered in wild grass, where people were gathered, some sitting on a fallen tree trunk, and few were properly dressed. Selvorne recognised Vugecarauk first, though he had only seen him briefly when introduced at Hartlehk – for he was tall and stood out from any crowd with his wild dark hair. Then he saw Nakla and Reklo, who unusually were not wrestling, but resting on the log quietly, neither man with a shirt. Rhede was there, sitting neatly, and Traglan was laid out on the grass asleep. Bitier and Orrikler were talking to each other and laughing, and Franek sat by himself on one end of the log, ignoring the others. All except Franek had removed their packs, jackets and any jewellery, and most of their clothing, piling all into a small cart. Many were dressed in undergarments, which for the most part looked just like ordinary trousers and shirts, but shorter on the arm and leg, and not quite enough for the cooler day. All had bare feet save one – a strange man who was there, well dressed, with dark hair. He seemed bored and idle, but when he noticed Selvorne and Rohy, he walked up to them and ordered them to remove their clothes.

"And who are you?" Selvorne asked, surprising all the others, who apparently had disrobed without asking.

"Roduil, guard, and right now, your commander. Disrobe!"

"And why are we disrobing?" Selvorne asked, concerned more for his possessions than modesty, for he did not want to place his clothes in a cart.

"You ask many questions for a new recruit, perhaps you would be better joining Franek over there, he does not have to disrobe, nor challenge orders again."

Franek was fully dressed, and had his pack, but looked miserable. Selvorne felt – not glad. Sorrow for him, for although he had not disrobed, he had removed his soft boots and his feet were swollen from the days of walking. Days of blistering, for nothing, if he was to be sent back to Tavalehk – if he was rejected, which seemed to be ... unless he alone was accepted, and they all were to be sent back.

Selvorne and Rohy disrobed as much as dignity would allow, Selvorne until he wore only his light linen under–trousers and his loose shirt, tied with the shirt cord, not his belt. Rohy was in a sleeveless and surprisingly fine light grey shirt, neatly buttoned, and linen under–shorts that showed his legs were quite pale, perhaps seeing the sun for the first time that spring. Both his garments had pockets in various places, though neither was meant to be worn on the outside. Once disrobed they went and stood with Vugecarauk.

"Do not mind him," Vugecarauk explained, waving at Roduil, "I have heard he can be cutting, at times. They want us to swim to the island out there," he nodded across the river, wide at that place, strongly flowing, but easily swam, and the island was not far, "we are waiting for the others, it is some kind of race. Though he said it does not matter who is first, only that all swim well."

Rohy seemed to grow tense as Selvorne nodded, and he was staring at the river – it was not that difficult, Selvorne thought, and he was more concerned with Roduil, who claimed to be their commander.

"Vugecarauk, do you know this Roduil? Have you met him before?"

"No," Vugecarauk admitted, "not seen him, I only know him by reputation, everyone does. He is the best, they say, the very best of the guards in recent years – new, fresh, very skilled, everyone has heard of him."

"Yes, that is nice, but it seems to me if everyone has heard of him, and never seen him, he would be the perfect person to pretend to be – to fool us."

Selvorne still had his clothes in a bundle, and stood before the others.

"Have any of you met Roduil before? Can any of you vouch that this is Roduil, and not some imposter? Some lanky, unshaven, badly–dressed imposter, trying to fool us and steal our greatly superior clothes?" Selvorne looked slyly at Roduil, half trying to appease him, insult him, tease him, see how he would react. He reasoned the real Roduil would be annoyed at the insults, but the fellow before him, at first angry, began to nod.

The youths looked at each other, but only Orrikler spoke up, "Yes, that is Roduil. I know him. I can vouch for him. He is always unshaven. I fear there is no cure for his sense of dress, neither wealth nor good advice seems sufficient. But he has the gift of making oneself look all the more attractive, if you take him along with you, when meeting young ladies of refined taste."

Roduil pounced on Orrikler and scruffed his hair terribly. "Now who looks scruffy!" he said, laughing.

"Not I!" claimed Orrikler, "Perhaps rough, ready and daring are a better choice of words!"

They joked a little more, thumping at each other, and Selvorne was satisfied that Orrikler knew him, and earlier the entire guard had identified Orrikler, including Temnere, so that was good enough. He still did not like leaving his clothes and boots in a cart, and liked it less when he realised his pack and all things owned by all the new recruits were there as well, brought down by boats, including his new spear. He sat down glumly next to Rohy, who was much the same – usually quiet, but he seemed strangely distant.

The others were talking in low voices amongst themselves, not sure if they were meant to be discussing the day or not. Apparently, everyone had a fight at the Axeman Inn. Everyone met a man drowning in the river. And everyone saved a boy from a stoning. Three tests, then, it could not be coincidence, all had faced them, but not all had met with the same success, and each went about matters in a different way.

Orrikler and Franek had gone first, and because Orrikler knew the town so well, he went straight to the inn, recognised half the people there, who nervously tried to start a fight with him as instructed – but did so badly, for fear of his father. It was an unsuccessful ruse, a poor test, though Franek still managed to insult several people and almost start a real fight.

Selvorne thought it a little harsh for Franek, for the men at the Axeman Inn clearly had been trying to start a fight, by orders or instructions, and ... if ... what had Orrikler said?

Afraid of his father. But that was not what Selvorne needed to remember – when first met, he had said his name. No, the guards had said it, introducing him to – no, not even that. Temnere and the guards had been introduced to Orrikler. Who had received them – Orrikler Ultainen. His father was the Lord of Hartlehk.

Breathing shallow, breathing slow. Breathing hardly at all, Selvorne calmed himself as the young son of the rival lord continued in a low voice, speaking of his day, making the others chuckle. Young? No, roughly the same age as Selvorne. Two sons of two lords – but Selvorne had been made more, he was heir to a town envied by Ruchten Ultainen – the forests, anyway. Why was a lord's son sent to the guards, it had to be to learn to fight. Or learn how the Waehdric guards fought, for some advantage in training their own town guards, perhaps. Or merely to learn how to survive, as a guard. Arnlausa had been a guard. Uhlsko had – Girradehn had – and though the brief thoughts of those he had lost was painful, Selvorne grew more curious of the young noble son before him, and whether he would be rival, equal, or friend.

Orrikler continued his tale, and did not soften words or feign politeness. Selvorne guessed that as a lord's son he rarely needed to feign anything. He had stopped referring to Franek as, "Franek, son of Ranek, son of Anek," and instead preferred to call him, "that idiot", or by his full title, "that idiot who keeps messing things up." Franek had truly annoyed Orrikler by trying to impress him with his name and – well, he did not even have titles, just names. It was likely something Orrikler had endured his whole life, grown sick of years ago, and even felt ashamed for having done the same thing in the past. So as he told his tale of the day, he kept putting Franek in his place – loudly, so he could hear, even sitting far away.

"That idiot who keeps messing things up would not wet his cloak for the drowning man, no," and, "that idiot thought the boy deserved to be stoned, and it would be funny to throw a few." Orrikler tore him down, and Franek was starting to wish he could go home at once.

Orrikler's anger was not merely contempt when he told of how he almost drowned trying to pull the man from the river – Franek did not help, he only ran to get help. Orrikler was furious, and at the stoning, wasted no time announcing his status and claiming protection for the boy, declaring that anyone who threw a stone – man, woman or child – would face the full wrath of the Lord of Hartlehk, which sent some to their knees. Even though they knew it was supposed to be a ruse.

Events for Bitier were equally a mess, at least for Traglan who was lost at each test. Traglan nearly fought the men at the inn, but Bitier stepped in and bought them more ale. And himself more ale. And pies. And he did so with their coins that he was lifting from their belts without them realising, until he got caught, and then he argued that actually, they had bought themselves ale with their own coin, which was not a crime, even in Hartlehk. He managed to get away with the pies, however, "knowing full well how good they are at that inn, and not at all poisoned, as some had suggested."

The drowning man was no problem, Bitier always had a cord at his waist, quickly unravelled it, threw it to the man who caught it, gave one end to Traglan to help, and began pulling the man in – until Traglan knocked him in the river, and then let go of the cord as he tried to reach him with his outstretched arm. Bitier was not a great swimmer, but not a fool, so he grabbed the man and floated downstream until it was safe, then came back to Traglan, who thought they had both drowned, and was being consoled by the previously wailing children.

"Of the stoning, I am most proud, but must admit I had an unfair advantage," Bitier said, "as I realised at once when I had assessed the situation. I simply tossed a small round pebble into the timer. When they pulled the lever to start, a small trickle came out, then it stopped, and they called the finish."

"How did you know that would happen?" Selvorne asked.

"Because, you see, I built the timer. It was something we used to sell, years ago, before these glassy, sandy ones came from Vonersehl."

"And – if it failed?"

"Kick it over! There is no rule saying you cannot destroy the timer. But if it is glass ... you would have to pay to replace it. A stupid custom for a foolish people. I assure you ... the show might have been a ruse today, but the law there is very real. Stupid river people. Wait until you hear what Reklo did, though, that was – "

Everyone turned to Reklo, including Roduil, who had been listening and pretending not to – but Reklo insisted Vugecarauk speak first, with Rhede, since they arrived earlier.

"Vugecarauk could not find the place," Rhede piped in, "eventually, I found it by running around, searching."

"I described it to you, but I have not been there in years, and it is a maze in that old part of town," Vugecarauk said in a deep low voice.

"All right," Rhede continued, as it seemed Vugecarauk was a man of few words, especially when telling a story about himself, which meant few had learnt much about him the whole day, "so, we went inside the inn, and everyone was frightening, well ... I thought so. When they saw Vuggy they all hid in their ale, which if you noticed, nobody had been drinking."

"Vuggy?" Orrikler asked, then laughed, but Vugecarauk glared at him and he was silent.

"Please, Vugge at least, or you sound like my mother," Vugecarauk insisted.

"I ... apologies," Rhede said, rather meekly, glancing at Bitier, who shrugged, "I thought ... your name is very long. Vugge? Well, we sat and ordered ale. And four pies. Each, thinking them small. But I could not eat more than one, and gave them to Vugge, who ate three and kept three."

"That is only seven," Selvorne pointed out.

"Did ... you eat four pies?" Rhede asked, and Vugge looked embarrassed, so Rhede continued, "We drank our ale which was not very nice, and left. When we stepped outside, some boy ran around from the back and told us to go to the boats."

"Well, that is not much of a test," Bitier said, "unless it was to eat many pies. Perhaps you failed?"

"The man drowning," Rhede continued, "I was halfway to pulling the rope off the rail when Vugge had removed his coat and was waving it into the water, then started walking into the depths, swinging his coat, trying to reach him."

"I was nearly there, also," Vugge said, "but must admit, I did not see the rope."

"So I took the rope, jumped off the pier and landed on his back, and threw the rope to the man. Who had stopped drowning, and started laughing as we pulled him back."

"I knew he was faking," Selvorne said, "what about the boy being stoned?"

"That was ... quite something," Rhede continued, as Vugecarauk began to blush, "When we determined what was happening, I wanted to run and get help, or cut him free, or something, but Vugge explained that would violate the law if we cut the rope. But not if you broke the yoke! So he took a large stone, and smashed the yoke, setting him free, and the boy ran away. And actually, not in violation of his punishment."

"Ahh ... what yoke?" Selvorne asked, "There was no yoke. He was tied to a pole."

"That would be because we broke it," Rhede said proudly, then added, "although, it is not as good as Reklo's story."

"Ooh, I truly do not want to tell it, my head still hurts," Reklo complained, so Nakla began.

"Very well, I shall tell it better anyway, for I use the facts, and also, recall it from the point of view of an intelligent observer," Nakla said, but Reklo was too tired and sore to retaliate, and gave a dismissive wave of one hand, "we had no idea where the inn was, having never been to Hartlehk, and now are not eager to return. Thinking it was a race, we started asking people the way, but on seeing our armbands, people refused to tell us."

"I thought that as well," Selvorne said, "did you take them off?"

"No! We grabbed a child, and said if he showed us the way, we would carry him on our shoulders all through the streets chanting his name like a victory procession. By the time we arrived, we had twenty youths following, that little trickster did not take us the direct way, you see, but past all the houses of his friends."

"Not bad, though a bit strenuous. What happened then?"

Nakla continued as Reklo shook his head in dismay.

"Well, we thought it our good fortune to be there so early and have a chance to sit and drink and eat. We thought everyone was meant to arrive, you see, a gathering, and that we were first, for we were the only recruits to have arrived. We thought it was just a fun race, not some test. So when a man came and took our drinks – "

"And insulted me, I might add," Reklo said, "he said I had rudely butted in, like a goat. And then he said you looked like the butt of a goat, something I tend to agree with. So I hit him. For you, my brother."

"He said nothing of the sort," Nakla corrected, "though he was very aggressive, glared at us, and stole our drinks, which we had already tasted, and without explanation."

"They likely were making up for the poor effort with me," Vugecarauk suggested.

"Hmm ... perhaps, anyway, it might have been pretend at first, but it soon was a fight truly, until one man alone stood up and commanded everyone to stop. Then he told us to go to the boats. He was angry at us, but I think also angry at the man we hit."

"He hit me first," Reklo clarified.

"He did not, you jumped up and pounded him in the chest."

"He hit me before I hit him the second time."

"I do not think that holds in a hearing. Say that, and I am not sure a lord would know what he was hearing, or what to say."

"He hit me hard where it hurts most, when he took my drink. That was worse than a hundred punches, and so deserving of several, at least."

"Well, a drinking lord might agree with you there. I do not think Arnlausa would fall for that, though," Nakla said, and Reklo shrugged, as though conceding it might be true.

Arnlausa ... to hear the name pained Selvorne deeply. Everyone assumed he was still alive, they had no reason not to. He wondered how well those two knew him, they said his name so casually – as friends, or perhaps they had once faced his judgement for unruly behaviour, hitting men in taverns over insults or ale.

"Anyway," Nakla continued, "off we go. And we are starving by then, unlike you lot, we had no pies, and the boat was very slow. We offered to row, planning to hurry to Senylehk, but the skinny fellow would not let us. And then he left us miles from anywhere – that was the same for everyone, was it?"

Everyone nodded.

"I told you brother, it was not my fault," Reklo said.

"Likely it was, I do not think the others had to run so far – we ran along the riverside, starving, wondering where this town was supposed to be. Reklo's bruise was swelling, and though it made him less ugly, our tummies were grumbling, we swore never again to venture out without food. Then we hear this child screaming, and we think – excellent! Perhaps he has some food – but some fool was drowning."

"He, however, had – "

"Now, first we think, this fellow needs to be saved, and we are about to jump in, but we noticed he was not truly struggling, and anyone with the breath to call out for help is not in any serious trouble, not yet. So we asked if he had any food."

"You asked if he had food?" Selvorne asked.

"Yes, because we were hungry, and reasoned if he was drowning and we saved him, he might give us a reward. That is when he stopped crying for help and started cursing."

"That, my friends, is a sure sign of someone who is not in trouble," Reklo noted wisely, wagging one finger at the men.

"Then," Nakla continued, "he starts swimming over to us, because we are rummaging through his bag, and the kids are yelling now at us to leave it alone. He was a strong swimmer, and had no problem with the current, however he was not strong enough to swim against the railing that Reklo pulled out of the ground and poked him with every time he came close to shore. Eventually he submitted, and said there were some pies in his pack."

"I think I gave him those," Vugecarauk said.

"Thank you, Vuggy, they were delicious," Reklo said, "I think he gave them up because I bopped his head with the rail."

"Let me get this story straight," Selvorne said, "you ran along beside a river, saw a drowning man, robbed him, and bopped him on the head with a railing?"

"I prefer to think we charged him a fee for use of the pier," Reklo explained, "well deserved after his deceitful ruse. We could have drowned saving him – or worse, starved."

"This story does not explain how the two of you got soaking wet?" Vugecarauk asked.

"Ahh, yes, well – after seeing how strongly he swam, we decided we would have a go swimming to the rock and back, racing against the current," Nakla explained.

"I won that one!" Reklo chimed in.

"You could argue I won it, spending a longer time swimming and fighting the current, than you did."

Reklo thought about it, and agreed it seemed a fair enough argument.

"Tell us about the stoning!" Rhede asked eagerly.

"I am not sure why you think that was the best bit," Nakla said, "for there were more pies at the pier. Anyway, we came to the village, saw what was happening, quickly realised it was not going to be as much fun as it first seemed, and came up with a plan."

"My plan, I thought of it!" Reklo declared.

"Yes, only a mad person could conceive of such a plan. And you might have thought of it, but certainly did not think about it, nor thought it through from beginning to end, or even the beginning, now I think of it," Nakla said.

"Right, well, I am telling this part," Reklo said, "and you will see the cleverness in the plan from the start, if it is well told, and not merely rambled, half recalled by one who did not understand it fully."

"You two are – " Selvorne began, but they both looked to him at once, their identical stares almost daring him to give insult, and he almost was that bold, "go on."

"First," Reklo said, "we could not fight the entire crowd. Not without a full stomach. We had eaten too few pies, and there were too many people who would get hurt.

"Second, we could not simply untie the rope, or cut it. We thought that would make us guilty of freeing him. What, then, to do? Time was running out. I considered stealing all the stones, but there were too many of those as well, and many people had their own stashed away in their pockets.

"Aha! And then it came to me. 'Fight crime with crime', I thought, and after a long difficult explanation to the painfully slow Nakla, we leapt into action. I grabbed the boy, who began to scream, drawing the attention of the crowd as planned."

"I do not remember that being part of the plan?" Nakla interrupted, "I thought that was an undesired consequence, not previously considered?"

"No, brother, that was a clever ploy to create witnesses to the crime. None there could not help but look – the boy was being taken clearly against his will. I picked him up, and he weighed nothing at all, so I lifted him high above my head – "

"And I took the rope and lifted it over the top of the pole," Nakla added, "which was far more difficult than lifting that waif, for the pole was very high."

"You could have used a stick, like I told you," Reklo said, "instead of jumping up and down like some crazed chicken trying to flee the coop – then, we simply took the child to safety. I mean, we captured him. Against his will."

"Actually, he was very grateful, after the shock," Nakla explained, "but by accusing us of the crime of capture, he was guiltless of the crime of escape, and the time had elapsed by the time we returned him."

"Because I flicked the timer lever on the way out," Reklo explained.

"Then he named the punishment for the kidnapping as a beating with a stick, and hit each of us in turn, but only softly."

"He might have hit you softly, but I have a bruise on my head," Reklo complained, rubbing his head.

"Serves you right for hitting that old man earlier, trying to swim, shame on you," Nakla said.

Selvorne thought they were quite amusing, rather reckless, but had everyone laughing. Even Roduil was grinning and trying to hide it, and Selvorne caught Franek giggling. He had to admit, it was a sound plan, and less risky than what he had done with Rohy.

When asked to tell their tale, Selvorne found himself having to explain his journey without Rohy, who was keeping to himself, and very quiet. He tried to be modest, even in praise of Rohy, who had done well in each trial. As had Selvorne, but he still felt foolish for leaping into the river without a knife, and not noticing the rope. None of it seemed as interesting, amusing or clever as the others, but at the end, and most of the way through, he received compliments, even applause.

"Nice work with the stoning, very dramatic, very brave," Nakla praised, who also congratulated Rohy.

"It would have been more exciting if they had started throwing stones, though," Reklo said.

"I think that might be number one," Bitier decided, "the best story yet. Who would have thought joining the guards would be such fun?"

"Well, I did, that is why I am here," Reklo answered.

"Not me, I joined to be rid of this one," Nakla replied.

~

They continued to talk and laugh, but Rohy was still keeping to himself, for quite some while before leaning over to Selvorne.

"Selvorne, I have a problem," Rohy whispered, "I cannot swim."

A joke, perhaps – but Rohy was not grinning. Grim, and ... almost afraid. Selvorne was not sure he knew of anyone who could not swim, except children, who were usually too keen to learn, rather than afraid.

"You mean, you think the current is too strong?" Selvorne asked.

"No, I mean ... I have never swum. Never in water above my waist."

Selvorne did not laugh, but looked thoughtful. He was not sure what would happen if Rohy could not swim – not drown, for he would not enter the river, and surely they would not force him – but he did not know if the guards would still accept him. Standing, Selvorne went over to Roduil.

"Hey lanky, I cannot swim. Is there a boat I can take to the island?"

Roduil glared at him, then grinned.

"So, you cannot swim. No problem! Get dressed and sit with Franek, no need to join the guards."

"Need or not, I am joining. Clearly the guards need me, being so poorly prepared that they did not arrange boats. What position is above commander, one who might organise such things well?"

Taunts. Not too bold, Selvorne hoped, but Roduil's stare suggested otherwise. No, the commander was not angry. Not mocked, and not displeased – Roduil narrowed his eyes just briefly, then spoke in a calm low tone.

"Need or not, want or not – if you do not swim, you will not join."

"Ha! Had you fooled," Selvorne said, almost at once, and tried to give the stupidest grin, "I can swim very well, thank you, in fact, I think I shall go for a dip now while we are waiting."

Selvorne started heading to the river, but Roduil stopped him. "Sit down and wait, or you are out. Swim when commanded – or you are out."

With neither nod nor smile nor idiot grin, Selvorne turned and went back to Rohy.

"We have a problem," Selvorne said in a low voice, "no swim, no join. No options."

"I have a problem," Rohy corrected him, "I will have to explain myself, or withdraw."

"Nonsense!" Selvorne said, "It is a small matter, it is our problem, and I have a solution – if you can keep your head. Can you?"

Rohy nodded, and Selvorne explained his plan.

~

Soon the others arrived – Toavel, Aigel, Igusli and Ragval. It seemed odd for four to arrive at once, apparently Toavel and Aigel had a terrible time, where Igusli and Ragval had simply walked through easily. Proud of themselves, they were directed to sit with Franek, and there they began to talk loudly amongst themselves. Roduil gave them a stern look as he approached Toavel and Aigel, and told them to disrobe. That amused Ragval greatly, and he sat there laughing, until Franek explained what it meant – at that he stood up and challenged Roduil.

"What do you mean, we are not accepted?" Ragval demanded to know.

"Sit down!" Roduil commanded.

But Ragval was in no mood to take orders, especially if he was not actually a guard. He could have sat down and sulked, or stood and brooded, or stormed off – if he wanted. No one knew why he chose instead to shove Roduil. Perhaps he thought his friends would stand by him – Roduil was just one man. Whatever the reason remained a mystery, for Roduil slipped to the side and was not shoved, and tripped Ragval to the ground as he tried, stomping on his back to drive his face into the dirt, then held him there under a tall boot.

"You have a choice – stay there in the dirt, crawl over to sit on the log, or stand up and get pounded down again," Roduil said, seemingly enjoying himself. All the other men had stood as well, and were watching, "and you can all sit down, too," Roduil added, removing his foot. Ragval crawled over to the log, and seated himself facing away from the others.

Toavel leant over to Selvorne, "Hey – what is going on here?"

Selvorne explained their situation, and asked if he could swim.

"Of course I can," Toavel whispered, "you ... did you have a strange time getting here? I mean, very, very strange?"

"Hey, lanky boy, are we allowed to talk a while? Or are we headed off now?" Selvorne yelled out at Roduil, who glared at him, looked at Toavel, then nodded, "Is that a yes we can talk, or a yes we are headed off?" Selvorne yelled again, and Roduil came over to them both and stared down at them.

"You can sit and be silent," Roduil said, then he turned to Toavel, "and you can tell your story, without interruption, and when you finish, we are leaving."

Everyone turned to Toavel and Aigel. Selvorne was about to speak, but thought better of it.

"Well I am sure Aigel could tell the story better than I," Toavel began, and Aigel nodded, but was silent, eyeing Roduil, "I will do my best."

Their story was perhaps the most normal of any, on a day that was far from normal. They never realised that they were being tested, both being from well run farms of Tavalehk, they just figured the other towns were full of strange people with odd ways.

Their altercation at the inn ended with them making a run for safety. After throwing insults. And ale in the face of one of the men.

The drowning man went well enough. Both could swim well, neither thought it wise to jump in when there was a rope hanging on the rail. They yelled at the children for being so foolish, claiming that if they live next to a river, they should know what to do if someone was in trouble. Again, they thought townsfolk were just stupid, those far from their homes in Tavalehk.

The boy being punished was a more interesting a tale, more worrying for them than the others, for they were convinced completely it was real, and did not know what to do. They tried to reason with the elders, to no avail. In the end, Aigel created a distraction by knocking things over in the square, Toavel ran around stealing the buckets of stones and ran away. Aigel pointed him out and some people chased him, then Aigel ran off with the timer and hid it behind a barn, under the hay. Seeing a chicken pen on the way back, he opened it and let them all loose, chasing them into the square. Toavel meanwhile had hidden the stones, but not all of them, just two bucketfuls, and returned to the square with the empty buckets, again to be chased out. Aigel returned with a herd of chickens, and as people chased them around, he used a broom to lift the rope from the pole, and then swept dust into everyone's eyes as the boy shook himself free from his bonds. Aigel told him to flee to Senylehk, Toavel yelled to Hartlehk, but the boy seemed to run through the village instead, to hide. It was not perfect, but it worked, and they ran away to meet again down the road, where they rested to catch their breath.

Toavel added that, when they later encountered Igusli and Ragval, the two of them made no mention of anything except the inn. There was no drowning man, no stoning of a boy, just a fight at the inn, and an easy walk by the river. An old man fishing, some children playing, a village that was cleaning the streets and chasing chickens.

"Very well," said Roduil, "enough of this. You lot, line up there. And you four, follow me."

Roduil took aside Franek, Igusli, Ragval, and sadly, Traglan. He said a few words to them alone, then sent them walking to the north, away from the river. Then he began checking each of the others for any items they should not have. That included knives, which he took despite their protests, insisting there would be no chance to whittle or danger of reeds, and certainly no meals to eat as they crossed the river.

"You can all swim?" Roduil asked, and they nodded, even Rohy, though nervously, "Good. See that island over there? Go swim to it. When you get there, head up the hill to the camp."

"What about our things?" Selvorne asked.

"They will follow in the boat, once I load them. I will bring them around the other side of the island, by the road. Now go!"

~

A swim – a test. Roduil had been more than stern when Selvorne had confronted him – all guards had to be able to swim. Head to the camp on the island – the final test, then, and with the others who were rejected being sent away, only the swim mattered, and it was assumed they could swim as well as march and run.

Selvorne watched as the others made their way to the water, some flinching at the cold. Reklo and Nakla dived in and began their race – not too far a swim, and with the current, across and downriver to an island. Pleasant enough, race or not. Others waded in across the pebbled shore. It was a gentle way to enter the river, and the current was not so bad there, but a long way to the island for anyone who could not swim.

"Ow, ow, my leg, it hurts," Selvorne yelled, suddenly limping along. He entered the water, rubbing his leg and complaining loudly, saying he could not swim with a cramped leg.

"I will help you," Rohy said loudly, making his way towards Selvorne, who leant on him. Together they walked into the river, carefully, and each time Rohy grew nervous, Selvorne yelped and rubbed his leg.

"Help me, Rohy, it is a cramp for sure," Selvorne lied, as the two were joined by others trying to help, but Selvorne waved them away. Soon, they were up to their chests, and the current was beginning to push them.

"All right," he said to Rohy, "keep your head up and breathe. If you go under, just hold your breath until you come back up. Only breathe above the water. You will go under, but the more you relax, the more shallow you will dip, so the sooner you will be back in the air. Try to look like you are swimming, but if things go bad – I can drag you along, unless you struggle. So do not struggle!"

Rohy tried to relax, but was fearful, for the deep river must have been like a cliff for a man who knew not how to fly. Selvorne, however, was a strong swimmer and managed somehow to drag him with one arm, swim with the other, and avoid being hit by Rohy's flailing arms. Roduil disappeared from the shore, so Selvorne began dragging Rohy without pretending, until they landed on the island, much farther downstream than the others. Rohy crawled onto the shore, exhausted and ashamed.

"That was a great effort," Selvorne puffed, looking back across the waters to where they had started. Roduil seemed to be running, then disappeared in the bushes. Other men were running after him.

"Thank you, I did my best," Rohy said.

"I meant me," Selvorne said, "a great effort for me. That was a long – "

Many men burst out of the bushes around them, and some jumped on Selvorne, pinning him to the ground. Others did the same to Rohy. Selvorne was being strangled and choked as he felt cords go around his feet and throat. Trying to twist himself free, they held his arms, then pulled them behind his back and tied them tightly – a cloth was shoved in his mouth, then tied behind his head. The men all withdrew, leaving him there, bound at both feet and hands, he lay like a snake in the mud. He wriggled, but it was useless. Unable to see, he assumed Rohy was also taken.

"We have caught two more!" one of the men yelled.

"Bring them!" came the reply.

"Argh – we bound their feet. Now they cannot walk, and I am not dragging them."

All Lives Ended

Selvorne was being lifted – bound, not helpless, he used his head to try and hit the man, and was promptly dropped, crashing to the ground. Then kicked in the stomach – warned – kicked harder, and heaved over the man's shoulder. There he was held as if a sack of grain, and he wondered if he should try to fight.

"If this is a test," Selvorne thought, "I am going to be very, very angry at the end of it."

Angry – but he hoped it was a test. He was helpless. Fight or not, try or not, he was captured and bound. Even if he could hurt the man carrying him, it would end with him on the ground, unable to do anything more.

He was carried along a path, each heavy step thudding on the dirt – through a camp, the smell of a fire and ... something else – he knew the smell, it was blood. Pigs blood, and ... clothes, on the ground. Why would there be clothes, in heaps, and ... wood for the fire, the smell of smoke and dust. And ...

An arm. Selvorne heaved his head around to stare, forced his neck to the side to see what he could – bodies. Parts. There was an arm, and near it, a sword. One of the men following bent to pick it up.

"I shall have that, thank you very much, my good fellow," the man said – then he kicked the arm aside, and began swinging the sword as though reaping a meadow of hay.

"Put it away or put it to use, there may be more," someone snapped at him.

"More? If there are any more, there will be no guards left."

The men laughed, and Selvorne was dropped without warning, crashing onto his side.

"Not there!" someone yelled, and he heard someone getting bashed, "put him with the others."

Selvorne quickly writhed around to see all he could – there had been a fire, not long ago, and there seemed to have been a battle. Many bodies were on the ground, and though the guards did not wear all the same clothes – he was sure they were the bodies of guards. Weapons lay about, spears were stuck in the ground, and poles stood tall with round lumps at their tops. A low tree stump near the fire had a huge axe stuck in the top of it, and a mound of clothes to the side. The whole place smelled like a butcher yard – smelled of pig blood – but Selvorne knew it was not.

And he knew what it meant – he had failed. Too confident, too reckless. He had vowed to go carefully. Safe – so he had thought. At the least likely time he was taken, when surrounded by guards. On the way to the main town, he had been ambushed. He, and all the new recruits, the guards, perhaps the administration – he hoped Dyneti went north. But all others ... they were being slaughtered. He had failed his father, Arnlausa, Girradehn, and himself. Too trusting of the guards, of their ability and judgement, their caution and planning. He had let his own guard down – and failed. Although ... he was not yet dead.

Seen on the ground near was a knife – he wriggled towards it, only to have it kicked aside – amusing, for those who had captured him, as was the kick to his ribs. He tried to see who the people were, but they were all wearing hoods that covered their head, hair and face, and some had their eyes peering out from dark leather masks.

"I like this one, he is good to kick," said the man, who kicked Selvorne again, "makes a good noise. Can we kill him last?"

"Just put him away," came the reply. Then another kick.

Selvorne was heaved up once more, thrashing until he was beaten with a stick on the arm. They carried him away from the camp, passing spears and poles, which were many – and there were heads impaled on each. Young men, none he knew, though it was hard to tell when hanging upside down, and he was not close to any. Poor strangers, likely other guards. But then ... he passed one pole and on the top he saw the pale skin and neatly trimmed beard of Temnere. Badly injured, bloodied, hair matted like straw – but it was him, he knew the beard and nose. Of all the horrors he had seen in the past week, that was the worst – the most cruel, the most heartless. Even though the others who died were those who he had loved the most – to make such a mockery of the dead made him sick.

"Aha! Look what we have here! A cartload of treasures!" someone called out. The man carrying Selvorne stopped, then turned around, and he saw a man pushing a cart along ... their cart ... their possessions, and on top – a body. The cart was being pushed a little too fast and the man doing so stopped it suddenly, so the body rolled off and fell lifeless in the dirt. It was Roduil.

"Argh, I want some of that!" the man carrying Selvorne said, then turned away from the cart and ran heavily along the path, away from the camp, before dumping Selvorne on a pile of people. He crashed down amongst the muffled anger of many who were there, groans coming from all around.

Selvorne had been dropped on top of an angry Bitier, and both twisted to see men laughing and leaving. When they were gone, Selvorne glanced around quickly, searching for enemies, finding none, only captives. All were there, he thought, the new recruits and another, an older man he did not know. None of the brigands were near, and none were watching that he could see. A woodland grove, though some men had landed to crush bushes, they must have been dumped beside the path in a small clearing. There was a slight rise in the path back the way they had come, and leading away it was downhill, but a gentle slope. On an island, the crest of a hill – all a problem, he could not possibly run to escape, let alone swim, even if not bound.

Bitier, Rohy, Toavel, Aigel and Rhede – each bound as he was, with gags and hands behind the back, ankles as well held tight. Vugecarauk on his side, tied to a rough pole. Nakla and Reklo were bound to each other, face to face, arms at their sides, and were struggling to see what was happening. A deep sounding bell kept ringing, as might be used for an ox, but was muffled somehow as it hung from Orrikler's neck. There was clunking – shackles of bronze, perhaps, also on Orrikler, and on the old man as well, who was sitting up against a tree.

Everyone was covered in mud, soaking wet and barely clothed. Everyone was helpless, but it seemed Bitier was trying to do something.

"Argh!" Bitier cursed as he writhed his way from under Selvorne, "I almost had it then!"

Bitier had somehow removed his own gag, and had been trying to chew through Aigel's bonds on his hands before Selvorne had been dropped on them both – Aigel was covered, so Bitier began on Selvorne's bonds.

Others were making noises to get his attention, it seemed everyone wanted to be freed first. None more than Rohy, who was making as much noise as possible, furiously thumping the ground with his legs.

"Be quiet!" Bitier hissed, stopping his chewing to speak, "If you make noise, they will come. I am not removing your gags, if I do so, they will soon know one of us is getting free. So silence! One at a time!"

Rohy persisted, though everyone else was silent. Bitier made a futile attempt at Selvorne's wrists. Frustrated, unable to free him, he turned to Rohy to see if he was any easier. Rohy kept moving his hands and grunting, until Bitier wriggled to clunk their heads together, bit hard on the cloth gagging Rohy, and pulled it far enough to slide it past his chin.

"What is it?" Bitier demanded, as Rohy spat and cleared his mouth.

"What I was trying to say," Rohy began, "is that there is a knife at the side of my shirt."

Bitier's eyes lit up, immediately he began nuzzling around until he found it. It was not truly a knife, but a small, flat piece of bronze that had been sewn into the shirt on his side, in such a way it would not cut him, but could be easily ripped free. Bitier managed to get it out, only dropping it twice before gripping it in his teeth, cutting himself a little, then slicing into the bonds on Rohy's hands.

Bitier cut as quickly as he could, but it was difficult even with the knife, and when he was halfway through, two of the men arrived – both masked, and began arguing about which one to take. They grabbed Selvorne, but said he did not look right, then grabbed Bitier, dragging him aside and to his feet, though once standing he almost toppled, for his ankles were bound together and he could not stand alone.

"This one will do, and he has removed his gag," one of the men said. The other laughed and agreed.

Bitier spat on the ground and tried to ram them, but one caught him and hoisted him over his shoulder, carrying him away kicking and yelling – abuse, then demands. Then – and it was not much later – pleading. Then screaming.

Rohy had found the knife Bitier spat out, but before lifting it, and as the screams grew louder from the camp, he spoke to everyone.

"Listen, I have the knife. I will cut Selvorne's hands, then he can take it and cut mine. Then we can cut each in turn, and anyone freed can untie the others. But we have to free as many as we can before we act. If they come, and you have been freed, do not let them see – if they know, they will stop us. And do not charge them. Our only chance is to all go at them at once, or to run, all at once."

Several nodded, though Nakla and Reklo were writhing around like a mad clumsy snake, struggling against their bonds. It was a good thing they were gagged, Selvorne could only imagine how much noise they would make otherwise.

Selvorne's bonds were strange to Rohy, it was as if two people had tied him, for when he cut through one cord, it loosened and he was left with a rope holding his hands half a foot apart, still behind his back. Selvorne thought at once he had been freed, but soon realised he was not – he managed to pull his legs through and get his hands around to the front, and he could use his fingers, even though his wrists were still bound. He took the knife and began cutting at Rohy's bonds, but even using his hands, it was not much better than holding it in his teeth, and the blade was rapidly going blunt.

Vugecarauk was making noise to get attention, and Selvorne, thinking he might have another knife, wriggled over and removed his gag.

"I think I can break this branch," Vugecarauk said, trying to bend the great branch he had been bound to. His arms were at his front, and the branch ran along his back. A long rope had been wound about him many times, to keep his body stiff and helpless, and his feet were bound separately. If it were not for the branch, he might have been able to stand and hop away, but the branch was longer than he was tall, and if he could stand, it would stick into the ground by three feet. Selvorne thought it looked as though he was a skewered pig, and had been carried along by two men, one at either end of the branch.

"If you can get the branch to stick somewhere, I can break it, I am sure," Vugecarauk said.

"He might be right," Rohy said, reluctantly, frustrated at how long it was taking to be freed, "he is bound like that so they can drag him easily, but the branch looks like he could break it."

Selvorne looked him over, not sure how he could trap the branch. It was greenwood and would have to bend a long way before it broke. Vuggecarauk's feet were bound, but had a long rope tail hanging from the knot, so Selvorne used that to tie the branch to his feet. Vugecarauk bent at the waist, straining, bending, then managed to crack it. He repeated the same, snapping and bending and working it loose from his bonds, and looked like he might get free.

Not wanting to get in the way, Selvorne began writhing around, removing people's gags, hoping someone had more ideas. He managed to free Toavel and Orrikler before Rohy noticed and told him to stop.

"If they come and see everyone ungagged, and Vugecarauk free, and your hands in front, they will secure us at once, or place a man to watch. Stop it!"

"Let me at them," Vugecarauk cursed, writhing to get out of his ropes, "and I will make short work of them."

"No!" Rohy said, "If you attack them on your own, you will fail, and we are doomed. You have to pretend you are bound until we are all ready."

From the camp there was the sound of yelling and screaming, and someone chopping wood, then a loud cheer. The captives began franticly trying to free themselves.

"What now?" Selvorne asked, "It is taking forever to cut these bonds, I think the knife is blunt." He looked about for a sharp rock, found none, and then inspected the shackles on Orrikler to see if they had sharp edges.

"Cut my feet bonds," Toavel said, holding his feet in the air, "they are just leather straps. It will be fast."

His feet were bound with thick leather straps, wrapped on each ankle, and joined with a loop of cord. The leather seemed it might be easier to cut than the cords. Selvorne felt a cold chill through his blood – they were the kind of straps used to hang dead pigs to bleed.

"What good is that?" Rohy asked

"Well, at least we can run away," Toavel replied, "if you can quickly cut our feet, we can run, hide, and cut the remaining bonds. It will give us time."

Rohy agreed, and Selvorne began to cut the strap on one foot. Rohy also chewed at Aigel's bonds, but then two of the men returned, carrying something in a bag.

"Hello fools! Your fool friend has returned to see how you are doing!"

Both men were wearing brown hoods like sacks with eye holes, which looked absurd and somewhat disturbing. Some wriggled to look and see what they were doing, except Toavel, Orrikler, Selvorne and Rohy, who tried to conceal their mouths to hide the fact their gags were removed – but Selvorne looked as best he could out of the corner of his eye.

No friend had returned – just the two men, but one held out a great lump of cloth in his hand – then pulled away the cloth to reveal the severed head of Bitier. Blood dripped to the ground, his hair was matted and wet, his face pale grey. The man took the jaw in one hand and made it move, as though Bitier was talking.

"Hello friends! Do not fear! You will join me soon!"

At that, the two men laughed.

Some felt sick, some enraged. Selvorne was furious and frustrated. Rohy seemed to go cold, and was staring at the bushes. Nakla and Reklo were savagely struggling, which made the men laugh more. Toavel groaned, but hid his face.

Orrikler, old friend of Bitier, jingled his shackles as he turned to them and spoke.

"I am Orrikler Ultainen, favoured son of Ruchten NohcTohm Ultainen," he began, "yes, that is right," he added, as they froze, "Lord of Hartlehk. He commands many men, and there will be no mercy. I assure you, wherever you go, whatever you do, you will be found, and you will be tortured, slowly, to death."

They were silent for a while, and it seemed they were scared. But then they burst into laughter, and one went to Orrikler, leant down to him and tinkled the bell about his neck.

"Well, then, son of Hartlehk," he said, "we had best make sure none of you live to tell what has happened, and none of your bodies are found. A pity, we would have enjoyed the ransom!"

"Strange," the other man said, "Temnere said that you were amongst them, and wanted to be treated like all the others. He also said you would bring a great ransom, if we kept you. Before he died miserably, he promised many things. I am not sure the ransom is worth the risk? Perhaps we should take him next?"

"Wait, then, how is it you have no gag?" the first man suddenly realised, and then, trying to replace the gag, Orrikler bit at his finger, making the man jump back, and look at the others, some of whom also had no gags.

"Well, so – some have removed your gags. Talk amongst yourselves while you can, soon it will not matter. Tell me if you want to be next! Nobody? Oh well, we shall choose."

They then grabbed Rhede, who still had a gag and gave muffled screams. They dragged him aside, but Vugecarauk sprung up, half bound in ropes that dangled from about him, and he lurched towards them. They were startled – standing, many ropes fell from Vugecarauk, freeing his body in part, but his feet were still bound and he fell, struggling on the ground. They took him instead of Rhede, dragging him away by the long rope from his feet.

Selvorne had moved to save Vugecarauk, but Rohy stopped him with a harsh whisper and shake of his head. Selvorne obeyed, but was not sure if it was fear or caution that held him back – he had only slight use of his hands, and there were perhaps thirty men at the camp. One yell could bring them all running, if he tried to fight. Even if not restrained by ropes, he would have to remain restrained by wisdom, at least until there were enough of them to have a chance. Roduil had been defeated and slain, and he was the best of guards – so it was said – fighting would be futile. Still, such caution was no comfort as Vugecarauk was dragged away, helpless and still trying to fight from the ground.

~

The stranger who was shackled with bronze restraints and a small goat bell was jingling as he chuckled behind his gag. Selvorne angrily writhed over to him, worked his way to sit up, and ripped off his gag.

"What are you laughing at?" Selvorne demanded, as Toavel desperately begged Selvorne back to finish cutting his feet free.

"Oh," said the older man, spitting gratefully to have had his gag removed, then nodding at Orrikler, "I am just laughing at him – if he is the son of a lord, he should have promised riches and ransom, not threatened death and pain. What did he think they would do?"

"He has a point," Rohy added, "and, who might you be, anyway?"

"I am a poor merchant in the wrong place," the man lamented, "well, actually, I am a rich merchant in the wrong place. I was providing ale to the camp of guards on this island, but when I arrived, there was this terrible scene, and I returned to my boat to leave, and they had taken it, then taken me, and taken the ale. They were quick to realise their luck, and took my coins, and my clothes. Only my promise of ransom from my brother has kept me alive. You saw what they did to the others?"

Selvorne nodded, cutting furiously at the bonds on Toavel's feet.

"No? What did they do?" Toavel asked, and he wished he had not as several answered that the heads of the guards had their bodies replaced by spikes.

"I think they are Vog from the far lands of the north," the old merchant said, "and hunt people for their heads. I think they do not care about our lives, but perhaps our coins and ale. I think you are all doomed, and now that you have threatened them – so am I. As they said, they cannot now afford anyone to know, oh Son of Ruchten."

Everyone was distressed, Toavel especially, who had seen no heads on spikes. They had heard of Vog, a distant people who lived over the mountains and had ferocious ways, almost like animals. But they were just stories from the olden times, not likely, and not ... but heads on spikes was not a thing Waehter people did.

"They are not Vog," Rohy said, "I wish they were Vog. They are nothing like Vog. I think they are brigands. And I think this is worse."

Rohy was certain, and gloomy, and growing tired of trying to chew through Aigel's bonds.

"How can you be sure?" Toavel asked, desperately urging Selvorne to hurry, by trying to move his feet against the bronze knife.

"Well," Rohy said, tired and sick from chewing, "they speak as we do. They dress as we do. They are not armed with swords. And the Vog do not cut off the heads of foes, except in duels of honour amongst themselves – between their lords and great men of fighting. They would not consider someone like Bitier worth the trouble. And if they wished to kill all of us, they would have done so at the start.

451

No, these are worse – these men are either questioning and torturing us, or keeping us alive ... to be prepared, one at a time, for food."

Toavel was finally free, kicked his legs, managed to stand with his hands behind his back, then looked around – his face was pale with fear, and he was trying to see if men were coming.

"Good luck!" Toavel said, then nimbly ran down the hill, away from the camp, and disappeared into the woods.

"What!" Selvorne exclaimed, stunned, "I thought the plan was to wait and all go together?"

Aigel started grunting to get them to cut his feet free, though Selvorne was reluctant, so he removed Aigel's gag.

"Cut my feet, I will not run," Aigel pleaded, "and will wait with you all. It is a good plan, if we can run into hiding, we can cut the bonds at will, on stones."

Rohy complained that it was a waste of time since his feet and Selvorne's were bound tightly with ropes. Nakla with Reklo were well bound together, and Orrikler was impossible to free. Regardless, Selvorne cut at the leather that Rohy had been chewing, and quickly sliced through it.

"I will not run," Aigel repeated, "I could not bear, that if any of you live, that I would be remembered as fearful, when you tell the story to others."

Selvorne had been holding on to hope that he would make it, until Aigel's words made him realise that perhaps he would not – someone might. He wondered if he should tell Dyneti's message to everyone, so someone else could pass it on to Tarbo. It might not matter, if the message was that brigands were amongst the guards – if all the guards were already dead. Too late, then, to deliver as a warning ... then he fell into gloom, realising he had failed her as well, and also, would never see her again.

Aigel did run, but not the way Toavel had headed. When one man came back to fetch another captive, looked over the area and grabbed Rhede, who was unfortunately still nearest the path – Aigel stood up, charged into the man, knocked him over and continued at speed – towards the camp.

Everyone was stunned – astonished that he had done it. Selvorne wondered if Aigel was hoping others would follow, only himself and Rohy possibly could. There were sounds of shouting and anger and chasing, and the man who had been knocked down, got up, looked over the captives to be sure no others were attacking him, then ran after Aigel.

There was a terrible noise of grunting and slapping of the ground coming from Nakla and Reklo, desperate to get attention. Selvorne crawled over and realised they had managed to writhe out of the ropes, which were unravelling at their feet. He pulled at them and unwound them in a tangled mess, they were soon free and removed their own gags.

"Finally!" Reklo said, unusually quietly, almost a whisper.

"Free at last!" Nakla said, also quietly.

"Do not do anything stupid," Rohy commanded.

"What, like all the stupid things you have been doing so far?" Reklo asked. He did not expect an answer, and immediately began trying to untie Selvorne's feet, as Nakla at once took to Rohy.

"All right," Nakla said as he tore at the knots, "this is what we must do. We cannot fight, there are not enough of us. We must get everyone walking, and now, and get as far away as we can, and find a rock to cut the ropes. Or use the knife that is not working very well. But we must go! And now!"

"You cannot cut nor untie my legs," Orrikler lamented, for he was in shackles.

Nakla and Reklo looked at the shackles, and each other. Their faces suggested they had not considered it.

"Can you carry him?" Nakla asked Selvorne.

"I think so, but can you do it? I think you are stronger than I am," Selvorne said, and they looked as dismayed as when they had first seen the shackles.

"No, we cannot," Reklo said, "you will have to do it."

Selvorne wondered why, when his feet were finally freed and he stood, stretching his back. His arms were still bound in front of him, though he could use them, and he felt like strangling his enemy with the rope that still joined one wrist to the other. It was about the right length. Rohy was standing as well, and soon Rhede, who immediately fled down the path Toavel had taken.

At that moment, one of the men appeared with his mask removed – he was a young man, very out of breath, and clearly had been running around. It seemed he had come to check on the captives to make sure they were secure, what he found instead was five of them standing, and two of them immediately charged. He turned and ran, but Reklo dived at him, caught his ankle and tripped him, then scrambled after as the man got to his feet and ran away.

"Argh!" Reklo grunted as he went after him.

"We will delay them as long as we can," Nakla said, grabbing the broken branch that Vugecarauk had snapped, "run, hide, be quiet, cut your bonds in silence, go to the river at night and float away. Good luck!"

His order was firm, but his eyes were desperate – he could not leave his brother, and ran after him. Selvorne wondered if it was their plan from the start, or if Reklo had been hasty in his pursuit. Either way, both men had to know they were doomed.

"Leave me here," said the rich merchant, "I think you are all going to be captured and killed, anyway, and I have my ransom to save me, perhaps."

Selvorne gladly left him, but heaved Orrikler to his shoulder and stumbled clumsily along the path. Orrikler held fast the bell so it would not jingle, and they all disappeared down the hill into the woods.

~

They were surprised at how far they made it before the noise of fighting and yelling disappeared. The woods were thick, old and wild, but the path was quite clear. Selvorne whispered that he wanted to leave the well–trodden way, but Rohy insisted the path would be best to move fast and make distance before disappearing, and so doing, widen the search.

Every so often when there was mud, Rohy turned to walk backwards, leaving prints that would confuse anyone tracking. At times they saw Rhede, far ahead, not exactly abandoning them, but only barely restraining his desire to get to the lake and swim away.

"Psst!" came a voice from the bushes – someone was hiding off the path, and everyone's heart jumped as they looked, "Psst! Hey, come this way," came the voice of Toavel, and they could hardly see him amongst the thick growth, "come this way, I have found a place to hide." His head popped out of the bushes briefly, and he waved his hands, that somehow he had freed.

"That is too close to the path," Rohy said, "they will find us."

"Not here, do you think me a fool?" he snapped back, still quietly, in a hissing whisper.

Toavel led them through the thick woods, Selvorne stumbling under the weight of Orrikler. Rohy continued ahead along the path leaving tracks, and returned walking backwards. He hoped they would follow Rhede at least for some distance farther as he fled – not fortunate for Rhede, but he was not supposed to flee alone.

The woods were thick, but people moving would easily be seen. Selvorne thought if they lay in the grass they could remain hidden, but not if they were walking – then Toavel, who was ahead, disappeared into the ground. Completely, dropping down much farther than a man could duck, before popping up again. He had found a hole, of sorts, overgrown with vines and bushes, it looked like an abandoned stone building, half set against a rocky outcrop – trees had fallen upon it to make a tiny hill, but from a distance it did not seem like an obvious place to hide. They all followed Toavel to drop into it. He took a sharp knife and began slicing through their remaining bonds.

"That is my knife," Rohy said, "where did you get it?"

"From their camp," Toavel replied, "they left it by the roasting spit."

Selvorne, Rohy and Orrikler stared, astounded – they realised Toavel had not fled at all, and he explained that he thought they knew the plan was to each escape in turn, hide, and free themselves. Rohy took his knife back, and though Toavel was reluctant to let it go, Rohy was much faster cutting with it, taking to the rope like a hungry man to a roast.

"I could not find a place to hide," Toavel said, "so decided to spy on the camp, and see if they could fight. Then Aigel appeared, racing through the camp and kicking things over. He did not seem he was escaping, but attacking, so I thought you must all be free and ready to charge. I almost charged, but soon realised he was alone. Then he ran away into the woods."

"Did he make it?" Selvorne whispered.

"I do not think so," Toavel replied, saddened, "perhaps, I think I saw him trip. They all went after him, and some are still searching through the woods. When they left, I quickly grabbed this knife, nobody saw me, and I disappeared, planning to come back to you all and cut you free."

"And then you did not return?" Rohy asked.

"I never truly left," Toavel said, "each time I tried to come back, another man had appeared amongst you. There was no way back to you except along that path."

"What now?" Orrikler asked, still glum, still holding his bell silent, "I cannot swim away, I will sink like a stone with all this iron and bronze."

"You could stay here," Rohy said, "they want you for ransom. They did not once try to take you, and that merchant has been there all day. You should be safe, if you hide, if they find you, you will live."

"Nonsense," Selvorne said, "he can find a log and float on it. Nobody is going to stay here."

"I am," Rohy said, "I am going to hide somewhere in the woods. I can lie in some ditch covered for hours – never move, and they will never find me. I am sure they are watching the lake."

Selvorne knew Rohy might have another reason for avoiding the lake, and realised it must be a thing very hard for him to face if he could not swim. Selvorne could not tow him, not when fleeing – he had thought to duck underwater for a long time and float downstream safely, only appearing with his face in the waves to breathe. But with Rohy it would be impossible.

"They are watching the lake," Toavel said, "and they likely expect us to go at night, so I think we should watch them, and when they are not watching, we go. Not at night. It is not far to Senylehk, and we will be in the town by nightfall. But very cold."

They all agreed that was a good plan, and after some discussion, decided to stay hidden in the hole, and if someone came – they would be quickly finished, silently, and the body would be hidden in the hole beside them. Rohy said he would be eager to kill them, but a much better idea would be to let them pass in silence, because if they thought they had searched the area, they would move on, but if one of them disappeared, they would be suspicious. So in silence they would wait, and when it seemed safe, venture out, separately, and make for the lake.

They were not entirely quiet, as planned. Rohy stood watch, or sat up tall to watch, as the others sat low, in gloom. Some could not help guessing at the fate of their friends. Selvorne suggested revenge, but was berated by the others for such a stupid idea at such a dangerous time. They wondered if Aigel had made it away, or if Rhede had made it past the river watch.

Selvorne hoped once more that he might survive, but he realised he might not, for it would be hard to escape, and easy to be caught. One of them might, though, and if he did ... he weighed up the idea of revealing a secret message against having it lost.

Dyneti never said what he should do if he was in danger of dying, she only said it was essential to get the message through as soon as possible. And to Tarbo, alone, and to tell no others – but he was about to tell others. Tell no others, tell no one – or reveal it to his friends in danger, in the hope it got through – or let it die with him. Guards were dead – clearly there were spies amongst them, or if not, it hardly mattered to dead men. Perhaps the message no longer mattered. Perhaps Tarbo's head was on a spike near the fire, and so he would not care to – but, oh, had he the message earlier, perhaps that would have saved him, and saved them all. If Tarbo lived, still – perhaps that message was essential, perhaps it would save him from something worse – save Dyneti, perhaps.

"Listen," Selvorne said, "I have a message that I am supposed to pass on, but if I do not make it, someone must do it for me."

He recited it and all the restrictions to the others, who were astounded and grim. He did not explain what he thought it meant, nor Dyneti's fears about spies, but he stressed the importance of secrecy, and saying it word for word. Toavel was baffled and wondered if it had to do with their current danger. Orrikler said he knew Tarbo was the High Captain and Commander of the guards – such a message must be very important. Rohy was silent. Selvorne felt a weight was lifted, and also that he had betrayed Dyneti, somehow, but he was doing the best he could, and wished she had explained his task better than giving it as she did, taunting him with jokes and messages of love for Demni.

After some while, when it seemed safe and no men had been seen, Toavel and Selvorne left to continue through the woods to the lake, not to leave, but hoping to find a log that Orrikler could float upon. They moved quietly, slowly, and watched for the men in the woods, and when they saw some approaching along the path from the lake, they froze, then gently slipped down amongst the grasses.

There were two men, one in a hood, and they were too far away to determine if they were armed, though of course they would be. After they passed by, one man in a hooded cloak and one poorly dressed, Selvorne and Toavel looked at each other in disbelief.

"Was that Rhede?" Toavel whispered, "Why does he not run?"

It certainly was Rhede walking with the hooded man, still in his short trousers and shirt, dripping wet, he must have tried to swim, but was caught. Selvorne thought on what might have happened.

"Captured at the lake?" Selvorne suggested.

"But he could flee now, he runs very well," Toavel said.

"But to where? The lake again? That must have gone badly. There may be dozens there."

"He might have bargained our capture for his release," Toavel whispered, his heart sinking as he realised Rhede and the man were headed back along the path towards their woodland hiding place.

"He does not know where we hid, though, so he could be lying, in the hope we rescue him," Selvorne suggested – defending Rhede, though he did wonder if it might be true.

"Or, it might be a trap to lure us out in an attempt to rescue him, and others might be watching, and Rhede knows that, and so does not run."

"Well, to realise all possibilities," Selvorne added reluctantly, "he might have been allied with them from the very start. But I am not going to assume that he was, and leave him to his fate – nor sit here wondering what danger there might be if we try to save him. I am going to try and take down that man with him, as quietly as possible."

Toavel reluctantly agreed and they began stalking Rhede and his captor through the woods, which was slow going, and at times noisy. They were in luck that the path wound around in a gentle curve, and they could move directly ahead through the bushes, hidden by a thick patch of woods, and reach a point on the path where they could jump out on the unsuspecting.

It was far from a silent ambush, but it was effective. As Rhede passed first, the man following found himself set upon by two charging youths from the bushes, filled with a day's load of fury. Selvorne hit the man first, grappling around his knees, and by force of weight shoved him right off the path into the bushes on the other side. The man let out a terrible yell, muffled as Toavel fell on top of his head.

Stunned, but skilled, the man wriggled free on the ground and clobbered Selvorne on the head, but could not stand because his legs were in pain. He began to shout "Stop! Stop!" – but Selvorne would not stop, and began pounding into his mask, the man striking back, so there were four fists wildly flailing as they rolled and tumbled in the dirt.

"Stop you idiot!" the man commanded, unable to fight on his side in the dirt, he covered his head with his arms. Selvorne rose, tried to pull the man's arms away to hit his face, and when it failed, he lifted the man, and began bashing his head down on the ground.

Someone grabbed Selvorne from behind and pulled him away, he spun around thinking he had been ambushed by more men. Ready to meet his defeat with a last, furious stand against them – he saw only Rhede.

"Selvorne! Stop! Look!" Rhede said, pointing at the man on the ground, who was rolling about in pain. Struggling to undo a fastener behind his head, he removed the leather mask and sat up glaring at Selvorne – it was Roduil.

Astonishment – then a moment of guilt gave way to a moment of joy, as Selvorne realised Roduil must have escaped, killed one of the men, taken his mask and was going to help them all escape. Or get revenge. But his excitement quickly turned to horror, as he thought Roduil and Rhede must have been involved. Then, confusion, and disbelief, for had he not seen Roduil's dead body, only hours ago?

"Get up and march back to the camp," Roduil commanded, rubbing his knee, and to Rhede, "you, help me up and help me walk."

Selvorne refused and Roduil left him there as he limped away with Rhede, who seemed to be having doubts, but left regardless with Roduil, who had no patience with Selvorne and did not explain anything. Toavel said he would follow at a distance and see what was happening. Selvorne was suspicious, and followed even farther behind.

~

Back they went – along the path to the camp of killers, and up the slope Roduil and Rhede disappeared. Toavel was far ahead when Selvorne passed the place where they had been held. The rich merchant was not there, and the ropes had all been taken away. There was laughter and shouts from the camp ahead, and a great smell of roasting, though he dared not think what it was. Toavel let out a shout of joy and ran – Selvorne cautiously continued after him.

There were forty men or more, laughing and joking, the mood had changed completely. Vugecarauk was there, easily seen amongst the others – with Nakla and Reklo. All were laughing at Bitier, who was in a conversation with a severed head that he held – identical to his own head – discussing all the lessons of life with himself, the merits of self reflection, then he put it on his shoulder and pretended to be a two–headed man.

"Is that a goat I hear? My favourite meal!" Bitier said as he turned to Orrikler, who was jingling furiously, trying to remove his bell from his neck.

Selvorne at first thought they were all in on some prank designed to make him look the fool, but as he approached and they welcomed him, he noticed some were still shaken, pale, and in shock. Others were laughing, Aigel was brooding. Rohy was silent as he looked over all the men at the camp, only half smiling when he saw Selvorne.

"Heads made of clay," Rohy said to Selvorne, "blood from a pig, freshly killed – there, roasting. These are the guards, and they have made us seem as fools."

"But we live," Selvorne added, his voice low, and his mood grim.

"Yes. But never again will I be fooled, or captured," Rohy said through gritted teeth.

One of the guards who was a much older man was sitting and laughing with the rich merchant. When he saw Selvorne, he suddenly stood and began counting, then blew a small horn with a couple of tweets. Every guard fell silent and began to form ranks around the fire. The new recruits were still making noise, but grew uncomfortable as they wondered what might happen next. Every guard there looked at the older man, so they did likewise.

He was not very tall, but he was solid and strong, in a large coat too heavy for the warm weather, and a wide–brimmed hat. He had a patch over his left eye, and his face was unshaven and bore a few small scars, half hidden by the stubble of what could grow to a great beard, should he let it. He walked with a slight limp and a staff, and his voice boomed with authority.

"Welcome, guards!" he yelled, and all the guards let out three great cheers, then were silent.

"This is your last chance to leave," he continued, "those who now realise they are not good enough to join, go over there, and we shall let you return to your ordinary life."

Nobody did so, though some looked like they might.

"Good. All wish to stay," he said, then came closer and looked at them each, "but you have until morning to decide. Consider it well. I do not want anyone here who is not willing to risk all, and will not obey."

"And who are you?" Selvorne asked, startling the man and creating a gasp of disbelief amongst the older guards. Roduil snickered – he was the only one sitting, rubbing his knee.

The old man turned to Selvorne and looked him in the eye. Selvorne did not feel intimidated, if anything he was furious for what they had been through, and ashamed that he had been tricked to reveal Dyneti's message against her orders.

The older man stepped back to address all the recruits.

"I? I am your new master. I am your new owner. I am your Lord, and Law. I am the High Captain of the Guards. I am Tarbo."

The guards let out a brief cheer, then all were silent.

Forgive and Remember

A rough lot were all the men. The older guards, who had done such deceits with masks and cloaks, struggling to bind men by the riverside – they were covered in sweat and dust turned to mud. The new recruits were far worse, and wearing only their undergarments in which they had swum. Selvorne did not care, for he felt a battle of anger and betrayal within him, and he was not sure if he was blameless for either. Tarbo seemed stern, but not displeased, and Selvorne wondered how that might change to learn that a secret message had been delivered to the wrong people. He had no time to dwell on it, for the High Captain of the Guards seemed ready to speak.

"First," Tarbo began, "the rules. You will not talk when I talk. You will not speak unless requested. If you do, you will receive a whack from this stick," he said, then waved his staff at them – it was as tall as he, and an inch thick, so would hurt quite a bit. They doubted he would hit them, and he must have sensed it, so he smacked Toavel on the arm.

"Ow! what was – " Toavel yelped, but when he spoke, he received another whack. He then was silent, brooding at the unfairness of it all. Unspeaking – and Tarbo smiled.

"Good! You are learning!" Tarbo said, then hit Aigel suddenly and hard on the arm. Aigel only bit his lip. Tarbo continued along the line of new recruits, hitting each in turn.

"Obedience is golden, but this staff is wooden, which serves just as well," Tarbo said, then chuckled at his own cleverness. Selvorne almost said something insulting, he could feel the urge to, but held his tongue.

"Speak and be hit. Drag out the night and delay these hungry guards from eating, and they will likely pound you to the dirt. Or instead, give you no food."

Suddenly one of the guards dashed out of line and ran to the pig, which nobody was turning, and it had started to burn on one side. He rotated it, sighed with relief, and Tarbo gave the others a dismissive wave, at which they broke from their lines and set about organising the camp and feast.

"You will not reveal any of today to anyone, ever. Not your friends. Not your family. Not – no, especially not your lady friends or wives, if you have them, for they gossip the most. Today is a secret of the guards, and – join us or not – if you reveal it, we will find you, and make you pay," Tarbo said, then he gave an extra large whack to Vugecarauk, who did not flinch.

Selvorne was last in the line to be hit, and he did not think it was too hard, but it was stern.

"You will not be angry at those who captured you, tricked you, hit you. You will not hold a grudge against these men who are your brothers, now. For they, too, suffered the same fate when they joined, and in time, you may do the same to a new group of men. This is the joining ritual, and must be endured."

Some of the new recruits did not seem convinced, and Selvorne wondered which of the guards toiling about the camp was the one who kept kicking him in the ribs, still sore, with worse blows than Roduil's punches. Selvorne had no anger against Roduil, if anything he was worried that the best guard might want revenge against himself. But the man who kicked him when he first crawled from the lake, that was not necessary.

"What, then is a guard?" Tarbo continued, "You are all guards, now, and all that implies – obedience, and initiative, self control, and reckless daring. To serve, and to lead, and bring honour to the guards in all you do."

Tarbo took a deep breath, and seemed solemn, as did the guards who were cooking and arranging the camp. A few moments, before they continued their tasks, and Tarbo spoke.

"What started long ago, as a gathering of angry men, intent on sweeping the lands of brigands – has grown to be the most noble group of men, united to serve the best cause of the lands. To bring justice, safety and help where needed. United under the wise direction of the Waehdric, loyal not to men, but to the noble spirit of their teachings, and the common laws – not to any one person, lord, commander, or town. You are paid by the Waehdric, you serve what they serve – their ideals, their truths, their wisdom. Not their leaders. Nevertheless, you must follow orders."

Tarbo looked to each of the men, and Selvorne could see in their eyes that anger was turning to pride. And Tarbo – though he was so stern he seemed almost angry – was also very proud.

"We are the reason there is no war – we are the reason there now is law. Orders we follow bring order to all. In defence of the lands, we are the wall."

Selvorne wondered how many more recruits they would have attracted at the festival, had Tarbo given the speech at Tavalehk. It was rehearsed, precise, likely given to every new recruit – but spoken with sincere vigour. The spirits of the men were lifting with pride, even those guards who were were busy organising the meal.

"I own you now, you serve me – but in truth I, too, serve – and we are as brothers. The same, equal. But, you will do as I say, for as long as you are in training," Tarbo shook his staff and some quivered slightly, "at least until I have knocked sense in and stupidity out of your thick heads."

Tarbo then grinned at them each in turn.

"There are no brigands like the days of old. Then, there were hundreds, perhaps a thousand, we drove them out with bloody fighting. I was there, I was young, at the end when all their leaders were slain. Now, only a few here, a dozen there, none know for certain – perhaps they have returned. We shall soon know, as we sweep through the southern woods ... "

Tarbo stopped himself and was silent for a few moments, watching their faces, then nodded.

"So, with fewer foes, apart from fighting, as guards you must serve in many ways – builders, harvesters, helpers, messengers. An army of workers to assist where needed, at any village or town. The best of you will stay and train others, or be commanders like Roduil, scouring the land for brigands, ensuring safety on the roads. Not all will fight, but all of you will be valued in the Brotherhood of Guards. Some will be runners – even a messenger can change the course of events, and live an honoured life of great service, without fighting a single enemy."

Rhede looked especially happy, as that had been his plan from the start.

"Some might learn to read, to build, to administer law, and move on to different lives than fighting men. All this will be available to you, should you show both interest and ability. Some might leave the guards, to become travelling merchants, making profitable journeys to distant lands, safe in your training and skill, like my friend here," he waved his hand at the rich merchant who had been bound as a captive. He was sitting on a log chewing on an early cut of the roast, and he waved it on the end of a fork when everyone looked at him. A friendly, casual gesture, not likely meaning to taunt their hunger.

"Others may become lords or administrators, and rule with justice and fairness, instead of terror and fear," Tarbo said, looking straight at Orrikler, who might have felt unfairly accused, for he seemed to stand awkwardly. If blamed, it was undeserved, for he was not his father, and not even the heir to inherit the town – his older brother Kyler had been trained as a guard, and from what Selvorne had heard from Bitier as they travelled, it had not changed Kyler all that much.

"What sort of person, then, makes a good guard? How do we find such people?" Tarbo asked, and his tone had changed from one of pride and promise to that of a curious instructor – almost, Selvorne thought, that of a Waehdric, teaching young children how to be wise.

"Strong, fast, enduring, healthy – these qualities are easy to find. A wrestle, a race, a swim, then choose from the best. Gentle, noble, fierce, kind, alert – willing to sacrifice themselves to help others – an eye for the fair and the good – these are harder to find, much harder to test."

Selvorne had to agree, and wondered if perhaps the better fighters might be the roughest, nastiest people, with few of those qualities – but he conceded that training such men to fight with even greater skill might not be a very good idea.

"Some of the greatest men of our time served as guards. Your own Lord Arnlausa, and the great Krogarve," Tarbo said, but paused as that name was spoken, and looked at them all, nodding as he did – all of the men were astonished, "yes, he was a real man, once. As was Torlor – more brave in life than told in poems. Perhaps just as clumsy, at times."

Some of the guards tending to the camp chuckled, then tried to look busy as Tarbo turned to them. Selvorne remembered his message – to be told to Tarbo, who would deliver it to Torlor. The man must still live. Rohy, Orrikler and Toavel also remembered it, and looked at Selvorne, then at Tarbo, wondering what it all meant.

"How can we find such noble people? How, when taking boys from distant towns? Do I know you? Any of you? Do I trust in your reputation – recommendation from others – your word?"

Aigel had Tarbo staring in his face for a moment and grew uneasy, until he realised he was meant to respond.

"Umm ... by testing them?" Aigel replied, remembering the trials of the day, and risking a hit with the stick.

"Yes, yes, the trials!" Tarbo agreed, obviously pleased with the trials of the day, which he likely had personally designed, "Temper, awareness, sensitivity, cleverness, sacrifice – I can teach these in time. I can take a rough boy and turn him into a gentle man, given time. Perhaps a week for some, or a lifetime for others. But I am old, and have no time, and that is why we seek people who seem to have been properly raised, and keep the ones who prove good.

"I do not know you, or you, or you," Tarbo said, pointing at each in turn, "and even if I did know you, how well would I know you? How well would you know yourself? Would you stop to save a drowning man? Would you risk your life to save a guilty boy, for justice? Or hide and let him suffer? Would you control your temper, if challenged by the drunk? The only way to know is to face such things, and there is not enough time to wait for such trials to present themselves. They never may. Or may, at the worst of times."

Tarbo waited, and some of the men nodded. Not all, and Selvorne wondered if some of the men agreed, but were so astonished they could do nothing but stare.

"Were you annoyed? Were they inconvenient? Confusing? Contrived? I assure you, the events of this day that you find so strange – they have all happened before. Not as a ruse, to guards, testing their character, some failing terribly. But truly, unprepared.

"The useless brawl in a bar, over ale of great quality, leaving two guards and four townsfolk dead. Guards have been unwelcome at that inn since – it did not happen at the Axeman, with their delicious pies, but at another inn. Ale there was fine, and expensive – worth the high price of coins – but not the lives of men. Not guards, not the rough men of the town – not the poor men who tried to ease them all to peace, and instead found death."

The men thought on it – some of them had come to blows, and for them it had only been a test.

"The drowning man, unnoticed by runners in a hurry, on a task – our own men. Too much of a hurry to investigate a weeping child. The poor man died, watched by his son, who had called for help and was ignored. We only learnt of that sorrow years later, when his son had grown to a man, and had his revenge. Bitterness taking years to become revenge – and we never knew the reason, until it was too late.

"The foolish boy, who killed a girl with a stone, a terrible accident, never intended – boys may do stupid things. But his unjust death, and that of his mother who tried to shield him – most horrible. Then the fury of his father, who returned from a distant journey, discovered the loss of all whom he loved – he burnt the village to the ground. Guards who were there could have saved the boy, but they had done nothing – and they were not there to put out the flames, many months later, nor save those who burnt. The village made its unfair law, but the guards failed to enforce justice."

Tarbo looked at them all again, and took a deep breath.

"Some of you failed!" Tarbo yelled, his voice unusually powerful and terrifying. Everyone at once began to think what they had done wrong.

"And so have been sent away!" Tarbo continued, and there was a sigh of relief.

"Arrogant, lazy, stupid – even cruel, we have no place for such men. Friends, were they? Remain friendly, if you must, but know this – those sent away are not guards, not your brothers, not your allies as we are to be – not good men. Not yet. Perhaps never. They are merely boys, or men, but not good enough to be guards – they are gone, forget them."

Igusli, Ragval, Franek and Traglan – only Traglan would be missed, but he would be a dangerous man to have as guard. He had proven it – almost started a fight at the inn, Bitier had said. Selvorne was not sure why the other three had been there at all. He did not like them, and was glad they were gone, except that in some strange way he felt sorry for them. Being rejected upset them, so they must have had their reasons to join. They would be made bitter – perhaps it would be better to have let them join. Had they stayed, it would change them – none of them could remain so arrogant, not that night, after being bound and facing death. Although ... perhaps they would not be standing there feeling proud to be accepted as guards, but seething with anger and revenge. Looking to the faces of the new recruits, Selvorne did not think any of them were bitter about being bound and facing death. Shaken, but not vengeful.

"Start no fight," Tarbo yelled, "against those who push – not for pride, not for pleasure. Not for glory, not for being a fool. Allow no man or woman in need be left without help. Allow none to punish unjustly, or do harm that may be stopped. So as guards you must do – at all times – and one more thing besides.”

Tarbo waited until they were all listening, which was not long, for they could do nothing else.

“Each day as guard you must know that death may come – danger – pain. And yet must face it, with fear or not – whether guards, or not – for all men this truth is the same. Most men prefer to give it no thought. But, as guards, you must know it – think of it – prepare.”

Selvorne was not sure if the others had considered that before or not – as guards, or not – they seemed solemn, but not completely surprised. Perhaps they had imagined life as a guard as being not so dangerous. Being well trained, they would elude death, avoid pain – embrace danger, knowing they would be victorious in battles. So they may have fancied that morning – but they had tasted defeat that day, and though all was merely pretend, at the time it felt quite real. All had resisted, all had been left helpless.

“Finally,” Tarbo continued in a low voice, “we need men, not boys. We need people who are young, but wise. What is a man? Does someone become a man simply by growing older? No!”

Tarbo was searching their eyes as he walked up and down the line.

“I do not want boys, in search of adventure, or fame, or pay. I want men, to serve as guards,” he said, passing Rhede, Bitier and Toavel.

“A man is a boy who has faced terrible fear, made the terrible choice, victorious or defeated – has drawn on the best of himself when confronted – and done his best,” Tarbo continued, speaking to them all, but he was standing before Vugecarauk and Aigel.

“Perhaps he fails completely – crushed, broken and dying – but he did what he knew was right, and he knows what matters to him most, and has touched on the best of himself,” Tarbo said as he stood before Nakla and Reklo.

“Perhaps he is victorious – gloriously thought of, by those who were not there, who only heard the tale of magnificent victory! But, inside himself, he knows it was close, and could have gone either way. Close to death, yes, he has known its breath at his ear. A man is he who no longer feels unbeatable, as a boy might do – and realises it was luck that separated him from defeat – whether that be the luck that he was prepared, the luck he was well trained, or the dumb, stupid luck of fate – the great joke of the world, played upon men, cruel and heartless, with no care either way.”

Tarbo looked over them all, but was at the end of the line before Orrikler, Rohy and Selvorne, who noticed some of the other guards at the fire had stopped what they were doing, nodding as they listened.

“You were not meant to win,” Tarbo said, “not to escape today, not to succeed. You were meant to face death, horror and loss. Sorrow, and fear. Because, as a guard, this is what you may face, one day. And every day you must know that, and not face it with doubt. You must be prepared, if not to escape, then to die with honour.

"Here, training, we may not have time to turn a person bad into one good – but we certainly have time to turn a boy into a man. You have known defeat. You are no longer boys, but men. Not just men, but guards. Noble guards – be proud!"

Cheers rose from the other guards, and a rush of pride ran through the new recruits – great grins for a few, wide, awkward smiles from others. Clearly some were wondering about the prospect of facing capture and death again – with real danger, not prepared carefully as a lesson. It frightened them, but focussed their fears, and Selvorne was sure each were thinking what they might do if it happened again. How to hide knives, how to fight, how to avoid capture. Determined to learn all they could, with a dedication that only came from fear. He certainly was thinking just that, and the promise he had made to Arnlausa came back to him – to learn to fight. He made it again to himself.

"So, you have all faced defeat, horror and death – and so have succeeded. But what a terrible lot you are," Tarbo said, mocking them with a gleam in his one eye, "I do not know if you are smart enough to train as competent guards, perhaps you will all end up as assistants, working indoors for administrators, fetching their things and bowing a hundred times a day."

Their pride fell, some were about to object, but, remembering the stick, they were silent. Tarbo waved it in the air, then shook it at Bitier at the end of the line.

"Bitier, next time, I suggest you choose one person to free at a time, and if they come for you, do not let them take the one person who has a knife, nor the people you have freed," Tarbo said, and Bitier nodded, agreeing, and seemed to be making a mental note of the advice.

"Vugecarauk, foolish boy, what did you hope to achieve? You should have let them take the other boy, and remained still, quiet, until you were completely free," Tarbo said, and Vugecarauk started to speak, but received a hit and was silent.

"Toavel, you should have told them your plan at the start so they could work with you. Then, returned immediately with the knife. What you did was dangerous, and stupid."

"Yes, captain!" Toavel agreed eagerly, earning himself an unexpected whack with the stick.

"Aigel, I do not know where to begin. What was your plan? Tire them as they gave chase? Wear them down, as they beat you to death?" Tarbo asked, and Aigel was silent. An insult, yet Tarbo seemed to have a gleam of respect in his eye as he thumped Aigel's shoulder.

"Reklo and Nakla, well done! You have achieved the record of quickest to get yourselves killed. Charging with no weapons into a camp of thirty armed men – it will be many years before someone beats that, I hope."

"We will be remembered forever!" Reklo dared say, bracing his arm for a hit, but Tarbo quickly stamped the staff down on his foot to make him howl, which earned him another hit on the arm. Nakla also received a hit, and then another as he complained it was not fair, for he had obediently remained silent.

"Work together, punished together. To work together does not mean foolishly following each other's lead. If he jumped off a cliff would you follow? I think you would, since you followed him to your certain death, just a few hours ago."

The brothers were distressed, but silent, and Tarbo changed his tone, patting their arms with his hand.

"Brave, but stupid. That will do. I cannot make someone brave, but I can teach them tactics, and planning. Then hope they are not completely stupid."

They grinned at the praise, but he thumped them both on the shoulder, and told them to keep their guard.

"Rhede, you obvious coward, you run and hide well, perhaps that is where you belong," Tarbo said, waving his staff towards the bushes. Rhede lowered his head, but Tarbo continued, "foolish boy – you had the best plan of all – to flee – badly executed. If anyone survived, it would have been you. You should be a runner, if you are so fond of running away. I think you are too weak to stand and fight."

Rhede looked upset, but said nothing.

"Oh, so you agree?" Tarbo asked.

"I should like to learn fight ... as well."

"Would you? Fight now, then, defeat any of these men, and prove me wrong."

Rhede looked to his friends, wondering who he might defeat, but as Tarbo turned slightly and waved one hand, he soon realised he meant his guards, who were all starting to face Rhede – who was at once uncertain and silent.

"I see. You should be a runner, for often the delivery of the message is the most important thing. Rhede – the most important thing. If I teach you to be deadly in battle, you must promise me to keep yourself alive. Had you escaped – had you disappeared, unable to be found, all would have changed. Perhaps the others would have been spared death, if the enemy knew one had escaped. Perhaps they would search for you, wasting time and giving hope to the others. Perhaps they would plan for ransom, or quickly flee with the treasure, hoping that leaving the others alive might spare them from the guards you fetch. Most grim, they might kill all captives, and flee – unavoidable sorrows. But you, at least, would bring word of what happened – save others from the same fate – killers may be caught. Do not underestimate the importance of the runner, it is the most important duty, often. Perhaps always."

Rhede had a big grin, so Tarbo hit him with the stick to keep him humble. Selvorne frowned, wondering if Tarbo had any idea that Rhede had wanted to be a runner, and had even ... tricked Tarbo into recommending it, for Rhede looked more satisfied than surprised. Tarbo did not notice, and turned his attention to the noble Son of Ultainen.

"Orrikler, your stupidity is matched only by your pride. Did it not occur to you, that if they were holding you for ransom, you could have demanded they spare the lives of your friends?" Tarbo asked, and Orrikler looked at the ground in shame. Selvorne agreed, it was foolish, and he wondered if it had occurred to Orrikler – and then realised it had not occurred to himself, either.

"You could have gone to the camp, alone, stalling them with negotiations. You may have kept them there for hours, discussing payments and conditions, long enough for anyone to chew through their bonds, run down the path and swim to Senylehk."

Orrikler was embarrassed and silent. The others were considering what was said, and though it was a test, had it been real, such an oversight would have cost many of their lives.

"You might want to be one of the others," Tarbo continued, "one of the men – but you are not. If people know who you are, you must use that to your advantage. They certainly will use it to their own. You want to be the same as the men? Congratulations, you have just killed them all with pride – and in death you are all equal. Do not let it happen again."

It was clear from Orrikler's face that Tarbo's words hurt more than a whack with the stick, so Tarbo only nodded before continuing.

"Orrikler, no man likes threats. They hate threats. They wound a man's pride. If made when danger is upon them – had you threatened them with a knife to their throat, perhaps then they would yield. But you did not. Men resent threats of danger that might come at some time later, uncertain, perhaps avoided – perhaps never faced. Intimidate a man in your town, there is no escape, for them – perhaps they may fear your father a little, even far from your home, but where is he? Not here, and no danger. In resentment, they take revenge in advance. If you threaten such men, you bring death upon yourself – perhaps quickly, causing your enemy to act in the haste of anger, or fear of being found. Then sit over your dead body in regret, for their stupidity in not thinking it through. As you would feel, for brief moments, as they ended your life."

Orrikler nodded, but was grimly silent.

"But – men love wealth," Tarbo continued cheerfully, "especially brigands. They do not risk their lives on the road for the fun of killing – they do it for easy wealth. If you promise it, and offer a way to get it, a way they believe they can achieve. A hope they might escape with great bounty, a negotiation that they see as a way to profit and run. Present to them a plan which seems flawed, in their favour – so they think they have outsmarted you – then you have them under your power. The Brigand Leader is he who can lead his men to wealth. Promises of riches is what they follow, such a man they will serve, be he killer, thief – or guard. Or noble son, if they believe you need them, or they can trick you. By promises you could lead them all, if you were well spoken and clever. Led by you and the desires that are aroused – offer them enough, and they will join your house as servants!"

Orrikler widened his eyes at the jest that such men might serve in his house, and Tarbo nodded. Perhaps it was not a joke, and Tarbo thought that enough wealth promised might bring them there – and delivered, keep them, to serve. If so, it did not seem that Orrikler agreed, at least not with the idea of keeping the men in his house.

"Fear will not save you," Tarbo said, putting a hand to Orrikler's shoulder, "but lust for wealth may. Do not let your pride get in the way of that, even if you think it is humble and good, to pretend to be one of the men."

Orrikler nodded, and Tarbo turned to the others.

"There was a clue there, you all missed – my friend here, a rich merchant, held for ransom. I hope that after training, you are all a lot more clever."

Many nodded, and Tarbo turned to Rohy.

"Rohy – you had a knife? You had a knife, in your shirt, hidden. Brilliant. Next time, make sure it is sharp. A real knife that can cut fast and let you run – because as soon as a knife is discovered, such men would use it to cut your throat."

Rohy stared back at Tarbo, then nodded.

"Also, why did you remain hidden in the woods, instead of swim to safety? Were you afraid they would catch you on the river? Or were you using the others to test the enemy watch, or as distractions to allow you to slip away, as they were caught?"

Rohy nodded and shook his head appropriately, silently, feigning shame at his own foolishness, to hide his true shame from Tarbo. He could not swim, and lied his way into the guards, but Selvorne thought Rohy was more furious with himself, than ashamed. He had let down his guard, had been caught and taken by surprise. The same thing had happened at the Axeman Inn, for Rohy's fear of the Horror Square, and the stump, where spirits of the dead might haunt the living. So unsettled, Rohy had not noticed the strange situation of the inn. Earlier, when they had been told to swim to the island, Rohy had been so distracted by the fear of swimming ... he had removed all his garments, and his sharp knife that Selvorne guessed was usually hidden in his boot. It was only good luck he still had the one in his shirt – and it could have been bad luck, if he had worn a different shirt. Good luck, and honour, for Rohy had planned for them all to escape carefully, and would not have done any of the things Tarbo suggested, using the others to create a distraction or test the enemy watch – honourable, perhaps foolish. To use people in that way might have been the only way any of the men might have escaped.

Tarbo turned to Selvorne, who immediately began to wonder what he did wrong.

"Selvorne – handsome young boy, well groomed when not covered in mud, well dressed in his strong fancy boots, but apparently, unable to untie knots. Who ties your boots, your mother? Your father?" Tarbo asked, but the expression on his face that was all taunting fell immediately to solemn, and he backed away from Selvorne's cold stare.

It surprised Selvorne. Not the fury he felt at the mention of his parents, nor the feeling of cold blood through his veins – but that Tarbo noticed so quickly, then stepped back without a moment's pause, softening his mocking glare. Selvorne eased, blinked, and was quite astounded that anyone could be so quick to read his anger through his eyes.

"So many chances to fight or run, you could have strangled the enemy with your bonds," Tarbo continued in a tone that was no longer mocking, "you could have run, but stayed, like a fool. You could have saved yourself, had you left the others. Next time you will know better."

Selvorne started to wonder if he was not being criticised, but praised. He thought about it – he was, for he had stayed instead of fled, to help the others. Yet Rhede had fled, and might have survived – Tarbo's attacks on everyone could have been cleverly disguised praise. Not for what they did, but why they did it. After all, he was accepting them to the guard.

Bitier had been clever and fast thinking. Vugecarauk bravely defended Rhede. Toavel, courageous, and cunning to get the knife from the midst of enemies, at the camp. Aigel, sacrificing himself, and bold. Reklo and Nakla, desperately trying to make time for the others – bravest and stupidest of all, for they were completely free and could have fled the other way. Rhede did flee, and in so doing he might have made it through to help, and he was not strong enough to fight, doing so would have had him killed, and so he was praised for being wise. Orrikler's heart seemed in the right place, though his foolishness had to be revealed – his failure was the worst of all, for his pride. Rohy was prepared in advance, Tarbo was impressed, despite the bluntness of the small bronze blade, it seemed a trick a trained man might do, or someone who often travelled the dangerous roads.

And Selvorne, perhaps stupidly, gave up many chances for himself to help the others – running and leaving them had occurred to him many times, but he simply could not abandon them. Although, he thought if it came to a fight, he would run away from the camp and hope to fight the enemy one at a time in the woods, not charge to fight them all at once.

Tarbo was silent, letting them all think on matters. The older guards prepared the meal and the camp, setting tents and moving heavy logs to sit upon. Some logs had been chopped and cut to make stools, and a long table was there, upon it were wooden plates for the food. A feast was being prepared, and a night of great mirth – had any of the new men harmed any of the guards, or even killed ... but no, the guards were not even slightly afraid of the new recruits. Though Roduil did not seem too happy to have been beaten so – what if instead Selvorne had Rohy's knife? A stone, a stick, or more skill with his hands – it could have been a very different night with one man dead. Even if one of them had swum away, perhaps drowning ... a very dangerous trial. All could have been so different.

And then Selvorne realised – all would have changed. That was Tarbo's meaning when he said Rhede should have fled. If just one of them had escaped, or even disappeared to hide, then true brigands would have to rethink all plans if one man was gone. No longer hidden by secrecy, they would have other guards coming to confront them – thoughts would turn to ransom or escape. It was Rhede who had ended the ruse when he made it to the riverside.

Tarbo was watching them, and seemed to notice Selvorne's blank stare. He stared back and frowned, seemed puzzled – then nodded. He could not possibly have known what Selvorne was thinking, could he? Selvorne looked to the other men – proud and grim, confused, and others were beginning to understand. But Selvorne more than understood, and he was not sure why so many things began to occur to him at once – a dozen thoughts of what he should have done, and why, and cleverness that had not come to him when needed, and yet ... a strange thought, also, that he should have known better what to do.

"You will all learn to fight!" Tarbo declared, his voice strong and loud, and the men were all startled, "Guards must be well trained to fight. A good fighter always stands guard, like this, or like this," Tarbo said, standing in various ways that were not quite casual, and were clearly alert to danger, "and so he is difficult to attack. In a tavern, he might stand like this, and anyone who wishes to challenge will think twice, for he is clearly ready, even when relaxing with ale."

The new recruits nodded at Tarbo's demonstration of how to stand – a dozen different ways, each seemed to have its merits. The older guards nodded when he mentioned the tavern and ale.

"So, too, the guards themselves appear ready, standing on guard. To see a man standing so – ready to fight. To know a man is a guard – by reputation of skill, he is feared and respected by both good men and bad. That alone prevents attack, and creates the authority of your position. Reputation of your abilities are your defence.

"If you are attacked, those abilities will be proven. It is not enough to merely be thought of as skilled. Reputation is your shield, seeming as strong as oak, but if seen to be made of reeds – the shield of all the guards is lost to your shame. So you must learn well to fight and not look a fool, and if you cannot – if we have wrongly guessed your ability, and you are too weak or frightened or clumsy – then you must become a runner, or assistant. Even so, you will be better men than you are now, better fighters than you are today, and if you are captured again, will be able to take the brigands, with skill."

There was joy on their faces, and great grins as all the new recruits thought about what they might have done, were they well trained to fight. Selvorne thought of all the punching he would have delivered, but when he saw Rohy's quiet stare, he wondered if he was thinking he would not have been caught in the first place.

"You will become faster, stronger – learn the staff, and other weapons. Also how to wrestle and punch. You will learn what to expect in battle, and how to adapt to what comes that is unexpected. To think like a brigand, and to outsmart them. To anticipate, or react, to work as a team, or alone. Perhaps even to infiltrate their ranks as a spy, or hunt them down in the woods, with silent stealth and cunning."

Selvorne was very pleased with all that he heard – he imagined the power he would have when trained, and what he could do with such skills. And with a few of the men, if he was back in the woods hiding in that tree, or in the ravine, waiting, then pouncing on the enemy. The brigands would not stand an hour, and most of that would be spent finding them – he would make short work of all foes. The others were all beaming, and he wondered what private thoughts they had, assuming most would be thinking of the day's events going very differently as they turned the ambush around and subdued all their enemies. Rohy remained quiet, and Selvorne knew well what he must have been thinking, planning and hoping.

"In one month," Tarbo said, "we will know where you fit amongst us. You will all train to be better than you are now – this is a promise. But, we cannot train all of you to be the best – the best you can be, no better is possible, and in one month we will decide what to do with you."

Selvorne had been pleased, at first, but when that was said he suddenly realised it was going to take some time. He had not liked the idea it would take a month to find Cienn and return – longer was a thought he had not truly considered, let alone that at the end of it they might not think him any good. He had hoped they would be training for a week at most, that it would somehow be all the training needed, then they would prepare to sweep the woods in the south. He had thought the aim of the call was to gather all the guard, numbers grown from new recruits, then, gathering at the last moment dozens of men from the town – march through the woods. Not train for a month – what if the brigands got away? If it was ... too late?

His thoughts were fast and distress within him rose before it softened and fell. One month – what could be done faster, he thought – nothing. It was days of travel merely to return home. Days to hunt brigands, who likely had moved already ... days to find them after the trail went cold, added to that the training, the gathering of guards ... weeks, at least – at the fastest.

Weeks, though, might be expected by men who had left a dead body on the road as a warning – brigands would be alert. For weeks. Not for a month, not as wary as the start – not for two months, if it took that long. Tarbo had some plan, Selvorne could see it in his unpatched eye – excitement grew in Selvorne as he realised what it must be. Train, grow numbers, then suddenly appear in force, unexpected. Brigands grown lazy, guards moved to position to strike.

"Look at poor Kurja here, he will never be the best!" Tarbo said all of a sudden, then he called over to a guard named Kurja, who reluctantly prepared to fight Tarbo with a stick. Tarbo swiftly disarmed him, then knocked him to the ground. He picked himself up, humiliated, bowed angrily and returned to the tent he was raising, complaining bitterly for all to hear.

"No matter how hard he trains, Kurja will never be great. He is good – make no mistake, better than any of you – but not the best. Now, Roduil – "

Tarbo yelled for Roduil, who was nursing his knee – he limped over with a stick and engaged Tarbo, who struggled, and though Roduil did not move much on his feet, he hit furiously, disarmed Tarbo and made him yield. He bowed politely, and Roduil hobbled away.

"Roduil is the best, and he will teach you. And replace me, when I am gone. Unless," Tarbo said, looking at each of them, "one of you is better than he."

Smiles from some of the men suggested they thought they might be, and Selvorne bit his lip to hide his own.

"So, after training, if you are good, you will join a group under a commander and head out to some part of the lands, and serve, and learn more. Although," Tarbo said, and he looked deadly serious, almost whispering as he stared with his one eye at each of the men, "you must train harder than any men before you. For you will go straight to battle, I think, as we sweep through the south. Other guards before you have had it easy, had time and ... those of you who can fight, will do so, earlier and more ferociously than all of these guards, who have had months, even years to prepare. They have enjoyed the quiet life of a guard, not the terrible danger of a guard's duty – of battle, which is upon us all."

Tarbo sounded ominous – Selvorne was pleased. Although, he wondered whether Tarbo would have said the same thing to any new men, even if there was no imminent sweep in the south. It sounded a little ... too well said. Frighten the new guards, to make them train hard. They had been captured, it made them angry – made them want revenge – but on who? The guards who kicked them, and bound them harshly? No. And anger was not towards brigands, who were unknown to them – but knowing such danger was coming soon, in mere weeks, perhaps – knowing they could face being captured by enemies – such a thought would make any man train hard. The brief, vengeful anger would last for many weeks, once it turned to dedication that came from fear.

So Selvorne thought, and he was not sure why it was becoming so clear to him. Perhaps it was another of Tarbo's ploys. The whole day had been arranged to take foolish, promising boys and make them into devoted guards. Selection by testing, then honing ambitions – but more was occurring to Selvorne, and he was not completely sure how.

"It is not all a hard life," Tarbo continued, and Selvorne thought everyone was beginning to wonder if he would ever stop talking and let them eat. The smell of the roasting pig was taunting them, and the testimony of its deliciousness was being shouted across the camp by one guard to another, behind Tarbo's back.

"Yes, you will work hard – building, harvesting, travelling. But you will receive good pay, go to many of the festivals, meet people, perhaps find love – not always once," Tarbo said, winking with his one eye, or perhaps he blinked, it was hard to tell, "and you can work the roads, or settle in a town. It is a good life, as a guard, you will see much that would otherwise escape you. So, think it over, and prepare to make your vow before the morning. And most important of all, eat!"

~

Tarbo turned and left them, and one guard encouraged them to cheer. They were starving and began to head to the feast, until several guards stood to block their path.

All the new recruits stopped – surely they did not have to fight their way to the food? But then one guard spoke quickly with Tarbo, waving his hand at the men – and Tarbo laughed.

"Before you eat," yelled the fair–haired guard – and Selvorne winced to think a fight was to be announced, "you should all wash. Look at yourselves!"

Selvorne frowned – then looked at the others. Undergarments, soaked from the swim, then crawling in the mud. Captured and dragged through dirt, rolling and fighting amongst leaves, and though sweat had washed some of the dirt from their faces – they were a mess.

"None may eat who are filthy," the guard yelled, "Kurja! Show them where!"

At that, the guard called Kurja put down his plate, furious, but obediently stomped his way past the men and ordered them to follow. They did, though some – Nakla and Reklo more than any – were reluctant. Away from the camp, down a path – not where Selvorne was captured, and not where the others said they had been – to a place where there was solid rock to meet the river, and good shallows to wash.

They bathed quickly and washed everything – clothes and hair, face and feet. Not by choice, but by order of Kurja – and not by his order, he explained, but if they appeared back at the camp with any mud on them, anywhere but their feet, they would be sent to wash again. None of the men wanted to delay their feast, so when they emerged from the river, Selvorne thought that although dripping wet, they were the cleanest young men he had ever seen.

At the feast the roast had been carved, and a line had formed as men were being served. The new recruits took back their knives for eating and changed clothes, then joined the end of the line, wishing it would move more quickly. Especially as those already served taunted those who waited, walking past and praising the delicious feast between mouthfuls. Sometimes between chews.

Selvorne waited in line, he was last of the new recruits, yet ahead of some of the guards, who had tried to push to the front and were turned back to wait at the end. They grumbled that the new men should be last, since it was not they who prepared the roast.

A blond, muscular, barefooted young man approached Selvorne with a grin and two plates – it was the guard who had suggested they wash. His trousers were tied high on his calves, his sleeves were rolled back, his shirt open and eyes twinkled as he stood before Selvorne, holding out two large wooden plates loaded with roast – piles of meat, and vegetables from the pot.

"Here, I brought you this," he said to Selvorne, much to the confusion of everyone else, "join me, if you will."

Selvorne took one plate, and as soon as he did there began an unplanned sharing with Reklo, who stepped out of the line to help himself – only to be reprimanded by the blond guard, who assured him there was plenty and he could wait. Then he turned to the men who were waiting and gazing at the plates with astonished longing. He gazed back at them all, then took a deep breath, as though preparing to sing – and almost did.

"So much food, you will fall down sick, from eating, and ill, needing care – and so be patient – and so take care – and enjoy these moments last, of tum–my, rumbling, before a night regretted, often, some ache, bubbling."

Strange words, loudly spoken to all. Some of the men clapped. The blond guard bowed over his plate, then led Selvorne away from the others – Reklo and Nakla applauded as well, and were staring eagerly ahead in the line.

"I am Torvor," the young man said as they sat on a log away from the others. The sun was close to setting, and it was growing cool away from the fire, but Torvor did not seem to care. Of course, he was dry, and Selvorne was wet, and finding everything so strange that a cold breeze was the last thing on his mind, even if it was the first thing he noticed. And then he frowned, puzzled, as he realised what the guard had said.

"Torlor?" Selvorne asked. The guard stifled what might have been a sudden burst of laughter, so that it made him cough.

"No, Torvor. Yes, it sounds like Torlor. No, that is not what it means, certainly not clumsy, far from poor in luck, I think. Yes, my father had a sense of humour, calling me that, and making my name rhyme with itself, indeed its double meaning is more poetic than a rhyme – Tor and Vor. No, it does not mean mountain-mountain, it is supposed to mean mountain revenge. And no, I do not know why it was so chosen, perhaps it was a joke. And yes, I have to explain my name – every time I meet someone. So perhaps the mountain revenge is on me, though why, I do not know, and the only vengeance is mounting, not mountain, and against my father for his cruelty in naming me so. Any questions?"

Torvor seemed a merry fellow with a sense of humour, though it was clear he was sick of explaining his name every time he met someone. Selvorne smiled back at him.

"Why have you brought me food?" Selvorne asked. Direct – for he was either a contact for Dyneti, or if not, he was a mystery, and Selvorne had no patience to play games.

"Aha, yes, well, see, I noticed you were beaten quite soundly as a captive."

Selvorne nodded, his ribs still sore from the kicking.

"Roduil hit me a lot, but I gave as good as I got. But someone kicked me on the ground, and it still hurts."

"Aha. Do you hold a grudge?"

"I do, it was not called for, I wonder who did it," Selvorne said as he looked around. Whoever did it was strong enough to throw Selvorne to his shoulder – some of the guards looked very strong, and he wondered if perhaps it would be unwise to pursue a grudge against them.

"Ah, well, the same thing happened to me," Torvor explained, "when I joined. So, I know what it is like."

Selvorne nodded, and thought he had made a new friend.

"Yes," Torvor continued, "someone saw me with my fine hair, and elegant clothing, and delicate ways, and they thought they would teach me a lesson with a sound beating, to wake me to the danger of it all, being a guard, and being captured."

"Did it work?"

"Yes, it worked wonders, it truly did teach a lesson. Which is why I promised them that I would return the favour when I had the chance."

For a moment Selvorne thought Torvor had revenge – waited patiently, and retaliated against the person who beat him – angry, as Selvorne was, waiting to ... get revenge ... and then he realised – Torvor was the one who had been kicking him. The favour returned was the lesson passed on.

"So, no hard feelings, then?" Torvor asked, putting down his plate and offering his hand. Selvorne shook it, but was not completely sure he had forgiven him, "I think I might have made a mistake, actually," Torvor continued, "from all accounts, you were some fancy man – laughing always, and so delighted by Dyneti. Hardly serious about joining the guards – some said you were only there for Dyneti, or Demni, or the maidens who were ogling the guards as they marched. I saw your well–styled hair and your fine undergarments, and I thought – here we go again. Nothing a few good kicks could not cure, either making you serious, or making you leave."

Selvorne wondered who it was that was saying such things about him – was that how he appeared to the other guards? As a fancy man? Perhaps that might work to his advantage – few amongst them could have been more serious or in as much danger as he had been. He grew pleased to think that he appeared as a laughing boy, not a threat, nor suspicious, not serious – not the man brigands wanted to kill – and at that thought, he smiled. Which made Torvor frown.

"What happened when you were captured?" Selvorne asked, thinking he could learn a lot about his new friend by hearing of his ordeal.

"Well," Torvor began, "I am afraid I did a lot of damage, and not just to their pride. They had guessed wrongly about me, you see, as perhaps ... I had you wrong. I might have looked the fancy man, but I already knew how to fight. I swam to the island, as we all did, climbed out – first to arrive, I believe. Covered in mud, I was kicked before they tried to bind me. That was his mistake, for I twisted his foot, dropped him to the mud, and bent his leg around behind his back, in a way most unpleasant.

"Roduil, though I did not know him at the time, pulled me back by the hair, but I spun around and punched him right in the nose, through the mask, and broke it. I do not think he has ever forgiven me for that, though others say it is an improvement, and that it is still rather straight.

"I looked and saw all my friends set upon and held, and many men running around. Alone, I would have swum away, but instead I pushed several over in the mud before they turned on me and chased me up the hill. This very hill," Torvor said, musing over the ground where they sat. Selvorne wondered how many times that very spot had seen that same deceitful ruse – then celebrations – then the forming of friendships amongst the guards.

"I did not know what was happening, or what to do, and had no time to think on it. And I like to know what is happening – such is the way to happiness, I find. Anyway, I ran straight into the camp here, nobody was ready, everyone was surprised, even Tarbo hobbled after me. I took a knife from the pig that had only started cooking, then I knocked it over, and the fire spread. I ran into the woods, as everyone tended the fire, but instead of hiding, I climbed up a tree to watch them."

"That does not seem a good idea," Selvorne said.

"Pure refined stupidity, with all wisdom extracted. At the time, it seemed the best of brilliance. As soon as I was up there I realised I could do nothing – if I moved, or came down, they would find me. I would not do that again – stay out of the trees, that is my advice. Nevertheless, no one suspected I was there, for to be there was madness – I could watch them unnoticed, and eating my apple, soon realised they were the guards, playing some game with the new recruits."

"You had an apple?"

"I took it from the pig they were preparing, a good one, too. Can you not taste the apple in the roast?"

Selvorne nodded, he could taste apple, but avoided the slices of it on his plate, assuming they were pieces of fat. He ate one, it was good, and he was glad to know of it.

"So I watched, and waited, and came down at the end."

"And then he captured Tarbo," another guard said as he walked past, "should I fetch you a trumpet, Torvor? Your own, perhaps?"

"None needed, just the facts, they sing for themselves, if it is music you want," Torvor said, adding quietly to Selvorne, "had I a trumpet to blow, you all should be dancing now. Yes, I caught Tarbo, holding him captive with the knife. I do not think he forgave me that, although we get along well enough, it was a huge embarrassment for him. I was not going to tell you that. He is good, he fights well, but stood no chance against someone who had been watching from above for hours, someone who knew that there was no chance of being harmed, knowing it was a ruse, and eager to get some small revenge. I would not be so bold amongst killers – it could not have ended well."

Torvor stood and called out to Tarbo.

"Hey! Tarbo! You managed to last a day without capture this year!"

Tarbo ignored him, but with a flick of his wrist sent what Selvorne thought was an apple core hurtling towards them, and Torvor almost caught it, but at the last moment decided to let it fly past.

"He still thinks I am some master of the woods, evading everyone for so long. I fear he will send me to kill a man, one day, and I will not know where to start!"

Torvor seemed to be joking, and was very merry. Selvorne was warming to him, but still annoyed at being kicked so many times.

"Well, if you were kicked and it did no good, why did you kick me so many times, and stomp on me?"

"I never said it was no good, the problem was doing it before I was bound. And I only kicked you once, to get you in the spirit of things," Torvor said, then looked thoughtful, "hmm ... I think I know who stomped on you, but I will not tell you who. I will have a word with him. Come to think of it, he was the one who told me about you ... actually, he is quite taken with Dyneti, as I recall. I see the pattern ... is it true you know her well?"

Selvorne explained his relationship with Dyneti, as much as he dared, as best he could, since he hardly understood it himself, except that he liked her very much and they often laughed together – and she trusted him, perhaps only him, with her message. Then he betrayed that trust – he was hardly going to say that to his new friend, though.

"Aha, lucky you, she is quite a stunning young lady. Though, I prefer golden hair, myself, perhaps red if it is fiery and bright. And I must say, although I enjoy a joke and jest and prank, of which she is fond, I prefer these to be few, saved for special occasions, and not always directed at me. Or at my expense. Mind her, Selvorne."

Selvorne nodded, and Torvor nodded as well – solemnly, as though to confirm he was not completely joking.

"Also, I would prefer my betrothed to not flirt with every single man out there, and a few wedded ones as well. No, any woman lucky enough to have me should be content with me alone – if not satisfied – if not exhausted!"

Torvor laughed, and Selvorne chuckled, though he did not like the warnings he was hearing. Some of it was in jest, surely ... and as they ate together, and others joined them with their meals, Selvorne was quite sure Torvor was fond of teasing and taunting.

People ate, drank and sang, and since the new recruits had been accepted as guards, and none of them seemed to want to leave, they mingled freely and made many new friends.

Reklo and Nakla challenged older guards to wrestling, trying to show how things should have turned out – none could refuse their challenge, so all offered them ale for each victory, until they lost eagerness for wrestling, for drinking, or indeed, for standing. There were many thanks given from one new recruit to another – for the heroic sacrifices some made – and a quiet understanding for those who had not been so brave. Not one of them expected Rhede to fight, he was too slightly built, but he vowed he would learn, and never again would be captured. The mood was merry more than grim, the taste of feasting and friendship was strengthened by the grisly taste of deadly danger – guards, as brothers, as allies against such peril. And it was coming – or, more uplifting – they were marching to bring it to an end.

Only Orrikler seemed sour, blaming himself for his failings, and he also vowed it would never happen again. The others made a similar vow, but there was something very stern in Orrikler's words. Selvorne thought all the new recruits had changed a little – from boys, to men, perhaps. Some more than others. Rhede very much, and perhaps Aigel and Toavel. Not so much Nakla, Reklo and Vugecarauk

– and oddly, Bitier seemed almost as though being captured and facing death was a weekly routine.

Rohy was not changed in the same way, he was neither afraid nor stern, but seemed quietly furious with himself, or perhaps ... he knew his terrible failing, his secret lie kept from all others – that he could not swim. It would have cost him a chance to escape, and though he might have somehow avoided needing to swim his entire life – as a guard, he might have to. As usual he said little and ate quietly, but he stared and seemed tense, and at times looked towards the river, where it could be glimpsed over the bushes down the hill.

Selvorne had changed as well, but for him the day was not the same as it was for the others – or perhaps one other. Selvorne had seen death – faced it – evaded it at the brigand's camp. And thought about it often, every day since. In that way he was not a boy, though in many ways he never was a boy, but a boyish son of a lord. He knew there were responsibilities to be a lord, and as a boy he had avoided them, for they were far away in time, for a boy, and not his concern, just his ... future. Not even that, when he learnt he was not to be lord. But he was aware of such matters, and after the killings on the bridge, his concern became only surviving and finding allies.

But something had changed when he faced death again in the trials. No, not death – it was failure. More was at stake than his life, and he did not know what. Perhaps nothing more than what he knew that would be lost with his life, enough to make his message of great importance. In some ways he was just a runner, and he should have fled when faced with death. Not only his message from Dyneti, no, that was not it – but the fact that only he knew what had happened to his father and Arnlausa. He had to reach Cienn ... and would – but he had failed that day, had they been killers, he might have been killed, and instead of learning a lesson in danger, to make him a man, he took it as a second warning – another chance. Regardless, he ached to think how he might have failed.

He breathed a sigh of relief as he realised not all would have been lost – not only he knew, Rerleden did. He had been a runner, and he knew well that more than one man should carry the message. He might have considered all such things, planning ways to ensure Cienn would hear the truth. Eventually. Perhaps a hidden letter in the town, in a location known only to other runners, or captains or lords – he had said as much. Perhaps he had sent messengers with poems or parchments to Cienn, or all manner of clever ways to ensure that the death of Selvorne – and the death of himself – would not mean the death of the message.

A relief, but fear of that was not what had changed in Selvorne, and he was not sure what it was, but in Orrikler's eyes he saw the same grim realisation. Boys to men – heirs to lords. That might have been it. All the others feared for their lives, and thought of their friends. It made them more serious, made them realise what it was to be a guard. But for Selvorne – and Orrikler – they had just experienced what it would be like for their men. For their guards, their townsfolk, if captured – if they let thieves and killers roam their lands.

That was it. That was what Tarbo had said to Orrikler, not in words, but in meaning. And that was the moment he had changed his face from angry to grim. Fear at capture – fury and threats. Frustration, and then – distress. Helpless, bound in chains and shackled, Orrikler needed Selvorne to carry him, but even when hiding in the woods in the hole, he was angry. And when the deceit had been revealed, he was more than annoyed.

But when Tarbo told Orrikler how stupid he had been – any idea of him being as the others, being an ordinary guard – avoiding the duties of a lord, or perhaps not before realising the responsibilities to his men – Orrikler had changed. None of the others knew it, they thought he was merely sulking, but Selvorne did, for he felt something of the same. It was one thing to think, as lord, guards might die – it was quite another to sit there as they were taken, and hear them be killed – and later to know it was his fault. It would always be his fault, if he commanded men to their deaths.

Even Orrikler cheered in time, for the men were drinking and making all manner of jokes. Teasing the new recruits grew dull, and taunting each other instead, the older guards became hilarious. Their mistakes when they were the new recruits were revealed to all, and though amusing, some of the new recruits wondered if they would have to live their lives with the tales of how they had failed. It made some uncomfortable, but all had to laugh at how proud it made Nakla and Reklo feel – not only because they had been brave, but because they had been so utterly stupid, and broken the record for getting themselves killed the quickest.

They swore they would serve no commander except he who came along and broke that record – and Tarbo laughed and said, to be strict, Roduil had been slain that day moments after they had finished swimming – so there was their commander. At that they bowed, and Roduil, though wounded and stern, grinned and nodded a bow back at them.

The mood was merry with laughter and ale. Selvorne drank little, and mostly water. He had to keep his wits, because he needed to speak with Tarbo alone, and though all the men were moving freely about the camp, Tarbo never left his old merchant friend, always had guards near him, and dismissed any attempt for anyone to speak with him alone – and many of the men tried regardless.

Torvor was Selvorne's main companion for the night, he was also sober, and did not fail to notice Selvorne drank little. Others laughed and slurred as they spoke, but the two of them spoke of the things Selvorne might learn – Torvor had great knowledge and skills. He showed Selvorne how to brace his hands together when being bound, so he may relax them later, loosening the ropes and making an escape – the secret being to make oneself larger when knots were tied.

"Or, if very muscular, like those two," Torvor said, waving a hand at Nakla and Reklo, who were lying on the ground watching the stars spin above, "you can flex your muscles and later, relax them – until you can slip out of the ropes. It takes practise, and calm. Much easier to do if strong, but not if fat – the fat man is strongly bound, with ropes biting deep to folds, but the strong man is only strongly bound so long as he holds his muscles tight, you see. And the thin man – perhaps can wriggle free, though that also takes practise. These are good tricks, but now, I always carry these," Torvor said, and he took out a tiny knife from each boot.

"Great work on the heads!" one of the guards said to Torvor as he passed, "They even fell for the talking one! Brilliant!"

The false heads of the fallen dead. Torvor had not made them, Selvorne learnt, but brought them down from the north. They were very well made, as convincing as any unmoving man might be, some better than others, and some disturbingly realistic. They were used in plays and as puppets, and Torvor had an interest in such performances on the stage – he was a tumbling, dancing entertainer from the north, from the town of Lodlehk, serving Lord Tordrum – someone Selvorne knew might be a trusted ally.

"How well do you know Lord Tordrum?" Selvorne asked.

"Very well, like a father. He is sponsor, and often writer, of our plays – and so he is as a father to all the performers, to many. Why?"

"I hear he is a good man."

"The best of men, a good lord, a talented performer himself. A great father."

"He is your father?" Selvorne asked, and Torvor laughed.

"He has many children – six well known – perhaps more! He is good to the ones he knows of, at least!"

Selvorne thought that was a lot of children, more than any family he knew, and wondered what it would be like to have had half of his small town as family – six children of his own, grown and wed – just four each more, as children grand – what was that, as much as thirty, including those they had wed. And then, their families – parents, brothers, sisters, whoever they wed and children they might have. His mind began to hurt to think of it – more family than his entire town, in just half a lifetime.

Torvor leant over and whispered, "And he is a great lord – a good lord. It is his skill – and vigilance – that keeps the north free of brigands. Not the northern guard, led by Taahr, who is praised for it – that is where I am heading. If you have a choice, join them and go north, they could use someone good, and you might be taken to join ... but at the least, doing so will spare you from Demni's command. If you think today was unpleasant, spend a week with her, and you will wish you had been captured by killers on this island."

Selvorne stared with wide eyes, not quite sure what to make of Torvor, who had praised one lord, insulted two commanders and given advice all at once, so seriously it was as though he was being given a deadly warning – then he leant back and laughed.

"You joke?" Selvorne asked.

"Oh, no – but she is not so bad! Still .... I envy you. Today. I am used to ruses, ploys, and deception. In the nature of my work – the plays, with all their performances, and then the mischief with the audience. Mystification, magic, fantastic escapes, and unexplained illusion. All to me are tedious, unless I see something truly new, which is so very rare. But today ... what a ruse – I remember it well, when it was my turn. Though it only lasted moments for me – I discovered in less than one hour that it was deception – the excitement was like nothing else. You will remember this day. Angry, fearful, laughing – wise. After today, you will never sleep the same again, always on guard, always prepared. Today your life has changed. You will not understand what I mean, until a few weeks have passed, then you will look back on it with fondness, instead of ... not anger, surely?"

"Not anger," Selvorne said, though he was not sure if it was completely true.

"Not anger. Fondness, in time. This is why so many guards are here to celebrate – they are remembering their time deceived, on this island. Sadly, it is a ruse that can happen only once. You will never again know the horror, the terror – and life will seem dull and grey ... but you will look back with fondness. And then, there is always a chance to play the ruse on others – and you will smile to think of what you might do, next time, as captor, not captive!"

A Fresh Parchment

Torvor excused himself, and said he had to prepare the boats. Selvorne was not sure what he meant, not by all that he had said, but especially about the boats, so he began asking others – to his dismay, he learnt that many of the guards were not staying the night, but leaving in the boats to return to the town of Senylehk and the main administration islands. The new recruits were to sleep on the island for several weeks. It would be sad to see them go, but it was the fact Tarbo was leaving that very night which distressed Selvorne – leaving, and then perhaps gone for several weeks.

Selvorne tried to be alone with Tarbo, but was refused a meeting. Even when he requested very politely to speak with him, instead he received the most impolite drunken laughter as a reply – so he asked Torvor how he might arrange it.

"Why do you want to see him alone? Are you leaving the guards?" Torvor asked.

"No, it is a personal matter."

"Can it wait? He has been drinking, and will not want to see anyone tonight, unless he has to. It has been a very long day for him, longer than you realise, for he was at Hartlehk this morning, and ran past you all to get here – his leg is not so good, and I had to row him about for most of the day, and now he is quite drunk and I hope he is not ill in the boat, for then I shall have to tip it over to fill it, and empty it after, and he never has the courtesy to do so at the beginning or end of the journey. I expect he will take the next few days to rest – and he might come back then. Will that do?"

Selvorne was uneasy, and not entirely sure what Torvor was saying, but the next few days were not good enough – he had to deliver his message at once. What had happened that day was a taste of how important the warning might be, and had Selvorne not learnt that Tarbo was leaving, he might have left before there was a chance to deliver the message. It had been only hours since he vowed to keep his mind on the task at hand, and already Selvorne felt he was being distracted and failing – again. He wanted to simply stand before Tarbo and tell the message, but Dyneti told him to make sure they were completely alone. True, he had made a mess of that already, but – and then an idea came to him.

"If I left the guards, would Tarbo take me aside to ask me why?" Selvorne asked, and Torvor looked astonished – then thoughtful – then suspicious. And then, oddly, he smiled, and Selvorne was sure he almost nodded.

"No, I think he would turn his back to you, and ignore you, and he would never speak to you again. I have seen it happen. You truly ... well, I guess, if you broke the rules, he would yell at you in front of everyone, then drag you away for what I have heard is a terrible beating – only using words, but lasting a very, very long time. You think he was long, boring and insulting when giving his speech? You have no idea just how long, boring and tedious he can be if you break the rules. Oh, how you would wish he would simply hit you with that stick ..."

Selvorne nodded – there was his plan – but he thought Torvor spoke from experience.

"What did you do?"

"Ahh ... well, it was at this very camp, I found the one who had kicked me, and stomped on his foot. That retaliation is not allowed, as you can imagine, if it was, none of us would be laughing now and feasting – everyone would be dead by morning. Or badly bruised. I apologised after Tarbo's stern talk, and the guard laughed because he knew what I had gone through, and thanks to him, here we are today!"

Selvorne looked thoughtful, and devised a plan, one that was simple and would almost certainly work. He smiled to himself, considering it had a delightful element of vengeance to it, and fairness, and cunning. So he took an empty tankard, filled it with water, marching straight up to Tarbo, who was standing and laughing with his merchant friend. Roduil was there, and glared at Selvorne, as he had all the night. They were preparing to leave, unannounced, gathering their few things. Selvorne stood until they all looked at him and stopped laughing.

"This is for you," he said to Roduil, holding out the tankard. Roduil reached for it, but Selvorne gave him a quick, sharp kick in the shin, and when he bent over howling, poured the water over his head.

"And that is for hitting me earlier."

With that, Selvorne began to stride away, but Kurja ran after him and dragged him back.

Tarbo was furious, and also a bit wobbly, even more than usual on his sore leg. Everyone was shocked, and Roduil had to be restrained from hitting back. Tarbo yelled abuse, and the whole camp went quiet. He grabbed Selvorne by the shirt and dragged him down the path where earlier the captives had been piled. Kurja ran after him to hand him a flaming torch, for the twilight was fading and the woods were growing dark.

The guards burst into laughter when they thought Tarbo and Selvorne were too far to hear, and the sound of them faded as they continued down the path. Past where the captives were held, down the hill, around wooded corners, and to a small grove, where they stopped. Tarbo turned to glare at Selvorne, his face furious by the light of the flame.

"What do you think you are doing?" Tarbo yelled, "I told you not to take revenge on those who captured you. That is the rule, that is what I said."

A mixture of concern, anger, discipline and confusion, all muddled by ale. Selvorne was more concerned with how distant they were from the others.

"Help! Help!" Selvorne yelled loudly, "Tarbo is fallen! I think he is ill!"

Tarbo, still drunk, but sobering, backed away and held the torch like a weapon. He did not have his staff, something he immediately seemed to regret as he raised one empty hand, and in the torchlight his face showed a sense of danger. There was no sound of people approaching.

"What are you playing at?" Tarbo asked, keeping Selvorne at a distance. Selvorne wondered if Tarbo thought he was a killer, who had lured him to his death – he certainly looked afraid.

"I just wanted to know if anyone could hear us."

Such a thing said to calm, hardly put Tarbo at ease – drunk, tired, alone – in the woods with a boy he hardly knew, he seemed to realise how stupid he had been, and began to circle Selvorne with the torch. Selvorne was also feeling in danger, but unlike Tarbo, he had good reason to fear the man before him. The woods were silent, apart from birds, bats, the burning torch, and their heavy breathing.

"Tarbo, I have a message for Torlor," Selvorne said. Tarbo looked at him with one wide eye. No longer threatening, he lowered the torch, using it to illuminate Selvorne's face.

"Well," Tarbo said, relaxing and slightly amused, "this is unexpected. Tell me the message, I will pass it on."

Selvorne repeated it exactly the way Dyneti had said it.

"There is a duck amongst the geese, the eggs all look the same. But some may be bad."

Any relief Tarbo felt quickly faded, and he looked ghastly. Turning, he waved the torch and found a log to sit upon, then collapsed onto it.

"What does it mean?" Selvorne asked, trying to make conversation, though also curious about the message.

"That is not for you to know," Tarbo snapped, then coyly, "what do you think it means?"

"Hmm," Selvorne said – he had some idea, but did not want to appear too smart, "from what I hear, duck eggs are very strong in flavour, and if a duck has nested amongst the geese, and is laying eggs, there to be collected unknowingly, it might be ruining the recipe. Although, it would have to be a very large duck, or a very small goose to confuse the two."

"Clever boy," Tarbo chuckled, "I can see why she likes you. Or did she tell you to say that?"

"I made it up myself. And I like her as well, very much."

"Careful, boy, she is not for the likes of you, no matter how clever you think you are," Tarbo said, standing once more, he waved the flaming torch dangerously close to Selvorne's face, "tell me this – does she trust you?"

"I believe she does," Selvorne said, and Tarbo watched his face closely as he spoke, "though I am not so sure about you. Or your men."

"And you are right to be suspicious, as is she," Tarbo added, then, as if suddenly realising, "you hit Roduil to get me alone?"

Selvorne nodded, then explained himself, and Tarbo seemed impressed.

"That was perfect. It gives us an excuse to be alone. You had a reason to hit Roduil after that brawl earlier. Everyone will think you are a maker of trouble, not a spy. If we meet again, it will be for me to interrogate you, for your bad behaviour. None will suspect. And if she trusts you, I can trust you, which means I have eyes and ears in the group. Brilliant!"

Selvorne was pleased, only a few hours ago he thought he might die without passing on the message. Then he remembered he had told Rohy, Toavel and Orrikler. He admitted it to Tarbo, whose mood grew grim.

"All right then, not perfect. Quite terrible ... to have told others. Keep an eye on those three. I do not know or trust them, especially Orrikler. Never trust the son of a lord who does not need to be here. Though, if he is a spy, it would be for his father, not brigands. My tests show whether someone is good hearted, courageous, brave and honourable – but they could just as likely be cunning, deceitful, determined – and warned of the tests in advance."

"Brigands?" Selvorne asked, trying to piece it all together.

"Yes, brigands. That is the message. Brigands have spies amongst the guards. And we do not know who they are. Possibly amongst you new men – but likely worse ... they are already here."

~

Tarbo fell back to sit on the log once more, placed the torch carefully so it stood in the ground, then buried his face in his hands. Selvorne thought he might be crying, but after a few moments he beckoned him to sit beside him, and turned so they faced each other, with the torch planted in the dirt near. Selvorne was not at all comfortable, and not only because the log was lumpy to sit upon, and the torch was unbearably bright. He noticed it was also unfairly positioned to the side of Tarbo's patched eye.

"Guards must do their duty," Tarbo said, "though they are tired, drunk, wounded – hurt. Afraid. A man must persist."

"I will," Selvorne said.

"Not you – me, you fool. I have been awake far longer than I should be, and did not sleep in a lovely inn."

"Nor did we, we slept on the grass."

Tarbo nodded, and Selvorne narrowed his eyes.

"And you knew that," Selvorne said, and Tarbo nodded once again, "why say otherwise, then?"

"Demni was ill?" Tarbo asked.

"Very, we – I mean, Dyneti looked after her, and she recovered."

"Poisoned," Tarbo said, and Selvorne felt his eyes widen.

"Poisoned – is she – Dyneti?"

"You suspect Dyneti?"

"I – what? Is she in danger?"

Tarbo nodded, but ... Selvorne was almost certain he was trying not to laugh, so he narrowed his eyes – and Tarbo chuckled.

"The poison of drink, my boy – that she truly should avoid. Ale makes her ill, wine does as well. But at least it makes her dance, first, before collapse. As for Dyneti – is she in danger? Likely, we all are, all the time. But not from ale or wine. No, that is likely in danger from her ... "

Selvorne sighed in relief, and Tarbo nodded – which seemed odd.

"I am drunk – not very, but enough to make me slow," Tarbo said, "and you have not touched the ale, I suspect."

"I did."

"Even worse, touched, but not drunk. Was this your intention?"

Selvorne frowned – Tarbo was testing him. Drunk – hardly – if that was Tarbo drunk, then sober he would have to be formidable. His mind was sharp and seemed ... he was leading Selvorne somehow, searching for answers he did not wish to reveal, and Selvorne knew where that would likely lead.

"Now you are concerned," Tarbo said.

"And being questioned. You think I chose this time to get you alone, to kill you?"

At that, Tarbo laughed – and seemed very drunk as he fell forwards and backwards, he leant on Selvorne to steady himself, which only made him laugh harder still.

"With ... what?" Tarbo asked, then chuckled.

Selvorne frowned – looked to his belt – no knife. But – had he not – there was the sheath. All the men had taken back knives from their things, they were needed to eat with. After washing they were dressed as before, and – Tarbo had removed it and stuck it in the log behind him. When Selvorne noticed it, Tarbo laughed again.

"Sorry," Tarbo said, "but it warms the heart of an old man to fool one so young – even when drunk. No matter, no matter."

Selvorne felt annoyed more than embarrassed – he had not expected someone who was an ally to take his knife, and so had not guarded it – and that likely was what made Tarbo laugh, though ... there was something else going on he did not quite understand.

"You are from Veksehl?" Tarbo asked, and Selvorne nodded, "Who of my men are from Veksehl that you know?"

"I – I do not know, I am from south of Veksehl," Selvorne replied. Fooling the other new recruits might be tricky, though they did not care where Selvorne was from, nor to hear of the wonderful sea – but fooling Tarbo – who would very much want to know everything – would be impossible. He took a deep breath and began to prepare to tell him everything.

"There is nothing south of Veksehl," Tarbo said before Selvorne could speak.

"Tawlehk is."

"And Tawlehk is not Veksehl."

Selvorne nodded.

"Have you met Tonuncia?" Tarbo asked, and Selvorne frowned.

"No, I – "

Tarbo raised a hand, and Selvorne stopped talking – an order that he knew well from his father. Tarbo seemed startled, stared for a while, then began nodding, and Selvorne was not sure what he might be thinking.

"Are you Varavahk?" Tarbo asked.

"Who?" Selvorne replied – and at that, Tarbo laughed, rumbling for a few moments where he sat, until he calmed himself.

"Well, that was much easier than expected."

"I do not understand, I – "

"Are you Untehra?" Tarbo asked, and at that – Selvorne felt insulted.

"Do I look like Untehra?"

"Yes."

Clenching his teeth, Selvorne stared back at Tarbo – who laughed.

"More amusing than expected, as well – some Untehra have fair hair. Fine clothes. Even good manners, as a man well raised," Tarbo said, and Selvorne frowned, "manners learnt, when young or old. Clothes stolen – borrowed, as they might say. And children taken – from families that are fair haired. Yes, you could be Untehra, on looks, and dress, and even how you speak – but you are not, or you would not be insulted. You know them and do not like them, though there are none at Tavalehk."

"There are at times," Selvorne said.

"Not that I have heard. No reports of them from my men just returned – and none from those always there. And you are beginning to seem the stupidest boy I have ever met."

"Why?" Selvorne demanded, but Tarbo raised an eyebrow – just over the patch on his eye.

"Because, my boy, just moments ago you claimed to be from Veksehl. Or Tawlehk. Where there are many Untehra – and yet were so quick to claim they were at Tavalehk. Had you any cleverness, you would claim you were one – once, now settled – and so explain who you are, and where you are from."

Selvorne bit his lip, and Tarbo chuckled.

"Fear not my stupid boy, if Dyneti trusts you, I shall let you pass – but you should consider your story a little better. Or at least learn something of the place you claim to be from."

Tarbo was right – and Selvorne felt hurt. He had given it all little thought, and though he had meant to tell Tarbo everything – thinking he had to, wanting to, wishing to deceive no longer – he felt more than a little angry that his ruse was so flawed. Taking a deep breath, he calmed his mind.

"South of Veksehl, south of Tawlehk, there is a quarry at the town of Vechransehl – the quarry there is rich in stone, the town no more. That is where I am from – hardly a town, and only a place to work. Stone is sent north to Veksehl, and east to Tavalehk. And every year I go to the Festival of Tavalehk – I am sick of the quiet life in the quarry. I have saved my coins from sale of stone, and decided to join the guards – for regular pay, and to learn what I may of the lands. A man was found dead at Tavalehk, and the killing on the road makes my old life seem far less safe than I had thought. Joining the guards seemed to solve many problems at once. And your talk today – although the trials were harsh – you have made me think of many things that before I had not. Only stone and pay and ale and savings. And before I had been fine to live under the stars, but now I wonder if – "

"My – if I had any hope of sleep tonight, that hope is fading fast. You do love to talk – that is a better story," Tarbo said, then he took Selvorne's hands to look them over, "and your hands suggest it is not a lie. Name three men of the quarry."

"Varumies, Daltamies and Faenith," Selvorne replied.

"Quickly – four more," Tarbo ordered.

"Aivosk – and myself. There are no more."

"That does not seem very many, then?"

"We work hard, sometimes others come, but never when I am there – you do not believe me?"

"Do you think I should? Believe you – without question? When you have already lied?"

Selvorne winced, and Tarbo nodded.

"Who is the best cutter?"

"Faenith, without question."

"Strongest?"

Selvorne felt awkward – many times they had said it was himself, though he learnt, as he grew older, they were teasing.

"Varumies – on a good day. His brother is, on a better day, but strength alone does not make a good quarryman."

"Nor fighter, but it helps – and is always known amongst the men. As it is amongst those of mines and quarries. Very well, I believe you. There is only one problem," Tarbo said.

"Yes?" Selvorne asked, astonished that the problems with his lie numbered only one.

"You speak too well for a quarryman."

Selvorne felt – he was not sure what – insulted? He had been complimented, though to claim one thing and appear as another was a stupid thing to do, so in a way he had just been called stupid. Again. But it was not that – Varumies and Daltamies spoke rather roughly. But Faenith and Aivosk were quite well spoken, perhaps not so well as ... his father and Arnlausa.

"The quarry carries sound well," Selvorne said, "and I fancy myself as a singer, and so practise, and have now a lovely voice."

At that, Selvorne began to sing – and Tarbo quickly stopped him.

"If you have even an ounce of mercy, please do not do that again," Tarbo said, drawing his mouth back in some terrible grin of pain. Selvorne felt more than a little hurt.

"Well, I sing better than the other men," Selvorne said.

"I will keep your quarry in mind if I wish to punish a man some day," Tarbo said, and he did not seem to be joking, "and ... does it truly carry sound well?"

"Yes."

"Then I will keep it in mind for Dyneti, as well. Your singing has made me ill."

Selvorne frowned and thought that a little unfair, but – Tarbo did look quite ill, and he winced.

"Not too bad," Tarbo said, "my family have a good ear for singing, and ... to me, appalling."

"Sorry. And my voice?"

"Speaking – tedious. You talk too much."

Selvorne nodded, and Tarbo smiled.

"Unfair. I meant what I said, you speak well. And you sing poorly. You have heard Dyneti – her voice is magnificent."

"It is – and I have heard Demni, she must be terrible to you, who is so keen of hearing."

Tarbo looked puzzled, then shook his head.

"No, her voice is odd, but no, she can sing well enough – different, but not terrible. And Dyneti, though magnificent – when she is here, none of the men can get anything done. When Demni is here – they all get things done. You like one and not the other?"

"I – very much like one, and the other ... not so much."

"Yet I say Demni is poisoned and you ask if Dyneti is harmed?"

Selvorne winced, and Tarbo nodded.

"You must realise," Tarbo said, "the situation I am in – Dyneti sends you, a boy who has lied, who has something to hide, to me – with a message that there are those amongst us with something to hide. Who lie. And spy. What am I to think?"

"Trust Dyneti?"

"I do. I think she has sent me a fresh parchment."

"A – what?"

"To send you as messenger is one thing, but for me to take you to the guards – that is another. You are not a spy – that is clear – not for anyone, unless it is the dumbest brigand, lord or ... "

Tarbo stopped talking, and Selvorne waited, but he did not speak. Instead he stared at Selvorne, and then, over his shoulder – so Selvorne turned, expecting to see someone there – but he saw only the woods. When he looked back at Tarbo, he was studying his face.

"Why did you not run?" Tarbo asked.

"What?"

"Why did you not run – when you were captured. You were freed – you could have run."

"We were running – with the plan to swim, once we were sure it was safe."

"All together?"

Selvorne nodded, then shook his head.

"One at at time, to increase our chances."

"Waiting for the others to all be free – to ruin your chance," Tarbo said, "despite the important message you had for me?"

"That I told to the others, should they live, and not me."

"Which you were told not to do."

"I – yes, against her orders. At the time ... we wondered who would live."

"None. Were it real – none would have lived. More likely, were it real – your escape would have been entertainment for a dozen men on the island with spears. A hunt of men. Did that not occur to you?"

Selvorne bit his lip – it had not. He thought they were doing quite well in escaping, though – it seemed a little too well. Stupid brigands, overconfident – actually, stupid new recruits, too confident they had outsmarted others who ... of course they would have let them run to chase them, for fun. A hunt of men. He had not been thinking as they might, and did not see it.

"You just realise this now," Tarbo said, "it shows on your face. So – not smart enough to realise it then – and you truly did think it best to try and go together rather than ... than use the others to distract your enemy. Which is what some men might do."

"Not me," Selvorne said, and Tarbo smiled.

"No – not you. So – trusted by Dyneti. For simplicity, perhaps – a fresh parchment. A badly crafted story of your past of which I think you are only half aware, and bold enough to defy the orders of a Waehdric, and yet ... did so to send the message, despite what I think was either sacrifice or stupidity – or a bit of both. Not deceit. Few men are so noble."

Selvorne was not sure if it was a compliment, so he smiled, and Tarbo nodded.

"And few others have the nerve to send me another without paying," Tarbo said, shaking his head, "yet here you are, and I grow weary. Very well. Do you – did they send you to try and learn who the spy was?"

"They?" Selvorne asked.

"Dyneti?"

Selvorne could have said yes – he wanted to find the spy. It might have earned him more trust from Tarbo, but he could not.

"No," Selvorne said, "but I am here to learn – and if I found a spy – what should I do?"

"Tell me," Tarbo said quietly, and Selvorne nodded.

~

Tarbo was quiet, and Selvorne grew uneasy sitting on the log, so he stood and began to pace. Tarbo seemed tired, and almost as though he might fall asleep where he sat.

"You truly are exhausted?" Selvorne asked.

"And when a man is, he is of little use. I should have questioned you when fresh."

"The answers would have been the same."

"The questions would not have been – Selvorne, I do not trust you yet, and am too tired to trick you that I do."

"So you admit it, so I might lower my guard?" Selvorne asked, and Tarbo chuckled.

"Not much of a guard to lower, my boy. No – I tell you not so you trust me, but so you realise you – and I – cannot trust anyone without care. She sent you – you are my contact with her, at times when no others may do. That might be often. A fresh parchment, that is all we can trust."

"I am not sure what you mean?"

"I mean – do not speak of this to anyone – you are the guard who defies me, who I must yell at and dislike. She is the lady you fancy, who all think is your secret love. Meet with me, meet with her, few may care – if I meet with her, many will care. You are the parchment we pass back and forth – though hopefully not with you reading every message out to anyone who might hear."

"Oh ... " Selvorne said. He did not like what he was hearing.

"Questions?"

"Ahh – what?" Selvorne asked.

"Do you have any questions? We should be back, I cannot say when I will see you next. Questions?"

Questions – yes, he had many. Too many to think of, but also more answers already than he had time to think about. The sweep of the woods – he wanted to know when, and whether it might work – but he knew that, roughly. Weeks, and across the south – it had to be, and likely there was a reason for the delay. He knew there was a spy, he knew not to trust anyone – he wanted to ask who he could trust, but that seemed a stupid thing to do, for it was quite clear the answer would be no one. What he wanted to ask was beginning to seem almost dangerous, so he thought of a way he might soften it a little.

"Who is Kludbo?" Selvorne asked – and at that, Tarbo tilted his head.

"What?"

"Kludbo – who is he?"

Was that a wink – no, a blink, but with one eye covered – and then another. It certainly looked like a wink, but Tarbo was not smiling.

"Did she put you up to that cruel prank?"

"Dyneti?"

Tarbo nodded.

"She – no," Selvorne admitted, "she ... told me not to ask about ... Torlor."

"And yet you did."

"Kludbo, not Torlor."

"Yet know the two names are the same person?"

"But at the talk earlier you said – "

"Torlor was real?"

Selvorne nodded, and was glad he was standing instead of sitting close to Tarbo, who seemed quite agitated.

"She told you not to ask, and yet you ask – and you knew the names were of the same person, and so thought to disobey by such deceit?"

"I only – "

"And are tense – so she warned you quite well. Interesting. Cruel, if her warning was a trick to make you upset me – kind, if she warned you to spare my feelings. Cunning if she did it to test you – as you are now proving yourself disobedient, deceitful, and think yourself clever."

"And also confused," Selvorne said.

"And she is blameless, whatever her intention. It is a trick of hers, Selvorne – nothing more. Torlor was real, as I said when I spoke to the men – never so clumsy in life. In the tales, a lesson in each of his wounds. Greatest swordsman, not so great if his sword is stuck in a tree," Tarbo said, and at that, he drew the knife from the log and stood, handing it to Selvorne, "the same goes for knives."

Selvorne nodded and took back his knife, and as he began to sheath it, he realised just how brave Tarbo was handing it over – had Selvorne been there to kill him, he could have done ... if he had been so clever to fool a man who likely had spent the whole time testing to see if he was that cunning. So he quickly moved the knife to Tarbo's neck – and Tarbo did not flinch.

"You are slow, tired, drunk – or very trusting," Selvorne said.

"A little of each. And you are a fresh parchment, but your face is never blank – you did that to test me, but are not sure how – pride, and astonishment I did not knock you down for it. I must say I am glad, in a way."

"That I would be so bold?" Selvorne asked, sheathing his knife.

"That you would be so foolish, and that it shows on your face. You remind me of Torlor, a little."

Selvorne winced, and Tarbo laughed.

"Enough of this, time to return. You stay on the island tonight, I must leave. They must think I was very angry to have kept you so long when so tired – better for you, if it spares you from Roduil's vengeance. You have done well to anger the best of us."

"Your best is not very good, then, to be beaten and angry from someone untrained."

Tarbo laughed.

"Indeed – I assure you, our best is very good, and is amused more than angry. Now, I am tired, but less drunk, and feel the aches of the day even more. I had planned a rest for a week, now I must ... quicken things. How stupid are you?"

Selvorne frowned, but Tarbo was waiting for an answer.

"I wish I knew."

Tarbo chuckled, and nodded.

"Yes – we all do, I guess. Others have noticed you and Dyneti – others will watch you."

"Oh – jealous men?"

"Jealous – what? No – spies, you idiot. Jealous?"

Selvorne bit his lip, and Tarbo shook his head.

"Well, now we know – quite stupid," Tarbo said.

"I ... yes, spies. You think they will be watching me?"

"You truly are an idiot, Selvorne."

"I know, I ... "

"Tell the message to three others you hardly know – half guessed its meaning, too – and yet that did not stop you."

"I am sorry."

"And disobeyed Dyneti, who told you one thing and you did the other, and why did you stay when you could have fled?"

"I realise that was a mistake, but – "

"And then hitting Roduil – even to get me here, a stupid thing to do. I warned you not to – "

Tarbo stopped – he sounded angry, but Selvorne could only apologise so many times.

"You are not making this any easier," Tarbo said.

"I am not sure what I can do – you told me all this before, I know I made mistakes, but this is new to me, and – "

"My – astounding! Can you truly be that simple?"

Selvorne frowned, sighed – then shrugged, and Tarbo began to shake his head.

"Selvorne – I am trying to make you miserable."

"Why?"

Tarbo stared at him – blinked, or winked – gazing with one eye, unable to speak. He took a deep breath, then relaxed.

"I am perhaps more drunk than I thought," Tarbo said, "tired, and vague of mind. Or perhaps you have the simple mind of a mother, clearly you have her looks."

"What?"

"Selvorne – think. Why are you here?"

"To join the guards, to – "

"Why – are – we – here – in – the – woods?" Tarbo asked very slowly.

The woods – alone. His punishment. Selvorne winced, as Tarbo nodded.

"Try to at least look a little miserable – if you go back with a great grin, what will people think?"

"They will think I am an idiot, and so will discover the truth," Selvorne said, and at that Tarbo laughed.

"Indeed. You are perhaps the only guard I know, but one, who takes insults with eager agreement."

"My father said insults true were lessons valued, insults false were the mistakes of others, and the only stupidity is to think one is the other, or to not care to discover which was which."

Tarbo, who was chuckling, stopped – was silent – then nodded once.

"Yes – that is wise. Did he also teach you how to look miserable when required?"

Selvorne bit his lip – he was not sure.

"Think of something miserable?" Selvorne asked, and Tarbo nodded, so he thought of hitting Roduil and earning his punishment, but he found himself beginning to grin.

"Perfect, now all the spies will know you are working in secret with me, whether they see you or hear how the new guard returned laughing at Tarbo's harsh words," Tarbo said, "is there nothing miserable in your life? Or is it all one great joke?"

Perhaps his father had taught him just that – to calm his mind, to change emotion. He did so when he shaved, and as Selvorne thought of it, his mood fell to nothing. Was there misery – yes. Much, deeply buried each morning when he shaved, though that morning had been most unusual. Horror of past not hidden, pushed aside by horrors present. The pain of it all must have showed on his face, for Tarbo seemed impressed.

"Good," Tarbo said, "very good. Keep the ruse – we are not to seem merry. Not warm, not friends."

"Not trusted," Selvorne said.

"Neither the other – but we are allies," Tarbo said, and at that, they made their way back to the others.

~

It was the bridge that Selvorne thought of – the killings, the anger, the misery. All at once, and though he did not want to think of them, it must have made his face look grim. The men seemed pained to see in Selvorne's eyes the anguish of enduring a long speech, which many must have known for themselves.

Misery and anger, frustration at the killings – and though his thoughts turned to Tarbo, there was some anger at him, as well. Despite his talk of alliances and trust, and danger, and shared enemies – Selvorne felt annoyed not to be trusted. And insulted. The two were keeping secrets from each other. Tarbo had no reason to trust him, that was true. But Selvorne had a reason to mistrust Tarbo, and that was because, although Arnlausa must have known him, he had said to only trust Cienn.

Selvorne greeted the other guards, who seemed almost to comfort him, more obviously once Roduil had left. Mixed responses came from the new recruits, once many other guards had gone – he had, after all, hit a guard in revenge when told not to do so. An unexpected maker of trouble. Reklo found it funny, Nakla thought it serious. Bitier liked the use of the ale to distract him – Rhede and Toavel were astounded anyone could be so bold. Aigel wished he had thought of it first, though why he had reason to hit Roduil was anyone's guess. Vugecarauk said nothing, and Orrikler merely shook his head. But Rohy ... he was strangest of all, for he nodded and did not smile. He – of all of them – must have realised Selvorne's true intent.

The night grew late and many of the older guards had started the day early, and had not planned to sleep there. Certainly not collapsed in the dirt in all their clothes, with wooden tankards for cruel pillows. The new recruits crept into their allocated tents – their homes, they were told, for weeks ahead. Orrikler had his own fine tent that was quite magnificent, large enough for a few men, but it was his alone, and Aigel wondered how that was in any way like being treated as all the other men.

Selvorne lay in the larger, plainer tent for the men – sober, tired, overwhelmed. The morning seemed a week ago, the day before, a month. The last time he had seen Dyneti – a year, or more – a lifetime. No, it was not ... but the next time he might meet her seemed just as far ahead.

Arnlausa. Cienn. One name – her, or whoever had replaced her – no others. Spies amongst the guards. Perhaps Arnlausa and Uhlsko trusted Tarbo once, they must have known the leader of all guards, even if only by name. But he had not been named as a man to trust, so perhaps they knew more of what was happening than either had said – Tarbo might be an enemy. Unlikely. But he might be compromised in a way that was a mystery even to himself. He had called Selvorne stupid many times – but to truly believe that, Tarbo would have to be an idiot. Selvorne had done stupid things – confused, pressured, fooled. He knew no better. But he was far from stupid, and what Tarbo had told him, though not in words, was that there was far more danger than was realised, even by himself.

Selvorne would have to be very careful in meeting with Cienn. He would have to mind what he said, and to whom – and he would have to train very, very hard to never again do anything as stupid as he had been doing. With all that in mind, he began to fall asleep. More danger than he had feared, closer than he had hoped, to others, not only himself – and worst of all – from enemies unknown.

~